Hester's *Hunt* for Home

TRILOGY

Three Bestselling Novels in One

LINDA BYLER

Hester's *Hunt* for Home

>>>———→

TRILOGY

Three Bestselling Novels in One

New York, New York

Library of Congress Cataloging-in-Publication Data is available on file.

Print ISBN: 978-1-68099-206-9
Ebook ISBN: 978-1-68099-207-6

Cover design by Koechel Peterson & Associates, Inc., Minneapolis, Minnesota

Printed in the United States of America

TABLE OF CONTENTS

Hester on the Run   1
Hester's Hunt for Home, Book 1

Which Way Home?   327
Hester's Hunt for Home, Book 2

Hester Takes Charge   681
Hester's Hunt for Home, Book 3

Glossary   1065
About the Author   1077
Other Books by Linda Byler   1079

LINDA BYLER

Hester *on the* Run

Hester's Hunt for Home
Book 1

CHAPTER 1

Outside, the rain fell steadily, splashing on the glossy green leaves of spring, sliding off in tiny rivulets, dancing from one leaf to another. The sky was pewter gray, the day's light dimmed by the heavy clouds of a rainstorm in spring. Beneath the great white oaks, the lofty maples, ash, and cedar trees, the undergrowth received the raindrops, spurring the lush grasses and bushes to renewed growth.

Nestled by the side of a sizable ridge, built to avoid the harsh winds of winter, a small house made of logs stood in the rain, the weathered shake roof glistening with moisture as the rain slid steadily from the edge, plunking like a curtain of water in front of it.

There were four small windows made of glass, with six small panes divided by a dark wooden framework. Only one of the windows glowed with a yellowish glow, beaming warmly through the muffled light, the dripping darkness of the thick forest surrounding the house.

The front door was made of oak planks with a chunky forged iron latch that was closed securely against the wild creatures of the night, or marauding Indians, the residents of the wild mountains of Berks County, Pennsylvania.

The year was 1745, and Pennsylvania was a land of forests, mountain ranges, rivers, and creeks, unspoiled and, for the most part, lightly settled by Europeans. Now a small community of immigrants was hacking away at the great trees, building homes, clearing land, making a life for themselves in the New World, America.

They came from Switzerland to escape religious persecution, their forebears having been called "Anabaptists," or "re-baptizers." This particular group was descended from Jacob Ammann and was known as "Amish."

Beside the glow of the oil lamp by the window, a young Amish couple sat side by side, their heads bent low, his brown hair almost identical to the color of his wife's. A heavy beard lay along his facial contours. His hair was cut straight across his forehead, falling to below his ears on the side and straight across the back of his head at his hairline. He had a wide forehead, high cheekbones, and full lips. A strong, swarthy man of twenty-nine, he was dressed in a dull, homespun shirt of unbleached muslin. Nine buttons held his broadfall knee breeches securely.

His wife wore the traditional white head cap, sewn in the old style adopted by their people in Switzerland. It was made of Swiss muslin, a wide band in the front with pleated fabric attached to it, and tied beneath the chin by wide strings of the same material.

Almost all of her head was covered. Only a thatch of severely combed hair, parted in the middle, remained visible. Her forehead was narrow, her nose a goodly size, but it was her eyes that dominated her features, the one beautiful aspect of her otherwise plain face.

They were large and the blue of a robin's egg, the color turning with the changing of her emotions, which happened as frequently as her words came. That dancing color of blue that went from indigo to the shades of blue sky on a sunny day, was what had captivated Hans.

And so Catherine had placed her hand in Hans Zug's, repeated her soft answer after his, at her place by his side in front of the Amish bishop in the Rhine Valley, and became his wife.

She was known as Kate.

She wore a linen shortgown, over a linen petticoat, as well as a linen kerchief and apron.

Barely visible on her lap was an infant, swaddled in serviceable blankets. Her thick, jet black hair shone almost blue in the lamplight.

When the baby turned her head, her small, oval face was the color of a red squirrel's ear. She was perfect, this tiny foundling.

Her eyelids were already beginning a curtain of brilliantly black lashes over the contours of her wide, flat eyes. The small brows arced like the symmetry of an eagle's wings. Her nose was a tiny bump, with nostrils so small, Kate feared for her ability to breathe normally.

Oh, she was so beautiful! Not of her flesh and blood, this foundling, but hers, all hers. And Hans's. At long last. Kate held in her arms her heart's desire after nine long years of waiting and hoping while her womb remained barren.

The desolation of sleepless nights, when the yearning for a baby of her own caused hot tears to squeeze between her eyelids, the ache in her chest a physical pain, were now things of the past.

She had gone to the spring swinging her wooden bucket, her step heavy but sure as she made her way down the path from the house.

That April, a sharp wind bore winter's reluctance to lighten its grip on the daily temperature. Kate held her shawl tightly around her neck.

A few dandelions waved their brilliant yellow heads, accompanied by the purple violets growing along the side of the spring. She had bent to gather a handful to grace the windowsill by her spinning wheel when she heard it. At first, she thought it might be the plaintive call of a catbird. A mewling sound.

She stopped picking violets and sat on her haunches, holding very still. There it was again. A kitten? But they hadn't brought any cats to America. Rocking back on her heels, she flattened a few dark green ferns, oblivious to anything but the beating of her heart.

When she heard the thin, wailing cry once more, she scrambled to her feet and stood motionless, holding her head to one side. A shiver chased itself up her spine, across her shoulders, and down her forearms, causing the hairs to lift across them.

Suddenly, she felt as if she was being observed. Making a turn to the right, she lifted her blue eyes to the surrounding wooded slopes, quickly scanning with her experienced eyes. More shivers sent an involuntary shudder through her, as her eyes raked the deep forest surrounding the spring. Was this small cry a trap?

Always, the Amish settlers needed to be wary of the Indians, the ones who had rightful ownership of this land. Always, there was the danger of meeting a group of hostile native men, in spite of William Penn's endeavors to keep the peace, as he offered more treaties to that effect.

When the cry came again, she knew it was not a bird or a kitten. It had to be an infant. Neither the danger of hostile red men, or anything else, could stop her now. Her mother's heart responded, and she became a woman possessed, weaving through the undergrowth, bent over, her arms thrashing, combing the ferns, grasses, and bushes with an intensity that sprang from her very nature.

She came up empty-handed and stood uncertain, the loud beats of her heart filling her ears.

When the cry came again, she lurched toward it, stumbled, slipped on wet rocks, then resumed her wild searching, raking aside the heavy ferns and mountain laurel that spilled across her face.

She gasped audibly when she came upon the small brown bundle. A fawn? Was it only a bleating fawn whose mother had been killed? The deerskin was so soft, it had to be from a young fawn. Tentatively, she reached out, touching the deerskin with trembling fingers. She bit down hard on her lower lip, and then a cry escaped her when she found the black hair, the brown face that scrunched up and emitted another mewling sound.

"*Mein Gott,*" she breathed. She sank to the ground, unaware of her full skirt trailing in the icy spring water as she put both hands beneath the bundle and lifted it gently onto her lap, crying now, laughing, chortling to herself.

In the dappled sunlight that played between the moving leaves of the forest, she saw the baby for the first time, and her heart swelled with an indescribable longing. The baby was beautiful.

Quickly, furtively, she stole a glance. Yes, it was a girl. A girl baby.

"*Ach, mein Himmlischer Vater*" (Oh, my heavenly father)*!* It was all she had ever wanted. Mumbling now, talking to herself, half in prayer, she examined the infant from her head to her tiny red feet. So perfect.

Again, her eyes swept the hillside, searching for answers. Would someone come to reclaim her if she took her to the house?

A strong smell came from the baby's furs, an unwashed, unclean scent that made her recoil. Her first instinct was to bathe her, rub her skin with oil of lavender, dress her in clean clothes, swaddle her with soft blankets.

The trees rustled around her; the spring bubbled and tinkled merrily over the rocks; the wooden bucket lay on its side, forgotten, with the clutch of purple violets beside it.

Quickly, she held the baby to her chest, and with a swift movement she was on her feet, glancing hurriedly behind her now. Gaining momentum, she walked fast until she was running, out of breath by the time she got back to the house, barring the heavy door behind her.

Only then, the thought came, what would Hans say?

In fact, Hans said very little. He stated, matter-of-factly, that very likely a scared young Indian maiden had left the infant by the spring purposefully, hoping the white people would care for it.

By the baby's features, he believed her to be of the Lenape tribe, often mistakenly called the "Delaware." The rich golden brown color of her skin. Her straight, thick, glossy hair. Her well sculpted eyes and brows. Yes, they would keep her, he said. He never doubted that God had heard their pleas for a newborn baby.

Kate's love for her husband sprang up, flowering into a new and beautiful thing, deeply appreciating his manly ways, this sure choice he made now.

She heated water in the heavy, black, cast-iron pot and swung it across the flames in the fireplace. She shaved small bits of lye soap and worried the warm water with her hands until bubbles rose to the surface.

When Kate placed the small brown infant into the water, she opened her eyes wide and became very still, and Kate giggled and laughed with the sheer joy of being able to bathe this wonderful little being.

That first night, they boiled a cloth to purify it, then dipped it repeatedly in warmed cow's milk, laughing together as the powerful little mouth suckled until their fingers hurt.

Kate would not lay her down, even after a soft burp came from her throat. She held her, possessing the baby, her face lit with a radiant fulfillment that came from her mother's heart.

They couldn't get enough of her. They wept together at her first smile. They marveled when she grew, her cheeks filling out from the good cow's milk.

Word got around, the way these things do, and only a few weeks elapsed before Kate's mother-in-law was at the door, tall, formidable, and completely disapproving. Kate clutched her precious foundling to her breast, a sick feeling mushrooming in her stomach.

Taking her outer wraps off in one jerked movement, the irritation on her face playing with her lowered eyebrows, Rebecca was a scary figure in Kate's life. Especially now. Bending to peer at the sleeping infant, Rebecca breathed out in a disdainful whoosh of annoyance, "She's red as a beet."

"*Ya*, Mam." It was all Kate could think of, a sort of agreement, a subservient answer, a bowing to higher authority that was deeply ingrained, the teachings of childhood branded into her conscience.

"What makes you think you can raise her Amish, with Indian blood?" Rebecca inquired, tersely, tight-lipped with disapproval.

"I don't know," Kate mumbled.

"She's a heathen child."

Quite suddenly, Kate broke out with a swift denial, pleading the infant's innocence, as her mother-in-law stood over her with fiery objection.

When the door latch lifted and her father-in-law, Isaac, appeared with Hans behind him, Kate's voice drifted off quietly, and Rebecca's features rounded into a caricature of pleasantness.

Isaac shook hands solemnly with Kate then bent to peer into the small wooden cradle Hans had just completed.

"*Ach, du lieva*" (Oh, my goodness), he murmured softly, quick tears springing to his nearsighted blue eyes, with the dozens of wrinkles and crow's feet spreading around them. *"An shay kind"* (A nice child).

Hans beamed, clasping his hands on his shirtfront. Kate blinked back the awkwardness of the moment, her mother-in-law's censure a cawing black crow stuffed into submission for now.

"So tell me how this all came about," Isaac said, kindly.

Willingly, Hans launched into Kate's experience at the spring, ending his story by surmising that a young Indian woman left the newborn there, intending that they would find it.

Isaac nodded, his blue eyes alight. "It's risky business, but perhaps Kate is right. Time will tell. Just be prepared to give her back if the mother would turn up at your door."

Kate sat up, opened her mouth to defend herself against the unlikeliness of that very thing, but glanced at her mother-in-law and decided against it, withering against the back of the chair she sat on.

"Do you have a name?" Isaac asked.

"Hester."

Hans spoke her name quietly, reluctantly. Kate looked down at her hands, clenched so tightly in her lap.

"Why such a name?" Rebecca said sharply. "No one is named Hester in the *freundshaft*" (extended family).

"It is the name Kate wanted," Hans said curtly, echoing Rebecca's own tone of voice and leaving her without a reply, since she had been taught to let male figures take the dominant role, even if they were younger.

"Why not Esther? It's a Biblical name. Queen Esther was sent by God to save her people." Isaac's voice was kind, so Kate could speak more freely.

"*Dat,* I had a friend in school, a French girl, named Hester Elizabeth. She was nice to me, in spite of my being Amish. I loved her a lot. And, well, I wanted my daughter to be called by her name."

"She's not your daughter," Rebecca spat out, saliva spraying across Kate's face, little wet pellets that made her draw back.

So Kate learned to live with the deepening gloom of Hans's parents' disapproval, although Isaac's kindness lessened the sting.

Each day was filled with a kind of heady gladness as she went about the tasks of running the house smoothly, interrupted only by the sweetness of little Hester's cries. Kate would go swiftly to her cradle, lifting her out, so glad she was finally awake so she could watch her perfect mouth lift into a smile, her black eyes sparkle with recognition.

She was at last a mother, like all her friends. She had a small gift from God, a benediction, a sign of his favor. Hans loved the baby so much, his love for his wife multiplied.

Spring turned into summer, and Hester grew into a healthy child with round cheeks and glowing skin the color of maple syrup.

Kate washed the baby's clothes in the great wooden tubs and wrung them out with strong, capable hands. She rinsed them in hot water with a dash of apple cider vinegar in it and hung them on the rail fence surrounding the house.

She scrubbed floors, the wide golden oak boards planed to a shining smooth texture by Hans's brawny arms.

She planted a garden, with Hester cooing from the blanket where she was placed. Curious butterflies flitted above her, the birds sang and twittered, diving around her, and Kate told Hans that she knew Hester's eyes followed the birds and other flying things. Hans never doubted her.

Hans had built their house against the ridge, which rose in back of it to the north. A gentle slope fell away from it, toward the south, down to the barn built of stone and log. The barn's sturdy roof was made of split shakes, overlapped from the peak to let the rain tumble down over them, keeping the cow and calf, the heifer, and two horses snug and dry in winter.

A split rail fence surrounded the barn, ensuring the animals fresh air in the wintertime. The large pasture was dotted with stumps from the trees Hans had felled and rose away beyond the small barnyard, up the side of another ridge to the east.

Little by little, Hans's acreage spread out, allowing him to plant wheat, rye, and spelt. In any spare time, he felled trees and split them for more fence rails or logs for neighbors who had use for them.

Hans was a good manager and a hard worker, squirreling away every coin he possibly could. His fields were planted, hoed, and harvested in time. He fed his horses well so they could work long days in the sun, tilling the soil, and harvesting what grew in it.

He was the blacksmith for all the Amish families of the settlement, spread out in a radius of fourteen or fifteen miles, give or take a few.

On the days Hans went *gile chplauwa* (blacksmithing), Kate enjoyed a sort of freedom that gave her a great and secret pleasure. She spent idle time arranging wild-flowers in redware cups, sometimes washing her hair and arranging it in different ways in front of the small wood-framed mirror above her sink.

Without her cap, her hair was soft and wavy, but she always pulled it back into a tight bun, jabbing combs sharply into the tight coils on the back of her head.

It was shameful to wash one's hair too often, a sign of pride. So she didn't tell Hans, figured he needn't know, for he was strict in some ways where she was concerned.

If her friend Naomi wore a new green shortgown, and she expressed her wish for fabric of such a beautiful hue, he would become quite angry, grasping her arm and giving it a small shake, saying she was going against God's will, being consumed by the lust of the eyes. So she learned to satisfy any desire for beauty when he was blacksmithing.

Once, she dyed a length of plain linen fabric with the juice of pokeberries, turning it into a delightful hue between purple and pink. She was so pleased with the results that she set about immediately sewing a curtain for the east window beside the fireplace. Wouldn't it turn into the color of wild roses when the sun arrived over the treetops, the rays piercing through the brilliant fabric, infusing the house with color?

Her disappointment was crushing when Hans said he would have none of her worldliness, ripped it off its rod, and took it away. She never found out what he had done with her handiwork, until she helped him shovel manure the following spring and discovered slivers of fabric that had once been brilliant, like the rubies Hester Elizabeth had told her about.

The stone in her chest had caused her great pain, but it had dissolved as she forgave her husband and berated herself for being so prone to cave in to her worldly desires. It was the way of it, being Amish.

But now, with little Hester, Hans changed completely when it came to dressing her as an Amish baby. He came home from Reuben Hershberger's with a swatch of blue linen the color of a bluebird's plumage, so blue it was a sort of purple. Smiling, his eyes alight, he asked Kate to sew a little dress for Hester. They would be taking her to church on Sunday.

Pleased, and convinced he would allow her prettier fabric, Kate set about sewing the small garment, her needle weaving in and out with tiny stitches that would hold for years.

She sewed a row of tucks in the sleeves that could be taken out to lengthen the sleeve as she grew. Around the hem along the bottom of the shirt, she did the same, thinking how this beautiful little dress could be worn for quite some time. She made a small muslin cap for her, too, much like her own. They tried the cap on Hester and laughed together when her thick, glossy black hair refused to remain beneath it.

Kate darned Hans's socks, but when a pair was no longer worth patching, she turned them into small black socks for Hester. Hans was so happy about her thriftiness, he told her that together they would turn this little homestead into a productive farm, a real place in the Amish community.

The gentle summer rains made her garden a lovely picture of growth, the pole beans climbing up over the crooked poles they tied together at the top, a tripod of support for the fast-growing vines.

Onions grew in straight rows, their tops reaching for the sky like scrawny fingers. Beets grew large and heavy, their red-veined leaves spread luxuriantly between the rows, adjacent to the field of corn and tobacco.

Kate kept the weeds at bay with endless hoeing. Every morning, before Hester awoke, Kate was in the garden, hoeing, collecting bugs, and drowning them in hot tallow, following well the ways of her mother.

She fed kitchen scraps to the chickens. She gathered the eggs and washed them, storing them in woven baskets in the cold cellar Hans had built behind the house. He'd take any extra eggs along when he made his horse-shoeing calls and then put any coins he received beneath the floorboards under their bedstead.

Somehow today she couldn't shake a disgruntled feeling about the brilliant blue dress for Hester. She had been delighted, reveling in the sewing of it, bending over her needle and thread with a gladness that was hard to explain. Why now, here washing the large, brown eggs, did this feeling creep over her?

Was it jealousy? Longing to have one of her own? Quickly, she scolded herself, muttering aloud. How childish. So shameful. Of course she must stop any such thoughts that crept in. They were of the devil.

Hans was the best father she had ever seen. How many times had she helped her friends with their screaming babies, or injured toddlers wailing out their indignities, and watched their husbands in animated conversation, oblivious to their wives' frustration as they struggled to take care of all the babies and young children?

No, Hans was exceptional, and it was only her own childish selfishness that brought on this gloomy foreboding. Or was it her woman's intuition?

CHAPTER 2

THE PENNSYLVANIA FOREST STRETCHED BEFORE them like an endless green sea, the trees as restless as the ocean currents, tossed about by a strong wind, setting the treetops into a sort of constant, ever-changing dance.

Hans urged the dependable driving horse, Dot, into an easy walk. The heavy leather strap, called the britchment, dug into her haunches as she leaned into it, working hard to hold the cart back, to keep it from careening down the steep, rocky incline. The road was barely visible because of the washouts from the thunderstorms of late spring.

Dot lowered her head, picking her way easily between the ruts as the cart bumped and swayed, sending Kate's shoulder bouncing against Hans's. She relinquished her hold on Hester, ignoring the ache in her elbow as she held the sleeping infant inside her brown shawl.

The morning was crisp and cool, the sun lighting up the deep greens into many various shades, from near black to joyful lime green. It was a bit chilly, with the wind whipping the small branches over their heads, turning the leaves inside out, worrying them frantically with each fresh gust.

Hans laid a thick hand on the top of his black felt hat and pushed down, ensuring the headgear's tight hold on his head, then turned to look at his wife. He could see nothing but the wide front of her cap, her face hidden behind its broad front piece. He knew her mouth would be set in a straight line of endurance, unwilling to admit how weary she was. They had come about three-fourths of the way, probably twelve miles, and her shoulders would be aching, he knew. They were on their way to church services, being held that morning in the home of Amos and Mary Hershberger, a distance of sixteen miles from home.

Soon the forest would give way to an open area, the fields and pastures having been cleared by Amos and his sturdy sons. The cart lurched, rocking from side to side as Dot picked her way carefully down the incline. When they came to a level area, the sun's rays changed the light to a yellow-tinged hue, a constantly moving play of light and dark colors. The road became a carpet of pine needles now, pierced only by a few wild black-berry bushes springing up from the acidic soil beneath the ancient pines.

Kate breathed in deeply, savoring the sharp odor of pine gum. Her eyes followed the movement of a red squirrel, chirring at the invaders from his perch on a low branch. Her full-fronted cap effectively obscured her side vision, which was perhaps the reason for its wide rim. The eyes of women should not wander or seem bold or brazen, but should be kept lowered in humility.

Today, Kate would need to pray for humility. Already her heart was thumping, her breath quickening at the thought of carrying her perfect child into the house, the women rushing to see, the gasps of admiration.

Hester was hers, all hers. Kate's moment of glory had come. They rode on in silence, swaying together in the cart. Hans had suggested the cart, because of the distance. It was lighter and easier on Dot.

Kate had given her consent, but after twelve miles, her back ached horribly, her elbow felt frozen into place, and she resented Hans's lack of forethought. They should have taken the box wagon, but Hans didn't want to exhaust Dot.

Soon, from the money he'd been saving from his horseshoeing, they could afford four new wheels. He would make a lighter cart himself, and it would be a fine one, she knew.

Kate turned her head, straining her neck to see the Stephen Fisher homestead. She was curious about Barbara's garden, the animals. Had their Belgian mare given birth? Barbara had spoken of the upcoming event in hushed tones two weeks ago.

The leaves on the trees obscured much, leaving Kate with unsatisfied curiosity, but since Hans did not speak as they drove past the Fishers, Kate thought it best to hold her words.

It was, after all, the Sabbath, the day of holiness. Let your *ya* be *ya*, your *nay* be *nay*, always, but especially on the Lord's Day. Her thoughts were to be on spiritual matters, not wondering about her neighbors' material worthiness.

Kate tugged at her flat hat, pulling it farther front, as if the width of it might ensure heavenly thoughts. She could not resist one furtive, backward glance, however, and much to her great triumph, she caught sight of a thin, blond, long-legged colt cavorting among the tree stumps in the pasture. So the mare had her colt. Kate smiled, well hidden from her husband's steady gaze.

"Oo-oo-ah." Hans began a slow chant, a bit above a humming sound. So, he meant to sing *fore* (be the song leader). He would lead a hymn today. That was good. Kate was glad. Hans had a clear voice that rose and fell like deep, chiming bells, a rich and full baritone. He was a good song leader, not one who stumbled and other men had to come to rescue, the way it was for some who were less talented.

The bundle on her lap began squirming, then tugging at her arms and heaving, before letting loose with a fine howl.

Lifting the flap of her shawl, Kate fumbled to loosen the baby's shawl, wrapped securely about her head, as the howls became more insistent. Shocked to find her beautiful baby's face bathed in sweat, the blanket around her neck already moist with it, Kate hurried to loosen the pins that held the heavy garments too snugly around her.

Frightened, Kate kept her head lowered, as Hester emitted stronger cries, her outrage building at being kept waiting.

Hans's singing stopped. "Can't you feed her?" he asked gently.

"I don't know how I would in this rocking cart. She was a bit too warm, I guess."

"Sit her up. Let her get some air," Hans instructed.

Kate wouldn't think of it and told him so. If a child perspired and then became exposed to frosty air, he or she could catch a cold. But when the indignant child's cries became quite frantic, Hans stopped the mare, told Kate to get her some milk now, because he could hardly see how she could survive under that heavy shawl.

Obediently, Kate tried to feed her the cold cow's milk, sitting beneath a great pin oak in the new grass by the side of the road, but Hester would have none of it. She turned her head and screamed her refusal. Kate lifted her to her shoulder, thumped her back gently, and tried again, to no avail.

Hans was becoming anxious, and the baby continued wailing. Kate wrapped her back into the shawl, stuck her unceremoniously beneath her own, climbed back into the cart with her eyes lowered, and rode the remaining few miles to church services under the fog of her husband's disapproval. There was nothing she could do. Why couldn't he see that?

When they finally reached their destination, Kate was exhausted from clinging to the crying infant, her nerves shattered by feelings of inadequacy. What had happened? Had their life been too perfect? Everything had gone so smoothly, but their first venture to take Hester away had turned into a nightmare.

She turned her head to search Hans's face, alarmed to find his eyes set straight ahead, the brows lowered over them as if he was enduring the misery of the infant all by himself. Did he really love the child so much?

Kate was reduced to carrying the still-crying infant into Amos and Mary Hershberger's well-built house.

Scurrying swiftly, she acknowledged helping hands gratefully, relinquishing Hester into Mamie Troyer's ample, old arms, who clucked and fussed and announced in stentorian tones that this baby was *au-gvocksa* (all tense and tight). Mamie proceeded to unwrap her, every head bending to watch as she lifted the baby.

Kate's dreams of Hester's first entry to church were dashed. Her beautiful child was red and perspiring, her eyes swollen from her painful crying, her little red mouth maneuvering grotesquely as harsh, nerve-jangling noises burst from it steadily.

Hester's beautiful new blue dress was soaked with saliva and perspiration, a dead giveaway about Kate's failure as a mother.

"Too warm!"

"The child is sweating."

"She'll get a cold, sure."

Clucks of pity, disapproval, wonder, whatever the reason, all served their purpose well, adding weight to Kate's utter sense of failure. She should have known better.

They all watched with approval as Mamie grasped the baby's left arm and right leg, bringing them together with a quick solid thump, producing howls of pain and fright. She did the same to the opposite arm and leg, then laid the child on the bare planks of Mary's kitchen table. She began to massage the tiny rib cage and underarms, as the baby's cries increased yet again.

Kate stepped forward anxiously, but Mary Hershberger caught her arm. "Let Mamie alone. She knows what she's doing."

Mamie's fat fingers kept moving up and down, while Hester arched her back and screamed. Just when Kate thought she would go mad, Mamie tugged the blankets, set the baby's arms by her side and wrapped her as tightly as possible, handed her to Kate and told her to "Burp her good."

Hester was limp as a rag doll, her face pale and exhausted, soft rhythmic burps coming up quite regularly. Kate's heart swelled within her as she held Hester close, thinking she might die of a broken heart if she let her loose, even a bit. Poor, poor baby. Precious child.

What a talking, then! These housewives may have been in Pennsylvania, but they spoke German endlessly the minute they were finally in the company of other women who knew the language, hungering to hear and to be heard.

"It was the cart ride. If you take a baby out before six weeks, they get an awful ache. The muscles are growing, and they ache. It's very painful. When I rub along her sides, it loosens them, and the burps can come up. Then the pain goes away," Mamie said, watching Kate's face intently. Kate only nodded, too close to tears to answer.

Barbara Fisher leaned her head to one side and said she'd never seen a prettier little one. That was met with a smile of approval from Mamie, and a bitter, awkward look from Hans's mother, followed by, "She's an Indian."

The women drew in their breaths, stiffened their shoulders, and crossed their arms as Rebecca's uncontested disapproval settled around them, poisoning the atmosphere with her taut words dripping toxins. Mamie gave Rebecca a level took, then said good-naturedly,

"Well, Kate couldn't leave her by the spring to die. That would be murder, wouldn't it?" Murmurs of assent rippled through the kitchen, leaving Rebecca isolated, but only for a moment.

"What do our English neighbors say? 'The only good Indian is a dead one.'"

The women gasped in disbelief and raised their fingers to their mouths. What boldness!

Mamie went right home and told her husband, Obadiah, what Rebecca said right there in the kitchen on a Sabbath morning. Obadiah told John Lantz, the bishop, and he said the statement bordered on hate, and that woman would have to be stopped.

Mamie took a secret glee in seeing Rebecca having to confess her sins in church two weeks later, that spiteful woman, talking like that about her own daughter-in-law, and the Amish being a loving, nonresistant people, at that. It was surely the end times, when a woman spoke such words. The Lord would not tarry very long anymore.

Church services were held in the barn, with straw scattered along the floor, the wooden benches set on top. Pigeons cooed from the rough-hewn rafters that were held together with wooden pegs, and shafts of dusty sunlight shimmered between the slats of a window set up under the eaves.

The horses stomped their feet and rattled their chains, while the slow-moving sound of the German songs rose and fell, as the congregation sang from the *Ausbund*, thick, little songbooks, each book shared by two members throughout the barn. The hymns had been written by Anabaptist prisoners, foreparents of the Amish held captive at Passau on the Danube River in Germany.

Kate sat on a bench alone, her baby settled in the house between two rolled up blankets on Amos and Mary Hershberger's bed. She'd go check on her, if need be, but now, she wanted to remain seated, her voice chiming in with many others, her heart swelling with praise to God, for Hans, for Hester, for her life here in America, for the freedom to worship God the way they chose.

And now she had Hester, a baby of her very own, and her battle to fight the good fight of faith was over. Likely she never would conceive, but that was God's will. It was all right. She had her beloved daughter. And Hans loved her every bit as much as she did.

When John Lantz rose to preach, she was reminded of the ancient patriarchs, Abraham, Moses, all of them. John was tall and wide, with bushy white hair springing into riotous curls, his beard circling his face, a bib of the same curling white hair, wagging up and down as he spoke.

His eyebrows were still dark gray, giving him an austere demeanor, as if the lowering of those bushy brows could decide your fate, godlike. His voice was low, well modulated in the beginning, but as he continued speaking, it rose to an emotional crescendo, instilling into the congregation the need to repent of their sins, that the day of the Lord was fast drawing nigh.

Kate sat, worrying her lower lip with her fingers, thinking how very much she hoped Hester could grow into a healthy little girl yet, before the Lord would return in the clouds with hundreds of thousands of his angels.

She wanted to sew her bright dresses and soft white nightgowns and braid her jet-black hair. She wanted to laugh with her and hear her speak and teach her the ways of the farm and the surrounding forest. But was that carnal thinking? Her own worldly views? She wished she had her mother or her sisters to confide in, but she didn't. They had all remained in Switzerland the day John Zug and his parents boarded the *Charming Nancy* and made the perilous journey across the heaving waters of the Atlantic.

She would write to them of her precious child, and she would receive a letter from her mother months later. She would be in favor of the Indian child, this beautiful baby who would grow with the Lenape nature of wisdom and *faschtendich* (common sense) ways.

Kate had no fear of the Native Americans. She often felt pity for them, without speaking of it to Hans. Deep in her soul, she found the arrogance of the Amish settlers disturbing. They were here first, these forest dwellers, their minds a wellspring of knowledge about so many things, especially the ways of survival. When winter and its bitter allies—wind, snow, and cold—threatened their existence, they survived in wigwams covered with bark, and they survived well. Their knowledge was beyond measure. They valued the land, worshiping the Great Spirit. Who was to say they were heathen? Kate didn't believe they were. The marauding, the murders, and massacres were the only way they knew to protect and keep the land they felt was rightfully their own.

When she felt a tap on her shoulder, she looked up into her young friend Anna Troyer's smiling face. "Your baby is awake," she whispered, then sat down smoothly, a smirk of accomplishment on her face. She had been the one to tell Hans *sei* (Hans's wife), Kate, that the little Indian baby was awake.

Quickly, Kate left the barn, hurried around the side of it, down the grassy slope to the house, where she found Hester cooing and smiling in Enos Buehler's wife, Salome's, arms. "What a pretty child! It takes my breath away," she said, lifting her face to smile sweetly at Kate.

"She is, isn't she? We're guessing she's Lenape."

"Oh, I would say so. She looks like them. Her rounded, high cheekbones, the wide, flat eyes. You are surely blessed."

Eagerly, Kate searched Salome's eyes, for truth, for honesty.

"Do you . . . Are you one of those . . . Do you think it's all right that we have her?" she stammered, uneasily.

"Why, of course. Kate, you couldn't let the dear child perish. Don't you think an Indian girl that was in trouble likely hid the baby for you to find? Who knows? They might be harsh in their punishment of loose girls, so, of course, what else could you do? Surely you believe she's a gift of God."

"We do. We do," Kate said, nodding her head. "But . . ."

"What?" Salome asked.

"My mother-in-law."

"I heard."

Salome clucked her tongue, shook her head, said she wished her much *gaduld* (patience). Kate nodded, but her lower lip was caught in her teeth, her eyes bright with unshed tears.

"Did you sew the dress?"

"Oh yes. It was a work of love. Every stitch was a joy. You can't imagine how it really is, after nine years."

Salome laid a kind hand on Kate's shoulder, gave it a squeeze, and went back to the service, leaving her alone with Hester. She marveled again at her perfect features, the little rosebud mouth, which opened into a smile that melted her heart every time.

Now she would have to grapple with the suspicion of men, or women, and what they thought of her. Of them. Of her and Hans and their decision to keep this little lost Indian baby and raise her in the Amish church. Mostly, they'd been supportive, but still. She'd have to wander among her people with the feelers of a cockroach, waving ahead, searching, checking attitudes, always fearful of a slam, a put-down, a glance of disapproval. Or would she?

Perhaps all she needed to do was hold her head high and be assured, proud of what they had done. So often that was hard to do, the lessons of humility, lack of pride, fear of authority, so skillfully imbedded in her soul, the teachings of the ministers a much-needed discipline. They were necessary, she knew. It was why the Amish stayed free of the worldly ways of excess and pride.

Just sometimes, she wanted to be free of the cross that was hers to bear, the fence that proved to be a two-edged sword. Safety and security, love, a feeling of community; on the other side, the indecision, fear of doing wrong, lack of backbone. Were these ways a safety or a handicap?

At home in front of a crackling fire, Hans lay on the bearskin rug and pulled her down beside him. He apologized for his impatience when Hester cried on the way to church. He stroked her face with his rough hands. He bent to place his lips tenderly on hers and told her he loved her with all his heart.

She returned his love, and far into the night they talked of her fears, her doubts, of Hester being Native American, of his mother's disapproval. She told him of her lack of resolve, withering under his mother's stern words.

He explained to her, then, about his mother. She had not been like other mothers, those of his friends. She was harsh. She punished him with a branch from a willow tree that sang through the air before it sliced into the tender flesh of his bare legs.

He rolled onto his back, his hands crossed on his chest. As he spoke, his voice quivered with the intensity of memories that he had not been able to successfully bury. They were pushed back, perhaps, but still alive, as he spoke of the iron hand his mother wielded over him, and still did.

Kate nodded, loving her husband with a new understanding. This, then, was why he loved Hester with such limitless feelings. He wanted a much better life for Hester than he had had, growing up beneath the stern rebuke of a woman who wasted no time in vaingglorying her children.

When the baby woke to be fed, they bent their heads together, a beautiful silhouette. In the background, a warm, crackling fire, the picture of perfection, a small family whose foundation was communication, love, and trust.

Hester wasted no time. She drank her milk, burped, and returned to the deep sleep of an infant. Her day had been strenuous, traveling to church with her parents for the first time. Kate tucked her in, kissed her cheek, and said a little German children's prayer, asking God to watch over her precious baby daughter.

They slept in front of the fire that night, and long after Hans was asleep, Kate lay on her stomach, staring into the red coals on the hearth. She relived each step of her day at the spring, the mewling cries, the feeling of being watched.

She prayed that God would watch over them, keep them safe from harm, and let the Indians know Hester was safe, all right, and in good care.

She thought of her mother, and the need to speak to her rose so strongly in her breast, she felt as if she would suffocate. "Mam. Oh, my Mam," she whispered, but no one answered. Only the cry of a screech owl reverberated through the surrounding trees, followed by the shrill, undulating reply of his mate.

Instinctively, she reached across Hans's back, wrapped her arms around his strong body, and felt exhaustion enter her mind. Secure in the sturdy log home, she soon fell asleep. A mouse emerged from the hearthstone and delicately lapped up the spilled cow's milk before scurrying back into its nest.

CHAPTER 3

KATE WAS PUZZLED WHEN A SUMMER VIRUS PERSISTED. She'd drunk the salted water from the oats she boiled, the way her mother told her. Unable to keep that down, she'd rolled onto her bed in the middle of the day, wave after wave of nausea sending the room spiraling counter-clockwise as she retched into the stoneware chamber pot by her bedside.

Today, she was looking for wild ginger. Hannah Fisher had told her there was nothing better for summer virus than ginger root steeped in boiling water. She combed the north side of the ridge with Hester in a sling on her back, her black hair visible above it, her bright black eyes following every moving object around her.

When Kate was outside, Hester was always quiet, completely immersed in her surroundings, leaving Kate free to go about hoeing the garden, pulling weeds around the cabin, or whatever she chose to do.

It was hot, much too hot to be walking all across the side of the ridge with a baby on her back. Her head pounded, and dizziness set in. She had the evening meal to think about and all the white laundry to retrieve from the fence, fold, and put away.

The heavy summer leaves stirred lazily above her as she sank to her haunches, squatting to take up a corner of her apron and mop her flowing forehead. Her eyes scanned the forest floor. Mayapples, way past their prime, a few mountain laurels, some dandelion, a few ginseng plants, poison oak, but no ginger plant.

She'd go back. Surely, tomorrow the nausea would abate. This was only the summer stomach woes, the way she'd often experienced. She had probably eaten too many onions with the fried rabbit on Sunday evening when Manasses and Lydia had paid them a visit.

The minute she stepped inside the door of the small log house, she knew she had been sloppy and left milk to sour somewhere. She sincerely hoped there were no blowflies on it. Sniffing, the nausea threatening to gag her, she lifted lids, checked the cupboard for spoiling food, but found none. What smelled so sour?

She sniffed Hester's cradle, lifted the little blanket and pillow and buried her nose in them. But she could not trace the sourness that hung over the interior of her house.

Shrugging her shoulders, she slid her baby off, sniffed her lower dress, then patted her and kissed the top of her head before placing her in the cradle. Immediately, Hester set up a howl of protest, which Kate had learned to ignore, and she soon quieted.

Taking up the poker, she stirred the coals on the hearth, poured water into the iron kettle on its swinging arm, and turned it above the hot coals. She'd boil some beans, adding a bit of salt pork. It was too hot to make a full meal. Hans appreciated cold soup, so she placed raspberries in a crockery bowl, added a dollop of molasses, broke some stale, coarse, brown bread over it, and pushed the bowl to the back of the dry sink. When the beans were finished, she'd add milk to the cold soup, and that would be his supper.

The smell of the molasses brought a fresh wave of nausea, which she stifled by holding her breath. She sank to the wooden settee by the fireplace, surveyed the line of white undergarments and sheets on the fence, and sagged wearily against the wall. She wondered if Hans would offer to bring in the washing.

Surveying the interior of the house, she noticed a few tired-looking cobwebs hanging limply from the ceiling, ashes scattered across the hearth, grease stains on her normally immaculate floors. Perhaps she would die. It had been two weeks, and if anything, the nausea was worse. The house needed a good cleaning, and she had absolutely no energy. It was frightening, suddenly.

There was that sour smell again. Getting up, she began her frantic sniffing, coming up empty-handed, hot, and frustrated. It had to be the hottest summer she could remember.

The beans bubbled in the pot, and she went to the barrel to slice off a bit of salted pork. When she lifted the lid, saliva rushed into her mouth, followed by a hot wetness in the back of her throat. She made a mad, headlong dash for the front door, where Hans found her straining and retching a while later. He put his arm about her waist, led her into the bedroom, and laid her gently on the crackling straw mattress. He said he'd go for the doctor, tonight yet.

No, no, Kate shook her head, desperately not wanting him to spend precious dollars on an unnecessary doctor visit. She assured him she would be fine after she found ginger root and they made tea with it.

Hans lifted Hester from her cradle, cooed and crooned to her, then slid the soft, white undershirt from her shoulders, saying it was too warm to wear anything in this heat. Such a small baby shouldn't be so uncomfortable.

Hester loved her new freedom, kicking and chortling, blowing little spit bubbles and laughing, while Hans stood and gazed down at her perfect little body, the skin a golden-brown hue. He had tears in his eyes when he told Hester that God had been too good to them. They did not deserve this perfectly beautiful child to have for their own.

Tears formed in Kate's own eyes, her overwhelming love for him filling her with an almost spiritual emotion. Hans was everything she ever wanted in a husband and father of her children.

It was her friend Lydia Speicher who finally drummed it through Kate's thick skull. They laughed about the episode for years to come. Kate had gone on her desperate quest for ginger root once more, after a few days of lolling about in the heat, sick, tired, and completely at odds with both Hans and Hester.

Finally, late one afternoon, when it was so hot the whole atmosphere seemed to sizzle, she stumbled on one lone plant. She dug it up as feverishly as a half-crazed man panning for gold nuggets, carried it home, and soon had a cup of the life-saving, fragrant tea.

She took a deep sniff of its fragrance, anticipation stamped on her face, illuminated by the glad light that normally played across her face. But her deep intake of breath turned into a surprised look of disbelief. Before she could swallow, she dashed to the front door and relieved herself of anything she had managed to keep in her stomach.

She would have allowed Hans to bring the doctor, had it not been for Manasses and Lydia's visit. They lived about seven or eight miles to the east along Irish Creek. They had two children, both boys with curly brown hair and wide-set brown eyes, named Homer and Levi.

Lydia was short and thin, with freckles splattered across her nose, as if God had had an afterthought and sprinkled her face with extra decoration, like a fancy cake. Her hair was mousy brown, her eyes the same color, and her nose was flat and wide. To hold more freckles, she told Kate, wryly.

Manasses was called Manny, for short, and he was of average height, with sun-tanned skin, a shock of brown hair, and eyes that were not really a color, just not white like the area around the irises. He couldn't grow a decent, manly beard, only a tuft of hair on his chin and a few discolored straggles along the side of his face, which was the source of endless ribbing from Hans.

When they drove their wagon down to the log barn, Hans jumped up eagerly, but Kate dragged herself to the dry sink to begin washing dishes in cold water, fast, before Lydia saw the dried food on them.

It was all she could do to keep from crying when Lydia walked through the door, but she wiped her hands on her apron, shook hands, and said she was glad to see them.

Lydia peered into her face in the fading light of evening and said Kate looked like something the cat had dragged in. In spite of herself, Kate laughed in short, helpless bursts, then told her she'd been sick for many weeks with an upset stomach. She guessed she'd eaten too many onions.

Lydia said nothing, just found the straw broom in the corner and began a thorough sweeping of the hearth. She scrubbed the planks of the tabletop, still saying very little.

Lydia always talked, always, so Kate asked her a bit timidly if she'd done anything to offend her.

"Not other than being dumb."

"What are you talking about?"

"Katie, you're . . ."

Her voice trailed off, as color suffused her face. She blinked, and more color deepened the blush on her cheeks. She stammered. She looked out the window and sighed.

Finally, Kate asked her if she had a serious disease. Was she going to die?

With a tortured expression, Lydia whispered, very soft and low, "You're in the family way."

Kate sat back in her chair as if she had received a blow. She blushed as red as the wild strawberries that grew along the bank by the barn. "I can't be," she whispered back.

But she was. Hans received Kate's stammered whispers with whoops and uninhibited yells. They had waited almost ten years for this, and now they would have two. Hester would be a bit over a year old when their baby arrived.

Hans helped her with the garden. He helped her pick the peas and beans and then helped to shell them. He planted carrots and beets, more pumpkins and late onions.

Slowly, the nausea subsided, her energy returned, and she tackled her chores with renewed energy.

They dug the carrots, turnips and beets, carefully placing them in the root cellar behind the house. She helped him make hay, hoe corn, and haul manure.

Hester, barely five months old, sat up by herself now, and Hans made a small wooden box for her. They placed her in one corner and adjusted a feather pillow around her. Everywhere they went, Hester bounced along, her brilliant black eyes shining below the thatch of blue-black hair.

When the hot sun shone down unmercifully, Hester never whined or whimpered. She sat bolt upright and viewed her world with eyes that missed nothing. Sometimes it seemed as if her skin absorbed every sight and sound and smell, keeping her fulfilled, occupied simply by watching the horses and birds, or smelling the outdoor scents of honeysuckle, ripe manure, and the sun-kissed earth. She loved to sit in the corn rows, playing with the dirt, sifting it through her little brown fingers.

Kate had watched when she'd taken her first mouthful. An angry expression crossed her face, and she let it all dribble back out. What stuck to her tongue, she swallowed dutifully, and she never tried eating it again.

Hans said she was a sensible child. Later in life, he predicted, she would be gifted with many talents, with the amount of things that kept her interested now. Kate agreed, secretly proud of her beautiful daughter. Then Hans brought another small swatch of homespun fabric home, this time a shade of rose, almost identical to the color of the curtains he'd torn down. She swallowed her anger like a bad tincture of herbs, smiled, and said she was pleased.

Dutifully, she produced another fine Sunday dress, placed the little white linen apron over it, and was glad. She asked Hans, though, why he never bought enough fabric so she could have a new shortgown and skirt.

When he became very upset, blaming her for being someone *behoft* (possessed) with lust of the eyes, she let the matter drop and never brought it up again. She did, however, keep a very small sliver of the fabric and tucked it into the letter she wrote to her mother, asking her if she knew where to purchase something of this shade that was less expensive.

The underarms of her only Sunday shortgown were wearing through, so she patched them, using tiny stitches so no one could tell. It was not unusual to wear the same dress to church for many years. But she felt as if everyone was whispering behind her back about wasting money on the plumage she put on that daughter of hers. Perhaps she was ashamed of Hans's adoration of Hester. Whatever it was, she wasn't comfortable carrying her brilliantly dressed daughter into church, knowing her own frock was in a lamentable state.

But it was a small thing. She decided not to fret or worry about something so insignificant. It was actually nothing.

In the early summer, they whitewashed the interior of the house. Hans mixed lime with water, and they brushed it over the logs and crumbling mortar, bringing a new cleanliness to the walls and a new white light over everything.

Kate's energy was renewed, and she cleaned the furniture with linseed oil, washing all the insides of the drawers, scouring the plank floors with hard lye soap, and loving her house.

She realized how happy it made her to be surrounded by the things she cherished. The woven coverlet on the wooden settee by the fireplace was a nine patch, washed many times, its colors fading to a sort of nondescript sameness, so she set about making another.

She lifted the brown homespun bag from the small attic she could reach by the sturdy ladder against the wall, heaving it over her shoulders as she stood on the top step, her memory serving her well. Every scrap of worn-out clothing went into this bag. She would sew the small pieces together to form a bed covering or a child's coverlet.

She would make a fine coverlet, a small one, to soften her seat on the bent hickory chair she always sat on to rock her baby to sleep. The interior of her house was so white, so clean and new, she would make a colorful coverlet like a bouquet of flowers she'd picked by the spring. Her mind darted rapidly from one pattern to another as she strained to remember the design she'd seen at Amos Hershberger's. It was multi-colored strips.

Could she cut and arrange a variety of strips into a pleasing whole? It seemed a bit daunting, especially now, with all the garden work. She'd have to do it when she found a few minutes now and then, probably mostly in the evening by candlelight. The gardening could not wait the way the bits of colored scraps of material would.

She cut some of the patches that morning though, guilt hampering the sure slices of the scissors, as she cut around the rectangular template made of wood. The blue fabric represented the joy Hester had brought into their lives. Yellow was the sunshine of summer, the warmth that drew the healthy plants up from the earth, fruits ripening, ears of corn maturing, beans hanging in heavy pods from the lush vines twined around the shaggy bark poles set in straight tripods along the rows. There was gratitude in the yellow, too, gratitude for God's sunshine, its warmth and nourishment.

Green was the forest, the mainstay of every settler's existence. The trees, the leaves, the abundant herbs and berries, the wild animals that provided them with food and clothing. The pine trees and mighty oaks provided shelter for all the creatures and enveloped the small log house with their bountiful green embrace, a protection sprung from the earth itself.

Kate frowned at the lack of red. Well, she'd take care of that later. Red signified the red bird's wing, wild raspberry bushes, the holly, and all dots of brilliant, glossy red. She'd dye some of the pale swatches of fabric with pokeberry juice whenever she had time.

The nausea had all but disappeared now, leaving her with an enormous appetite. Everything she had not been able to eat before, she ate now in large quantities. Great piles of beans, sizable slabs of fried meat and eggs, all

disappeared from her heavy redware plate, followed by
sips of creamy buttermilk or milk laced with molasses.

Hans watched his wife's head bent over her plate,
shoveling food into her mouth with quiet efficiency, a
sudden urgency to fill the great grasping stomach that
seemed to be constantly empty. She developed a bit of a
double chin, and her neck and shoulders became rounded, fuller, along with the rest of her.

But she kept the garden weeded, helped in the fields,
and whitewashed the small log house, cleaning it until it
shone. He had no complaints. If his wife put on a pound
here and there, it was no big concern of his. She was a
good woman.

Soon the attic would fill up with the harvest, onions
heavy and white, braided together by their tops in a long
string, mounds of orange pumpkins, turnips, and squash
laid out on the floor for the winter's use. Kate grunted
a bit as she bent over to pick the yield, Hans opposite
her in another row, and his good-natured teasing made
her laugh.

Hester was crawling fast now, so quick that Kate
could hardly keep up with her, grabbing at the little dress
as she came close to baskets of beans, pulling her back
from the edge of the chair she always loved to sit on.

Kate's whole world turned into constant color and
motion: Hester's bright black eyes, her brown skin, the
orange of the pumpkin against the changing leaves of the
forest, all red and yellow and green. The whitewashed
log walls inside the house brought out the rich, brown
hues of the wooden furniture. Kate mixed strong apple
cider vinegar with a bit of beef tallow and polished all of

it with a bit of soft cloth, rubbing it into the wood grain to produce a luxurious sheen.

In the evening, when the light of the betty lamp shone in the windows, the fire leaping and dancing on the hearth, and Hester sound asleep in her cradle, they sat talking, making plans. Kate's needle wove in and out of her patches, and Hans's voice rose and fell. They were truly content. God had blessed them far beyond measure, allowing them to become parents again, even after the gift of little Hester. They felt unworthy of God's goodness.

Hans worked on a new springhouse, set by the flow of the cold waters that bubbled out of the ground at the base of the ridge, fed by the runoff from the surrounding mountains. Kate was thrilled to think of having a cool place to set her eggs, milk, and cheese.

She watched Hans lift the heavy limestones, his massive shoulders straining at the seams of his shirt, the constant way his hands lifted and cut, fitting the stones tightly, building this sturdy little house that would help keep food cool in summer. The well-placed structure would greatly ease Kate's burden of cooking and preserving.

Manny Speicher came to help when the stone walls became taller than Hans. Together they formed a scaffolding of stumps and planks and lifted the stones onto it, as Hans kept laying the stones to the eaves.

He made a small window at each end, one to the south and one to the north, and then built a sturdy shake roof over the top. The spring flowed through small openings on each end, keeping the stone interior cool and moist.

Hans built a trough made of stone and mortar so that the running water would not upset the heavy crocks filled with milk. They marveled at the occasional buttermilk they could have, no matter how warm the days would become.

Kate's springhouse was the envy of the whole community. More than one housewife was guilty of serving her husband soured milk with his breakfast porridge, raising her eyebrows in practiced meekness, saying sweetly that a springhouse built the way Hans Zug had done would take care of any milk spoilage. They came by the wagonload to view this wonderful springhouse. Kate beamed with pleasure, her full cheeks blooming with color, her blue eyes radiant upon her husband.

Hester sat on Hans's knee, her bright eyes missing nothing, always alert but seldom smiling, although her black eyes twinkled, enhanced by her thatch of straight black hair.

When the November winds swooped down off the ridge and blew the tired, brown leaves to the ground, the beautiful red, yellow, and orange ones came along with them. Hester sat outside, her nose red from the cold, and played in the leaves, crawling among them, sometimes holding so still she was like a stone child. She watched a curious chipmunk scamper close then sit as still as Hester as they eyed each other, neither one showing any fear.

Kate wondered at this. Were Indians trained in the way of the forest, or did these traits flow in their bloodlines, as much a part of them as the color of their skin or the growth of their thick, black hair? Kate had never realized a baby could be so perceptive, so curious, black eyes missing nothing, constantly darting here and there, the unsmiling little mouth beneath them expressionless.

Yes, she was an Indian, and an Indian she would likely remain. That was all right with Hans and Kate. They would take her to church and raise her within the religious tradition they knew would shape her and bring her to God, the Amish way of life instilled in her heart.

Yes, they would dress her modestly and simply, in clothing like that worn by grown women. She would be baptized upon her faith, and all would be well in the end. They were devout, believing that through the blood of Jesus Christ they were redeemed from their sins. They practiced a godly lifestyle and prayed for their sweet baby girl every day.

And now she would have a sister or brother very soon. Kate's heart was alight with anticipation. Hans made a trundle bed, a low, small bed that could be shoved beneath their large bedstead during the day, made of the same sturdy pine boards.

So the cradle stood, awaiting the next little occupant, empty and quiet, the rocking stilled for now.

CHAPTER 4

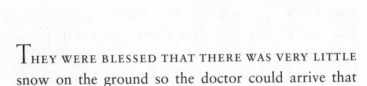

THEY WERE BLESSED THAT THERE WAS VERY LITTLE snow on the ground so the doctor could arrive that February.

Hans drove Dot like a madman. The doctor clutched his hat and prayed out loud, his prayers peppered with exclamations of surprise and astonishment that they came out of that gully or over that rock in one piece.

Hans's face was as white as the few inches of snow that dusted the road and surrounding woodland. His eyes bugged from his face in genuine panic, and he leaned forward until his nose almost touched the walloping haunches lunging ahead of him, as if that position would get him back to the house sooner.

Dot was wild-eyed, lathered with white sweat, her sides heaving, when the wagon careened to a stop by the barn. The doctor sat still as Hans launched himself from the wagon, instantly loosening the traces, his hands shaking.

Tugging at his hat brim, the doctor told Hans very courteously that he was, indeed, extremely fortunate to be among the living, let alone steady enough to attend to his wife, and he hoped he would never again have to sit in the same wagon Hans did.

Hans paid him no mind, just waved a hand as if to rid himself of a fly, and asked if he intended to sit in that wagon the remainder of the evening.

Elizabeth Hershberger was already there, the neighborhood matriarch who attended mothers at a time like this. Everyone called her Lissie, a tall, round woman of roughly seventy years, well trained in midwifery, although she usually worked with a doctor, if possible.

Lissie was a widow, Dan having been knocked over by the tree he had felled, miscalculating its crash to the ground. They found him pinned underneath, his skull crushed. Lissie buried her man, took up the reins of the fat brown mules, and kept the farm going with the aid of her two sons.

Lissie was not one to be soft-spoken or humble. Her voice rang out with a deep, bell-like sound. Unlike many Amish women, she knew her own mind and spoke it without fear of being corrected.

"What took you so long?" she asked, as her way of greeting. The doctor was not overly fond of Lissie, having been scolded many times by her tongue-lashings. His nerves were already shot, and he was in no mood to tangle with her self-appointed position as head coach.

"Look, Lissie, if we would have been here before this, we wouldn't be here at all. So keep your nose out of it."

Hester began to cry, this loud exchange from strange people frightening her. Hans scooped her up, kissed her on her soft face, and held her the remainder of the evening until her head drooped against his chest. Then he changed her into the heavy nightgown she wore on winter nights and tucked her into the trundle bed, setting it carefully into the shadows.

Lissie made tea, strong and black. She spread cold biscuits with apple butter and swung the kettle of beans over the fire until the house was filled with the aroma of browning beans.

Dr. Thomas Hess was a gentleman with refined ways. He had graduated from a college of medicine in England, so he did not take kindly to Lissie's slurps and rumbles of appreciation as she tucked into the food.

He watched her large fingers grasp the heavy handle of a cup, lift it to her lips, gulp, and then grimace, her eyes squeezed shut in endurance as she swallowed the hot drink. She dipped her biscuit into the bowl of steaming beans, then opened her mouth wide to shove half the bean-laden biscuit into it, leaving a trail of apple butter on her greasy dress front.

"Now, then, Dr. Hess, why aren't you eating? It's *wunderbar goot*" (wonderful good), she chirped, her small black eyes dancing with pleasure.

Dr. Hess thought of his wife lifting a china teapot to pour tea into a china cup for him, but he didn't mention that. He just said politely that he would have a cup of tea, which was plunked in front of him with more enthusiasm than good manners.

For the second time that evening, Dr. Hess thought he might not live, swallowing the boiling hot tea from the scalding cup. When the pain on his tongue became unbearable, he went outside, scooped up a handful of snow and considered it a great and calming luxury to bury his stinging appendage into it. Lissie chortled to herself at the doctor's discomfiture. The smarter a man was, the less common sense he had. So much for college, if he didn't think a redware cup was hot.

Kate delivered a fine son. Dr. Hess pronounced him "strapping," already able to plow the fields. He was pleased to say that with feeling as Lissie whisked the baby away for his bath.

The doctor puzzled over Hans Zug's expression, or the lack of it, for a long time. Finally, he shrugged his shoulders and let it go. Clearly, something was wrong.

Hans looked at the pale face of his son, the too wide forehead, the swollen eyes, the pouting red mouth, and searched desperately for any inkling that someday he would have hair. There was none. Only a whisper of pale, red down, or was that his imagination? To think that his own flesh and blood, his offspring, would look like this shook him to the core of his being. He always imagined his sons would be handsome. He asked Lissie if there was something wrong with him.

"What do you mean, Hans Zug? Why, of course not. He's the finest, sturdiest baby I've seen in a coon's age. You better not mention one word of this to your wife, or I'll clout you with a wooden spoon. Shame on you."

And Hans was ashamed. He cringed, turned red with embarrassment, and gave Lissie a whole ham instead of giving the doctor the other half, to get back into her good graces. He sincerely hoped she wouldn't speak of this to anyone.

After his son's bath, the baby looked clean, but not much better. Hans watched with a sort of mistrust as Kate held their son, her face shining with a mother's love, cooing and whispering to the baby, saying he was so beautiful. *"So an shay kind"* (Such a beautiful child).

Hans tried to smile and share her joy as he bent over his wife. But his smile was thin and wobbly, his eyes dull with disbelief.

"What do you want to name him?" she asked, her voice soft, her eyes luminous in her wan face.

All Hans could think of was Ham. Wasn't he one of Noah's sons in the Old Testament? He looked like someone who could be named Ham. What he did say was, "It's up to you, Kate."

"Oh, but a father should name his child. Especially his first son. Remember, I named Hester." Kate's voice was soft and quivering with emotion.

Hans couldn't think of anything except Ham, but he didn't say it. Noah was Ham's father, and a man of God with that ark building and all, so he said, "I like the name Noah." He hoped his voice came out reverent and loving, without a trace of Ham in it. He sighed with gratitude when Kate smiled up at him, her eyes full of love, and said that was a good name, a sound and reasonable name from the Bible.

Lissie was pleased with their choice, although she told them they should have named their son after Hans's father, Isaac. But Hans didn't want Lissie to know he wasn't overly fond of his father, who had let his youngest brother Shem have the farm back home in Switzerland.

He looked Lissie square in the eye and said his name was Noah. She shrugged her shoulders and thought she was glad Hans wasn't her husband, with those bugging eyes and pushy demeanor. "You need to name one son after your father, you know that," she said, tartly, packing her things in her square, black bag.

Hans was tired, sleepy, and disagreeable, so he merely asked her why. She said it was the *ordnung* (law) of the church. Hans said he never heard of such a thing, whereupon Lissie lifted her finger and shook it at him, and told him if he wanted to know he could ask John Lantz, the bishop. It was only common sense and good manners, and it brought a blessing to a family to name a son after the father.

Andy Fisher's Ruth was their *maud* (hired helper), arriving before breakfast, a small, narrow-faced girl with brilliant green eyes and a small sliver of red hair showing around her cap. Kate would stay in bed for ten days and be waited on for everything she needed. Ruth was capable, and the household was run smoothly, much to Hans's delight.

He felt sorry for Hester, the poor, dear child, not able to understand any of this, Kate in bed with the new baby that she was so jealous of. She held out her arms and wailed for her mother, but Kate was not allowed to hold her because it would take too much strength.

So Hans spent a lot of time with Hester. He taught her to take her first steps, watching her face as she concentrated on keeping her balance. Her black eyes lit up with the challenge as she wobbled toward her father, giggling gleefully as he swooped her against his chest in a loving embrace when she succeeded in taking a few steps alone.

From her bed, Kate's eyes shone, watching Hans with their daughter. Yes, he was a wonderful father, so good with her, the dear man.

As she fed their son, she held him close, running the palms of her hands across the small, bald head and marveling at his beauty. He was so different from Hester. Of course he was. He was white, and would likely be blond when his hair came in, but he had Kate's blue eyes and a strong nose. This baby was already sturdy and well rounded, his hands and feet large. She envisioned him walking behind the plow, his hands clenched on the wooden handles, his bare feet coming down solidly, crumbling the earth. These hands would wield an axe, fell mighty trees, clear land of his own, continue the way and heritage of the Amish.

Ruth was so good with Hester, entertaining her with stories, twining string around her fingers, and playing "Hide the Thimble," so that Kate's recovery was a time of contentment and bliss.

During the second week, when she got dressed and sat on her rocking chair, resuming light household duties, she was bothered by a niggling doubt. At first she could push it away successfully, but later, as the days marched on, she confessed to herself, it was beginning to be a worry.

Hans's lack of attention to his son loomed above her, a real adversary she had to face. He still had not held him. He very seldom looked at him. Usually the baby was sleeping, but still. Was this normal? He hadn't been this way with Hester. Not at all. He still wasn't. Why wouldn't he hold his son?

Before Kate could control them, thick tears leaked from her closed eyelids, and her chest felt as if it would cave in on her stomach. She simply could not rise above a feeling of deep despair.

Hans found her in the rocking chair, crying. Kate would not say what was wrong, but after Ruth was asleep behind the curtain that was placed at one end of the small house, Kate confided in her husband, haltingly at first, but her voice gained strength as she continued.

Hans was guilty, ashamed, and caught red-handed, possessing terrible thoughts about his newborn son. He begged Kate to forgive him. Kate said of course she would and assured him that Noah would grow hair and his looks would change as he became older. She slept dreamlessly that night, so glad the little talk had changed her worst fear about Hans as a harsh and uncaring father.

The following day, Hans held his son for the first time, and Kate's heart overflowed with joy. He looked down on Noah's sleeping face, smiled, and said, yes, he would be a strong and husky boy some day. Then he didn't pick him up or acknowledge his presence for three days. Kate finally decided to let it go. Perhaps this was more usual behavior than she was aware of.

When company began to arrive on Sunday, Hans hardly let go of Hester. She was always ill at ease around strangers, but when the house became full of visitors, she clung to Hans, her black eyes darting from one face to another, as if surveying the room for her own safety.

Many of the visitors commented on Hans's devotion to Hester and thought it was truly a sign of a caring heart, the way she wasn't even his own child. Kate smiled and nodded, glad Hans loved the little Indian child. When she confided in Lydia about Hans's lack of affection for little Noah, Lydia pooh-poohed the silly notion and said lots of fathers didn't pay much attention to newborn babies.

"They don't know how to hold them. They feel awkward and think they look stupid. They can't feed them, so they act as if they don't even know a baby is in the house. It's normal." She held a finger to her lips, held her head sideways. "I'm sort of surprised, though. He's so good with Hester. I mean, look at him, she never leaves his lap."

Kate nodded and met Lydia's eyes, but neither woman said more about it.

Spring came late and slowly that year. Some of the mountain laurel didn't bloom till June, and many buds froze, so that the pink flowers seemed to be scattered randomly across the bushes, as if they had been forgotten but tacked on at the last minute.

The wind was harsh and the earth cold as Hans and Kate plowed the garden. Hans ran a harrow across the heavy clumps of soil that had rolled away from the plow.

All around them the woodland was coming to life, buds pushing out of branches, small green leaves unfolding under the sun's caresses, wild daffodils popping out of the moist layer of leaves. The weathered log house stood solidly against the backdrop of trees and hills, a cozy home surrounded by rail fences, the shake roof almost black with age now.

Kate had planted a lovely wild flower on either side of the door, and small pine trees dotted the area around the house. The cows had kept the grass down very well, so it was coming up green and smooth. The slope to the barn contained many dandelions and purple violets.

The new springhouse was more picturesque than ever, now that Hans had built an arbor for the wild grapevines. There were glossy leaves and pink buds where he had trimmed the vines, and Kate was looking forward to making wine in crocks. Her mother had always done that at home in Switzerland.

The barnyard was alive with calves, two new lambs, and a white calf named Ruth. Hester toddled everywhere. It was impossible to keep track of her, she was so quick, darting in and out of buildings or the surrounding forest. Like a mouse, Hans said, a little brown mouse. Kate smiled, then laughed out loud. She really did look like a field mouse.

Kate was so busy she did not notice the nausea when it returned. She just knew she wasn't hungry, and not once did it occur to her that another child might be on its way until she began losing her breakfast in the woods behind the house. Wiser now, she didn't undertake a frantic digging for ginger root. Grin and bear it, she told herself.

She didn't tell Hans, afraid of what he might say. She knew he was busy getting the tobacco in. He had no time for his son, who at almost five months, was grabbing at anything he could catch and stuffing it into his mouth. His hair was still not there, as reluctant to grow as Kate had ever seen anything. Hans always spoke to

Noah when he returned from the fields, hot, tired, and overworked, but he seemed reluctant to pick him up even now. Kate paid close attention, her anxiety decreasing whenever Hans would take him up and hold him for a few minutes before a meal was ready. But always Hester was the one he held, whose plate he filled while talking in silly, childish tones. She shrieked with glee, imitating his voice.

When another son arrived, they named him Isaac. He looked very much like Noah, except for a nice amount of brown hair growing mostly along the top of his head.

Lissie was in attendance once more and told Hans this was very nice, naming his son Isaac the way he should. Hans merely said he was glad she approved and left it at that.

He did, however, have to take her home after the *maud* arrived. He did it with the same speed and lack of caring he'd used when driving Dr. Hess the last time. Lissie careened around on the seat, her full cap sliding around on her head, her hip hurting with each teeth-rattling bump over rocks and ditches. She got down stiffly, faced him, and said if they ever needed her again, she'd bring her own horse and wagon, that if he didn't have more sense than he had just demonstrated about how to drive a horse, why then, she'd just drive herself.

Hans was deeply ashamed. He hadn't wanted her to think that way about him. Old bat. Maybe they wouldn't need her for a while.

With each child, Kate seemed to spread out around the hips until she was quite ample. He felt ashamed of the fact that he didn't want his wife to look fat like Mamie Troyer.

Well, at least this son had hair. That was a huge relief.

Kate was so busy she had to employ every skill she could muster to get all her work done. Hans's mother, Rebecca, was pleased they named their second son Isaac, so she made the trek across the hills and ridges quite often to lend a hand wherever Kate needed her, which gave her a boost. She baked sturdy loaves of satisfyingly chewy bread, which they sliced and ate alongside chunks of pork, cooked with some parsley, and salt.

Rebecca said new things were being discovered, different seeds. How would they like to have watermelon? She had planted some, so hopefully, till the end of summer, they would be eating this succulent fruit.

Isaac was a cranky baby, fussing after each feeding. Mamie Troyer treated him, but he remained fussy. Hans said she needed to stop breastfeeding and put him on cow's milk, but Kate resisted. When Hans stomped out to the barn, slamming the door, she began to cry, but not for long.

She lifted her head and decided Isaac was not fussy because of her nursing. He was cranky because that's just how he was. So she fed him, changed his diaper, and told herself that if he preferred crying, that was up to him. Noah was not walking at thirteen months, so Kate's shoulders and arms became strong, enduring many hours of lifting and holding her heavy sons.

Hester was two years old, a happy child and able to entertain herself endlessly outdoors. She ran just for the joy of running, her thin, brown legs propelling her down the slope to the barn at an alarming rate. She could also

sit quietly for hours, watching butterflies and bumble-
bees or listening to the voices of the many kinds of birds
singing from the treetops.

That summer she imitated the crow, the cardinal,
and the turkeys that gobbled ceaselessly in the evenings
behind the house. She began to talk in garbled German.
She could not quite master the "r" sound, which always
came out as "w."

Hans was completely enamored of his winsome
daughter. Although Kate had her moments of wishing
he would pay as much attention to the boys, she held her
worries inside, bottled up against his anger and denial.
It was easier that way. Submission was necessary as a
wife, and she had been taught well by her mother. So she
let Hans's undivided attention rest on Hester, while she
tried hard to make up for his lack of interest in Noah and
Isaac, devoting her time and attention to them.

Sometimes meals were a disaster, with Isaac screaming and Noah clumsily shoving great amounts of food all
over his face. Hans was always quick to smack his hands,
which resulted in great howls of protest and Noah's large
mouth spilling food all over the table. Hester sat, her
black eyes taking it all in, her mouth giving away no
feelings. When Hans turned to smile at her, she did not
always smile back. Sometimes she would go around to
Noah's chair after the meal was over and wrap her thin
brown arms around him, lay her cheek against his back,
and close her eyes briefly.

One night after the children were in bed, Kate saw
an opening to approach Hans about his lack of fatherly
affection. Hans became contrite, ashamed, yet again.

"Have patience with me, dear Kate. I don't mean to be partial to Hester. I really don't. It's just that I feel so much more for her than I do for my sons. Perhaps I was raised that way. Maybe it's normal. I do like my sons. I do. Kate, Hester is just different. Do you think it's because she was abandoned? A poor foundling?"

His face was so earnest, his eyes clear and searching, that Kate's heart melted within her. She put her arms around her husband and loved him. Of course he was sorry. He was doing the best he could.

Their nest egg grew as Hans carefully placed the dollars from his blacksmithing jobs into the jar. He bought more land and planned to build an addition to their small house before winter.

Kate thanked God for a hardworking husband who provided well for them. She put her worries aside, threw herself into her work as never before, and tried to keep away every unsettling thought that entered her mind.

The women of the community didn't know how she could manage so well with three little ones. Her house was clean. Her picturesque garden produced many fine vegetables. Her bread was light. She churned butter with great skill so that the wooden dasher pounded the milk into gobs of butter. Her arms grew strong and muscular, and her figure expanded with the many pats of good, rich butter she spread on thick chunks of brown bread. And Kate did like her ham.

CHAPTER 5

At Christmas-time, the snow lay deep and heavy, covering the log house with the new addition, burying it up to the windowsills. The snow had come down steadily all night long, and a whole day before that.

Hans stepped out of the house, surveyed the white world, and thought they'd be able to make it to his parents for the *Grishtag Essa* (Christmas dinner), an annual event, long-awaited and looked forward to.

He'd get the bobsled and clean it well with the straw broom. Yes, hitched double, Dot and Daisy could make it. He went to the barn, fed the livestock and polished the harnesses, swept the bobsled, then went to get Kate's opinion.

Her eyes were cloudy with doubt, but at his persistence, she placed bricks in the fireplace and began to dress the children. It would be all right to travel the eight-mile distance as long as the wind did not pick up, and it was too early to tell about that. The snow had just stopped.

Hurriedly, they ate cornmeal mush fried in lard, along with bread and butter. Hans rinsed the dishes while Kate pulled on the warm underclothes she would need to stay comfortable, then dressed in the old linen Sunday short-gown and apron she always wore. She did have a freshly washed linen cap, which looked quite neat, so she tied the strings under her chin, jutting it forward so it fit better.

She dressed Noah in warm undergarments, then placed his linen shirt and vest and knee breeches on him.

Little Isaac still wore a dress, which he would continue to wear until he was two, or close to it. He looked angelic with his bangs cut straight across the forehead and locks of light brown hair hanging below his ears in the traditional "Dutch Boy" haircut.

Noah had some very fine blond hair, but you could still mistake him for being bald from a distance. He was husky, large for his age, and a bit pigeon-toed, but he walked and ran as if he'd been doing it for quite some time.

When everyone was bundled into their outerwear, Kate pulled on her cape, wrapping it around herself, tied a heavy scarf around her head and across her mouth, flung the shawl across her shoulders, and secured it with a straight pin. She put her flat hat on last, pulling the front well past her face.

Hans placed the hot bricks wrapped in cloth at their feet. When they were tucked in below layers of bearskins and coverlets, with the horses hitched to the singletree, they were on their way to *Doddy* (Grandfather) Zug's house.

Kate was unprepared for the winter wind's cruel bite. She bent her head to the spray peppering their faces from low-hanging branches and from the horses' hooves kicking up the powdery snow as well. Chills crept up her spine. She shivered then set her mouth in determination. She would not whine, neither would she complain. It was her wifely duty to abide by the wishes of her husband.

Behind them, Noah was not visible, he was so covered with a heavy layer of robes and skins. Hester, however, had managed to extricate herself from the confines of the heavy covers and sat, her eyes two dark stars of wonderment, peering out over the sides of the bobsled, dodging the spray of snow from the branches, or lifting her face to it, her tongue catching the cold wet particles.

The wind was definitely picking up, and it was only mid-morning. A stab of fear shot through Kate, but she only glanced at Hans, his face resolute beneath the heavy black hat, as he urged the horses forward.

When they arrived at the top of an especially steep incline, Hans pulled back on the reins and said, "Steady, there, Dot. Easy, Daisy."

The bobsled creaked across a few rocks then dipped at a dangerous angle as they started down over them. Kate pushed her feet against the dashboard to stay seated. She clung desperately to little Isaac and prayed to God that he would see them safely through this dangerous trek to her parents'-in-law home.

She was thankful for Hans's skill as a blacksmith, as the horses' haunches backed against the britching, holding the bobsled back, keeping it from careening madly down the rocky incline.

A break in the trees revealed an awesome world of brilliant white, puffs and layers of snow piled on every pine, their jutting, dark green needles accentuating the brilliance of the snow. The sun was obscured by a mass of cold-looking gray and white clouds, and Kate bent her head as a shower of snow blew across her line of vision. There was no doubt in her mind that there would be high winds, and how were they to remain safe? She knew well the roaring of the wind that blew in after a long snowfall, driving great walls of loose, powdery snow ahead of it, creating drifts that could be up to ten feet high.

She swallowed. "Hans," she said, "the wind is picking up."

Hans did not answer. He was occupied with the task of getting his family safely down the treacherous mountain road.

A thin, high wail sounded and increased steadily as Noah was thrown from side to side, sliding under the robes and then out of them.

When Kate could turn, she found Hester on her hands and knees, her black shawl flapping in the strong wind, her voice crooning, comforting her brother. "*Na, na, na, komm,* Noah. *Net heila*" (Don't cry).

Noah heard his sister's voice and calmed down as her mittened hand patted his back. She was not much bigger than he, but she thought of herself as his little mother, taking him under her wing, a two-year-old biddy hen.

Kate's shoulder slammed into Hans's as the wagon swung hard to the right, straightened, and then continued its descent. Steam came from the horses' nostrils in small gray puffs, their exertion showing now in the dark, wet hair around their harnesses.

When they finally found level ground, Kate breathed out as she let the rigid set of her shoulders slump, glad to have navigated that long, steep downhill safely.

The roaring of the wind in the treetops increased now. The snow was only little bits hitting their faces, but as the tree tops lunged and swayed, showers of snow whipped across them, the horses bending their faces along with them, to avoid the stinging.

Hans leaned forward, urging them on, calling loudly. The horses responded by lowering their backs and giving a strong lunge against their heavy collars so that the bobsled whispered through the deep snow.

Whether they hit a rock, or one runner went into a ditch, or one of the horses slipped, Kate could never be sure. She knew only that there was a sharp thud as if the bobsled had slammed against a tree. She heard a resounding crack of wood splitting and felt herself falling sideways, her only thought for Isaac, her sleeping son.

Everything turned into pandemonium after that. Horses whinnied in terror, unable to understand the jutting of the broken singletree that pulled their heavy collars taut to their sweating neck muscles.

Hans cried out as he lost his grip on the leather reins, although he managed to cling to the seat of the bobsled as it turned over on its side. Kate cried out hoarsely once, then remained silent as she lay in the deep fluffy whiteness. Noah screamed and kept on screaming as he was dumped into the snow, his wide, red mouth filled with it. He choked, coughed, and then resumed screaming.

Hester flew off the bobsled, landed in deep snow, sat up, and blinked. She watched Hans leap and flounder through the snow, his face red, his mouth open, screeching and threatening as the bewildered horses thrashed and kicked in their traces. They panicked as they became thoroughly entangled, their eyes rolling.

Hans yelled and yelled. Kate lay in the snow, her shoulder sending out red-hot stabs of pain. She gritted her teeth against it, willing herself to stay conscious as the cold, white, whirling world spun around her. Isaac, wakened by his rude dive into the snow, cried loudly, matching his brother's screams.

Hester blinked again. No sound emerged from her mouth. She lifted herself to her feet, waded through the snow to comfort Noah, and then went to her mother. Bending her head, she touched Kate's face. *"Mam?"*

Kate struggled to sit up. The children needed her. She had to rouse herself. Leaving little Isaac crying in the snow, she managed to push herself onto her side with one hand. Her shoulder was fiery with pain. She was able to move her fingers, as well as bend and turn her elbow, so she figured her arm and hand were all right.

A heavy wall of snow came roaring through the trees, the massive trunks creaking and bending. Kate struggled to see Hans and the fleeing horses then bent her attention to her throbbing shoulder.

She concluded that nothing was broken. She was likely bruised, the joint having taken the brunt of her weight as she fell off the bobsled. She would be all right. Gritting her teeth against the pain, she bent to retrieve poor little Isaac, his teeth chattering with cold and fright. She held him against her body beneath the heavy shawl, hunching her head to the flying snow, then searching the wild, cold, unrelenting winds for her remaining two children. Hester was visible in her little black shawl and hat as she crouched over Noah, who was still crying out in terrified howls.

"Hester!"

Her word was whipped away by the wind. Kate realized in that instant that their situation was dire. She fought down the fear that threatened to take her common sense away and replace it with stupidity, tempting her to try walking through the snow and the drifts that would certainly and rapidly form.

Hans would calm the team. She watched as the broken bobsled lurched, lifted, and then fell over and over, as the kicking, galloping horses drew it steadily away from them. Hans cried out as he plunged clumsily after the frantic animals.

They had to have the horses. Could they possibly get to *Doddy's* house without them?

Kate turned her head to view the long, steep hill they had just traversed, inch by dangerous inch, and now here they were on level ground, but with a useless bobsled.

Thank goodness, Noah stopped screaming, calming under Hester's motherly words. Only the wind, the retreating sounds of the galloping team of horses dragging the overturned bobsled, and Hans's cries brought Kate harshly to her senses. They were alone.

Kate calculated the distance back to the house. Somewhere between two and three miles. Between here and there was the long incline. She had two babies and a two-year-old. There was her painful shoulder. She had nothing but the wagon robes and the deerskins. They would freeze here. Hans needed to take care of the team. She would have to provide for the children.

Laying Isaac carefully in the snow, she moved her left shoulder gingerly, telling herself the pain was, indeed, subsiding.

Hester stood in the whirling whiteness, her black eyes peering from beneath her hat's rim, watching her mother, saying nothing, waiting to hear what she would say.

"Hester, can you walk home with me?" Kate asked, her words catching in little gasps of pain.

Hester blinked. *"Ya."*

So Kate made a sled of sorts by gathering two corners of the wagon robe together and then laying the babies on it. She shushed Noah, bunched the corners of the robe in one hand, and then bent to its weight, walking briskly as she struggled through the snow.

She assured herself that Hans would know she was heading back to the farm. She had to. It was the only rational thing to do. They never should have started out in the first place. Anger at Hans washed over her. Jealousy stabbed her heart. Tears of rage and weakness boiled up from her pain, thinking of Hans's undying love for his mother. Skinny, meticulous, ill-tempered, old . . .

Kate caught herself, guilt stopping the flow of Adam's nature that she knew caused these thoughts. She knew how much she resented Rebecca too much of the time.

Her anger propelled her straight up the hill, her babies' yowling and bouncing only adding to her strength. She was glad for her strong legs and wide backside, her powerful shoulders, her muscles tempered like a man's from the lifting of her sturdy sons, the washing, the gardening, the cleaning.

She stopped to catch her breath, swiping a wet, mittened hand across her running nose, her streaming eyes.

"Mein Gott, vergebe mich meine Sinde" (My God, forgive my sins), she whispered.

Her thoughts were of the devil, she knew, and he must be overcome by the power of Jesus Christ, she knew, too. And so she did her utmost to repent, her inner spiritual struggle matching her strides, hampered by the incline and the snow.

"Hester, are you coming?" she called back to the small form, struggling to place her footprints in those of her mother, the dragging blankets making it much easier for her to walk.

"Ya."

Hester's voice was calm, unafraid. She was simply going about her duty, following her mother back to the house. She had to place her feet carefully, but she could do it.

Love for her beautiful little daughter welled up in Kate as she leaned forward, pulling her sons steadily up the incline, picking her way carefully among the rocks and through the ruts where rivers of rain had furrowed deep ditches down each side.

"Do you want to sit on the blanket awhile?" Kate asked, turning to Hester.

"Nay. I can walk."

"Are your legs tired?"

"Nay."

"Can we go on?"

"*Ya.*"

Hester scooped up snow with her mittens, brought it to her mouth, and took big mouthfuls. The child was thirsty, Kate realized. How did she know enough to eat the snow to slake her thirst? For the hundredth time, she marveled at the child's common sense, the way she knew things far beyond her years.

There was no time to contemplate these things, she had to get her babies home. Their cries of terror had turned into pitiful whimpers, sniffles, and an occasional cough, so Hester plowed on.

The bare branches of the trees were increasingly whipped about by the force of the wind, the snow thick and whirling around them. Kate was not as frightened as she had been when they were going in the opposite direction. She knew exactly where she was and the distance she had to cover. Her shoulder had settled into a dull, pulsating pain, bearable now, and she knew she would make it home.

When Hester lagged behind, Kate stopped, rolled her sons more tightly in their cocoon of deerskin, and then kept on going. Her hands were numb with the cold, her toes like blocks of ice, but she had no time to worry about that now.

Chickadees fluttered by the wayside, crows cawed overhead. A red bird called from a bush nearby, and Kate did not know Hester stopped walking until she turned to see, her daughter now a small black dot a hundred yards away.

"Hester!" she called, impatient.

The call of the red bird was repeated, over and over as Hester resumed her little steps through the snow, her eyes alight, snapping brilliantly beneath her flat hat.

"*Rote birdy*" (Red bird), she announced.

Over and over, she repeated the call.

"Aren't you cold?"

"*Nay.*"

When a particularly strong gust of wind whipped the snow into a fast-moving white cloud, enveloping them inside, Hester merely sat down and buried her face in her shawl. She didn't look up until the stinging snow had slowed, then she pushed herself to her feet and looked at Kate, as if to say, "All right, let's go."

Long before the small, gray house came into view, Kate dreamed of it, longed for it, felt as if she would never lift the heavy iron latch and stumble through the door.

At first, when the house came into view, Kate could see only the walls, and then just a part of them was visible. The roof held a layer of drifting snow; the windows were frosted with snow flung against them. She felt a little crazy, as if the cabin had changed in appearance, having turned into a half-buried cave, cold and white and wet with snow.

When she lifted the latch with frozen mittens clinging to her cold fingers, she heaved the burden of blankets and babies through the opening and collapsed beside the makeshift sled after closing the door behind Hester, who stomped the snow off her boots, imitating Hans.

She breathed fast, then got to her feet and went to the fireplace. She uncovered the red coals, digging around in them with the poker. She added a few small sticks of wood and went to attend to her shivering, half-frozen sons. Hester walked to the fire, removed her mittens, held her hands to the warmth, and imitated the call of the red bird once more. She lifted her face to Kate and smiled the sweetest, calmest little grin she had ever seen.

Kate bent, grabbed her daughter and smothered her in kisses. "My sweet, darling little Hester. You did so good. I love you so much. You are the very best daughter I have."

Hester giggled, then turned to place both palms against her mother's cheeks inside the dripping hat. She placed her lips reverently on Kate's, a solemn vow of love.

Somehow, as long as she lived, Kate would remember this.

Hans recovered the team, his lungs on fire from yelling, drawing on every ounce of his strength as he plowed through the snow and roaring wind.

Dot, the intelligent horse, regained her sense of calm first, which helped Daisy slow her headlong plunge through the snow. The bouncing sled hampered their progress, so Hans was able to catch up with them after less than half a mile. He had to spend considerable time freeing the still-struggling horses from the broken sled. He cut his hands and pinched his fingers, but with heroic effort, he eventually freed the heaving, sweat-soaked animals from the terrifying confines of twisted harness and bouncing sled.

He stroked Dot's neck, praised her and calmed her down, then looped the reins across her neck and flung himself on her back, leading Daisy.

He figured he'd find his wife and children huddled beneath the blankets. He planned on continuing the trek to his parents' house on horseback, which might have been better in the beginning anyway. He was shocked to find no trace of his family. He sat on the horse's back, peered through the whirling whiteness, and did not know what to make of the situation.

Where had she gone? She couldn't carry three children. Then he saw the indentation, the wide path through the blowing snow, all but obscured in some places. What was wrong with her? She couldn't return home.

He peered up the steep hill they had just slid down and thought he'd find her, that they'd resume their journey to his parents' house. His mouth watered, thinking of the wild plum pudding, the roast turkey and stewed rabbit, the potpie made with squirrel, the applesauce and cream drizzled over the berry pie.

The whole way home, his ill temper worsened. Kate never heard him put the horses in the barn. She didn't know he was at home until he burst through the door, lifting the latch in the same second, a heavy, clunking sound that made her jump.

"Kate."

"Yes?"

"Why did you come home?"

"What was I supposed to do? I couldn't sit in the snow with two babies. And Hester."

"We could have ridden the horses to my parents' house, Kate. You know that. I'm disappointed in you."

Kate hung her head. "I'm sorry."

"I want to go."

"But . . ."

Kate floundered. She lifted her eyes to the window, the now whirling whiteness never letting up.

"Hans, I don't feel it is wise to take these young children out in this blizzard. God has spared us this time. If we were foolhardy enough to try again, he might not."

Slowly, Hans's anger abated, and he shrugged off his steaming coat. Going to sit by the fire, he acknowledged Kate's words with a nod of his head, but barely.

Kate kept more thoughts to herself as she bathed both sons in very warm water, gave them chamomile tea, and dressed them in heavy flannel nightgowns before putting them to bed.

Silence hung invisible, a spirit of martyrdom on Hans's part, a deep shame on Kate's. How much of her wrong decision had come from her hidden jealousy of his mother? For it had been a wrong decision, if Hans, her husband, had wanted to go.

She made fried mush and *fishly*, the best cut of deer meat fried in lard, steaming hot and crispy, a pot of bean soup with *rivels*, the flour and egg dumplings thick and heavy in the scalding milk to cheer him, but he said he was not hungry. Instead, he watched Kate lean over her large bowl of soup, spooning it into her mouth with studied intensity. He felt an emotion close to disgust, but he read his German *Schrift* (Scripture) to resist it.

Only Hester could elevate his dark mood, playfully grabbing his shirt and hanging on like an agile little squirrel.

Kate washed dishes, listened to their play, a smile on her face. Yes, God had sent the darling girl into their lives to fulfill them. Already she was weaving her special magic in the family, a little mother to Noah, a ray of sunshine to Hans, a blessing to Kate, who needed her now, more than ever, as the familiar nausea welled up yet again.

CHAPTER 6

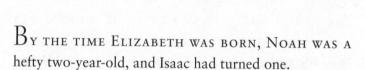

By THE TIME ELIZABETH WAS BORN, NOAH WAS A hefty two-year-old, and Isaac had turned one.

Elizabeth was called Lissie, after the midwife who attended the birth. Never pronounced "Lizzie," in the refined manner of the English, she was known as "Lissie," with the German pronunciation. A fair child with a thatch of thin brown hair and her mother's blue eyes, she was welcomed into the family with gladness.

Hans held her, became more familiar with her than he had with his newborn sons, but it wasn't long until he largely ignored her.

Hester was three years old, almost four, although Kate and Hans never knew the exact date of her birth. They calculated she may have been six weeks, perhaps a month old, when Kate found her at the spring. So on the first of March they celebrated her birthday with a sweet cake made of molasses and brown sugar.

Little Isaac had come down with an alarming fever and cough after Kate's trek through the snow. Onion poultices and Lissie Hershberger's knowledge pulled him through. He remained sickly throughout that summer, crying endlessly with wheezing little breaths from his damaged lungs. Finally, at summer's end, Mamie Troyer made a tincture of herbs learned from an Indian grandmother who was traveling through, and he became stronger.

Noah, however, ate ceaselessly, developing a fine physique at a very young age, although his hair was still thin and very blond. He followed Hans about the farm wherever he could and did not think anything was amiss if Hans kept him at bay, barely noticing or speaking to him, rarely acknowledging him and often smacking him. He learned to wait his turn for food, to stay out of Hans's way, never to speak unless he was spoken to, and to sleep when he was put to bed.

With his mother, he could be more lively, ask more questions, be more playful. He never thought much about it that Hester was always granted favors and never spanked. It was simply the way of it, through a child's eyes, his life accepted without question. He loved the dark-eyed Indian child and was too young to know she was anything but his older sister.

By the time Rebecca arrived, Lissie was a little over a year and a half old, and Hester was already learning her numbers. From her bed, Kate taught Hester the alphabet, nursing little Rebecca as the *maud*, Ruth, went about running the household smoothly.

Lissie Hershberger, however, returned to visit with Kate when Hans was out shoeing horses. She brought a box containing pennyroyal tea for Kate to drink and a determination that Kate needed to hear what she had to say. The varicose veins in Kate's legs were not *goot,* and she needed to look after herself.

Lissie sat in the hickory rocker, drank cup after cup of peppermint tea, held little Lissie, and told Kate she had a beautiful family, she really did, but now she needed to take care of herself. She asked where Hester was. Kate told her she went with Hans to shoe horses. Lissie squinted her eyes, pressed her lips in a straight line of disapproval, and asked why Hans didn't take Noah. Kate lowered her head as a small blush crept across her tired features. "Noah gets in Hans's way," she said. "He's too small."

"Hmph!" Lissie snorted, which set little Lissie to giggling, reaching up to touch Lissie's face. "That's no excuse. Kate, I have to say this. Either you love your husband beyond all reason, or you're just plain dumb. That Hester of yours is spoiled beyond control. Does she ever get punished for anything she does? It's unnatural the way all of you dote on her. Believe me, your harvest will come with these poor, needy boys. Oh, don't talk, Kate. Let me finish. I've been here at all the births, and nothing ever changes. Hester gets five times the amount of love and attention the rest of the children do, and you don't notice at all. That Hester will bring you down, you mark my words."

Kate dropped her eyes and kept them lowered as wave after wave of color chased over her features. She plucked at the woven coverlet on the bed with work-worn fingers, pleating it nervously. Finally, she sighed, heavily.

"All right, Lissie. If you promise not to speak of this, I'll talk. No, I'm not dumb. Yes, I know Hans is partial to Hester. He always was, but I figure there's nothing I can do to change that, and to punish Hester for his unfairness will only make the situation worse. He is my husband, and I have promised to obey him. His will is my will, Lissie."

"Well, good for you."

The words were short and hard, pellets of mockery now. Kate watched her fingers methodically pleating the coverlet, as if her own hands did not belong to her.

"All I can say is, be careful with that child."

Kate nodded.

The subject was dropped, conversation flowed to easier subjects, and they spoke of community news and the band of Lenape Indians who was traveling through the area and had stopped to trade furs at the trading post on Northkill Creek.

"You know, they are peaceable people, the Lenape. I don't believe they'll ever make much trouble for us, except perhaps if we push them out of their land. Too much of that going on as it is." Lissie spoke her thoughts out loud. "I'll make dinner for you, before I leave," she said, suddenly, getting up and asking what Kate was hungry for.

Kate was grateful and said she would love a good pot of deer stew—fresh venison, onions and carrots, thickened with cornmeal, just a bit—to eat with bread and molasses.

Lissie rumbled and buzzed around the house, teased the children, complimented the housekeeping, and then brought Kate a bowl of the fragrant stew. She filled one for herself and sat beside Kate's bed to eat it. Ruth fed the children. The house smelled wonderful when Hans stepped through the door, Hester's hand clutched firmly in his own. Seeing Lissie, the smile on his face became crooked, then disappeared entirely, as he let go of Hester's hand.

Hester went to sit beside Noah to peer into his bowl. She took a bite of his bread, licked the molasses off her lips, then took another bite, a large one. When Noah protested loudly, Hans gripped his shoulder and gave it a shake.

"Let Hester have some, Noah."

So Noah watched silently as Hester finished his bread and molasses. Isaac dropped his spoon, yelled loudly about it, and was given a smart rap on his shoulder from Hans. By that time, Lissie was visibly shaken, but, wise woman that she was, kept spooning up her stew, her eyes lowered.

Hans filled a bowl of stew for himself and one for Hester, then asked everyone to bow their heads in silent prayer. Lissie shot him a look of disrespect, yet she set her bowl on the small table beside Kate's bed and bowed her head. But she didn't pray, pretty sure the prayer wouldn't be heard under these circumstances, when she felt like a teakettle ready to explode from the buildup of steam.

Isaac and Rebecca came to visit, clearly pleased, their faces wreathed in smiles at the arrival of the little namesake. She was short and plump, measuring only nineteen inches long, her eyes big and blue, her skin pink and healthy. Rebecca was so pleased, she unwrapped the baby, counted her fingers and toes, then, alarmed, quickly counted them again.

Kate watched the consternation on her mother-in-law's face.

"She . . . Wait a minute."

Then, quietly, a mere whisper, "She has six fingers on one hand, Hans." She said this to Hans, not Kate, as if he could do something about it if she told him first.

Hans moved swiftly to his mother's side. He looked, his lips moving softly, his brows lowered.

"Yes, there are six."

Kate didn't care if she had seven fingers on one hand, she was a dear baby, another girl, and her love only expanded and wrapped itself about this newborn, same as all the others.

Hans's eyes found Kate's, accusing, begging her to fix it. He certainly did not want a disfigured child. She would be *fa-shput* (mocked). "Can you do something?" he asked quietly.

Her face white, Kate shrugged, holding the baby tightly to her breast as if to reassure herself they could not take her away because she had six fingers. Who would notice?

Rebecca would not hold the baby after her discovery, after seeing the extra finger. She had decided that Rebecca was, indeed, disfigured, unclean, as if she had leprosy.

The remainder of the evening crawled by, stilted, miserable. Kate wept after Hans's parents left, but quietly, so he wouldn't see.

After the children were put to bed, Ruth cleaned the kitchen and retired to her bedroom, quietly whispering a polite goodnight. Hans asked her how she enjoyed the new addition. Ruth blushed and said it was nice to have her own room.

He had built the addition because of his forethought, his wanting to provide well for his growing family. He had even built a second stone chimney for that time when they could have a small stove from England, the way wealthier families had. He had also constructed a long cupboard against the wall to hold the children's clothes, another well-thought-out plan on his part.

Kate had so many things to be thankful for, how could she fret if Hans showed a bit of partiality among the children? Kate let her loyalty to Hans edge out Lissie's warning, bolstered by her resentment, too, that Lissie had intruded into their private lives.

Lots of families lived with unequally divided love. Kate remembered that her sister Fannie, a year younger than herself, was most certainly favored by their mother as her skilled fingers produced one work of embroidery after another. Sometimes you had to accept life for what it was and not what you wanted it to be.

Hans came to Kate's bed and lay down beside her. Quietly, he held her hand, his thumb caressing the back of it over and over.

"Kate," he said softly, "I really want to know if there's nothing to be done about the extra finger. What caused something like that in the first place?" His voice quivered like a little boy's, and Kate turned her head to watch her husband's face. There was real fear in his eyes when he turned toward her.

"Is God punishing us for something we have done, that our babies are not perfect?"

"What do you mean, Hans?"

The firelight played across her husband's features, creating a dancing yellow light in his eyes, changing their color and expression, fascinating her.

"I feel I have sinned, that our baby has six fingers."

"Why?"

"I don't know. Sometimes I have impure thoughts."

"Oh, Hans, confess to God. He will forgive if you are truly contrite."

"I don't know why I carry this burden of guilt, but I do."

"If it helps, you can confess to the church. I'm sure John would help you with your confession."

"Oh no, no. I can't do that. It's only fleeting. It's not that bad. Sometimes it seems as if it raises itself, and I can't stop the thoughts that go through my head."

"Pray about it, Hans. Ask God to help you."

"I will."

When he leaned across the baby to kiss her, an involuntary shudder passed through her, and she turned her face away, his lips reaching the formal presentation of her cheek.

When Hans rolled on his side and slept, Kate's eyes remained wide open, her thoughts racing, unable to sleep. Why would Hans have this trouble? Was it Ruth, the hired girl? She'd have to keep an eye on her, for sure, but she'd never noticed one single flirtatious move from the dear, shy girl. She was so hardworking, bless her heart.

Kate's thoughts traveled across the community, the young women and girls, none of them holding the least bit of suspicion even for a second. Oh, well, perhaps it was only a passing thing. Hans was young, and the devil strode about like a lion, seeking whom he may devour, she reasoned. She would be sure to perform all her wifely duties well, obey him in everything, and God would bless them.

Sometimes she could hardly grasp the fact they had been childless all that time. Nine and a half years. And now she was thirty-five years old and had five children. If this continued, she'd have five more by the time she was forty. My, oh.

She hid a smile now. Poor Hans. Why did he think that sixth finger was so awful? His parents were given to myths and old wives' talk entirely too much. Rebecca had told her once that when the moon was full, people lost their minds much easier, and that bad skin came from eating grapes before they were ripe.

She'd ask Lissie. She'd know.

And Lissie did know. She laughed out loud, said she must be getting old. How did she miss that extra finger?

Well, it was no problem whatsoever. She plied the limp finger gingerly, testing its strength, then took a length of string and tied it firmly at the base, saying it would fall off in a few weeks.

Kate nodded. She knew it would not cause the baby pain, and Hans would be relieved of his burden of guilt. The poor man, he worked so hard to support all of them; he certainly did not need the added load of wrongdoing.

When Baby Rebecca was six weeks old, summer was upon them once more. Kate was rested and energetic and threw herself into the work of cleaning her house thoroughly. She sent the children outside to play, then opened the windows, shaved strong lye soap into buckets of steaming water, and scrubbed and swept and polished and waxed until the house shone with cleanliness. It was their turn to have church in two weeks, and Kate was in a frenzy of activity. No one was going to come to their farm and find anything unkempt or slovenly. Not the barn, surrounding fields, the garden, or the house.

Hester and Noah pulled weeds, crawling around the rows of beans and corn, throwing weeds into the wooden bucket Kate gave them. They worked all morning, stopping only to imitate the calls of birds or to watch a timid deer walk across the field with its tiny fawn.

Hans praised Hester's efforts warmly, then tousled Noah's hair with the palm of his hand. Kate's heart ached to see Noah's face light up by this one infrequent gesture, almost an afterthought, but it was a crumb of blessing Noah grasped eagerly. His father had touched him, and it was a benediction, a feeling that was almost holy in a way only little boys know.

Hester was pleased for Noah as well. She was always glad when Hans was nice to the boys, her heart pure and unselfish, the way she'd been since the day she arrived.

As Lissie had predicted, the extra finger on Rebecca's hand lay in the cradle one morning, leaving a funny looking spot on her hand. Kate took up the tiny finger, buried it in the woods behind the house, put a salve on the place where the finger had been, and never spoke of it to anyone after that.

When the first cart drove around the turn in the road and came to church services at Hans Zug's farm, the men's practiced eyes appreciated the amount of forest Hans had cleaned since last time they'd had services, the green of the cornfields, the size of the tobacco plants.

The women gazed at Kate's garden and wondered aloud to their husbands how that busy woman got all her work done the way she did. Did she get up at four o'clock every single morning? She wasn't getting any thinner, said the more mean-spirited ones. Those who held a generosity of spirit were quick to praise, asking Kate, indeed, how did she do it?

Kate blushed and became quite pink and flustered. She said her children were good and helped in the garden, which sounded dumb to her own ears, but she hardly knew what else to say, since praise of any kind was a bit foreign. Not that that was Hans's fault. Of course she knew he appreciated her efforts most of the time.

Hester appeared especially pretty, wearing a new dress in a light shade of green, setting off the caramel hue of her skin. Her eyes were darker than ever, the dress that was buttoned around her neck giving her skin an almost olive hue.

Old Mamie Troyer watched the Indian child and clucked internally, her expression giving nothing away. Why wouldn't Lissie and Rebecca have a dress of the same color? Or Kate, for that matter? Perhaps Hester had an indulging aunt or cousin who presented her with these brilliant shades.

None of it was any of her business, so she would let it alone. That was best. Her eyes followed the graceful, fawnlike movements of the child, caught the glistening blue of her black hair, and thought if she was Kate, she'd pull that white cap front further over her hair. But maybe it was Kate herself who dressed her in that finery.

The sun shone warmly, and the green leaves of the trees dappled the earth as the women walked solemnly to the barn, where Hans had spread the clean straw and set the wooden benches. The barn below was also as clean as a whistle, without a trace of manure anywhere.

Silently, the women filed in, their heads bent, eyes lowered in submission, and sat down, spreading their skirts smoothly across their laps, setting their bare feet neatly on the floor. They never crossed their legs or bounced their knees or feet. This was the Lord's Sabbath, and they were to respect it as such.

When the strains of a man's baritone reached their ears, they waited respectfully until the first line was finished, then joined in, their high soprano voices blending well with the men's deeper voices.

The summer breezes played with the golden straw, as Hans sat with his sons by the opened doorway. Flies buzzed about, a bumblebee droned by, a butterfly made its crazy way along, wings fluttering as it veered left and right.

Hester was making her way to her father between the benches, sliding her bare feet along in the slippery yellow straw. Her eyes caught the butterfly's movement, following it until it was out of sight. It was only then that she completed her walk to Hans, who pushed Noah over to make room for Hester close to him. He bent his head and smiled at her, receiving her smile in return. Isaac leaned forward, smiling at his father, but the smile Hans gave Hester never reached Isaac, disappearing as Hans focused on Hester. Isaac sat back, sighed, kicked his bare heels below the bench, clasped his hands, and looked for something else to hold his interest.

Rebecca was crying, so Kate took Lissie's hand and walked to the house beneath the waving maple trees overhead. The slow, undulating chant of the German words swirled about her, filling her heart with gratitude for this warm day, the sunshine, the fair weather, and the added blessing of having services in their barn, the mothers making their way back and forth to the house with crying babies.

God was in his heaven, as Hans would say, sending his love in the form of nature, the wonders of it abounding everywhere she looked.

Rebecca had cried herself into a red-faced screaming frenzy, so Kate was at the cradle in a few long strides, raising her to her shoulder with the blanket trailing after her, patting and crooning until the baby quieted. She sat down on the rocking chair to feed her. Looking around the house, she was glad the walls were whitewashed, the furniture polished, the floors clean and gleaming, her expertise at housekeeping so evident.

Her close friend Sarah emerged from the bedroom and said it would be wonderful to have a new addition put on her house. Kate was fortunate to have a hard-working man like Hans. Sarah spoke wistfully, her fear of being overheard evident in the slant of her eyes, the discreet touch of her hand to her mouth.

Kate let all the blessings of her life soak into her heart, saturating it with a bounty of gratitude. She loved Hans with all her heart, his four sweet children she had borne, and adorable Hester, the jewel in Hans's crown. If his love and devotion was a bit lopsided, she could overlook it, no matter what that suspicious Lissie tried to instill in her, whittling away at every bit of faith she had in her hardworking husband.

And so she smiled at Sarah, acknowledged her praise with a thankful heart, and assured her friend that, in time, she would have a larger home as well. Sarah's eyes shone warmly, her smile genuine, but with a veil of sadness that alarmed Kate. It was transparent, but barely. Kate looked deeply into Sarah's eyes, lifting her eyebrows in question. But Sarah shook her head, pulled her upper lip down to catch it with her lower one, drawing a curtain of privacy in front of herself as she did so.

Kate had to be satisfied with the puzzlement she carried with her in the coming weeks.

CHAPTER 7

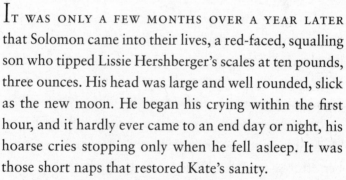

It was only a few months over a year later that Solomon came into their lives, a red-faced, squalling son who tipped Lissie Hershberger's scales at ten pounds, three ounces. His head was large and well rounded, slick as the new moon. He began his crying within the first hour, and it hardly ever came to an end day or night, his hoarse cries stopping only when he fell asleep. It was those short naps that restored Kate's sanity.

Rebecca remained small and thin, a sickly child who lost her appetite easily and was prone to high fevers. So when the winter winds slammed against the little gray house, shaking it to its teeth, Kate stirred up the fire on the hearth and added more logs, keeping fear and panic at bay by telling herself the fever was coming down now.

For days, she'd lain, her little Rebecca, the fever causing her to cry out with chills, feeling as if she were frozen. Then she'd kick and scream when the heat from her fever became unbearable.

Kate washed her little body with cool vinegar water and fed her echinacea and garlic. She soaked strips of elm bark in boiling water and gave her the cooled liquid, but nothing seemed to help.

Solomon kept on fussing and crying, sometimes reverting to short gasping screams, his face turning purple with the noise.

Kate held her mouth in a thin line as she moved through the small house from one to the other. The rest of the children played around her, sometimes squabbling, but she could usually nip the uprising in the bud by a firm twist of an ear or a pinch of forearm flesh between her strong fingers.

Hans was away much of the time, shoeing horses. Kate wondered if that was really what he was doing, but she reasoned that Solomon's crying was very hard on Hans, that his nerves simply couldn't take it. The poor man seemed not to be able to put up with such a racket, and her own ministrations were simply not enough to make Solomon stop crying. She would need to redouble her efforts, to make Hans's time in the house with his family more pleasant.

Hester was a big help now at five years of age, growing taller, her jet black hair as straight and thick as a horse's mane. Kate wet her hair down, drew it back, braided it into severe braids, and then coiled the braids around the back of her head as tightly as possible. She unwound and combed her hair only once a week.

Her eyes were large, if anything a bit elongated like almonds, her nose tiny and flat, with delicate nostrils, her mouth wide and full, her skin a beautiful brown hue. Everyone noticed Hester, including visitors to the Amish church. Some of them stared, others gasped, and then felt ashamed at their lack of good manners. Kate was accustomed to this and found it mildly humorous, sometimes a bit disconcerting, but she never felt afraid. What harm could come to her beautiful child? For that was all she was, a child.

That evening when Hans came home, he went straight to Solomon's cradle, picked him up, and held him. He looked into his face and told Kate he was changing his looks. He believed he resembled her more and more.

Kate was so pleased. She made sure the ham was done to his liking, fried in the cast iron skillet, then steamed in a bit of water to soften it. She sliced cabbage and cooked it until it was meltingly soft, made hominy from the dried corn, and blushed to the roots of her hair when he grabbed her in a darkened corner of the kitchen and planted a wet kiss on her face. "My *gute frau*" (good wife), he chortled, warbling jubilantly.

To what did she owe this attention? She felt elevated, lifted out of the daily cares and rituals of her ordinary life, and thought she could do anything with that kind of praise.

Rebecca's fever came down that evening. Kate held the shockingly thin body, stroking the brown hair away from her fevered brow, and sang, softly.

> *Oh, Gott Vater, in Himmelreich,*
> *Un deine gute preisen.*

Hans hummed from his seat by the fireplace, smiled at Noah when he recited the German bedtime prayer,

tucked Hester's hand in his, and put the children to bed.
Kate felt as if she had a visitation from God himself.

The harsh winds of winter moaned and shrieked
around the eaves. It slapped loose a shake on the roof
until it made a buzzing sound as Kate lay beside Hans,
sleepless. Between them, little Solomon lay, snoring softly. He had just been fed, and she should have lifted him
for a burp, but it was too warm and cozy under the
covers. She'd let him burp on a remnant of cloth, where
she'd laid him on his stomach.

From the wooden trundle bed, the sound of thin,
fast breathing chilled her through and through. The
breathing was Rebecca's, her fever in its second week
now, and Kate wanted Dr. Hess. She no longer had the
audacity or good faith or whatever you wanted to call
it to think that all these remedies she'd tried would heal
her now.

The tip of her nose stung, the prelude to quiet sobbing. She could not bear to think of losing one of her
babies. Not one. They were her whole life. She gave them
all her love. Her day's work was centered around her
little ones. They were, pure and simple, a part of her.

But Hans would have to agree about the doctor. She
dreaded approaching him, with all the good humor he'd
been displaying, splashing it about the small log house
with abandon, coloring their world with new and vibrant
hues. It would cost money, but she believed the amount
Hans had had significantly increased now.

Rebecca's fast breathing was accompanied by a hoarse
rattle. Terror filled Kate's chest. Outside, the wind flung
twigs and leaves against the small six-paned windows.

Kate shivered and then left the warmth of the bed to check on Rebecca.

The sick child was so hot, she was flinging her arms about. Kate drew back, gasping, then stumbled to the bed, grasped Hans's shoulder and shook, clenching her nails into his muscled arms, whispering, "Hans! Hans!"

He sat up, his brown hair disheveled, his eyes swelled with sleep, his face shiny with night sweat and unwashed skin. "Hans! Please. It's Rebecca. She's very sick. What should we do?"

Hans put a palm to the side, pressed down to lift himself up and away from the bed, pushing little Solomon into the straw mattress. He began grunting, snuffling, and then crying, which soon escalated to shrieks of fright.

"*Ach.*" Hans got out of bed, pulled on his everyday knee breeches, bleary-eyed, his brain still foggy with sleep. He passed a hand across his eyes, rubbing the sleep from them, and said to the crying infant, "Here, here. Hush!"

They let him cry as they hovered over Rebecca, the same silhouette as years ago when Hester entered their lives, and everything had been like a dream, too good to be true.

Now with each passing year, a new baby had entered their lives, leaving them no time for silliness or games or lazy afternoons spent by the creek. Too often, if they had time to give relaxed attention to their children, it went primarily to their one foundling, Hester.

When Hans saw his wife's tears, sliding down her cheeks, he was stung into action. "I'll go," was all he said. Kate lifted her eyes to his with raw gratitude.

"Oh, *denke* (thank you), Hans," she whispered.

A small form appeared in the doorway, then padded noiselessly across the floor, and climbed up on the bed, tugging efficiently at Solomon's blanket.

"Sh. Sh. *Net heila*" (Don't cry). Hester sat on the bed, her legs dangling over the side, her arms wrapped around the crying baby. She lifted one hand and allowed the baby to suckle on her finger, which quieted him immediately.

Hans said goodbye, a thick form in his heavy overcoat, a scarf tied across his head to cover his ears, his heavy black hat set firmly on top.

"Take the wagon," Hester said.

"Certainly."

How long he had been gone when Rebecca went into *die gichtra* (seizures) Kate did not know. She screamed in fright when the small body convulsed, the soft, pliant form becoming stiff as a board, the back arching, the head thrown back as her blue eyes turned up in her head.

Hester sat holding Solomon, her black eyes alive, dancing in the firelight, erect, unmoving, waiting to see what her mother would do.

"No, no, no, no," Kate moaned softly, her mother's heart unable to grasp what her head knew with uncanny intuition was to be.

How many hours, how many minutes? Was it only seconds until her little tongue curled back into her throat and shut off the tiny passage behind it? Her fever had been too high, the infection raging unchecked through her lungs and then into her bloodstream, taking her life.

When Rebecca choked, Kate cried out again. With superhuman effort, she tried to save her little daughter, but there was no use. She was gone.

Gone to a better place. A little angel in heaven. A flower in the Master's bouquet. All of these comforting phrases pushed themselves into her mind and then were sent away by her own refusal to accept the fact that Rebecca had died.

Oh, she had willed her to live. She'd done everything. She'd had Lissie Hershberger more than once, tried all of her herbs and tinctures, the foul-smelling concoctions that spread their vile odor through the house, and nothing helped.

When Hans returned with the doctor, he found his wife on the floor on her hands and knees, rocking back and forth, her eyes squeezed shut as a high, keening sound rose and fell from between her clenched jaws.

Hans went to her but drew back before he could touch her, raising terrified eyes to the doctor. The good doctor assessed the situation by the dim light of the dying fire and shook his head, his mouth grim. Bending, he touched her back. "Kate."

The word cut through Kate's grieving, opening the possibility that she might live rather than die with Rebecca. She had never felt such despair. A great yawning abyss had been before her, beckoning to her. It had been easier to think of simply slipping away into it than to keep fighting.

The doctor helped her up and onto the other side of the bed. He gave her a double dose of laudanum before turning to Hans and the body of the child.

"Hm." His experienced hands felt along little Rebecca's throat, her limbs, her stomach. He realized the suffocation was brought on by her convulsions. It was not unusual. Children died from "the fevers" or "lung fever," as the condition was frequently called.

This baby had never been as hardy as the rest of the family. She'd been pale since the day she was born, her cry a thin, mewling sound like a newborn kitten.

Baby Solomon was in good hands, Dr. Hess knew. He was more concerned about Kate. Sometimes these women who bore a child every year seemed strong and capable, fulfilling their duties without one word of complaint. But they were extremely fragile on the inside, and a sudden shock, a terrifying incident, changed them forever. Dr. Hess said none of this to Hans. He believed Kate was strong, a fighter. She'd come back.

Hans had no tears. Grief was written all over his face as he bent low, talked to the Indian child, then took Solomon from her and laid him gently in the cradle.

He went back to Hester and talked in soft tones, pointing to Rebecca, lifeless and still, laid down tenderly by her mother. Then he took Hester up in his arms and buried his face in her thin shoulder. Soon hoarse sobs began, a manly sound of grieving the doctor had heard many times. It never failed to chill him.

He watched as the little Indian girl's arms went around her father's neck, her little hands patting his thick shoulders. *"Do net heila, Dat,"* (Do not weep, Dad) she said, for all the world like a capable grandmother.

The doctor finally concluded that Hans derived condolence from his small daughter as he held her, the grieving child clinging to her father for her own support. It was, indeed, something to see.

Word spread through the community after Hans rode to tell his parents, who sent their son, John, to other Amish families.

Hans Zug's little one-year-old Rebecca had died of *lunga feva* (lung fever), and Kate wasn't good, were the furtive whispers, the knowing rolling of the eyes. This would get the best of her.

The doctor left a large brown bottle of laudanum, with the precise instructions of a dedicated doctor, more worried than his professional manner allowed.

The wagons began to arrive, Isaac and Rebecca first, dressed somberly in brown from head to toe. Rebecca's eyes remained dry, but her mouth twitched and her chin quivered for just a moment. She felt as if this was a bad omen, her very own namesake, Rebecca, dying like this. God was calling loudly, and she needed to heed his voice.

Isaac's kind blue eyes filled with tears, and he shook his head up and down, saying the young child was *goot opp* (well off). She would not have to go through this sad world with its many trials and temptations.

Rebecca asked Hans why they hadn't sent for her. He said Lissie Hershberger had been there twice.

"Piffle!" Rebecca snorted.

Hans looked sharply at his mother.

"What does fat Lissie know?"

Hans lifted his shoulders and then let them fall.

When Solomon began wailing, Rebecca took him from the cradle, and handed him to Kate, shaking her awake with powerful hands.

"Your baby needs you," she said, sharply.

Kate pulled herself up, shamefaced, then looked at her mother-in-law with eyes that were chillingly empty. She reached for Solomon, fed him as if each movement was too hard to accomplish, keeping her eyes dry and giving nothing away.

They came to help, close friends as well as those who were acquaintances, all sharing the common bond of being Amish and attending the same church services. The depth of friendship didn't matter at a time like this. A child had died, linking them all together within the *bund der lieve* (bond of love).

The neighbors who weren't Amish came and the friendly Indians, the Lenape from the trading post on Northkill Creek. They brought gifts of beads and tobacco. The Shawnee were less confident than the Lenape, not as comfortable in the presence of the Amish, but they came, too.

People cleaned the house and the barn as well. They set up the little brown, wooden coffin on sawhorses. The women sewed a tiny linen dress.

It was Kate's duty to dress the lifeless body of her child. She accomplished this stone-faced and rigid, her eyes dry, with the help of her mother-in-law, Rebecca, who sobbed and cried, alternating between hiccups and nose-blowing.

Noah and Isaac stayed in the background, out of the way, not making any noise, barely whispering. They ate when they were told and sat down where they were told to sit, watching everyone with large eyes that did not seem to understand what was going on around them.

Hester helped with the care of baby Solomon, watching the people coming to the house or leaving it. She offered to find kitchen utensils or cloths for cleaning up, anything she could do to be helpful, amazing the women of the church with her grown-up wisdom.

Lissie Hershberger sat in a corner with a huge slice of apple pie (she hadn't time for dinner before she came) and wagged her large head from side to side.

"See iss an chide kind" (She is a sensible child).

She licked the pewter spoon clean, then asked who made the apple pie. No one seemed to know, so she polished off the whole slice and sent for another, making no excuses except to say she hadn't had apples for too long. How can you make apple pies without apples? Hm? You can't.

No one laughed, or smiled, for this was the day before a funeral, a quiet, holy time, but a few hands were put up quietly, gently placed across mouths that twitched up at the corners.

They dug the small grave with pickaxes and shovels, the frozen, stony soil reluctant to give the child a resting place. Brawny men of the community hacked away at it, inside the rail fence where twenty-five bodies lay buried in their wooden coffins, returning to the dust from which they were formed, and God the judge of their souls.

Funerals were not uncommon. It was the way of it. Folks took sick and died for various reasons. Snakebites, lockjaw, childbirth, whooping cough, accidents, many maladies. That was life in the 1700s.

They cooked a sizable slab of pork, sliced yellow and white, strong-flavored cheese. They fixed carrots and grated cabbage, seasoning it with vinegar and store-bought sugar. They cooked dried apples, plump and full, to be eaten after the meal.

Mamie Troyer said those prunes put her to mind of the *auferstehung* (resurrection). Dried, dead, and dusty-looking, but the minute they were boiled, they returned to life, plump, juicy-looking, and quite tasty.

Lissie Hershberger choked on her hot, black tea, and said Mamie better stop saying those unholy things. It wasn't funny. This was a funeral.

Then they sat together like two fat, black hens, their faces drawn and somber, with due respect to the *hinna losseny* (the ones remaining). But their eyes twinkled and sparkled every time they thought of what Mamie had said about the prunes.

Kate washed and dressed in her best shortgown, skirt and apron. She pulled her cap well over her head and tied the wide, white strings beneath her chin. Then she dutifully received the grieving members of the community and was comforted by them. But she remained strangely dry-eyed, compliant, agreeable, and without emotion of her own.

The graveyard was situated on top of a rise, on a plot of land that was only partially cleared. Sturdy pine trees swayed in the bitter cold, the bare branches of the oak and maple trees creaked and bent by its force.

As Kate stood, hearing the sighing sound of the wind through the pine needles, a wrenching sadness gripped her soul. Her tears began to flow, a warm steady stream that welled up in her eyes and dripped steadily off her chin, falling on her black shawl and splattering on the frozen earth, a baptism of the Pennsylvania soil with tears of a mother's sorrow.

Hans stepped closer to her when he saw her tears, and she drew comfort from his solid presence. She leaned back slightly against him.

They set the house to rights, packed the food away, and resumed their lives as best they could.

Baby Solomon quit his endless crying. He sat up and noticed the world around him, and even smiled at Hester. A restful atmosphere fell across the weathered little house in the woods.

Three more babies were born, in the next four years. Daniel, John, and Barbara. Hester was nine years old when Barbara arrived in June of 1754. She was a capable little maid, used to hard work at this tender age.

Her arms were round with muscles, her legs strong and slender, as lean as a willow. She rode any horse on the farm without a saddle or a bridle. She just flung a rope around its nose, tied it with her own special knot, and was off.

Noah was her best friend, with Isaac coming in second. The three were inseparable, skilled in many ways for as young as they were.

With seven children to feed and clothe, Hans and Kate remained constantly busy, working from dawn till dusk, the children working side by side with their parents as much as possible.

Kate was nearing forty, and she carried her spreading hips and midsection with a certain sense of submission. She accepted all childbearing as a duty, her God-given ability to fill Hans's quiver with arrows. Children were a heritage of the Lord, a blessing, truly.

Hans accepted his wife, grateful for her understanding of him. He indulged her appetite for ham and eggs and great bowls of thick porridge. She loved buttermilk when they had some, aged cheese, drizzles of milk over fruit pie, and homemade bread. She fried cornmeal mush in lard, spread the thick, greasy slices with apple butter, and ate slice after slice, sometimes frying another panfull while she washed dishes in the wooden tub that hung on the wall by the dry sink.

Rebecca eyed her daughter-in-law's burgeoning figure, drew her mouth down, and tightened her grip on the disapproval that threatened to escape. Why couldn't she control her appetite? When Hester was older, she'd be ashamed of her mother. She watched the beautiful child grow tall, muscular, and slender and noticed the innocence of her devotion to her two brothers who were not her brothers at all. Rebecca wondered how long it could last.

Hester was not just beautiful, she shone from within with a goodness, a purity of heart. Love flowed from her, unhampered, the generosity of her spirit endearing her to each member of the Amish community.

"Hans Zug's *glay Indian maedly*" (little Indian girl), they all called her. They watched her light-footed comings and goings, unable to hide how much she charmed and captivated all who knew her.

CHAPTER 8

ON THE TENTH DAY OF AUGUST, WHEN HESTER was ten years old, Hans decided it was time the children had some schooling, and he set about enrolling them in the *Englishe schule* (English, or non-Amish classes). It was a miserable little clapboard hovel five and a half miles away, with old Theodore Crane as head schoolmaster.

Many of the children were Amish, with a few half-Indians, and two or three rowdy sixteen-year-olds. Crane kept his school with a rigid eye and disciplined with unrelenting harshness. He had to. If he didn't, the boys would throw him out and thrash him within an inch of his life.

When Hester, Noah, and Isaac met Theodore Crane, they were dressed primly in clean Amish clothes dyed with walnuts. The boys held their broadfall knee breeches up by a strip of sturdy rawhide when they were too thin around the middle to keep them up otherwise. Their straw hats were yellow, made with fresh straw that summer. Kate made all her family's straw hats, soaking the straw in water until it was pliable enough to be braided, shaped, and sewn together.

Hester's hair was pulled back so tightly, her eyes were raised up at the corners, giving her a slightly foreign look. Her dress was dyed a light purple, her brown legs and bare feet emerging from beneath the hem.

Hans knocked on the door of the school, and Theodore opened it from inside, the latch wobbling to one side after he let go of the knob.

To Hans, it seemed incongruous that there was a knob on that wooden door, broken and muddied as it was by children's boots. But he said nothing about it or the broken windows and stick siding that was warping away from the wall behind it. Instead, he said, "Theodore? I am Hans Zug."

Theodore's bushy black eyebrows shot straight up, his Adams apple rose high and immediately plunged much lower. "How do you do, Mister Zug?" he asked in a high-pitched voice that scared both boys. But Hester was so mesmerized by the bushy eyebrows, she didn't notice the voice.

Hans said he was fine and hoped Theodore was the same. These were his three children, Hester, Noah, and Isaac.

Whereupon, Theodore Crane's eyebrows rose and fell, his Adam's apple bobbed from under his chin to below his tightly buttoned shirt collar, and he squeaked like a mole. "Oy! Oy!"

He was looking at Hester. "This one is not yours."

"Yes," said Hans. "She is ours."

"But not . . . um, you know, your own."

"Yes, she is our own."

Up shot the eyebrows. He hooked a forefinger across his very prominent nose, and a wise rumbling came from somewhere near the vicinity of his throat. The subject was never spoken of again, not once, although Theodore Crane surmised plenty, thought more, but kept his mouth closed.

He tipped his rail-thin body from his heels to his toes and back again, still rumbling in his throat, his narrow, green eyes still surveying Hester. A full-blooded Lenape if he ever saw one.

"Well, do come inside. Please do." He stepped aside and swung both hands to usher them in, still rumbling and clicking his heels.

Hans was appalled at the dark, odorous interior of the classroom. The floorboards were rotting, the old cast iron stove rusty, the desks merely hard, splintering, wooden benches. Field mice scampered across the filthy, leaf-strewn floor. The teacher's desk was more like a box pegged together with wooden pins than a desk.

"How many students are enrolled?"

"This year, if your three come, we'll have twenty-nine."

"That many?"

"Oh, yes."

"Don't you think the school needs a few repairs?"

"Well, yes, but the parents think not. There's no money."

"Would you accept help if we came?"

"We?"

"The Amish."

"If you promise not to convert me. I don't hold with your principles."

Hans Zug found that humorous. It was not the Amish way to try and persuade other people to conform to their ways. They believed they had enough to do, staying on the straight and narrow themselves.

Hans told Theodore this and made a true friend, right there in the middle of the dilapidated schoolhouse.

So a work bee was called for the following Thursday. Theodore Crane had never seen anything like it. The wagonloads of people with little heads sticking out all over was downright heartening. He didn't know these Pennsylvania woods held so many people.

After the first five minutes, he gave up his impeccable manners. He had his hand shaken so hard his teeth rattled, while clammy palms slapped his thin shoulders with the force of a sledgehammer, until he sincerely hoped he'd just met the last hearty Amish man.

The women started a roaring fire, roasted sausages, and then served them with thick slices of bread. One woman brought a wooden crate lined with a tablecloth that was stained with grease and asked him if wanted a fatcake.

He didn't know what a fatcake was, so he said, Yes, he would try one. It was round with a hole in the middle, lighter than a small cake, and coated on the outside with a sort of sugary glaze. He found it delicious and told a woman named Elizabeth, who very much resembled a fatcake herself. He would not like to pay for all the fabric it would take to make a dress for her, but then, he wouldn't have to by the looks of things. They all had husbands.

They whitewashed the walls, scoured the floor, fixed the siding, built long tables in front of every bench, added four new windows, and then sanded and rubbed the stove with lard to keep it from rusting.

Theodore ate a roasted sausage and two fatcakes, marveling at these women's ability to cook, or however they made those fatcakes. He met many of the children who would be coming to his school. At one point he stood and called for everyone's attention.

"I want to say thank you for all you have done here tonight. I hope we will have a successful school year. I look forward to working with you." His eyebrows rose and fell at an alarming rate but never simultaneously. He tipped forward and backward so fast, everyone seemed ready to spring to his assistance if he should happen to tip over.

Lissie Hershberger was quite taken with him, telling the other women he was *sodda schnuck* (sort of cute). Much clucking and eye-rolling followed that remark, but Lissie was quite unabashed. She went over to Theodore and struck up a most interesting conversation, telling him all about little Hester, found by the spring.

Theodore nodded and nodded, rocked on his heels, and stroked his chin with long, thin fingers. "Yes, yes. She was found. Yes, I agree. Hm. Yes, obviously, someone wanted Kate Zug to take the baby. Yes . . . I would say an unspoken pact was made, wouldn't you? Oh, yes. And she's such a winsome child."

Hester sat on her haunches, her purple skirt tucked modestly around her legs, cooking a sausage and staring at the fire. The night was warm and humid, too hot to be sitting so close to the fire, but she was hungry. Noah had wanted her last sausage.

She didn't like this school. She didn't like all these people, but she didn't know what to do about it. Her father was making them go to school, so she was reasonably sure she'd have to obey. She didn't trust that tipping schoolmaster with the dipping eyebrows. She wanted to tell him to hold still, but she guessed she'd better get used to him.

Hester sighed, her eyes flat and expressionless. Why did she have to learn about books? It was worthless, as far as she could tell. She could ride any horse, muck out the stables better than Noah, weed the garden, do the washing.

She could imitate every bird call, knew every bird's own distinctive call, could tell a frog species just by listening—a high trill, a low garrump, a fast whirring sound. She could milk a cow and catch chickens, easily. Even roosters. She was able to change Barbara's diaper and feed Daniel. What else did she need to know? And why?

Far away across the ridge, she heard the yipping of a coyote, the thin, high wail of a distant wolf. The moon was sliced thin, the new moon, when the night was very dark and the whip-poor-wills called best. When the moon was full, their cry was a bit furtive, afraid. Those birds were afraid of their own shadow, silly things. The high call of an elk, bugling frantically, turned the men's heads.

"*Harrich mol sell*" (Listen to that)! shouted Aaron Speicher.

Whoops of elation followed, smiles widened, beards wagged as the men's adrenaline flowed, reminiscing, recounting tales of the hunt for these magnificent creatures.

Bats dove and swerved through the trees. A night hawk set up its plaintive screech.

"Screech owl."

"No, no. Not a screech owl!" Noah shouted.

Hester grinned in the shadows, her eyes expressionless. Good boy. Not a screech owl.

"Is, too!"

"Nope."

"Yes, it is."

"No. I said no. It's a night hawk."

"Here. Here." Hans hurried over, lifted Noah by one arm, and conveyed him to the wagon, reminding him not to argue. It was not polite, especially for children, who should be seen and not heard, especially in a crowd.

Theodore Crane viewed this scene with hopeful eyes.

Sure enough, the last week in September found Hester, Noah, and Isaac on their way to school, their bare brown feet moving swiftly along the path that led to the newly renovated classroom.

Hester carried a round wooden pail containing the bread and butter for their lunch. The boys were dressed in linen shirts, long-sleeved, and homespun knee breeches, also Sunday ones, kept for church services but assigned for school use now.

Hester's hair shone in the sun's rays that pushed between the brilliant foliage, the large bun twisted on to the back of her head and secured with hairpins only suggesting the amount of straight black hair on her head.

Her usual good humor was not in evidence, her brows lowered, her eyes expressionless, her mouth a straight, firm slash in her dark face. Her brothers had to scramble to keep up with her. They paced off the five miles in quick footsteps without any words.

Hester did not want to go. Kate had done something highly unusual that morning, chastising Hester's disobedience with a firm slap on the side of her head when she refused to allow the comb to rake out the snarls as she did her hair for school.

It was the first in a long time that Hester had displayed any sort of self-will or rebellion. An alarm was set off in Kate by the violent jerk of Hester's head, the flat eyes that hummed with silent defiance. Kate stood her ground, however, admonishing Hester with strong words and sending her out the door with motherly warnings, words of wisdom, and no pity. These things had to be nipped in the bud.

Theodore Crane presided over his twenty-nine students with a good balance of authority and friendship. His eyebrows raised and lowered busily according to his words.

Enrolling was simple. Each child stood, stated his or her name, birth date, and age, then sat down, either blushing, blinking, or showing some sign of discomfort.

When it was Hester's turn, she stood, announced her name, "Hester Zug," her age, "ten," and then stopped, still as a stone, her eyes boring into the opposite wall, black with defeat.

She had no birthday. Kate had never spoken of it.

The silence stretched like a rubber band, taut, dangerous.

Theodore Crane waited, then swallowed. What to do?

Instantly, he thought of Lissie Hershberger's kind words. This girl had no idea at ten years old? He was angry at Hans and Kate suddenly. Why hadn't they provided this girl with a birth date?

What he said, was, "That will do." His Adam's apple rose and fell as he swallowed again, moved on to the next pupil, and vowed to have a word with Hans Zug.

But it was too late. The damage had been done. The two sixteen-year-olds, Joash and Obadiah, had found a delightful new plaything, the angry Indian girl with no birthday. They teased her without mercy, conjuring up myths and old wives' tales of how she appeared at Hans Zug's house.

Hester stood, her head bent, the purple dress billowing behind her where the black apron parted, her sleeves too short, thin arms contracting at the wrists as she clenched and unclenched her capable fingers. That was her only movement, the ripple of purple, the leaves overhead rustling as the early autumn breeze moved them about.

"Your Mam found you, huh? That's because a ghost left you there."

Raucous laughter followed, the smaller boys tittering behind their hands. "*Schpence* (ghost)*! Schpence!*" they yelled, looking eagerly for the big boys' approval.

Where was Theodore Crane when all this was going on so close to the classroom? He was, in fact, tutoring young Isaac Zug, who had to stay in for recess and go over some of the numbers that he always wrote backward.

The sounds of yelling and calling were all common-place, hovering on the edge of Crane's knowing, but not penetrating it, so the merciless ribbing continued.

When the bell rang, they all went to their seats and sat obediently.

Hester sat down, bent her head to her black slate, lifted the dusty white chalk, posed it above the slate, and waited for instruction, showing no outward sign that anything out of the ordinary had taken place.

The numbers and letters required of her all swam together in a hopeless mish-mash, a sort of vegetable soup of undecipherable shapes and lines that made abso-lutely no sense.

It took her a few weeks to remember the letters in her name. She could not grasp the concept of using letters to form simple words or doing addition problems. All numbers cavorted around in her head like mayflies, and she could never quite grasp them correctly.

Now the teasing included a new name. *"Dumkopf* (dumbhead). She can't spell, she can't write, that's because she's not quite right!"

Over and over the children continued their brutal chant, and as children will do when something cruel gets started, especially when it's led by the "big" leaders of the playground, the children who felt kindness toward Hester couldn't bring themselves to stop the cruelty, not wanting to be unpopular.

Noah and Isaac played with the little ones and knew vaguely that their sister was being teased, but they fig-ured she was capable of taking it. They thought it was all in fun, and there was no harm in it.

When Hester became withdrawn, Kate reasoned it was due to her dislike of school. She went about the never-ending job of being a mother to her brood, cooking, cleaning, washing, and helping Hans in the fields. Hester's moods became no more than an annoying thought.

So, Hester took matters into her own hands. She roamed the surrounding forest, looking for the perfect branch that was sturdy yet pliant enough to cut and shape. She climbed trees, took Hans's hatchet, and whacked away at a suitable branch, only to have it split down the side, making it useless.

It was months until she finally finished her weapon. The hardest part was procuring a long length of rubber for the part of her slingshot that would launch the rock. Rubber was rare, a precious commodity, but she knew Hans had a small square of it stored away in the chest where he kept his horseshoeing supplies. So she waited for the chance.

The teasing had quieted, somewhat, from a novelty to an occasional uprising from two or three of the more mean-spirited children who thrived on hurting their classmates. Hester brushed it off like bothersome horseflies.

It was the ones who'd started it, Joash and Obadiah, whom she remembered. In her mind, sixteen-year-old boys who are almost men and who resort to bullying a ten-year-old girl need to be put back a notch.

One morning, she told Noah and Isaac to go ahead, that she needed to heed a call from nature. They went on to school without their sister, talking animatedly, innocent of anything out of the ordinary.

Hester slipped into the woods, took a running leap at a low branch her sharp eyes had discovered a week beforehand, caught it deftly with both hands, and swung herself up into the tree. Her purple dress billowed up and out, her bare feet latched onto the rough bark like a squirrel.

A small grunt, and she was up to the next branch, her hands and feet quick and sure. She took the slingshot from the large pocket sewn into the seam of her dress and draped it around her neck.

She stopped. Her dark eyes peered through the brownish-red foliage of the white oak tree. Unsatisfied with her vantage point, she moved quickly to the opposite side of the tree, her eyes moving from side to side, evaluating the distance and the clearest view.

Lifting the small homemade slingshot, she reached into her pocket for the largest, smoothest stone. She rolled it between her thumb and forefinger, savoring the perfection of it. She knew her aim was uncanny, completely without fault. She'd practiced behind the barn for weeks, sliding the slingshot into her pocket whenever footsteps approached.

Her breathing was steady, her muscles bunched, rigid as iron, her feet wrapped about the thin branch as she squatted, her back leaning against an adjoining branch. A group of children approached, walking fast, low words rising to Hester's ears, but she made no move to acknowledge them. A horse and wagon followed, rumbling by beneath the tree. Still she waited.

Then she spied both forms strolling into view, stalling for time, wanting to be the last ones into the schoolroom, to see what Theodore Crane would make of it.

Joash wore a brown straw hat, which made it more difficult as a target, so she chose Obadiah's instead. Skillfully, she fitted a smooth stone into the strip of rubber, drew back, and let it fly, picking Obadiah's light-colored straw hat expertly off his head and setting it neatly in the tall, dry grass beside the road, where it swung on the grass tops, then slithered from view.

"*Voss in die velt*" (What in the world)? Obadiah stopped and lifted his face, his mouth open in astonishment. Before he could retrieve his hat, a stone knocked Joash's hat neatly off his head.

"*Voss geht au*" (What's going on)?

Shaken, their faces blanched now, they bent to retrieve their hats, only to be hit simultaneously on their backs by hard objects that caused them to cry out, each grabbing at the spot that was already smarting.

When a high-pitched ghostly yodel followed, an otherworldly, weird quality in the awful sound, they scrambled around on their hands and knees, grabbed their hats, and with a wild-eyed glance at the treetops, took off running, unable to resist a few backward glances as the high, undulating wail continued.

When Hester saw a knot of boys in the schoolyard, listening with rapt attention and large, scared eyes as Obadiah and Joash gesticulated with their hands, she turned away, her eyes flat and expressionless.

When the teasing stopped, she said nothing. When she heard Obadiah say there was an old legend about a ghost in the hollow where they had their hats knocked off, her mouth twitched.

For months, the men discussed this happening at church and every other gathering. Always, for a long time afterward, they lifted the reins, brought them down on their surprised horses' rumps, and moved through that hollow at a smart clip, keeping their eyes straight ahead as they rumbled past the haunted tree.

Hester never turned when she felt Obadiah's and Joash's eyes boring into the back of her head.

CHAPTER 9

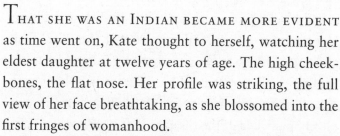

THAT SHE WAS AN INDIAN BECAME MORE EVIDENT as time went on, Kate thought to herself, watching her eldest daughter at twelve years of age. The high cheekbones, the flat nose. Her profile was striking, the full view of her face breathtaking, as she blossomed into the first fringes of womanhood.

She was still a girl, a child, and yet there was a difference. She moved with a supple grace, her footfalls without sound. She moved through doors, opening them only wide enough to allow her slim body to slip through, as if opening them wider would allow too much wasted space.

She often seemed to experience the house as an uncomfortable place of detention, causing her to become restless, often pacing from window to window and back again.

With the horses, she was phenomenal, showing no fear and much patience. She exercised a skillful authority that usurped Hans's own expertise. That was why she often accompanied her father on his horseshoeing forays, able to assist with the mean-spirited ones.

On this day in early summer, Hans had asked Kate if it was all right to take Hester, but Kate had demurred, saying the blackberries were ripe, and they needed all they could get to make jam. Hans protested, becoming quite upset, but Kate refused to budge. The family numbered ten now, after the births of Menno and six-week-old Emma.

In the rocker by the hearth, Kate rocked the baby, the chair almost completely hidden by her voluminous skirts, spreading over her ample hips and long, thick legs. Her swollen feet protruded from beneath the heavy skirt, her soiled black apron reaching only a bit below the knees. Her arms were thick and capable, her shoulders fleshy and soft, a home to the dear babies God had been kind enough to allow them to have. That was a thought she still clung to, grasping it with greedy fingers as she completely panicked at the thought that kept trying to push its way into her knowing.

Her life was often a bit more than she could handle. She tried steadily to tip the scales toward accepting children as good blessings, at least they were supposed to be.

Kate struggled. She loved a clean house. She liked her washing done on time, the whites as white as possible. For that, she scrubbed the laundry in water that was almost unbearably hot, using a knife to scrape cakes of strong lye soap with a vengeance.

She carefully folded and put away the wind-blown wash as soon as it was dry. She liked to have a weed-free garden, the walk and floors of the house swept.

But when the babies came every year, the workload increased tenfold. The pounds on her tall frame kept adding on until, when she came to the age of forty, her bones creaked in the morning, her back hurt by evening, and still the babies cried. The weeds multiplied in the garden, and Hans could hardly keep up with the farm and all the horseshoeing.

Kate slung little Emma across her back in a large cloth tied around her shoulders. She told all the children to come along, to gather up the wooden pails by the springhouse, and to climb the ridge behind the house with her.

Hester helped with the little ones, carrying Menno piggyback, her strides effortless, until she pulled far ahead of everyone else.

Kate grabbed a young locust tree, lowered her head, and gasped for breath, the pain in her chest suddenly smothering her. She coughed and wheezed and put a hand to her throat. She watched the little ones cavorting about the low grass like energetic rabbits and remembered wistfully the time when she, too, frolicked so effortlessly.

Quite unexpectedly, an unexplainable rage gripped her. She lifted her head and screeched at Hester in a thin, whining sound of reprisal. "Hester! Stop! You're going too fast, and you don't wait on the little ones!"

Impatient, Hester turned without saying anything, her eyes flat, dark slits. Menno was asleep on her back.

Mopping her streaming forehead with the edge of her dark apron, Kate saw her young daughter looking like an Indian princess—haughty, superior, capable—and the first nibble of jealousy crept into her heart, a subtle invasion, a harbinger of maladies.

Oh, she looked astounding, this child who was no longer the small baby she had found. Her hair was like the wing of a raven. She had perfect form, the ability to climb any mountain or tree, ride any horse, and impress Hans with all of it.

Of course, it was Hester who led them to the black raspberries. They were even better than the blackberries. At the edge of a natural clearing, the bushes grew in such great abundance, it was difficult to remain calm.

The children squealed in delight and were soon covered in purple stains as they tore the berries off the prickly bushes and stuffed them into their mouths. They savored the sweet juice on their tongues, forgetting their steady diet of turnips, cabbage, carrots, deer meat, and pork.

They filled every pail heaping full. Then Hester took off her apron and filled it with the succulent berries. Bees flew lazily by, sated with the sweet juice, and butterflies hovered over the vast growth, sipping their own portion of summer's bounty.

Noah stopped, lifting his face as three crows wheeled across the sky, their raucous cries a warning to his trained ears. At the same moment, Hester pointed, mute.

A black bear and her cubs.

Hester and Noah acted in one accord, herding the children silently, efficiently, out of the clearing.

"Mam, you must come." Noah's voice was a whisper but with much urgency, a tone that Kate completely missed. Loudly, she said, "This bucket isn't full yet."

Noah held a finger to his lips, grabbed the baby from her sling, and ran into the safety of the woods where Hester had herded the remainder of the family.

Intent on filling the one pail to the brim, Kate turned back to the bushes, her wide back to the heavy black brute that was now raised up on its hind legs, its nose snuffling, sniffing the wind. Its small brown eyes rolled from left to right, searching for the intruder with the strange smell.

Kate turned at the cawing of the crows, subconsciously aware that it was never a good omen. At the same time, the bear dropped on all fours and moved toward the trespasser in her berry patch. Kate turned and froze. The black bulk was moving fast in its lopsided, shuffling gait, the hulking body propelled by the bear's desperation to save her cubs.

A high wail of despair tore from Kate's lips, and she raised her arms up over her face, instinctively shielding herself from the black onslaught. The mother bear hit her with terrific force. Its stinking hot breath was the only thing preceding the slashing, red hot, ripping sensation as four sharp teeth embedded themselves in the soft white flesh of Kate's shoulder, shredding the homespun fabric with ease.

She didn't know if she was screaming or the bear or her cubs. She only knew that a blood-curdling bellow went on and on as she lay, waiting for the subsequent bites and her death. She knew the end was here as she cried out in the German language of her forebears. She remembered her parents in Switzerland and the loss she realized when she left them, knowing she would never see them again.

"Mein Gott, ich bitte dich, hilf mihr" (My God, I beg you, help me)!

She begged for mercy, at the same moment she accepted her fate.

"*Dein villa geshay, auf erden vie im Himmel*" (Yet, oh blessed Lord, your will be done on earth as it is in heaven).

The screaming went on, the wild howling accompanied by thumps, someone beating, beating.

Kate knew the bear had gone when an eerie quiet hung over the clearing. She lay on her side, her bloodied shoulder on the ground. Slowly, she rolled on her back and grimaced as she struggled to sit up.

Immediately, Hester was there, her dark eyes taking in everything—the shredded dress, the punctured shoulder, the dark blood pumping out of it, slowly running down her arm and across her dress front.

"*Komm*" (Come). Hester spoke calmly as she helped her mother to her feet. They both knew the importance of getting to the house as quickly as possible. To save her mother the added burden, Hester transported baby Emma in the sling and carried two pails, while Noah and Isaac brought the remaining berries, the other children between them, their eyes wide with fear.

No one complained or lagged behind, and few words were spoken as they made their way off the mountain. Often Noah looked back or to the left, then to the right, keenly aware of his surroundings as Hester took the lead. She strode swiftly down the steep incline, scrambling over rocks and between trees, her only objective to get her family back to the safety of the house.

They poulticed Kate's bleeding shoulder with ground red pepper, eliminating the heavy flow of blood almost immediately.

Noah slung his powerful body across the back of the swiftest roan and rode headlong to Lissie Hershberger's house. She was in her garden, busily tying up her pole beans, hot, red-faced, and ill humored. She sincerely hoped that crazy rider was not someone needing assistance. She was dead tired and so sleepy her whole head felt fuzzy. Midwifery wasn't easy, and she wasn't young anymore.

Hans Zug's Noah. What did he want?

He told her, breathlessly, shaking the blond hair away from his face. Lissie gave herself up right then and there, but she couldn't help grumbling to herself, imagining that fat Kate, so greedy for berries to make all that jam to put on her many slices of bread. Her own fault.

Ach no, she reasoned. Forgive me, *Herr Jesu.* I have sinned.

Lissie settled the cloak of love securely about her shoulders, buttoned it well with the virtue of duty, hitched up her own horse, and drove recklessly to Hans Zug's, her leather case of tinctures and salves rattling along on the back seat of her wagon.

She entered the house amid crying babies and wide-eyed little ones. Kate was propped up on pillows, grim-faced and pale.

"*Voss hot gevva*" (What gives)?

Kate blinked, then ground out through tight lips, "A mother bear. Picking raspberries."

Lissie peered over her round, gold spectacles and lifted the thick square of cloth.

She clucked like a hen, sucked her teeth, and said, "*Eye, yei, yei.*"

Kate lifted worried eyes and asked if she'd be all right.

"Oh, *ya, ya.* But she got you good. It's a wonder she didn't finish you off."

"She would have, but for Hester."

Lissie stood still.

"Hester?"

"*Ya.*"

"What did she do?"

"Oh, she screamed and carried on."

"She banged on the bear with a big branch, kept it right up, yelling the whole time," Isaac offered, his eyes bright with excitement.

Lissie turned to Hester, who sat on the wooden rocker holding the baby, dipping a cloth into warm milk, satisfying its constant need to be fed for now.

Hester ducked her head, and Lissie was presented with the sheen of black hair.

"Hester! My, oh," Lissie said.

Hester volunteered nothing, so Lissie turned to her bandaging. She washed the wound with hot water and lye soap, then laid comfrey leaves over it and held them tight with clean cloths, watching as Kate's lips compressed, gritting her teeth as Lissie pressed the remedy against her skin. She'd be fine, Lissie knew. This woman was strong.

"All right?"

Kate nodded.

Lissie knew her remedies. Chickweed salve and a clean compress with strips tied around her chest and beneath her arms, comfrey tea, and comfrey leaves to help with infection.

Lissie marveled at Kate's size. My goodness, she was a lump. Now who would take care of all those raspberries, with her laid up from that bear chomp?

"There you go, Kate. Now don't do anything for at least a week. You could tear those puncture wounds, and you don't want to start up the bleeding. Do you need help putting away the raspberries?"

Kate tried to smile, but it turned into a grimace. "Hester can."

"By herself?"

"I think so."

From her seat on the rocking chair, Hester raised her head. Lissie watched the dark eyes glisten in the noon light, slide away from her mother's face, then move back again. This time, a new and darker light shone from those mesmerizing eyes, and Lissie stiffened, her small blue eyes going rapidly from Kate's face to Hester's.

Was there *ztvie dracht* (divisions)?

Turning to Hester, Lissie raised her eyebrows.

"You look tired. You have things to do. I'll manage," Hester spoke quietly.

Lissie looked dubiously at the little, dark-skinned girl, at the nine children surrounding her, the weary Kate, the six pails of raspberries, the apron thrown in the corner with dark purple juice leaking out of its bulk, spreading a purple stain across the scrubbed oak floor. And Lissie made up her mind. She'd stay.

Hester placed the sleeping Emma in the cradle by the hearth, sliced a loaf of sourdough bread, spread it with wild pear butter, and sat the children in rows on the benches pulled up on each side of the long plank table.

Lissie poured cups of spearmint tea and laced it with molasses. The children ate hungrily, and then the littlest ones were put to bed for their naps. Kate fell asleep, snoring softly.

Noah and Isaac went down to the barn to finish cleaning the cow stables. Lissie set to work.

Hester was a fast learner. She washed the berries and put them to cook in the large cast iron pot.

Lissie tried to get Hester to talk, in the manner of mother and daughter. She soon discovered that Hester was not comfortable with too many questions. Yes, she got along well with her mother. Yes, she enjoyed the babies. Yes, she worked hard. Yes, she liked it.

Finally, Lissie's round form shook with laughter. "Can't you say anything except yes?"

Hester's head dipped, but her eyes sparkled, and when she raised her head, Lissie felt as if an angel had visited her. When she finally looked Lissie full in the face and smiled a full, wide smile, her eyes danced with humor.

Where would this young girl's destiny take her? She was, indeed, a special girl, a gift of God for Hans and Kate. But after nine children in ten years, did they remember? Or was Hester turning into an unpaid servant?

She mentioned Hans, and Hester's face lit up.

"Dat likes me. He's very nice to me. He buys me things special. He tells me to hide it from the others. Especially Noah and Isaac."

Lissie's eyes narrowed. She stopped stirring the raspberries. "He does?"

Hester nodded happily.

"Look!"

She ran to the adjoining bedroom, and Lissie heard the scraping of a box on the wooden floor. Hester returned with a necklace of turquoise stones, draping it across her fingers, lifting them to move the exquisite lights of blue green. "Isn't it beautiful?" she whispered.

"But it's jewelry. From Indians. We Amish don't believe in adornment of the body. Hester, Hans should not have given it to you."

"Oh, it's just for pretty. To keep. I have to put it in my box under the bed."

Lissie nodded, her eyes wary. Well, suspicious or not, real Christian love would accept and believe the child's story, so she did, for at least five minutes. Then she blurted out, "But he didn't ask you to wear the forbidden jewelry?"

Hester shook her head, her eyes averted.

When she looked up, Lissie's eyes questioned the shaking of her head, but again, Hester's eyes were flat and expressionless, so Lissie shrugged it off once more and changed the subject.

Hester, however, enthused by the rare peek into her dearest thoughts, told Lissie how Hans had draped the necklace about her neck, just to see what a true Indian looked like. "He doesn't *schput* (mock) my dark skin, the way some others do. He is a very good father. He is kind."

Lissie lifted the heavy square of muslin, bulging with steam and hot cooked raspberries, and squeezed so hard the juice burst out of the cloth. She burned her fingers and whistled.

"*Häse*" (Hot)! she chortled.

Hester laughed out loud, a sound like the tinkling of cold spring water tumbling over mossy stones.

Lissie realized why the sound shocked her. Hester rarely laughed, and certainly not out loud.

They added precious coarse sugar to the steaming raspberry juice, then set it to boil in the big pot over the low burning embers in the fireplace, filling the whole house with its summery fragrance.

Lissie set about mixing lard and brown flour, wetting it with vinegar water, her capable hands kneading and mixing. She thumped the wooden rolling pin across the lump of dough under Hester's watchful eye.

Not one bit of the raspberries went to waste. Lissie poured the pulpy mush out of the muslin square, added a bit of sugar, and thickened it with more flour. Then she dumped the mixture into the waiting pie crusts, slapped another rolled pastry on top, and set the pies on the table while she got the brick oven going.

Not too far away from the back door, Hans had built a bake oven for his wife. The low building was large enough to contain a sizable brick oven with a cast iron door built into the opening and room for a roaring fire. A large wooden paddle hung on a hook beside the oven. When the fire had died down, and the coals had been raked out of the oven, Kate placed pies and bread on this thick paddle, inserted it into the vast interior, or slid it beneath them when they were done baking and pulled them back out.

The bake oven was not in the kitchen because of the heat in the summertime. Kate was as proud of Hans's craftsmanship of the oven as she was of the springhouse he had built.

With the addition built onto the house and the many acres Hans had cleared through the years, the little gray house and weathered barn were turning into a farm, a place where hard work and skilled traits were in evidence.

Kate lay in her bed enduring the pain, half listening to Lissie Hershberger and Hester. When Hester laughed out loud, Kate strained to see, catching a glimpse of their bent heads, Hester voicing her admiration of Hans.

Wearily, Kate closed her eyes and let her head roll back and sink mercifully into the softness of the feather pillow. That bothersome old agitation about Hans's admiration of Hester was too wearying for words. Lissie didn't need to be nosing into their life this way. It really was none of her concern. But here Kate was, unable to work, Lissie's capable hands *fa-sarking* (caring for) all the raspberries, and she was having contentious, selfish thoughts. She was ashamed. She fell asleep with humility coasting through her dreams.

Hans listened to the children's tale of adventuresome raspberry picking and fussed over his bedridden wife, his face filled with loving concern. Kate gazed into Hans's face, his round cheeks gleaming in the light of the fire, and let the love she felt for him hover between them as her eyes stayed on his.

Yes, he was a loving husband, a good provider, a man clever with his tools, building her a bake oven and springhouse, so why would she fret about *kindish* things like a small bauble he gave to Hester?

Lissie was out at the bake oven wielding the heavy wooden paddle. She removed the piping hot raspberry pies, muttering her grievances to herself, and mumbled her way into the house in time to see the loving exchange between husband and wife. Guilt-ridden, she decided to drop her suspicions then, considering her thoughts nothing but evil surmising, a horrid sin.

Hester tucked the turquoise necklace into the wooden box beneath her bed and felt confident that she had made a friend, a trustworthy one, at that.

CHAPTER 10

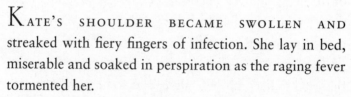

Kate's shoulder became swollen and streaked with fiery fingers of infection. She lay in bed, miserable and soaked in perspiration as the raging fever tormented her.

Hans brought Dr. Hess. He lanced some of the most infected parts of her shoulder, wrote instructions for the care of it, and left, leaving Hans pacing the floor, his head thrust forward, his hands clasped behind his back.

He was worried about Kate. How could he manage with ten children if something happened to her? Would she be laid to rest beside little Rebecca in the damp earth of that lonely, forsaken graveyard?

He shivered, the shadows around him becoming living things, raking at him with dark, transparent claws.

His breathing became labored. Beads of sweat formed above his lips. He stopped pacing. The suffocating shadows immediately clambered over him with nerve-wracking accuracy. A roaring began in his ears. He stopped the sound with forefingers pushed against them.

Lunging against the door, he fell out onto the pathway in the cool night and lowered himself to a stump in the yard, trembling. He turned, slid to his knees, lifted his hands in prayerful supplication, and begged his God for mercy. *"Mein Gott, Mein Heiland!"*

Tears rained down his face as he prayed for Kate's deliverance. When he opened his eyes, the twinkling white of the stars blurred with the silvery leaves that were bathed in moonlight. The low-lying dark barn rose in stark contrast to the surrounding fields. He thought of the growing herd of cows, the pigs. Who would milk them? Who would make butter and cheese? Who would make bacon and sausage?

Kate's worth rose above him, leaving him reeling with the need to keep his wife alive, and so he prayed on, far into the night until he was completely spent.

The robins set up a raucous chirping before the sun had even begun its ascent over the mountaintop. Hester closed the door of the log house quietly behind her, padding noiselessly on bare feet down to the barn. She stopped to listen to the saucy chirping of the robins, smiled to herself, and moved on. Ambitious birds. They always got the worm first, waking up before anyone else.

"Guten morgen" (Good morning)! Hans greeted her cheerfully. She nodded at her father, a smile parting her lips, as she found his direct gaze.

"Hester, if it's not too much for you, I guess you'll have to milk the two cows your mother normally does," he said, leaning against a rough-hewn post as his eyes surveyed her face.

"How is she?"

"Not good, I'm afraid."

Hester nodded, alarmed at the pain in her father's voice. She was spare with words, as well as emotion, so she chose to leave it at that. She reached for the wooden bucket hanging from a nail in the barn, next to the cows' stalls.

She supposed she could ask Dat if Mam would live, but he didn't know the answer. No one did. So she became very quiet within herself, sat down on the dirty stool beside Meg, the Brown Swiss cow, and began to milk.

She pulled and squeezed, her strong brown fingers capable of producing jets of warm, creamy milk into the wooden bucket. But by the time the third cow was milked, she wasn't sure if she could ever open or close her fingers properly again. She rubbed one hand over the other, her face pinched with exhaustion, her mind jumbled with Noah's inability to milk. And Isaac's for that matter.

When Hans met her at the barn door, she asked him why she had to milk alone.

"I milked two. Why can't Noah?"

"He's too young."

"He needs to get up early and learn to milk if Mam isn't well."

Hans was surprised at Hester being so outspoken, finding it a bit unsettling. Well, the boys weren't capable like Hester. Besides, he enjoyed the peace and solitude while milking. Hester was quiet and soft-spoken, and those boys would be yakking on about their *dumb heita* (foolishness), disturbing his morning. He didn't need them in the barn.

Hester had never cooked breakfast by herself. She came into the kitchen hungry, her fingers dulled by pain, her mother a large form beneath the coverlet, and baby Emma screaming from the cradle. Menno, awakened by the baby's cries of hunger, let loose with a loud yell of indignation. For a moment, Hester was overwhelmed with inadequacy, a tiny form in the face of a huge, unscalable cliff.

She looked around, her eyes large in her brown face, her dress hanging loosely on her thin frame, tendrils of straight, black hair draped over her forehead and into her eyes.

The house was in disarray. A greasy white tablecloth hung sideways on the plank table, unwashed dishes scattered over it. The redware jar with lilies of the valley that Barbara had picked a fortnight ago was perched precariously on the edge, half full of murky brown water, the small white flowers drooping and half-dead. The floor was strewn with bits of string and corncobs, wooden spools that were empty of thread, colorful pieces of cloth, hay, mud, and dirt.

A rancid odor came from a redware plate in the middle of the table. Hester picked it up and shooed the blowflies from it. Slimy yellow maggots had already hatched from their eggs where the half-cooked rabbit had begun to spoil.

She took the smelly mess to the door, opened it, stepped out and away from the house, and flung the spoiled food angrily into a briar patch. Let the vultures find it.

She stood very still, lifting her eyes to the rising sun. She let her gaze wander across the beautiful green ridges that fell away on each side of her, over the sturdy, gray, log house, and the barn below it, the stone springhouse, split-rail fences, the lush pasture with grazing cows behind it. The sky was lavender, the rosy-hued sunrise turning into a heavenly color.

She turned to the sun, the yellow orb warm on her skin. The Creator made the sun, the land, and her. She felt a part of the waving grass at her feet, the moving leaves over her head. She was here. This was her home. She couldn't separate herself from the forest or the sky or the sun. God had made it all, set her here with this family. They were hers.

Taking a deep breath, she lifted her face to the sun, letting the pores of her skin absorb its warmth, receiving its strength. The rustling of the leaves from the great oak tree whispered its resilience against drought and storms and hordes of insects. The morning breeze lifted loose strands of her hair, caressing her smooth brown forehead, and she felt the breath of her Creator. She would be strong. She would do her best. In the face of all the obstacles, she would be able.

In the house, she changed the baby's cloth diaper, swaddled her in a warm blanket, and then set Isaac to work feeding her. In clipped words, she ordered Noah down to the barn, telling him he should have been down there since five when she went. He cast her a red-faced look of shame, but she already had her back turned, retrieving the heavy, cast iron pot from its hook.

She wrinkled her nose at the residue of burnt beans, then carried the pot outside and sloshed tepid water into it from the bucket on the bench beside the door. Better let that soak. She'd watched Mam soak burned beans.

Daniel and John were awake and already quarreling, their long nightshirts stained from too many nights of being worn and too few washings. Their hair was stiff and tangled, their eyes heavy with sleep and the inability to understand.

"Solomon, get the boys' knee breeches," Hester called, from her station by the fireplace.

"Where's Mam?" he asked.

"Asleep."

"Why?"

"She's sick."

Climbing to the top cupboard on a kitchen chair, Hester got down her mother's recipe from the pile she kept there, then snorted, a balled up fist on each hip when she realized she could not read the recipe. Well, she'd watched Mam.

Taking up the clean, cast iron pot, she filled it half full of water, added a handful of salt, hung it on the heavy, black hook, and swung it over the fire. Grabbing the heavy poker, she stirred up the coals and barked a command to Isaac, who laid the baby in her cradle, where immediately she set up an awful howling. Unsure what to do, Isaac hesitated but was immediately pressed to a choice by Hester's second set of orders. She wanted wood for the fire. She wanted it now.

He dumped the wood on the glowing ashes, which sent up a shower of sparks. But Hester chose to ignore that as she sliced bread on the dry sink.

She put Lissie to work cleaning the dirty dishes from the soiled tablecloth, telling her to shake the cloth, replace it with a clean one, and set the table with clean, redware plates. She put down redware cups and a spoon with each plate, then placed a pat of butter on a small plate in the middle. The breakfast table was set.

Hester stopped, hearing her mother's soft cries. Swiftly, she went to her and bent low, listening. Her anxious wails were punctuated by hiccups, her ramblings unintelligible. Hester placed a hand on Kate's forehead, then drew back, catching her lower lip in her teeth, surprised by a sharp intake of breath.

Her mother would die. Already her festering wounds were odorous.

Hester ran with the speed of the wind, breaking into the cow stable where she found Dat, who looked up, surprised.

"You must come. Mam is very . . . she's burning hot."

With an exclamation of dismay, Hans let the pitchfork in his hands fall to the floor with a dull thud. He followed Hester from the barn, then flung himself by his wife's bedside, groans of despair wobbling from his loose, heavy lips.

"The doctor. The doctor!"

Hester looked at her father sharply. It was not proper for a girl to ride, but she had no choice. Her mother would die.

Lifting agonized eyes, Hans said, "Noah. Go."

Noah, terrified, shook his head. "I don't know the way."

"You have to go."

Hans was wailing, his teeth bared, as his lips drew back in unaccustomed fear.

Hester mulled the way in her mind, the forks in the path, the ford across the river. Already her heart pounded, knowing she would be the one to go. Hans couldn't. His beloved Kate might die in his absence.

She pulled on a pair of Noah's patched knee breeches, whistled for Rudy, the blue roan, caught him easily, and slipped the halter on his head and the bridle with the smallest bit attached to it. Then she stood aside, grasped a handful of the coarse mane, and flung herself up onto his back.

Rudy lifted his head, wheeled, and was out of the barnyard through the gap in the rail fence and onto the road that led to the doctor's house in Irish Creek.

Dust rose in little puffs as Rudy's hooves thundered down the grass-covered road. Deep ruts were cut into the road where spring thunderstorms had poured buckets of rain on the hilly landscape, sending gushes of muddy water down every incline. Rudy was surefooted, but Hester kept a watchful eye for especially deep and treacherous grooves, ducking her head, her face against the flying mane whenever a low branch loomed ahead of her.

The first fork in the road was a surprise, but she knew enough to stay left, and they thundered on. A small branch, like a whip, caught her forehead. She felt the sharp sting but let it go. When she put her hand up, her fingers came away sticky with blood that seeped from the wound.

The trees were thinning now, just as the road turned to the left yet again. When it headed steadily downhill, she knew they were close to the river. She remembered the boatman at the ford the last time she'd come to the trading post with her father.

When the road leveled off and Rudy's hooves sank deeper into the sandy soil, she caught a glimpse of the sparkling water, sunlight glinting from its wavelets, the water dark green, gray, and brown all at the same time.

She pulled back steadily on the reins, her dark eyes peering ahead into the unknown, a troubling scene that was the river and its ford, a large raft, a rope, and a boatman with a long wooden pole. A woman alone was never good, and she was only a girl. She'd heard Hans speak to Kate about this ford and the questionable characters that regularly took too much money from honest travelers, or worse.

She had no time to decide her plan or the action she would take if the boatman was dishonest. She had no money. She had forgotten the coins she'd need, overcome as she was by wanting to save her mother.

At a trot now, Rudy broke through the line of trees, Hester low on his back, her eyes downcast. She had seen the boatman and was fully aware of his flaming red hair, his youth. She could only try.

She pulled Rudy to a stop. His nostrils quivered, his sides heaved, sweat stained his odd, bluish-gray, cream-colored flank.

The youth was tall, thin, and dressed in a clean linen shirt and knee breeches. His feet were brown and bare. His face was dark-skinned, his freckles barely visible, his eyes green. His head looked as if it was on fire, his hair was so red.

He looked up, said, "Har."

Hester said nothing. She sat still as a stone, her black eyes watching his green ones.

It gave him the creeps, so he said, "Har," once more.

She nodded her head, then continued to stare.

He jerked his thumb in the general direction of the river.

"You want across?"

"Yes."

"Five cents."

"I don't have money."

"Then yer gonna haf to swim." Rudy snorted, turned his head at the small tug from Hester's hand, and started down the embankment to the waving grasses at the water's edge.

"Hey! I didn't mean it."

"Say what you mean."

The youth watched as she turned her horse again, then slid off with the ease of long practice. She was just a slip of a thing. Couldn't be older than fourteen. Maybe even thirteen.

"You shouldn't be by yerself."

"My mother is very sick. I'm going for the doctor."

The youth whistled. "That's a long way off."

"So."

"Why don't you go to Trader Joe's? Indians all over the place."

"I'm not going for an Indian."

"Why not?"

"I want Doctor Hess."

"You're an Indian, ain't you?"

"I'm an Amish Indian."

"A who?"

"Take me across."

"S' wrong with yer ma?"

"She's . . . She was . . . She has wounds. They're festering. She has a fever."

"You don't need a doctor. You need Uhma. She's a herb healer. Sort of like a witch."

Hester looked at him, wide-eyed, her face revealing nothing.

"Did you already have the doctor?"

Hester nodded.

"I figured."

The youth stood looking across the water, then turned and looked back the way she had come. He seemed to be considering something. He looked at Hester finally.

"Look. Is your ma dying?"

Hester shrugged her shoulders, her eyes flat, giving away nothing.

"Can you stay here and let me take your horse?"

"No!" The sound was an angry outburst, a vehement refusal.

"Then you're going to have to let me up on your horse's back. I can't give you directions. I have to take you to Uhma's house."

"Your mother?"

That question showed the crack in her steely resolve, and he said quickly, "No. Everyone calls her Uhma. She's an old, old Indian woman that mixes herbs and stuff. If your ma was bit and has a fever, ain't much Doc Hess is gonna do, trust me."

He watched the young girl's face. Nothing changed in it. Her eyes didn't blink or her lips part or anything at all. Her answer was merely a dipping of her head, the glossy black hair visible instead of her face. Was she Indian or wasn't she? She sure was pretty, he thought, but odder than a two-headed calf.

"Come," she said, suddenly.

In one swift movement, quicker than he had ever seen anyone mount a horse, she swung up on her horse's back, looking down at him. He met her black eyes, a question in his, and she nodded. He had to grab a handful of the horse's mane, but she sat firm as he flung himself up, his left arm raking across her middle.

He pointed to the narrow trail following the river, and she goaded Rudy into action, his hooves pounding the wet sandy earth with dull thunks as they sped along the river bottom, skirting willow trees, honeysuckle vines, and great arches of raspberry and blackberry bushes hanging across the trail.

Blue jays screamed their hoarse cries as they flew out of their way. Fat groundhogs sat up, listening, then lowered themselves and waddled out of sight at their approach. Turtles sunning themselves on half-submerged logs slid silently into brackish water, and frogs briefly stopped their endless croaking, starting back up again after they passed.

The road led up from the river bottom into dense forests of pines and briars so thick, the road became only a trail. Jagged rocks protruded from the pine needles, and the pines thinned to a few dead, old trees, charred from some long-ago forest fire. Seedlings sprang up everywhere, the sunlight filtered through the dead trees giving them life.

The trail became steeper with rocks jutting out over it. Hester slowed Rudy, afraid of the sharp edges. She lifted her head. She heard water. She remained silent, thinking the youth would speak if she needed to know something.

Rudy continued climbing up the trail at a fast walk. They rounded a bend, and Rudy lowered his head to pick his way carefully as the trail turned steeply down.

The sound of water became more apparent, a sloshing, tumbling sound. Birds called, a myriad of sounds that surpassed anything she'd ever heard. It seemed as if hundreds of birds were warbling or singing, whistling and calling, all at once. The trees around them were alive with the colorful songsters.

Emotion that had no name rose in Hester's chest. The plaintive calls and whistles evoked the nameless call of the Creator. He was alive and had made her and the life around her. He had formed the youth with the flaming hair that sat so close behind her. She felt bound to a great and Higher Spirit, a power far beyond her years.

The trees thinned once more, the trail smoothed out, and the light became brighter with shafts of sunlight piercing the branches. Hester breathed deeply. The dry summer smell of the forest had changed to a rich, wet smell, the way a quick thundershower in summer gave out a clean scent.

Suddenly, they broke through the trees into a natural glade where strong sunlight poured through the gap in the forest. Hester quenched a gasp of pure astonishment.

The youth behind her said, "Stop your horse."

Mute, she pulled steadily on the reins, remaining seated, unable to move. She had never seen or experienced any place of beauty such as this. An outcropping of limestone created a shelf high up the side of a steep cliff. Pure, clean, silver water tumbled off the rocks and splashed against more stone before it fell into a deep pool, so clear it was the same color as the trees and the sky and the earth beneath it.

Great masses of dark green ferns moved restlessly, either by the breeze or the droplets of water that sprayed endlessly from the moving water. Lilies, orange, yellow, and white, grew in abundance, great colorful clusters of them everywhere she looked.

Hester was aware of the youth's hand lightly on her waist. "I guess you still remember yer ma."

Shaken by the strong feelings, the response to all this beauty, Hester could only nod and slip quickly from her horse's back. She was brought back to the moment by his voice. "See that goat? It's Uhma's. Best tie yer horse."

Hester dropped the reins. Patting Rudy's neck she said, "He'll stay."

She caught the sunlight in the youth's green eyes and was amazed to find they were exactly the same color as the deep pool of water where the ferns grew out over.

CHAPTER 11

"FOLLOW ME."

Obediently, she fell in behind him. His quick footsteps led her along the outskirts of the glade.

The white goat grazing by the pool lifted its head, chewing rapidly before bleating its high-pitched sound.

Hester laughed out loud. "Silly goat." Her voice was a caress, that of a lover of animals. Her laugh was a waterfall, a human tinkling sound of spring water, but more refreshing. He'd never heard any sound of laughter like that, ever.

They rounded the falls, becoming silent as the power of the water stilled them. Another bower of rocks and ferns, a few young trees, and they came upon a wooden hovel tucked beneath a pine tree so large it seemed to reach all the way to the sun. It was mostly made of bark with a round top that was all one piece. Moss grew over it in some places to the north like an old tree. Plants were growing everywhere. Vegetables in sunny areas—beans and corn, squash and pumpkin. Many different flowering plants tumbled over and about one another in colorful profusion. More goats were tethered close to the peculiar little house.

As they approached, the youth called out. Instantly, a white head appeared at the door, the face beneath it as brown and craggy as the bark surrounding the door. Two white braids hung on each side of the face, the black eyes hooded by layers of loose skin, wrinkle upon wrinkle folding themselves beside the eyes, up the side of them and down along the cheeks. A shift hung loosely on the narrow shoulders, but the hips were wide, the skirt hanging in gathers over the width of the old woman.

She did not smile. She spoke only in broken English, her speech soft, as if it came from deep in her throat. "You." That was her way of greeting.

Her black eyes examined Hester with the intensity of a magnifying glass. She spoke another language very fast, then came over to Hester and touched her hair, her face. A strong grassy odor enveloped Hester, like when a pitchfork lifted newly mown hay that had been rained on and partially dried.

"Lenape," she kept repeating, nodding her head, her tongue clicking against the roof of her mouth.

The youth watched Uhma, looked at Hester, and waited. Finally, he stated his purpose.

"What bite?" Uhma asked, her black eyes boring into Hester's.

"Bear. Mother bear. A black one."

"Ooo. Ooo." Pursing her lips, she nodded, then disappeared into the bark-encrusted hovel.

The youth told Hester that meant she knew why the infection was there and what had caused it. She would know the mixture of herbs, the medicine they would need.

"I have no money," Hester said, quietly.

"She won't take any."

Hester nodded.

They waited. Silence hung over the peaceful little area except for the songs of birds and the distant waterfall. So many scents wafted through the air, intensified by the misty wetness of the falling water.

Uhma's return brought the bleating of the littlest goat, and she turned, scolding, chiding, in another language.

She handed them a package, a small one, wrapped in skin and tied with string. Her sharp eyes confronted Hester, boldly telling her to stay still and listen.

"This." She pointed to the package. "This. Steep in boiling water. Pack on bite. Hot. Change every four hour."

Producing another package, she held it up. "This. Steep in boiling water. Give to drink. Every hour. All day long."

"What is it?" the youth asked.

In answer, Uhma shook her head, solemnly. "I die, packages die with me."

She straightened, her eyes seeing faraway, further than the mere earth and trees and sky. "The Lenape. Common people. There is no separate. The land and the people are one. No longer. I die. I go soon to my Creator. I have been here awhile, now soon I go. I have knowledge. It go, too. Too many new worlds come. One foot in old, one in new. Not good. Now go. Heal girl's mother."

Hester put out her hand in the manner of the Amish to shake Uhma's hand, a way of thanksgiving, of gratitude, "Thank you. *Denke schöen.*"

Uhma's hand was cool and calloused, the skin paper-thin between them, her grip firm and sure. Her eyes kindled with an ancient recognition of her people, her lips parted in a smile. "You Lenape girl. I die, you come."

She swung her hand in the direction of her little hut, the goats and herbs, the falling water. "You come. Get wisdom. I write."

Her black eyes shone, the wrinkles deepening around them. Hester felt as if she had been given a blessing, just like the way the bishop, John Lantz, would say so lovingly, *"Ich vinch da saya"* (I wish for you a blessing).

A current of understanding passed between them, fully understood by Uhma, still innocent and unaware by Hester. *We are one people, one culture, the same blood flows in our veins, no matter what the white men try to take from us. We had a proud heritage, we are one with the land.*

When their axes bite into the trees of our forest, they bite into our souls. Our heartbeats are one with the Creator, our responsibility the care of the earth.

Young Lenape girl, your blood will be Indian forever. Destiny can take you where it chooses, but your Indian heritage will remain. Go in peace.

The return trip found the youth reluctant to let go of her. He tacked it up to his long days of loneliness as a boatman, shrugged his young shoulders, and tried not to think more about it. But her black hair that blew in wisps across his face was a sensation that stayed with him during the remainder of his time at the river. He slid off the horse with an acute sense of loss. She sat straight, keeping her eyes on the trail ahead, not moving a muscle.

"Thank you," she whispered.

"Will you be coming by again?"

She shook her head. "I am not allowed to speak to outsiders. Especially men."

"Yes. Well."

He wanted to keep her there, so he reached out to stroke Rudy's neck, who promptly lowered his head and nuzzled his shirt front. "You like horses?"

She nodded.

"Do you go to school?"

She nodded again.

"You don't know my name, and I don't know yours."

She became very still.

"I'm Padriac Lee. Paddy."

"Paddy is a girl's name."

"It's Irish."

"Oh."

"What's yours?'

She hesitated. Her mother would not be happy, knowing she spoke to Padriac Lee. "Hester Zug."

"Zug? Boy, you are Amish. Only people around with that name."

She hesitated. She was not used to sharing her feelings or her background and certainly not the fact that she was so different from her family.

"Are you an Indian?"

She shrugged her shoulders.

"You're a Lenape. They're good people, most of them. Same as the Amish."

She smiled.

"I have to let you go."

The overwhelming need to go with her, to protect her, was completely mystifying. He wanted to fling himself up on that horse, put his arms around her, and keep her safe for the rest of his life.

He touched the leg of her trousers and looked up at her. "Goodbye, Hester."

She nodded. Her eyes shone darkly as she lifted the reins. Rudy sprang into a gallop immediately, kicking up little clumps of sandy loam, leaving deep footprints in the earth and in Paddy's heart. The remainder of the day, he sat on an old wooden crate, his chin in his cupped hands, and stared across the water, her black eyes etched on the back of every object he saw.

When Hester returned, Kate had roused from her stupor, but the fever still raged, the infection still foul-smelling.

Hans met her at the door, the afternoon sun full in his face, his skin greasy and unwashed, his eyes intense with fear and worry.

"Where's the doctor?" he pleaded, anxiety edged in his voice.

"I didn't go to the doctor."

He raved and ranted. He tore at his hair with both hands on either side of his head, lifted his face to the ceiling and cried like a baby. He scolded Hester. He lifted his hand to smack her face, but couldn't bring himself to do it. The children cried, Noah walked to the barn, grim-faced, the look in his eyes much older than his years.

Hester calmly prepared the poultice and the tea, moving about the whitewashed rooms, talking to Hans quietly. Under her voice, he regained his sense of direction, wiped his streaming face, and set about helping Hester with her administrations.

Far into the night, they fed Kate the strong tea by the spoonful. They changed the poultices and lowered their faces to sniff the wounds, afraid to hope there was a difference.

Toward morning, when the sky was darkest, just before the light streaked the dark clouds of night, Kate began to cough, slightly at first, then with more effort. Hans was alone, Hester lying by the fireplace, her eyelids refusing to stay open.

At Hans's cry of alarm she scrambled to her feet, aware of her surroundings in an instant. She heard Kate coughing, then retching miserably, the strain tearing at her wounds.

When morning broke, Hans went to milk the cows. Hester changed the poultice once more, placing a hand on her mother's wide forehead. She was streaming with sweat. It beaded on her pale upper lip and ran from her forehead, soaking the nightdress she wore, the sheets beneath her, and the coverlet spread over her.

The breathing was very soft, almost indistinct, as her chest rose and fell evenly, her eyes closed as still as death. Through the fog of her weariness, Hester wondered if indeed she would die in spite of the night's vigil, the endless hours of spooning the tea into her mouth.

How patient Kate had been! So obedient, forcing herself to swallow when it took all of her strength to open her mouth. A new, stronger love for her mother welled from Hester's young heart, cementing the bond between a mother and her foundling. Perhaps they were not of the same blood, but heartstrings can be inseparable.

Hester replaced the bitter herbs every four hours steadily. She spooned tea endlessly into Kate's obedient mouth. She continued to perspire, then slide away into a sleep so deep Hans cried out for Hester to come. Had she died? Was this really the moment when he would need to give up his beloved wife?

All during that day and into the night, Kate slept. Toward morning, she began coughing again. Hester lay on her coverlet by the fireplace, hearing the rasping sound as if it was too far away, too unbearable to bother with. So it was Hans who bent his head to hear Kate's words.

"I want water."

Joy pulsed in his veins as he brought her a glass of cold water from the springhouse, stumbling over tufts of grass and his own shoes, bent over, scuttling, muttering to himself like a man possessed, unable to grasp the realization that God had, indeed, heard his pleading.

Kate's recovery was slow, but in a week's time, she sat on the hickory rocker, much thinner, weak and pale. As she held little Emma, her white face took on a shining gratitude.

Hester threw herself into the work, doing her best at the numerous tasks that needed to be done every day. Kate spoke in quiet tones, instructing Hester. How hot the water should be for the washing, how to smooth the wrinkles out of them before folding them and putting them away, how to bake the bread, boil the cornmeal mush.

The weeds in the garden took over, and Noah and Isaac were sent to pull them. They worked together as a team, and life went on. Visitors arrived, wagon loads of curious well-wishers bearing covered dishes of fruit-breads and nut cakes, *schnitz und knepp* (ham, apples, and dumplings).

Kate sat, wan, youthful-looking, almost beautiful, her blue eyes bearing an inner light of gratitude that had not been there before. Hans hovered over his wife in gentle servitude, bringing her a drink of water, a handkerchief, eager to do her bidding.

Hans's parents came, Isaac and Rebecca Zug, wanting to know more about the rumors that circulated through the community. Some said an Indian woman had cast a spell. Others said it was *hexary* (witchcraft).

Still others said Hans had prayed. A real miracle. *Unser Jesu* healed her.

Lissie Hershberger said Dr. Hess gave her enough laudanum that she slept it off, the infection.

So they came, talked and talked and talked, formed their own opinions, and went away *unglauvich* (unbelieving). Hans spoke plenty, his face red with effort, his beefy hands spread wide for emphasis. He showed them the herbs in the deer leather parcels, asked Hester to tell her story. Hester refused.

The air in the log house was stale and stuffy with the scent of mens' puffed up knowledge, their opinions permeating the very oxygen with their foolishness. The wagging beards, the wobbling chins, the endless solil-oquizing, surmising, backbiting about the old Indian woman. Some said they heard she lived and moved as one with the earth and its Creator, a witch.

Hester stayed still, silent as a rock, her large black eyes moving restlessly from face to face. When Rebec-ca laid the tablecloth on the long plank table to serve the food people had brought, her mouth was stern with rebuke. Hans and Kate sat up to the table, ate the good food obediently, and didn't address the subject.

They ate the *schnitz und knepp*. Rebecca piled the plates high with the boiled ham cooked in dried apples and dropped dumplings over the sweet and salty ham and apples, an old Amish favorite. Rebecca, watching her son ladle in huge mouthfuls and chew with great enjoyment, his cheeks round and rosy, was pleased. Here was her favorite son, his wife healed by his prayers, his children around him, his quiver full of good, strong arrows, able, sturdy workers who would be a great help as he journeyed on his way to prosperity.

She served the *schpeck und bona* (ham and green beans) with a flourish, basking in Hans's lavish praise. The cobbler and walnut cake came next, with a heavy redware pitcher of milk to drizzle over the mound of sweet baked goods.

The children squealed in appreciation. Kate smiled and ate small portions, remembering to praise her mother-in-law's cooking skills. Hester ate, aware of the change in atmosphere as the visitors took their arguments smelling of rotten sulphur out of the house. Isaac and Rebecca, too, had voiced differing opinions, but they had chosen to drop the subject, "letting each man to his own thinking," which was right and had cleaned up the air.

After the good meal, they asked Hester to tell her story. Hester shook her head no. Kate watched her eldest daughter and knew that Hester would never reveal the secret of the old Indian woman. She would rather die. Hester was an Indian in so many ways, and no one could change that.

Hans tried, at the milking in the morning. He leaned over the back of the cow she was milking and implored her to tell him so he could thank the old woman.

Hester pictured the silver, splashing falls, the ferns and the goats, and recalled the scent of the pure water. But she knew hordes of mocking people would search for her with their scornful curiosity, and she shuddered.

"No," she said. "No."

Hans promised her a trip to the trading post. Perhaps to town. Would she like to go to town, buy a new dress?

The answer was the same. "No."

He told her she was a disobedient child. What if Kate took sick again and needed herbs?

"Then I'll go," she said into the bucket of milk at her feet.

"Look at me." It was a command.

The steady milking stopped. Obediently, she raised her head. Her father's eyes held a new expression.

"Disobedience is not allowed in this household, Hester. 'Spare the rod and spoil the child,' our Lord says."

She lowered her head, resuming milking as if she hadn't heard him.

"Hester."

"What?"

"You are openly disobeying your father." The words were a taunt, a bold announcement cushioned by something that allowed for a seed of rebellion.

"Tell me."

"I said, no."

Still, Hans leaned on the cow, and Hester bent to her task. By now, her hands had become accustomed to the hard work of extracting milk from the cow's udder. Milk came down in thick, heavy streams, creating dense foam close to the top of the pail, muffling the sound of the jets of milk. Hester's hands stripped the last of the milk from the cow's udder. She held very still, her head bent, hoping her father would leave.

He didn't.

"How did you find the Indian woman?"

With the speed of lightning, Hester was on her feet. Frightened, the cow lifted her right foot, kicking the bucket of warm, creamy milk to its side, sending a gushing stream all over the straw-covered floor of the stable. Rivulets of milk carried pieces of straw into the corner.

Hans jumped back, the fury in Hester's black eyes as lethal as the whirring of a disturbed rattlesnake's warning. "I told you no."

Her voice was barely raised above a whisper, but Hans felt as if an arrow had pierced his chest. He slunk out of the cow stable without looking back. Hester retrieved the filthy milking stool and straw-covered pail, patted the next cow and sat down to milk, steady as a rock, her eyes holding no recognizable emotion. Enough was enough. Obedience was one thing, betrayal another.

Kate sensed the change almost immediately and wondered what had occurred that Hans watched Hester with a certain meekness.

She asked Hester.

Hester looked up from her dishwashing, dried her hands on her apron, and came to sit at her mother's feet, elegantly folding herself onto the tiny wooden stool. She lifted dark liquid eyes to Kate's blue ones and waited.

Kate lifted her eyebrows.

"I wouldn't tell him where I got the herbs."

"Why can't you tell us, Hester?"

She told her mother the real reason. Kate received the words, nodding her head. Quick tears sprang to her eyes as her foundling described the place of beauty, the old woman's words, the awareness of the kinship she felt with Uhma.

Kate recognized the spirit of belonging and was humbled. Would they need to give her back someday? The thought was unbearable. This was her beautiful daughter whom God had entrusted to her care! Afraid to mention the frightening subject, Kate smiled, marveling at Hester's words. She kept hidden the fear of her ever leaving and returning to her people.

From that day, Hester felt a real kinship with her mother. Something so genuine, it clothed her with a sense of belonging, as though it was a valuable garment worn beneath her Amish dress, lightening her days. She had a home, a mother, a place where she was needed and wanted. She loved the constant work, she learned many things, and her days were filled with purpose.

She kept a wary eye out for Hans, however, unable to forget his threats and the way he had purposefully goaded her to anger, inciting that rich fury that had possessed her. No matter how hard Hans tried to change things, Hester's childish trust had vanished like the straw carried away by the streams of spilled milk.

Chapter 12

In the fall, Kate had still not regained her usual strength. Hans had a talk with Theodore Crane, the schoolmaster, and they agreed that Hester would no longer attend school. She was needed at home.

Almost thirteen years old, she was unable to read very much of anything. She could only decipher easy addition and subtraction. And that was the extent of her schooling.

Noah and Isaac begged to be allowed to go to school, however, eagerly moving ahead of their classes in every subject. Book-learning was a wonder to them, and Kate said that was straight from Hans and his mother, Rebecca.

On Saturday, Kate said she was tired of the deer meat and salt pork. Wouldn't a mess of brown trout be a wonderful supper? So Hester, Noah, Isaac, and Lissie carried their poles to the tumbling waters of Maiden Creek.

It was a warm kind of day for autumn. The leaves hung in great bunches of red, gold, orange, and yellow, undisturbed by even the gentlest breeze. The air was golden and dusty, thick with the scent of goldenrod, fiery with sumac.

Little puffs of dust rose from their brown bare feet as they walked briskly along the path that led from the road to the creek bottom.

Lissie had learned to whistle and kept up one annoying trill after another, swinging her fishing rod into the tall grasses by the path, sending shivers of dust and seeds from them. She imitated a cardinal, then the call of a crow, finally settling on the lullaby Kate sang to baby Emma.

"Lissie, shut up," Isaac growled.

"We're not allowed to say that," Lissie countered.

"Well, be quiet then."

Hester's thoughts were far away, wondering how far Maiden Creek flowed until it reached the river. She only remembered the red-haired youth sometimes—when she didn't want to. But she couldn't keep his presence from pushing its way into her mind.

She wanted to forget him. What a name—Paddy! It seemed like a dog's name. Or maybe a doll's. And his red hair! She wondered if he was still shuttling people across the river. He had been kind to her.

She wondered how many English people knew about the old Indian woman.

Her thoughts were interrupted by a singing sound, loud and off-key, a sort of rambling chant.

> *"Yugli vill net beer shiddla*
> *Beer vella net fall.*
> *Yugli vill net hundli schlowa,*
> *Hundli vill net schtecka chawa."*

"That's not right!" Isaac screeched, swinging his fishing pole in her direction.

"Is too! *Yugli* would not shake the pear tree, and the pears wouldn't fall."

"The dog and the stick aren't supposed to be yet."

"How am I supposed to know?" Lissie fell behind, pouting.

She certainly had the right name, that Lissie, Hester thought. She was every bit as independent as Lissie Hershberger and about as outspoken.

Lissie Hershberger had visited the house quite often after Kate's near death. She lay no stock in the Indian woman's herbs, saying she'd have come out of that fever all right without those stinking weeds. Everything the Amish needed to know they'd brought with them from Switzerland. They certainly did not need some heathen savage to tell them what to do.

Hester had shriveled up deep within herself, remaining quiet as she went about her work, wondering how grown-ups thought about and understood these things. She shrugged her shoulders as she remembered Lissie Hershberger's generosity while her mother was so ill. Lissie gave her that impression, but Hester didn't want to carry it too far. It was better to stay quiet, or soon she would be just like the visitors, her mouth going and going and going, her own knowledge held high for everyone to examine, quickly looking like foolishness. Yes, the Amish were her people, and they had brought many fine recipes and lots of wisdom with them when they crossed the Atlantic Ocean.

Lissie Hershberger had butchered two nasty geese that tried to chase her down at the barnyard. She had gone to the stone water trough to give her old horse a drink and spied these two geese coming at her like two devils with black eyes, hissing and honking worse than a *schpence*. She vowed to rid Hans Zug's barnyard of his evil fowl.

She told Hans it was she or the geese, and if he planned on keeping the geese, why then, he'd just have to *fa-sark* his own sick wife. Hans had shrugged, gone off to sharpen his axe, and caught the geese with his long, steel hook. Lissie heated the water over a roaring fire and stuck the flopping carcasses into the boiling water, plunging them up and down in it over and over. She chortled to herself about how they would never slam into her leg again, their beaks strong enough to break a limb. Here she was now, safe, but with a nasty bruise swelling on the thick part of her leg behind the knee.

Unfaschtendich, that's what.

She butchered those geese, cut the meat into pieces, and rubbed them with garlic. Then she rubbed them with a salt, pepper, and ginger mixture and put them in the large crock in the springhouse till the next day, when she'd set them to boil with parsley from the garden.

She made a gravy with the broth, put *knepp* on top of the meat, and served it all on a huge platter she got down from the top of the cupboard. It was called *Gaenseklein*, or goose with gravy in English. It was so good that Hester could almost stop feeling sorry for the fate that had befallen the poor things. You had to understand geese, that was the thing. They were only protecting the barnyard, same as the black bear with her cubs. Animals had a territory they claimed as their own, a natural order of things, and when human beings stumbled onto it, they could get hurt, if they weren't watchful.

Lissie started in again, now, on her way to the creek, singing the annoying song, whacking at the grass with her fishing pole.

"I'm going to catch the biggest trout," she yelled, when everyone chose to ignore her obnoxious singing.

Hester smiled to herself and turned to watch as Lissie poked the tip of her fishing pole into Noah's back.

"Ow!" Noah whirled and was off. Lissie screeched worse than a coyote as she ran to save herself from her brother's clutches.

Isaac went ahead, not bothering to find out what the end result would be. But Hester stopped, turning to watch. Lissie was sturdy, but no match for Noah's tall muscular legs. He caught her in due time, whirled her around, and knocked her to the ground where she yowled like a cat.

Dust-covered, but her face shining with glee, she bounded to her feet, slapped her hands together, sending dust flying everywhere, and squealed, "Hoo-hee!"

Hester dug a fat earthworm from the bucket at her feet, wove its slimy, wriggling length in and out of the hook, and set it flying across the water of the creek. She hoped to land it exactly in the middle of the shaded pool beneath the willow tree around the bend where the creek widened.

These trout were finicky. It seemed as if they didn't want any bait unless it was close to the surface, so Hester was perfecting a way of drawing the wriggling worm toward herself. She kept the bait moving, which was sure to attract the trout in less time.

Lissie still hummed the *Yugli* song, nodding her head in time to the imagined beats, weaving the hook on the end of her line into the wriggling worm.

Noah and Isaac had gone farther downstream, hoping to get away from Lissie's constant yodeling, who seemed blissfully unaware that she was causing anyone a disturbance.

They eventually caught the trout, six large, fat ones, just waiting to be cleaned. Over the fire in a kettle they would go, dredged with butter and spices, until flaky white chunks of meat fell off the white, pliant bones.

The return trip was uneventful, except for sighting a snapping turtle sunning himself on a flat rock, then silently disappearing before they had a chance to catch him. Turtle soup was "awful good," as Lissie put it. Carrots and leeks cooked in a brown broth with the turtle meat was just awful good.

They reached the barnyard, dusty, with the fish flopping from Noah's tired arms. They met Hans, who was walking behind two horses, his straw hat pulled low.

"What's going on?" he asked, without a smile.

"Mam sent us fishing. She was hungry for a mess of trout."

"Oh, she was? Well, what about the corn picking? She didn't say anything about that, heh?"

"No." Noah was red-faced, nervous. Isaac stood still.

"The next time you go fishing, ask me first. I spent all afternoon picking corn by myself, which is not necessary. I have big boys to be picking corn with me, not wandering off fishing like that."

Hester's and Lissie's eyes were held to the ground and their bare toes, anywhere more comfortable than Dat's eyes boring into them, accusing them all of laziness.

The trout were prepared by Mam's own hand, perfectly done over the fire in the hearth in just a short period of time and then laid on a bed of watercress. They ate the fish along with a big pot of bean soup. For Saturday night, this was a wonderful supper. Normally it was just bean soup.

Everyone had to have their bath on Saturday night in the gigantic wooden washtub behind the makeshift blanket Kate strung across a corner of the room. Church clothes had to be laid out and the wrinkles smoothed away so that in the morning, the chores, breakfast, and getting dressed could all be done, and they could still get to church on time.

Kate was extremely weary, so she allowed the girls to wash the dishes as she sat cuddling baby Emma, hoping to have more energy when it was time to bathe the little ones. She remembered, wistfully, the days when she could work hard from sunup to sundown, without as much as a sore muscle. Now, by mid-forenoon she was tired out.

She looked up, surprised to see her husband in the house at this time on a Saturday night.

"Girls." His voice was stern.

Lissie turned, her eyebrows raised, her sturdy body poised, as she tapped the dishcloth against her side. Hester chose to ignore him, washing dishes steadily, her back turned.

"Hester, are you listening?"

In answer, she stopped washing dishes, her back straight, her eyes boring into the log wall ahead of her.

"Hester!" The shout was a command.

From her seat by the hickory rocker, Kate's grip tightened, her eyes flew to her husband's face. What was this?

Hester turned, her chin lifted in defiance, her black eyes pools of nothing.

Kate shivered and held the soothing body of her baby closer.

"When I speak to you, I expect you to listen. I don't want you riding horses anymore. Not you or Lissie. It's not proper, wearing the boys' trousers. Do you understand what I am saying?"

Lissie's eyes flew to Hester's face, which seemed etched in stone, then back to her father's clouded eyes.

"Dat! You can't do that!" The protest was out before Hester had a chance to retrieve it. Too late. The damage was done, and she awaited her fate as Hans's eyes clouded over.

Hester spoke quickly.

"What is your reason, Dat?"

"If you had never learned to ride, you could not have gone to the old Indian woman that day. Now you are caught in her ways. They are not God's ways."

Accustomed to having her father on her side, Hester felt confused, as if directions about how to proceed were eluding her, leaving her scrambling wildly for a foothold in a world gone dark.

"But the herbs healed Mam!"

Hester's words broke from her, driven by desperation. Life without riding Rudy was as unthinkable as breathing without air. An impossibility.

"It was not the herbs that healed her, and you know it. I prayed long into the night, and God answered."

Hester's heart jumped and took off racing, draining the blood from her face. Her nostrils flared, her eyes dilated as she drew to her full height. "You. You do not know that."

Kate rose in one swift movement when she saw Hans raise his large hand and draw it back. She stood between them, wobbling a bit on legs suddenly gone weak.

"Hans, don't do something you'll be sorry for later. I beg you. What has gotten into you?"

Kate began crying weakly, a soft sound like a kitten. Hans lowered his hand, strode from the house with footfalls like booms from a cannon, slamming the door until the windowpanes rattled in their wooden frames.

Much later that night, Kate lay awake. Resolve flooded her open eyes. Reaching across, she shook Hans's shoulder, hard, until he awakened.

"Hans."

"What is it, Kate?"

"Hans, what has gotten into you? Hester was always your favorite. So much so, that I was afraid it wasn't natural. She is not of your flesh and blood, or mine. But she never did wrong, my husband. Now she does nothing right. This is very hard for her."

"She defies me, refusing to name the Indian woman or her whereabouts."

"Why do you need to know if you don't believe the herbs healed me?"

"She's going to go back, that's why. She'll get mixed up in those old remedies that are nothing but witchcraft."

"When we found Hester, we saved her life. It is up to her, now, to choose what she wants. We cannot force her to stay or force her to go. If the ways of her people are what she chooses, that is her decision."

"But her soul will be lost. She'll burn in hell. She has to remain here among the Amish where she can learn from the ministers how to live a devout religious life. The Indians are heathen."

"Are they, Hans? Are they?"

In minute detail, she told her husband what Hester had described to her about the old Indian woman and warned him of the error of his ways.

"Hans, if you love me, you'll see that she needs to be set free, to decide what she really wants. Please."

Hans lay on his back, his breathing deep and easy, his mind in turmoil. How could he?

He loved Hester as a beloved daughter. He needed her beauty. How could he set her free to go? The only way he knew was to remove all earthy obstacles and expect her to obey. He would lay down rigid rules and see to it that she followed his expectations.

He felt the divide between him and Kate, a chasm, growing even as she spoke, her hands restlessly caressing his chest, her words whispered close to his ear.

Ah, but this precious foundling, so beloved, her price above gold, suddenly growing into a young woman with a mind of her own, the thing that frightened him most.

And now, his own wife was caving in to these heresies. What was wrong with her? Yes, she had been healed, but by his prayers alone.

The corn turned dry and brown; the ears hung heavily from the rustling stalks. Temperatures plummeted. The winds whispered of frost. They carried the cabbage and turnips into the mound of earth that had been dug by Hans's own hands and finished with a sturdy, wooden doorframe.

The carrots stayed in the ground, their tops covered with straw. When Kate needed a carrot or two, she'd send the children to the garden to uncover them.

The pigs were fat, waiting on colder weather. Then Hans would bring his rifle to his shoulder, aim, and fire, while the children were still in their beds.

Kate did the housecleaning scrupulously. Not a windowpane, a coverlet or a floor, went unwashed. She emptied the straw ticks, washed their covers, and filled them with fresh straw. She made new pillows and stuffed them with feathers from the geese they had eaten after one had bitten Lissie Hershberger's leg, although Kate thought the bruise was not a bite, just more like a hefty tweak.

She and Hester disposed of every spider or ant in their path, making sure that the insects' homes were destroyed. They scoured the floors white with lye soap, then buffed them to a dark sheen with linseed oil.

Hans brought home a calendar from the blacksmith shop in Berksville, and Kate hung it proudly by the kitchen table. Next to it was the clock, its wood wiped clean until it shone.

Hester worked side by side with Kate, accepting her admonishments to give herself up to Hans's wishes.

Hester spent hours down at the barn cleaning the stables and caressing her beloved horse's face. Not once did she fling herself up on his back, her obedience to her father intact.

Kate had told her many times that obedience meant sacrifice, but that there was a blessing in it, even if it was hard. Hester nodded and understood, yet she struggled with many ill feelings toward Hans's increasingly rigid rules.

Noah and Isaac continued to ride Rudy especially, their best horse, which was almost more than Hester could bear. Still, she remained obedient and true to her mother.

At butchering time, when two lifeless hogs hung from the rafters, the snow lay heavy on the ground, and the wind whipped around the corners of the barn. Hans stood with his father, Isaac, heating water in great iron kettles over a roaring wood fire. They scraped the hogs clean, then cut them into pieces—hams, ribs, and *seida schpeck,* the meat that would be cured for bacon and other trimmings for making sausage.

All day, Rebecca and Hester worked, seasoning and grinding, cooking and canning. The boys tended fires while Hester cleaned the entrails, the casing that would be used for sausage. This had always been her job, and she became accustomed to it, gamely scraping the casings clean.

Lissie was put to work alongside her. She entered the forebay in the barn as if she was going to her execution, martyrdom shrouding her face, her eyes liquid with self-pity.

"It stinks."

"Yes."

"I'm not going to do this, you know."

"You are."

"Who said?"

"Dat."

"He won't know if I don't help, if you don't tell him."

"Here." Lifting a trailing, grayish mass, Hester held it out to Lissie, telling her to lay it down, take the blunt edge of the knife, and scrape out the whitish substance that clung to the inside, explaining how they would fill it with ground, seasoned meat.

Lissie watched, holding her nose, and pronounced the whole process unfit. She jumped to rigid attention, however, when Hans came over, his face red from the heat, to ask Hester how it was going.

"Good," she answered without lifting her head.

"Lissie." The word was a command.

Dutifully, Lissie faced her father, found his gaze, and said, "Fine."

"Good, good."

Isaac hurried past, carrying a large, bloody portion of meat. Lissie swallowed and set to work immediately afterward, the sight of her saintly grandfather spurring her into action.

When Rebecca came to the barn to season the sausage meat, all eyes turned to her.

"Where's Mam? Where is Kate?"

Rebecca shook her head, her lips compressed, and Kate was forgotten.

Hester knew. She'd heard her being sick again. It had not frightened her at the time, but as her mother's full figure continued to decrease and the color in her face diminish, Hester knew the time was coming when she would need more strength than she had.

She bent over the entrails of the hogs and scraped with a vengeance, her strong brown arms rippling with young muscle. She set her mouth in a straight line, as tightly guarded against the sprout of rebellion and dislike of her father as a cast iron key turned in a lock.

The love she had felt for him was a thing of the past, which she remembered only fleetingly. When had the tide turned? When she was no longer a child and had developed a mind of her own. It had all started with the herbs in the brown packages.

CHAPTER 13

W<small>HEN</small> H<small>ESTER WAS FOURTEEN YEARS OLD,</small> K<small>ATE</small> died in childbirth at the age of forty-four.

The day was gray with rain coming down in slanted, cold sheets, reflecting the misery of the huddled family, hovering about with empty faces, unable to grasp what was before their eyes.

Hans lifted his face to the rain and could not understand God's ways. The little ones cried, snuffling into Hester's shoulder, clinging to her skirts, and whining like little lost lambs.

Noah and Isaac shed solemn tears, even while they squared their shoulders, shoved their hands deep into their pockets, and tried their best to look manly. But tears of grief swam across their eyes, ran over, and coursed down their cheeks, falling on their linen shirts. They blew their noses, blinked, and were finished.

Hester moved about the house as if in a dream. Nothing seemed real. Everything was without clarity. A fog of disbelief left her feeling lethargic, as if nothing mattered. Her dark eyes glistened with unshed tears.

She had cried before. Kate had told her, as her body wasted away, the once ample arms becoming thinner as the months wore on, that she would try her best. But deep inside, she felt as if God was telling her she needed more strength than she could find.

"Perhaps my time has come, Hester. I'm counting on you, though, to keep the family together, if . . . if something should happen to me."

"Mam, don't."

But Kate had pushed on, speaking words like slaps from her hand, words Hester could not bear. She had tried, but she failed to hold back the premature sorrow.

A sadness so heavy lay over the graveyard, crushing Hans, even as the sun shone down on them the day of the burial. Kate and her unborn child were lowered into the wet earth beside the tiny gravestone inscribed with "Rebecca Zug. Daughter of Hans and Catherine Zug."

The community rallied around them, powerful in their kindness, bringing food and labor and sympathy. Love flowed among them, binding them together with its strong ties, and Hester was comforted by these gentle well-wishers who wanted only the best for her.

That she had so little schooling was something they took into consideration, but Hester refused to budge. School held no promise for her. Memories of being mocked formed like clouds on her inward horizon, and she remained obstinate about going back.

Baby Emma was one year old and cried incessantly for her mother. Barbara and Menno wandered around without understanding, and Hester took them under her wing like a fledgling mother hen.

Hans refused to eat or drink, saying he needed to fast and pray, which Hester respected. She eyed him with a new reverence and was thankful she had shown so much obedience. For Hans blamed himself for his wife's untimely death. He had prayed for her life now, and God had not heard him. He was sure his sins were piled around his head, and he sat in the proverbial sackcloth and ashes, repenting of his misdeeds for three days.

He'd charged John Lantz too much to shoe his two mares, and him a bishop and a man of God. He was caught in avarice.

He'd tasted the whiskey at little Reuben Hershberger's house, becoming quite merry, if it came right down to it. He had taken strong drink and guilt rattled his very soul.

He had not listened to the quiet voice of his wife, when she tried to persuade him of the goodness of the old woman and her herbs. He had gone right ahead and despised her all he wanted and was beset by the sin of hatred.

Oh, the list went on and on until he smote his breast, lifted his eyes to the heavens, and implored God to be merciful to him, a sinner. He grieved with many sighs and silent tears. He stood with bent head as kindly men expressed their sympathy. His future loomed before him, frightful with the inadequacy of being without his Kate.

Hester cooked and cleaned, washed and mended. Her grandmother Rebecca came and advised her about rearing the children. Lissie Hershberger hitched up her doddering old horse and stopped by every day for almost a month, helping Hester by sewing clothes, darning socks, churning butter, tending the lamps.

Hester was a fast learner, and although the cornmeal mush burned sometimes, and the beans were under-cooked, she forged ahead with every duty Kate had always done.

With Lissie's help, she folded Kate's things and stored them in the attic. Lissie urged Hans to write to Kate's parents in Switzerland, explaining her death, telling them about her life beforehand. John took the letter to the trading post and came home with tales of the Indians who were gathered there, coming in for supplies, saying the winter would be long and hard.

Hester's eyes glinted in the firelight as chills crept across her arms and jangled their way up her spine. She thought of the acorns piled on the forest floor. The muskrats' heavy coats. The early flocks of blackbirds and geese flying low and fast. She wanted to go to the trading post. She wanted to see if the old Indian woman would be safe if the winter was too harsh.

All these thoughts she kept hidden away as she turned her lithe form from the fireplace to the bake oven to the table to the shelves, providing food for the always hungry children, their stomachs growling before each mealtime. Lissie was a help in her ten-year-old way, which sometimes was worse than no help at all. But Lissie could make Hester laugh. Out loud, too. And that was worth something.

On the morning of the first storm, no sunrise was visible, only a heavy white hoarfrost that clung to every blade of grass, crunching beneath Hester's brown leather boots as she made her way to the barn. She knew there would not be enough eggs to go around, but if she stirred them well and added milk, along with some stale, torn bread, the mixture would set up well if she cooked it over the fire. She'd make fresh bread as often as she could, too. They had some maple syrup to pour over it, which Hans was especially fond of.

When she returned to the house, she hung her heavy black shawl on the hook by the door. She was surprised to see Lissie standing by the fire, spreading her hands to its warmth, grumbling to herself.

"What?" Hester asked, a smile already forming.

"I froze in my bed. Mam always put extra coverlets on. You didn't do it."

"I don't know where they are."

"I don't either."

Hans strode into the kitchen, shivering, and went straight to the fireplace, holding his hands to the fire beside Lissie.

"Good morning, Lissie. Why are you up so early?"

"I'm cold. I almost froze in my bed."

"Hester, haven't you *fa-sarked* the extra coverlets?"

It was the way the question was spoken that rankled her. As if she was expected to know everything and carry it out unfailingly.

"No."

"Do you know where they are?"

"Yes."

Hans watched Hester's face, her black eyes giving away nothing. If anything, she was becoming even more beautiful, her face losing its childish roundness, replaced by more chiseled cheekbones. She was tall, now, he guessed at least five and a half feet, her body shapely beneath the loose dress, the black apron tied about her slim waist.

She wore a kerchief too much of the time, but he didn't know how to approach her about that. Again, for the hundredth time, he wished for Kate's wisdom and foresight.

Winter roared in across the Pennsylvania mountain ranges, bold and brash, reaching across the land with fingers of ice and snow, winds lashing the bare branches without mercy. Snow piled in tightly packed drifts, blown against the buildings by furious winds. The cows, horses, and sheep that were unable to be housed in a barn or shed died of the cold that winter.

Farmers built lean-tos, temporary sheds to give their animals a break from the endless wind that drove snow and bits of ice from every branch and raised bit of land. The snow pooled into the hollows, densely packed, so that many a team of horses floundered up to their collars in snow, unable to draw their sled or wagon an inch farther. Red-faced men carried shovels so they could loosen the frightened horses, freezing their ears in the process.

Finally, toward the beginning of January, they admitted defeat. They had no church services for more than a month. No one went to visit anyone else, except for a few hardy teenagers who possessed snowshoes. They brought tales of emaciated deer, unable to move about and starving, all over the mountain.

For Hester, one day blurred into the next, an endless stream of days punctuated by nightfall when she tumbled into her bed, weary and heartsick, the endless responsibility of nine children too heavy on her young shoulders.

Hans brooded. Some days he sat, a great hulking figure, by the fire, staring into it with somber eyes, his spirits so low he could barely lift his head. Noah and Isaac accepted this, even flourished in the face of their father's silence. They had never been used to having a father who cared about them much.

Hans did what was necessary, providing their clothes and food, instructing them in the ways of the farm, but supplying no emotional support. It was Hester he cared about, just as he always had. Now, although he was sternly dictatorial to her, he still watched her with brooding eyes, trying to imprison her with his will, looking out for her welfare in his own way.

Meanwhile, Noah and Isaac grew mentally and emotionally by relying on and reacting to each other. They shared and spoke together about everything. The barn rang with their merry words, chiding, teasing, laughing, and jousting harmlessly, two boys who loved life and each other. They never hated Hester for what she was to Hans. It was just the way of it, a part of life.

The longer the snow piled around the house, the further Hans declined into his pit of grief. He missed Kate's presence so keenly, it was a knife between his shoulder blades, a constant hurting, a deep, dark thing that followed him wherever he went. He tried valiantly to shake this unspeakable misery. He prayed long and loud, his voice raised to the rafters of the barn as he implored God to help him. He tried to conjure Kate's face, but it was only when he dreamed of her that he found a miniscule amount of solace.

One storm followed another, days without end, it seemed to him. Was the end near? Had God lost patience with the sins of the world and said it was enough?

Whether encased in the small, dark house, shoveling his way down to the barn, to the outdoor privy and the bake oven, or carrying wood from the adjoining shed, his spirits steadily worsened until his face became slack. His rounded jowls hung in limp folds. His cornmeal mush went untouched.

Hester saw all this, her large dark eyes observant. It stirred up fear, this unnamed malaise. Hans didn't care enough to scold her anymore. He didn't care about anything.

Increasingly, Noah and Isaac shouldered more of the workload, their faces calm as they carried wood, milked cows, mucked out the stables, carried water, and shoveled snow. School was out of the question, so they studied the books they had available, mostly in German. They learned to read fluently and discussed the Bible endlessly like two youthful prophets, their blond heads bent together in front of the fire.

Little Barbara and Menno clung to Hester, and her arms encircled them, her heart open to the lonely children who remembered their mother but were too young to understand what death meant.

Baby Emma simply crawled into Hester's arms, sighed, and from that day on, claimed her as her mother.

Solomon, Daniel, and John understood Mam's departure. They had a view of heaven, placed their mother in it, and were comforted. They ate the food set before them, accepted Hester as their mother, and went about living their lives the way children do. When they quarreled, Hans shook himself out of his black reverie long enough to mete out due punishment, then returned to brooding.

Sickness entered the house like a gray specter, stealthy, frightening, demanding more from Hester than she had thought possible.

She strung a makeshift clothesline across one corner of the kitchen. It was always pegged with white clothes, either sheets or pillowcases, and long rectangular pieces of muslin that had been smeared with strong, odorous salves and then wrapped around swelling glands, now washed clean.

So many of Kate's words were seared into Hester's memory as she cared for the sick children. Cleanliness was important for a sickbed. Lye soap had the power to wipe away the residue of disease. Kate wasn't sure how, but it made a difference, she always said. Onion and mustard poultices worked well for the croup. Often Hester thought wistfully of the Indian woman and the stored knowledge in that head crowned with white hair.

What would she do when Menno was red with heat from the awful fevers that ravaged his thin body? Which herb of the forest had the magical power to fight the fever? Hester felt sure that somewhere, all over the land God had created, there were remedies used by her people. The ancient old woman's people. Hester's own people.

She wondered during that long winter who her people really were. She had never been an Indian. She was only born one. The only Indian she had ever met was the old woman. She had experienced a fierce kinship, a need to defend the old woman. She'd felt in awe of the beautiful place and wanted to know everything she spoke of. But she felt no sense of belonging.

Here was her home. The Amish way of life was her way. It was all she knew. And yet, she wondered. Someday she would go to the trading post. There were always Indians there. Someday she would meet one or two. Perhaps someone her own age who could speak English. Who knew her own mother and father. Maybe her mother had died in childbirth like Kate.

And so her thoughts went on and on as she stirred yet another load of clothes in the boiling hot water, lifted them, rinsed them, and turned them into twisted ropes, squeezing the water from them before pegging them to the line across the corner of the room.

Baby Emma toddled through the water that had pooled around the clothes, where bits of wood chips, straw, and ashes were turning dark as the water ran in little rivulets.

Grabbing a piece of heavy toweling, Hester swiped at the puddles, then opened the door to shake out the wood chips. For only a moment, she breathed deeply the gray-white purity of the snow and the storm. Bits of snow and ice hit her brown face, but she lifted her eyes, reveling in the cold and startling power of the wind.

Behind her, Solomon coughed a rasping croak, followed by a whine for *vossa, vossa* (water). A sharp reprimand from Hans followed. When she turned, after settling the latch securely, she felt his dark eyes on her, angry and displeased. Keeping her head low, her face averted, she brought Solomon a drink of good cold water from the springhouse. She patted his shoulder as he lay back, his blue eyes so much like Kate's, watching her face intently.

"Why did you stand there with the door open, letting in all that cold?" Hans asked.

Hester chose not to answer him. Whatever her reply was, it would be the wrong one, she knew.

"Answer me."

"I was watching the storm."

"And letting in the cold."

"Yes."

"You're old enough to know better."

"Yes."

It was the answer he wanted. Total servitude. Absolute obedience. Compliance. A deep bowing to his will. When she acknowledged her own stupidity, he was satisfied. Anything else would only have been met with more sparring, a hopeless exchange of words, gone awry without a smidgen of common sense.

And so he brooded, staring into the fire, lifting his eyes only momentarily to absorb the one thing that kept him grounded, his appreciation of Hester's beauty. For he still loved her as he had loved the young Indian child. Only now he was intimidated by her. She was growing away from him, and the experience left him rife with hopelessness, inadequate and afraid.

She moved about the room like a princess. Her figure was tall and perfectly proportioned, her neck long and slender, her face a display of emotion as she bent over

Barbara with her long, slender fingers, healing, soothing. Her eyes were large with a fringe of heavy lashes shading them. Her eyebrows were like the wing of a raven in the distance. Her nose was small and straight but wide at the top, built out between the perfection of her eyes, different from the Swiss and German faces Hans was accustomed to. Her mouth was full, wide, and in absolute symmetry with her eyes, the chin beneath small and round.

He needed to speak to her of her soul. In a year or so, she would be expected to become a member of the church. How could she, if he was certain she couldn't read very much? How much did she really understand? This weighed heavily on Hans's heart, as the storm blew itself out, leaving the sky blue for only a short period of time. The wind returned in an awesome display of furious clouds, spewing forth a blast of frigid winds that gathered in the north and swept over Pennsylvania.

The sturdy log house shook and shivered in the winds' power. The gray shake shingles tore loose on the barn, and snow sifted down onto the backs of the animals, melting slowly, marking their hides with dark streaks. Hester set wooden buckets when yet another drip appeared in the house, until Hans roused himself and set about making more shingles. He placed a ladder against both buildings and set their roofs to rights.

When Hester overcooked the dried beans, leaving the soup thick and mushy and the bread a paste, he let her know in soft-spoken tones that she had better be more watchful of the time when she set the beans to soak.

She agreed, her eyes hooded, giving nothing away. When the bread was not kneaded long enough, he mentioned it immediately. When it crumbled away from the freshly churned butter, he did not hesitate to speak of it as well.

Hester didn't always understand the ways of bread. Sometimes she could knead the heavy brown dough until her shoulders ached, and it would not rise or turn out light and spongy. Other times, she gave it a few good rolls, patted it, put it to rise, and it turned out light and chewy, in perfect harmony with the tasty butter. But she said nothing to Hans, only to Lissie, who looked up from the sock she was darning, her blue eyes sizzling with indignation, and said if Dat didn't like his bread the way Hester made it, then she guessed he needed to make it himself. Hester laughed out loud, a sound heard infrequently. She relished the thought of Hans bent over the dough tray, kneading and kneading, the bread crumbling away at the touch of the butter knife.

The children regained their health, the storm blew itself out, and Hans left the house to change a few of the box stalls in the barn.

When spring arrived that year, hearts everywhere celebrated. Housewives sang joyously, and men walking behind their plows watched rolls of fertile soil turn over and whistled praises.

Swallows wheeled in the sunshine. The air was heavy with the scent of honeysuckle vines and wild strawberry blossoms. The grass grew thick, the sheep and cows gorged themselves on the tender new growth, becoming fat and contented. The cows' udders bulged with new milk, and Hester made butter. She packed the excess away, and Hans took it to the trading post to sell, coming home with coins weighing down his pockets. He emptied them furtively into the redware cup by the fireplace.

Hester also collected buttermilk, which she set in the springhouse to keep cold. Now and then, when more had accumulated than she could use, they sold it, too.

When the hens occasionally laid more than usual, and the family could spare some eggs, Hans sold them by the dozen at an exorbitant price.

The gray mare produced a fine colt—a bay foal— which had its mother's fine, long legs. This fine animal lifted Hans's spirits to a higher level than they had ever been since his beloved Kate's death.

Hester laughed aloud at the antics of the new calves and chased them about the pasture. She gathered great armloads of wild iris and honeysuckle and fitted them into earthenware bowls, filling the log house with a scent that was unmatched by anything Hans had ever smelled.

It evoked a sadness in him, an unnamed longing for someone to call his own. He would need a wife in the future, a mother for his children, a helpmeet to share his life. The thought terrified him and made him feel very small and ashamed of who he was. Only a man, with nine children, no, ten, counting Hester. Who would be willing to give him her hand?

CHAPTER 14

Ever since the local school had resumed in March, Theodore Crane was dreadfully behind with the year's lessons. His stomach soured from his nervous tics, and his eyebrows jumped unceasingly as he passed about the classroom like a caged lion.

When a line of children stood side by side in the front of the room to read from their small, hardcovered readers, he tipped forward and backward so fast, Noah's eyes widened to Isaac, and he jerked a thumb in the schoolmaster's direction. Isaac bent his head behind his slate, desperately striving to keep a straight face.

Theodore called a school meeting for the parents and asked for any available volunteers as tutors to help the little ones with their work, a plan that seemed excellent to him at the time. When Lissie Hershberger volunteered, raising an ample, well-rounded arm and stating her eagerness to help, he floundered like a catfish caught on a hook. What a woman.

Anyone, simply anyone else, would be fine, but not Lissie. He turned his head very slowly at the meeting and acknowledged her raised hand with one shaggy, gray eyebrow climbing halfway up his forehead, the other one refusing to move.

"Yes. I believe you are Elizabeth Hershberger. Is that correct?"

"Yes. You can call me Lissie. I would be willing to help three days a week in the afternoons." Her voice was low and rich; it carried well across the room.

Theodore pulled on his Adam's apple with his thumb and forefinger, adjusted his stiff, white collar, and cleared his throat in a rattling fashion before blinking two or three times.

"Ah, yes. Elizabeth. I believe I can . . ."

Here he broke off with a terrible coughing spasm, lifted his right leg, fished around in his pocket for a clean handkerchief, and proceeded to finish coughing into it.

"I do beg your pardon."

The occupants of the room were unsure exactly whose pardon he was begging, so ripples of acknowledgment spilled across the many faces.

Lissie, however, believed he was speaking solely to her and replied loudly, "You are so pardoned."

Theodore felt as if he had been led to his own execution, with his fate changed by Lissie Hershberger, but he coughed a while longer to erase all that.

"Yes, yes, Elizabeth, I accept your kind offer. I thank you very much."

He felt like a traitor, untrue to his own heart, but he could not bear to hurt the lady. She was a hard worker and sincere, and he was also quite sure she had a good head on her shoulders.

But my, she was so large. It seemed as if those yards and yards of fabric gathered across her bounteous hips would scrape the smaller children right out of their seats. She was like a great ship plowing steadily through the sea, her sails all unfurled. It was a bit frightening.

The evening closed with a discussion about the older boys' behavior. They were almost never on time in the morning, or they loitered unnecessarily at the end of the school day. Comments came from one of the boys' parents and then another and another. Finally, they voted unanimously to discipline their children to try to make his workload easier. They agreed there were only six more weeks of school and much to be done in that short period of time.

And so it was that Lissie drove her well-fed, old horse down the road through the lush green forest to school. The shoulders of her cape came well down the sides of her arms, and the cape was pinned closely and modestly around her neck. Her cap was white as snow and pulled well forward over her thick ears. She parted her graying hair severely in the middle, and then greased it back in a small roll along each side of her forehead. Below the sleek sheen of her graying hair, her blue eyes sparkled in anticipation.

Here was a challenge, something new. Hadn't she changed enough diapers and swept enough dirty houses? Hadn't she slaved over stinking farmknee breeches soaking in lukewarm wash water when the soap no longer formed decent bubbles, with her arms too tired to stir or pound the dirt out properly?

She'd tended to ailing mothers and screaming babies, comforted the dying and smacked the newborns' backsides. She'd cared for her own husband and children besides, and then lived through the shock of his death and the deaths of two of her children.

She thought it was time for a change, so she took great care with her appearance. She turned this way to catch the light on her forehead, then another way to see that her covering was just so.

Yet, she still owned some snap, so she did. She deemed herself quite agreeable, perhaps even charming.

Theodore opened the door at her knock, stepped aside—very far aside—and ushered her into the schoolroom. She sailed through with the light, quick step of a much younger person, smiled at him, and said, "Good afternoon, Theodore."

"Good afternoon, Elizabeth."

He showed her the classes she would have and introduced her to the first-, second-, and third-graders who smiled guilelessly, genuinely happy to have Lissie Hershberger for their teacher. Everyone knew Lissie. She'd been to all their homes many times.

Theodore watched from his vantage point in the back of the room as Lissie launched into her first assignment, explaining multiplication to the third graders, German alphabet to the second, addition with three numbers to the first. She was thorough, well spoken, and patient. She smiled often, encouraged the slackers, never intimidated by the strongest.

However, when the last pupil ran yelling out the door, she lingered, exactly what he was afraid of. He wanted nothing to do with this outsized Amish widow. It was only his impeccable English manners that kept him from telling her so.

She spoke only of the children—who was capable, who was lagging behind. It seemed she knew each household intimately, knew what the problem was if a child seemed insecure.

He was beginning to fidget, thinking of his chores at home in the small brown house by the trading post not quite six miles away. He was hungry. He had stuffed only a portion of cold corn pone in his haversack that morning.

Lissie heaved herself to her feet, the yards of fabric swishing—why did he always think of a ship?—smiled up at him, and said she'd made ginger cookies. "I brought you some in a bag."

She sailed through the door and across the schoolyard to her wagon, bent to retrieve the cookies from beneath the seat and sailed back, her wide face radiating happiness. "Ginger cookies."

He opened the cloth sack immediately and came out with the largest, thickest ginger cookie he'd ever seen. It was like a small, round cake, dusted liberally with sugar and ginger. The first bite was ambrosia, chewy, soft, and fragrant with spices. He closed his eyes and chewed appreciatively, his eyebrows jiggling with the movement of his jaw.

Lissie watched him, waiting eagerly.

"The best," he said simply.

"Thank you," she answered, turned lightly on her heel, went to her wagon, untied the old horse, and was gone.

He should have offered to help, but he was too busy stuffing ginger cookies into his mouth. Besides, he was glad she had left.

Lissie rode home in the late afternoon sunlight and thought that Theodore Crane was just a bit *schnuck* (cute), the way his eyes came alive when he spoke.

But he was English, perhaps a Catholic or a Protestant, so that meant he was quite worldly, and likely she'd not be able to think of him as a potential husband with the difference in religion.

Her golden years stretched before her, bereft of a close relationship with a husband, something she had cherished, nurtured, and appreciated. She liked to set a good table, cook wonderful meals, try different recipes, loving to see a man eat.

Ach well, he was very English. He couldn't even say Lissie. It came out "Elizabeth."

As different as day and night.

Noah was the first to notice. He told Hester that Lissie Hershberger dressed awful particular to teach school. Hester said teachers were expected to dress in Sunday clothes, and Noah said it wasn't just her clothes, it was the way she seemed to watch the schoolmaster with a bright face or something like that.

Hester shrugged her shoulders, and went back to the butter churn, lifting the dasher, plunging it up and down, the muscles in her young, brown hands tireless. Now that Lissie had taken the job of tutoring, Hester was on her own. Hans was a big help with the garden and the planting, and he put the boys to work as well, helping carry wood and water, hoe the garden, and perform any chore that saved Hester's endless hard work.

She had little time to spare. Forbidden to ride her horse, she had no other activity to think about, so she became a young mother years before her time.

All that mattered to Hester was being able to feed everyone and keep the laundry done and the house decently clean.

The sewing, however, was another matter. She could sew strips of cloth by hand with tiny stitches, but she had no idea how to go about sewing a dress or shirt or pair of knee breeches.

All the boys' knee breeches were much too short, and she had applied patches to them over and over. Sewing the patches on with firm, necessary stitches, Hester had whipped the needle in and out, her mouth set in a determined line.

They all needed clothes to wear. Without Kate, where should she begin? Noah's and Isaac's knee breeches were creeping up their legs, but no one thought anything of it. Lots of boys wore their breeches short, before they were handed down to the next younger brother. But Hester knew something needed to be done before school started in the fall.

She approached Hans, finally, when the spring warmth had turned to summer's heat, when the corn was already knee-high and the hay was ready to be cut. It was late, after the children were all in bed. Hans noticed Hester's reluctance to retire for the night, so he sat watching her. She folded a small coverlet and put it across the back of the rocking chair, then picked up a few playthings and placed them in the basket by the fireplace. She stooped to pick up a washcloth someone had left on the bench, folded it across the wooden rack by the dry sink, her back turned, straight and still, for too long.

She was not wearing a cap again, and here she was, fifteen years of age. Hans knew the matter needed to be addressed.

"Hester." The voice was not unkind. But it was authoritative, jolting.

"Yes." Hester's voice squeaked, and she stammered a bit.

"Why aren't you wearing a cap?"

"I don't like them."

"But you were taught to wear a cap in the manner of our people."

"Yes."

"Then not liking it is no reason, when the *ordnung* of the church requires it."

"Yes."

"You must give yourself up as Christ did, dying for our sins. Do you think that was easy for him, our Lord and Savior?"

"No."

"Then wearing a cap is a small thing, is that not so?"

"Yes."

"Then you must begin to wear it."

"I have only one, my Sunday one."

"Who knows how to go about getting fabric? Or making it?"

Hester shrugged, her eyes lowered.

"I'll speak to my mother," Hans offered. "You might also want to consider more sewing. All the boys need knee breeches and shirts. The girls need dresses."

Suddenly Hans's face became very soft, his eyes warm and moist. "Ah, yes, Hester. That was the joy of my life when you were small—buying the fabric to make little dresses. Colors of wild roses, the blue of cornflowers. You were like a colorful little fairy."

Hester lifted her eyes, surprised to find the emotion that memory brought to his face.

Hans met her gaze.

Hester looked away, uncomfortable, now.

As quickly, Hans said gruffly, "So, you'll promise me you'll wear a cap?"

"If I have one."

The truth was, she hated to wear a cap while she worked. They were big, and the strings tied below her chin were itchy and warm in summer. Besides, what was the point? If she said that to Hans, he would never get over her flagrant display of rebellion, so she dusted the corner of the table with the tip of her apron, a movement so graceful it reminded Hans of a dancer he had watched as a young man in Switzerland.

"Go to bed."

"Yes. You will see to it, about the fabric?"

Hans only nodded, his eyes hooded. He turned from her as something black and frightful, like a shadow of fear, rolled across his features.

"*Denke*" (Thank you).

She slipped through the door to her bedroom, closing it softly behind her.

Far into the night, Hans sat. He was tired, his legs aching from the long day of loading hay after cutting it with a scythe. His thoughts were tumultuous as he tried to decipher his own rush of feeling for Hester. It was the little girl he loved. It was not appropriate to feel any fond emotion for her at this age. Somehow he needed to tread carefully and be the father she so desperately needed.

Sleep eluded him. The wolves' spine-chilling song added to his loneliness. An unnamed fear of the future tormented him as he thought of Hester. She was a young woman now. Who would be a fitting husband for her? His mind traveled, resting on each young man of the community. Jacob. David. Abner. Joe. All of them were either too short, too immature, too lazy, or had no character. *Ach,* it would be a few years yet.

He wanted to buy her yards and yards of beautiful hued fabric, but that was no longer a luxury he could allow himself. She needed to be restrained and come to understand the way of the cross. It was best for her soul.

He got down his heavy German Bible and immersed himself in the words he found between the leather-bound covers. Slowly he relaxed. He prayed for strength, the will to do what was right. As he prayed, he began to realize that Hester's beauty was a thing he cherished, even held with pride. And pride was wrong.

"Forgive me, Father, for I have sinned." Again, he sank deep into spiritual ashes, imagining gray sackcloth covering his head completely. He emerged some hours later, knowing the joy of his life would remain with him, the young Indian maiden named Hester.

It was only a matter of ridding himself of the pride he carried.

Rebecca came, stern and overbearing. She swooped through the log house like a hawk, her sharp, beady eyes missing nothing. Everything was out of place. She meant well. She just came to teach Hester how to be a better housekeeper.

She sewed a white cap for Sunday. She placed the used Sunday one on Hester's head, tying the wide strings beneath her chin.

Hester stood, her soft brown chin lifted, her eyes flat and black, veiled by lowered lashes. A hatred so intense built up in her chest until she felt as if she was on fire. Abruptly, she turned on her heel and left the house, walked swiftly to the spring, and climbed the ridge behind it. She moved in strong, hurried strides, on and on, over rocks and through brambles, until her breath came in short gasps. Her heart pounded with her swift ascent. Clambering up the side of an outcropping of limestone, she crawled out to its edge and flopped onto her stomach, folding her arms beneath her chin.

She had no tears, only a knot that was so hard she felt as if she had swallowed a large, mysterious object. Hatred for Rebecca swam in her veins. She wanted to chase her out of the house like a vermin-infested dog, drive her across the yard and down the road until she disappeared, then send the stodgy old horse and wagon after her.

It felt good to acknowledge and finally understand the emotion that rocked her. Hatred was wrong; it was evil. She knew it inhabited her mind and heart. All her life, she'd sat in church services and heard the Amish ministers speak of heaven and say that the only way to go there was through Jesus Christ. The way you went to hell, they said, was not to believe in him as your own personal savior.

So where was Jesus? What did you do if you accepted the fact that you were such an awful sinner but you
still wanted to drive your grandmother down the road?
Besides that, you hated your cap.

Slowly, Hester lifted her head. The summer's heat
radiated from the rock she lay on. It shimmered and
waved above the multicolored green of the treetops,
which waved and rolled away as far as she could see,
blending into the distant purplish-blue haze that was
Hawk Mountain. There was no break in the sea of green.
The sky was the azure blue of summertime with fluffy,
fat clouds lazily floating along.

She became aware of birdsongs and butterflies. Suddenly, she sat up, untied the scratchy strings, tore off her
cap, and placed it carefully on the rock. She lifted her
hands to the back of her head and pulled out the hairpins. She ran her fingers through her heavy black hair
and shook her head to loosen it.

Leaping to her feet, she lifted her arms, spread them
slowly, then flung them out, on her tiptoes now, her bare
feet lifting her body as high as it could go. She threw her
face to the sky, her eyes closed, as she absorbed the movement of the trees below her, the rustling of the branches
around the heat of the sun, the rolling of the white clouds.

Here I am, God. It's just me. You created me, you
made me who I am. I know I sin. I know it's wrong, but
alone, I cannot do everything I should.

A puff of wind caught her black hair and lifted it,
sending it rippling behind her.

I am flesh and bone. An Indian. My skin is a different
color. I am different. Why am I here?

Slowly, she lowered her arms and dropped her head with the grace of a ballet dancer.

Overhead, a shadow crossed her. She lifted her head and caught sight of a bald eagle as it soared directly above her, so low she could see the strength of its intense yellow eyes, the strong curve of its noble white head, the great lift and swell of its massive wings.

Cold chills washed over her as tears squeezed from between her thick black lashes. She felt alive. She felt the spirit of the eagle, inseparable from God. God was the eagle, and the eagle was God. He was so big, her mind could not accept it. He was so strong, she could not fathom it. Everything was possible, everything was wonderful. She had nothing to fear.

She stood on the limestone rock, the sun blazing down from the summer sky as the great bird soared, circled, dipped, and lifted on swells of air, her heart following its movement.

Strength flowed from its wings. Redemption immersed her yearning heart. She understood that God had created her, knew her nature, knew every cell in her body. She was his. He alone could guide her, save her, by sending his Son to die for her.

If someone had asked her to put her heart's song into words, she could not have done it. Words were untrustworthy. God was not. Humbled, satisfied, her spirit rejuvenated, she turned. The wind caught her hair and blew it across her face as she lowered her eyes to find the offending cap.

Quite suddenly, the corners of her mouth lifted, and she sat on her haunches to retrieve the hairpins. The eagle's head was white, too. God had made him in that fashion. She would wear the cap. In her heart, it signified the strength of the eagle. She would live the life he required of her, a small price to pay.

Gathering her thick black hair, she twisted it into the usual bun, placed the cap on her head, and tied the strings loosely. Then she knelt, lifted her face to the sky, and said, very soft and low:

"*Denke, Gute Mann*" (Thank you, good Father).

I am a child of his, and he will give me courage and strength for each new day.

She would certainly need it.

CHAPTER 15

W<small>HEN</small> H<small>ESTER</small> <small>RETURNED TO THE LOG HOUSE, THE</small> air had become stifling in the hollow surrounding it.

The bake oven radiated heat, so Rebecca must be baking bread, she thought. She was surprised to find the family gathered around the table for the noontime meal. Had she been gone so long?

Hans pushed back his chair, rose hurriedly to his feet, then stood, uncertain, stifling the strong feeling that rose in his chest as he faced Hester, who had returned unharmed.

Rebecca's sharp words rang out. "Where were you? Disobedient child."

Hans's tortured eyes went to his mother's sharp features, and he folded into his chair, trembling before the familiar sound of his mother's temper.

"I went for a climb up the mountain."

"Why? With all you have to do here?"

"I don't know."

"You don't know." The words were a mockery, a bald-faced slur that hung in the room like a stench.

Hans sat up, opened his mouth, his eyes going to Hester's face. He wanted to protect her. He wanted to keep her from the grinding, twisting wrath of his mother.

Hester sat down when no more words were forthcoming. Noah poked Isaac's thigh with his forefinger, and he slid down the bench to make room for her. She sat close to Hans, whose unveiled eyes revealed everything Rebecca needed to see.

Rebecca's breath hissed between her lips as she lifted the spoonful of bean *schnitzel* to her mouth. Well. So this was how it was.

Hans praised the bean *schnitzel,* saying he had never eaten a better seasoned dish than this one. The mixture of cut green beans, bacon and onion cooked in butter was a combination he had always loved. All she said was, "You have onions in your beard."

Hans's face flamed.

Rebecca reveled in his discomfort. A talk would be in order.

They all bent their heads to the fried salt pork, the cooked turnips and the *knabrus,* the dish of buttered cabbage with onions, and no further words were spoken. The children were not allowed to speak at the table. They were expected to eat everything placed before them and to remain completely silent. There was no asking, no questioning about the amount of food each one was given. They accepted the food, receiving it as nourishment, and that was it.

When Rebecca served the warm *Lebkuchen,* the silence was broken by Hans's gleeful laugh. "Did you make the sauce, too?" he chortled.

"Yes, I did." Rebecca placed large squares of the moist, warm cake on the scraped-off plates, then poured the sweet brown sauce over it. There were walnuts and dried apples in the cake—a very special and infrequent treat. Every spoonful was eaten with gratitude, plates scraped noisily, and spoons licked clean.

Afterward, they bent their heads in prayer for the second time to thank God for what they had just received. Then they sat around the table, drinking cold mint tea sweetened with honey.

Rebecca told Hans he needed a bigger house. He needed to buy a new stove, the kind she had heard about. She knew he had money, so why not use it to the children's benefit?

Hans smiled, his round cheeks glistening with sweat, his stomach overly full, and stroked his beard. "If I build a house, it will be built with stone."

"Ooh." Rebecca was impressed. A son who built a house of cut limestone was, indeed, prestigious. Someone of high status.

Hans smiled at his mother with benevolence in his large, dark eyes. Yes, he had money put by. The farm was growing, the pile of coins accumulating.

Before Rebecca took her leave, she cornered Hans in the barn. Wasting no time, she told him it was high time he sought a wife. She told him the children were running wild, that Hester was incompetent, the house was dirty, the clothes unwashed, the sewing undone. He needed to find someone.

"I don't want a wife."

"No, you want Hester."

Hans recoiled from his mother's words. He could not help the heat that rolled across his full cheeks or the accompanying confusion.

"No, no, no."

Rebecca waited, haughty, enjoying her son's floundering.

"No, Mam. No. Not in that way. She is my daughter."

"Piffle. She's not your daughter, and you know it."

"But I have no feelings for her in that way."

"Then get a wife."

"Who?"

"Annie Troyer."

Hans's eyes bulged with disbelief. "Mother!"

"Don't 'mother' me. If you're going to compare every available woman with Hester, you'll never get anywhere."

"Mother!"

Later, swinging the scythe through the tall, waving grasses, the sweat rolling from his wide forehead and down the sides of his cheeks, he thought about his mother's words. Yes, she was right. But, oh, the thought of someone replacing Kate was unthinkable. *Mol net die Annie* (Certainly not Annie). Honeybees buzzed through the grasses, crickets chirped and hopped, crows wheeled and cried their unnerving squawks, but his mind was far away.

No, it was not true. Hester did not leave the house dirty or the clothes unwashed. None of it was true. Perhaps not to Rebecca's standards, which were ridiculous. She was one of those Swiss women who scrubbed her doorstep every morning, living in a house so clean you could eat off the floor.

Hester did well. Not like Kate, but good enough. He wondered idly why Hester had taken to wearing the cap. She had put it on for his mother's sake today, perhaps.

His ears burned as if she had cuffed him the way she always had when he was a boy. He cringed within himself. That was not true, either, that outright lie about his feelings for Hester. His mother had always had a sharp tongue, unguarded, as loose as a flopping fish. Of course it wasn't true. He loved Hester only as a daughter, that was all.

He prayed for guidance, for strength in the coming days, as he rested on his scythe there in the middle of the hayfield in the blazing sun.

A few weeks later, Hans made up his mind. He polished the leather harness until it shone, instructed Noah to wash the spring wagon, and curried Dot and Daisy until their coats shone. They were going to the trading post, then to Berksville.

Hester's heart beat rapidly, her eyes snapped and sparkled as she washed dishes and laid out the children's clothes. She picked the cleanest, least-patched knee breeches for Solomon, John, and Daniel.

For herself, she chose a dress of bittersweet, a rust-colored hue. She loosened the small drawstring in the back of her cap, then tightened and retied it. There. That was better. The cap did not have to hide so much of her straight, black hair. She liked the way Mary Fisher's cap fit much better than the one strict Rebecca sewed for her.

They did the chores, ate a quick breakfast of porridge with bread and milk and got everyone dressed and combed before seven o'clock. The sun was a red orb of resplendence, already giving off heat for the day. Hans wore his long-sleeved linen shirt, vest and knee breeches, and a wide-brimmed straw hat, placed squarely on his head.

The horses sensed a long drive and trotted gaily, their heads lifting as they followed the dusty, sun-dappled road between the trees, down steep inclines, and up more hills and turns. After an hour of steady traveling, Hans stopped the team beneath a tree, threw the reins across the dash, and let the horses rest awhile. The children scrambled off the high spring wagon, stretched their legs, and raced in circles, chattering like a flock of colorful birds.

Hans smiled. He looked at Hester beside him holding Emma. What was so different about her today? Beneath the shade of the oak trees, she was radiant with beauty, an inner light making her brown skin glow, her large dark eyes like liquid fire. He looked away.

"Come, children," he called, his voice choking.

When the road led down to the river, Hester caught her lower lip between her teeth and her upper one. Padriac. Would he be there? She could smell the river, the wet bottomlands, where the dusty, crumbling earth turned to soft black mud that squished beneath toes and smeared easily across skirts and breeches.

A row of thick bushes almost hid the raft, but Hester spied it long before they reached the crossing. An old, grizzled man unfolded from his seat on a wide stump, a blade of grass dangling from his teeth. His hat was a questionable shade of brown, made of felt, the brim waving and flopping around his face. His stained, col-larless shirt was open at the neck, his knee breeches held up by a sturdy rope with frayed edges.

He removed the blade of grass, spit a stream of green juice, and rumbled, "Howdy."

"Hello, there."

"Goin' across?"

"Yes, we are. If you'll take us."

"Sure thing." Going to the rope that circled a sturdy post, he unwound it slowly, then coiled it and laid it on the raft. Picking up another rope, he hauled the large, flat raft to the bank, secured it, and went to Dot's bridle.

"Horses skittish?"

"I doubt it."

Hans lifted the reins and clucked to them as the old man tugged at the bit. The horses stepped gingerly, bend-ing their heads as they walked across the planks and up onto the raft.

Hans got down out of the wagon and went to stand next to the horses' heads as the old man poled them away from the bank. The children's eyes widened with appre-hension, but they remained seated, obedient.

"These all yours?" the man asked, looking directly at Hester.

"Yes," Hans said, gazing across the water.

"Where's your wife?"

"In heaven."

Up went the old man's eyebrows. "Can't beat that."

"No."

"When'd she die?"

"It'll soon be a year."

Hester looked straight ahead, clutched Emma on her lap, and remained silent. She knew the wizened old man wanted to ask more, but he chomped on the blade of grass, watched Hans, busied himself forming his own opinions, and kept his questions to himself.

When Padriac returned the following day, he told him about the Amish man and his wagon load of kids, his wife dead. "Either them Amish allowed young wives, or that oldest daughter wasn't his," he mused. "Them Amish is odd," he finished.

Padriac watched the old man's face intently, but he only nodded his head and asked if they had come back in the evening. Frustrated, he kicked the raft, balled his fists, and stalked off, leaving the old man looking after him with questioning eyes, shrugging his shoulders and shaking his head before sitting back down on his overturned, wooden crate. He pulled his felt hat down over his eyes and leaned back against a tree. Young chaps nowadays!

The trading post was a long, flat building made of logs. Two windows with a door in the middle looked like eyes and a nose, Hester thought. The hitching rail in the front was strung with horses of every size and description, some carrying saddles, others without. Men lounged against the front wall, eyeing them curiously. Hester sat very straight, looking neither left nor right as Hans guided the team up to the side of a hitching rail. He tied them with the neck rope, then told the children they were allowed off, but to stay with him.

Inside, the light was so dim, Hester had to blink her eyes to be able to see anything. After a minute or so, she could see the long, high counter along the side, the form of a man behind it, and a knot of Indians talking in low, guttural tones.

The smell that assaulted all of them as they stepped inside came from the great pile of furs in a corner of the room, tied in bundles with heavy string, a great stinking heap of them. Noah and Isaac held their noses, rolled their eyes, and made gagging sounds, until Lissie plucked at Hans's sleeve and whispered to him about the boys' bad behavior.

Hester had never seen so many objects in one place. Her large, dark eyes roamed every wall, taking in the bolts of fabric, rope, plowshares, lanterns, hooks, utensils, tools, rakes, pitchforks, dishes, books, long rifles, and evil-looking pistols.

There were barrels of molasses and herring and pickles. Drums of vinegar, barrels of sugar and flour and salt. Tentatively, Hester reached up to touch her cap and adjusted it slightly.

One Indian who caught sight of Hester stopped and stared. Speaking rapidly to the others in his group, they all turned and stared, their black eyes keen, their bodies held very still.

They were tall with straight black hair tied with lengths of rawhide. They wore linen shirts, leggings made of deerskin and brown, beaded moccasins on their feet. Heavy ropes and necklaces made of bear claws, bear teeth and shells hung from around their necks. Each had many bracelets of Dutch beads strung around both wrists.

Hester lowered her head. Her stomach flopped when one of them approached the family. He spoke to Hans, who spread his hands and shrugged.

"Come." The Indian led him to the counter and began a series of rapid-fire questions, which the owner of the trading post translated to Hans in German.

Yes, Hester was an Indian. A foundling. She was fifteen, maybe older. They had never been sure of her birth date. Yes, she was Amish.

After this had all been translated back to the Indians, they nodded eagerly and became quite excitable. They came to stand close to Hester, examining her with their eyes, reaching out to touch her, but stopping before they actually made contact.

Hans fought to remain calm, the looming fear of losing her seeming like a sudden reality.

The Indians were quiet, well-spoken, and strong. Their bodies were honed to perfection by long hunts, their travels through the forest, their way of moving constantly.

Hans thought they were likely of the same tribe as Hester as he observed their stature, the contour of their faces, the way they walked.

When he felt it was polite, he pointed Hester toward the fabric, in spite of the Indians' interest in her. They chose bolts of linen to make knee breeches and shirts, shortgowns and dresses for the little ones.

Hester could not help but look longingly at some purple fabric, too, the shade of violets nestled between their waxy green leaves in early spring. Her eyes begged Hans. At first he shook his head no. But when she bent her head gracefully, the thick lashes sweeping her cheeks, and when a painful blush crept across the swell of her face, he caved in, sinking like a man caught in quicksand.

He bought a plowshare, a length of rope, and a new axe blade. He bought hard candy for the little ones. Lissie pouted prettily until he bought a beautiful square of fabric for her.

They sat beneath the shade of a great locust tree behind the trading post. Hester spread a cloth on the ground, and they ate bread and some dried deer meat.

It was very good. They were all hungry, so everything tasted especially fine out in the open air, away from the pile of furs, thinking of the new colorful fabric they had just bought. The dried venison was salty and tough. They chewed it for a long time, finally washing it down with spring water, which Hester had put in a wooden pail with a tight-fitting lid, then wrapped in heavy coverlets to keep it cool.

It was a wonderful day.

Hans asked Hester how she felt about the Indians who were so like her. She kept her face averted and said she didn't know. She couldn't sort out her feelings yet. It was too soon. The Indians had not repulsed her; neither had they attracted her.

She knew her skin was the exact same shade of brown, her hair straight and sleek and thick. God had created her an Indian. And he loved her. He loved her enough to have her be discovered by Kate, a childless mother whose arms had ached to hold an infant of her own. But then he'd taken Kate away. She'd figure it out later. Today was too perfect.

They traveled on to Berksville, where a group of houses huddled in tired rows lining a dusty street, like maids trying to appear as wealthy women.

Hester knew now why they were called false fronts. A lot of Amish people had false fronts—perhaps English people, too—appearing to be a lot more than they really were. Behind the fronts were the brownish, gray-weathered lumber buildings that looked exactly alike, but people couldn't see that. Only God did.

In Berksville, Hans bought a great copper kettle that cost a lot of money, he said. He also said it was a necessary item, one that would pay for itself at butchering time, and in the fall, when they cooked apple and pear butter.

The children saw a livery stable, a hotel, and a drunken man who was weaving in and out of other pedestrians' paths, singing a ribald song at the top of his lungs, hiccupping in between his off-key words.

Hans's face became set and severe, thinking how he'd brought his innocent children directly into the maw of the world. What if Noah and Isaac wanted to try that? Well, he certainly couldn't say he had always abstained. But that was in the days of his youth, when the Amish leaned toward tolerating youth who sowed a few wild oats before they were ready to settle down.

They met an English couple walking arm in arm, chatting happily, their faces turned toward one another, and Hans experienced such a pang of pain, he thought he would fall down in the dusty street. How he missed those moments with Kate! Hunched over on the front seat, he became weary of life with such an uncertain future before him. Yes, he needed a wife, a helpmeet, a fine Christian companion. The thought settled into his brain, bringing a kind of hopelessness he hadn't thought possible.

He glanced over at Hester, who sat like stone, her perfect profile etched into his heart, impossible to remove and as lethal as smallpox.

He heard the children's noise in the background. Lissie was seated in the copper kettle, wagging her head in time to the song they were punching out in various keys. He smiled to himself.

The sun was not yet setting when they crossed the river again. Hester watched for the flaming head of Padriac, but only the old man rose from the stump he was seated on, shuffled over, and poled them across.

It was not yet dark when tired Dot and Daisy pulled the spring wagon up to the barnyard. They stood with their heads drooping, eagerly awaiting the removal of the heavy leather harness and a long, cool drink of water from the trough, a fine pile of oats and corn, and a forkful of hay thrown across the stable door.

CHAPTER 16

ALMOST TO THE DAY, A YEAR AFTER KATE'S DEATH, the deacon, Amos Eash, announced the upcoming nuptials of Hans Zug and Annie Troyer.

The well-trained congregation remained in their seats, faces solemn, showing no emotion. The number of the last song was given out, and the slow rhythm of German singing followed. No one cracked a smile.

The children had been told the evening before. Noah's face closed like a book. Just folded up, unreadable. Isaac searched Noah's face to see what his own reaction should be. Finding no clue, he shrugged his shoulders and figured Noah would let him know sometime.

Lissie jumped up and down and clapped her hands in excitement. Then upon finding out who the bride was, she wrinkled her nose and said, "Ew. Why her?"

The three boys, "the stair steps," as they were often called—Solomon, Daniel, and John—said it was all right and that it would be nice to have a mother again.

The three little ones jumped up, eagerly imitating Lissie. But they were confused by her nose-wrinkling and went outside to play.

Hester said nothing. She watched Hans's face, and thought he had done well, asking Anna Troyer. She was young, never married, slim as a rail, and probably prettier than Kate had ever been. She had brown hair, the color of most white people's, and a round, comely face, if not beautiful. Yes, Hans had done well.

Like a stone rolling off her young shoulders, the burden of keeping house, the washing, the baking, just everything slid off as she thought of having a mother in the house.

The wedding could not be soon enough for Hester. The Amish neighbors gathered around and planned a "sewing" for Hans's family.

One day after another marched by in quick succession, unraveling life as Hester knew it.

After a year on her own, she was the one in charge. She decided when to do the washing, when to light the bake oven, when to put in the bread and cakes. The wood was chopped and carried in under her supervision, the bedding washed in her time.

Now and then Rebecca swooped into the house, a great beaked crow of disapproval, shouting at the children, simpering with pleasure at Hans's appearance, and sending Hester to do the meanest tasks she could think of. The farm had to come up to Annie Troyer's standards, and she was fastidious, Rebecca said. She came from Germany, where the people worked hard, lived clean, and never shirked a duty. The children would have to live up to her standards now.

The day arrived when Hans brought Annie to meet the children, only a few hours after Rebecca prodded her horse down the road, the house cleaned to her satisfaction.

He unhitched Dot with Annie's help, who seemed flushed, radiant, and eager to help. Together, under Hester's watchful eye, they entered the house, Hans stepping aside, a hand on Annie's back, to introduce her to the children.

She was thin as a rail like a young sapling. Her skirts hung straight and full, touching the heels of her shoes, her cape pinned close under her chin, falling across her shoulders, revealing not the slightest hint of a womanly figure. Her eyes were large and set far apart, her whole face quite comely except for the uneven row of teeth that revealed themselves when she smiled.

Hester watched warily as she shook hands with Noah, then Isaac, saying softly, hardly above a whisper, "How do you do?" The boys nodded awkwardly, the late afternoon sun's rays illuminating their tortured eyes as they searched Annie's face for signs of approval.

When Annie reached Hester, she put out her hand yet again, grasped Hester's in a firm grip, and said, "Hester." Hester's eyes met Annie's with a flat, expressionless appraisal. She held her lips straight and taut. Annie was struck by her beautiful face, crowned by a sheen of black hair, while noting that her cap was too far back on her head. Hester's eyes were like the eyes of a cat, mere slits, awaiting its prey, Annie thought. Her knees went weak.

Hans saw. Ah. Hester didn't like Annie. A fierce possession welled up in him, and he was strangely comforted. His heart was a tangled mass of knots, a disorderly jumble of feelings he was struggling to unravel. The display of animosity in front of him only heightened the tension by far.

His heart pounding, he smiled untruthfully while showing Annie the remainder of the rooms. He sat with her at the clean plank table and laid out his plans for a new stone house. When the children gathered around shyly, Annie lifted little Emma onto her lap, and they resembled a family.

The wedding was held at Dan Troyer's, and a fine one it was, everyone said.

The great house was emptied of its furniture. The summer kitchen filled up with women, who, although dressed in their Sunday finery, cooked and stewed and baked as the wedding guests were seated in the main house on hard, wooden benches. The gathered community listened to the traditional sermon as the minister spoke of creation, of Ruth and Samson and Tobias of the Apocrypha.

Hans was large and dark-skinned, his full cheeks flushed with color, his eyes bright with renewed vigor. His Annie sat beside him, meek, quiet, her eyes lowered, dressed in a navy blue dress and black cape and apron, pinned snugly about her neck. Her white head covering hid most of her brown hair.

It was a solemn occasion. The children were in everyone's thoughts and were being closely observed. Poor motherless little ones. The women sized them up, clucked their tongues, said the little boys didn't look happy. *Ach,* Annie would be good to them, poor little boys.

That Hester. Good luck with her, they said, shaking their heads. Annie would have her hands full with that one. Well, they never should have raised her. She was, after all, an Indian. Mark my words, she'll bring sorrow on the family. So the talk drifted in half-whispers behind palms held sideways, as people are wont to do on occasions such as this.

Hans ate turnips with dark streams of browned butter running from a pool on top of them. He ate large spoonsful of *roasht,* the traditional chicken filling, with rich brown gravy, and shredded cabbage mixed with vinegar and sugar.

There were cakes and pies, cookies, stewed apples, and apple butter bread.

Annie smiled, her eyes sparkling as she looked at the tools people had brought as gifts. She gazed at her new husband and felt a lucky girl.

Hester sat with her friends but remained strangely silent most of the day, except when she answered questions or lifted the corners of her mouth in a half-hearted attempt at gaiety. This was not what she wanted. She wanted Kate, her mother. Her loyalty, her love, was with Kate. Why had they gone that day? If they never would have picked raspberries and disturbed the mother bear, Kate would still be here.

The wedding songs rose and fell as the guests sang lustily. The children ran outside to play, eating all the cookies and doughnuts they wanted with not a care in the world.

Hester thought of the old Indian woman and wondered if she was still alive. Suddenly, she had an overwhelming urge to see her and to visit the magical place. She knew without question that she must go. She needed her in a way she could not understand.

"Hester?"

She looked up.

"Come. The girls are getting ready to go to the table."

Hester shook her head.

Annie's sister, Barbara, questioned her with lifted eyebrows.

"I'm not sixteen."

"Oh, but you may go to the table with a boy."

"Going to the table" meant standing in a group with other white-faced, nervous girls, waiting for a single young man to reach for her hand, then lead her to the table and join in with the hymn-singing. She wouldn't be able to participate, being an Indian. No boy would choose her to accompany him to the table.

She shook her head.

"Come on."

"No."

"Please?"

Hester lowered her head. "No one will want me."

Barbara was shocked.

"Oh, but that's not true."

"It isn't?"

"Why, no."

Hester wanted to believe her. Her friends prodded until she gave in, standing miserably behind the rest of the colorfully clad young women who giggled and made small talk, trying to appear nonchalant when, in truth, they were bordering on hysterics.

Who would ask for their company? Would anyone? Would it be the one they preferred, or one they could barely tolerate?

Hester's heart pounded as she stood in the room upstairs. The young men would come trooping up the stairs, their hearts pounding as well, jostling, joking, combing their hair, bending to check their appearance in small mirrors, held discreetly.

Hester almost elbowed her way out of the room. She wanted to flee, to run and run and run out of sight, away from this ghastly wedding, this disturbing, unnerving day, when her father took this questionable, skinny girl to be his wife, her mother.

The first young man appeared. Gigantic, wide-shouldered, his head scraping the low ceiling, his hair as black as midnight on a rainy night, his eyes as brown as a shelled walnut.

One glance, and Hester's eyes fell.

His eyes surveyed the room from left to right and back again. He stepped forward. Softly, he made his way through the over-eager young girls, parting them, his eyes telling them to step back.

Hester could not look up. Her eyes were held by the hem of the dress in front of her. When the skirt moved aside, she saw a white sleeved arm, a large brown hand extended, the fingers long, tapered, the nails clean and cut evenly.

She hesitated, unsure. She waited for another girl's hand to take the one that was offered. When none appeared, she looked up, afraid of making a mistake. The brown eyes looking down at her were the gentlest thing she had ever seen.

Slowly, trembling, she placed her hand in his. She was led away, the girls parting for them, faces showing the extent of their congratulations or misery. He took his time, walking slowly, holding up his hand so she could easily descend the narrow staircase.

Heads turned at the first couple's approach. There were broad smiles of approval, eyes following their every move. This was a wedding, and matchmaking and romance swirled in the very essence of the room.

Other couples followed, but Hester was guided to the bench by the wall, facing the wedding guests.

Gracefully, she slid into her place on the bench beside him. Her shoulder touched his solid one. Quickly, she leaned away, lowering her eyes, folding her hands in her lap. She felt as if her breathing brought no oxygen to her body, as if her heart would lose its power to keep going. There was no way she could speak to him.

He propped his elbows on the table. His shoulder came solidly against hers, and he kept it there. "Hello," he said, very softly.

Hester only nodded. She had no power to speak.

"Can you say, 'Hi'?" he asked, so gentle, so easy.

She nodded again.

"All right. That means 'Hi.' Do you speak Dutch?"

Again, the nod of her head.

"I'm William."

When the singing began again, it was easier to look at him. She felt as if the guests were watching their hymn-books and not her, so she lifted her head, turned it slightly to the left, and opened her eyes. Her lips parted in a soft smile. Gladness rose in her dark eyes, and she said, simply "Hester."

He could not answer. He had not thought this feeling possible. The welling of unexpected emotion that rose in his chest brought tears to his eyes. All his life he had prayed. When he reached his twenty-sixth birthday, he stopped asking God for a woman he could love. He fought bitterness, sure that God had forgotten him.

Thinking she had been too bold, Hester bent her head, misery suffusing her face.

"Esther?" he asked, finally.

"No, I am Hester."

"Hester."

"Hans Zug is my father."

"The groom?"

"Yes."

"Forgive me, but are you his daughter?"

"No."

"I didn't think so."

"I am a full-blooded Indian." She turned her head, and he drank in her beauty—the glow of her cara-mel-colored skin, the perfection of her nose, her mouth. Her eyes were sad, too old. She couldn't be more than eighteen. Perhaps he had no chance.

"Why are you Amish?"

"They found me as an infant. Kate did."

"Kate?"

"My mother. The one that died."

"Oh."

The sweet treats that were offered, the cider that was served in redware cups, turned to sawdust and vinegar for Hester. She could not eat or drink, for she had been held captive by kinder eyes than she had ever thought possible. She wanted to hold his eyes with her own, drain all the caring from them, and hold it in her heart forever.

She wanted to keep that gentleness so that she was rooted to something, no longer floating between the fractured family she belonged to and the distant calling of the old woman's heritage.

"How old are you?" he asked, when he was able to speak.

"I am fifteen."

The disappointment was so heavy, it left him speechless, yet again. Too old. Too old. You're twenty-six. The words in his head mocked and shamed him. He could not rise above it.

"*Ach,* you're a slip of a girl. I'm twenty-six."

From the weight of his letdown, his spirits soared to unnamed heights when she shrugged her perfect shoulders.

"What does that mean?" he dared.

Anything she said would be too bold, so she remained silent. While she knew she was risking straying out of her rightful place, she desperately wanted to reassure him that twenty-six was perfectly acceptable. Sometimes she felt older than that. So she looked at him. She looked into his dark brown eyes, realized the perfection of the contours of his face, the rightness of it, and let her eyes tell him what she could not say.

How could they leave this hallowed place that was only a hard church bench?

Quickly, he told her he was from Lancaster County. A group of Amish had migrated there from Chester County. His name was William King. His father was a brother to Annie. He was the youngest of ten children, four of them dead from smallpox. He had just bought one hundred acres of land.

She listened, nodded, then whispered, "I am nobody."

"Don't say that."

"I am. I don't know where I belong."

You belong with me, his heart cried out. How to let her know? In answer, he reached over, gently pulled her left hand away from her right, and held it in his own.

No one else would have to know, just them.

Unbelievably, he felt her fingers slip into his own like a trusting child. If he had no more from her for the rest of his life, this was enough. The moment would be etched into his mind forever, a gift of God to the end of his days.

> *Seeye, der bräutigam kommet*
> *Gehet ihm entgegen.*

The words of the German wedding song rolled through the house, its joy rising to the rafters, the house filled with goodwill and forbearance. For the lonely widower had found a wife, the children had a mother, and that oldest daughter would have her workload taken from her.

God was in his heaven, and all was good in the fledgling Berks County Amish settlement.

William looked down at Hester, trying to absorb the blue-black of her hair, the perfect part in the middle, the white, white cap, like an angel. He memorized the way her black lashes fell heavily on her glowing brown cheeks, the high cheekbones tinged with the whisper of a blush. Her lips were more than he could ever hope of touching, but he could remember them.

He shuddered, thinking of his Aunt Annie and her family, the ragged tear that was so desperately hidden, the pride, the blatant lies.

He couldn't stay quiet. Bending his head, he leaned his shoulder solidly against her.

"Hester."

"Yes."

"Promise me if things don't go well, you'll let me know."

"What are you saying?" Frightened, she lifted large dark eyes to his.

He drew in his breath. "If Annie proves to be less than, well, how can I say this without disappointing you? I'll just say, if Annie is hard to get along with, if she hurts you, will you let me know?"

"I can't. I don't know your address."

"I'll give it to you before the day is over."

"I think Annie will be kind. She seems nice. I just want a mother and not a stepmother."

William nodded. "Do your best."

How could they explain the agonizing loss at leaving a hard wooden bench, their time together? Years stretched before them, she too young, he too old. How many young men would want her first? And him so far away. He almost wished he'd never settled for the one hundred acres. But he had, and he would remain true. He could not let an Indian girl's beauty derail him like this.

The remainder of the day was nightmarish. He only wanted to be with her. He couldn't find her. He thought she'd gone home. Beside himself with fear, he rose a head above the crowd, his eyes searching anxiously, but she was nowhere to be seen. He left the wedding heartsick.

He stayed at his uncle's house for the night. He was tempted to ask for a horse and ride out to Hans Zug's house, but he thought better of it and decided to let his fate rest in God's hands.

Alarmed at the feeling of losing her, of never seeing her, he felt the memory of her like torture now, an agonized longing that threatened to send him into despair. What color was her dress? He didn't know.

All he knew was that he understood, at long last, what it meant to be in love. That secret no one could fully express made young men do silly things, made them forget the ordinary daily world and dwell on utterly useless things.

Ah, but it was priceless to be able to savor this once in his life. He could wait, placing his trust in the One above.

A cold fear gripped his heart as his Uncle Dan yelled at his wife, then followed his words with a quick fling of a shovel in her general direction, leaving her scuttling for the house and muttering to herself. When William came to talk to Dan, he gave a quick start. A smile spread across his lean face, his blue eyes crinkled in pleasure, and he said jovially, *"Da Villie!"* his favorite nickname.

William kept his manners, held them in front of himself like a shield, but a foreboding gripped his spirit. He wanted to ride to Hans Zug's, grab Hester, and ride away with her, a knight in armor.

CHAPTER 17

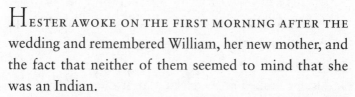

HESTER AWOKE ON THE FIRST MORNING AFTER THE wedding and remembered William, her new mother, and the fact that neither of them seemed to mind that she was an Indian.

She stretched, luxuriating in this new and astounding discovery. She had never imagined being accepted in this way. Every word they spoke, their every touch, were like drops of pure gold, covering her whole being with grace and love.

She rolled over, buried her face in the pillow, and allowed the happiness to overtake her. She would never again have to wonder where she belonged. It was here with her family and her sweet new mother, whom she would learn to love in time. When she was old enough, she would marry William King, her newfound beau.

She got up, dressed, and went to the dry sink to wash her face.

"Hester!" The sharp word caused her to jump instantly.

She stopped, water dripping from her face. She lowered her hands slowly to the edges of the dry sink and gripped it tightly.

"Hester!"

"Yes?"

"Do not! I repeat—do not ever let me catch you washing your face in the dry sink again!"

"I'm sorry," she whispered, shocked into a low voice.

"Just so you know."

Unsure what to do, Hester turned to the right slowly, afraid the sight of her dripping face would only inflame Annie further. She sidestepped like a crab out of her eyesight, then rubbed her face dry with her apron.

Unsure of exactly what was expected of her, she turned, meaning to ask Annie what she should do to help.

A stack of plates came crashing down in front of her. "Wipe these."

Hester looked at the clean plates, the shelf they had rested on, and then Annie's face.

"What? Weren't they washed?"

"Of course. But an open shelf? Think of the dust."

Nodding, as if it was perfectly understandable, Hester began wiping, placing the dishes on a stack. Then she went to the pantry to retrieve the tablecloth that they always used two or three times before washing it.

Instantly, Annie was by her side, fingering the tablecloth, then whisking it out of her hands. "No. It's dirty. Always use a clean one."

Hester obeyed, quietly placing the plates on the clean tablecloth. Then she stood uncertainly at the corner of the table, one hand placed over the other.

"Don't you milk?"

"I do in the spring. Four cows are dry now, so Noah and Isaac milk."

"That's a girl's job. You should be at the barn."

"I can go if you want me to."

"Yes. Go."

Uncertainly, Hester entered the barn, meeting Noah and Isaac, who were letting the cows out to pasture. When they asked what she had come for, she said that Annie thought she should be milking, not them.

Hans walked in on their little huddle, his face set grimly, boding no good for any of them.

"What?" That was his way of greeting.

"Annie told Hester she should be the one milking, not us boys."

Hans eyed Hester, shrugged his shoulders, and said it was all right with him. "If Annie wants to make breakfast by herself, that's all right with me."

The first meal together was a lesson in Annie's way of life. Everything was perfect. The eggs were cooked just right; the *ponhaus* (scrapple), cut not too thick and not too thin, was fried crisp. The tea was hot and sweetened with honey, the milk cold, the water chilled as well.

Annie was an expert housekeeper, but she avoided Hans's intense eyes. Her conversation to him was civil although a bit stiff, containing none of Kate's closeness. Hester reasoned that a marriage was not created in one day.

But the minute Hans was out the door, Annie turned on Hester, berating her for not setting the water on to boil so she could properly wash the dishes. Had Hans not taught her the ways of a household?

Hester thought Annie had already heated the water. She figured if she told her that, she'd not accept it as a valid answer, so she simply bowed her head, set about filling the water pot, and swung it over the flames of the log fire.

By the time the children were off to school again, they were glad to go. Annie was trying to be a good mother, but she was a new one, one they were not yet comfortable with. School was their refuge, a place familiar, old, and dependable, like Theodore Crane, the schoolmaster, and his helper, Lissie Hershberger.

They loved school, every one of them. They loved the order of their days, the hard work, the lessons they learned. Lissie enjoyed the lower-graders immensely, especially the little Zug children. Poor motherless babies. That Annie Troyer was like a scarecrow, she thought. Good for nothing except scaring away birds. Whatever ailed that Hans she'd never know, but she kept her thoughts to herself, knowing gossip did no one any good.

She watched Lissie closely. Her face was like an open book, revealing everything that was on her mind. She asked her questions when she thought Solomon or John or Daniel looked white-faced and peaked. And she confided in Theodore, who had become quite accustomed to her solid, comfortable presence. He concluded that she wasn't after him at all. She simply enjoyed cooking and baking, which was a profound relief.

Today she offered him a pie, saying she would enjoy a slice with him, bringing out two pewter plates, two forks, and two cups. Had he ever eaten her pumpkin pies? No, he shook his head, no, never.

She cut him a high, wide slice, then served it shivering and custardy on his plate. He cut into the very tip with the side of his fork, brought it to his mouth, and chewed with his eyes closed as he savored every creamy, spicy bit of it.

She leaned forward, her eyes expectantly on his face, then clapped her hands high in the air, a child's yelp of glee following. "Yessirree! Yessir!"

Theodore was not known to burst into spontaneous laughter, being a solemn man and not given to any emotion, but at the sight of Lissie's unabashed delight, he burst into an unusual croak of loud laughter.

He ate the entire slice of pumpkin pie, then another. He became quite talkative, bolstered by the energizing pie, and told Lissie where he lived and why he lived alone. He'd had a sweetheart once, but she had died before they made it to the altar, and his vow to remain single was still as sincere as the day he made it.

"*Ach,* yes, yes," Lissie answered. "But you know, Theodore, you don't know what you're missing, living alone like that. You have no one to eat with, no one to laugh with, no one to wash your clothes."

"Yes. Yes, I do."

"Who?"

"Some old Indian woman, who comes to the trading post."

"Piffle."

"What does that mean?"

"Just piffle, I guess."

He almost laughed again but caught himself and remained decorous.

"Well, I guess if you enjoy living by yourself, that's none of my business. I guess you've been on your own long enough to know what you want. And look at that

Hans Zug and his children. You'd never know it, but mark my words, those children have a hard taskmaster now. I'm afraid Hans was swayed by that Rebecca and his own loneliness."

Theodore nodded wisely. "Indeed. Indeed."

Outside, the leaves began rustling dryly as black clouds piled up to the north. The door swung back, groaning on its hinges as it was swept outward. Theodore got up to close it and latched it firmly, leaving them together in the confines of the classroom.

The room darkened as the sun slid behind the bank of clouds, and Lissie heaved herself to her feet, gathered up the plates and the remainder of the pie, and put it all in her cloth bag.

Stopping, she held her head to the side, considered, and yanked the pie back out of the bag. "Yes, I will have another piece." Expertly, she slid her fingers beneath the wedge of pie, brought it to her mouth, and ate half of it in one hearty chomp. She chewed reflectively, then asked if he liked fried cabbage.

Yes, he certainly did.

Well, why didn't he drop by on Sunday, and she'd make him fried cabbage.

"I go to church on Sunday."

"So do I. After church."

Theodore thought of his dusty old Sundays, when his bones ached as he got out of bed, padded around his cluttery, cobwebbed little rooms, made his eggs, and ate them with salt and pepper. He listened to the minister, helped sing a few songs, and went back to his disorderly home to eat boiled cornmeal mush.

Dinner with Lissie seemed like a bright possibility, but he eyed her warily and said he slept a lot on Sunday afternoon, which did not deter her in the least. She informed him quickly that he could eat at her table and then take a long afternoon nap.

Theodore considered this, but in the end, he declined. What great juicy fodder for gossip would that be? Lissie getting company on a Sunday afternoon and the schoolmaster asleep in her bed! Well, he would be every bit as bad off as that poor fellow who was caught by the old maid when he was stealing her valuables, and she cried out, "At last I have a man."

So Lissie drove home beneath the gathering storm clouds, but she did not despair. She was making progress. She couldn't wait till the time came when she could call him Ted. Or Teddy. She chuckled and then slapped the old horse with the heavy leather reins, whose only response was the flicking of his left ear.

The storm lashed Berks County with unprecedented fury, driving a cold, slanted rain from the north, battering every structure with high winds that bent the trees of the forest, laying flat the ones that were not deeply rooted.

Lissie barely made it home before the rain sluiced against the log barn. It was cold and wet against her face as she hurried to the house, her flat hat slapping her face. She was glad to enter her cozy kitchen, the fire burning low on the hearth, the white linen tablecloth a welcoming beacon.

She lit a betty lamp to ease the darkness away from the corners, then put the pot on the flames for a cup of spearmint tea. She thought she still had enough bacon to fry up with some dried string beans, brown bread, and apple butter.

Theodore arrived home well ahead of the storm, the fire out and mice munching the crumbs on his table. He whacked at them with his broom, then went out through the wind to cut kindling, shivering as the icy rain blasted straight through his trouser legs.

He bet someone like Lissie could make the winter nights quite comfortable, then was overtaken by an awful attack of coughing, so that he choked and had to go to the pump for a drink of water.

The Zug house was warm in the middle where the leaping flames from the fireplace gave out a steady glow, but the corners were drafty. Hester reached for a small shawl to wrap around her shoulders, then sank into a rocking chair. She pulled Emma onto her lap and cuddled her beneath the warm folds, bending to kiss the top of her fair head.

She was weary, and a few minutes with Emma were a good reason to sit. She watched Annie from the corners of her eyes, turning her head slightly so Annie wouldn't know. The late afternoon sun cast a square of yellow light on the oak floor. The light from the fire illuminated the remainder of the house in a warm glow, reminding Hester that a house was a home, as long as there was a group of people in it.

She was trying hard. She scrubbed floors, wiped walls, washed bedding and blankets. She took on the hardest tasks, trying to win her stepmother's affections. Her shoulders were wide and capable, her arms rounded and muscular. The seams of her dresses strained beneath the power of her arms as she hoed the corn, cut it with a sharp scythe, and carried it to the barn for bedding.

As the winds became colder, rustling the last of the clinging, brown oak leaves, she was in the fields. With her ungloved hands, she ripped the ripened ears of corn from the stalks and threw them on the wooden wagon, her nose red from the cold, a warm scarf around her head.

Lissie was helping her. Noah and Isaac had gone to help Hans with the foundation of the new stone house. The corn rustled in the wind, a dry brittle sound that spoke of the coming winter. The mound of golden ears was reaching above the wooden walls of the wagon. Hester's stomach growled.

She lifted her face, searching for the sun, but the gray clouds had reduced it to a shaded, white light. It would rain. The clouds in the evening sky had resembled fish bones, a sure sign of rain, Kate had always told her.

Thunk. Thunk. The ears of corn flung into the wagon made a satisfying sound. This was sustenance for the horses, as well as the family. They would roast the ears of corn in the bake oven, then shell the corn into the wooden dishpan. The next step was to grind the kernels into a fine, golden meal, set it to cooking with water and salt so that it bubbled slowly in the black cast iron pot hanging above the fire, then pour it into pans. The cornmeal mush would set, so that it could be sliced and placed carefully in sizzling lard, where it was fried to a rectangular piece of crisp goodness.

Or Annie would dish the bubbling corn pudding from the pot, lace it with molasses, and pour rich, creamy milk over it. Sometimes she made cornbread. It was all very good.

Thinking of it made Hester swallow, her eyes searching the clouds yet again. Surely the dinner bell would soon ring. Unaware of any changes, Hester continued stripping ears of corn from their husks, flinging the cobs onto the wagon, a mindless repetition, until she called to the horses. "Dot! Daisy! Giddup!" Dutifully, the horses leaned into their collars, tugging the wagon through the emptied cornstalks, until Hester said, "Whoa."

It was only then that she noticed Lissie's absence. She stooped, her eyes searching the cornstalks. "Lissie!"

"Hm."

"Where are you?"

"Here." Lissie lay on her stomach, her face in her cupped hands, her feet kicking the air above her.

"What are you doing?"

"I'm lying on my stomach."

"Why?"

"Why do people lie down? Because they are tired."

Hester laughed quietly. "Come, Lissie. It's almost dinnertime."

"I'm starved. I'm falling-down tired. I can't pull one more ear of corn."

Hester knew she meant it. Lissie was young to be husking corn all day, but Hans had said he felt the hurry in his bones. Winter was going to catch them this year if they didn't stay steadily at the husking of the corn.

There was no doubt about it, with Annie as his wife, Hans's stride matched hers, side by side. He began laying the foundation for the new stone house after digging the cellar with shovels. Neighbors lent a hand, with Noah and Isaac helping after school.

Annie was the taskmaster, the one wielding the scepter, barking orders, shoving the family into a regimen of good management. Where Kate had been relaxed, her work done well and in an orderly fashion, content with her log house and small farm, Annie's goal in life was getting ahead, attaining status and wealth. Of course, she never spoke of it, but Hester knew by the narrowing of her eyes and the lift of her chin when they drove into Amos Hershberger's farmyard, that she aimed to have a house like Mary's, and soon. So Hans took his place beside his thin, energetic wife and met her requirements.

It was only at times, at unguarded moments, when he sat pensively staring into the fire at night, that Hester saw the longing, the remembering, and she wondered. Did he really want this stone house?

Some things, you never could know, but as the days grew colder and Hans redoubled his efforts, laying one stone upon another steadily, week after week, his cheeks became gaunt and lost their rosiness. His shoulders stooped with tiredness, and his eyes glittered with a strange light. Hester shivered. Where would it end?

In due time, the house was built with frolics, those days when men swarmed into the farmyard with wagons and carts, their able bodies a boost to Hans as they bent to the task of cutting and laying the good, solid limestone.

Before those days, Annie and Hester worked from dawn till past sundown, preparing food for the hungry men. They made *Leberklosschen,* the dumplings made of chopped liver and onions, boiled in a good, rich, beef broth and served with pungent mounds of sauerkraut from the crocks in the cold cellar.

Annie made the most wonderful chicken they had ever tasted, serving the dish on a big redware plate with creamy chicken gravy poured over it. There were great dishes of *Schpeck und Bona*, beans cooked with ham, a salty, savory dish served with cruets of vinegar for those who liked the beans strongly flavored. Filling out the tables were stacks of homemade bread and apple butter.

Annie loved to cook, using her mother's recipes whenever she could.

Hans proudly hosted these wonderful meals for the men who came to the frolic. He urged the men to fill and refill their plates, and he ate two platefuls himself. But never once did anyone see him lift his face to find his wife or speak to her as she darted from oven to table and back again, holding her head just so, a bit to the side, away from him.

Isaac observed this, beginning to understand his son's empty eyes. A great sadness lay like a heavy stone on his chest and his breathing, so intense was his pity. And when he observed Hans's eyes on Hester's face, a look that struck Isaac with the force of a sledgehammer, he knew the power of his prayers were more necessary now than they had ever been before. He knew the way of life with a woman like Annie. Rebecca was so much the same. He knew the sacrifices his son would need to make.

Yes, a man gave his life for his family. It was in the Word of God. For years, Isaac had struggled with this monumental sacrifice, this giving up of a close relationship, a shared intimacy, the relaxed and loving way of a wife.

He had much, Hans had. A mother for his children, a willing and able worker, a manager, a zealous woman, but one who left him with an empty heart, a longing. And there was Hester. Isaac shook in his shoes.

CHAPTER 18

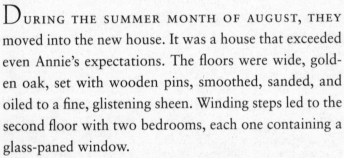

DURING THE SUMMER MONTH OF AUGUST, THEY moved into the new house. It was a house that exceeded even Annie's expectations. The floors were wide, golden oak, set with wooden pins, smoothed, sanded, and oiled to a fine, glistening sheen. Winding steps led to the second floor with two bedrooms, each one containing a glass-paned window.

Large pieces of furniture held all of Annie's blue and white dishes, which she had brought from Germany.

A fireplace was located in the center of the house, with a wide hearth for cooking.

Noah and Isaac cut wood for cooking and for heating the rest of the house from the fireplace, the back wall of which jutted into a large room for gathering opposite the kitchen.

Annie kept the floor of the big room swept clean. And when visitors came, she often put down some hand-sewn rugs she had made. The chairs were always dusted, just in case someone would drop by. She hung some of her favorite coverlets over the backs of the chairs to add warmth to the room. She liked doing needlework and wasn't shy about displaying her skills to others.

It was a fine house, with closets built under the stairways and little pantries built in nooks off the kitchen. One of the pantries contained a small window that Annie always left open in winter, which was a wondrous idea. That kept food from spoiling for a week at a time, but no one needed to go outside to bring it in. Water from the spring stayed cold in the large, covered bucket inside this pantry, as well as many foods.

Annie was always pushing for more. She thought a black stove would allow her to do more efficient cooking. And she had heard talk of a pump in the house, which would bring in water at the lift of a handle. Hans knew how expensive these conveniences were, but he kept thinking about the possible depletion of his saved coins, plus the burden of owing a debt to his father. How he hated to ask his own father for money. He eventually had to admit defeat and allowed himself to ask for help to keep his new wife content.

He trembled under his mother's wrath. "Neither a borrower nor a lender be," she said, the words like icy pellets ingrained into his conscience.

"Yes, Mam. But I did not have quite enough money to finish."

"Hans, it's all right for you to have this big house, but not with our money." To have a son who was well-to-do was one thing, but to give up her own pot of coins was quite another.

"He'll pay it back," Isaac offered.

Rebecca chose not to answer. She leaned against the doorframe, crossed her arms, lifted her chin, and asked, "How's it going, son? With Annie?"

"Good. Everything's fine."

Rebecca's eyebrows shot up, disbelief lifting her upper lip. She snickered. "Well, good."

That was all she said, but Hans felt as if his mother had seen straight into his soul, leaving him struggling to put up the shield of happiness he had been accustomed to holding. "She's a good cook."

Isaac nodded.

Rebecca said, "That's about it."

Hans left his parents' house with higher resolve. He would work harder, hide his feelings with more ease, and become the son his mother expected.

When the new house was finished, Annie turned on Hester. She rarely performed any given task properly. The washing was not done to her specifications. When she cleaned, she left dust in the corners. When she washed windows, they were streaked. Her sewing had to be ripped apart and done over.

Hester could not cook, she was told over and over, until she believed it was true. She avoided the kitchen as much as possible and took on more and more of the boys' chores.

For reasons beyond Hester's understanding, Lissie seemed to be able to fulfill Annie's expectations, spending hours in the kitchen producing cakes and biscuits, bread and cookies, with Annie's assistance. It was only Hester who rankled her moods.

Hester climbed the mountain to her rock, as she thought of it now, the great ledge of pure limestone that jutted out over the hillside allowing her a view of the hills surrounding her home, her community of Amish people, the only way of life she had ever known.

She was almost seventeen now, so she was allowed to go with the youth. But so far, she'd chosen not to socialize with them. There wasn't anything she wanted there except to be with her girlfriends, whose inane giggling set her teeth on edge.

Her eyes took in the sky, the heat shimmering above the restless, green trees. She watched a few brown birds wheeling in the sky, those daring swifts that flew so gracefully.

She drew up her knees and laid her head on them, closing her eyes wearily. She felt beaten today. Finished. Surely there was more to life than this endless round of disapproval. She woke up to it and went to bed with it, a knowledge of all her shortcomings. She was never quite enough in Annie's eyes.

The next day, Annie asked Hester to cook a huge kettle of apples, so none went to waste. She had built a good-sized fire, burning hot, so the apples would finish cooking before it was time to start supper. She was struggling to lift the heavy kettle onto the hook set over the fire, but she bumped it when she swung the loaded pot up and over the bank of flames. Determined not to ask for help, Hester pulled the kettle back again with a broad arc of her arm, balancing herself carefully so as not to have the sparks that were racing across the hearth catch her skirt.

But as her elbow flew back to its highest point, Hester felt a burst of heat at her feet. Her skirt had swept the edge of the hearth, and flames ran quickly across the width of her hem.

Determined to achieve the perfection Annie required, Hester landed the pot of apples onto the hook over the crown of flames. Perspiration formed on her forehead and beaded on her upper lip, but she didn't slacken her pace once.

She bent to smother the flames on the bottom of her skirt before they could race up the threads, consuming her weekday clothing. But as she stooped to stamp on the smoldering cloth, a stinging slap connected firmly with the side of her face, then another. "You're just a strong-willed, insolent Indian," Annie hissed, her wide eyes alive with the anger she felt, never acknowledging the danger Hester had been in.

Hester escaped in the only way she knew how, straight up the mountain to her rock, the only place of solace she knew.

Today, she did not see the eagle, as she often did. Where was her God? Did he hear when she prayed? It seemed as if God had hidden his face from her, the way he had allowed Annie into her life.

It was the endless, mind-numbing disapproval she felt continually. She tried and tried, doing her best each day, but she guessed Indians must be like that. What other explanation could be valid? Indians were incapable, untrustworthy, slackers who shirked their duty, unable to perform the way white people did. At least that's what Annie wanted her to believe. But did she? Her thoughts jumbled and twisted painfully. Stuck in self-hatred, she examined each of her flaws and cringed before them.

Yes, she was unworthy, but there was nothing she could do to help that.

Gott im Himmel (God in heaven), she prayed. I know we are not supposed to ask for signs, but today, when I am not sure if you are there, please show you care about me. I need something or someone to show me how to be a better person.

The sky remained blue and bright and empty. The leaves whirled and danced, the thin, brown branches waved in the summer breeze. A curious green lizard scuttled out on the edge of the shelf of rock and watched her with wide red eyes, its sharp, forked tongue darting in and out so rapidly, Hester could see only a blur. Bees hummed past on their way to a certain type of nectar from a flowering bush.

Hester lifted her head, her eyes searching the great blue sky so empty today, devoid of one puffy white cloud. She sighed, straightened her legs, and propped her shoulders by extending her arms behind her.

A clear, melodious whistle entered her consciousness. Not a bird, certainly. She held her body motionless, a part of the limestone. The whistle was clear, a melody, a song, although she didn't know the tune or the words. Who would be here? Noah or Isaac? It was a beautiful tune. It sent chills down her back. Had God heard her? Was this an angel? In the German Bible she had learned to read, a visitation from an angel was always frightening. Should she be afraid?

Slowly, the whistling faded away into the distance, leaving Hester frustrated, longing to know.

Sighing, she prostrated herself on the rock, hid her face in her hands, and thought of William King. What a name! Worse than the red-haired youth named Paddy. The King of England, this one.

Yes, it had been nice, and oh, he was handsome. A fine man. But if she harbored thoughts of him, it would only lead to heartbreak. She could never have him. She wouldn't be white enough, with skills to do housekeeping properly.

A butterfly hovered over her, then danced through the sky with its fluttering, erratic pattern of flight. Perhaps she was like this butterfly, made to be the way she was. Hadn't God created her? John Lantz, the bishop, had explained it very well. God had taken a rib from the man he created and formed a woman. That was a wonderful idea.

Hans was not like Annie. He was a good person. Perhaps all men were better than women. She knew that thought was incorrect. Kate had been the best person Hester had ever known. And Lissie Hershberger. She smiled. Local gossip swirled around the portly woman and her tall, skinny co-worker, Theodore Crane.

She strained to hear the whistling, unafraid, curious, but there was no sound except the leaves rustling, distant bird song, the faraway cawing of crows.

Hester sighed. She did not want to go back. If she stayed here on this rock, would she suffer much if she didn't eat or drink for days and days? Now that was only being foolish.

One thought became very clear to her. She would find the Indian woman who gave her the herbs to heal Kate's wounds. She sat very still as the thought saturated her being. Yes, she would go. Somehow she would find her way, perhaps only to the river, but perhaps Padriac Lee would go with her.

She felt a clear direction, a newfound purpose. The old woman would help her in much the same way she had healed Kate's wounds. Lifting her hands, she felt thankful for the direction. It was a simple thought, but a belief so strong it was like an object she could hold.

She drew a sharp breath when a doe stepped out of the trees, followed by a fawn, its white spots already disappearing. The doe's ears flicked forward, her large, dark eyes examined Hester quietly, then she lowered her head and lifted her feet delicately, disappearing into the surrounding trees, the fawn at her heels.

Again, Hester lifted her hands, then flung her arms to the sky. Freely, her spirit worshiped the Creator. She praised him; she thanked him for sending the deer and her fawn. She would go to the Indian woman.

Revived, she didn't dread her return to the house like an unwanted chore. Everything was possible. She could survive, even prosper, under Annie's disapproval.

Later, when she retrieved the twice-washed bed linens from the line, she lingered by the emptied washline, the courage she had felt earlier in the day slipping away from her. Footfalls behind her made her stand erect, at attention, waiting for the harangue that was sure to follow.

"Hester." It was Hans, the soft word a boon to her flagging spirit.

"Yes?" Turning, she faced Hans with tired eyes.

"I need horseshoeing supplies at the trading post. Annie says it's a waste of time in the busy month of August to go after them. Would you please go with Noah?"

"Tonight?"

"Tomorrow."

He watched the expression across Hester's face. Suspicion, fear at first, then acceptance, and what else? "Hester, are you doing all right?" he asked suddenly.

"What do you mean?"

"Is Annie too hard on you?"

She wanted to tell him. She longed to let him know how unkind Annie was but knew it would only make her life worse. Hester shook her head. She would not look at Hans.

"Why don't you go with the youth?"

"What do you mean?"

"You don't try to attend the hymn sings. Why not?"

She shrugged her shoulders.

"The only way . . ." Hans's voice trailed off. "Hester, the only way out of here is to get married."

Anger sliced into Hester like a knife, catching her unprepared, unable to control herself. "Oh, marrying would be a fine kettle of fish. Who would have me? Not an Amish person. Every last one is self-righteous and pious beyond belief. The day Kate picked me up, she should have dropped me in the spring and let me drown like an unwanted cat."

"Hester!" Hans was shocked.

"Don't 'Hester' me!"

"You have no right to talk this way."

"Yes, I do. She hates me."

"No, no, you have it wrong. She's just like that. Annie means well, Hester. She's teaching you the ways of a housewife."

Stepping closer, Hans was overcome by his strong feeling for the Indian foundling, the sweet baby he had helped Kate to raise, appreciative of her grace and beauty. "It's all right, Hester. She treats me the same way. You must forgive her if she seems harsh. She really does mean well."

His hands went to her shoulders. She bent her head, letting go of her anger.

"Promise me, Hester."

She nodded.

He stepped back, feeling more alive than he had in months.

From the front living room window, Annie moved to the kitchen, just in time to see Hans place his hands on Hester's shoulders. Her eyes turned to pools of jealousy; her lips tightened into a fierce line of determination. Hester would have to go.

Energetically, she began cleaning the new stovetop, her anger giving her all the speed and force she needed. She served warm wild plums and dumplings for supper, along with a pitcher of cold, creamy milk. She praised Hester's fried rabbit until her face burned with embarrassment, not knowing how to tolerate the wrong, the treachery in Annie's voice.

Annie approved of Hans's plan to let Noah and Hester take Dot and the wagon to the trading post, making it unbelievably easy for Hester to get away. She guessed that if God cared, he made things possible, and that was the truth.

Hester's face was flushed with excitement as she pinned the black apron around her red dress. She took great care in combing her thick, black hair. Tying her white cap strings beneath her chin, she hurried out of her bedroom, down the stairs, and across the living room before Annie's voice caught her unexpectedly.

"Hester, here are two quarter pieces to buy yourself something."

Hester stopped but would not look back.

"Your father said you can use them for a dress."

"I don't need a new dress."

"He said you're supposed to."

"I'll get one for Lissie."

"He said it's for you."

Turning, Hester faced Annie, summoning the courage to look into her eyes. Reading nothing, she reached out her right hand, and Annie placed the two coins into it. Hester folded her fingers around them, then reached into her pocket to leave them there.

"Aren't you going to thank me?"

"I thought they were from Hans . . . Dat."

"They are."

"Then I need to thank him."

"We are married, Hester. To thank me is to thank him. Although, I'm sure I won't place my hands on your shoulders the way he does."

"Thank you." Her face burned yet again, humiliated by Annie's evil surmising. Hester stumbled through the door, wiping at her swimming eyes with the backs of her hands, hardly able to breathe for the gigantic lump in her throat.

There was no getting away from her. Well, she was on her way, so Annie's jealousy would be of no consequence. She would tell Noah where she wanted to go and hoped that Padriac would be at his post, taking people across the river.

So far, God had been with her. Or had he? Could she bring herself to question her reason for being on earth? Should she return to her people, the Lenape? Could she adopt another way of life after living the white way for so long?

The mockingbird's song from the hemlock tree reflected the scornful voices within her, telling her she could never be white nor Indian. She should have drowned as a small, helpless infant.

CHAPTER 19

SHE TOLD NOAH.

Noah nodded his head, listened to her, then his lower lip trembled, and he begged her not to leave them, telling her she was the only one he could depend on anymore. "Dat and Annie are married, but she can't stand him, and he goes around pretending to be happy. It makes me sick."

Hester nodded.

"Don't leave, please don't." Noah's large green-blue eyes pleaded with her, but all she could do was nod her head. One little slip of her iron control, and all would be lost.

She genuinely loved Noah. In spite of having lost their mother, he had done a great job of dealing with all of it, including Annie's ambitious cruelty.

"You have Dat."

"You mean what's left of Dat."

A small smile lifted the corners of Hester's mouth. "You mean, a pair of shoes and his straw hat and nothing in between."

Noah's loud roar of laughter frightened Daisy, who leaped, jerking the wagon up and forward, flinging their heads back against the seat.

As the wagon bounded across the rutted road, veering left and right, Noah fought for control, still chuckling to himself.

When they arrived at the river, Padriac's bright head of hair was visible on the water as he poled the raft across with a lone rider on it. He caught sight of their wagon and waved his hat.

"He knows us?"

"Yes." Hester said the simple word, but her heart was pounding.

Noah climbed off the wagon, his youthful face watching Padriac intently. He gave a low whistle. "Look at the way he poles that raft across. I bet he could wrestle anyone down."

Hester smiled. Her knees felt soft and weak, as if she had been running for a long time.

Leaving the rider on the opposite shore, Padriac poled back in a short time, his face showing his eagerness. "It's you! Hello, there!" he called, long before he reached the shore.

Noah was puzzled, looking from Hester to the youth with the flaming hair.

Padriac went straight to Hester, took her hand, and bowed over it.

"My Amish Indian princess," he said, so soft and low only Hester heard him.

She looked into his blue eyes, so open and honest, so completely without guile, it was like a refreshing drink

of water on a very warm day. "I have a favor to ask of
you."

"Gladly. Anything, anything."

She told him.

Plans were made. They would ride together while
Noah went to the trading post. He would return, waiting here till they returned. If anyone came along, they
would have to wait to cross, or if Noah was here, he
could navigate the raft and its freight. His eyes shone
with anticipation, thinking of poling that raft across
the river.

It was so easy being with Padriac. He was confident,
at ease with the world around him, carefree and lighthearted. He responded to questions in a way that left a
smile on Hester's face.

The way was longer and more complicated than Hester remembered, but his horse was surefooted, taking the
streams, ravines, and hills easily, picking his way along.
Padriac kept up a steady flow of words, while trying to
keep his arms from going around her slim waist. As he
watched Hester's white cap bobbing up and down just
by his chin, he wondered what she would look like with
that thing off her head.

Again, it was the birds' cries, their warbles and whistles and liquid trills that gave Hester an otherworldly
sense, as if she had stepped into the *Paradeis* (Paradise)
that John Lantz spoke of in his sermons. The pine trees
were as mighty as she remembered, the waterfalls even
more so. The flowers were startlingly unreal, their splendor completely unmatched. Why had no white man ever
stumbled on this place? she asked Padriac.

"Oh, they did. A bunch of people know this place is here. Only they're scared of the old woman and her powers. Some say she's the devil; others say she's a witch. Everybody's just glad to let her be."

"Where are the goats?"

"She must have penned 'em up to milk them." Padriac stopped his horse, slid off, and reached up to help her down, then tied his horse to a sapling, returning to her with a smile-chiseled face.

"Ready?"

She nodded.

"I'll leave you alone with her as long as you need to be, okay?"

Again, she nodded, letting her eyes thank him.

Except for the birds and the sound of the falling water, everything was eerily hushed as they made their way down the narrow pathway. They came upon the hut covered in bark. Padriac called out once, then again. Hester was aware of her pounding heart and a rushing in her ears.

"She must have left."

There was not a sign of the clean, white goats. The door of the hut was closed. Padriac tried the latch, pulling on the knotted rawhide, then pushed the door in on its creaking, rusted hinges.

The smell was overpowering at first, but after a minute or more, she was aware of the odor, an earthiness, a scent infused with herbs, dried and preserved in whiskey.

It was so dark, they both waited by the door until their eyes adjusted to the stingy light. Slowly, objects came into focus. She was not here, but her house was filled with the essence of her. A bed on the floor with skins to lie on and to cover her comfortably when the nights were cool. A betty lamp, a fireplace of sorts, an assortment of boxes and crates containing bottles and skins.

Arrowheads, turquoise jewelry, spears, a tomahawk, pipes, dried plants hanging from every available inch of wall space, the floor littered with dried, broken leaves.

Hester's eyes fell on a leather-bound book. A section of brown skin lay across it with Hester's name scrawled in large shaky letters. Hester gasped.

Padriac hurried to her side, bending his head to see. Slowly, Hester reached out to remove the skin. She meant to toss it aside, then decided better of it, folded it tenderly, and placed it in the wide pocket of her dress. A feeling of awe enveloped her as she opened the cover of the book.

"I can't see."

Padriac led her outside and pulled her down on the grass beside him. They bent over the ancient volume.

"It's in English."

"Some of it isn't."

"To my companion, Hester."

"Companion?"

"She probably meant 'friend.'"

"I have gone deep into the forest to die. My time is here. The Great Spirit is calling me. I told you I would leave these ancient herbal remedies, which tell how to cure sicknesses of every kind.

"You will come again to question me. My time is not long, and you have not come. You are misplaced, a sheep among goats, a bird among bats of the night. But you cannot return. You are raised in the way of the white man, and you will never be a true Indian.

"I am very tired, and cannot go to the post to have the schoolmaster help me. The remedies are written as best I know how. To find further instruction, go to the schoolmaster.

"Your God is mine, and my Great Spirit is yours. We are bound to the Great Earth. It is our duty to protect it, care for it. The Earth gives us its food and its animals of the forest. The way of the Lenape will soon be lost as time marches past swiftly, day by day. To prosper, you must trust your own instincts. In our veins runs the pure blood of the Lenape. Courage and strength are your virtues.

"Stay with your people. They have been kind. Do not let the evil slay you. Let the Great Spirit lead you. When the night is dark, the path is hidden. Wait. Wait on the eagle who rises up in due time.

"I will leave now. My heart is very slow. Do not look for me. My body will return to the earth, from which it was made. Someday, we will meet again."

Hester was not aware that she was crying. She didn't know the wetness that fell on the brittle pages was from her own eyes.

She consumed the words the way a starving person ravenously gulps food that is finally available.

She lifted the leather-bound book to her breast and bowed her head over it, as pent-up emotions propelled the tears in an endless, satisfying stream. She was not aware of Padriac's arm around her, of the comforting touch of his hand on her shoulder. She knew only of the wonderful gift she held in her hand.

She dragged the back of her hand across her dripping nose, sniffing, then leaned against Padriac as a fresh wave of all the sadness and pain in her life swept over her. She felt guilty for her revulsion at the odor of the Lenape, her own tribe, coupled with the great chasm between them, accompanied by the betrayal of her mother's dying, and now Annie's hatred, if that's what it was.

The words of this Indian woman were a rope thrown to a struggling person.

John Lantz would not approve of this, but he had not been born an Indian, adopted by the Amish. He would say the Bible is the only true road map. This thought made her sit up, look at Padriac with streaming eyes, and say, "Do you have a handkerchief?"

"Not a clean one."

"Doesn't matter."

Grateful, she took the crumpled piece of cloth, frayed at the edges, and blew heartily. "Thank you."

"How come you're crying so hard?" Again, his eyes were blue and clear and guileless, the question in them kind and honest.

"You wouldn't understand."

"I bet I would, in a way. It can't be easy, born an Indian an' bein' Amish with them strict, bearded, old men hovering over every move you make."

"It's not like that."

"Huh."

"What does that mean?"

"Nothing."

Hester took a deep breath, then held the book out to Padriac. "Just go ahead, read what you can of it."

He was finished long before Hester thought it possible. Reading was still very hard for her, and she took a long time to decipher any words.

She looked deeply into his eyes, taking from him everything he had felt while reading it.

"This must be absolutely profound for you."

"What does 'profound' mean? I'm Dutch, you know."

Patiently, he said, "It must be amazing, meaningful."

She nodded.

They sat in this way, a comfortable silence between them, only the birds' voices in the distance. A sense of belonging, coupled with reverence for the Indian woman's death—the intriguing way she had departed, giving herself to the earth from which she was made—left them in awe.

What faith and simplicity, Hester thought.

"Are you going to the schoolmaster?" Padriac asked.

"Yes. Oh, yes. I know him."

"Is he Amish?"

"No."

"What's his name?"

"Theodore Crane."

"That skinny nervous guy? Bounces his eyebrows?"

"That's him."

"Can I come with you?"

Hester looked at him. "Why?"

"How else am I gonna see you again?"

"If you're thinking about . . . you know, courting, you better not. Amish girls are only allowed to date Amish boys."

Padriac thought on this blunt statement. "I could be Amish."

"Probably not."

"What's the difference?"

Hester shrugged.

"Not much."

"More than you think."

"Yeah, well, I'm Irish. Red hair, blue eyes, a temper. We're all Catholic."

They rode back in silence, Padriac regretting his own Catholic life, the Irish way, vowing to give it up. He wasn't steadfast at all. He never confessed his sins to the priests, figured it wasn't their business. No, he was not devout about anything—not Amish, Catholic, or the Indian's Great Spirit. He just wanted Hester Zug. He wanted to be with her every hour of every day, make her life happy, and protect her from every stepmother and father that treated her wrong.

Could love transcend every culture? He didn't know. He knew those Amish men were some sour-looking individuals. He bet if some of them laughed, their faces would break like glass. The women didn't look much different, except for their white caps or bonnets or whatever you called them. They didn't dance or play musical instruments, so things would be pretty flat. But he'd make it.

Again, Padriac felt a devastating sense of loss when they reached the river. Noah was sitting patiently on the stump. Daisy was unhitched and chomping on great mouthfuls of lush, green grass. Padriac helped Hester down, looked longingly into her deep brown eyes, drinking in the loveliness of her face, and stepped very close to her. "Please say it won't be almost two years till I see you again."

"I can't tell."

Noah sauntered over and began firing questions. His mouth formed a perfect O of astonishment at the book, vowing that between him and Isaac, they could decipher the ancient remedies, couldn't they?

Hester said they could try, laughing her rippling laugh as she helped him hitch up Daisy and left, a cloud of dust obscuring them at the edge of the forest.

Padriac paced the bank of the river, mumbled nonsense, and vowed to appear at Theodore Crane's door, even if the man's eyebrows drove him nuts.

For reasons of her own, the leather-bound book inflamed Annie's hatred. She found it beside Hester's bed, picked it up, and confronted her immediately, her face white and pinched, her breath coming in small gasps of agitation.

"You may as well go back to your people. You are nothing to us."

The words were rocks raining on Hester's head. Her hands went up to defend herself from the pain.

"You think Noah and Isaac and Lissie love you. They don't care a lick what happens to you." Annie stood, her thin fists held to her gaunt hips, leaning forward at the waist, her face only a few feet from Hester's.

"You think Hans cares for you, too. You think your pretty face will have everyone bowing to you. Well, you are about to be surprised."

Hester began to tremble. Like a leaf in a storm, she was shaken by Annie's words. Unable to form any words of her own, she cowered beneath the onslaught of displeasure. But she did not cry. She stood, her arms at her sides, her fingers playing with the folds of her apron, her head bent so that Annie could only guess at the expression on her stepdaughter's face.

"Another thing you need to understand. You won't be able to find a husband here among the Amish. Who would want to have the impure blood of an Indian in their *freundshaft*? So don't go around harboring ideas about this handsome boy that had you at the table at my—our—wedding. He didn't pick you to go to the table. You don't know that boys make bets. They earn money taking the unwanted girls to the table."

Breathing hard by the force of her words, Annie fell silent, glowering.

Still, Hester would not raise her head.

"Look at me!" Annie shrieked, her voice a hoarse whisper.

Hester obeyed. Her eyes were half-closed, expressionless, her mouth a straight, perfect line, her caramel-colored skin flawless, shining with an inner light.

"Look at me!" Annie whispered.

"I am looking at you," Hester said, soft and low.

"Open your eyes when you do, you rebellious Indian."

Hester opened her eyes.

"You see this book? It's full of witchcraft. It's evil and must be burned." She shoved the precious, leather-bound book into Hester's face, forcing her to turn her head away.

"Now I'm going to burn it." Gleefully, Annie held it just out of Hester's reach.

Hester knew if she protested or cried out, it would serve to goad Annie's fury to new levels, so she stayed still.

"Do you want to put it in the fire, or shall I?"

Still Hester remained as still as a stone, immovable.

The front door opened, and Hans entered the house, followed by Noah and Isaac.

Quickly, Annie lowered the book and lifted her lips into a caricature of a smile. Her eyes widened, her eyebrows lifted, and she stepped back, laughing a low, mocking laugh.

"My, Hester, this book is full of drivel, isn't it?" Annie looked at Hans, her face contorted with the effort to swallow her anger.

Hans stopped, taking in the scene in one glance. "Give her the book."

"No."

"Give Hester the book."

"No, Hans. It's full of witchcraft. If this book stays under our roof, evil will befall us."

"Annie, stop. You have no reason to say such things. It is a book containing old herbal remedies and medicines. It is worth a lot to Hester, who needs to learn some of these things."

"It will not be in my house." Annie said evenly.

"Give it to Hester."

Annie would not. She crossed the room slowly and placed it on top of the warm kitchen stove. "I mean to burn it."

She said the words to no one, her back turned to them all, her thin shoulders held squarely.

Hester moved so quietly Annie did not hear her. With speed borne of desperation, she grabbed the book off the stovetop, clutched it to her breast, and stood aside, her eyes alive with hope as she searched Hans's face.

Whirling, Annie snatched the book from Hester's clutching hands.

"No!" The involuntary cry was wrenched from Hester as she gave up the book.

Hans stepped forward, took his wife by her thin shoulders, wrestled the book from her grasp, and handed it to Hester. "Take it away," he barked, his eyes like black fire.

Hester ran through the door, down the slope, and into the green forest, silently holding the precious book to her chest, her only link to hope.

CHAPTER 20

FROM THAT DAY, HESTER'S FATE WAS SEALED.

She was an unwelcome addition to a family that was changing under Annie's tutelage. As subtle as an approaching change in the season, so was the web Annie wove among all the members of the family.

When did Noah and Isaac begin to keep their distance from Hester? She couldn't be sure. She just knew they no longer talked openly and unashamedly around her, the way siblings do with each other. It seemed to Hester they harbored a suspicion of her behind a wall of mistrust she did not understand.

Lissie remained the same for some time, but her ego was so swelled by Annie's praise that she soon formed an air of superiority over Hester that she may or may not have been aware of. Her cookies were soft and moist, her bread light as a feather. Annie taught her how to make pumpkin pies. Hans's eyes shone at his daughter as he praised her baking, knowing he could enter Annie's graces by doing so.

Hester began losing weight. Her dresses hung loosely on her thin frame, her facial contours became more pronounced. If anything, she was more beautiful than ever.

Hester hid the book away under a stone below the limestone overhang of rock. She wrapped it carefully, put it in the wooden box, and never looked at the words again. They were imprinted on her heart.

To live without love is one thing, but to live with suspicion and displeasure is quite another, she soon found out. Even Hans seemed to stay away from her, avoiding her at all costs, afraid of Annie's wrath.

One Sunday in late autumn, Lissie Hershberger placed herself squarely in Hans's path when church services had just come to a close. He was surprised to see her large bulk obstructing his way and stopped, his eyes wide.

"Lissie."

"Hans."

They shook hands, in the way of the Amish. They spoke of the weather, the crops.

Lissie wasted no time. "Hans, what is going on at your house? Hester is not well."

Her eyes bored into his, quick, alert, and knowing.

"What do you mean?"

"You know what I mean."

Almost, Hans broke down and told this capable woman all his troubles. Almost, he told her of the division that tore Hester from him, the fear of Annie driving Hester away. Almost, he confessed that the only reason he soothed Annie by agreeing with her disapproval of Hester was to make it possible to continue living as her husband.

"Oh, it's all right, Lissie," is what he said.

"It's not all right, Hans, and you know it. What will become of Hester if someone doesn't intervene? She's looking thin and sad, and I know Annie is mistreating her."

"Lissie, everything is fine. You stay out of it. Hester is happy. She really is. She just had a summer spell."

There was nothing to do but step back and let Hans continue on his way.

When Theodore Crane began attending the Amish church services, he was met by looks of disbelief, suspicion, and then acceptance when they saw he was making an honest effort to learn the German language.

He was respected by the community as the industrious schoolmaster who kept unflagging order in the classroom, taught the three Rs thoroughly, and went to eat Sunday supper with Lissie Hershberger. That was all they knew.

They didn't know everything about Lissie, either—the merry whistling that accompanied her swiftly moving hands as she kneaded the biscuit dough on the floured dough tray. Her lighthearted singing late on Sunday afternoons as she cut up the carrots, thickened the chicken broth, and dipped out cream to drizzle over the berries.

Neither did they know the anticipation Theodore felt as he drove his rickety black cart with the gold stripes painted on the wheels. He had never known a warmer, more caring person than Lissie Hershberger. She never failed to administer a kind word to a failing student, hand a hungry child her own lunch, or give a word of praise to a discouraged one.

She was large and soft and filled with goodness. She infused sunshine into his world until he no longer felt old and rickety and dried up, even when his bones hurt with the cold and his cough heaved from his chest when he rose from his chair to add a few sticks of wood to the cranky, low-burning fire in his fireplace.

Every Sunday, she made roast pork and sauerkraut, or a chicken or some beef if she had them. She often fixed stuffing, stirring in broken chestnuts if they were in season. Sometimes she made duck *und* kraut, which was one of his favorites. She made so many different pies, he didn't know if he liked one any better than all the others. Raspberry, strawberry, pumpkin, custard, apple, they were all delicious. He would tuck his napkin into his shirt collar, lean forward slightly, and eat two or three wide wedges of pie, never failing to praise her with flowery words.

And yet Theodore spoke neither of love or marriage. That was all right with Lissie. She chuckled to herself as she mixed up a cake with brown sugar crumbled over top. She thought the dear man couldn't live without her, he just didn't know it yet. Give him time.

It would be wonderful to cook his breakfast and wash his clothes, to sit with him in the morning and discuss their day, to refill his cup with steaming coffee and bend to kiss the top of his head. She would sew his shirts and wash them. He could learn enough of the German that he could understand the sermons in church. He already knew each family, having taught their children. He knew the Amish ways, so it was only a matter of time.

It was on a blustery evening, as the pumpkins lay rotting on the dry, brown vines and the yellowing corn stalks rustled in the gale, when Theodore thought he heard a sound in the wind. He put down his fork and looked at Lissie, who stopped chewing, held very still, and thought perhaps this was the moment when he would finally propose. But what he did was hold up one finger and tilt his head to one side so he could hear better. Lissie's blue eyes watched his face intently, then cut into the pie she was eating once more.

"Sh. There it is again."

Lissie heard nothing. She resumed eating her pie.

"I hear a sound of whistling in the wind."

"*Ach* piffle, Theodore. Who could tell? It's so windy that everything flaps and whistles, howls and roars on a night such as this."

Theodore shook his head, lowered his eyebrows, then raised them again, before bending to his pie. He drank two cups of hot milk, putting off going out to his cold cart, cranky horse, and weak lantern light. The thought of entering his cold, disheveled-looking house gave him a decided case of the blues. How would it be to rock without interruption in Lissie's chair by the fire on a night like this? He could stay here and would not have to go out and hitch up the ill-tempered beast or light the smelly lantern hanging on the cart's side. He just did not want to do that.

Sometimes he wondered if there would be any room left over on her fluffy, goose down mattress, if he ever decided to ask for her hand in marriage. She was a large woman. More and more, he found thinner women quite unappealing compared to Lissie. Take that Annie Hans had married. My goodness, she was like peanut brittle.

Oh, he just wasn't sure. For years, he didn't think about women, didn't even notice them. Then Lissie pushed herself into his life, cooking all this food, and he felt himself slipping, losing his handhold on his vow to remain alone all his life.

Abruptly, he said, "Lissie, you know I don't hold with shunning."

In answer, Lissie laughed, her stomach shaking up and down. "What makes you say that?"

"Well, this ban and shunning is not something I would hold to."

"Why would you have to? You're not a member of the Amish church."

"But if I were."

"Why would you want to be?"

Feeling the noose tighten about his neck, he said gruffly, "Oh, nothing."

When he left, Lissie whirled about the kitchen, singing and whistling, scouring pots and pans, her cheeks pink and shining, her eyes snapping. He was surely thinking about something, that Theodore was. Coming up with that statement out of the clear blue sky. Yessir, he was thinking of joining the Amish church. There was not one other reason on earth to make him pop up with that statement.

She thumbed through the greasy, dog-eared, old book that contained her recipes, planning next Sunday night's supper. Dried plums. She'd never served them to him. Or would dried apples be better? He'd never eaten them either.

She set the old recipe book aside, placed her hands across her rounded stomach, and thought of Hans, his evasive manner, and Hester, that poor, unwanted soul. What kept her in that house?

Hester wrapped her black shawl expertly around her thin shoulders, shivered, drew her knees up to her chin, and laid her head on them, as she sat perched on the limestone rock that jutted out over the side of the steep mountain. Beside her lay the opened book, bound in leather, the one the Indian woman had left her. It was her heritage, the link to something true and real, an object that gave her direction. Over and over, she read the words of wisdom, memorized them, spoke them to herself.

Here on her rock, she felt as one with the earth and its Creator, exactly the way Uhma had written. She could identify with ease the things Uhma portrayed on these pages.

She had never had a chance to visit the schoolmaster. Never had a chance, or was she too ashamed?

She had a constant companion now. Everywhere she went, she imagined herself carrying a handicap, like a growth on her back or one leg too short to walk properly. She was an Indian. Ingrained in her mind, for everyone to see as plain as day, the color of her skin marked her as strange, inferior, less.

The small changes had grown steadily, fueled by Annie's distaste for the Indian. Savages, she called them.

Hester kept the book hidden away, opening it only in rare moments when she could get away without being seen or needed.

The rock had become a place of worship, an altar, a place she came to be comforted, to feel as one with her Creator.

She so wanted to find the secrets of the book and understand the way of the Lenape, which she carried as an unexplored longing in her heart. The old woman had written instructions for her, it was true. She had told Hester to stay among the white people because they were kind. That was not true. They were no longer kind, so that would give her the right to leave.

Hester had a birthright. She had the right to search for her beginnings. A place where every skin was the same color as hers. "My people," she said aloud to herself. The thought brought a thrill, an intense desire to be among them, to live with them in peace and harmony so she could experience a true and pure sense of belonging.

She remembered the distasteful smell permeating the interior of the trading post on the day she had finally encountered the men from the Lenape tribe. Could she learn to live in this primitive manner, now that she had lived all her life in the German culture of cleanliness and hard work?

And there was Jesus, her Savior, who redeemed her from sin. There was her promise to the Amish church to be baptized and live by their rules, to help build the church, to be honest and good and obedient. Like Kate. Like John Lantz, the bishop. And like Hans and Noah and Isaac used to be before Annie came into the family.

Why did Annie dislike her so? For the thousandth time, the question tormented her. Annie's dislike was deeper than the color of Hester's skin.

She did not want to leave her family. Not now. Winter was coming. She wouldn't survive. If she stayed, she would have food and shelter.

Well, she would try harder. She would work more, do everything better. Perhaps her family would change again.

Hester went home and threw herself into every task required of her, again.

She spent days husking corn, forking manure, hauling hay with Noah and Isaac.

When the snows came, the woodhouse was jammed with expertly cut wood, probably half of it done by Hester. She directed all the frustration and loneliness in her life at the cut log pieces, the blade of the axe biting skillfully, severing the pieces easily. Hans praised Noah and Isaac, telling them they were tremendously capable of sawing and splitting wood.

Hester left it at that, lowered her eyes, and swallowed her pride. Annie's mocking eyes laughed at her.

Every Sunday when they had no church services, Hans gathered his children around his chair, and they took turns reading from the great German *Schrift* (Scriptures). Noah and Isaac were fluent, rattling off one difficult sentence after another, but Hester stumbled over the words, mispronounced them, or sat silent, feeling the sneers behind her heavy eyelids. Hans was always patient. Once, when she dared lift her eyes, she found his dark ones on her, brooding, mysterious, containing an expression she did not understand.

Reading and writing had always eluded her, but since she was older, she was getting better at words. That was why Annie told her to go to the schoolmaster for awhile.

"What a dimwit! If you'd sit with Theodore Crane for awhile, he could knock some sense into your head," she said one Sunday after a particularly grueling session of German reading. Suddenly the atmosphere in the house was stifling. Hester got up, wrapped herself in her shawl, and headed out the door.

No matter that she slipped and slid, Hester pulled herself up the side of the mountain by any young tree that offered itself. She was gasping and heaving by the time she reached the rock. Falling on her knees, she dug frantically, her breath coming in quick puffs of steam, searching for the box.

Her mittens were soaked, her fingers icy, her arms aching with effort when her heart leaped. It was there! Pulling out the wooden box, she grabbed eagerly at the volume inside wrapped in cloth. She held it to her body and calmed her breathing.

A clear whistle edged into her senses. The tune was as melodic as the first time she'd heard it. She froze. The sound was undulating, a series of warbles, chirps, and whistles, a liquid, tumbling sound like the waterfalls near where the Indian woman's hut had been.

Slowly, Hester turned her eyes, searching the surrounding forest. The trees were bare and black against the mounds of drifted snow beneath them. The sky was whitish-gray, almost identical to the snow, with a weak winter sun shining faintly as if it was veiled. There was no wind, no sound. A few chickadees scattered a dusting of snow from berry bushes, twittering and chirping to themselves.

Her eye caught a movement beneath the trees. A small brown form, leaning a bit forward as if stalking his prey, moved through the trees. He was too far away to calculate his age or his size. When the whistling began again, she could see that the figure was clearly its source. Hester watched, holding as still as possible until the form moved farther along on the side of the mountain. It was only then that she allowed herself a deep breath, turned, and made her way carefully down the side of the slope.

Neither Noah nor Isaac would accompany her. They said she'd be safe on her own. She asked Hans if she could ride. With all the snow, it would be better. He said no, so she threw the harness on Dot, hitched her to the wagon, threw a few furs across the seat, and left without looking back.

The lump that wanted to rise in her throat was an unhandy thing and served no purpose but to bring on the hated self-pity. She swallowed, resolved to forget there was a time when Noah and Isaac would have helped her hitch up, accompanying her eagerly anywhere she wanted to go.

Lifting the reins, she slapped them down on Dot's rump, relishing the fast trot that ensued, reveling in the dangerous swaying of the wagon as it slid back and forth. Fiercely, she hoped Hans had seen. In the past, she would have pushed such thoughts back, but now there was a difference.

Out of the sneering, the life-draining disapproval that she eventually experienced from each family member, came the small steady flame of Hester's independence. If the wagon rolled over, crushed its shafts, and broke a wheel, there was no one to worry. She felt a freedom somehow. Perhaps a lonely kind of freedom, but she was breaking away from the chains of self-loathing.

The icy air hit her face like a slap, yet she lifted it to the elements, savoring the cold and the pure white world around her. A red bird flew away, its dipping flight pattern carrying it aloft, followed by his dull red-brown mate. Dot clopped along, throwing snow from beneath her hooves, her head held high as she pulled the wagon through the snow.

She passed Amos Hershberger's, the smoke from the chimney wafting in gray plumes into the metallic sky. Looking up, Hester noticed the sky was turning darker. She brought the reins down on Dot's back, who answered with a flick of her ear and an accelerated pace.

When she pulled up to the schoolmaster's house, she was alarmed to see dark windows with no smoke coming from the chimney. Perplexed, she sat in the wagon, unsure.

The light was fading fast, the graying clouds bringing along clumps of snow that had not yet fallen but would come swirling in from the north before the night was over. Uncertainly, she stepped from the wagon. Her black shawl was in stark contrast to the snow. The steaming horse enveloped her in a gray cloud, the white of the sky behind her.

Theodore Crane stretched and yawned, pulled himself up out of his chair, scratched his ribs, peered through the glass at the darkening world outside, and yelped. Surely that was not a ghost.

He peered again, blinking his eyes as Hester moved through the fading light, the steam, and the snow. She pulled the horse and wagon to the hitching rack and threw a blanket across the horse's back. It was only then that he recognized the dark face beneath the large flat hat. The Indian girl. Relieved, knowing it was not a ghost, he opened the door before she had time to knock.

Hester was as relieved as he was. Her quick smile showed the appreciation she felt, and she was promptly drawn into the cold, cluttered house, with Theodore's affable words of welcome. He fiddled around with the fire until it roared up the chimney, filling the small room with radiant heat and light.

She took off her shawl and hat and held her cold fingers to the raging fire, while watching two mice nibble on a bread crust beneath the table. She smiled hopefully at the schoolmaster.

He voiced his enthusiasm when she produced the Indian woman's book and nodded his head in understanding. He said that all the English she had written she had learned from him, and, yes, he would love to try to decipher everything else she had written in the book.

CHAPTER 21

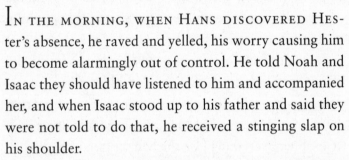

IN THE MORNING, WHEN HANS DISCOVERED HESter's absence, he raved and yelled, his worry causing him to become alarmingly out of control. He told Noah and Isaac they should have listened to him and accompanied her, and when Isaac stood up to his father and said they were not told to do that, he received a stinging slap on his shoulder.

Annie was terrified. She had never seen her husband so irate. She didn't know what to make of it and set about frying bacon and stirring up biscuits, as if the sight and scent of her breakfast would mollify this awful yelling.

Hans would not eat. He told Annie to feed the children, he couldn't eat, not with Hester gone. He yanked on his boots and fur coat, smashed his felt hat down on his uncombed hair, and lumbered through the door, still accusing Noah for not accompanying her. Were they aware that she might be lying at the bottom of a ravine, dead and frozen?

For one searing instant, Annie felt cold dread, guilt piling in on her as she remembered all the times she wished Hester ill.

Lissie cried, and Annie felt worse. What had they done? Oh, surely God's judgment would be swift! She trembled in her shoes but kept her fears hidden from the children by firmly reprimanding them to sit up and eat, Hans had gone to fetch her back. One terrified thought after another crowded itself into her mind, and she wondered if she would be accounted for a murderer in God's sight. The Bible plainly said that to hate someone is as bad. Annie wasn't sure if it included humans of another color or not.

Hans searched every ravine, his eyes combing the surrounding trees as terrible thoughts of Hester's demise ran rampant through his fevered brain. The snow was coming down in earnest, hard, stinging little pellets of misery that raked across his face beneath the wide brim of his hat.

He found himself talking out loud to Kate, telling her he was sorry. Memories of the two of them, the perfect child between them, became a fine torture, the denial of his love for Hester an exquisite pain.

A shower of snow enveloped his head as it fell from a weighty pine branch. It knocked his hat into the deep snow, leaving him wailing and floundering, searching desperately for the necessary headgear.

By the time he arrived at the schoolmaster's house, his teeth were chattering, his hands were stiff with cold, and his toes felt like ten chunks of ice. He flung himself off his horse, pounded on the door, rattled the lock, peered in the windows, then paced the small porch, his hands behind his back, his face thrust aggressively in front of him, muttering questions and answers to himself.

He looked off across the falling snow and tried to come up with a plan. Had she arrived here at all? He looked wistfully in the direction of the trading post, wondering if the proprietor had seen her go.

But where was the schoolmaster? Oh, at school. No, this was Saturday. He should be at home.

Finally, he lay down his pride, shouldered his resolve, and pushed through the deepening snow to the front porch of the trading post. A handful of slovenly looking men stepped aside, allowing him to enter. He nodded shortly without meeting their eyes and walked quickly up to the counter where a youth with red hair looked down on him, a good-humored grin on his freckled face.

"What can I getcha?" he asked, without any greeting.

"Have you seen my daughter?"

"What's she look like?"

"She's Indian."

"Yeah. I bet. Move on. Next? What can I getcha?"

When Hans realized he was not going to be helped, he walked back and forth between a bale of furs and some fencing tools, muttering, trying desperately to come up with some way of locating Hester. He tried talking to a stolid Indian wrapped in blankets but was glad to get away from his penetrating, black eyes.

He walked back to the schoolmaster's house and rattled the doorknob before sinking onto the snow-covered bench. Where could she have gone? Was the schoolmaster with her?

He retraced his route, a tortuous journey of fear and indecision, hoping to find her, afraid to look down rock-slides and ravines.

He reentered his house around noontime and was met with questioning eyes. He shrugged his shoulders, then tore off his hat, peeled off his wet coat, hanging it across the back of a chair, and sat, starved and dejected, blaming Noah and Isaac, then Annie. Even Lissie had a turn, blamed for her baking skills.

Hans wept openly. His hands shook as he lifted the cup of scalding tea laced with whiskey to his quivering mouth. He refused any food. Annie stayed out of his way, finally understanding why she disliked him so much.

He hitched a fresh horse to the cutter, the small sleigh that whispered through the snow, and made his way to his parents' house, pleading with them for help.

Isaac told him to sit down, think rationally, calm himself. Had he prayed? Was he seeking the face of the Lord to help him? For without faith, nothing was possible.

Out of his son's mouth, then, came the tale of misery—Annie's hatred of Hester, his fear of Annie, the entire family's mistreatment of Hester—leaving Isaac without a trace of surprise.

Rebecca nodded, her mouth prim with the knowledge of having seen this all along—where had Isaac been?— but she said nothing until Hans's voice wobbled into silence, accentuated by the shaking of his shaggy head, left to right.

Finally, Isaac spoke. "Well, Hans, perhaps this is meant to be. It is better for your household with Hester gone. You know that, and I think you know why."

"Why would you say such a thing?'

"Hans, face it. You feel for Hester what you should be feeling for Annie."

Hans's denial was so emphatic, his outrage so complete, that Isaac apologized in the end, saying perhaps it was incorrect to put it that way.

Rebecca turned her back to hide her feelings, then asked if he had checked the widow Lissie Hershberger's house. Rumor had it that Theodore Crane spent Sunday evening with her.

"Why would Hester be there?"

"It's worth a try."

"No. Fat Lissie doesn't have to know."

"Perhaps she has returned to her people, the Lenape."

Up came Hans's red face, shock and disbelief written all over it. One single word was forced from his mouth, in a wail of denial. "No!"

Rebecca stepped up to Hans then and spoke her piece.

In the end, he drove his horse through the snow to Lissie Hershberger's house and found the wagon in front of her small barn, Dot munching oats in the box stall beside Lissie's horse. He fell on his knees there in the hay-strewn barn and thanked *der Herr* over and over for guiding him to Hester. Relief pulsed through his veins; redemption shone from his dark eyes. He adjusted his hat, blew his nose, took a deep breath to steady himself, and walked sedately up to the porch of the little log house.

Lissie answered the door.

"Good afternoon, Lissie. I came to get Hester." He hoped his tone of voice was normal, his countenance calm and friendly.

Lissie pulled herself up, glowering from her blue eyes. "She's not here."

"The wagon is."

"Well, she's not."

"You're hiding her from me."

"I sure am."

"Lissie, I beg you, let me see her."

Lissie considered, then stepped aside, motioning him in with one hand.

Hester was seated at the small linen-covered kitchen table with Theodore Crane, steaming bowls of thick soup in front of them. Hester rose, holding onto the back of the chair, her eyes so large and dark in her thin face, they were like dark, turbulent pools.

With a glad cry, Hans moved swiftly across the room, gathered her against him, and held her there. He bent over her, crooning as he would to a small child, murmuring words of endearment, jumbled with soft apologies.

Uncomfortable, Hester tried to extricate herself from his embrace, her face a mirror of Lissie's own.

Theodore choked on his soup. His eyebrows began raising and lowering themselves of their own accord, but he remained seated, unable to watch.

Hans let Hester go, but his eyes remained on her face as if he could not bear to let her out of his sight. Finally, he realized how he had lost control of his emotions in Theodore's and Lissie's full view, lamely telling them how precious the small babe had been, this foundling who had made his and Kate's home complete.

Lissie nodded, her mouth a slash in her round face. "If you like her as much as you say you do, why would all of you mistreat her, then? What explanation do you have?"

"Mistreat?"

The question quivered in the air, a bubble of hope, Hans's desperate wish that Hester had not spoken of her life as she knew it since Annie had become his wife.

"You know what I mean. Hester went to Theodore's house for tutoring in the German language and stayed with him, unable to bring herself to go home, that's how bad it is. So you're not getting her. She's staying right here with me, and this time, I mean it."

"Oh no, Lissie. You're mistaken. Hester comes home with me."

"She stays here."

"She's my daughter."

"Tell that to the ministers when they come to call on you."

"*Ach* now," Hans's tone became a whining, nasal plea. "Let's work this out like two Christians should."

"How?" Lissie demanded.

"Hester, you want to come home, right? To Lissie and all the others, your own bed, all the good food Annie prepares for you. Please return with me now, and this will all blow over. No one needs to know that any of this occurred." His voice rose an octave, his eyebrows elevated, his tone becoming eloquent in his earnest desire for Hester's return.

They all stayed silent, looking to Hester for an answer. She stood behind her chair, tragic in her beauty, her eyes sad and much older than her years. Quietly, she began to speak.

"I'm not sure what I need to do. I can't go back with you as long as Annie is your wife. I'm not sure if I want

to return to my—to my people, the Lenape tribe of Indians who live in the Pennsylvania forests and mountains.
I have the book from the Indian woman. She says to stay
among my people. They are kind.

"And you aren't anymore. Annie is cruel. I'm not sure
who I really am. I partly belong to two peoples, to two
ways of life.

"When Kate was my mother, I never wavered. I
became Amish; I was Amish. It was a good way to live
life on this earth. Annie takes all that away, making
me wonder why I am here. Maybe my life as an Indian
would be better. I would be accepted."

"You are accepted by me, by the Amish community,"
Hans broke out, spreading his hands wide for emphasis.

Without wavering, Hester asked coolly, "Am I?"

Hans floundered, said he'd talk to Annie, but Hester
shook her head.

"Annie will not change."

Hans knew the truth of her words. He knew, too, that
he was caught. He could not turn his back on Annie, but
he would suffer unspeakably without Hester.

"I suggest that Hester stays here, away from Annie,
until she chooses which direction she will go," Lissie
said, testing the situation.

"But she has chosen. She is one of us. She professes
to be part of the church."

Around and around the dizzying conversation swirled
like clouds of wearying gnats that only served to heighten
tempers. Hester saw this and knew it would be unwise
to stay with Lissie. For the sake of peace, for Hans, she

would return. He had given her a home when she was a helpless baby. Now she would return.

She told Hans she would go back, then proceeded to dress in her outdoor clothes and never said another word. She walked woodenly through the drifting snow, lifted the reins onto Dot's back, and moved off, a dark, lone figure wearing a large, flat hat that hid her face completely.

Hans followed in the cutter, resolve in the way he smashed his hat onto his head, memorizing the speech he would give to his family.

The speech was never delivered.

Annie's face was radiating her disapproval, her body taut with it. Her arms moved like jerking sticks as she loudly derided Hester's behavior.

Fear of his angry wife crowded out Hans's words of bravery. He kept his eyes hidden from Hester as she hung up her shawl and hat, and he tried not to see the puzzled expression on Isaac's and Noah's faces. He was a man caught in the middle between two women, indecisive and afraid.

No one spoke.

Hans cleared his throat.

Annie thumped serving dishes of creamy cornmeal mush on the table top and poured water in redware cups so fast, it splashed on the tablecloth. Her mouth quivered. Her hands shook with repressed fury.

Hester took her place, choked down a small amount of the mush, and drank a sip of water while the rest of the family bowed their heads and ate hungrily. Hans kept his face averted, talking only to the small children. He never looked straight at Hester or Annie, the unresolved issues hanging between them like an invisible partition.

The snow piled around the stone house, mounded on the roof like heavy frosting, loading the pine trees with its weight. Upstairs, one lone window shone with a dim yellow light, barely visible through the white semidarkness of the night.

Hester sat on her side of the bed, Lissie a lump beneath the covers. She was bent over the open book, one forefinger placed beneath the English word Theodore Crane had written below each word scrawled in Uhma's handwriting.

Carefully, her tongue catching between her teeth, she read slowly in whispers, storing the words deliberately in the deepest recesses of her memory.

"For Fever. Take one pound of the bark of the yellow birch tree, half-pound sweet flag, half pound of tag elder bark, two ounces thorough wort, two ounces tansy dry. Boil down with water to a liquor. One dose every two hours till shakes come on."

She stopped, staring wistfully at the black, cold rectangle of the window, wondering. Would Kate have survived had she been given these ancient remedies?

"For Weakness."

"To Strengthen the Leg and Feet."

"For Coughing Blood."

"For the Lungs."

"For the Pleurisy."

"Burdock leaves, white root, unkum root, pennyroyal tea, bud of lobelia, skunk cabbage, Indian turnip, chamomile flowers, seed of the silverweed."

Hester knew all of these.

She wrinkled her nose at the prescribed "ox dung, mixed with yarrow, half part Jacob's ladder."

Sighing, she held the book to her breast, bent over it, and thanked her Father in Heaven for Theodore Crane's assistance. She smiled, remembering the way his blue eyes danced with merriment, reciting the old Indian ways of healing.

"Mouse dung mixed with the lard of a boar"?

"Coltsfoot snake root"?

What was "gravel"? "A glass of the juice of onion tops" to cure the "gravel"?

Theodore said he believed that "gravel" meant kidney or gallstones. Hester nodded, wrote it down carefully, asking how to spell kidney.

They laughed together at the remedy for dull sight. "The skunk's musk bag steeped in boiling water." The laugh they shared was so genuine, Hester felt as if she had made a lifelong friend.

Theodore was so polite that night as he scurried around, seeing to her needs. He spread a clean, white sheet on his bed and turned the pillow over. He insisted that he would be fine rolled up in a coverlet by the fire.

She'd slept in her dress, for there were no partitions for privacy. He assured her he would leave the house when she crawled into bed, but she wanted to sleep in her dress. He lay awake, blinking into the red embers of the fire, thinking how strange this was to have a woman, no, a girl, in his bed, something that had never occurred before.

For Hester, there was only a sadness, a fondness.

He could not fathom what would become of her. He had no doubt in his mind that she could survive on her own if it came right down to it. He knew she was treated only slightly better than a slave, and that happened because of the base nature of the woman Hans had the poor fortune to marry. Well, he'd take her to Lissie. She'd know what to do.

Hester's life continued much as before. She counted the days by Xs inscribed in the old book of Indian remedies. She took the hissing, scolding voice of her stepmother like a bitter potion, swallowing it, hiding her pain.

She put on the same serene face for church every two weeks, dressed in brilliant dresses covered by a white cape and apron. Her face was as undecipherable as everything else about her. Refusing to go with the youth, she had no friends. The few girls who coaxed her to go to the hymn singings and Saturday evening hoedowns dwindled down to one, and finally she gave up.

Hester roamed the woods on those days when other girls were preening, dressing themselves in their finery, making plans and giggling, their main interest the boys who would pick them up in their wagons. She found the plants and roots she searched for, held them, cradling them in the palms of her hands. She sniffed them all appreciatively, storing each scent in her memory.

When the snow melted, leaving old, wet undergrowth exposed but patches of snow still lay beneath the pine trees on the north slopes, she searched the woods with new desperation. She dug feverishly at the roots she believed would be needed, and soon. Her keen eyes had observed the involuntary quivers in Annie's hands. Often the plates she carried to the table rattled without reason.

Sometimes, when Annie sat at her spinning wheel, she would suddenly throw the thread of flax, but her foot would cease its pumping, bringing the whirring sound of the wheel to a stop. She would shift her hands between her knees, bend forward, and rock over them, her lips twisted in frustration.

Hester believed she had palsy of the hands. She would need a concoction of sage mixed with mustard root, stirred into boiling water. She should soak her hands in this mixture as often as possible to get relief.

Would she be able to redeem herself in Annie's eyes, Hester wondered, by the cures from her ancestors? She thought of it, dreamed of healing Annie's hands. Perhaps Annie would be able to forgive the color of her skin, the alien brown hue that forever marked her.

Hester stored the herbs in the box, separating them with scraps of stolen skins. She read the old volume scrupulously now. Very seldom did she sleep before the clock struck midnight.

She found the flax plant and tore it excitedly from the earth. Mixed with ewe's milk, it was a powerful source for healing swollen, painful joints. She thought of Hans sitting before the fire, rubbing his right knee, his brows lowered, a grimace on his face at times when Annie was out of the house. Once he'd looked up, saw Hester's eyes on him, and kept her gaze for only a few seconds before removing his hand from his knee. He got up, went to the wooden peg holding his straw hat, slammed it on his head with unnecessary force, grabbed the door handle, and let himself out, not looking back.

Hester folded the tablecloth she was holding. Years ago, she would have approached him with the remedy and gladly administered the poultice. Hans would have gratefully accepted it, but now, with the poison swirling among them in the form of Annie's displeasure, she did not know how it could be possible anymore.

CHAPTER 22

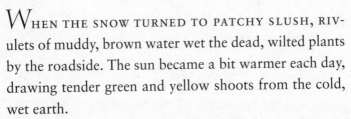

WHEN THE SNOW TURNED TO PATCHY SLUSH, RIVulets of muddy, brown water wet the dead, wilted plants by the roadside. The sun became a bit warmer each day, drawing tender green and yellow shoots from the cold, wet earth.

Hans was sharpening his plowshares and oiling the heavy leather harnesses in preparation for the long, hard days of stumbling behind the plow. Noah could work with the harrow, preparing the soil for the corn and the tobacco. Hans wanted to clear at least five more acres this summer. More, if possible. Hester would be able to harrow. He'd put Noah instead to work felling trees.

He shook his head as he thought of Noah. That homely baby, that clumsy boy who ate at the table with fewer manners than a dog. What, indeed, had happened to his son? He was powerfully built, a great hulk of a boy, with shoulders that strained against the seams of every shirt he owned. Narrow in the hips, with powerful legs and feet that filled shoes a size bigger than Hans's own shoes, he was clearly in awe of his son. Now that he was grown beyond the awkward stage of boyhood, Hans wanted to have a close relationship with Noah, but he felt shamefully inept.

Hans shivered, thinking of his oldest son's clear, light eyes mocking him, the slight upturn of the left side of his well-shaped mouth, so like Kate's. Why did he always feel as if Noah was disgusted with him?

Isaac was not like that. He was still awkward, shy, and not as powerful as Noah, with a merry spirit, quick to laugh, easy to control and advise. A shadow crossed the doorway, darkening the plowshare he was holding. He looked up. It was Noah.

"Too wet to plow?" The voice was low, rough, gravelly, a sound that sent shivers up Hans's spine.

"*Ya.*"

"What does today look like?"

"Well, I'd like to clear at least five more acres this year. If you think it might be dry enough, you could start."

Noah nodded and walked off. Hans heard him sharpening the axe. How did one go about starting a friendly conversation? He wanted to. He wanted to ask him how many trees he could fell in a day, for there was no doubt about it. Noah could fell a tree twice as fast as Hans, cutting into the wood with unfailing accuracy, the tree crashing within a foot of where he wanted it to go.

Hans was irked, jealous at first, then grudgingly proud. He wanted to convey some sense of this to Noah, but always, his tongue remained tied. Ah, he had never expressed much interest or love to his sons from the time they were born. Hans knew he rarely acknowledged their presence. It had been Hester. All Hester. As it was still. A flush crept up past his linen work shirt and hid behind his thick black beard, which was already turning white along the side.

It was only the Bible's teachings, his obedience to the church, to God, to John Lantz and Simon Yoder, and to the memory of Kate that guided him. He remained distant from his sons and now subservient, obeying Annie's will.

In his own mind, Hester belonged to their family and to the Amish, no matter that the blood of the Lenape flowed in her veins. He knew many good Indians. But since Annie harbored a firm and unrelenting distaste for every native man, he kept his opinion to himself.

He could accept his life and appreciate Annie's house-keeping skills, her management of the household, the mothering of his children. He had to give himself up to her treatment of Hester. As long as Hester remained with them and he could see her, that was all that mattered. It was enough.

He knew Annie deserved much of the credit for his prosperity. The great stone house was finished and contained many things other Amish women envied. It stood sentinel, surrounded by clearings, the trees felled by the sweat of his and Noah's brows. The barn had been elongated and held a fine herd of six cows, twice what other landowners possessed.

Annie had shown him what hard work and perseverance could accomplish, no doubt. With Kate, there had been a contentment, a peace in gathering around the hearth, going on picnics in the summertime, attending every frolic or get-together in the neighborhood. No matter that the barn was piled high with manure, or the calf had not yet been weaned, or the rabbits were getting into the beans in the garden.

He remembered his Kate, large and soft, laughing as she collared the errant creatures and hauled them out of the garden, only to have them return the following day. Yes, his life had changed.

But now he was someone. He was a highly respected member of the Amish community, a man others went to for advice and looked up to. His ways were esteemed. That was another reason he kept the true nature of his household well hidden.

He could grind his teeth, thinking of Annie's swollen ego, her big mouth, the speed with which she voiced her young, inexperienced opinion. He often wanted to smack her, doubling his fists beneath the wooden family table, swallowing his anger for his pride's sake.

All the while, he watched Hester bloom into the full beauty of her womanhood, sweetened by her rare sense of innocence.

It was when the wind carried the scent of violets and honeysuckle, and the hollows on the south side of the ridges grew thick with spring morels, those delectable mushrooms that camouflaged themselves among wet winter leaves, that Theodore Crane, the stern and capable schoolmaster, opened his heart to thoughts of love. He was riding in his cart, a nice bunch of morels in a redware bowl at his feet, on his way to Lissie's house. He had dropped the "Hershberger" name from his mind a long time ago, thinking of her only as "Lissie."

His thoughts of her surpassed fondness now. He wanted to be with her each hour of every day. He was not quite sure how to go about the next step, but he believed she would be willing, perhaps even eager. His eyebrows went up as a smile creased the lines around his eyes. Yes, Lissie would make him a fine companion.

She met him at the door, her usual welcoming smile especially wide. She threw up both hands at the sight of the large, succulent morels as she chortled with pleasure. "My dear man! Where have you found them?" she asked, her round face pink and creased.

"Oh, I have my places. I try to keep it a secret."

"Well, they will certainly go well with the greens I'm cooking."

The squirrel, fried in the pan and finished in the oven, fell off the bones, seasoned with plenty of salt and pepper. The greens swam in a thick, brownish white sauce topped with bits of dried beef. The accompaniment of the stewed morels was superb.

They bowed their heads over the ample table, Theodore's mouth moving with his whispered silent prayer, Lissie's eyes closed tightly, her hands folded neatly under the table as she thanked God for the food they were about to enjoy. She added a footnote to her prayer, requesting that God please let today be the day. For how many springs had gone by, and Theodore's thoughts still had not turned lightly to thoughts of love, the way young men's often did.

She ate with great relish, enjoyed the morels with satisfaction, and brought out the cake and applesauce, saving the plum pie for last. She reveled in Theodore's praise as she always did.

She had her spoon in the cup of coffee and was stirring it when the conversation flagged, and the comfortable silence between them settled softly through the small house. It had been a wonderful meal, truly one to be remembered. Theodore cleared his throat. She looked up.

His eyebrows stayed perfectly level, and he said very soft and low, "I don't want to go home tonight."

At first, she thought he'd meant the cranky, obstinate horse or the lack of good lantern light, so she just shrugged her shoulders and asked why not.

"I've come to dread the ride home."

Still, Lissie missed what he was trying to convey. "You need to get a better horse."

Sadly, he shook his head. "No, I don't believe that has anything to do with it."

"Maybe a new seat."

"No, no," Theodore said, shaking his head sadly.

Lissie was genuinely puzzled.

"No, what afflicts me is far more complicated than acquiring a new horse or wagon seat. I am caught in a serious malady that often attacks much younger men."

Afraid suddenly, Lissie gasped. "Theodore, whatever is wrong? Surely it isn't consumption or pleurisy?"

"Oh, no, no. Much worse than that."

In answer, Lissie flung her apron over her face, unwilling to allow him to see the tears forming quickly in her tender blue eyes.

She froze when she felt his hands grasp her soft ones, and when she lowered her apron, could hardly believe the sight of Theodore bending toward her, his thin face earnest, a new light radiating from his eyes.

"Lissie, my malady is love. I believe I love you. Will you be so kind as to consent to be my wife?"

Lissie didn't wait, not even for the space of a heart-beat. "Yes." The word was out, as breathless and as eager as she felt.

"Thank you, Lissie. I will try and be a good companion."

Lissie leaned forward and placed a hand on each side of Theodore's face. Her eyes shone into his with a warm light. "*Ach* now, my man. You will be more than a companion to me. You will be my husband." And with that, she gathered him into her lonely arms and kissed him soundly.

He blinked, his eyebrows danced madly, and they got to their feet, where he promptly embraced his beloved Lissie. Moving his feet, he took her slowly around the kitchen in time to the music in his head. She rested her round head on his small shoulder. His long, thin arms went about her bountiful waist, and the little house was suffused in a soft yellow glow of love.

At last, Lissie's lonely heart was filled.

That Sunday in church, John Lantz spoke eloquently of marriage, the raising of children.

Theodore and Lissie kept their heads bowed, then walked out as soon as the last prayer was read from the German prayer book. Before the congregation realized the fact that both of them had gone out, the deacon, Manasses Yoder, announced in stentorian tones that he wished to let the congregation know that two souls had agreed to become man and wife, Theodore Crane and Lissie Hershberger.

The closing song was a rousing rendition of God's love, fueled by the anticipation of the wedding day to be held in the community. As soon as the last strains of the old hymn had died away, the sedate service turned into mayhem. What a fuss! The women shrieked and giggled, threw their hands in the air, and said the fact that Theodore had joined the church should have given this away.

"*Dumbkepp* (Dumbheads), that's what we are!" laughed Mary Troyer.

"Oh, I thought about it. Those two were together longer than we knew."

"Every Sunday night, no?"

"No, just for supper."

"Oh, well, she took the route through his stomach."

This brought howls of laughter.

Hester sat alone, her face impassive, at the long table holding the Sunday lunch that accompanied Amish services. She spread a slice of bread with the home-churned butter, then speared some dried apples with her knife, the only utensil provided, and chewed quietly.

Around her, girls chattered, planning the afternoon's get-together. Babies cried. Children ran, calling to one another, stopped suddenly by mothers' firm grasps of their arms.

Hester took a sip of her water. She turned when she felt a touch on her shoulder. It was Ruth, her friend. "Would you like to go with me this afternoon? Davey will take us to Bertha's house if you want to go?"

Quickly, Hester shook her head.

"Hester, please come. You can't always remain alone."

"I'll talk to you after I'm finished eating."

She told Ruth there was no point in joining the youth's activities, being Indian and of different blood.

Ruth assured her that made no difference, but Hester held steadfastly to the conviction Annie had successfully branded into her consciousness.

She was different and still unsure which way her life would go. For now, she was content to have a roof over her head and be a servant to Hans and Annie, daily storing in her memory vast quantities of information about the Indian way of healing with plants and herbs.

Sometimes she thought of Padriac, the ease with which they communicated, or the hand of William King, which she had held discreetly beneath the wedding table. And always, she dismissed both of them. She could never taint a *freundshaft* with her Indian blood. It would not be fair to future generations.

To have a husband, she would need to return to the Lenape. The whistling youth had perhaps been sent by God. He would grow up to be her companion, aiding her return to the people of her birth. Today she had no doubt. The whistling had moved her deeply, bringing a sense of her own longing for something she did not understand.

In spite of her many unanswered questions, she did have the leather-bound book of Indian wisdom. It would remain with her wherever she ended up.

She had convinced herself that it was right to leave the Amish people. This thought had been brought about by Annie's hatred, but now, as she bowed to Annie's will, she wondered if everyone in the tribe of Lenape was kind. Wouldn't there be unkind ones among them? Certainly. They were part of the human race. She began to wonder if leaving one group of people for another might not give her the answer she hoped for.

She was surrounded by mountains, great hills, and valleys, an endless schoolroom containing a vast store of knowledge.

She knew which birds migrated south and when. She knew where the mother fox hid her kit. She had found all the plants and trees and roots mentioned in the book, easily identifying them. She watched the bald eagles build their nests and knew where the spotted fawns were hidden. She could tell by the swallow's flight when a storm was approaching. The beavers' houses told her how harsh the winter would be, as did the thickness of the acorns scattered on the floor of the forest. The jay's screaming heralded the approach of another animal or human being.

She was an expert marksman with the handmade slingshot she'd fashioned while still in school. She supplied the household with rabbits and squirrels and an occasional pheasant. Many deer had fallen when one of Hester's arrows lodged in precisely the right spot, bringing them down with a minimum of suffering.

She always thanked God for giving her meat for her family, then dragged the deer to the side of the barn, where Hans or Noah or Isaac would *fa-sark* it. It was an unspoken secret, for nothing inflamed Annie's seething temper like the thought of Hester's hunting or Hans admiring her skills. Annie never knew who killed the wild animals.

Theodore and Lissie's wedding was held at Hans Zug's because his and Annie's stone house was the largest in the community. Annie and Hester had scrubbed and washed, painted and toiled, until the place was perfectly groomed and shining. Already, the additional five acres had been half cleared, with the stumps burned.

Because it was springtime, many families offered a chicken for making *roasht*. There were plenty of turnips, and even some celery and cabbage. They added fresh greens with hot bacon dressing. The women made *schnitz* dried apple pies instead of the traditional pumpkin that was made during the fall of the year when most Amish weddings were held.

The wedding guests were duly impressed by Hans Zug's fine farm, his wealth, his hardworking children. Strapping sons, they said. What a fine child, that Lissie!

Tongues clucked over the Indian girl. What a pity. The prettiest girl many of them had ever seen, but her eyes contained a pool of unnamed sadness in their black depths. What would ever become of her?

Theodore and Lissie, however, eclipsed every guest's happiness, their joy shining visibly through their otherwise reserved demeanor, which was fitting and proper for a sober Amish wedding. They stood side by side, their hands placed in the bishop's as he pronounced them man and wife.

Sadie Fisher told Mamie Troyer that Lissie was twice as wide as her husband, but Mamie frowned at Sadie's remark, ruining the festivities for Sadie entirely.

Well, Mamie thought Sadie was making fun of Lissie, and everyone knew Sadie prided herself by maintaining her trim figure, which wasn't right in the sight of God, or at least, in Mamie's.

They ate vast quantities of *hinkle dunkus*, that good, rich, salty gravy that was ladled generously over the *roasht*.

Lissie leaned over and told Theodore that her own bacon dressing was better, although she wanted to remain appreciative. Theodore smiled at his radiant bride, agreed wholeheartedly, and thought himself the most fortunate man on earth. To think of having a good hot breakfast, with the scalding coffee she drank every morning, was a luxury he could not begin to imagine. The long cold nights spent shivering in his bed would be a thing of the past, as well as eating burned toast and poorly cooked eggs with the mice, that pestilence that dogged every day of his life.

The warm touch of his beloved Lissie had already taken up a place of wonder in his heart. The pure enjoyment of being in her company, the way she touched his arm, his shoulder, his cheek, the way she cooked his supper, he wondered why he'd waited so long.

Lissie's smile faded and then melted away when she caught sight of Hester standing off by herself, dressed in the traditional blue wedding dress, a black apron around her slender waist. She was indeed, by far, the most beautiful person in the room. The most tragic as well.

Lissie pursed her lips, laid a hand on Theodore's leg, leaned into his shoulder and jutted her chin in Hester's direction. "Look."

Theodore followed Lissie's gaze. His eyes found Hester. "What?" he asked, unsure of what she meant.

"She's so alone. Couldn't we find a young man for her on this, our wedding day? Wouldn't it be perfect?"

Theodore nodded. "But they do not pair the young people at a small wedding like ours, do they?" he whispered.

"No, you're right."

They watched as the young men filed in, observing carefully the way they behaved as they sat across the table from Hester. They all watched her discreetly, as she kept her eyes lowered to the German hymnbook placed on the table in front of her. Her lips moved along with the singing, but not once did she look up or as much as lift her face an inch.

At the next table sat her brother Noah, a blond giant of a boy, his face darkened by the early spring sun. His shoulders pushed at the white fabric of his shirt; his black vest fit seamlessly. His hair was cut shorter than the suitable *ordnung* for young men.

Some said Noah was "turning wild." Some said he'd spoken of joining the lumber men, those crews of rough men without scruples who felled trees as fast as they could, hacking away at the forest with nothing in mind but making as much money as they could.

Noah had the most unusual eyes. They were not quite blue or green. Hans had dark brown eyes. His mother Kate's eyes had been an astounding shade of blue.

Lissie watched, her eyes narrowed. Not once did Noah acknowledge his sister's presence. He spoke to the young men beside him, smiling and laughing, but Hester may as well have been invisible for all he cared.

Yes, Hester may as well disappear for all that family cared about her, and it was all Annie's doing. All of it. For the rest of her life, Lissie would remember her perfect wedding day, filled with love and anticipation, containing only one gray cloud named Hester.

Poor, darling Indian foundling. Surely God had a purpose.

CHAPTER 23

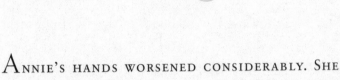

ANNIE'S HANDS WORSENED CONSIDERABLY. SHE could no longer lift the heavy crockery without using both hands. She hid this fact from Hester's eyes repeatedly, covering one hand with her apron whenever Hester was in the kitchen.

One summer day when the heat and humidity had lifted, mercifully cooling the damp earth, Annie was in a better state of mind. She allowed Hester the luxury of ironing instead of hoeing corn, which she had done every other day of the week from sunup to sundown. Calluses formed on her hands where the dreaded blisters had been, which eased the pain and made the hoeing bearable, in spite of the fiery sun beating down on her head.

All girls strove to keep a pearly white complexion, devoutly wearing a straw hat to work in the garden. Annie required that Hester wear a hat as well, although she reminded her many times there was no use trying to keep her white since she never was and never would be. But it was the *ordnung* of the church, and no child of hers would be seen in her garden without a hat.

The minute Hester entered the back field, she untied the hated straw hat and flung it to the ground. All day, till she heard the dinner bell, she hoed, listening to the bird calls around her, identifying each one, as her hoe rose and fell and sweat trickled off her forehead and down her back.

Today, she cleaned up after the noon meal, washing all the dried food off the plates and forks while moving as quickly as she could. Annie watched with narrowed eyes as she quietly dried the many dishes and put them all back in their places.

Turning, Annie lifted a heavy crockery pitcher, gasped, then screamed shrilly, as the pitcher crashed to the oak floor, a wide pool of milk spreading across its gleaming surface. Instantly, it was all Hester's fault, but she had expected that and didn't reply. Bending, she lifted the broken pieces, went to the pantry for a rag, and began to clean up the milk. Annie turned away, her tirade finished, satisfied that Hester had taken the blame.

Little Emma voiced her opinion with Barbara's support, whereupon they were both paddled firmly and told to sit on the bench until they were sorry for their *grosfeelich* (proud and cocky) ways.

When Annie became agitated, her hands were always worse, causing her to clench them together, her fingers interwoven, her shoulders held erect.

Suddenly, Hester stood, having cleaned up all the milk and holding the bucket of soapy water she had used. "Annie, I believe I know a solution that would help your hands," she said firmly.

Annie snorted. "Out of that devilish book, I suppose."

Hester did not answer but simply took the bucket
to the back porch and flung the water over the steps.
Immediately, a bevy of geese came waddling, their necks
outstretched, lifting their wings in warning.

"Can I mix a few herbs and steep them in boiling
water?"

"No. You'll kill me with that witchcraft."

"It's not to drink. It's to soak your hands in twice a
day."

Annie scowled, and the vertical furrows on her forehead deepened as her narrow face took on a look of
undisguised suspicion. She pursed her lips, smacked
them with an unappetizing sound, turned away, and
said, "No."

"Please."

"What kind of herbs?"

"Sage and mustard seed."

"We don't grow either of them."

"I know where the wild plants are."

Suspicion was replaced with hope, but then pride cast
its shadow across her face, and she turned away. "No.
And don't mention it again."

Hester returned to her ironing until the basket was
empty, with the ironed garments hanging from the back
of a chair. She folded the rows of white shirts and then
put them in the wardrobe for Sunday's use. She sewed
missing buttons on knee breeches and searched all the
everyday work breeches for holes and patched them.

Annie ran a terribly efficient house, every hour of
every day producing something worthwhile. She had
no use for any person who shirked a distasteful duty,

all heavy people who ate more than was necessary, and anyone who spent a penny without considering the true necessity of the purchase. Hester knew she was too frugal to visit the doctor in Berksville, so she decided to bide her time, to let the matter drop for now.

Hans found Annie watching Hester with a wary eye. There was a difference in the way she looked at her, with a hesitation of sorts. For one hopeful moment, Hans wondered if Annie was indeed changing her opinion of Hester before he discarded the thought as foolish. He knew his wife's ways all too well. She did not budge once she formed an opinion.

What did the scriptures say? Ah, but it was unthinkable. As he watched Annie hide the shaking of her hands with her apron more than once, he brought a fresh resolve to be more patient, more understanding of her tense moments with Hester.

Annie sent Hester to bring Noah and Isaac for the evening meal. Unsure about the borders of their property, she asked Hans where they might be.

"You'll know. You'll hear their axes."

Annie asked loudly how she could traipse all over God's creation and not know where the property line was.

"I know where the east and west borders are. I'm just not sure of the north."

"You'll find them."

It seemed odd to Hester that anyone would be sent to fetch the older boys. Didn't they always come in when dusk ushered them home? No one seemed particularly worried about their absence or their return. She decided to use extreme caution and keep her eyes and ears open. Annie had proved to be as untrustworthy as a wolf or a cornered rat, although neither of those descriptions suited her really. Hester knew she was more cunning than either one.

Walking through the cornfield, she entered the woods, staying on a straight course to the north. The land sloped uphill gently, then abruptly changed to a steep incline at the top. Undecided, Hester stayed still, evaluating the terrain. Yes, she'd been here many times. She'd always imagined the property line would be the top of the incline, along the crest of the hilltop.

She heard the ringing sound of an axe meeting solidly with wood. Clunk. Clunk. Clunk. A steady rhythm, faster than Hester thought possible, and then a cracking, ripping sound, a moment's breath, a fearsome sound of branches breaking and cracking. A giant oak disappeared from view, coming to rest in a newly created clearing.

Noah stood hatless, his blond hair stuck to his head by the perspiration that soaked his body. One hand was coiled loosely around the heavy, wooden handle of the axe; the other rested low on his hip as he watched the tree's descent. His feet apart, his strong legs made him appear a ruthless giant, taking control of every tree's demise, destroying the pristine forest as if he were God himself.

Hester felt an inexplicable sadness, a tender pity for the great tree that stood so proud, its green leaves shading the forest floor, providing homes for woodland creatures. How could Noah spend his days whacking through the forest, cutting the beautiful trees without a thought in his head? Hester visualized the bald mountains and ridges littered with dead growth, the good, rich soil washed off the hillsides by torrential rains, the creatures of the trees having no home.

The old woman had informed her about the way of the Lenape. To fell a tree was unthinkable. Wrong. The Creator had placed trees on the earth for shelter and protection, and they should not be disturbed. They were sacred.

Suddenly, a rage so violent it was physical lent wings to her feet. Silently, she moved, swiftly hurrying down the incline, sliding, grabbing small trees, making only a minimum of sound. Noah looked up at her approach, his face masked. When he saw the agitation on her face, he stepped back, watching her uneasily.

On she came, her chest heaving, her fists balled tightly by her flowing green skirts, her black eyes flat with displeasure. She strode up to Noah, raised both hands, and thumped her fists against his wide, solid chest.

He stepped back, catching her hands, but so powerful was her dislike of him, she wrenched them free, delivering another blow to his upper arm. "Hey! What is wrong?"

In answer, she flung her head back, her black eyes snapping her anger. "I guess you're happy to spend your days ruining the sacred forest!" She spat her words.

Isaac stopped, watching his sister intently.

"Oh, come on, Hester," Noah said, grinning.

In answer, she reached up and smacked his face, hard. "Don't you make fun of me! You mark my words. The time will come when you'll regret this. All of you will."

"Stop acting like an Indian. We are only obeying our father's wishes. We need the land."

Hester raised herself to her full height, her black eyes conveying her contempt. "Believe me, the time will come when the white people will need the land more than they do now."

There was nothing to say to this, so Noah looked off across the woods where the tree lay in his path.

"Annie says supper is ready."

Instantly, Noah loosened his grip on the axe, letting it fall to the ground. Then Isaac led the way up the slope, their heavy boots crashing through the undergrowth. Hester followed soundlessly, a few steps behind her brothers.

At the evening meal, Hans watched his two oldest sons with new respect, seeing the way they stayed silent, shoveled the hot food into their mouths, thanked Annie, and left the table immediately after the second prayer was said in silence.

Hester ate very little. She kept her head lowered except when she helped Barbara with her meat or spread butter on a biscuit for Emma. Hans sensed agitation and wondered what had occurred, if anything.

A new thought snaked its way into Hans's mind. Had the boys behaved unseemly toward Hester? A great and palpable fear entered his heart. He had no clue how he could ever approach these grown boys with his fear, his suspicion. It was unthinkable.

He could not talk to them of his feelings on any subject, so how could he approach them about Hester? He would need to be her guard. Every waking moment of every day, he would need to look out for her.

The thought placed a crushing responsibility on him, so he shared it with his wife, who watched her husband's face go from red to white and back again as he spoke of his concern about the boys growing into men, perhaps thinking of Hester in ways other than merely being their sister.

Annie listened gamely, choosing to keep her face averted, unable to meet her husband's too-bright eyes. Yes, she agreed, it was a reasonable concern, but she was certain the boys would not think of her as anything other than an Indian and want nothing to do with her.

"Unlike you, Hans," she added.

For Annie was shrewd and watchful, her skill at deciphering looks and attitudes honed by her years of surviving a family that had hardly been better than a battlefield of wills.

Hester would have to go. How to go about that was a challenge she had not figured out, at least until now. No matter how she was treated, Hester became more of a servant. Annie would need to figure out another way.

These thoughts were all hidden as she watched the display of emotion on her husband's face. Her husband. Hans. The Hans who did not love her.

Well, the rejection, the denial, could operate both ways. With her lips compressed into a thin line, her eyes doe-like, her head nodding in agreement, her will given to her husband, Annie plotted a plan that would not fail.

The trees continued to fall. Black smoke poured from the stumps that were removed. The boys had lit them on fire, and they were so thick and heavy that they burned endlessly.

They hauled firewood into the lean-to, and Hester took her turn with the axe. She walked behind the cultivator, following the harrow; she planted corn and helped with the tobacco through the cool spring days.

The sun turned warm. Soon they had spring onions to place on the table, along with freshly churned butter, which the family spread on thick slices of wheat bread. Annie served great wooden bowls of greens flavored with a hot dressing made of eggs, vinegar, and bacon, seasoned with chives. They ate sugar peas, small and green and limp, flavored only with salt, a dash of black pepper, and a touch of butter. The greens grew tall and thick. Annie cut them in bunches, gathered them into her apron, and then cooked them in a cream sauce with nutmeg. The table was laden with the gifts of the earth, Annie said demurely, often noting the plentiful rains, the goodness of God.

Even the women at church noticed the change in Annie and wondered at it. Some said Hans was good for her, and so she could act kindly toward Hester, noting that she was not even his own child. He was certainly good to his own children, something you could plainly see by the way they sat so quietly beside him in church.

And so the family prospered, growing substantially in prestige, their status among the Amish steadily improving. For Hans had really made something of himself with that Annie by his side. Look at the way those children behave themselves in church, they said. Hans just had such a nice way about him.

Hester came to believe that times were, indeed, changing. Annie displayed a new tolerance of her knowledge of plants and their ability to heal. Annie even allowed her more time to pursue her interests, so Hester often found herself on the rock, her favorite place of meditation. She never heard or saw the whistling youth again, although she kept her eyes and ears alert, curious.

Annie asked Hester and Lissie to see if the trout had spawned yet. She was hungry for a mess of fish. They would eat them fresh and salt the rest in barrels for winter meals. Hester's heart leaped unexpectedly as she thought of the creek's emptying into the river, close to where Padriac shuttled traffic across on his raft. Would she be able to speak to him again?

Hans decided to take the day off to accompany the girls and help them with the net. When he asked Solomon, Daniel, and John to ride along, his request was met with whoops of joy as they clambered onto the back of the spring wagon with Lissie. Hester sat on the front seat with Hans, wreathed in smiles. The color of his face brightened, and his eyes sparkled.

Annie stood on the porch, waved a thin, shaking hand, then turned, her hand on little Emma's head, letting herself in the door slowly. Once safely away from anyone's prying eyes, she clasped her hands behind her back and paced, her mouth working.

Before they knew it, fall would be here, and with it, winter close behind. Hester could not leave in winter because she would freeze or fall prey to wild animals, and Annie could not live with the guilt of having her blood on her hands. Yet this plan was going entirely too slow. By all appearances, Hans loved his wife, and his mindless infatuation with Hester was completely disappearing. But Annie was running out of patience. She wanted Hester gone.

She swept the kitchen, her agitation causing her to draw the broom stiffly across the well-worn floor, her thoughts in turmoil.

When Padriac spied the spring wagon with Hester seated beside Hans, he didn't try to veil the all-encompassing joy that shone from his blue eyes. "It's you!" he shouted, making a mad dash for the spring wagon, holding up his hand to help her down, holding the small, well-formed fingers in his own entirely too long.

Hans felt anger rise within but told himself it was his fatherly instinct wanting to protect his eldest daughter.

Padriac showed them where the trout were heavy with roe, some of them sleepy. He caught the huge, fat trout with his bare hands, his enthusiasm rolling with his easy laugh, a sound so genuine it was infectious.

Hans had not heard Hester laugh so often or so freely since she was a young child. Lissie giggled and floundered about, soaking her skirt and the front of her dress as she came up, gasping, with yet another trout.

The afternoon was filled with the smell of fish, the blazing sun, the skittish dragonflies hovering over the tall grass on the bank of the creek. The low-hanging branches trailed their leaves in the water, as Padriac and the girls dragged the net through the still, green pools.

When Padriac had to leave to ferry a team of horses across the river, Hans watched Hester as he walked to the small building, an expression he had never seen etched on her lovely face. Well, he would have to nip this in the bud. This fellow was not Amish, and Hester knew it.

Cold fear of her disobedience wrapped its stifling tentacles around his heart. His breath came quickly.

What would such a romance do to his pride? How would it appear to the Amish community if one of his children went off with an *Englisher*? Such an occurrence would only flaunt his failure at raising the Indian foundling in God's way so her soul would be saved and she would go on to lead a true Christian life by choosing the way of the cross.

Hans called a swift halt to the afternoon's activities, his face pinched and white, his eyes darting furtively from Padriac's open, joyous demeanor to the blush on Hester's perfect cheeks.

Quickly, he threw the flopping, dirt-encrusted fish into the wooden barrels, tied them securely to the sides of the wagon with strong hemp rope, called his children, and told them it was time to go home. The children wailed their disapproval but climbed onto the back of the spring wagon obediently, where they sat smelling like fish, wet, bedraggled, and tired.

Hans hitched Dot in anxious jerks, snapping the traces hurriedly to the singletree, his eyes going repeatedly to Padriac and Hester as they stood aside. He couldn't hear what Padriac was saying. He just saw that Hester's eyes never left his face. When Padriac reached with his hand to clasp hers, Hans became inflamed like a man possessed.

"Hester!" He shouted the word once, harshly.

Hester responded as if she'd been shoved. Without another word, without a backward glance, she ran to the spring wagon, leaped lightly to the seat, and spread her wet skirts carefully around her feet.

Before Padriac realized what was going on, Hans held the whip aloft, brought it down on Dot's back, and startled her into a wild plunge up the slope and away from the river, the wooden barrels swaying and creaking against the heaving sides of the fast-moving spring wagon.

The children clung to the sides and to each other as they bounced and swayed from side to side, leaving wet spots when they moved from one location to the next. Lissie became angry and yelled at her father in her brash manner. Hans told her to close her big mouth. Hester hung on, braced her feet against the dash, pulled her cap strings forward, and thought surely Hans didn't have to be in such a hurry to start the milking.

When they clattered into the barnyard, Dot was soaked with sweat, the lather white against her black harness, her sides heaving, the pink nostrils dilated, her eyes rolling behind the blinders on her bridle. Noah straightened from the water trough, ran his fingers through his soaking wet hair, and watched with narrowed eyes.

Isaac opened his mouth on one side and said with certainty, "Dat has seen a *schpence*."

Noah only shook his head, his mouth grim, his eyes slits against the brilliance of the late afternoon sun.

CHAPTER 24

From that day on, Hester became uneasy with Hans's behavior. He dogged her footsteps. Some days it seemed she was never out of his sight. He popped up in the house when she least expected him. He hired Noah and Isaac out, putting a much larger workload on Lissie and Hester. Even Annie took her turn in the fields, forking hay and chopping thistles.

When Hester realized the new kind of prison that had closed its talons around her, she resigned herself to whatever God, the one who controlled her life, would allow. She had long ago reasoned to herself that he was the only one she could trust. Her people called him the Creator, the Great Spirit, and he was the same to her.

She had found an uneasy truce, as well, between the Amish and the Lenape. In her heart, she no longer tried to divide them. They were all God's handiwork, the same as the tall pine and the lofty oak, made according to his purpose. In the Indian tribe, there was good and evil. In the Amish community, there was the same. Human nature contained tempers that flared, jealousy that reared its poisonous head, covetous folks, and dishonest ones.

There was kindness, so much goodness, pity, and compassion, plus a spirit of helpfulness, all things that kept her within the culture in which she was raised. Deep in her heart, she believed that to be among the Amish was a privilege. It was a blessing to be shown that you needed Jesus Christ and the power to overcome the nature one was born with.

Of course, people were imperfect. Even Annie had good qualities—her discipline, the way she managed her family's duties, her financial outlook.

Hester tried without success to gauge Hans's odd behavior, then decided to give in and stop thinking he was unreasonable. He was concerned about her welfare, that was all.

It was in the evening, when the katydids and locusts were already in full symphony, their whirring, chirping chorus the music of the forest in Hester's ears, when Hans approached her.

Dusk was only a few minutes away, the light was slowly leaving the front porch where Hester sat shelling pole beans. She popped the pods with her thumb and caught the heavy beans in the palm of her hand before dropping them into the wooden bucket beside her chair.

He stood above her, his breathing hard, his hands held loosely by his sides. Hester could smell the soil on his shoes and see bits of earth clinging to the rough fabric of his trouser leg. He smelled of straw and warm grass, of honest perspiration after a day's work in the field.

"Hester."

She remained seated, the urgent note in his voice keeping her face lowered.

"Hester."

The word was not a question or a command; it was more a sound of desperation. Why was Hans so frantic on an evening such as this?

"Yes, Dat."

She hardly ever called him that, so why now?

For reasons beyond her understanding, "Dat" seemed necessary suddenly, the proper word, the needed fence around her.

"Look at me."

She obeyed.

"You know I have loved you as a father should from the day my beloved Kate found you by the spring. I have given you a home, fed you, raised you in the fear of the Lord in the Amish way."

Hester dropped her gaze away from the wrong in his. In one jolt of awakening, she understood. She sat still, as if she were part of the stone wall behind her, except for the white of her cap, listening to the words he said, his breath catching on phrases, his eyes boring into the top of her head.

"Promise me, Hester. Promise me you will not begin a courtship with this Irish heathen. For you are preserved among the Amish. God would not want you to consort with the Irish."

On and on, his voice rose and fell, the words true and Christian, fatherly and caring, the motive behind them another thing entirely. Hester was no longer an innocent child. The knowledge of Hans's caring and Annie's hatred—all of it—suffused her mind and heart like a white-hot iron, branding her with its pain. Hans knew, as did Annie, that he loved her in the way a man loves a woman, in the way God designed that two people fall in love, and that, as time went on, it would become harder and harder for Hans to deny this. This Annie knew, as well.

A great pity welled in Hester's heart for the thin, hurting Annie with the palsied hands. Ah, how Annie must hate her! She loved Hans, Annie did. But his love eluded her, and she saw the reason why.

Before Hester now lay the great unknown, a vast new world without the safety of the Amish fold. There was only one remedy for this situation, and that was for her to disappear. Hans must never know what had become of her. Unlike Joseph in the Old Testament story, she would leave behind no evidence. All this flashed through her mind as Hans talked on. Bits and pieces of what he said pierced her consciousness, but nothing mattered, nothing was of any consequence.

"You were more precious to me than my own sons," Hans spoke heavily. His hand came down on her shoulder, the touch like that of a viper.

Leaping to her feet, Hester scattered the bean pods. She kicked the wooden bucket to one side as she stood erect, facing Hans squarely. Her voice was low, well-modulated, but terrible in its depth. "Don't you touch me ever again, Hans Zug. Your words are righteous, but your foul breath contains the wrong that battles in your chest. You will never have the right, from this day forward, to tell me how to live my life. You are living in hidden adultery, and you know it."

She was crying now, with the weight of his wrongdoing, the uncovering of his intentions. His betrayal was a blow so crushing, Hester dealt with it in the only way she knew how. With her foot, she kicked his shin again and again. She pummeled his forearms with her fists, then fled around the corner of the house as he watched her go, helpless as she unveiled his innermost secret.

She slammed through the back door, found Annie at the hearth, grabbed her forearm, and spun her around. "You will never have to look on my face again after this night. I wish you and Hans a long and blessed life together with his children gathered around your table."

Annie's mouth opened, then closed. When it opened again, a mere squawk emerged. She stopped and licked her dry lips with an anxious tongue.

Hester had already gone to the stairs, her feet pounding up the steps. Annie stood stiffly, her breathing so rapid she felt lightheaded, listening to the sounds overhead. She heard Hester take the wooden box out from under her bed, then slide her feet across the floor. She opened and shut the wardrobe.

Hans came into the kitchen. His face searched Annie's. "Where's Hester?"

Silently, Annie pointed to the ceiling.

"What is she doing?"

Annie shrugged, her face chalk-white, her eyes dilated with the stark fear that was wreaking havoc in her conscience. What if Hester died? Quickly, she moved to Hans and grasped his shirtsleeve with nervous fingers.

"Hans, the winter is coming. She won't survive."

"What are you talking about?"

"Hester is leaving."

"No!" The cry exploded out of him. He was completely unable to stop himself from that burst of fear. He leaped up the stairs, two at a time, and tore open the door to Hester's room, begging her to stay.

She didn't know how it happened; she just knew her fury and disgust propelled her across the floor. The great banging and thumping that ensued was Hans's heavy body falling backward down the stairs, the breath leaving his body in drawn-out "oofs" and "ahs" of pain before he lay sprawled out on the kitchen floor at Annie's feet, doubled up in hurt and humiliation.

Hester grabbed the sack she had filled with her earthly possessions, with the only coat she owned stuffed on top, and lunged down the stairs after him. Without a word of goodbye, she let herself out of the house and into the deepening dusk to the sound of the katydids and crickets.

"Hester! Wait! Where you going?" Little Emma came flying across the yard, her strong young legs propelling her.

A groan escaped Hester's lips. She dropped the sack she'd slung across her shoulder and bent to reach for Emma, the true little companion she loved. Lifting her, she held the small body close to her face, kissing her over and over as hot tears pricked her eyelids.

"Goodbye, Emma."

"But stop! Where are you going?" Emma's voice was raised in concern, her lisp pronounced.

"I'm going away. I'll be back soon."

"How soon?"

"Soon."

"All right. Stay safe." Wriggling, Emma wanted down, satisfied that Hester would be back soon.

Hester held her tightly, kissed her one last time, and set her on her feet.

"Bye!" Emma called, running across the yard to the house. Hester stood at the edge of the forest and lifted her right hand, a small smile on her face and tears coursing down her cheeks. It was almost Hester's undoing, this saying goodbye to little Emma.

She knew nothing of the world she was about to encounter. The forest, the surrounding mountains were not alien or terrifying. But she was leaving a world that was safe and cloistered, where ministers led her in the way of righteousness, parents made decisions, and her identity was taking shape. But she had to go. There was no other way. Annie was Hans's lawful wife, his wife in God's eyes.

Still she hesitated, her eyes taking in the stone house, strong and magnificent in the evening light. The green slope fell away to the long stone and log barn, surrounded by split-rail fence, keeping the animals safe from predators.

Long, straight rows of vegetables lay in perfect symmetry with the rows of trees, the springhouse, the new corn crib. Each year, the Hans Zug farm prospered and grew.

She would leave all this and become no one, a runaway, hiding, always moving, for she had no home now.

She stood tall, her green skirts lifting, blowing slightly, her hair barely visible beneath the starched white cap.

Her face shone with an inner light; her eyes contained immeasurable sadness. Her posture was erect, upright. Her heart beat strong in her chest. The blood in her veins sang the song of the Lenape.

She would go now. Etched forever in her heart was the stone farmhouse, the ways of the Amish, the Bible, the work she had learned, the preserving of food, the cleaning and cooking, the way to keep clothes pure with lye soap made of wood ashes.

Down in the shadowy hollows below the barn, a cow bawled for its calf's return. A horse thumped against the wooden gate, causing the hinges to creak. All common noises of the farm, dear, familiar. She would carry them with her in her heart forever.

Turning, she faded into the overhanging branches of a maple tree, into the Pennsylvania forest that would be her home.

The End

LINDA BYLER

Which Way Home?

Hester's Hunt for Home
Book 2

CHAPTER 1

NIGHT WAS COMING ON.

All around her the thickets turned to shadows, the crickets' song heralding the approach of darkness when the light would fail her. She'd need a place to rest or at least stay still. Alert, perhaps, but definitely still.

Now more than ever, she needed every ounce of her Indian heritage. Was "heritage" the right word? Or was that knowledge simply in the blood that flowed through her veins? Had she been born with the Indian way?

She guessed "heritage" fit more with the Amish, the people who found her when she was only a few days old. Or was it weeks? She would never know. She only knew that she was a full-blooded Lenape who was found by a white Amish woman. The Amish brought her up, these plain people who migrated from Switzerland to avoid religious persecution.

This afternoon, after a long-overdue confrontation, Hester had packed a few possessions in her haversack and left her family and the prosperous farm, built by their years of hard labor and good management in the

wooded valley of Berks County, Pennsylvania. Her father's affections for her had ignited her stepmother's jealousy, until the situation escalated to the point of misery
for Hester, Hans, and his new wife Annie.

Now Hester was on her own. She had always roamed
the familiar forests of her childhood. Her own special
rock, a large, flat limestone, jutted from the steep incline
on the mountain where she spent entire afternoons. She
went there as often as she could for some solitude, away
from the ten siblings born after Kate had found her one
morning by the spring. She loved the hills, knew the way
of the forest, and was instinctively adept with a slingshot
and a hand-crafted bow.

But now this was different. She had no large stone
house to hold its protective arms around her at night.
There was no fireplace, no cookstove. She no longer had
a home.

Hester Zug had gone to school for a short period of
time, but letters and numbers got all mixed up for her
like a pot of vegetable soup. She could decipher some
words, enough to get by, but numbers she had no need
for. What she couldn't grasp in book-learning, she made
up for by knowing the forest and developing acute skills
with her weapons.

She stopped. Everywhere on the darkening hillside,
there was laurel, thickets of it. Underbrush, tangles of
vines, sharp blackberry shoots—almost impossible to
navigate—stopped her ascent. She had wanted to reach
the crest of this sharply inclined ridge, but since night
had darkened the path, she would stay where she was.
Lowering the haversack from her back, she sank to the

ground, then rolled to one side to tear at the brambles that pricked through her skirt. She pulled the cork from the handled crocking jar, took a few greedy swallows of water, and replaced the cork. She had found no spring, no creek, so far.

Through the deepening gloom, she kept looking for a bed of pine needles, knowing her chance for a night's rest increased if she could lie on that natural carpet. But finding none, she'd have to make do. Leaping to her feet, she bent her back and rid the ground of stones, thorny bushes, any obstruction that would bother her during the night. Then she spread the cleared area with dead grasses, leaves, anything to cushion her night's rest.

Her stomach growled, and her whole body felt pinched with hunger. Sleep would be long in coming if she ate nothing. Reaching into the sack, she pulled out a long, flat piece of deer jerky, inserted one end into her mouth and tore at it ravenously with her teeth. She swallowed before the section was properly chewed, struggling to make it go down before tearing at it once more. The salt and grease increased the natural flow of her saliva, so she slowed down, chewing longer with relish before trying to swallow.

She disciplined herself. She would need that in the coming days. Another sip of water and her evening meal was complete. She would have loved a warm bucket of water to soak her feet and wiggle her toes, to slosh about extravagantly as she used a bar of homemade lye soap to scrub the dirt from under her toenails.

In summer, Hester was always barefoot. She detested the restriction of shoes, especially those heavy shoes from the traveling cobbler. Her mother allowed her to wear homemade moccasins, light and supple, at home, but to go to Amish church services, she was made to wear the cumbersome leather ones. Her feet were calloused, the healthy blue veins showing through the brown of her skin, capable of walking over any terrain. She wore no shoes now.

In her haversack, she had packed a pair of moccasins, one shortgown, more dried meat, and the journal of recipes from the old Indian woman. It was filled with directions for making the medicines and herbal remedies, the Indian knowledge of healing which she had entrusted to Hester before her death. That was it, except for the slingshot, a knife, and a ball of twine. She would need the sturdy string to make a bow.

The slingshot would serve her well for small animals, but before winter arrived, she would need to kill larger animals. She would need the skin of the deer. She would also need a shelter first, though many miles would need to separate her from her former home before she put something up that could be easily spotted.

She had no idea where she would go. She was headed east and perhaps a bit to the south. She had heard of the great blue waters, the Atlantic Ocean, and wondered how long she had to walk before she came upon it. For now, she knew there would be an endless string of hills, valleys, and rivers, all covered in woods. These were Penn's Woods—Pennyslvania—where William Penn had signed a treaty and worked constantly to maintain an unsteady peace with the Indians.

She figured Hans would try to find her. He'd stomp around for miles, his face flushed with fear and the fever of his longing. Hester's mouth was a compressed slash in her face. Her large, half-moon eyes were flat with disgust, clouded with remembering her own sense of innocence through the years when all the signs of his hidden torment had eluded her.

He'd send Noah and Isaac, his oldest sons, to find her, the sons born after Kate had discovered Hester, a newborn crying at the spring. The sons he ignored, so taken was he with Hester from the first day he held her in his arms.

Noah and Isaac had come to expect their father's neglect. They had each other. They sat beside their father in church, swinging their bare feet, content to be with him and unaware of his lack of attention, not knowing they needed a father's love.

They thought fathers always loved daughters more. Until they grew in age and stature. Their outward obedience had served its purpose. But an inward seething pot of rebellion, a fire stoked by Noah's intelligence as he absorbed the supposedly well-hidden thoughts of his pious father, only grew. Hester didn't know about this.

But Hester was confident that Hans would not find her. He was not taught well in the ways of the wild. He thrashed around through the woods with his heavy workboots, awakening or alerting every shy creature for miles. Sure, he was a hardworking farmer and a good manager, but he wasn't worth a lick at tracking or shooting.

He posed no threat. Besides, Hester knew he would not leave his wife for any extended period of time. He held his status in the community close to his chest like a priceless treasure, tending it lovingly.

Hester felt a fresh wave of hatred. It boiled through her veins, a foreign thing. She had never hated. She knew dislike, annoyance, irritation, but nothing like this. She had learned from her Amish community to be honest about her weaknesses, her sins. But how should she regard her father, who was held in high esteem by his fellow Amish? She imagined him wearing some kind of rich robe of righteousness, while inside he was crawling with maggots of lurid thoughts and consumed by wrong desires not yet acted upon.

Hester was past the age of twenty, but how far, she wasn't sure. She had come to believe that her own simple mind had failed to grasp what more intelligent girls would have seen years before. She had accepted the faith of the Amish. She had been baptized and had become a member of the church, promising to live for God since being saved by Jesus Christ. She had vowed to denounce the devil.

Yes, she had promised. She knew that the hatred driving her was wrong. She could not realize the promise of heaven when she harbored such intense dislike of Hans Zug, her father.

Hester was beautiful, and for that she took no credit. She was created in near perfection by God alone. A gift that might have been a blessing had turned out to be a curse, or so she thought. It was many things—the way she carried her tall lissome figure as graceful as a dancer; her thick, straight, jet-black hair; her dark eyes containing a myriad of lights; her small, straight nose; her full, perfectly curled lips, behind which a set of brilliant white teeth would occasionally appear. When they did, it was a delight to anyone who beheld her, so pure, so total was her charm. And so achingly guileless.

Many young men had been enamored, smitten by the young Indian woman. William King from Lancaster, tall, dark, taking her hand to accompany her to supper at her father's wedding to his second wife after the death of his first. Padriac Lee, the young man who poled travelers across the river on his raft, his red hair and easy Irish charm the source of her daydreams. But nothing had ever come of either one's attention. Hester had always been elusive.

Too many times she was labeled an outsider because of her Indian blood. She had developed no real relationships outside her family. Even her friendship with other Amish girls was sparse, cold, restrained, and reluctant. Now here she was, alone in every way.

She wondered how long it would take until hatred separated her from the God she believed in. Or might God understand the intensity of her disgust? Hester understood well that to be forgiven, she had to forgive. But an overriding sense of hate, and the resentment she carried for having to leave the home she loved, ruled her.

She was born an Indian. Her very being was of the Lenape tribe. The Amish called them *faschtendich*. Sensible people who roamed the forests of Pennsylvania, taking care of the land and worshipping the Great Spirit. But don't get on their wrong side. They don't forget, Hans always said.

Hester twisted her body until she lay on her side, drew up her knees, placed both hands beneath her cheek, and closed her eyes. A shiver ran along the top of her shoulder and slid down her back. The night air was cooling down. Well, there was nothing to do about that. She had no quilt, no blanket to ward off the chill of the settling dew. She drew her knees up farther.

The crickets and katydids kept up their night music, but Hester didn't notice. At home, with the upstairs window open, the same sounds sent her off to sleep every night. She knew the call of the screech owl, the barn owl, and the night hawk, the yip of the foxes, as well as the baying of the wolves.

She shivered at the high, primal scream of the wildcat, hoping she'd never encounter one alone in the wild. Noah had. He said they were shy creatures who would slip away unnoticed much of the time. When they were hungry or threatened, they were dangerous, however, so Hester learned to keep her eyes and ears on high alert when she was alone during the day.

The trees overhead hid most of the stars, but a few twinkled like friendly beacons between the leaves. As far as she could tell, there was no moon. She'd put a notch in a soft sapling branch every day to record the moon's rising as well as waning.

Small scurrying sounds reached her ears. Little night creatures snuffled their way through the thick undergrowth, she knew. Mink would be slithering about, their long, thin bodies sleek and supple. Bright-eyed deer mice rustled as quietly as possible, their lives dependent on the ability to escape the largest creatures.

Hester swallowed, thinking of a squirrel or rabbit cooking over a spit, the hot fire roasting the dark flesh to perfection. She'd find some blackberries in the morning.

Sleep would not come. She was cold. Sitting up, she reached for her haversack, pulled out the clean blue dress, and spread it across her legs. Removing the remaining items, she draped the heavy sack across her shoulders. Ah, that made all the difference. She couldn't believe a summer night could turn so cool, when at home, up-stairs, it was so uncomfortably warm. The last thing she remembered was one star wishing her good night from its perch on the lacy pattern of leaves above her.

She woke with a start. The sound of crashing under-brush assaulted her senses. She lay perfectly still. The sound of her heart swelled in her ears, the thumping in her chest painful, as if it would increase its beating until it exploded.

If she got to her feet, she'd be no better off. The thick-et, the thorny branches, the laurel, all the undergrowth would not allow her to run. She estimated the time it would take to gather her things and attempt to crawl through the heavy growth. Rolling her eyes, she estimat-ed the distance to the nearest tree. She knew if it had low enough branches, she'd be able to draw herself up out of danger, but what if there were no branches she could reach? Then she'd only be revealing herself.

She thought of the white-tailed deer. The old bucks, the wise ones that grew the biggest antlers, often eluded hunters by bedding down in impenetrable undergrowth, especially laurel. She'd stay.

She estimated the cracking of twigs to be a few hundred yards off. Not close. If it was a large animal, it would have to be a bear, and a very careless one at that. No deer made that amount of ruckus while moving through the forest. A cat was even quieter.

Humans? Was Hans on her trail? She knew she was capable of leaving little or no sign of travel, especially in her bare feet. He would not be able to track her. He was far too clumsy.

Noah? Or Isaac? Real fear gripped her whole body like a vise, clenching her insides until bile rose in her throat. She fought it down, swallowing repeatedly.

Realizing that Noah would be able to follow her crowded her like an onslaught of defeat. She knew his way. He was her brother. As children, they roamed the woods, the surrounding hills their playground. Hester taught Noah where the redbirds built their nests and where the squirrels hid their cache of nuts for the coming winter. She taught him how to track an animal by pointing out one leaf turned on its underside, one section of bark peeled unnaturally from the side of a tree.

But would Noah accompany Hans? With all the hidden drama, this sordid battle of Hans's nature, would Noah be perceptive enough to grasp the underlying truth of what was happening? As she lay in the undergrowth, Hester reasoned that Noah was someone she was barely acquainted with.

He was her brother, her playmate. But after their mother passed away and a stepmother entered their lives, Noah became a young man she no longer understood. He grew to towering heights, his shoulders widening into thick, powerful muscles that could fell a tree much quicker than Hans could. Rarely did he speak, and he never acknowledged her presence.

Sometimes Hester imagined he was a mute, perhaps deaf or not quite right, harboring a brain disease.

Or perhaps he simply disliked her because she was an Indian. She didn't know. She supposed if Hans ordered Noah to accompany him to find Hester, he would obey.

She could not go back. There were no options there. The breaking of small branches drew closer. Hester curled herself in a fetal position, completely motionless. Had she made the wrong decision?

Suddenly, the crashing stopped. Hester's heartbeat was the only sound, the steady, dull thumping in her ears and in her chest. Had it been an oversize, clumsy black bear that had bedded down for the night? These bears were the reigning authority over a vast area of Pennsylvania's mountains.

Would he catch her scent? The air was from the southwest, behind her, the way it mostly was on warm summer nights. The bear, as she now called the noise, was a bit south of her perhaps to the east, which meant she would be downwind of him. He would not catch her scent readily.

As she lay, hope infused her, along with the realization that all would be well after all. Black bears were fat and lazy in summertime, gorging themselves on berries and the fish that would be spawning thickly in the clear, gray-green waters of the many streams that flowed to the Susquehanna. The bear would go to sleep. And at the first streak of wan daylight, she'd be on her way, skirting the laurel by a wide margin, giving the bear plenty of territory.

When the crashing sound resumed and she heard the frustrated, whining sound of her father's voice, it did not penetrate her understanding at first. She thought the bear had spoken. But when she heard Hans' high-pitched yell calling to Noah, then to Isaac, she knew he was after her. He had so much power over his grown boys.

A great calm enveloped her, folding around her neatly like a freshly washed quilt ready to be put in the cedar chest. She'd stay. They wouldn't find her in this thicket. Hans hated pushing his way through any brambles, often saying that nothing in a mess like that was important enough to put yourself through the pain.

She calculated the distance between them. Perhaps a hundred yards.

On they came now. Hester remained in the same position. Thoughts of being taken back to the farm entered her mind. She could go if she had to. She'd go. But she would walk all the way to the bishop's house. John Lantz was a kindly man, stooped and aged, wise and loving, the best man Hester knew. She'd tell him about Hans. Bring down the golden castle of his pride.

Then, just as quickly, she knew that was an impossibility. Hans had done nothing wrong. His denial of wrongdoing would be accepted long before anyone would take her word. He actually had never acted on his thoughts.

Hester began to shiver, then to shake uncontrollably, her teeth chattering and clacking together, a riptide of her fear overtaking her. The sound of breaking twigs, the scuffling of leaves came closer. Would they be able to smell the fresh earth where she had torn briars away, moved stones and branches? Noah might, or Isaac, but not Hans.

Another shout. So close, Hester brought the tips of her fingers up to cover her ears, pressing in on them so hard they hurt, as if that course of action would shut out the men.

"Noah, *shtup*!" There was no answer except for the stillness, the ceasing of breaking twigs.

"There is no possibility of Hester traveling through this laurel," Hans said, his voice high with irritation, fatigue, and anxiety, a voice Hester knew well.

Someone continued on, making less noise. They were so close. How could they see to move? They must have had lanterns, or perhaps only torches.

Then Hester heard breathing. Only when she took her fingers away from her ears did she realize how close either Noah or Isaac had stumbled. Another long silence, and then Hans directed his boys to retrace their steps.

The space of a few heartbeats seemed like an eternity. She heard level, even breathing, the raking aside of thorny branches. She did not move a muscle. If she were found, she'd have to go. But she'd devise another plan. Reasoning, calming herself as best she could, Hester remained motionless. Then she heard the breaking of the underbrush, the stillness as the breathing went away.

Hans bawled out another order to Isaac as the three men made their way down the side of the ridge, leaving Hester weak and so powerless she thought she might die of sheer relief. She remembered to thank God with one small, German prayer from her childhood, which made her feel a bit as if she should be caught and hung for treason. For how could she hate Hans and thank God?

Did God hear the prayers of someone like her? Or did he look upon her with mercy, understanding her plight? She didn't know. She only knew that she needed to increase the distance between her and Hans as fast as she possibly could.

The racing of her heart would not allow her to relax, so she lay awake under the dark canopy of trees, trying to devise a plan. Should she avoid settlements? Or find a group of people and blend in among them? She had heard of the large community that started in Lancaster County east of her. Acceptance there seemed out of the question. Everywhere she traveled, she'd be an Amish Indian. An oddity. If she chose to dwell among civilization, she would have to desert the ways of the Amish. She'd need to stop wearing her muslin cap at least.

Weary, her thoughts upsetting, she decided to take one day at a time. Surviving was the most important thing. She'd travel fast, getting as many miles away from Berks County as possible. That was the best solution.

God would provide, or at least she hoped he would remember to look after her, walking through the wilderness in her bare feet without her muslin cap and with a heart filled with disgust for her father.

CHAPTER 2

When the first streaks of pink light separated the dark blue and gray of the early-morning sky, Hester was on her feet, the haversack bulging on her back, her eyes searching for the best route around the laurel. She was strangely exhilarated. She stepped out, moving swiftly as the light strengthened. She could see pine trees now, but who could have known they were there in the fast-fading light of evening?

She skirted the laurel, making her way over rocks and around thickets, but steadily up the side of the incline. On top, she ate some of the dried deer meat, drank sparingly of the water, and made her way quietly down the opposite side.

She guessed there was a creek, perhaps a spring, at the bottom of this ridge. She was surprised to find only a deep gouge containing layers of old leaves. A perfect place to sleep, but that time was not now. The sun was rising, a hot, red, shimmering orb of heat. Flies droned everywhere; bees hovered by the raspberry bushes.

Raspberries? Excitement pulsed through her veins when she realized how thick the raspberry canes stood along this small clearing. The purple berries grew profusely. Hester walked rapidly, plucking greedily at the sweetest berries. She lifted them to her lips, gobbling them like a starving bear. She ate until she could hold no more, thinking how berries satisfied hunger and quenched thirst at the same time.

That day, she calculated she'd walked a distance of fifteen miles. It was only a guess, but she knew she was in country she'd never seen or heard about. Tonight she'd start a small fire. But first, her water was all gone. She needed to find a stream. On top of the mountain, she'd figured there'd be a spring somewhere, but she'd been unable to locate one.

She knew the book of Indian medicines contained directions about how to find water using the forked branch of a peach tree, but those trees weren't around, and besides, she wasn't certain it would work.

She made her way down the mountain, clinging to small trees to lower herself. Thirst spurred her on. Her tongue was dry and heavy, her lips parched. She should have brought more water, should have known it was the dry summer season, and that water might not be as easy to find as she'd imagined.

A snake slithered across a flat rock, scaly and dry and brown. She was not afraid of snakes, finding them to be shy as long as they were undisturbed. The backs of her legs ached from the rapid descent, but she tried to ignore the pain, knowing the most important thing at the moment was to find a source of water.

The steep mountain leveled off a bit; the trees grew larger and farther apart, as if they received more nourishment to grow to this resplendent size. Hester smelled the river long before she saw it. It smelled of sulphur and iron and moisture. It smelled of mud and wet grass and dragonflies and butterflies. She increased her speed, her breath coming in gasps. Her mouth was painfully dry, her throat on fire. Ahead, the trees thinned even more.

Remembering caution, she slid soundlessly from tree to tree, her large eyes searching her surroundings for any sign of human habitation.

The clearing was surprisingly hard to get through, the thick grasses overgrown by wild rose bushes. Her feet were bleeding by the time she slid down the muddy bank of the river, plunging into the clear, brownish-green water like an otter and submerging her tired body completely. Then, rising to the surface, she cupped her hands and drank deeply, over and over, until the fiery thirst was gone.

She wished for soap. She rinsed her hair, clambered up the bank, and shook herself like a dog, then inhaled the pure, wet air, the pleasurable sensation of being without thirst. She felt alive, in control of her situation. What did she want for supper? Fish or wild game?

Schpeck and Sauerkraut? Stewed chicken and carrots?

Hester smiled, remembering the long plank table and the great bowls of food passed around to the thirteen hungry people. Saliva pushed into her mouth. She swallowed.

Efficiently then, she took stock of her situation. She'd have to stay beneath trees and away from the clearing. There was no sense in being a sitting duck. Why be free picking for unsavory characters? Or for bears that decided they had had plenty of fish for the summer?

She found a natural alcove with the trunk of a great tree at her back, the upturned roots of a fallen one beside her. It was perfect, shielding her from sight and protecting her from animals. All she needed was a roof.

No, that was not possible. She had not put enough distance between herself and her family. She must stay rational, no matter how homey this natural little wonder appeared to her. She set about piling soft materials into a small hollow. She found grass, soft bark from the fallen pine tree, moss, and wonder of wonders, great sheets of old bark that she could peel from the dead tree. Perfect for a sleeping cover.

Squirrels chirred from the tree branches, so she bent swiftly, retrieved her slingshot, found a smooth stone by the river, and let fly an expert shot at the nearest, especially saucy one. Triumphantly she picked up the nice, fat, gray squirrel, one of the biggest she'd ever seen.

The round, orange sun was hovering just above the mountain to the east when Hester cleared a small area, then gathered dry leaves and very small dry twigs. She found a healthy hickory tree and pulled off the lowest, small branches. Then she began to rub them together, squatting on her haunches above the small pile of dry leaves.

She'd often done this and had shown Noah and Isaac the way of it. There was a trick to attaining enough friction, in the proper span of time, with the right amount of dry leaves to catch those first few sparks. But now she was hungry and tired, and her arms felt soft and pliable when she had rubbed for only a minute or more.

She continued, faster and faster, her shoulders hunched, her teeth pressed together as she concentrated on starting a fire to cook the squirrel.

She could not stop the friction to check how hot the branches were becoming. Her breath came in rapid puffs, and the muscles in her arms knotted, sending up spasms of pain as her fingertips heated up. Good. Faster now. Only a while longer.

A thin, white plume of smoke curled up from the peeled hickory branch, followed by a few orange sparks. Hester moved her hands even faster. More sparks fell on the dry leaves. A gray curl of smoke blackened the edge of a leaf, then another. Still Hester's hands flew back and forth, as more sparks showered on the dry leaves.

Suddenly a bright orange and yellow flame danced to life. Quickly, she flung the hickory branches to the ground and sifted dry leaves over the small, orange flame. Her eyes lit exultantly when the flame grew large, licking greedily at the dry twigs Hester placed on top.

As soon as the fire was started well, she surrounded it with stones, then fashioned a spit from green branches. Taking up her knife, she cleaned the squirrel with a few expert slices, then cut off its head, legs, and tail, drawing the skin down and away from the carcass. She impaled the prepared squirrel on the green branch, hung it low above the now crackling fire, and lay down on the bed she had made for herself to wait hungrily until the meat was done.

As the shadows lengthened across the river, the trees' reflections became longer and darker, the water no longer friendly the way it had been with the sun glinting on it. When sun shone on water, it created light, like ice. Sometimes the light was blue or yellow or clear, but it always brought light and joy to Hester, no matter if the day had turned into drudgery.

She wanted to stay here by the river always. She picked the hot meat off the bones, crunching it with her fingers and in her mouth. She ate every scrap of meat, sucking it off the tiny, fragile bones, then chewing a few of them and eating the small bits of marrow. Marrow was life-giving, filled with iron and other good minerals, so she ate every morsel she could find.

She threw what little remained of the squirrel back into the fire, took a long drink of the tepid river water, and settled herself comfortably for the night. The river ran silently toward the east. Only occasionally, Hester heard the splash of a leaping fish in the distance. A loon called its ribald laughing sound. Another answered, then another. Bats wheeled and drove through the evening sky, marauders after every flying insect. Mosquitoes buzzed in Hester's ears. She slapped at them, then drew her hair across her ears to keep them away.

Exhaustion filled her mind and her body. Sleep overtook her, and she knew nothing more until the first light of dawn played across her brown face.

She scratched the red coals back to life, added dry twigs and small pieces of wood, then went to the river to wash.

The day was cool and fresh, the grasses hanging heavy with drew. Her bare feet were soaked by the time she reached the river. She stood on the bank of the slow-moving water, stretched her arms over her head, and caught the light of the sun's first rays, as tenderly warming as the heat from the fireplace on the winter mornings of her childhood.

She caught a fat, slow, brown carp beneath a tree root with her bare hands, a skill she'd developed along with her brothers. She cleaned the fish, grilled it fast over the hot fire, and ate all she could hold. The fish was not very tasty, but Hester knew beggars can't be choosers, as Annie would say. She did not know when she would eat well again. She considered spending the day catching fish and drying them, but then thought better of it. She needed to keep moving as fast as possible.

She continued along the riverbank until she found an area of the river that appeared shallow. She began to pick her way across, her bare feet feeling for rocks that were sharp or holes that appeared unexpectedly. There was nothing in her sack that could not get wet if she needed to swim, except for the volume of Indian medicines. She could not have it destroyed by water or stolen. Nor could she lose it. The book contained the only wisdom she could use to make her way in the world.

She would apprentice to a midwife. Or a doctor. She'd figure it out, once she had put enough distance between her and Hans Zug.

She reached the opposite side without mishap and kept moving straight up the mountain without looking back. She knew she would not find a cleared spot again like the one where she had spent the previous night. She had covered the area with grass and rocks so that every trace of the fire was gone. She had put the large piece of bark back on the tree. No one could tell that it had been pulled off and served as her cover. Even someone following her would not know.

A cold chill chased itself up her spine. She looked back over her shoulder. The morning light barely penetrated the covering of leaves, leaving the mountainside dark and wet with the night's dew. She glanced over her shoulder again. She stopped, caught her breath, then resumed climbing. Up, up, she went as the sun rose, too, heating the side of the mountain. Perspiration broke out on her forehead and trickled down her back, yet still she climbed, her steps long and even, her breathing hard but steady.

She looked down the way she had come. Why couldn't she shake the feeling of being followed? She stopped, turned slowly in a half-circle, and assessed her situation, trying to calm herself. There was nothing but rocks, trees, bushes, and the usual mountainous terrain. Nothing out of the ordinary. A blue jay called its raucous cry, but that did not necessarily mean anything. It was big and bold like blue jays are, leaders of the bird world, or as they imagine themselves to be, crying out about everything, even a big, green, walnut letting loose and crashing to the forest floor. She climbed on, then stopped to uncork the jug of water and swallowed large, thirsty gulps, before stopping herself.

Now on top of the mountain, she laid down her sack of belongings and looked for a tree with low branches. She swung herself up, hand over hand, pulling herself from branch to branch until she came close to its top. She had found a panoramic view of the river and could see down the way she had come. Perhaps this would take away her unsettled feeling. The sun was white hot, the air shimmering with heat and humidity. Falling away as far as she could see were tree-covered mountains and hills, like little bumps of green—the dark green of the pines, the lighter green of oak, maple, hickory, ash, and chestnut, the pale green of locust—all these millions of trees.

Hester had no idea how much a million was, or a thousand, for that matter, but she figured it would take an awfully long time to count them all.

Her eyes located the small clearing, the edge of the forest where she had slept. For a long moment she kept her eyes on that spot, never moving them. The grass was pale green, almost yellow. Along the edge of the sparkling brown river, the cattails were darker. Absolutely nothing appeared to be moving. She was probably too far away to tell.

She checked the branch below her, ready to descend, then looked one more time out over the trees below her. A part of the pale green grass had a dark spot. One she had not noticed earlier. A rock?

As she watched, the dark spot moved toward the river, then stopped. Hester knew it was not a black bear or a deer. It was a man. Who, she could not tell. Her eyes narrowed as she evaluated her situation. He may not be following her at all. He might just be a traveler, too, searching for a way across the river like she was. She had no reason to be alarmed.

She had a long running start away from him if he was following her. He'd have a hard time keeping her trail, as far upriver as she'd gone away from the shallow water. Confident now, she climbed slowly out of the tree, dropped to the ground, and landed squarely on her feet. She picked up her haversack and continued down the other side of the mountain.

By late afternoon, she was hot, tired, and hungry. She found two creek beds filled with rocks and small, yellow, locust leaves that drifted down from tired, dry trees. But not a drop of water. She drank sparingly, just enough to keep the misery of thirst at bay, and kept walking fast.

She picked her way among rocks now, coming to a hill covered with dead, fallen trees, where sharp limestone rocks were piled one on top of the other. The place appeared to be cursed, as if nothing green were blessed enough to grow there.

She stopped. The heat waved and shimmered, a thing alive, pressing down on her head and her lungs, burning her back with its power. Her whole body cried out for water. She uncorked the jug, took a swallow of the warm river water, then forced herself to put the cork back in its place.

Bent on all fours now, she crept along the rocks, her feet shaping themselves to the formations, her hands steadying her progress. When she came up over a rise, she gasped. So this is what happened. Lightning had struck, starting a fire. From blackened stumps and gray ash, tender green trees were emerging from the burned ground. The rocky area had stopped the raging fire.

Hester walked through the acres of destruction, wondering at the power of God, the way nature reinvented itself. She found a perfect pink rose growing on a vine that wound its way around a black tree stump. Stopping, she bent to pick it, held it to her nose, and inhaled deeply. This beauty among ashes. It was so lovely Hester could hardly bear the thought, the pink rose so alone, lighting the destroyed world with its presence.

She found a narrow cave beyond the burned area. She wanted to stay for the night, but there was no water, so she continued on her way with long, even strides that ate up the ground. She followed the side of a ridge, then turned downward, hoping to find a creek or a spring—just a trickle of water. She thought of Hans's springhouse, the cool, wet interior that housed the cold, creamy milk, mint tea, ginger beer. She had to find water.

She calculated the distance she'd come. Probably ten miles since morning, but that was only a guess. She hoped she had traveled far enough that anyone who searched for her had given up.

The light faded now. She lifted her face to look at the sky and saw black clouds rolling and tumbling. The wind rustled the leaves above her head.

Hester did not try to find shelter. She sat beneath a sparse old tree and lifted her face to the glorious, wind-driven, pelting raindrops. The flashes of lightning and ear-splitting claps of thunder evoked no fear in her. She cupped her hands and caught the pure, clean water, licking it up like a dying animal.

She winced when hail bounced off her head, then covered herself as best she could with the coarse haversack. On her hands and knees, she raked crazily at the small bits of ice, stuffing them into her mouth and chewing them to pieces. She could not get enough. Shivering, she kept swallowing, opening her mouth to the driving rain that followed the hailstorm.

The trees bent and swayed. Lightning flashed in jagged streaks across the sky, followed immediately by loud claps of rolling thunder. Not once was she afraid. This was the way it was. Nature punched and bounced itself around upstairs, throwing lightning down with fiery swords. But in all that clatter, the gift of rain followed, saving withering fields of corn, assuring anxious house-wives another chance at preserving enough vegetables for the coming winter.

Her thirst slaked now, Hester remained beneath the aging tree. She thought of looking for a sapling so she could strip the bark and gnaw the tender inside lining like a rabbit, but she was afraid her stomach would rebel because it was so empty. The last thing she needed was to get sick.

She was cold, shivering, and so hungry she decided to eat a whole strip of the jerky. She had to keep moving. The storm was a big help, the way it would wash away her tracks, but she could not relax or become sloppy or inattentive.

She filled the crockery jug full of water from the tumbling little brook that appeared in the crevice between two steep banks. Heartened, she walked swiftly along the dripping forest, thunder grumbling in the distance.

The land was leveling out now, becoming almost flat. She climbed another tree and was amazed to see a large clearing just ahead of her. Would there be people living close by? Her steps increased then, until she was panting a little, so eager was she to see what was in the clearing. A house? A town?

She ran shaking fingers through her long, unkempt hair. She looked down at her torn skirt, the blackened front of her shortgown, and decided to change into her clean one. Raking her hair back from her face, she snapped a piece of string from the ball in her haversack, then tied it securely. Washed clean by the rain, Hester decided she was presentable, just in case she did stumble onto another person. Or people.

She walked eagerly now, realizing the happiness she would feel in meeting anyone—a family, perhaps, or a couple alone. She traveled the entire length of the clearing, her head swiveling, searching, without seeing one building or a small soul. Well, so be it then. She'd likely find a spot to spend the night, then kill a small animal for her supper. She was not thirsty, she was reasonably clean, and she still possessed enough strength to care for herself.

She'd start a fire, although that thought gave her a scare, but only as long as she let it. The man by the river was very likely uninterested or unaware of her presence. Probably both.

In the shelter of the trees, she repeated the previous night's ritual, although this supper was even tastier. The clearing popped with healthy, brown rabbits barely smart enough to hop away at the sight of her. She ate the succulent, browned meat, made a mild, tasteless tea with catnip from the meadow, then fell into an uncomfortable, restless sleep. The ground was wet and dripping. Her only cover was the sodden haversack and her soiled shortgown.

During the night, every fox and coyote in the mountains must have come down to the clearing to hunt rabbits. The yipping and barking and squealing were enough to wake the soundest sleeper. Finally, wet, uncomfortable, and chilled, Hester got up, poked the coals of her fire to a small flicker, then set the crockery jug on a hot stone to heat the catnip tea.

Sitting cross-legged, she lifted her face to view the vast panorama of stars in the night sky that was washed clean by the afternoon's hailstorm. Every one of those stars looked as if they had had their faces scrubbed, they were so bright and shining.

Alone in the vast universe without the base creature comforts she had always taken for granted, Hester sensed a wild elation growing in her chest. Her senses were freed like an eagle in flight, and her spirits soared. Ah, yes. "They that wait upon the Lord shall renew their strength; they shall rise up as eagles."

"Here I am, God. Please look after me. Amen." One star blinked, smiled, and bowed to her.

CHAPTER 3

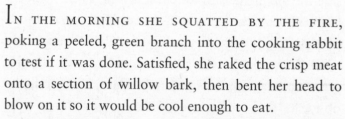

IN THE MORNING SHE SQUATTED BY THE FIRE, poking a peeled, green branch into the cooking rabbit to test if it was done. Satisfied, she raked the crisp meat onto a section of willow bark, then bent her head to blow on it so it would be cool enough to eat.

Ravenous, she ate in great, tearing gulps, her strong, white teeth ripping the meat away from the bones. It was good even without salt. She tested the wild artichokes roasting in the fire, rolling them gingerly before popping a section into her mouth.

After she had eaten, she packed the haversack, set it aside, then kicked dirt on the fire, replacing the natural order of growing grasses as best she could. She lifted her face to the sun and walked toward it. East. Always east.

In long, loping strides, she covered the clearing and entered the surrounding forest. Her strength bolstered by the rabbit cooked over the fire, she was tireless. The air was crisp and clean without the pressing humidity.

The day passed the way the previous two had. She climbed ridges, then slid down the opposite side, hunger and thirst her only company. She found pokeberries, wild leeks, and a few tart strawberries that made her mouth pucker. Later on, a stomachache forced her to sit beneath a tree to rest. The wild creatures watched her approach, then slid noiselessly into the underbrush and behind fallen logs.

The sun had already dropped behind the high mountain ahead of her, the shadows lengthening to create a long twilight on the west side of the mountain. As usual, she was thirsty. She knew the best place to find water was at the base of the mountain, so she'd stay on this side for the night. She searched as long as the light befriended her, then stopped in defeat. Well, she'd survive till morning. If there was no water, she'd just rest for the night. Her stomach felt as if it would cave in, shutting off her airways with its deflating. There was nothing to do for it.

She did find a patch of liverwort. She knew the flat-leafed herb grew only in moist places, so she bent her back and spread her fingers through the crumpled edges of the leaves. The earth beneath the herb was damp, but not wet. She looked for a sturdy green branch, shaved the tip to a digging tool, then walked downwind to a place where the slope fell into a crevice.

Here she began to dig, repeatedly inserting her hand to feel for moisture. Her tongue clung to the roof of her mouth, her head buzzed with fatigue. When blisters formed on her palms, she pitched the pointed stick angrily to the ground and flopped down on the forest floor. But she did not give into the weakness of women. She did not cry. She merely gave up, fixed a bed of leaves, and dropped off into a fitful sleep. The sliver of moon that rose above the trees gave no light. It just hung in the sky above the endless green of the forest, a slice of peace and tranquility, a small thing of beauty, completely unnoticed by the sleeping Hester.

Another morning brought thirst like cotton fibers in her mouth. She thought of digging deeper, then looked at the angry red spots on her hands where the water-filled blisters had popped, leaving the tender skin exposed and burning.

The sun already dappled the way as she hauled the haversack on to her shoulder and set out. She would not attempt this mountain, even if it was a low one. She would walk north until she found water.

She tried not to think of water. Or tea, or any cold, frosty drink from the springhouse. She swallowed, then swallowed again. She coughed, a dry, rasping sound that surprised her.

When she broke out of the forest to a clearing lush with yellow tangled grasses, raspberry bushes, thorny wild roses, burdock, thistle, and locust seedlings, she stopped, sniffing the air warily. This field may have been tilled at one time.

She remembered Theodore Crane, the schoolmaster, telling her how the land reclaimed itself after settlers moved on. One of the most invasive plants were wild rosebushes, their roots multiplying underneath the thick, unkempt grasses. They and the locust seedlings.

Warily now, her thirst forgotten, her large, dark eyes roved the clearing, searching for buildings, piles of stone, split rail fences, any sign of human dwellings.

She stood as still as a stone. Nothing moved except the strands of loose hair that straggled across her forehead and the black eyes beneath them. She sniffed, then turned her head to sniff once more. Yes. Unsurprised, she caught the faint smell of woodsmoke. Turning back the way she had come, she glided noiselessly to the safety of the trees.

She'd skirt the clearing, remaining hidden. She would watch. She moved stealthily now, bent forward, dashing from tree to tree, lifting her head to breathe deeply. Ah, yes. The smell of smoke. She was surprised at the sharp sensation of homesickness. She smelled the smoke that had curled down from the stone chimney even in summer, when the cooking and baking needed to be done.

How her stepmother grumbled on humid mornings when the smoke hung over her laundry, infusing the spotless, sweet-smelling linens with its earthy scent. She conjured up the thought of breakfast cooked in cast iron kettles over the fire—fried corn meal mush with dried beef, plenty of eggs, and thick slices of good bread spread with churned butter. And all the water she could drink in the redware tumblers.

She felt lightheaded now. The forest spun, tilted to the right, then at a crazy angle to the left before righting itself, allowing her to keep moving. The smell of smoke was sharp and suddenly acrid. She froze when the deep baying of a hound dog began. Another voice chimed in. The high-pitched wail ended on a much higher note, stopped, then began all over again.

Hester's eyes searched for low branches. She found some pines, swung herself up into the lowest one, and climbed rapidly, her bare feet curling around the scaley extension, the pine tar harsh to her nose.

When the hounds' baying increased to a frenzy, she peered beneath the bough of the great evergreen to find the source of the woodsmoke far below to her left. A small gray house built of logs, with a weathered roof made of split shingles and covered in heavy green moss on the north side, stood at the edge of the clearing. Like a humble, squat soldier, it presided over the tangle of weeds and brush that covered the clearing. There were no out buildings, no barn.

The house had a porch on the gabled end to the north, where the cool shade of summer provided a place of comfort away from the blazing sun. A small section of the porch contained an uneven pile of firewood, stacked, but not efficiently. A stump in the yard hosted an axe sunk into its top, along with various articles that didn't appear useful.

She spied the hounds. Skinny, ungainly creatures, their bawling mouths wide, their lolling tongues waggling as they howled, their noses turned in her direction.

A door slapped open, then shut. A stout man appeared, but he was too far away to determine his age or the color of his clothing. He yelled something unintelligible and the hounds slunk away, their tails curled beneath them, cowering.

Hester remained in the tree as the man went back into the house, slamming the door shut behind him. She weighed her options. Her thirst became the deciding factor. She would ask for a drink, ask to have her jug filled, then move on fast. She'd risk being attacked by the hounds.

She lowered herself, branch by branch, until her feet hit the soft bed of pine needles. Shrugging her shoulders, she adjusted the haversack and stepped out of the forest, thirst taking the place of common sense.

As she had hoped, the shrill baying of the dogs brought the man to the door immediately, yelling orders in a language Hester did not understand. As before, the dogs slunk away, lowered their bellies, and crept beneath the porch. Startled, the man watched her coming across the edge of the clearing. He waited, a thick hand on the rough post supporting the roof of the porch.

A few bare spots held back the soiled tufts of grass among the rusted junk and various tools that spoke of times when someone tilled the soil. A few bones, lengths of string, pieces of bark, and clumps of dirt, rocks, and leaves littered the area surrounding the cabin. As she drew closer, she saw the man's beard was flecked with gray, the mustache drooping above it gray as well, yellowed, and uncut. His hair was long and tied back with a thong of rawhide, his clothes of undetermined origin, color, or cleanliness. Hester guessed his age to be around fifty, perhaps close to the age of her father.

Her words were a croak, unable to be understood. Hester tried to clear her throat but was unsuccessful. She stopped and pointed to her dry mouth, her pride pushing back the desperation she felt.

"Wal, wal."

The man's eyes were kindly, crinkled in a weather-beaten face. Eagerly, Hester watched him turn, go into the cabin, then emerge with a large metal dipper with a long curved handle, precious water dripping from it like diamonds. Muttering like a person gone mad, Hester reached for it, lifted it to her lips, and drank sparingly before lowering it.

His eyes approved, then he spoke to her in a foreign tongue. Hester did not reply. She lifted the dipper and swallowed once more.

"Where?" he asked.

She shrugged. He watched her savor a few more swallows, then turned and motioned her to follow. But she remained on the porch, standing uncertainly against the post, still cradling the dipper, greedily possessing it.

He came back out and offered her a crust of dark bread and a piece of soft cheese. His hands were darkened by hard work or soil, the nails black around the outer edges. A sour smell, an aura of soiled clothes and unwashed skin, surrounded her, making her shrink away, her eyes lowered.

"Don't be afraid." His words were halting and heavily accented.

When Hester lifted her eyes and saw his kindness, his will to please, she reached out and took the food from him. She gulped the coarse, nutty-flavored bread, washing it down with insatiable gulps of water that ran down the sides of her chin. She ate the soft cheese that tasted a bit moldy.

She handed the water dipper back to him and he refilled it, watching as she slurped thirstily. He brought more bread and cheese, which she ate ravenously.

She would not sit down or enter his house. In halting English, she told him she must move on. She had learned to speak it in school, but her time there had been so short and often sporadic, so that she had to concentrate to come up with the right word.

"Where you going?"

"I don't know."

364 Which Way Home?

"Why?"

She shrugged.

He invited her to stay. He said he would not harm her. She did not believe him. She stepped off the porch and bent to pickup her haversack, meaning to be on her way.

His voice behind her stopped her. "You need water. I will give you more bread."

She turned, hesitant.

"Come."

She followed him inside. At first, the dim light disoriented her, but she soon made out the shape of the fireplace, a table and chair, a bed in the corner, unmade. The logs inside were brown, not gray or weather-beaten like the outside. There were mounted deer antlers, skins stretched from peg to peg, and a shelf containing dishes and heavy pans. A few rumpled cloths covered with dirt lay in front of the fireplace.

Hester smelled the aroma of cooking and saw the black pot above the red coals. Her mouth watered. She watched the man warily, unable to scale the wall of suspicion. Mistrust left her pacing the room like a caged animal.

He brought a brown parcel and held it out to her, his eyes watching her face. "Take it."

She did, quickly, before he changed his mind. She turned to place it in her sack, then straightened, ready to go.

"You want soup?"

She nodded.

"Sit."

He hurried to draw up a chair, then cleared the bullets and skins away from her, leaving the table bare. Going to the fireplace, he ladled the thick, brown soup into a bowl, then placed it carefully on the wooden table. He brought a pewter spoon, as big as a tablespoon.

The soup was thick and rich, with a flavor she couldn't identify. She raised her eyebrows and pointed to the dish. "What is it?"

"Turtle."

Hester nodded. She had made soup from the gummy, white flesh of the snapping turtles from the pond in the lower field. It had to be boiled for hours, until the thick chunks turned into threads, then flavored with fresh herbs, carrots, and leeks. This was good. It filled Hester with strength, giving her a bright, new start, returning energy that had flagged to the point of exhaustion.

"Thank you," she said.

"More?"

She nodded gratefully.

He filled the bowl a second time. Smiling, she emptied it, then reached down to lift the haversack.

He stepped forward. "I want you to stay."

She shook her head. "I must go."

"Mountains all, if you go north."

She stopped, but kept her back turned.

"East, land will be flat. Towns. People. Lancaster."

She turned, despairing. "No. I don't want."

"Go north."

"No."

"West. No Lancaster."

She watched his face closely. She did not want to re-trace her footsteps. Neither did she want to be among her people, the Amish. It was unthinkable. They would not accept her, an Indian. She hesitated.

"Stay," he said.

She turned to watch his face. Still kind. Still open, honest, without cunning.

"You my daughter. I have one. She die. Wife die. In river when it is high."

"What river?"

"The Susquehanna."

"Am I close?"

He nodded.

Her mind worked fast. She would get to the river and away from the mountains. She would meet her people, the Lenape. They were by this river. She had to leave.

His sad eyes followed her for days. She could have stayed, but she knew it was unreasonable. How long would she remain his daughter? As long as Hans had her for his daughter?

There was no use courting temptation. She knew many lonely trappers, who, shunning society, took Indian women for their wives, but that was not for her. Maybe someday, if she lived, she would be glad to be a wife to one of these men, for she was nothing of value. Her skin was the brown color of the Lenape. That would never change. So she was close to Lancaster County and William King. How many ages ago had she harbored enough sense of well-being to imagine the handsome, dark-haired youth one day asking for her hand?

No, she would go to the Susquehanna, the river of her people. Determined, she turned south. She walked fast now. The land was flat with many creeks, some of them dry, but always there was another. The thirst she had experienced the first four days of her journey had not returned.

She kept walking south through forests and over small hills and ridges, but no tall mountains presented the endless challenge of finding water. For this she was grateful.

She fashioned a bow from the sturdy branch of a willow tree. She spent one whole day making arrows from sharp stones, twine, and straight, green branches which she peeled with a knife. She slung the bow across her back, carried the arrows, and resumed her journey.

Her eyes roamed the world around her, constantly searching for danger, watchful of small changes in the appearance of harmless trees and underbrush, observing clearings for any harm.

One day she noticed the first curling of the leaves. She felt the chill in the air at night. Locust leaves were beginning their dizzying spiral to the forest floor. Soon the large leaves of the oak and chestnut and maple would follow, turning the brown-hued forest into a world of vibrant color, the foliage taking on a blaze of glory before dying.

Winter would come riding in on the winds of hoarfrost and icicles, bitter elements she'd find hard to withstand alone. If she did not come upon her people by the Susquehanna and chose to reject Lancaster County altogether, would she be able to survive by herself? Adrenaline rushed through her veins. A greater challenge had never presented itself. Now it was served up on a platter of sheer fear. She shivered. She would need a shelter. She was hardly capable of building one alone.

And so she planned, her thoughts keeping her company as she traveled. She practiced her routine well. Evenings were filled with the chore of staying alive. She had become more experienced in starting fires. She learned to let the coals become hotter, without flames bursting from them, when she roasted animals. The meat was more edible and not as blackened and stringy.

She learned to roast wild yams, simply tossing them into the fire, then juggling them in her hands until they cooled. She gouged out the insides and ate them with crisp, wild garlic, sliced. She found chives and fennel and tucked them into her haversack so she could season roasted pheasant, whose meat she found fit for any dinner table.

When she came upon a wild crabapple tree, she wished for a pot to simmer the fruit in water, cooking it into applesauce. She thought that if she could find mallow, she would sweeten it. She had no pot, however, so she learned to eat what was possible and not wish for anything she could not have.

Sometimes she sang songs of the Amish church, the slow, mournful plainsong in German verse. Other times she merely walked, clicking off her strides in long sharp steps that ate up the ground.

She smelled change in the air. She smelled mud and the rolling brown water of the Susquehanna, she believed. Had she skirted Lancaster County entirely?

Excitement sluiced through her, tingling in her stomach. Would she find her people living in long, low houses covered in bark? She imagined the smell of cooking fires—and belonging to people of her same color.

Eagerly, she pressed on. Between the trees, she sensed movement now. Water? Her steps became soundless. She held her breath. Lowering her body, she peered from beneath a fir tree. Before her lay a sight she had never seen. A clearing so large she could not define the end of it. There was no river, no mud. Only the rattling of wheels as a team of four horses pulled a harrow, its teeth tearing up the moist, brown soil, preparing the land for a fall crop.

Hester lowered her head and laid her cheek on the floor of the forest, letting the rich, earthy scent comfort her as disappointment and exhaustion consumed her. She had stumbled directly into the settlement she was determined to avoid.

Mein Gott, she whispered. Now what? She would be mocked, turned away. Back in Berks County, life was far different. There, she had been accepted as a newborn, a crying foundling saved by the lonely, childless young woman who had been her mother. Could she stay here somehow? Perhaps she could, with her vast knowledge of herbal remedies and cures for sick people. Winter was coming on.

She watched the horses' heads bobbing up and down, their great hooves coming down, lifting up. She saw the farmer guiding the horses as they pulled the wooden plow through the ground, the iron piece cutting through the soil and releasing its rich, earthy smell. The ache of remembering was more than she could bear. She was a young girl again, her white cap strings waving delicately, her face lifted to the sun, her legs strong, her balance complete, as she stood on the plow, the smell of disturbed earth rich and sweet to her senses.

She wanted to retrace her steps and rid herself of the burden of survival, of making decisions on her own.

Would she be defeated if she returned? Could she speak to her stepmother, try to reason with her father?

Perhaps if her face was disfigured, or if she became handicapped, she would be safe. All she wanted was to live within the sturdy protection of the stone walls of the great house and eat the food that always appeared three times a day—a wonderful thing, until now never fully appreciated. And so she cowered behind the veil of the forest, homesickness, fear, and doubt her only companions.

Chapter 4

She retraced her steps, finally, sensing with certainty the one move that would prove to be futile. She would be Amish no more. The thought of approaching the man with the plow was terrifying. She knew he would see her as an Indian, not a member of his own plain sect.

She had debated within herself. The Pennsylvania Dutch she spoke might convince him, but if *he* did not accept her, there were hundreds more who would not. Outwardly they would perhaps say they did, but they would not with their hearts. They would warn their sons. The German heritage should stay pure.

So she slipped into the forest, her only home. She walked aimlessly now, without caring. The land was almost flat except for an occasional rise, a small slope, a hollow. The trees were sparse where logging trails crisscrossed through the bush. She smelled woodsmoke, spied gray, weathered buildings and soft yellow ones, where the lumber was so new it had not yet aged.

Dogs barked. The lowing of cattle sounded unexpectedly. She heard voices in the distance. She imagined she was making her way through Lancaster County and would soon reach the great river, the Susquehanna. When the heat of the afternoon waned, Hester knew she would have to exercise much better surveillance, now that she would spend the night so close to other human beings.

She heard the barking of a dog in the distance. Realizing this might be her biggest challenge yet, she zigzagged through the dense, green forest. She could make no cooking fire. She would conserve her energy and drink very little of the tepid water in her jug. Earlier than she normally did, she prepared a bed of leaves and moss behind a large, uprooted tree, where the residue of past years had blown beside it, leaving a comfortable place of rest.

A chipmunk streaked across the log, then turned to watch her with bright eyes, its tiny cheeks bulging with a cache of nuts, the fruits of its energetic foraging. A garter snake slithered soundlessly through the leaves, its small eyes alert, the wee tongue lashing out repeatedly. A bumblebee droned past, then came to rest on a white flower, the columbine that grew profusely in low areas.

Perhaps she could find a few berries, so she heaved herself to her feet and was off in search of anything to ease the emptiness in her stomach. She soon found it was too late in the season for berries of any kind, but she came upon a tangle of wild grapes. They were turning purple, although most were green. She would have been cautious, but her hunger was a driving force. She pulled the clusters from the sturdy vine and devoured them, her thirst and hunger both easing as the sour juices puckered her mouth.

Sometime during the night, Hester awoke, a fire in her stomach. She rolled onto her side, drew up her knees, and shivered with the cold and the clawing pains in her abdomen. Too late she realized her mistake.

She remained by the log all that night and into the next day until her body had rid itself of the unripe fruit. Twice she had fainted from the scourge of pain. She cried aloud for water, her body dehydrating as her stomach expelled its contents. She lay by the log, finally deciding she would probably die because she could not bear the pain. She was too weak to sit up. Too weak to travel in search of water.

In the afternoon, the pains subsided and she slept. Jolted awake, she struggled to sit up, alarmed. The forest floor spun crazily, tilting at impossible angles, but she stayed erect until the dizziness passed.

She pushed herself to her feet, then sagged against the log, finally willing herself to move. Stumbling through the forest, her thirst a clenching fright, she weaved from left to right, her dizziness directing her feet. Then she smelled water. She had reached the great river!

With her remaining strength, she surged forward, her tongue cleaving to the roof of her mouth. Again, like her hunger for the grapes, her thirst overrode the restraint she needed. Breaking through a line of trees, she came upon a meandering waterway, a wide, sleepy creek. On its banks, green willows, turning yellow with autumn's approach, swayed above the deep, grey current. Rocks jutted from shallow places where the cool water ran against them, rippled around the obstructions, and sang merrily on its way.

Hester slid down the bank, her foot collided with a rock, and she was thrown into the water like a fish. Uncaring, with her thirst taking away any sense of danger, she sat on the pebbly creek bottom, drinking and drinking, then becoming as sick as before, her stomach resisting the onslaught of cold water.

She did not smell the cooking fires or the dogs or see the longhouses. She simply lay on the banks of the creek, heaving, wet, and too sick to care. They took her haversack and burned the contents in their cooking fires—including her cherished volume of remedies from the ancient Lenape woman. She was too sick to save it. The fat women that found her by the creek trundled her wet, feverish form home to their settlement, washed her, and dressed her in a warm dress made of soft, pliant deerskin, with colorful beads woven into an intricate design all over it.

They washed her hair with the herbs and flowers that they grew, while gabbling and laughing. They shooed the men and children away when curiosity drove them into the longhouse where Hester lay, barely conscious. They gave her bitter medicines, and she slept so long she didn't know how many nights she lay in the hut, or how many days.

She dreamed of Kate, her mother, dressed in white. She dreamed of white, blinking stars and lovely pastures where Lissie and Barbara beckoned to her. She dreamed of Hans, strong and mighty, shouting at her. And always on the outskirts of her subconscious, in an area she could not quite penetrate, the voice of someone she had known, someone she recognized but could not remember.

When she awakened fully, it was nighttime. Hester lay on her side, able to look around with one eye. The beating of her heart in her chest was loud in her ears, like drums that came from within. She rolled on to her back and stared wildly at the ceiling. A roof. A low bed of coals in a hole in the ground. Muffled sounds of breathing. Dark shapes of various sizes. A smell. A scent of animals, food, earth, skins, an overwhelming odor of something she could not name.

Someone had rescued her. She ran her hands along her body, touching the foreign garment. Her fingers found the beadwork, felt the texture of the deerskin, and knew. She had the explanation for the smell, the bed of coals. She was with the Indians, her people.

Fear overrode every other emotion. Her people were talked about as savages. Uncivilized. Uncouth. She had not been raised the way they lived. She wanted Kate, her soft, clean touch. She wanted wooden floors, lye soap, hot water, clean bedding, scrubbing brushes, white laundry strung on lines, flapping in the breezes.

But she was here now. Here in this building constructed in the way of the Indians, her birthplace. Every terrifying bit of gossip filtered through her mind—the massacres, the scalpings, the Amish women's tongues wagging endlessly with gruesome tales of the savages.

Not here, though. Not in Lancaster County and the surrounding areas. William Penn had lived peacefully among them, trading woolen blankets for the precious wampum and teaching them to cook in heavy cast iron pots.

Hester relaxed, breathing in the scent of the skins beneath her. The heavy robe covering her could hardly have been from a deer, its bulk weighing her down like the good, warm sheep's wool of home. The skins had an earthy, dry, smell. Not rancid, but surprisingly pleasant.

She reached her left hand out, but drew it back in alarm. She was not on the ground. She sat up in the heavy blackness. Her eyes searched the interior of the dwelling, but all she could be sure of were the holes in the ground where red coals glowed softly, illuminating only a bit of the darkness around them.

So she was on a raised platform, higher than her bed at home, it seemed. She was aware of the company of sleeping people—deep breathing, an occasional snoring sound, a cough. Someone stirred. It seemed as if the movement came from above her, but she couldn't be sure. Darkness did that sometimes, turning the world every which way.

An animal snuffled from outside the wall to her right, then moved off into the night. A child whimpered and began to cry, but the sound faded away quickly, either because of its mother's care, or because it had gone back to sleep.

Hester rolled on her back, snuggled deeper into the skins that kept her warm, and tried to go back to sleep. But she was awake for hours, her thoughts tumbling endlessly as she wondered what she should do or where she should go. Perhaps she should stay with winter coming on. She could adapt, if they would receive her.

In the first gray light of morning, Hester awoke, her eyes wide. Directly above her was a row of saplings bound together with long ropes made of bark. Slowly, she turned her head to find that she was lying on a raised platform, lashed to the sturdy poles that supported the domed roof of the Indian dwelling, the longhouse.

She raised herself on one elbow, making no noise. What she saw was incredible. She had never been in a house this large with so much open space. First she saw the number of poles on both sides of the structure. They held sleeping platforms—one lower one and another above it—the entire length of the longhouse. Raised mounds of skins dotted these platforms where the Indians lay sleeping.

She supposed if there were no barn, no cows or sheep or pigs, there were no chores to do. So perhaps they all slept later than Hans or Annie did.

As the light became stronger, her eyes focused on many items strung from the poles of the platforms. Bows, quivers made of reeds or skins, baskets made of different materials, beads, gourds, cooking pots.

The floor below her was bare, yellowish-brown earth, dry and compacted by the many feet that walked over it.

Flat rectangular stones held stone bowls with heavy pestles. Bags of dried corn sat beside them. She had heard that corn was the staple of the Indian diet.

When a grunting sound came from close-by, Hester lay back down in a flash. Feet hit the ground and lumbered past. The hide by the doorway was pushed back and then flapped down with a soft swish as the footsteps faded away.

Another set of feet thumped the hard earth floor, followed by another. A low tone of voice reached her ears, but Hester did not understand anything that was said. The words were garbled, as if they were swallowed, the sound of syllables she had never known existed.

Cooking fires were stirred into flames as more of the Indians awakened. Some squatted by the fire; others went outside immediately. A baby's thin, high wail sounded through the gray light.

Should she get up? Offer to help? Her heart beat rapidly as the full knowledge of finding herself in this situation confronted her. She had no reason to believe they would hurt her, and no reason to think they wouldn't.

She was gathering courage to rise when she became aware of breathing directly beside her. Her eyes flew open. Two woman stood looking down at her. The fat one, her eyes glittering black in the folds of her dark face, her small mouth moving as the words tumbled from it, pulled the heavy robe off from her shoulders. Loud exclamations and finger pointing followed. The younger woman reached out to touch Hester's hair and her eyes, then tugged gently on her nose, her eyes revealing her intrigue.

Words tumbled over one another, every one as foreign as the next. A few children came to peer at Hester like bright-eyed mice, half hiding behind their mothers' skirts.

The fat woman began motioning with her hands. Hester understood that she wanted her to come, so she threw back the heavy robe, which she now saw was buffalo, swung her legs over the side, and stood on her feet. The longhouse tilted to one side and spun crazily, so she held on to the pole beside her until the dizziness passed.

The beckoning continued, so Hester followed both women to the deerskin flap hanging over the door, bending to follow them outside into the crisp, fall morning.

The longhouse was built close to the banks of a creek, a slowly moving one that wound among the willows, deep and clear and quiet.

The women motioned for her to follow until they stood on the creek's banks where the tall, green, willow branches swept the earth like giant dusters, swaying slowly in the shivery little breeze. Hester watched suspiciously as they urged her with their hands to bathe in the creek. The fat woman motioned to the east where the sun had already risen, then to Hester to remove her deerskin dress.

"No. No."

Hester shook her head, her arms wrapped tightly around her waist. She had never undressed for anyone to see. Once a month—more often in summer—she and her sisters and brothers had bathed discreetly one by one in the great agate tub behind a heavy blanket in the farm house, all using the same scalding hot water. They had always been taught that bodies were to be covered, from their necklines to the soles of their feet. It was shameful to see even a bare ankle exposed.

The fat woman's eyes glittered with anger. She spoke to the younger one, who made more motions for Hester to bathe in the creek, pointing to the sun.

Why the sun? Suddenly it dawned on Hester that they wanted her to bathe each morning. Surely not. She refused again, shaking her head with even more conviction.

With lightning speed, they reached for her in one motion, lifted her and swung her down the bank. Hester felt the rough scrape of the willows before the cold waters of the creek washed over her. She had never been under-water before. Creek water filled her nose and her mouth and poured down her throat. Instinctively, she flailed her legs and arms as she propelled herself to the surface, her mouth opening, gasping, and gurgling, before she felt herself slide under the water again.

There was a fire in her chest as her lungs strained for oxygen. The muddy water, churned up by her struggling, filled her nostrils. Again, she rose to the surface, desperately sucking in air, only to choke and gag on the creek water.

She had heard about going under a third time, heard enough about people drowning. She lunged once more, kicking out with her feet, her arms slapping at the water that threatened her life.

One toe hit a stone. She threw herself in the direction of it, found a toehold, and then another. Gasping, with water streaming from her nose and mouth, she lifted her face above the surface of the water, grabbed the life-saving branches of the willow tree, and hung on with an iron grip.

But when she floundered up the wet, slippery bank and heard the women's raucous laugh like mocking crows, anger consumed her. She had almost drowned in that cold creek, and there they were, slapping their knees, bent over with the force of their scornful laughter.

Lowering her head, with her breath coming in short forceful bursts, Hester threw herself, catching the fat woman by surprise. A powerful cuff sent her wobbling sideways down the slippery bank and into the creek. The younger woman was prepared, but Hester grabbed her by her shoulders, easily overpowered her, then rolled her down the muddy bank after the other one.

She stood, breathing hard, her feet planted apart, feeling more alive than she ever had. Perhaps it was the near-drowning, perhaps it was fear, but she shivered with her newfound power. All of her life someone had ruled over her, bent her will to their own, including her brothers, Noah and Isaac. Once, when they had fought to gather the most walnuts, Hester had gotten angry. She kicked Noah's bucket over, scattering all the walnuts into the tall grass. He had wrestled her to the ground, held her hands behind her back, and cuffed a sound blow to her shoulder. She bit his hand. Surprised, he yelped, then looked at her as she raised herself from the ground, her eyes flashing dark fire.

In his eyes was an expression close to pride, or was it admiration? It was a new light. He had walked away, and things were never the same between them after that. It was as if he practiced the Amish way of shunning her, then, which often bound her to a great and stifling sorrow.

Now she watched as the two women sliced expertly through the water like large, dark fish, scrambled out, and came steadily toward her. Hester stood firm, her hands curled into fists, ready to roll them down the bank another time. But they were laughing. They punched her arms playfully, flexed their own muscles, stroked her hair, and made a fuss about her face, her strength, lowering and raising their eyebrows as they garbled away in the foreign tongue.

They took her into the longhouse, dried her, and then threw woolen blankets about her shoulders. They cooked corn cakes on a thick, flat stone and brought her meaty stew, steaming hot, in a maize-colored gourd. They hung around as she searched for a spoon or a fork, all the while making motions for her to eat.

Gingerly, with one thumb and forefinger, she fished out a portion of dark meat, her fingers burning. Quickly, she deposited it into her mouth, her lips an O, as she breathed in and out to cool it. She nodded, smiled, and licked her fingers, which brought a happy shout from the women.

The meat was rich and salty. Eagerly, she grabbed another chunk, cooled it, and chewed hungrily. The corn cake tasted like unsalted mush, which it was, she reasoned. She dipped it into the stew, which brought more happy shouts of approval.

She guessed she was a hero now, or a princess, the way the children adored her, touching her face and her arms like inquisitive little chipmunks, and every bit as cute.

A bright-eyed papoose hung from its cradleboard securely fastened to the supporting pole along the bunks. Hester wanted to free him from the confines of the leather rope that bound him to the flat board so she could cuddle and hold him the way she had held Kate's babies. She knew it was the Indian way to keep them confined till they were seven or eight months old.

The men came into the longhouse, their height and powerful builds frightening. She had never seen a man without a shirt, so she kept her eyes downcast to the earth floor. A conversation ensued, the fat woman flapping her hands, pointing, and finally laughing. Bright, flat eyes focused on her.

She could not know how perfectly beautiful she appeared in the half-light of the longhouse. More than one of the men watched her, already planning a marriage ceremony in their hearts. One of the older ones could speak passable English. He squatted by her side. She turned her eyes to him, finding his black eyes expressionless, his nose hawkish, his black hair greased and tied back with braided thongs of rawhide. She did not look at his bare shoulders or his chest, it was too shameful.

"I Naw-A-Te."

Hester nodded, then said, quietly, "Hester Zug."

"You come?" He waved his arm, questioning her whereabouts.

"Berks County Amish settlement."

He lowered his fine eyebrows and closed his eyes as if trying to remember, then nodded slowly. "You live here with us? No?"

Hester kept her eyes lowered, shrugging her shoulders.

"We are the Conestoga. The last of the red man in Lancaster. All our brothers have gone west." He threw his arm disdainfully in that direction, as if the west was a loathsome destination.

"We stay. Conestoga our water. We are here. Mine."

Hester nodded. She understood his need to portray the ownership of this allotted space. She knew the Indians were constantly driven west as settlers poured into this region of Lancaster.

In the waning autumn, Hester stayed with the Conestoga Indians on the banks of the sleepy creek named for them. The days were golden and filled with light, the dusty air alive with the sounds of rasping black crickets.

Brown grasshoppers catapulted themselves from the tall grasses as her feet approached.

She helped harvest the Three Sisters—corn, beans, and squash—in the vast garden. She loved the work, falling easily into the steady rhythm of the season, reminding her of harvest at home on the farm.

She became accustomed to her early-morning bath in the cold waters of the Conestoga. It was such a new and unusual ritual, but now one she relished, submerging herself in the invigorating waters before starting her day. She found the term "*dreckichy* Indians" to be quite untrue. They were not unclean, the way she had believed them to be. In fact, the infrequent bathing done in Amish homes was likely less clean, in spite of the Indians' earthen floor and the skins.

She learned to scrape and dry buffalo, deer, and mountain lion skins. At first she had found it a revolting chore—the stench overpowering—but she kept on scraping with a flat, sharp piece of limestone and eventually, got used to the smell.

The wild animals sustained the tribe. They were their clothing, their food, their tools. The large shoulder blade of the buffalo was lashed to a straight branch with willow bark, which functioned as a sturdy shovel, turning soil in the garden. The smaller shoulder bone of the deer was turned into a hoe in much the same way.

Hester marveled at the ingenuity of these people. And when the golden days of autumn turned into the bitter winds of November, she was grateful for the shelter of the longhouse.

CHAPTER 5

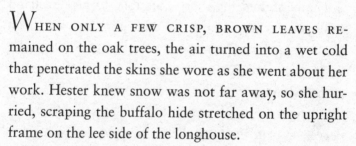

WHEN ONLY A FEW CRISP, BROWN LEAVES RE-
mained on the oak trees, the air turned into a wet cold
that penetrated the skins she wore as she went about her
work. Hester knew snow was not far away, so she hurried, scraping the buffalo hide stretched on the upright
frame on the lee side of the longhouse.

The men had been on a successful hunt, ensuring food
for the coming winter months. A celebration of dancing
and eating had followed, the children alive with renewed
energy and joy, waving the bean-filled gourds gleefully.

Now the women must hustle. The snows were hovering over them, spurring them into action, or at least
those who were willing to perform their assigned duty.

The fat woman was named Clover, in English. They
all had Indian names in three syllables. When Hester
couldn't pronounce some of them, Naw-A-Te gave her
their English names.

A young woman named Beaver, who Hester imagined
to be about her own age, did not enjoy work of any kind,
wandering off or shirking her duties whenever she could.

Today Beaver was cold, cross, and lazier than usual. She cowered beneath two woolen blankets, her teeth chattering, her eyes boldly challenging the older women to do something about her lack of working.

Soon jabbering arose. Clover walked over, carrying her large, round form like a barrel on her stocky legs, her face like a thundercloud. When she lowered her face directly in front of Beaver, a tirade followed, finished by a smart thump on the side of her head. Beaver fell sideways, sent up a heart-rending yowl, and then became silent.

Hester shifted the sharp limestone to her left hand and kept on scraping the white membranes away from the buffalo skin. She glanced sideways at Beaver, who lay perfectly still. After a while, Hester could see she was sound asleep.

A younger woman, named Otter Run, came over to Beaver, crouched in front of her, then put the back of her hand to Beaver's forehead. She jumped back and began an excited tirade of words to Clover, who immediately laid her palm on Beaver's cheek. "I, yi, yi, yi, yi!" she yipped shrilly.

Together, they bundled Beaver off into the longhouse, put her to bed, and returned to the chore that needed to be finished before the snow began to come from the east, driven hard by the first icy blast of winter.

Clover did everything she could, but Beaver became deathly ill, her fever spiking in the evening until she writhed and gabbled, pointing to the hallucinations that tormented her. They covered her with heavy woolen coverlets they had received from the settlers, traded with the precious wampum, and still her teeth chattered from the cold. Sometimes she flung the covers from her miserable body until she shivered from the cold yet again.

Hester desperately longed for her book of Indian remedies. She could see these Conestogas did not have the knowledge and wisdom of the old Indian woman of the forest in Berks County. They danced around Beaver and shook various rattles and gourds to drive away evil spirits. They concocted many different herbs with vegetables and meat dishes and brewed teas, but nothing seemed to help.

They allowed Hester to try plasters made from onion, mustard, and wild garlic, which seemed to soothe her rasping cough. When angry red pustules appeared on Beaver's feverish skin, Hester knew what was wrong but kept the knowledge to herself. When the pustules turned yellow with pus, she bathed the thin form with a mixture of warm water and soothing spearmint.

Hester lay awake when the young child Corn Mouse came down with the same symptoms. She had to do something. She rose from her sleeping bunk and woke Naw-A-Te by shaking his heavy body relentlessly. He followed her past the sleeping tribe, through the flap of deerskin that served as a door.

The thin layer of snow dusted the earth the way Kate used to dust her cakes with granulated sugar. A sliver of white moon hung in the cold, black sky, surrounded by the blinking stars of early winter. Hester's breath was a white vapor as she spoke. "Naw-A-Te, you must bring a doctor. The little one has the same disease as Beaver. It is smallpox. They will die."

For a long time, Naw-A-Te remained as still as stone, his face shadowed by the night and the waning moon. Straight and tall, unhurried, he stood. Finally he spoke. "When all else fails, we go back to the Creator. We return to the earth from which we were made." He remained standing, his face in the shadows.

A thin wisp of woodsmoke curled from the hole in the rounded roof of the longhouse. Across the frosty lowland, a screech owl sent out its high rattling sound. It was answered by another.

Hester spoke. "I have heard of the smallpox. Indians die. It is given to them from the white people."

Again, Naw-A-Te remained mute. Hester watched his face. When he spoke, his voice was rough. "Which is worse? To die from the sickness, or to be driven from our land by the white people? The time is coming."

Hester spread her hands. "But you have to do something. Many will die," Hester cried. "They will die soon."

Naw-A-Te grabbed her shoulders roughly. The move was so sudden, his fingers digging into her arms so powerfully, she gasped and turned her face away, thinking he meant harm to her.

Slowly, his grip lessened, becoming tender. The tall Indian gently drew her against him. Hester heard the beating of his great, stout heart beneath her cheek. The deerskin he was wearing was soft and pliant. She was strangely moved by this gesture. She felt bound to him by a kinship, a bloodline that spoke the same language.

"It is well. It is good you are here."

Hester stayed very still.

"We are the few ones. They will not let us live. Soon they will kill us. Or drive us away."

Hester drew back. "But you don't know!" she cried. "I know. My heart knows."

Sadness so thick it choked her crept into her soul, and she bent her head and wept. She cried for the Indians, for their ways that would eventually be lost. She cried for the unfairness of life itself. A small part of her railed against God for allowing these two cultures to meet in this blessed, rich land, completely unable to exist side by side.

The white man's goals were the opposite of the red man's—to clear the forest, cultivate the land, grow in knowledge, invent new things, while constantly moving forward for wealth and earthly gain.

The Indians were content to roam the forest, holding the trees and animals sacred, believing that they were given to them by the Creator. They did not understand the passion for wealth and power, the greed to own land. They fanned their fires with the wing of a wild turkey for hundreds of years. They grew corn, beans, and squash, content with the earth's gifts. If a week or a month went by in sunshine, and the grass grew brown with drought, they watered the corn, but made no effort to innovate or change the course of nature. For it was inseparable from the Creator.

When Naw-A-Te spoke softly, Hester listened. "You come to us with your beauty. You will live. The Creator has made you. The white man nurtured you as a small baby. Now he has a plan for you." Hester stayed very still.

They returned to the longhouse and their own bunks, each falling asleep, comforted in the still, frosty night.

Hester tended to the sick all that winter. Beaver died late one night with Hester holding her thin, cold hand.

The ceremony for the dead was performed, a foreign thing, the spirits and animals conveying Beaver's spirit to the Creator. Many of the children became ill. Mothers squabbled, the tension thick and filled with static.

A storm blew in from the northeast. Naw-A-Te held up one hand with three fingers spread out, showing there would be three months of snow. The young braves hunted on snowshoes to replenish the meat supply, dragging in thin, starved deer. But there was plenty of dried corn and beans, dried fish, and berries.

Often Hester walked along the Conestoga Creek, her legs encased in heavy leggings, her skirt sweeping over the snow. She filled her lungs with the fresh, cold air, watched the cardinals and chickadees flit from the snow-laden bushes and trees, and saw fish lying silent and dormant beneath the ice.

She remembered skating on the creek in Berks County, sliding around with boundless energy after being cooped up in the stone house too long. She scooped up a handful of snow and tossed it into the air, remembering snow fights with Noah and Isaac. Lissie was too young to do much harm, but like a buzzing fly, could become bothersome, sometimes having to be dealt with by a good face-washing with snow.

Would she ever be able to return to her childhood home? Would she ever have a home of her own? Two of the young Conestoga men had asked for a marriage ceremony, but so far, she hadn't been able to bring herself to accept this strange way of life.

In her own mind and heart, she wanted a husband, her own man, to love and to cherish, but she'd come to accept the fact that this wasn't possible for her among the Amish in Berks County. Here with the Conestoga, it was possible, but her whole being shrank from it. The communal living, the sleeping arrangement, the sharing of life with so many was not the way she imagined her future. And yet, what other choice did she have?

The snow drifted down through the tree branches as the wind moved them back and forth. Little gray birds flitted from one snowy branch to another, their busy little chirps lifting her spirits. She watched a brown rabbit strip the bark from a green sapling that was almost covered with deep, powdery snow. The rabbit eagerly chewed the tree's soft inner lining.

She was hungry, her stomach hollow and empty, but the corn and beans were rationed now. Naw-A-Te had spoken the evening before, saying the worst storms were still to come.

Sighing, she stopped, breathed deeply, then turned to go back the way she had come. She walked slowly now, her legs pushing the snow away with a soft sh-sh-sh, the cold finally penetrating her feet. She did not exactly want to return to the smoky interior of the longhouse, but she had nowhere else to go.

Lifting the deerskin flap, she went inside, her eyes adjusting to the gray half-light, the pungent smoke of the cooking fires. She sat cross-legged, watching Clover string beads on a sinew, then took up the dried reeds herself and began to weave a basket the way Clover had taught her.

The little ones were coughing. In a corner, Running Bear worked on his arrows, precisely carving another sharp head. He looked up, his piercing black eyes in his ruddy face boring into hers. Quickly she looked away and began weaving faster, the reeds moving through her fingers smoothly.

She felt him beside her before she actually saw him. He nodded to her to follow him outside.

Hester shook her head. He frowned and refused to move. He picked up the basket she was working on and moved it aside. She watched as his hand came down to take hers. He pulled gently. She looked up at him, his dark, dark eyes beckoning to her. How long could she keep saying no?

From the opposite wall, Clover looked up and giggled, holding her hand to her wide mouth. Soon enough, Hester would be prepared to become Running Bear's wife. Soon she would begin the wedding dress.

When the Chinook woke Hester one mild night, she felt a joy in her heart again, a sensation she could barely recall, a forgotten illusion. Had she ever been happy?

She would have to leave or marry Running Bear. The decision was hers, but she knew it had already been made. It would not be long now. After the scourge of smallpox, there were only seventeen remaining. The children slipped away, one after another, except for four of them.

Death among the Indians was understood the way other hazards and unfortunate happenings of nature were accepted. There was a sadness, but a soft, gentle receiving of what the Creator had done, an uncomplaining yielding of something they had once possessed.

Hester had cried for Beaver, but alone, in the privacy of her bunk. She was in awe of the loving acceptance she witnessed, so completely in tune with the Creator. Death was a passing, a turning of the wheel.

So many things among these people were good, but so many things were wrong. In the spring, when the thaw came, she would slip away. She would survive. She had done it before.

The snow melted into the earth, turning the banks of the Conestoga into a quagmire. The interior of the long-house was dense with the lingering smoke of cooking fires.

Running Bear killed an elk, a huge antlered animal that had miraculously survived the deep snows. The people ate ravenously, tearing at the stringy meat like dogs and gnashing their teeth as grease dripped from their chins and fingers, staining their shirt fronts. They leaped and danced. Running Bear fell into a stupor, his head lolling like a broken doll.

Hester was seized with horror when the chanting began. Would this mean she would be given to him, the brave hunter? Her breath came in quick gasps. She looked around wildly. Darkness had fallen, which meant she could slip away unseen. A great cry rose from the feasting when Naw-A-Te stood, holding up both arms and calling for silence.

Hester did not wait. Slowly, as if she wanted to step outside for only a short time, she moved toward the door while every eye was stayed on Naw-A-Te and his upcoming announcement. Silently, like the smoke that disappeared through the hole in the roof, she slipped through the deerskin. Her heart racing, she stayed just out of sight, straining to hear what the eldest among them would say.

There was the distant sound of drumming. Had they already begun their celebration? No. Naw-A-Te was speaking. Distracted by the sounds in the distance, she could not hear his words.

She slipped to the ground and pressed her ear to the wet earth. The unmistakable sound of hoofbeats shook the ground. The full realization of the oncoming riders hit her like a sledgehammer. With a small cry, she raised her head, then sprang to her feet with another. Running at full speed, she immediately disappeared into the evening light as a posse of men from the town of Lancaster bore down on the lone Indian village.

They waved torches in orange flashes of destruction. Hoarse, hate-filled cries carried through the wet woodland by the creek.

Hester ran, zigzagging among the trees, finally hitting one with her bent knee. Pain exploded through her head as she fell to the ground. She heard the cries of the men, and then the hopeless wails of the Indian women. The torches had already lit the longhouse, an eerie orange glow placing each tree in silhouette.

Hester clung to a tree, her knee a throbbing appendage now. She must run. She must. The baying of a hound dog behind her sent her into a mindless dash. She felt no pain from her knee as she crashed through underbrush, weaving in and out of trees. The toe of her moccasin caught on a grapevine, and she was flung to the ground. Her head snapped back with the impact. She bit down on her tongue, tasting blood.

The hound gave its eerie, high-pitched howl, sending chills of fear up her arms. Through the dark, behind her, she heard more than one dog coming. She'd never get away.

The night was filled with orange light as the long-house went up in a roaring inferno, and the cries of the Indians mixed with those of the men who took them captive.

Hester looked back once, then turned sharply to the left. She slid down the muddy bank of the Conestoga Creek, lifting the branches above her head before succumbing to the mind-numbing cold of the snow-fed waters. She could not stay in water this cold. She would freeze. But she dared not get out, either. The dogs would lead the posse to her.

After a while her legs became numb, completely without feeling. When wave after wave of drowsiness overtook her, she knew she would freeze, so she had to take her chances with the dogs. The instant she dragged herself out of the frigid water, she knew she'd made a mistake. The baying began immediately, rising to a high pitch she could only describe as horrible. She ran on legs she did not know were there. Her only goal was to widen the distance between her and the dogs.

On they came. To the right now. She veered left. She became aware of thundering hooves and waving red torches bearing down on her. Still, she continued running.

The torches illuminated a pile of blackened brush. Bending low, she dived straight for the tangle of branches and weeds, then lay flat on the ground, panting, as the dogs and riders closed in. She kicked with all her strength, as the skinny, spotted dogs pushed their snouts through any available opening.

The horses slid to a stop. She smelled sweat and leather, heard the horses' nostrils quivering as their breaths came rapidly. Men dismounted. They flailed the bushes with their rifles, calling out to one another, their voices high with excitement. "Got 'em! Got 'em!" one man kept yelling in a strained, whining tone.

Hester stayed where she was, alternately kicking the dogs' noses and slapping at their jaws. She put up such a fierce fight that it took two men to drag her from her hiding place. One dropped his torch, which sizzled out in the cold, wet earth when she bit down on a hairy hand as hard as she could, sinking her teeth into the fleshy thumb.

Its owner howled a high-pitched screech of pain and anger. Hester felt an explosion of pain in her head as the man brought down the butt of his rifle, and mercifully, darkness took the world away.

Billy Ferree was nosing around the livery stable on Water Street in the town of Lancaster, much too late at night for a schoolboy to be out and about. He found out most of what was going on when the men came out of Carpenter Tavern and tried to hitch their horses to their buggies, which sometimes they did successfully and sometimes they didn't. When they had had too much brown ale, Billy offered his services. He had already squirreled away a plentiful stash of coins in the wooden box beneath his bed.

Tonight, though, he'd hid. That bunch of Indian killers coming through the door was enough to make him pop off and jump into the grain bin. He saw them dump a sack behind the bin where the straw was kept. Billy figured like as not, it was a dead Indian, which gave him the woolies.

He'd heard they were gonna get rid of Indiantown, the last of the Conestoga Indians' villages. Too many of the townspeople did not want them red men skulking about. Harmless, they were, in Billy's opinion, but then an eleven-year-old boy with a thatch of carroty hair couldn't go up against town council.

He waited. Some of the oats in the bin had gotten between his shirttail and his trousers, itching him terrible. He figured he'd better not scratch till that gang was gone.

Slowly, he raised his head above the top of the bin. His gray felt hat drooped and hung in all the wrong directions, the holes in the crown sprouting red hair. Beneath the floppy brim, his blue eyes rolled to either side of the stable before he slowly pulled himself up. He scratched heartily, then sucked in his stomach and shook both knees back and forth to rid himself of the stray oats.

He thought he'd better check on that sack of Indian. Looking back over his shoulder, he tiptoed softly to the spot he reckoned they'd dumped it. He didn't want to be too loud in the presence of the dead. He reached up and took off his hat, letting his red hair fall loose. It went every which way, as long as it was and uncombed.

Cautiously, with thumb and forefinger, he drew back the sacking. Oops. Feet. Wrong end. Softly, he tiptoed to the opposite end and pulled aside the sacking. He bent down to peer very closely in the weak, flickering light from the oil lantern swinging from the beams.

He whistled, a soft whoosh of astonishment. Boy, oh boy. This was no ordinary one. Had to be a girl. She was still as death, so he guessed she was gone.

He kept looking though. Just looking and looking, and thinking what a waste of life. A girl this pretty. A huge dark blue bruise. They'd walloped her good.

When a soft moaning sound reached his ears, he jumped so hard his teeth whacked against one another. He bent his ear to the girl's chest and heard the steady thud-thud of the faint heartbeat. Well, this was one for Ma, no doubt. If he could get her out of here, leastways.

CHAPTER 6

THE SOFT MOANING SOUND WAS FOLLOWED BY another. The head turned a wee bit to right. Straw was getting stuck in her hair, so he brushed it off with his dirty little fingers. He'd run home and get the wagon if she woke up. In the middle of the night, no one would know, and if they did catch sight of him, they'd think he was hauling feed for the horse.

She turned her head, getting more straw in the heavy wet tresses. Billy brushed it away, tenderly. He talked to her then. He told her she should try to wake up if she could 'cause his ma could watch out for her real good. Her name was Emma, Emma Ferree. She was a widow. Enos Ferree died from the lung fever. Now Emma took in any weak or poor or starving person, but she'd never taken a dead one yet, so far as he knew, so she better wake up.

When her eyelids fluttered, he stayed right where he was and kept on talking. When she looked out from be-tween those black eyelashes and groaned, he lowered his face and asked her to repeat that sentence, please, that he hadn't rightly heard just what she meant.

He kept on, patiently trying to bring her to consciousness, but in the end, he decided to run the whole way home for the *seck veggley* (sack wagon). When he got back, he stopped at the tavern door and pounded on it with his fists until the black cleaning man came to the door, his eyes rolling up white into his head, he was so scared. "Come and see this awful-lookin' girl that got dumped in the alley," he begged him.

He obliged Billy, but could only assure him that no, she weren't dead, at least not yet. He said, "Laws, Laws, Laws a mercy," over and over so many times that Billy didn't know why he was calling on the law now. It wouldn't help much, seein' as she probably wouldn't be living till morning.

Billy trundled off down the deserted street with his burden covered in sacking, his step jaunty. But he was a frightened boy whose heart was knocking against his rib cage like a pigeon that wanted out.

Billy lived in a group of houses called Lancaster Townstead, located about a mile from the Conestoga Creek. James Hamilton, a socially prominent lawyer, laid out the plans for the town. Local folks thought Hamilton was foolish, planning the town so far away from the Conestoga Creek with no other good waterway. It was hilly and hampered, too, by the large Dark Hazel Swamp. Mostly German people lived there, and in time they overcame the less than friendly environment, creating businesses, and putting up row after row of wooden houses along the streets.

These Pennsylvania Dutchmen from Germany claimed that they didn't understand the fee the township required for them to live there. So they left their rents unpaid, their stoic, unchangeable ways driving the property owners to distraction. They said they'd paid enough rent the day they occupied their lots and refused to pay more. They were required to build a substantial house within a year, made of wood, with a good chimney, among other requirements.

Hamilton reasoned that if he kept out unskilled lower classes, the town would prosper with merchants, builders, and other professionals. Lancaster Townstead became a thriving community in the mid 1700s, with well-laid-out streets lined with lots and houses built to accommodate the mostly German population.

Emma Ferree's ancestors may have been French, but she'd say she was as "Dutch as they come" and proud of it. She was an extremely short, portly woman, her small feet propelling her stocky legs through the rooms of her house in a floating motion, her wide, gathered skirts brushing her scoured oak floors, her dark hair tucked beneath the white *haus frau* (housewife) cap she always wore. Her eyes were mostly hidden beneath puffs of flesh resembling good bread dough, but her bright, glinty gaze missed nothing, her eyes darting back and forth, often filling with quick tears of sympathy.

Beneath her homespun housedress, behind the row of fashionable buttons, her heart beat quick and sure, burdened only with the unfortunate circumstances of her people, which meant every person she encountered. She took in the sick, the beggarly, the cold, and the hungry.

She handed coins to the poor and ladled out her thick bean soup to anyone who was in the need of sustenance.

That was the main objective in her life, now that Enos was gone, may he rest in peace, she always said. For Enos had been a good man, following the plow and working the land until his knees wouldn't take it anymore. Emma persuaded him to purchase a lot in the town of Lancaster, and he set up a successful peddling business, buying cheese and butter from the country folk, then distributing them to the townspeople.

Oh, she missed Enos terrible, so she did, but she stayed busy and kept her grief at bay. Billy was not hers, he was *aw gnomma*. She never could bring herself to part with the three-year-old waif with the flaming red hair. A young Scottish girl, her husband killed on the front line of the never ceasing French and Indian War, with three little ones, two of them younger than Billy, and no way to support herself, had lived with Emma until she ran off with a British huckster, taking the two youngest and leaving Billy.

That was all right with Billy, who stuck to Emma like a small burr from the day she'd wrapped her soft, warm arms around him and kissed the top of his dirty red hair. He had been much like a bad case of lice to his tall, skinny mother, driving her to madness with his antics, his red hair, and his temper. All he knew from his mother was constant scolding, followed by stinging slaps across his face or shoulders or backside. He attached himself to Emma, and that was that. He never missed his mum, called Emma "Ma," and went right ahead with his life as if nothing out of the ordinary had ever occurred.

From the tavern, Billy pulled the wagon through the wide tracks made by horses' hooves and carriage wheels. The night was damp and cold, the light gray from the few sputtering gas lamps on iron posts. The snow hampered his progress, but he persevered, both hands curled around the iron handle of the wagon, his sack-covered burden lying perfectly still, a bag of feed by all appearances.

He was slogging his way up Water Street, then he'd turn left on Orange Street and right on Mulberry to the second house on the left. He leaned forward, his gray, felt hat pulled down to the tops of his eyes and over his large ears, his red hair bouncing with each tug.

The streets were quiet at this hour. The houses lined the streets like strict Quakers, tall and dark and silent, not even one welcoming orange glow from a black, rectangular window. That was all right with Billy. Coming home past midnight with a sack of feed might raise a few questions, as if he'd stolen it from the livery. The only thing that kept Billy on the straight and narrow (which was wider for him than for some) was the thought of being clamped in those formidable stocks on the square in front of the County Courthouse, where thieves and pickpockets, liars and frauds were stuck for days, while jesting onlookers made fun of them or threw tomatoes or eggs at them. Billy was afraid if that happened to him, and he couldn't get out to avenge himself, he'd explode from his fiery temper. So he better watch out, he reasoned.

He stopped the wagon by the front doorstep, dropped the handle, and pounded on the door with his fists. He waited, then pounded again, harder, looking over his shoulder. When the door creaked open and his ma peered around the flickering yellow light from the candle flame, he was weak with relief.

"Ma. I got us someone needs help."

"*Ach, du lieva. Grund a velt*!" As usual, Emma exclaimed in Dutch, set the candle down on the half-round, wooden stand in the hallway just behind the heavy oak door, and lumbered down the stone steps to peer beneath the sack on the *seck veggley*.

"*Mein Gott in Himmel*, Billy, now what have you got? A dead one, sure. An Indian. Oh, *mein Himmlischer Vater, ich bitte dichi, hilf mir*." She was half praying, half crying, and her ever-present tears were already pooling in the soft folds beneath her eyes. She stroked the black hair and lifted the white face for further observation beneath the weak light of the gas streetlamp.

"*Ein maedle, Ein shoe maedle. Oh, du yay. Du yay.*" She wrung her hands, helpless in the rush of love and pity that consumed her.

"Ma, you need to shut up now," Billy said, not unkindly, but looking furtively over his shoulder, feeling keenly the possibility of being stuck tightly in those wooden stocks.

Emma hoisted the girl's shoulders in her capable hands as Billy lifted her feet. Grunting and exclaiming, Emma's breath coming in short puffs of steam in the gray, damp night, they hoisted the girl up the steps and into the candlelit hallway of the house.

Carefully, they lowered her onto the multicolored rag rug. Emma straightened, her chest heaving beneath the yoke of her linen nightgown, one plump hand going to her breast as if to control the thumping of her heart.

Emma whisked the sack away and rolled it into a ball, the dust from the feed wafting to the floor. She'd deal with that later.

Billy held up the candle as Emma bent over the cold, inert form clad in deerskin. Her hands and feet were blue with cold; blood had congealed and dried on her legs and hands. Billy was used to seeing injuries and starved folks, but he'd never seen a mess like this. The girl had been pretty, but the one side of her forehead was bulging with a huge blue-black bruise, oozing blood, the texture like sausage. Her eyes were hidden behind the gross swelling, her nose widened with the fluid that seeped from her injury. Her lips were chapped and bleeding, although much of the blood had dried black.

"*Ach, mein Herr Jesus, Du Komm.*" Praying now, Emma felt the need of her *Gott*. Hardly ever did she feel in need, as she capably tackled ministering to the wounded just as she handled the rest of her life.

Tenderly, she used her fingers to examine the wound and feel the cold limbs. They traveled over the young woman's body, searching for more injuries, broken bones, open wounds. Clucking her tongue against the roof of her mouth with small sounds of sympathy, she finished her inspection, straightened, and began to bark orders.

She lit two lamps in the kitchen. Then she stirred up the fire in the fireplace, added a hefty, split log, and swung the black, cast iron kettle over the fresh flames. She moved rapidly with single-minded purpose to the sitting room, there lifting the heavy, warm coverlets.

Then she was back in the kitchen, yellow with lamplight and the flickering flames beneath the pot of hot water. She spread the coverlets by the fire, then together they laid the girl on the soft warmth, so gently, so carefully. Billy put a down pillow beneath her head, and Emma drew up the heaviest coverlet to her chin.

While the young woman slept, they poured warm water into a crockery bowl, shaved lye soap into it, then dabbed at her wounds. Billy silently took a homespun cloth, patted the scratches on her feet and legs with it, then applied the comfrey leaves from the warm water in another bowl.

They worked together efficiently. They'd done this many times. When the wounds were sufficiently cleaned they applied bandages. Emma administered the smelling salts, wafting them back and forth beneath the girl's nose. When she did not stir, Emma bent to lay an ear on her chest, nodded, and kept waving the evil-smelling salts. Shaking her head, she sat back.

"She gonna make it?" Billy asked, his eyebrows raised.

"We should get her awake." Grimly she shook the thin shoulders, but her head wobbled back and forth on the pillow like a rag doll. This was beyond Emma's knowledge. She looked at Billy and then at the door, as if she were trying to decide.

Finally she went to the tall cupboard by the opposite wall, took down a redware bowl of tea leaves, placed them in two cups, then dipped boiling water from the pot over the fire with a long-handled copper ladle. She poured some water in each cup, then handed one to Billy who took it silently, wrapping his cold fingers around the heavy mug. He lifted the jar off the white cone of sugar, but Emma was too fast for him as she reached for the shears and clipped off a chunk of the expensive sugar. Her German frugality allowed her only a small snip for herself and a small one for Billy.

"Ma, that ain't enough for half a cup."

"*Ich glaub. Ich glaub.*"

Billy had to be satisfied with the hot semisweet tea, but was heartened when Emma set a cloth-covered bowl of biscuits and a small crock of jam beside him.

"So no, Billy. *Sage mihr.*" In fluent German, Billy told his story, relating his forays into the livery down by the tavern. Emma shook her head with consternation, blaming herself. She was far too easy on the boy. He should be at home in bed, not allowed to tramp about the streets, and certainly not near the tavern. But she knew about his stash of coins, knew, too, that he would aid her work in helping the poor, so how could it be so bad? That Billy had a head on his shoulders, so he did. He always had. The way his mother batted him around, it's a wonder he had a grain of sense.

She looked down at the bruised, sleeping girl, then to Billy as if he could help her make a decision. She spread her third biscuit with *hulla chelly* and licked her fingers well, the sweet preserves sustaining her flagging spirits. "Billy, *voss sagsht?*"

Billy shrugged as he looked down at the girl.

The lamps burned steadily, a waste of expensive oil. Heaving herself to her feet, Emma lowered her face and pursed her round lips, giving a hefty, whistling blow, extinguishing the lights.

"Let's try and get some rest, Billy. I'll check on her every hour, all right?"

The heat and the scalding hot tea were making him drowsy, so he nodded. Lifting the mug, he emptied it, placed it back on the table, and went upstairs to bed, unbuttoning his knee breeches as he went.

It was the pain in her hands and feet that woke her. At first she was aware of a ripping, tearing sensation, an awful thing she could not overcome. She moaned and turned her head, but an explosion of pain stopped her from doing anything. When she went to lift her hands to her head, giant pincers of pain gripped every finger. She tried to cry out, but found she had no voice.

She held very still, as wave after wave of tingling pain coursed through her feet and up her legs. She shivered with cold. She could not remember anything and had no idea where she was. She was terrified, suspended between a place she could not remember and a void she could not grasp. She had no focus and no sight, only the clawing, ripping pain in her feet and hands.

Slowly, she became aware of a persistent yellow light, a flickering through the blackness of her torment. She would open her eyes. It took all the strength she had, like lifting two huge stones.

The pain in her head exploded into something so white and hot she could not tolerate it. She whispered, then moaned. She tried again to open her eyes. This time, before the pain overtook her, she saw the source of the flickering yellow light. A fire.

She receded into unconsciousness, a blessed place of knowing, of feeling nothing at all until the painful sensation in her feet brought her unwillingly to the frightening knowledge that she was alive. All she knew was that she was somewhere between certainty and a vast area she knew nothing about, as if she were hurtling through a dark tunnel without end.

With her entire being and the full strength of her will, she tried to focus, to find a foothold somewhere. Painful as it was, she lifted both eyelids, willing herself to find an object, something nearby that would help her make sense of this unbearable hurting in her feet and hands.

A fireplace. A floor. Relief flowed through her veins. A floor. A wooden floor. She knew what that was. She knew the fire. A wetness ran down the sides of her face and she knew why. She knew she was crying. She knew her name now. Hester Zug.

When the rustling of skirts came near, she closed her eyes. When she heard the voice of someone saying words in German, she wondered if she was at home in the large stone house in Berks County with Hans and Annie. She wanted to see Lissie and Daniel and all the little children. She wanted to talk to Noah and Isaac the way she always had before they shunned her. *Ach! Ach, du lieva,* the crooning continued, mixed with prayers and pleadings, all in the Pennsylvania Dutch Hester knew so well.

She tried to tell this person about her pain. Her mouth opened, then closed and opened again, but she could not speak. She felt tender hands and willed them to her feet.

A squawk of recognition sounded from the region of her worst pain, now. *"My grund! Die fees. See Fa-fieer."* Over and over, she heard the exclamations about her feet being frozen. Then a slap, and the loud voice of the speaker berating herself. *"Dumkopf, Vot a dumkopf!"*

Steps retreated hastily, a loud, urgent calling ensued, and then another person joined the Pennsylvania Dutch–speaking woman. Together, they placed her hands and feet in cold water. The pain worsened, and Hester cried out, then bore it uncomplaining. She knew about frozen toes and fingers, and so she allowed the work that Emma and Billy were doing.

They gave her a shot of Enos's home-brewed whiskey or tried to, but with Hester unable to swallow, they wiped away the dribble from her chin, and what fell on the pillowcase, and gave up.

Her feet were still frozen but tingling with a milder sensation. And when the morning light shone through the windowpanes, Hester was able to focus her eyes, despite her swollen eyelids.

She saw a strange, round woman, wearing the English cap favored by the non-Amish. She saw a boy with riotous, long hair the color of fire and copper. She saw a kitchen, a fireplace, a cupboard and plank table. She could read a few words of a stitched sampler on the wall.

She remembered God, the hand that delivered her to this house. She thanked him softly.

They brought warm water now, further decreasing the pain in her thawing limbs. She tried to let them know how she longed for water to drink. They brought a bowl with a rag and let her suck it greedily for the cool water. As she swallowed, she choked and coughed, grimacing from the pain in her head. But her thirst was so strong she continued to work her throat muscles, finally receiving life-giving water into her body.

She told them her name in halting whispers. She learned theirs—Emma and Billy Ferree. These weren't

Amish names. Or Indian. Hester was confused. The woman spoke Dutch. Why was she not Amish?

It took far too much effort to ask, so she closed her eyes and slept. She slept for days, waking only to drink water.

It was early one afternoon when she finally awoke, her senses clear, her mind refreshed. She still lay on the oak floor, in the kitchen by the fire.

When Emma found her awake, she threw her hands in the air and yelled for Billy, who, she'd forgotten, had gone to school. "*Guten morgen, guten morgen!*" Emma kept repeating. Then she proceeded to heat water, thinking she could finally get this poor, striking girl out of that Indian dress made of deerskin. She could just picture the lice and fleas that must be crawling all over Enos's mother's best sheep coverlet.

When Hester tried to sit up, she couldn't make it the whole way, lying back down twice before she could stay erect. The pounding in her head increased each time, but she remained sitting upright, propped by the pillows Emma placed against the back of a chair.

Emma washed her hair when Hester felt up to it, gently but thoroughly, and more than once. She bathed her like a small child, dressed her wounds, and put her in a heavy linen nightshirt that had been Enos's. She put his woolen socks on her feet and made a warm, honey-sweetened porridge with milk, feeding it to her by the spoonful and talking the entire time.

When Billy came home from school about two hours late, she scolded like a hen whose eggs had been snatched from beneath her. But Billy didn't seem bothered by it, merely eating a slice of bread, tearing off the crust, and watching Hester, curiosity plastered all over his face.

"Hester. Hester Zug," Emma said. "Amish settlers in Berks County found her, an Indian baby at the spring close to the log house where they lived."

Billy's eyes lit up, recognition shining from their depth. "You're like me!"

Hester smiled, a small widening of her mouth that caused her eyes and nose to feel stretched, it had been so long since they had been exercised in this way.

"Your second mom better than the first?"

Hester shook her head.

"Well, you ain't got a thing to worry about no more. Ma's the bestest there ever was."

Hester watched Billy's face, his natural kindness as beautiful as a wild rose or a sunset, a reflection of the good in humankind. But she wondered what Theodore Crane, the schoolmaster, would say, if he heard that grammar.

CHAPTER 7

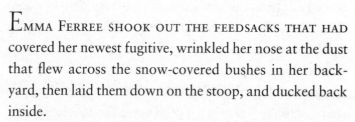

EMMA FERREE SHOOK OUT THE FEEDSACKS THAT HAD covered her newest fugitive, wrinkled her nose at the dust that flew across the snow-covered bushes in her backyard, then laid them down on the stoop, and ducked back inside.

It was cold, too cold to hang out clothes, but the sun was bright, the air was fresh, and she wanted to wash those union suits, both hers and Billy's. When long underwear got to itching, it was time to wash it.

She filled the gray wooden tubs, shaved lye soap into one, dumped in a pile of light-colored things, and began to stir with a well-worn wooden stick, swirling the thick, heavy undergarments around and around. The small room off the kitchen was thick with steam as she took up the wooden washboard and began to rub, her upper arms flapping in time to the furious scrubbing she gave the items she was washing.

Why, she'd sat beside Rhoda Denlinger down at the church house on Sunday and endured all that itching in silence, until she declared there must be insects in unreachable areas of her outerwear, as well her as underwear. She was in so much misery during the service she hardly heard a word the minister said, and all that week it seemed as if her soul needed food, which she couldn't find just by reading her Bible.

It was the way John Evans spoke, so true, so pleading. It just filled her soul with grace. And now she'd have to go hungry all week, where spiritual food was concerned, all on account of her insect-infected clothes.

She wrung the cumbersome garments with hands turned red from the hot water, then wrapped up in a too-small shawl, tied on the *vesh pettsa sock*, threw a heavy scarf across her head, took up the basket of washing, and ventured briskly into the frigid morning.

She shook out Billy's union suit and had just pegged it firmly to the line when a deep voice shouted her name. That dreaded voice was the very reason she didn't wash her long underwear more often.

Turning calmly, she answered in what she hoped was a level voice, her mouth flat, her face expressionless. "Why, Walter Trout." She didn't say it with a twinge of welcome or excitement, not even a smidgen of gladness. She meant to convey just a simple recognition, albeit grudgingly — as, Oh, there you are, and I wish you weren't.

"G' day to ya, Emma! Wonderful morning! Wonderful!" The beaming man on the opposite side of the fence could only be described as vast. His face was wide and florid, alive with color and good humor, his shoulders, back, and stomach twice the size of any other man. He wore no coat or hat. His pink head was circled with a

U of gray hair, as if a squirrel had taken up permanent residence around his noggin.

Emma was in no mood to take his sugary description of this frigid winter morning, when she was just about to hang up her undergarment shift which he could easily examine. So she turned her back, bent and picked up the basket, and returned to her washing, slamming the door unnecessarily.

Nosy, overfed man. If he'd stop eating all that tripe and liverwurst. Well, she was not hanging out her shift. She'd dry it inside. It dripped all over the clean floor, so she waited till he had himself back inside, then scuttled out the back door, her head lowered. She looked neither left or right as she brought the wooden clothespins down hard on the offending garment now hanging on the washline.

She had just reached down to retrieve a petticoat when a stentorian voice made her jump all over. She nearly dropped the garment, took a deep breath, and turned. Her supply of good Christian patience was awfully low, the way she'd missed most of John Evans's sermon, but being the kindly person she was, she said smoothly, "Why yes, Walter?"

"So, then, neighbor. Had a bit of a goings-on the other night, heh?"

"I don't know what you're talking about."

"Billy had a load of something or other on the sack wagon."

"Oh, that. Yes, yes, that."

"What was that?"

"Oh, that. Well, yes, it was that."

"What was it?"

"Well, don't you know what a sack wagon's for?"

Oh, he hadn't meant to offend her. Of course, a sack wagon was for hauling sacks. He thought that's what it looked like. He smiled widely, and the squirrel around his head moved upward a few inches, making Emma shiver, it looked so real.

He hung his florid face above the fence, like a red full moon, she thought grimly, and told her she had nothing to fear, he understood if she hauled things in her sack wagon that were not sacks. Then he giggled in the most obnoxious manner. Emma gave him a stare that surpassed the frigid morning air and said if it was all right with him, she'd be pleased if he stayed to his own business, thank you.

She went back inside with what she hoped was a courteous, regal walk. But Walter Trout saw the hat she was wearing backward, the hairpins hanging dangerously close to leaving her head altogether, then saw her near-slip on the icy doorstep. A resounding laugh came from way down in his rotund belly as he shook his head from side to side, thinking of the delightful Emma Ferree.

Hester was surprised to find Emma's angelic demeanor changed into one of red-faced fury when she finished the washing. Did she dislike that chore so thoroughly? Hester decided to offer to do the washing. She had always loved it, even in winter when her fingers became so cold she had to blow on them.

Emma hung up the clothespin sack, clapped her hands a few times, then ladled hot water into a mug, added tea leaves, cut a large square of molasses cake, and chewed methodically.

Hester sat by the fire in a worn rocking chair lined with coverlets. The bruise was not large, her dark eyes no longer slits in the purplish swelling, although she still faintly resembled a burst piece of fruit, in Billy's words. She watched Emma in silence.

Suddenly Emma burst out, "Some days I long for the farm. The idea of being townspeople may have appealed to me at one time, but this thing of hanging out my shifts for the nosy next door neighbor to see just *gricked my gase!*"

It hurt Hester's head to laugh, but she had to, the body-shaking sound rolling out of her before she could stop it. "Oh, that felt good to laugh," she said, breathlessly. "Kate used to say something 'got her goat'!"

Emma nodded, then reached for the pewter knife, measured another large square of the sweet, brown cake, and plopped it happily on her plate. "Tell me about Kate. Tell me about Berks County. Have you ever been to Philadelphia?"

Hester talked, slowly at first, then faster, as if she wanted Emma to see the woods and the stone house, Kate and the sweet babies that arrived so soon after they found her as a tiny newborn. She told her about Kate's dying, the ensuing misery when she was replaced by the hawkish Annie, how Noah and Isaac shunned her, and the reason she left, leaving her fate in God's hands. The reason she left, she said, was Annie's mistreatment of her. She never mentioned Hans.

Why? It made her head hurt to think about Hans, for she still wrestled with self-blame. He had been good to her. He had provided a home, shelter, food, a way of life. It was Hans who showed her the discipline of the Amish, the way of the cross. Could she always blame her leaving on him alone? Some things were best left unsaid. The whole thing made her tired, made her head ache.

Emma watched the battered Hester gimlet-eyed, missing very little. Who was this girl? What was behind the sadness in her swollen black eyes?

The good food Emma placed on the plank table nurtured Hester's body and spirit in the winter days after their talk. Billy came and went the way a ray of sunshine slips between puffy, gray clouds, illuminating a room with its brilliance. His red hair waved and straggled about his head like copper-colored flames. His blue eyes shone with mischief, curiosity, and an appetite for life that only small boys possessed.

He often wolfed down his evening meal, then roamed the streets of Lancaster Town, as he called it, claiming ownership to far more than he could in reality. He was the bearer of news, gossip, truth, and untruths. He soaked up tidbits like a dry sponge, then poured it forth at every evening meal, the only meal they ate together.

Tonight, Emma had made *Hootsla*, a quick, filling dish that Hester had never tried. Emma had cut stale bread into cubes, toasted them in butter in a heavy skillet, then poured a mixture of beaten eggs and milk over top. She had also made *Schmierkase* from the whey stored in the cold cellar, a spreadable cheese Kate had sometimes made. Hester bent her head to her plate of nutritious food and ate every morsel.

Emma watched her with satisfaction, noticing the color of her dark skin as the bruises healed. She could see Hester's unusual beauty emerge, the fine contour of her high cheekbones becoming more prominent.

"Hey," Billy said.

Hester carefully spread the remaining cheese on a slice of bread before looking at Billy, who was energetically shoving a crust of bread along the rim of his plate, the way Hans had taught all the children at home.

"They're saying." He paused until Emma stopped chewing and gave him her full, undivided attention. "They're saying there's no Indian safe in the town of Lancaster. Nary a one."

Hester held very still, absorbing the words, fighting down the panic.

"You know they got only thirteen of them at the jail-house. They're saying some men from Harrisburg want rid of 'em. Just wanna bushwhack them out of Pennsylvania entirely."

Hester nodded. She understood Naw-A-Te's words now. She could still feel the frosty air and see the sickle moon of that haunted evening. Yes, her people were leaving. Had left. Or been killed. Well, they'd done plenty of killing themselves, the settlers' hearts quaking with terror as they heard tales of the marauding Indians on the western frontier. A heavy sadness followed these bits of news, darkening Hester's life like an angry black cloud that hid the sun's face, whenever the threat was mentioned.

"So, you better not go out till this thing blows over," Billy finished, sticking a knife into a quivering custard pie before jerking the handle up and down like a saw.

"Now watch it there, Billy." Emma looked up from her *Hootsla*, her eyebrows lowered as he maneuvered the shaking pie onto his plate. "You have half of a pie there."

"The other half is for you."

"Hester?"

Billy eyed her, then said she didn't eat pie, like as not.

Hester laughed, but the sound was hollow, a false tinkling sound like a distant cowbell that someone was shaking foolishly.

Her thoughts churned, disturbing the normal flow of her mind, wondering, watching Billy's young face. If she was not safe here with Emma, would she ever be safe anywhere? Or safe, perhaps, but unwanted?

A part of her wanted to rise from the table, gather a few belongings, and be on her way, but on her way to where? Back to Hans and Annie? The days stretched before her, dark and mysterious, swelling with gigantic questions, unanswered now.

She had one thing, and that was her faith. God would protect her, go with her. Hans had taught her this. The imperfect Hans. How could she believe a word he said after he betrayed her with his well hidden ardor? Could she continue to believe in a God presented by Hans?

Naw-A-Te was true. He was faithful. He could press her head against his chest, and she could hear the steady beating of his heart, and nothing seemed wrong. If Hans would have tried the same gesture, it would have been vile, revolting. Should she have stayed and married Running Bear? Wen-O-Ma? A visual image of his face, slick with grease, was as real and as repulsive as ever.

Emma Ferree finished her pie, sat back, and watched the display of emotions, fanned by her troubled thoughts. Well, if she had anything to say, this battered Indian girl would suffer no more if she could help it, and she fervently believed she could. A fierce, protective feeling welled in her chest. Hester had suffered enough.

Emma's eyes narrowed shrewdly as her brain churned with possibilities. She'd have to let go of her pride and have a talk with that fat Walter Trout. She would find a way.

Walter had just tucked into a delightful stack of buckwheat cakes soaked in butter and drizzled with maple syrup, a large white cloth stuck in his collar to protect his shirt, when there was a rapid knocking on his back door. Thinking how unusual that was, he became a bit hasty, heaving his oversize body from his kitchen chair so that he knocked over his coffee.

Letting it go, he clucked mournfully at his loss but hastened his bulk to the back door, pulling it open and waving an arm with a flourish when he saw who it was. Emma Ferree!

She brushed past him, saying pointedly, "Take your bib off."

He clawed at it hastily, the red of his face turning to an alarming shade of purple as he rolled the cloth between his fingers, unsure if he should tell her it was not a bib but a cloth napkin which the gentry always had at their disposal. What would a German know about napkins?

So he drew himself up to his full height of five feet and five inches and told Emma in clipped tones that it was not a bib but a napkin. She answered tartly that he could call it what he wanted but it was still a bib.

She walked into the kitchen ahead of him, eyed the stack of buckwheat cakes, and to her horror, her mouth began to water. She swallowed. She had never seen better-looking buckwheat cakes.

She pulled at the ladder-back chair. Instantly, Walter rushed to her side, pulled the chair out, and asked her to be seated, but found he could not push the chair at all after she was on it. He observed the ample pile of skirts on each side of the chair and pretended not to notice when she bumped the chair up to the table herself. "Now, then, Emma Ferree, could I interest you in some buckwheat cakes?"

Emma swallowed. My, from down here they looked even better. "Perhaps you could," she said pointedly, feigning disinterest. But when he served her a stack of three cakes dripping with butter and a coating of syrup, made her a cup of tea, and handed her a cloth napkin, she didn't have the slightest idea what to do with it and laid the thing beside her plate.

So that Emma wasn't as high up as she thought. But he enjoyed her obvious delight in the buckwheat cakes and didn't mind when she licked her fingers, then brought up a corner of her apron to wipe her mouth. Such rosy cheeks, so well rounded, he thought. What a healing of his sad heart for her to grace his table.

She asked the favor of him. Did he not own land outside the town? Down by the Amish somewhere? Near Coatesville?

Yes, yes, he did.

Was there a possibility that he could keep a secret, then?

Oh yes, yes, of course.

His head was shining in the morning sunlight, the reflection bouncing off the mirror hung by his wash bench, illuminating the skin to the highest sheen she had ever witnessed. The circle of gray hair looked thinner in the unforgiving light, not entirely like a squirrel, she thought. Perhaps just part of one.

"And on this land you own," Emma said, pursing her lips and drawing out her question, just enough to keep him on edge.

"Yes?" he asked, eager to help Emma accomplish her goals.

"There is a dwelling?"

"Yes. Oh, quite a presentable house. One built of log and bricks."

"And there is someone living there at present?"

"No. No. Jonas Fisher has inquired, but finds the rent too steep for his pocket."

"Well, then." And Emma launched into a vivid account of Hester's arrival, keeping Walter mesmerized, for he had truthfully never expected the sack wagon to hold anything quite that frightful. At worst, he'd imagined Billy to have pilfered some hay, which he figured only served that Simon down at the tavern right.

Emma wanted to move out there with Hester until these threats against the redskins died out. Billy would go with them, of course, and she'd school him at home. It was unthinkable for Hester to stay indoors in the town for such an extended period of time. When spring arrived, she would need fresh air and sunshine.

Oh, absolutely, Walter agreed over and over to Emma's plan, nodding his head so hard his chins wobbled and waggled as if they had entire lives of their own. Emma grabbed her own chin, tugged a few times before deciding, yes, definitely, she had only one.

When he walked with her to the back door, he briefly rested his hand on her back, which made her stiffen and lower her voice a few degrees in iciness, but he paid her no heed. She was very German, and he had his napkins, after all.

Hester was seated at the kitchen table, a small pile of rye straw in front of her. Emma noticed the new look of concentration, a purposeful demeanor, as she began the basket she would make.

"*Wunderbahr*!" Emma exclaimed, her spirits high, her cheeks flushed from the buckwheat cakes.

Hester smiled. "I learned from Clover and Beaver. You wait!"

Emma clapped her hands like a small overgrown child. "So exciting. Hester. Our house will be graced with your *kaevlin*!"

"You say *kaevlin* for 'baskets,' too?" she asked, her face alight with understanding.

Emma sat across from Hester, explaining her visit to her neighbor, then told her she had nothing to fear, that she would be taken care of, not just this day or even this winter, but always. She told her she would be the daughter she never had. Walter was willing to let them stay at his house, where she could roam the woods and adjoining fields among the Amish, who would never harm her. They could raise a sow, have a flock of chickens and a cow.

Hester's eyes glowed with happiness. She wiped her tears hurriedly and said she'd do her best to help make Emma's life easier.

Emma was so touched by Hester's declaration of loyalty that she patted her shoulder with her soft, puffy fingers and said she must never fear about the future from this day forward. She, Emma Ferree, would look out for her, same as Billy would, for as long as she needed their protection.

Over and over, she repeated herself, until Billy said he'd be the man of the house, but what was he going to do for excitement if they lived in the country? Without the tavern and the livery, and his band of friends to roam the streets, life was going to be dull beyond anything he could imagine.

Hester could easily explain the ways of the country. Water to haul, firewood to chop, animals to feed, garden to tend, the list went on and on.

Billy listened, his eyebrows drawn down as he thought about Hester's words. "Well, I know, but if *you* do all that work, there's not a whole lot left for me to do." Emma told him he needed his ears boxed.

Hester was happy to move to the country. She hoped her gardening skills were sufficient, as well as being able to keep house the way Emma required. The German Emma was always scouring floors, washing, and carefully smoothing out clothes and bedsheets, even linen towels and doilies, as if one speck of dirt would never be allowed to exist on anything washable.

Hester wove the rye straw expertly, drawing the rows tightly with strips of willow bark, a basket style whose origin was half-German and half-Indian. Emma was amazed. Billy fell silent, his bright eyes watching Hester's fingers like an observant hawk. Hester began to talk of her time with the Indians, about Naw-A-Te, Running Bear, Clover, and Beaver, the ways of the longhouse, their weapons and primitive tools. She spoke of her inability to stay, sometimes still not understanding the choice she had made.

Billy snorted. "Seems you didn't have much choice there toward the last."

Hester laughed easily, her eyes shining dark pools of appreciation. "No. No. I didn't."

"You were sorta dumped into the feedlot by the livery, and if I remember right, I found you, dead as a doornail."

Emma broke in, "Now, now, Billy she was alive."

"Barely."

Hester nodded, her face serious. "I would have died."

Billy told her if those men found her, he knew she'd been better off dead.

When a pounding on the front door exploded the homey atmosphere of the kitchen, they jumped, sat erect, then looked at one another with questions in their eyes, all fearfully recognizing that Hester might not be safe.

Emma was the first to think rationally. For someone of her size, she moved with lightning speed, opening the cellar door and beckoning Hester. "Into the potato bin. Cover yourself."

Hester knew she must obey. She asked no questions, merely slipped down the narrow, steep stairs backward, holding on to the railing on each side until her feet found the uneven, earthen floor. It was pitch black, but her hands fluttered in front of her until they found the stone walls, the shelves, the meat hanging on hooks. She stifled a cry as a large rodent scuttled across her woolen sock–clad feet.

CHAPTER 8

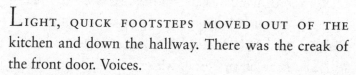

LIGHT, QUICK FOOTSTEPS MOVED OUT OF THE kitchen and down the hallway. There was the creak of the front door. Voices.

Hester moved blindly, her hands roaming the walls of the cellar.

Heavy footsteps, the solid clunking of big boots thundering down on the oak floor like an avalanche of boulders. Emma's voice.

Hester moved faster, her hands raking the wall. Where was the potato bin? It had to be here somewhere.

She heard the rough voices of men. She heard Emma say they could look all they wanted. She had seen no Indian running away.

She heard the steps of the men going upstairs. For one heart-stopping instant, she believed they were lowering themselves into the cellar. If they found her here, she had no way of escape.

The steps were muted, far away now. Hester imagined them upstairs, enormous, dark bodies, massive white faces outlined with black beards and filthy, smelly hats of fur and leather, glittering, greedy eyes, their single-minded goal to rid the town of Lancaster of the last of the redskins, the Conestogas.

Hester thought of the jailhouse, the hunger and filth she heard of there where she would be taken to join the small band of surviving Conestogas. When she heard the muted steps returning down the stairs, she moved frantically, the potato bin seeming completely unreachable. Surely it was along a wall. Perhaps not. She began swinging her arms wide, searching, when one hand slapped against rough lumber. Thank God.

With both hands, she found the square box. Bending over, she felt a large mound of potatoes. More loud footsteps sounded overhead. Her mind rushed faster. She had no time to cover herself with the small vegetables. It would take too long. Could she squeeze beneath the bin? She measured with her hands.

Emma was talking, talking, her words following a calm, relaxed march of ordinary words as she acted the part of a round little housewife, a *dumbkopf*, asking silly questions about the Indians that had nothing to do with this night or this mission.

Hester found enough space, she thought. Lowering herself, she flattened her body, wriggling and clawing with her hands. She felt the unhealed bruises on her head being squeezed. Dust and dirt slid past her cheek and filled her nose and mouth. Inch by inch, she pushed into the narrow crevice beneath the wooden bin containing the summer's potatoes.

The voices overhead continued. Hester could not understand the words.

She could go no farther. The floor rose in a mound beneath the potato bin. With every ounce of her strength, she pulled her hips and knees further into the opening. She stopped, guessing her skirt was hidden away. She had to leave the rest of her fate to God. If they came down the cellar steps and found her, then her life would surely be over.

It was hard to think of dying, but harder yet to imagine the hunger and torture of jail. As she thought of her life being in the hands of these swarthy, uncouth men, she inched her way into the crevice a bit more.

The dry, rasping sound of a snake. She stifled a cry as its heavy body slithered across her hand, then down across her knees.

The cellar door opened. A rectangle of flickering yellow light shone directly ahead of her. The men lost no time, coming down the steep stairway backward the way she had come. Hester heard the scurrying of the rodents.

She realized she had squeezed beneath the potato bin from the wall side, away from where the men had planted their feet. Had she come from the front where there was no opening beneath it, she'd have never found her hiding place.

She felt a cough begin in her throat. The veins in her neck swelled, her eyes squeezed shut, her mouth worked as she tried to abort the raucous sound that ached to be released. I will not cough. I will not cough. She swallowed over and over, finding with each contraction of her neck muscles that the sensation was receding.

Loud voices, footsteps on the packed earthen floor. "There ain't no Injun down here."

"Snake!" A bawling sound, a howl of mocking laughter and another one of glee as a man ran straight up the stairs.

She heard Emma. "I told you there ain't nothing down them steps."

"Potatoes."

"*Ya, wohl!* I work hard to dig them *Katufla*. You let them be."

Hester heard voices.

"You hear?" Emma shouted.

When there was no answer, Emma warned them once more, her tone strident but relaxed. After all, she was only an ordinary housewife protecting a summer's bounty, an important staple for the winter.

A rude reply rasped directly in front of Hester. She shivered and felt tears of panic begin to form. Now they were reaching into the bin, the candle held aloft, rolling the potatoes and laughing. They compared sizes, filling their empty pockets with the vegetables.

The men were so close she could hear their breathing. She smelled horses, stale sweat, deerskin, leather, tobacco. Hester's throat worked as she swallowed her fear.

Emma shouted down the opening of the stairway. "You leave them *Katufla* be. You let them down there for me and Billy. I'll tell the constable about you making off with my stuff. You hear me?"

There was only a rude mocking sound in reply. That, and a boot kicking the corner of the bin. A fine layer of dust from the potatoes filtered down on Hester's face. It felt cool, smelled like Annie's garden. Before she could think, a sneeze tore through her nose. She pushed her tongue against the roof of her mouth and willed the rush of air to be compressed.

A sound squeezed out, but it was overridden by another clattering of heavy boots on the stairway. Breathing rapidly, her nostrils filled with dirt, Hester lay beneath the potatoes and thanked her heavenly father for keeping her safe. The image of John Lantz, the Amish bishop, his hair white, his blue eyes piercing, saying, "*Gott sie gelobt un gedankt,*" filled her mind. She repeated the saying over and over, the treasure of the words' meaning increasing fourfold now.

The choking dirt that filtered over her face took her back to the dust and heat of August, as she bent over a row of beans or hoed newly planted beets. She could see the flight of the butterflies above the purple blossoms, erratic little upward flutterings, only to zigzag sideways, or plummet ungracefully to hover over blossoms before moving dizzily on their way. Butterflies were beautiful creatures but without smooth flight patterns, which birds and other airborne insects had.

She could hear the clatter of the iron-clad wooden wheels of the wagon bouncing over the rutted field lane. Hans was driving the faithful, plodding team, while Noah sprawled on top of the hay, his hair as light as the hot, white sunshine, Isaac beside him, a darker shadow.

When Kate was alive, they would have waved, called out a silly saying. Hester would have straightened her back, waved, and answered, a smile playing around her perfect mouth, her spirits lifted.

When Annie became their mother, she spread her venomous jealousy to Hester's brothers, her staunchest friends, and they no longer acknowledged her presence in the garden or the barn at milking time. Nowhere ever. Hester carried that great and awful pain like a growth close to her heart that cut off her capacity to feel joy. Her brothers' love had carried her through the rough spots that occurred in her life, her grafting into the Amish community softened by their protection.

Lying beneath the bin of potatoes in Emma Ferree's house in this strange Lancaster town, Hester wondered at the twists and turns in the uncertain path of her life so far. Maybe sometime she'd be able to go back to Berks County, back to her childhood home where butterflies flitted blue and orange and black and yellow, and the dust was filled with the scent of honeysuckle and wonder.

Hester longed for that lost sweetness, savoring the sights and smells of that time when she had been filled with belonging, the serenity that came from knowing her place in the world.

All this flashed through her mind as Emma's staccato voice berated the men who had searched her house. She told them God would hold them accountable for stuffing their pockets with a poor widow's potatoes. She hoped their horses would all get hoof rot and their wagon wheels would fall off. She banged the door after them, then sagged against it. The color drained out of her face and a sheen of sweat appeared on her forehead as she yelled at Billy to bring the smelling salts. She was sure her heart was not going to take this.

She moaned about poor, poor Hester down in that cellar. Oh, what had she gone through? Tears puddled and dripped from her doughy cheeks as she rained down other wishes of deep trouble on those *schtinkiche men-na*. For what she felt responsibility for, she fiercely loved and protected and passionately esteemed as her own, sometimes to the point that Billy wished she'd stop saying all those flowery speeches. A fella didn't need to hear all that. But his eyes shone with the goodness of Emma's love and spread right out of his own heart to others, without him even realizing it.

The next day, all the Indians that were held in the county jail were murdered. Fourteen of them were hacked to death by a group of men that called themselves the Paxton Boys, led by a minister who was a zealot. The town of Lancaster and the area around it had effectively been freed of any Indians, they believed.

Hester heard the news, but her face showed no evidence of distress. She just folded in like a withering plant and did not speak the remainder of the evening. Emma watched Hester closely but decided to leave her alone to mourn, to sort out her feelings, to absorb this terrible deed done against her people.

For weeks, Billy arrived, breathless, with one gruesome story or another. Hester gave no sign that she heard one word, simply bowing her head to her basket-weaving without a single tear or acknowledgment of his presence.

Emma and Billy discussed the moving. It would be odd to move their belongings in the dead of winter. People would talk. They stoked the fires, cleaned the house, cooked their meals, always watchful as they went about their usual routines.

Every Sunday morning Emma dressed in her Lord's Day finery, combed Billy's rebellious mop of hair, pinned his high collar amid furious grimaces as she worked. Then they set off for First Reformed Church on Orange Street.

Hester had to stay behind for safety's sake. Emma was well aware that other Indians were still in the area, some of them hired out as slaves, serving wealthy families without wages, but she took no chances. Helen Denlinger told her there was talk of an Indian girl having escaped the jail the night of the massacre and that she was living with Emma Ferree. Then Helen looked at her with too-bright eyes and a knowing smile. Emma waved a hand, dismissing her entirely, then turned to speak to her neighbor, Walter Trout, who became so gratified by the widow Emma's attention that he began to stutter, something he hadn't done since he was eight or nine years old.

Hester sat by the crackling fire, enjoying its warmth, then got up to look out the many paned windows, watching the carriages and wagons moving up and down Mulberry Street. In winter, most folks were hidden inside their carriages, but frequently an open wagon would rumble by, the wagon's inhabitants blobs beneath layers of buffalo robes with even their faces obscured. Pedestrians walked off to the sides of the streets through the snow, ladies lifting their skirts daintily as carriages rattled by.

All going to church, Hester thought. She had never seen the huge brick church houses Emma described, or the stone ones. Everyone went to church. There were so many different ones, it was dizzying. Why, if they all believed in the same God and his son Jesus, were there so many different ways to worship? It was more than Hester could figure out, so she stood hidden by Emma's spotless, white curtains and observed the people. Always she stayed alert, her senses tuned for any peace-crushing blow delivered to the sturdy oak door that led to the street.

Hester turned away from the window, then sighed restlessly. Going to the small mirror above the hall table, she examined the wounds on her face in the light from the snow and sun. She found a redness, but very little besides. That pleased her immensely. She wandered back to the window and saw a tall, top-hatted man walking sedately, a lady's hand on his arm, her skirts spread below her coat like a yellow flower. What unthinkable finery! So out of the Amish *Ordnung*, the stringent rules that kept them obedient, that held them within the promise they had made to be faithful.

Hester had always been accustomed to wearing a huge cap and hat pulled well past her face with a heavy, black woolen shawl pinned severely over her shoulders. If she wore her Amish outerwear, she would not be taken for an Indian, but the Amish did not live in town, so that would be stranger still.

An oddity yet. An oddity all her life. Well, she wouldn't look too far ahead, which was like welcoming a whole nest of wasps into a kitchen. It did no good, brought a load of unnecessary anxiety, and in the end, a stinging pain that had to be daubed with care, same as memories that were painfully colorful.

She looked forward to spring, the time when they would take their belongings and move to the country, close to the Amish. Today was the Sabbath, so she would not work at her baskets. But she felt restless, a longing for something she couldn't name. If she had wings like an eagle, she'd fly above this house and all the others that looked exactly the same.

In row upon row of wooden houses with brick chimneys rising from their middles, gray smoke waved endlessly, coming from the heating and cooking fire in the *shuba*, the soul of each house.

Hester sighed again. She sat down, reaching for the *Heiliche Schrift*, the great German Bible Emma delved into constantly, reading out loud to Billy, who, like as not, was fast asleep or carving a small object from a stick of wood.

Hester looked at the intricate black and white pictures and tried to read in *Mattheu*, but so many of the words eluded her. Reading in English was difficult enough. Reading German was like climbing a tree without branches. Hans had taught all his children well. He brought out the catechism every Sunday morning as regularly as he milked cows. Noah and Isaac were brilliant. Hester could read only haltingly, but Hans had praised her nevertheless, his eyes warm and brown, staying on her face too long. She could never remember hearing him give a word of encouragement to Noah or Isaac. And they so deserved it.

In one quick, fluid movement, Hester rose, a fierceness in her change of position. Taking the German Bible in both hands, she dropped it on the floor solidly. Her breathing came hard. Noah and Isaac had been slaves, working—no, toiling—from the time the sun appeared above the mountain, till it sank below the opposite one. And always, always, she had received flowery words of gratitude for the smallest endeavor.

Well, she'd gotten what she deserved, she supposed. Reaped richly the suffocating jealousy of her stepmother, after, like a slow-witted opossum that's so easily trapped, she finally saw Hans for what he was.

For a moment she was tempted to compare herself to Joseph in the Old Testament who had been persecuted because of jealousy. But he was good and holy and found favor in God's eyes. She, too, had a coat of many colors laid on her shoulders, in the form of colored linen made into her Sunday dresses. And when other little girls had one Sunday dress, she had three.

Ah, but he had loved her—she tried to convince herself—in the proper way a father loves a daughter. It was she who had done wrong. Perhaps. But how?

She paced the confines of the house accusing herself, but for what? Her past was like rain—life-giving, sweet, and generous in its abundance of things that were good. But if she lingered too long in this rain, she became cold and uncomfortable and needed to retreat to a place where the rain could not touch her. And yet, it still did. The rain penetrated her heart, filling it with sadness for Noah and for Isaac. They were such noble young brothers, working endlessly to Hans's and Annie's specifications, until they built the farm from a lowly log house and a few cleared acres to the status of a homestead belonging to Hans and Annie Zug. They were regarded as the best managers in Berks County, owners of a large stone house and barn and of the finest herd of cows in that area (if not in all of Pennsylvania), plus a couple of Belgian horses and a blacksmithy.

Hans had it all. Hester's eyes narrowed. Yes, he did, but by his shrewd wife's manipulation and the sweat of Noah's and Isaac's brows.

Perhaps it was better that she wasn't alone too much, the way these thoughts rushed around in her mind, creating ripples of pain. Why did she remember her brothers so keenly now? If only she could talk to them and make things right. She wanted to tell them that they were the ones who deserved to be exalted, lifted up, encouraged. Just look at me. Please look at me. Talk to me. I need to tell you these things.

Hester was relieved when a quiet rapping sounded on the door. She quickly scooped up the Bible she had let fall, then hurried to slide back the bolt on the door, allowing Emma and Billy to enter. Emma's face was flushed, two purplish spots appeared on either cheek, her nose looked bruised from the cold, and her green hat was sliding to the back of her head. She resembled a frenzied bantam hen at home in the barnyard when a skunk raided her small, neat nest of eggs.

"We're getting company!" she said.

"Rufus and Helen Denlinger. And Walter Trout," Billy crowed, already divesting himself of the noose other people called a collar.

"But?" Hester was bewildered.

Emma was sliding the wool cape off her rounded shoulders, her eyes flashing beneath the folds of skin, now heightened to an alarming pink color. "Now, Hester, you don't worry. If Helen is nosy, then she's going to have the surprise of her life. You are my new maid from Virginia. A slave. Here." She stopped Hester, handed her a ruffled housewife's cap and an apron that was so over-sized it was ridiculous, but since Emma didn't seem to mind, Hester didn't either.

Emma fried salt pork, the pan so sizzling hot it was only a miracle the kitchen didn't go up in flames. She peeled potatoes while Hester laid the table with a plain white tablecloth, serviceable ironstone plates, pewter utensils, and clay tumblers.

They served the sauerkraut with dumplings, the salt pork with pickled watermelon rind. The potatoes had a whole lake of brown butter on the mounded top. Like a volcano, the butter spilled down the sides, pooling around the edges of the serving bowl.

Emma served the chilled chow-chow in a glass dish. Pats of homemade butter gleamed and shone by the tall candles. Thickened elderberries sat alongside the butter, making a perfect marriage of fat and sweet to spread on thick chunks of crusty German bread.

Helen Denlinger was a bit stout, although she girded herself so severely that she appeared slender, at least in the proper places. As she ate and ate and ate, her face grew steadily more colorful, her eyes decreased in size, and her breathing became decidedly more labored, like a plodding horse pulling a plow in the spring.

She mentioned the delightful way the Germans served their bread, in a thin, gasping voice, before reaching for another thick, crusty chunk, spreading it with a greedy portion of butter and the marvelous berries. Her husband ate like a starving wolf, lowering his head and shoveling it in without the good manners of taking time to answer the smallest inquiry.

Walter Trout sat at the end of the table where there was plenty of room, cut his salt pork with knife and fork, poised like a perfect British gentleman, slowly chewing the neat squares of meat with his mouth closed. His small mouth, moving up and down in a grinding, circular motion, completely entranced Billy, who thought it amazing the way that small opening could be the only door for so much food.

To his knowledge, Walter had never tasted German cooking. He found the dumplings on the sauerkraut blissful, the salt pork heavenly, the turnips absolutely divine.

Billy rolled his eyes at Hester. "I can tell you come fresh off a sermon," he quipped.

Emma was so mortified she didn't know what to do, but when she looked at Walter and he was rolling from side to side, trying to repress his good-humored mirth, she spluttered, then gave up and lifted her hands, howling with unladylike glee that Helen Denlinger found ill-mannered. And since she had to struggle to breathe, she certainly could not waste precious air in laughing. That Billy Ferree needed to learn manners, to be seen and not heard.

Hester hovered over the Sunday dinner, the ruffled white cap hiding her sleek, straight hair, enhancing the simple beauty of her large dark eyes. She filled and refilled water tumblers, filled the sauerkraut dish twice, and made sure the dumplings were moist and hot. She brought out a chocolate cake, loaded with walnuts ground to slivers and topped with crumby brown sugar. She served applesauce and golden pears, glazed with honey.

Helen looked up from her plate and watched Hester intently. "Emma, your Negro is light skinned. Is she a mulatto?" she asked, watching her friend shrewdly.

Emma's face was kind, soft, and benevolent, the steel beneath her skin well hidden. Her remark was courteous as well. "Why, yes. Helen, she is, in fact, of mixed origin. I believe they said Jamaican, when I bought her at auction."

"But," Helen spluttered, wrestling with curiosity, "I had no idea Enos was so well-to-do that you can afford a servant."

Emma batted her short lashes and lowered her eyelids humbly. "Oh, Enos was a man of means. Indeed he was. But so modest, so very unassuming."

This remark set Helen directly on the path of acquiring a girl to serve her food, no matter what the cost. Never once did she imagine that Emma had taken in an Indian, the way some people claimed. Why, she was so well-to-do she had her own servant. But then look at the way that woman has given, casting her bread upon the waters in more than one area. God rewards people like that, she told Rufus.

Walter Trout took one bite of the chocolate cake and figured it was among the best things he'd ever been fortunate enough to taste. He watched Hester's impeccable manners, her quiet serving of this delicious meal, and wondered if he could possibly be called to Sunday dinner more often. Even when they'd be living out in the country and all. His warm heart felt a great longing to erase the sadness from the young girl's eyes. He looked forward to being able to sit at Emma Ferree's table again.

Billy watched Helen Denlinger's face turn steadily darker, her breathing light and quick as she consumed her cake, and thought how much she looked like a catfish after you take it off the hook, gasping for air the way they did.

CHAPTER 9

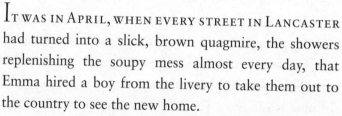

It was in April, when every street in Lancaster had turned into a slick, brown quagmire, the showers replenishing the soupy mess almost every day, that Emma hired a boy from the livery to take them out to the country to see the new home.

She was worried about Hester, so lifeless and thin. She had no appetite and said very little. Even Billy could not get her interested in anything. When the carriage pulled to the door, Emma hustled both Hester and Billy out, shooting uncomfortable glances Walter Trout's way. He had hinted broadly that he could accompany them, seeing as how he owned the property and all, but Emma said there was no need, they'd be fine, and dismissed him easily. He watched them go through an opened curtain, then thought perhaps it was best that they go without him since the carriage looked pretty narrow.

Emma heaved herself into the carriage, taking the livery boy's hand as an aid. She meant to touch it lightly the way the younger ladies did, filled with grace, but she pushed down on the slight boy's hand so hard he had to hold it up with his opposite one. His face grew red with exertion, and he considered himself extremely fortunate to have any room at all beside her on the front seat. Emma did think that if the time ever came that Walter would accompany them to the country, they would need a sturdy wagon, not a weak carriage. They made them so flimsy these days.

She set her hat squarely on her head and tied the thin scarf down over it securely beneath her one soft chin, then sat back to enjoy the ride. The air was wet, filled with scents of rain and standing water and dripping new plants that seemed to be bursting with happiness. The sunlight was weak but getting stronger each day, holding the promise of heat and humidity, a coming season of plenty.

They passed the wheelwright's shop, a row of houses, and the livery. Soon they could smell the open fields, the forest, the clean new grasses that waved and bowed by the muddy roadside. Their progress was slow. The horse lowered his haunches and leaned into the collar, pulling the carriage through the ruts made by all kinds of traffic.

Hester sat in the backseat, her face hidden by the broad brim of a large, blue bonnet, an old one of Emma's, who had carefully adjusted it to hide the color of her skin. Beside her, his new straw hat pushed to the back of his head, Billy hooked an elbow over the back of the carriage, whistling and warbling and chirping to his heart's content. His blue eyes followed the soaring of the birds, the way they dipped and wheeled in the blue sky, smudged by streaks of white clouds.

Hester asked if he knew the fish bone clouds, the ones that appeared in the east when a good rain was coming the following day.

"You can't go by that," he said airily.

"Sure you can."

"Nah."

"So tell me how you can predict rain."

"Go out and see if it's raining. That's easy."

Hester laughed.

Emma turned, so glad to hear this sound.

Hester smiled at Emma and said there would be so much she could teach Billy about nature, the garden, the herbal medicines she prized. Emma said probably not just Billy, but her, as well.

Their first view of the house was a disappointment. It was in lamentable shape. A moth-eaten dress that looked suitable from a distance, but the damage clearly visible as they approached.

Emma almost fell out of the carriage in her eagerness, while the boy who brought them stayed sitting in the exact same spot. There was no way he was going to put his life in danger and help this lady down.

Emma rushed to the front door, her small feet pattering across the wet grass, giving the illusion that she was floating, as if wheels propelled her smoothly along.

The door was attached by only one hinge, allowing creatures access to the house. By the looks of it, plenty of them had taken up residence. The rooms were filthy, the kitchen black with smoke.

"Now, how can this be? Walter said there was a couple living here, but they couldn't afford the rent." Emma's voice was thick with despair, almost a whine. Billy had spied a snake already and was off across the wet grass. Hester stepped through the door, turned her face left, then right, sniffed, wrinkled her nose, and pronounced it livable.

There was a fairly large kitchen in front, the first room of the house. Half of one wall was filled by a vast fireplace, a wide beam placed across the top, the stone and mortar disappearing into the ceiling in the middle of the house.

The floors were oak planks, wide and sturdy but littered with rodent's waste, bits of nutshells, grass, dead flies, and other insects. The sitting room took up the whole left side of the house, a tiny, circular stairway going out of a corner of it to the upstairs. There were only two bedrooms. The ceiling was the underside of the oak roof shingles.

Everything was covered with the remains of free, scurrying mice and rats. Likely mink, otter, opossums, and skunks, too, Hester thought.

"Let's just stay in town." Emma's voice carried genuine tears, ill concealed. "*Du yay. Du yay,*" she kept lamenting.

Hester said nothing. She realized her position as the person who was the recipient of this kind woman's charity and didn't wish to appear bold. Her whole heart longed for this space, the fields and grasses, the trees and water, clean and fresh and free. She wanted to stay here in this unused dwelling, away from the fear that dogged each day, the feeling of being stalked, her spirit repressed, unable to go outside and smell the scent of the town. Without that, the very atmosphere seemed secondhand, as if the air had already been breathed by someone else, and her allotment had been spare.

Emma had started on her other excuses, reasoning that at her age, there was no sense in working like this, and she was fairly certain that fat Walter Trout wouldn't lift a finger to clean this place. Hester thought of Kate saying, "The pot shouldn't call the kettle black," but said nothing.

Quickly, Emma shot out, "Hester, what do you think?"

"I want to stay! Please, can I stay here? I'll clean, I'll do everything. I don't want to go back."

Emma's eyes widened, popping in surprise. "You do?"

"Yes! Oh, yes! I love it here!" She swung her arms toward the surrounding hills, the grasses heavy with good moisture, the soil beneath it so rich, so fruitful. She explained where a garden could be made, a horse and wagon kept in the adjoining barn, a fence built for a pasture, perhaps in time their own plow, more than one cow, a nice flock of chickens.

When the doorway darkened, Emma lifted a hand to her mouth, her eyes wide with fright. She squeaked helplessly. Hester stayed still, her back rigid, without looking. It was best this person did not see her face.

"Hello." The voice was deep with a demanding quality.

Emma's chin wobbled a few times before she could speak. "Yes, yes. Hello."

"I was riding across the field and saw the carriage parked by the barn. I was curious, is all."

"Oh, of course." Emma stepped forward, her natural goodness of heart shining as usual as she thrust her plump hand in the general direction of the tall, dark man.

He bent to take it and shook politely. "I am William. William King."

"Emma Ferree. Enos was my husband's name."

"The cheese peddler?"

"Why, yes, yes, he was a peddler. Cheese. Yes!" Delighted, Emma gabbled away like a silly turkey being chased by its peers, recognizing her words had no merit had she not been connected to Enos.

The tall young man was very good-looking, Emma summed up, and she was always a bit tongue-tied around *selly goot gookichy*. This one might be Amish, though, since he was wearing those wide suspenders and that flat-looking hat.

He lifted his chin in Hester's general direction. "And her?"

"Hester? You mean our Hester?" Too late, Emma realized her mistake. Hester moved swiftly. Like a wraith, invisible, she melted away through the half-open back door.

William King's face blanched. He looked as if he had, in fact, just encountered a *schpence*. "Who? What is her name?"

His eyes were terrible in their intensity. Emma's plump, pink hand went to her throat to still the fluttering. "It is Hester. Hester Zug."

"No!"

In a few long strides, he pushed Emma aside, tore through the door in the back of the house, and lunged down the steps. Hester heard his name. She heard his voice. All her own shortcomings, the color of her skin, Hans, her past, rose directly in front of her, roared and crashed and clawed their way past any hope of meeting him again. She could not look at him. He must never see her. She ran, lifting her skirts. The rush of air caught her hat, swinging it off her head. It hung by its wide strings, flopping, bouncing like a terrified bird, a parody of her heart. She increased her speed when she heard strong footsteps behind her.

"Hester! Wait! Wait!"

She looked back, wildly.

"Please stop. I just want to talk."

On she ran, determined that he must never see her.

He overtook her, then reached out and caught the flapping bonnet. She slid to a stop, her chest heaving, her hands balled into fists.

"Hester. Oh, Hester." The words were a caress, a coming home, a believing of the impossible, the accepting of a miracle.

"Don't. Don't." She whispered the words harshly, her eyes downcast. She would not lift them.

"Hester, it is you."

She felt his nearness, heard his breathing.

"Look at me, Hester."

"I can't."

"Try. Please try."

What kept her from allowing him to see her eyes? All the shame of her past. The greedy, clutching self-loathing that choked her and tamped down her eyelids.

She felt his strong, calloused finger reach out and lift her chin. "Hester?" he whispered.

Tears squeezed through her closed eyes. She caught her lower lip in her teeth to suppress the emotion.

"What is it?" he whispered.

"I am not who you think I am."

"Who are you?"

Her eyes opened, revealing black, liquid pools of pain and uncertainty. She saw the tall, dark form, the black hair cut squarely across his forehead, falling below his ears at the side. She took in the blue of his eyes, the chiseled nose, the perfect mouth. "I ran. I ran away. I am with the English."

The disappointment that darkened his face was hard to watch, so she lowered her eyes.

"Why?" he grated.

"You remember the wedding?"

He nodded, eagerly.

"Annie didn't like me. It didn't work out."

"If I remember, I warned you."

"Yes."

Emma was walking toward them, her calling reaching their ears. For a long moment, he drank in the face kept alive in his memory, so much as he remembered, and yet so different. Fear clutched at his heart. Why had she left? What had she done?

Emma's short form was so unwelcome William King had to visibly rearrange his features to accommodate her breathless appearance. Fat little *gwunder* nose.

"Oh, oh, oh." Emma's voice made puffing sounds, like a small, fussy locomotive.

"Hester. Hester, my love."

Stopping, Emma looked from one face to another, her sharp eyes boring into the mask of impatience across William's, the raw despair in Hester's, a vulnerability that brought sharp words of rebuke to her small, red mouth. "Mister, you are upsetting Hester. You should not have run after her this way. She has been through an ordeal. Now you just go easy on her. I mean it."

His anger was ill disguised. It rippled along the muscles in his cheeks, turning the brilliant blue of his eyes a shade darker, an orange flame appearing only one second before evaporating. "Oh. I didn't mean to upset Hester. I am not aware that I did."

Oily words. Emma was quick with her tongue. "Then, I would suggest you leave her alone."

William drew himself up to a magnificent height, his eyelids falling to a level of condescension he was accustomed to exercising over his peers. He cleared his throat. "Hester and I have met before."

"Really?" Emma's tone was flat and as uncompromising as a stone wall.

Hester became agitated. A hand went to her throat. "William King and I met briefly at my father's wedding. He does not know my story."

"If you will please allow me to continue my conversation, perhaps she can tell me in her own words."

"Oh, no, she ain't. You want to talk to my Hester, you ask her if you can come calling, like any gentleman. And for now, we will be busy, too busy, in fact, to have you around."

Before he could reply, Billy popped out of the high grass, his gray hat pulled down so far he didn't appear to have a face, only an opened collar and a chin. "Hooo!" he yelled. "Frogs ain't easy to catch."

He tilted the grimy hat back out of his eyes, releasing a curtain of copper hair, sized up William with his blue eyes, and blurted, "Who're you?"

William's smile was genuine, his white teeth lighting up his face as he bent to extend his hand to Billy's, grasping it firmly with a solid shake.

"William King. Nice to meet you."

"You, too."

Billy wasn't used to meeting men—strangers—that were ten feet tall, he guessed. His hand felt as if it left the wrist it was attached to, but he figured it was still in working condition, once William King let go of it. Together they walked back to the house. William did most of the talking with Billy injecting his flow of words with boyish remarks.

Emma's face looked like a thundercloud, her eyes snapping blue sparks, her mouth a compressed down-turned slash of disapproval.

Hester walked beside William, making no sound except for the gentle swishing of her skirts in the unkempt grasses.

"Hey! You know we're gonna move out here? Oops!" Billy's hat slid off the back of his head when he lifted his face to watch William speak. He grabbed it off the moisture-laden grasses and clumped it back on his head, shoving it down hard with both hands, then jerking on both sides of the brim, enlarging the tear on the left side of the crown.

"We hafta move on account a Hester bein' a Injun. You know they killed 'em all now. Lancaster County don't have any Injuns no more."

"Good. You can't trust them."

Emma jerked her right shoulder, walked faster, but kept her peace.

"Yeah," Billy said, nodding his head rapidly, unsettling the loose hat once more. He grabbed it with his right hand, pulled it down over his ears, bobbed his head a few times to ensure a good fit, then walked solemnly ahead, digesting this new way of thinking about "them Injuns."

When they reached the house, Emma turned to William. "Good day."

William searched Hester's face but found only hidden eyes beneath lowered lashes. "I'll be on my way then. If you need help, I'll be available. My parents' house is only a few miles across these woods as the crow flies."

Hester lifted her eyes to watch his retreat. She thrilled to the set of the shoulders, the way he loped easily. Like a wolf, effortless.

Emma fumed and steamed, fussed and stewed, worrying herself to the point of hysteria. She told Hester that man was up to no good, and if she knew her place, she'd have nothing to do with him.

Billy said, "Why not, Ma?"

Hester watched the figure on the horse, a striking rider, disappear into the row of trees. Confusion rode uncomfortably on her shoulders.

Well, first things first. Saying nothing, she left Emma and Billy to their own little war of words, slipped through the front door, and assessed the damage, the things they'd need. She made a mental list, then returned to the front door, preparing to leave. They did need a man to help them, certainly. Walter Trout was a bit dubious with his weight and all.

But Walter proved to be a wonderful help. His face was covered by the wide brim of a straw hat, his thick red suspenders holding up the homespun kneebreeches very well, the clean linen shirt bunching over the top of them as he wielded a hammer, pulled a saw, swung an axe. He whistled, sang, or talked, one of the three, all day long. He could only be described as a jolly soul. Hester found him to be a storehouse of amusement. It rolled out of him the way spring water bubbled out of the ground. Spring water was like that. It you tried to stop it, it squirted out the side, stronger than ever.

The May sun was warm. It heated the house with its fresh, yellow light. Even the dust turned into specks of gold, floating through the air like bits of magic.

Hester's hair was covered in an old kerchief, her dress smudged and torn, the gray apron tied about her waist layered with the dust that clung to everything.

Walter's whistling was infectious. She began a tune of her own, low, a sort of humming of an old song Kate would sing to the children. She slapped at the low ceiling with her broom, dragging a net of cobwebs with it, blinking and sputtering as chips of old whitewash fell into her eyes.

Walter straightened from fixing a hinge on the front door. "Mercy, mercy, child! You're raising more dust than the cavalry marching through town."

Hester laughed, swinging her broom in his direction. "You want to do this?"

Walter's eyes twinkled at her, the good humor crinkling them like a fan closing until they were mere outlines with lashes. "Good to see you so happy, girl! Never saw you with a full-size laugh on your face."

Hester laughed again, which brought tears of joy to Walter's eyes. They repaired, swept, whitewashed, scoured floors, and scrubbed cupboards and closets all through the mellow month of May.

Sometimes William King would appear, his offers to help always met with Emma Ferree's icy denial, which riled Billy considerably. He genuinely liked William.

Hester wanted him to help but would not step over the boundaries her benefactor had placed for her. Emma was the authority in her life now, and she respected her requests.

William caught her alone, scouring the wide oak planks of the small upstairs. She was whistling softly, the hot water reddening her hands as she worked on the floor with a wooden scrubbing brush. She held completely still when he whispered her name.

"Hester."

"Yes, William?"

"Why did you leave the Amish in Berks County? That question haunts me, keeps me awake at night."

"It's a long story." Hester placed the brush in the bucket of water, sat back on the wooden floor, her knees tucked beneath her.

"Tell me. Please. Emma is outside."

"She doesn't like you."

"I know. I can't say that I care much for her, either."

"My story is long, a bit complicated. Annie was not a good companion, as you pointed out to me."

"Yes, we are in *die freundshaft*. There is a cruel streak," William said, saying the words slowly, as if he handpicked them with great caution.

"The situation became unbearable. She didn't like Indians."

"Well, I don't either. They're savage. Wild men that deserve to be pushed west where they can live their un-civilized lives, roaming the wilds like the heathens they are."

Hester drew a deep breath to steady herself. Every fiber of her being rebelled against his coarse speech. Was this the same William who held her hand beneath the Amish wedding table, made her heart beat, sent shivers of joy sluicing through her veins? How could he say these things?

"I am an Indian." Her words were firm, the syllables deliberate, as if she cast them in stone and held them up for him to see.

"You may have been born one, but the Amish saved you from being a dirty heathen."

William watched her chest heave with the force of her emotion. He watched as one work-reddened hand went to her apron front to still the upheaval she felt. Her eyes became blacker still, widening with the force of her words.

"The Amish had nothing to do with saving me, as you say. Hans Zug and his wife Annie have clabbered my spirit like soured cream, poured me out to soak into the cracks of their parched Berks County earth, leaving nothing but a smelly odor in God's nostrils."

William shivered beneath the dark truth in her eyes.

CHAPTER 10

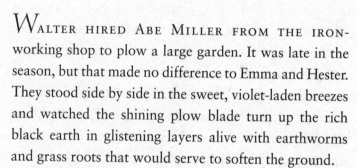

WALTER HIRED ABE MILLER FROM THE IRON-working shop to plow a large garden. It was late in the season, but that made no difference to Emma and Hester. They stood side by side in the sweet, violet-laden breezes and watched the shining plow blade turn up the rich black earth in glistening layers alive with earthworms and grass roots that would serve to soften the ground.

An Amish man by the name of Amos Speicher brought wagonloads of manure from his cowshed. Walter decided not to climb up on the wooden bed of the wooden-wheeled wagon because of his age. Emma rolled her eyes and held her hands in front of her own over-size stomach, making meaningful little dips with her eyebrows to show Hester it was his size, not his age.

Billy wrinkled his nose, but jumped right up and helped Amos fork the manure on to the harrowed ground. They dragged the harrow through the manure again and again, the sturdy Belgian plodding faithfully until they had a perfectly prepared plot of soil to raise the vegetables they'd need.

They placed onions into rows and sowed tiny carrot seeds in shallow trenches. They planted beans and then prepared poles for them to climb, once the bean shoots broke through the soil.

One morning Walter's face became an alarming shade of purple. He spent half the day with his straw hat tipped back, mopping his streaming head with a wrinkled, red handkerchief. Emma shook her head at his frequent lapses of effort, her own perspiration running freely down the side of her pink face. She swiped at it with the tip of her apron, discreetly, as if she could hide the fact that she did any sweating at all.

Hester heaped the good, loose soil over the seeds, her heart beating strong and sure, the love of the earth infusing her nostrils with a heady scent. She would search the surrounding forest and swamps for the plants in her memory—yarrow and licorice and comfrey, mullen, sorrel, and fennel. She worked ceaselessly, her bare brown feet treading the earth, her spirits soaring with the wings of an eagle.

Billy remembered nothing of living in the country before his life with Emma, but the small garden they dug by hand in the town of Lancaster had kept him occupied in spring. The house sat beneath two maple trees, squat and weather beaten, but as clean as a whistle, windows gleaming, floors smelling of fresh soap and lumber.

There was a front porch with a sagging roof that Walter had repaired, balancing his bulk on a seemingly inadequate ladder, until even Hester dreaded the approaching accident. Which, of course, never occurred. It was just his size, Walter said.

When moving day arrived, they hired the same man to drive and haul their possessions out to the homestead, still being careful about Hester's Indian blood. They left the china cupboard and some of the folderols they didn't need. The plank table and straight ladder-backed kitchen chairs fit so nicely by the fireplace, with shelves built along the low kitchen cupboard they brought, that Emma hopped up and down with excitement, spread a clean cloth on the table immediately, and brought out the *Schtick* she had painstakingly prepared for this long-anticipated day.

She sliced bread in substantial slices and spread them with pungent, yellow butter, freshly churned and packed into a small, shallow crock. She placed thick slices of salty ham on one slice of bread, topped it with more yellow butter and another slice of bread, then arranged the sandwiches on a pewter plate.

She fished hard-cooked eggs from the red beet brine that had turned them a delightful shade of red, placed them on a smaller plate with a salt shaker close by, a mound of pickled red beets among the eggs.

That done, she set out the square pan of gingerbread, the chilled bowl of clabbered cream to spoon on top, and the biggest treat of all, a sparkling jar of spiced peaches from Helen Denlinger, as a gift in appreciation of their Sunday dinner. It was very nice of Helen to present them with the peaches. Helen's gesture brought great relief to Emma, who had worried about Helen lapsing into heart failure, laced so excruciatingly into her corsets as she was during that Sunday dinner. Emma had given up trying to wear those torture devices as soon as she had snared Enos.

Now Emma poured hot tea into earthenware mugs and called Walter, Hester, and Billy to her table. Billy reminded her about the moving man and Amos Speicher, which sent her immediately to the door, yoo-hooing and making other ridiculous outbursts of sound, which served their purpose, bringing both men to the table.

Hester kept her eyes lowered but felt the curious eyes of both men on her face. Amos tried to engage her in conversation, which brought a quick look from the dark eyes, a nod of the head, but a minimum of words.

In the late afternoon, lazy, white smoke curled up over the stone chimney, the small cooking fire giving away its existence. The fresh white walls were clean and bright, the floors homey with bright rag rugs, the redware and pewter arranged on the shelves in straight sensible rows so they could be reached efficiently.

In the parlor, the corner cupboard stood sentry, a sturdy piece of furniture indispensable to their needs, holding anything from tablecloths and towels to buttons and thread. A few comfortable chairs, one armless, were pulled up to the window. A chest containing blankets and coverlets was pushed against the north wall.

The small bedroom along the back was Emma's. The sturdy wooden bedstead was loaded with a straw mattress and feather ticking on top. A tall handmade closet held her changes of clothes, high-topped shoes, and hats. Emma hung a serviceable white curtain across the window. You never knew, she said.

Billy shared the narrow attic with Hester. They strung a sheet of homespun cloth between them, down the middle of the room, for privacy. They set up a narrow rope bed on either side, plus a chest for Hester and a small wooden box for Billy. A window at each gable end let in sufficient light, but Hester knew the approaching summer would bring the stifling attic heat. First they learned to endure it, and then eventually accepted it as the summer days wore on.

Walter pronounced the reclaimed house and garden unbelievable. He praised Emma's work with lovely words of approval, holding his straw hat by the tips of his fingers, his freshly wiped head shining pink in the late- afternoon sun. Emma accepted his praise graciously, of course, but the thought ran through her mind that she'd probably like him so much better if he was not quite so pink. But then, bless the man, God had made him so. Or maybe not. All that eating was his own doing.

She remained unmoved about Walter Trout, being the stubborn, independent German that she was where men were concerned. Enos had won her heart, but it had taken him a while. Walter had always figured perhaps that was the reason for their childless state. Emma tended to be a bit brittle. Certainly not, though, to the poor and the suffering, the orphans and the destitute.

To Emma, men were an irritation, mostly. Take that William King. Now there was a winner. She'd as soon smack him as talk to him, with his making those sheep's eyes at Hester, his suave good looks, and a high-minded attitude that irked her every time he opened his mouth. But if Hester chose to allow him to court her, she'd have to let her go.

Walter rode home in the black buggy with the gold pinstripes, pulled by his fine, serviceable horse. He held the reins loosely in his pudgy fingers, his head bowed, the straw hat slightly askew, the breeze flapping up the front brim.

Emma Ferree was a hard worker who liked her things in order, but after all these days of labor (which had seemed but one sweet hour of devotion), she had not softened toward him at all. Ah, but wait. Had she made such a fine *schtick* for only hers and Hester's benefit?

He lifted one finger, holding it aloft, as he said out loud, "Now those were the finest, most hearty sandwiches I have ever come across." And who knew? Perhaps the peaches and the gingerbread and the pickled eggs were all prepared with him in mind. No, the battle to win Emma Ferree's heart was, indeed, not over.

Billy was milking the new brown Guernsey cow with Hester giving him instructions. In the adjoining stable, the brown mare gazed at them with her blue-brown eyes, the heavy black lashes blinking slowly as she watched. She was a small horse, but sufficient, Walter had told them, content to let them buy her from him at a low price.

Hester finished the milking. Billy stood nearby, flexing his fingers with overly exaggerated motions, his mouth open, his tongue hanging from it like a dog. "That hurts!"

Hester laughed. "I used to milk five cows at home."

"Don't see how you could!"

"You get used to it."

Hester straightened, then bent to retrieve the bucket brimming with frothy milk, when the soulful eyes of the brown cow caught sight of Billy's red hair. She kicked out with her right hoof, caught the edge of the wooden pail, and tilted it at an angle, spilling all of the good milk into the straw.

Hester shouted, but she was too late.

Billy yelled, then bent over double, howling with glee, slapping his legs over and over, as tears coursed out of his eyes.

The brown cow merely lifted her head, switched her tail from left to right a few times, before placing her cloven hoof in the center of the spilled milk.

Wiping his eyes, Billy chuckled the whole way to the house, walking beside Hester, who swung the empty pail by its handle.

They worked in the yard that evening, mowing the grass with a scythe, raking it with a wooden rake, and taking it to the barn for the animals.

They named the cow Flora, after Billy suggested Kicker or Thumper, laughing uproariously at his own cleverness. The horse they named Frieda. Emma said she'd always wanted a daughter named Frieda, meaning peace, but she'd never had a daughter until now, and she was already named Hester. She held Hester's hand warmly and thanked her for all the hard work she had done around the place.

Hester reminded her that they would not have had to move if she had not come to their house in town. Emma said it was high time Billy got away from that tavern. The coins he hoarded in the tin box weren't worth the danger he put himself in.

They slept in their clean, new beds that night, the windows opened to the sounds of night insects, the call of the owls, the whippoorwills, and the coyotes. A three-quarter slice of moon bathed the small house in the middle of the clearing in silvery shimmering light, casting black shadows on the north side and under the maple trees. The rectangular patch of newly planted garden needed a fence, but that would soon be done, Walter promised.

An opossum scuttled out from beneath the porch, poked its pointed snout into the ground, shoveled out a few onions, sniffed them, and let them alone. It moved to the barn, snuffling along the walls of the cow stable, its beady eyes taking in the night landscape, digging up tasty grubs along the back wall. Suddenly, it stopped. Like a stone, it held still, its nose twitching, then flattened itself against the wall of the shed.

A dark figure emerged from the woods, bent over, as if the person were aged or had an arthritic back. The person wasted no time in crossing the field, still crouched but running. The opossum stayed still, watching. The person straightened, flattening himself against the north side of the house where the shadows were thick and black.

The moon inched across the sky. A nighthawk screeched his unsettling call. The opossum stayed low against the wall of the shed, scuttled forward, stopped to listen, then disappeared into the thick grass. Still there was no movement from the deep shadow by the house.

In his sleep, Billy coughed softly. He groaned and stretched. The ropes beneath his straw mattress creaked in protest. Hester slept on, deep and dreamless.

They discovered a pear tree on the outskirts of the forest. Emma found wild raspberry bushes, then lamented her loss since the fruit had already been eaten by wild creatures.

"*Hembare! Oh, meine hembare!*" Over and over she wailed and groaned and recited the recipe for raspberry mush. They found *hulla* elderberries, but they were not quite the same.

Hester spent all her spare time in the garden. The onions popped out of the soil, succulent spears growing an inch every week. The wispy little tops of the carrots grew and sprouted like feather dusters, spreading their lacy tops across the fertile black soil. Red beets grew their tender green leaves, the red spines spread across them like blood veins. Emma cut the beets when they were new and heated them with butter and salt. They ate them with hard-cooked eggs and grated, cooked turnips.

Hester was in the garden one hot summer day as the afternoon sun was beginning to slide down the bowl of hot, quivering sky. Her hair was a mess, she was overheated, sticky, and a bit disgruntled at Billy's refusal to weed. Emma was too easy on him. She grabbed a stubborn dandelion and yanked, breaking off the root with the snap she knew too well, threw it aside with disgust, and stamped her foot impatiently.

A low laugh behind her made her jump. She whirled around, hating to be caught unaware. She always had thoroughly disliked the feeling of being exposed when she should have been able to discern the slightest movement.

It was William King. She watched him warily. She felt light-headed now, the way her pulse fluttered at the base of her neck.

"You don't like dandelions?"

She did not smile, just shook her head no, evasive, mistrustful.

"Why do you dislike me? Am I like the dandelion? A weed that threatens to take over your well-organized life?"

"I don't dislike you."

"Is it Emma?"

"No."

"What is it, Hester?"

"It's nothing."

"I have asked my father permission to court you."

"You didn't ask mine."

"May I come see you on Sunday evening?"

The toe of her right foot shoved into the loose soil. Her head was bent to watch the earth fall away from her toe's movement. "I don't know."

"What kind of answer is that?"

"Exactly what I said. I am not sure."

"My father said no."

"So why are you asking?"

"Hester, I have passed my thirtieth year. It is time I think of taking a wife."

"But if your father said no?"

"I'm past the age where he can dictate my choices."

Hester nodded.

"May I come see you?"

His voice was warm, eager, kind. His face was open and earnest, his black hair falling on either side, his obedience to the *Ordnung* so evident.

Hester's future stretched before her, an undulating plain of doubt, the road disappearing into a pit of fear and despair. With William, she could find happiness, she believed. They would take their time as they allowed the Amish community to accept their union. But did she truly want to go back?

"Yes."

Stepping forward, he caught her hands and held them to his chest. His blue eyes shone with the intensity of his feelings.

"Thank you, Hester. At last, I can say those words."

She smiled, a fluttering, shifting, stretch of her lips.

"I'll tell Emma. Do you want to come with me?"

She shook her head.

He walked off with an easy, loping gait, swung himself up on the porch, and rapped eagerly on the door. Hester watched as the doors swung inward and the stout form of Emma stepped aside. William bowed slightly, then began to talk. Emma's gaze hung over Hester like a two-edged sword, the way God's Word was described in the Bible. She felt as if Emma could see into her very soul and know her past. The part for which she was to blame.

Hans might never have had those thoughts and intents if she had been smarter. A dumb Indian. How often had she heard those words? She was dumb. As *Schtump* as a rock. She found the German language difficult, but English was like climbing a chalk cliff. And here she was, chasing dumbly after William King.

As she thought, Emma moped about the house, then unleashed a fury of words against William King, hurling them into the air so that they smacked against the walls and the sides of Hester's head.

Emma held her head and rocked back and forth, then cried copiously into her wide, white apron, spluttering and sniffing and saying it was all because she loved Hester more than she knew and she was so afraid she'd be mistreated by the Amish people. She didn't know these Amish from Adam, and she'd been in a bad situation before. What was Hester thinking?

"*Oh, du yay. Hester, du yay. Mein Kind.*"

A part of Hester wanted to obey Emma's dire warnings. But to live her life here for the rest of her days, never having experienced marriage or having someone close to her heart, without spending life together with a family, was unthinkable as well.

"Emma, I am not getting married now. I promise to spend only one Sunday evening with him. Only one. If I feel he is not the right man for me, I will end it then. I will."

Through her tears, Emma nodded her head, the chin wobbling, her cheeks wet with fresh pathways of more tears before wiping her face with a white handkerchief.

Billy stuck his head in the door and left again, shaking his head and muttering dire predictions about all women.

By August, the heat lay so heavy over Lancaster County that the cows stood in any available waterhole to cool themselves down. Heatwaves shimmered across the hot earth, pressed down on one's shoulders like a wooden yoke, causing Emma to sit gasping for air, her mouth opening and closing like a bluegill as she waved her apron in front of her face.

She sat on an upturned bucket, although very little of it was visible, beneath the still leaves of the maple tree. The air was thick and brassy. The bees' droning sounded tired, drained of energy: the cicadas clung to tree bark as they gasped for breath themselves.

"Hester! Get out of that garden!" It took all the reserve energy Emma could muster to raise her voice loud enough to yell.

"Why?"

"It's too hot."

Hester laughed the sound of a rippling brook, her white teeth flashing in her dark face. She laid down her hoe, lifted her head, and came toward the maple tree. Tall and little, she moved without sound, effortless, her Indian blood enabling her to travel great distances without tiring. Emma never got weary of watching her daughter's graceful, fluid movement.

Hester threw herself into the grass at Emma's feet. "I love the garden, Emma."

"If you stay out there, you'll melt like a lump of butter."

"No."

"I wish I had a springhouse."

"Oh, you should have seen ours in Berks County." Hester's eyes lit up with enthusiasm as she launched into a vivid account of the wet, cool, dripping stone house Hans had built so cleverly over the cold mountain spring water.

Emma watched Hester's face shrewdly, observing the animation. Did Hester miss her home so much? Obviously, there were good memories. There was a time when Hester had been happy, innocent, content.

"And my brothers? Remember I told you about Noah and Isaac? They loved to drag a bucket into the cold spring water, run ahead of me on the path I was on, quickly climb a tree, and then dump the cold water all over me."

Hester laughed at the thought, then became closed, pensive.

William had taken her to view the Amish community in Lancaster. They rode in his well-made wagon that was comfortable enough for a drive in the warm winds of

July. She had been intrigued by the Amish in this area, and interested, but in a halfhearted way, as if she were tasting soup and one important ingredient had been left out, but she didn't care enough to figure out what it was.

The farms were prospering, carved out of the woodland by swinging axes that bit into trees that were sacred to the Indians. They thought that a tree belonged to the Creator and not to any particular person. They couldn't conceive of owning tracts of land since all the land belonged to the Creator as well.

When the white men came and tried to impose their views, many of these peaceful, roaming tribes became furious, marauding in their defense without mercy.

Yes, she told William, the Amish and Mennonite settlers were amazing. They had a fierce work ethic. Like Hans, they thrived on hard, physical labor. Their goals were to make money, expand, get ahead.

They argued that time. He did not back down but kept his attitude, resolutely holding it within himself by the set of his jaw, the sparkle in his blue eyes a glint of determination.

She felt his superiority—and her inferiority and inefficiency. Her way of thinking lay fallow. It was dead, old.

He had what it would take to get this country going. It was called forging ahead.

CHAPTER 11

THAT LANCASTER COUNTY LAY DIRECTLY ON UN-usually fertile soil was evident in the growth of its crops. Its forests were also thick and green and dense, the oaks growing to majestic towers, their thick branches bearing a canopy of leaves so heavy it was like a roof.

Amish men cleared the land by the sweat of their brows, side by side with the Mennonites, the Dunkards, and the Quakers, to name several of the "plain" denominations who had settled in the area.

There were Scots, Irish, and English, too, many of them Roman Catholic. Churches sprang up in the town of Lancaster to accommodate the influx of people seeking to make a living on these fertile grounds and needing spiritual sustenance as well.

All her life as a child in Berks County, Hester had been used to attending services in Amish homes, with a simple meal served afterward. It had seemed odd to skip religious services on Sunday after she came to live with Emma. But because she was afraid to show her face in Emma's church, she simply did not attend any services.

She often thought about her childhood, riding to church in the wagon with her siblings. Hans would be practicing his songs, the way he always did, with Kate sitting soft and wide beside him, clutching yet another little one on her lap, the large hat pulled well forward past her pleasant face.

Going to church was a warm and comfortable ritual, like porridge for breakfast. There was an order to Sunday mornings that began with getting up from her bed in the chilly darkness. Kate would stand so close that Hester could feel her warm breath on the top of her head as she drew the heavy-toothed comb through the snarls in her thick, black hair, pulling it so tight her eyes felt slanted, like she was from Asia. She had once seen pictures of the Chinese with wide, flat eyes in a book that Theodore Crane, the old schoolteacher, had. In fact, she told Kate that her hair was so tight she was going to turn into an Asian. Kate's soft, rounded stomach had shaken up and down as she laughed quietly, then she'd held her head against Hester's for an instant, and said, "Ach, my dear daughter."

That she was loved was never a question. Love had been in abundance in that narrow little log house. It bubbled from rocks in the spring and hovered over the steaming bowls of oatmeal and corn and beans that Kate set on the table. Love was everywhere—in the sky and the birds and the distant mountains, the sights that made her heart swell and swell until she had to laugh or cry, she felt so much love. She missed it all now.

She sat on a chair she had carried outside, the rough, wide boards covered with a cushion, her bare feet hooked on one of the rungs. Already it was hot as the morning sun climbed into the bold, glaring sky. It was too humid to call the sky blue. Instead, it was white all over, shimmering with heat supplied by the orange sun.

In the pasture, the cow stood beneath an oak tree, her tail swishing endlessly back and forth, dislodging troublesome black flies that made her life a misery. The horse, Frieda, stamped a front foot, then a hind one, swishing her tail in the same steady rhythm as the cow's. Their heads drooped, as if they already had prepared themselves for the heat of the day.

Billy was off somewhere in the woods. Hester knew fishing was forbidden on the Sabbath, so Emma made sure he did not sneak off with his fishing pole. But Hester was almost sure that if she went to the barn to check, the pole wouldn't be there. She smiled.

Emma was inside taking her after-breakfast-Sunday-morning nap, her bare feet turned up, her ample hands crossed over her stomach, her breaths coming with quick, soft regularity. Her opened Bible lay beside her, a tribute to her Sabbath day's devotion.

Hester had read portions of her own Bible as well, but nothing seemed to satisfy her longing for a deeper knowledge of God's will. She skipped over verses, paging through the Old Testament and then the New. She read the words of Jesus but felt no sense of wonderment. Maybe she was too lethargic to be able to sustain her spiritual body, as if the heat and humidity stifled her desire to learn about God.

She reasoned and thought on these things. As she had been raised Amish, the days in her weeks were repetitive, an order to each one. Her clothes portrayed the *Ord-nung* or rules for living, agreed to by the Amish community. Her cap was a sign of meekness, symbolizing a subservient attitude toward the men in her life—Hans, her father, and if she should marry, her husband.

She had stopped wearing her cap. Her hair was now her glory, as the Bible said. Thick and black, it was so straight it resisted combs and hairpins, shining and so glossy it appeared to shimmer with blue. The feeling of being half-dressed had disappeared after a few months, until she felt no need to wear something on her head.

William had brought up the subject recently, allowing a sliver of guilt into her conscience. He told her God would not hear her prayers unless her head was covered, since she was a member of the Amish. She had promised to live, stay, and follow Jesus in that church, so who did she think she was?

Instantly, rebellion had raised its head, a hooded cobra ready to strike. Angry words filled her mouth, ready to fly forth. Her heart beat heavily, but at the final instant, she bit them back, her mouth wide, compressed.

She believed William wanted to marry her someday. Why would he be courting her otherwise? Yes, she thrilled to see him, but it was troubling, the instant, all-consuming resistance that rose in her when he spoke of so many things—the *Ordnung*, the Indians, Emma Ferree, almost everything.

Maybe the devil had control of her thoughts now that she had made a stand against Hans and Annie. Perhaps that had all been wrong. Should she have stayed and remained a true and honorable servant all her life? For now she was of the world. She was worldly. It was hard to always know if you were doing the right thing.

Had she picked up the heathen ways of the Indians, as William had said? But they were not heathen. They weren't. Would she say one thing and mean another all her life?

Oh, she'd stood up to William when his voice brought the usual uprising, the resistance that filled her. She'd told him how she felt about Hans and Annie. But what did she really believe about them, and what was right for her to do?

She leaned forward and dropped her dark head in her hands. She felt as if she were being torn in two directions. Two sides were pulling her in opposite ways, upsetting the peace and stability of her life with Emma and Billy.

She heard a sound that was not birdsong. It was a bit liquid and trilling, like the sound of birds, but. . . . Wait a minute.

Up came her head. She held so still she seemed built into the chair. Unmistakably, the whistle held a tune. Lightly, but it was there.

Now she heard the chirring of a gray squirrel, the call of the meadowlark she could see plainly, perched on the rail fence.

There it was again. Someone, somewhere, was whistling. Rapt, she remained seated, her senses keen, expecting the whistling to come closer. Instead, it faded away, leaving her feeling deprived, as if a wonder had occurred but been taken away before she could grasp it.

The feeling of melancholy, a lowering of her spirits, remained the rest of the day, until she realized it was almost time to prepare for William's visit.

Emma made no pretense about hiding her displeasure. She told Hester outright that she had no time for William King, but if she insisted on letting him court her, then she would stay out of the way.

Hester eyed Emma from her place at the oval mirror above the washstand, small and round as she was, her face beet-red with indignation, bristling with disapproval and something else. She wound her hair into a loose twist, held it fast with sturdy pins and combs, then turned to Emma, her eyes large and dark. She had no idea how beautiful she was, how pure and unspoiled, a magnolia in the midst of dandelions, Emma mused.

"Why do you dislike William so?" Hester asked breathlessly.

"I just do."

"I'm sorry if you feel bad about me spending the evening with him, but just let me try, all right?"

Emma's answer was a significant whoosh of forced air through her nostrils, a sharp turning on her heel, with her wide back floating across the room and out the front door, leaving the room empty of a spoken statement.

Hester felt as if she were violating Emma's goodness of heart. How could she be so set in her mind? Emma was the angelic figure who rescued poor children, wet dogs, and injured cats, who handed out food and money to dubious bedraggled recipients, who, more than likely, were not worthy of her generosity, spending it on cheap apple whiskey or frittering it away on senseless sins of a different nature.

William arrived in his shining wagon, the lap robe tucked beneath the seat, the horse black, his neck arched and his tail flowing, pawing the ground impatiently. Hester's heart fluttered as if a canary were caged inside her chest. A high song of happiness propelled her down the steps and out through the short grass surrounding the house.

His eyes found hers and stayed on them. He drank in the caramel color of her fine glowing skin, the black liquid stars that were her eyes, and vowed to himself that he would make her his wife. He would rescue her from the heathen nature of her origin and pull her out of the quicksand Emma Ferree had set for her.

Love beat strongly in his breast. He marveled that God allowed this wonderful creature, this child of sweetness and innocence, into his life. That outburst about Hans and Annie had all been Emma Ferree's poison, not Hester's own thinking.

Secure in the knowledge of his own intelligence, William lifted the reins, and they were off in a cloud of heat and dust. Behind them, a florid, sweating face peered around the corner of the brown house, and an arm was flung angrily in their direction. Her small feet carried Emma into the house, where she cut herself a wide wedge of custard pie, followed by another as large as the first, before she looked at the clock and wondered where that Billy was. It was getting late.

The wagon wheels made very little sound as they followed the country road away from the house. The magnificent horse trotted smoothly, its black mane flowing in the breeze. William's hands were strong and brown, with long, thick fingers holding the reins easily, skilled at the art of driving a fine horse. His profile was so handsome, his yellow straw hat set square and low on his forehead, the way she remembered Hans's.

He was kind and attentive, pointing out the Amish farms that dotted the cleared fields. The farm belonging to his parents, Elias and Frances King, had a stone house so much like her own in Berks County that she gasped. It was almost identical, including the grayish color of the limestone.

The windows were few, tall, and paned with many separate pieces of glass. The wooden sashes could be raised and lowered, allowing for breezes when the weather was warm and protection against cold winds and snow. The barn was built along the side of a hill, allowing easy access to the second floor. The animals were housed snugly against winter's frigid winds on the first floor. A vast orchard lay to the south, with apple and peach and cherry trees, sentinels of hard work and excellent management skills. The corn was tall and heavy, a deep green color that spoke well of Elias King's farming know-how. Hester imagined the hayloft bursting with mounds of loose hay and straw, the corncrib full.

Her heart beat firmly and steadily. Here in this fertile soil was her destiny. Here she could work tirelessly side by side with her handsome William. Finally she would be free of the creeping certainty that she was no one, always hunted because of the color of her skin. The Amish were held in high esteem, hard workers that tilled the land, and she would be one of them.

If William King wanted her for his wife, the Amish would come to accept her in time. She would prepare herself for the ridicule, which was as sure to come as rain. It was the nature of men, just as certain as the changing of seasons or the lightning that occurred by the powers of God. But she would belong. She would etch out a place for herself as William King's wife. Respect and honor would follow.

She would bake the lightest bread and the sweetest pies. Her garden would yield vast quantities of vegetables, enough to share with the neighbors. Like Kate's, the wooden cradle would always hold an infant.

Hester glanced sideways at William, noticing the neat angle of his nose, the perfect jaw, the set of his mouth.

"Here, Hester, is what I will inherit." William waved a hand in the general direction of his parents' farm. Hester's large eyes were round with awe.

"Of course, my father and mother will live in the *doddyhaus* on the same yard, but I believe, in time, my mother will come to accept you. She can teach you how to work."

"I know how to work. I was taught first by Kate, then by Annie. I doubt very much whether your mother knows more than I do."

"Oh, ho! The voice of inexperience, Hester! My mother is held in high esteem all through the valley. She is unequalled in just about every housekeeping skill. She makes her own *ponhaus* at butchering time, saying no one else's is fit." William laughed, a superior sound of exulting that eclipsed Hester's happiness and her plans for the future, turning her awe of the beautiful farm to a gray hue of uncertainty. Hester fell silent after that laugh.

William told her he would not introduce her to his parents just yet, adding that it would be nice if he had a magic potion that would turn her skin white like his.

Hester smiled, but it was a mere lifting of the corners of her mouth, a small, trembling mock of gaiety.

He stopped the horse by a tumbling brook, then turned to her in the glow of the evening light beneath a canopy of green leaves that made a soft rustling sound, as if they were settling themselves for the night. Somewhere a robin set up a short, raucous bedtime call, gathering her fledglings in. He let the reins dangle at his feet after loosening the horse's neck rein, allowing him to lower his head and pull at the thick green grass.

"Hester, I have loved you since I first saw you, so shy, so set apart among a group of girls at that wedding. I have never forgotten you. You have remained in my heart and in my mind. It is only by God's grace that he allowed you back into my life. I know this is very soon, but I hope to marry you by November."

"But." Hester was completely taken aback.

William held up a hand. "No, don't protest. I know I'm moving too fast. I love you, Hester. My love for you is a beacon of hope I carry in my heart. I want you for my wife. My mother needs to have me marry now."

Suddenly she was caught in his arms, held against him in a viselike grip. Clumsily, his lips sought hers, then found them. Hester had never been kissed. It was so sudden, so powerful. She had no time to resist, to attempt to loosen herself from his grip.

When she thought perhaps she would suffocate after all, he released her just as suddenly. His eyes shone with a new and triumphant light as he reached for the reins.

Hester wrapped her arms around her waist as if to steady the quivering in her stomach. So this is how it was. No one had ever told her. It was bearable. There were worse things. To belong, she could endure being kissed, held in that painful grip. It was good to feel as if she belonged.

Again William turned to her. "I love you, Hester. Will you marry me?"

Hester nodded. "I will."

Later, she remembered that she had not said she loved him. Or that he had not thanked her for accepting his offer of marriage. She did love him, she reasoned. Enough to marry him.

She spent her days without telling anyone of William's proposal. Emma clucked and worried when she left her soft-boiled egg beside the toasted bread at breakfast, then ate every morsel after Hester went to do the washing.

Billy started back to school that week, an unhappy red face spouting many bitter words of resistance beneath his new, scratchy straw hat with a decorative red band that matched the stiff collar on his starched new shirt. His riotous red curls were cut and plastered into subjection with hard strokes of wet palms against his head. Emma's threats to bring in a nice slab of wood from the woodpile were mere whistles above his furious little face.

Billy told Hester he was going to run away. He'd stay in the woods with the crickets and katydids like she had. Then he walked stiff-legged with fury the whole way out the lane—a grassy dent called a lane—turning right toward the schoolhouse two miles away, swinging his lunch pail angrily at a passing sparrow.

Emma chuckled and chuckled at her Billy. What a display! Like a bantam rooster, he was. *Ach, du yay,* she thought, shaking her head. Yes, and what good did school do for a bright boy like him? Why he made as much money down at that livery stable as some grown men. He was smart, her Billy. His brain was as quick as a whip. Oh, he'd grow into a fine man, but he needed schooling. It was the order, the discipline, that did him good.

All that week, every morning, she wet down his short red hair, packed his lunch pail with bread and butter, ham and cheese, stewed apples, and crumbly sugar-sprinkled cookies made with molasses. And every morning he stomped around like some dangerous little man, vowing to run away, making Emma chuckle and laugh, her round stomach jiggling with her efforts to restrain it.

When Emma served platters of beans with chunks of pork, roasted cabbage, and fresh mint tea, and Hester only picked at a few beans, Emma finished her third helping of roasted cabbage, wiped her mouth with the back of the tablecloth, sipped her mint tea, and turned to Hester. "Now, Hester dear, you're going to have to tell me what's wrong. You can't hide it. Tell me."

Silence hung between them, a curtain of irritation for Emma, a necessity for Hester, as she desperately searched for the courage to explain what was going on.

"I'm being married to William. In the winter. In November." Her voice was weak and whispery, but they were words, and Emma heard each one correctly.

"But, you can't!" she burst out immediately.

"He loves . . . me. He said so. He wants me for his wife."

"*Mein Gott. Oh, mein Gott. Oh, du yay, du yay.*" Up went the apron over her face as she rocked from side to side. "*Gook do runna, Mein Herr und Vater.*" Praying aloud in German, she beseeched her heavenly father to look down on Hester.

"Why? Oh, why?" Lamenting and exclaiming, perspiration forming rivulets of moisture down the side of her wide forehead, she rocked back and forth, as if Hester's announcement were too much for her rounded shoulders to bear.

"I told you, Emma. He loves me. He is taking me to live on his farm with his parents."

"Do you love him?"

"Yes." Firmly the word sealed her future. Surely now she would return to the fold and be welcomed with open arms, her life full and running over with purpose and belonging.

She would be exactly like Kate. Laughing, telling stories, her children about her like jewels, each one more precious than the last. William would love her as Hans had loved Kate. She would win Frances's love. She thought of Hans's mother, the abrasive Rebecca, who, like a stiff brush, had hurt Kate. But, that, too, would be the price she would pay. In exchange she would experience a great and wonderful sense of belonging.

Emma remained unconvinced that Hester could ever be accepted into William's family—and she said so. Not willing to hear Emma's tirade of words, Hester thought back to William's kiss. Was that how it was? She almost asked Emma, but she didn't want to listen to more agonized wails of wrongdoing.

Perhaps the tenderness would come later, like the way Hans would slip an arm around Kate's soft waist or whisper a word in her ear, making her face light up with happiness. No one had ever given her the slightest sense of romantic notions. Hans's tortured eyes and touch had been swept beneath the rug of denial now, where they belonged. It was nothing. It never had been. Whatever little bit that occurred had been all her own fault.

William would be like Hans was with Kate, filling the stone house to capacity with love. You couldn't separate love and belonging.

"Hester, you don't have to look for a place to belong. You belong here. With me and Billy." Emma began to cry, real sorrow running from her eyes so nearly lost in the folds of her round face.

Billy put up an awful fuss. He said William King was all right, he guessed, but not as her husband. She didn't need a husband as long as him and Ma were around, and besides, once he grew up, *he* was going to marry her. Which started Emma on another round of sorrow mixed with laughter, until her voice rose to a squeaky pitch and she became a bit hysterical, which served to turn her face into a purple color that stayed all evening.

Hester remained unmoved, stoic, steadfast. William talked to his parents and to Joel Stoltzfus, the bishop of the Lancaster County Amish congregation, who called a secret meeting with his *mit dienner*, and then met with John Lantz and his group of ministers, who said yes to the marriage. Hester grew up in Berks County, John confirmed, but why she suddenly ran away from her Christian home and joined the worldly people in the town of Lancaster they would never know. Hans and Annie Zug were prominent members of their district. They must be told that Hester had been found.

The leaders set about doing this, arriving late one evening at the Zug home to share this news. On the way home, Rufus Troyer told Amos Fisher that according to their beliefs, shunning Hester was right when she lived in the world—but why was Hans refusing to have anything to do with her now, when he should be wanting her to return to the fold?

Amos Fisher said likely Annie had something to do with it. What he didn't say is how he noticed blood draining from Hans's face. Something was a little mysterious there. Something you did not talk about.

Rufus said, yes, no wonder Noah went off to the war.

CHAPTER 12

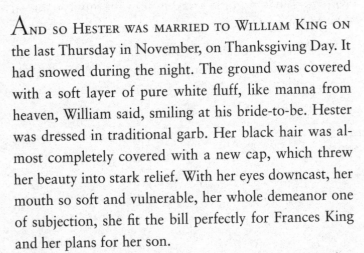

AND SO HESTER WAS MARRIED TO WILLIAM KING ON the last Thursday in November, on Thanksgiving Day. It had snowed during the night. The ground was covered with a soft layer of pure white fluff, like manna from heaven, William said, smiling at his bride-to-be. Hester was dressed in traditional garb. Her black hair was almost completely covered with a new cap, which threw her beauty into stark relief. With her eyes downcast, her mouth so soft and vulnerable, her whole demeanor one of subjection, she fit the bill perfectly for Frances King and her plans for her son.

The stone house was filled to capacity, the benches set in long lines in rooms cleared of furniture. This was a wedding, so everything that couldn't be sat on had to go. The preparation had been a work of many hands.

Emma Ferree threw her hands in the air and said she was having no part of this. She asked Walter Trout for a group of helpers so she could move back to her house on Mulberry Street in short order before winter came on.

She did not approve of William King and let everyone within earshot hear her opinion.

She went right back to Mulberry Street and began to minister to the poor. Billy went back to the livery stable and began collecting coins in his tin box. He found a straggly little terrier he named Hester, who lived beside the fireplace on a cushion, shivering with fright for weeks after they took her in. But they never quite got over the disappointment of losing Hester the young woman to William King.

The Kings' Amish neighbors gathered their cabbage and beans, beheaded their fat chickens, baked wedding cakes and pies and cookies, cleaned the house at Amos Speichers', and had a wedding.

Susie Fisher, a single woman, did the sewing for Hester. She had always hoped William King would ask for her hand, but had given up on that, seeing as she had already turned thirty. She liked *sell Indian maedle* and wished them the best. She measured and pinned, talking all the while in rapid Pennsylvania Dutch, exclaiming about Hester's dark hair and her skin.

Hester sat at her wedding table in the traditional corner with William's brothers and cousins as part of the bridal party. William ate great quantities of the festive wedding food from the fine china plates he had given Hester to be used on their wedding day.

He could not take his eyes off his lovely bride, a fact that was duly noticed by his mother, a keenly observant woman, tall and spare, with the same loping ease of movement as her son. Good. That bode well for the future.

William's five sisters had all married before him and were quite happy to finally have him married off, even if it was to an Indian. They had been afraid he'd run off with an Englisher yet.

Hester's eyes shone with happiness—the excitement of the day, the headiness of being the center of attention. In a few months' time she had gone from being a refugee and living in the country away from prying eyes, to becoming a young wife of a handsome, older Amish *rumshpringa*, a youth who was overdue for a wife.

Far into the night, the wedding guests sang old German hymns, passed food and drink, and ate with great relish. Over and over again Hester and William shook hands with friends and family, accepted their blessings, and acknowledged their kind words and good wishes. Their wedding gifts were substantial, but then, everyone knew this poor Indian girl had no wooden hope chest piled with bedding and linens, towels, and other necessary items stored away for this day, the way other Amish girls did.

Hester was taken to the stone farmhouse and made her home there. William's parents were housed securely *ins ana end*, literally, "the other end," the phrase meaning, the apartment built on for the older folks on the homestead.

So many things reminded her of her home in Berks County. The hearth for cooking, the way the washing and cleaning were done—everything she had been taught came tumbling back.

With sturdy arms, she washed the whites to a shining clean that was almost blue. Her mother-in-law's approval rang in her ears like bells of much-needed esteem. She reveled in William's praise of her meals as well, as she turned out succulent roast beef, fluffy mashed potatoes, crisp corn mush, and creamy porridge.

She sewed carefully and scrubbed floors with speedy precision. She was accepted by William's family, which gave her the prestige she needed to be received well by the remainder of the congregation.

Two years went by. The wooden cradle stayed upstairs beneath the eaves, a beautifully carved work done by William's own hand. Often Hester would climb the stairs when William was in the fields. Today the weather was dreary, the rainwater running in rivulets down the mossy oak shingles. It dripped off the edge and splattered at the base of the house, creating thin indentations in the grass, soaking the scattered brown leaves and the acorns.

Hester shivered from the chilly dampness of the upstairs. She wrapped the thin shawl around her shoulders before reaching for the cradle. She dusted it with the tips of her fingers, then rocked it gently with her right hand. She prayed in broken whispers. She pleaded for the blessing of a child. She thought of Hannah in the Old Testament at the temple, lamenting for a child until onlookers thought she was drunk. Ah, poor woman.

As Hester threw herself on the unforgiving oak boards, sobs wracked her shoulders. No one could see or hear her. No one. "Let the rain pound the shingles. Let the water slide down the side of the roof. My tears will be like the rain," she said aloud to herself. For William and his mother and father were running out of patience. Their *gaduld* was wearing thin.

She often thought of Kate. If only she could have one conversation with her to ask her what had happened so that she was able to have children. Her table was filled, her heart and hands busy with the hundreds of duties of love that had brought so much enrichment to Kate's life.

Perhaps, Hester thought, it was her fault. William loved her well, but he never understood her shrinking away, her inability to welcome his ardor. She had finally admitted to herself that his kisses were an onslaught. It was a long time before she acknowledged the warnings of Emma Ferree.

But she was William's wife, and she loved him as best she could. She endured bravely, nodding her head in agreeable perplexity to William's question about her inability to conceive and answering Frances King's impertinent questions honestly.

Lying on the wooden floor, she cried until her spirit felt battered and brittle, as if it could easily break into thousands of pieces. Then she was finished. She got to her knees, folded her hands in supplication, and asked God to bless her one last time, before pushing the wooden cradle back under the eaves and making her way slowly down to the kitchen, where she dried her eyes, washed her face, and put on a bright smile for William's evening meal.

How she longed for him to fold her into his arms tenderly, carefully, whispering words of love and assurance. But that was not William's way.

Hester knew he had too much to do. He needed to hire a *Knecht*, a youth to help with the milking and the harvest, but he felt it was money unwisely spent. He often wolfed down his supper, barely noticing what he ate.

Tonight, though, it was raining, which allowed him some free time in the barn, repairing a harness and cleaning stables, jobs that had been pushed back during the harvest. Hester had prepared a special dish, the one he favored above all the hearty meals she set on the snowy white tablecloth. Lima beans and potatoes cooked together with milk and butter and a generous douse of black pepper, thickened to a creamy consistency, served with fried chicken and applesauce.

Before every meal he washed, combed his thick black hair, and then sat down at the sturdy plank table full of Hester's cooking. They bowed their heads. His lips moved in silent prayer. He raised his head, filled a plate, handed the dish to Hester, then served himself, usually without speaking, his thoughts on the cattle, the crops, or some other important matter. He would lower his head and shovel the food into his mouth, clearly hungry and sometimes ravenous. Hester learned to eat in silence, knowing he would talk later.

"The cake all gone?"

Hester nodded, her dark eyes lifted to his.

"You haven't had time to make another one?"

She spooned applesauce into her mouth. Swallowed. "Yes, I had time but thought perhaps I should spin wool upstairs."

"Upstairs? You go up there to moon about that cradle, working yourself into a frenzy about being childless. That's what Mother says."

Hester's eyes were black with rebellion when she raised them to his blue, mocking, appraising eyes. Her performance fell short. Unable to fill that cradle, she left William's quiver empty for the whole of Lancaster County to see.

"Hester, you need to read your Bible more. Get yourself in the *Ordnung* better. I see your cap tied loosely, your hair just a bit more worldly than I would like. You know God cannot bless us if we are inclined to rebel against the laws of the church."

"But I wasn't aware that I do!" Hester cried out.

"Oh, but you do. It's the Indian in you."

If William would have reached out and delivered a resounding blow to her face, it would have hurt less.

"The Indian in you." Always, she carried that flaw like a monstrous growth, a defect.

William got up, pushed his chair across the wide oak boards, and stood by the fire, chewing on a sliver of wood, his blue eyes waiting for her response.

When there was none, he watched her rake dishes off the table and carry them to the dry sink. To her back, he said, "Mother says to try pervinca."

Hester stopped washing dishes. As still as a stone, she stood facing the wall. When she turned, William flinched against the sizzle in the black depth of her eyes. "'Mother says. Mother says.' William, I am your wife. For over two years, I have been your wife. I bow to your wishes, as well as your mother's, which is my rightful place. But when you hurl insults, I do not feel it is my duty to keep bowing beneath them. Has not *Unser Herr* instructed us in the way of marriage? Should you not love your wife?"

"*Schtill!*" William's command was powerful. His voice rang out harshly as he flung the toothpick into the crackling fire. Two steps—long and deliberate—and his hand snaked out and spun her around to face him.

Lowering his face, his breath hot, he rasped, the words slow and methodic, branding into her conscience. "God has ordained from the beginning that your will is subject to mine. I am the head of the house. What I say is truth. You are to think as your husband. Your will is gone now. You are my wife."

Up came Hester's face, her eyes blazing. "Then you need to love me, William!"

"I do love you, Hester. I love you more than you know. But you are disappointing me in more ways than one."

As you are failing me, Hester thought.

"I do not believe pervinca has much to do with my needs. I have a storehouse of knowledge about herbs. When I was younger, I had the good fortune to meet an old Indian woman who wrote many cures for all kind of diseases in a book."

"Indians have no written language."

"She learned from Theodore Crane, the schoolmaster in Berks County."

"So you're saying you know more than Mother and I?"

Hester drew herself up, clasping her hands behind her back. "Yes. I believe I do." One eyebrow was lifted as William emitted a short, contemptuous laugh.

"I highly doubt it."

Hester returned to her dishwashing, the set of her shoulders giving away the fury that raged in her breast. She knew that continuing this conversation would prove futile. She would sin, pushing her words onto her husband, where they would only slide away from his hearing and disintegrate into the floor, contributing nothing to either one of them.

Frances dried and pounded the herb called pervinca, mixed it with whiskey, and brought it to Hester a few days later. Hester was folding wash. The sun shone through the small windowpanes, providing the light she needed to smooth out William's clean shirts before expertly folding the homespun fabric.

Today, there was a lightness in her heart, a song on her lips. The golden light streaming through the window, the November chill removed by the glowing fire, the dull gleam of the cupboard with the white agate pitcher containing sprigs of orange bittersweet, the white ironstone plates stacked neatly on the shelves above it all, pleased Hester, providing beauty and a sense of accomplishment. Imperfect she may be, but she was William's wife.

Frances never knocked on the door, saying that was for *die Englische*. Amish were family; there was no need to be formal, including knocking on doors. When Hester looked up, Frances was standing inside, startling Hester so that she jumped, surprised that Frances could open the door so quietly.

"Hester." It was Frances's way of greeting.

"Mam! You startled me."

"And you an Indian? You should be the one sneaking up on me."

Hester let that one go, squelching a retort.

"Here. Pervinca. One dram every morning and evening."

Obediently, Hester reached out, took it, and set it carefully on the cupboard by the bittersweet. She noticed the pale green color, how the light turned it to an olive shade, the orange bittersweet beside it.

"You will obey?'

"Yes."

"Good. You heard? Amos and Sarah Speicher have been blessed with their first child. A son. They named him Abner."

Hester's face softened, her eyes became moist. "Oh? That's good news! I must go see her. That's wonderful. God be praised."

"Yes. I am so glad for a successful birth. Always a sign of God's blessing."

Hester nodded, picked up the shirt she was smoothing, repositioned it, and prepared to continue.

"So, will you visit soon?"

Puzzled, Hester lifted her eyes to her mother-in-law. "Why?"

"Oh, you should go soon. Sarah is such a shining example of purity for you. She has obviously acquired the blessing that God is withholding from you."

This statement left Hester pondering, uneasy, exploring avenues of release from the condemnation in Frances's words. Why would God bless Amos and Sarah, when he would not fill William's and Hester's arms with a bundle so precious it would fill them with joy?

Kate had always told her that the moment when she first held Hester in her arms, she experienced a joy as great, if not greater, than when she held Noah less than a year later. God had not blessed Hans and Kate for nine whole years, then, unexplainably, he had. Who could figure that out?

Had Kate submitted herself more fully to Hans' wishes? Had she drawn her cap well over her hair, covering herself more convincingly with humility and subjection to Hans? But with Hans, subjection was not a hard yoke nor a dead weight slung on Kate's unwilling shoulders. Hans was easy-going. He had laughed, pulled her wide covering strings, and told her she was getting fat, but in an approving way. His was an attitude lined with the comforting pillows of love on which Kate could rest and recline, her spirit exulting in the constant stream of his approval.

It was the approval. Hester smoothed the shirt over and over, long after the wrinkles had been rubbed out. Her thoughts turned to memories of longing, to a desperate hunger for approval, the kind that would allow her to be free, to move along with lightness like a dandelion seed, effortless, carried along on soft summer breezes of love.

She sighed. In the stillness of her kitchen, the bittersweet blurred into the waxy, dark green leaves as tears stung her eyes. For the first time in over two years, she longed for the safety, the haven of approval that was Emma Ferree. And Billy. Dear redheaded, mischievous boy. She should have listened to the words of warning.

But she had a whole life ahead of her. She would be brave. She was an Indian, fearless and stout-hearted, so she would summon her courage and live her life with William as she had promised the day she married him. Perhaps she could yet soften him, molding him into the kindness she longed for.

William was a good man. He was. She would try harder. She would be blameless. Then perhaps God would bless her and give them a son, another generation to till the fertile black soil of Lancaster County.

She swallowed the whiskey-soaked pervinca. She prayed, endured her husband's kisses, obeyed every wish. Often while he slept, she wondered at the ways of a man, that God had wrought such a difference.

William told her repeatedly that it was the woman who had sinned in the Garden of Eden. Not Adam. Eve had taken the fruit of that tree, that forbidden apple. Worse yet, she had enticed her husband into senseless betrayal as well. So it was her lot in life to suffer, to subject herself to her husband. Did he not do his duty, cutting trees, tilling the soil, keeping weeds at bay? The sweat of his brow was the price he paid to provide for his wife, the weaker vessel.

Yes, she said. Yes.

She threw the heavy harness on the brown driving horse named Fannie. It was Elias's horse, but hers to drive any time she wanted. Fannie was a small brown mare with liquid eyes the same color as her black mane, except for the green and purple lights in the irises. She was gentle and easy to hitch to the buggy so that Hester could manage the task by herself.

Fannie stood content and patient as Hester lifted the wooden shafts, then backed into her space with only a minimum of calling. Hester fastened the traces and then the backhold strap to the britching, gathered the reins, and looked up.

Frances stood, not ten feet away. It was uncanny the way that woman crept up on her, drawing irritation the way lobelia drew pus from a wound.

"You're off to see Sarah and the newborn?"

Swallowing her words of inflammation, she nodded. A semblance of a smile, to be polite, formed around her mouth.

"Where is your shawl?"

Hester threw up her hand and pointed to the buggy seat. "It's hard to throw a harness on a horse's back wearing a shawl."

"Not on Fannie. She's small."

"I'll put it on."

"Make sure you do. Some of the young girls have taken to wearing a coat without a woollen shawl. Serves them right if they freeze." With that remark vibrating in the cold December air between them, she turned on her heel and walked away, as stiff and formidable as an axe.

Hester climbed into the buggy, reached for the required shawl, thrust the heavy steel pin through the wool, then flung the corners over her shoulder, making driving easier. She flung Frances's words over her shoulder as well, then remembered her unacquired blessing of a child as the guilt piled onto her shoulders.

The road that led away from the Elias King farm was well traveled this December day. The ground was frozen, making the going easier. The first snow hadn't yet appeared, which was very unusual. William said the Bible spoke of the latter days when unusual weather would occur, and these were definitely the latter days, now, weren't they?

The earth lay cold and fallow, a time of dead, frozen cornstalks and wind-whipped grasses that grated together, brittle-brown, waiting for snow to cover their uselessness. Holes in the frozen road were covered with ice, broken where heavy steel-covered wheels had crashed through.

The sky was gray, the wind a bone-chilling blast from the east. It would begin to snow during the night if not before. William wanted to get more corn fodder into the barn before it fell, so he frowned when she'd said, over fried mush, that she wanted to visit Sarah and her new baby. He clapped his hat on his black hair and stalked out without further words.

She had opened her mouth to tell him if he needed help, she would be available, then thought, no she'd see Sarah today. Sarah Speicher and her little Abner.

Her heart sang in anticipation. *"Schlofe, Buppli, Schlofe."* She sang every verse of the old lullaby. She could see Kate, large and warm, her wide face serene and content, singing yet another baby to sleep. Oh, she'd loved her babies! Nurtured them, rocked then during the night, cuddled and loved and adored them.

Hester could still feel the warmth from her large body, feel her breathing above her head, the soft palms pressed on either side of her face, a reverence between them, a benediction. Kate's love, a remembered treasure, was still sufficient. But only sometimes, like now, did she really experience Kate again. Hester moved along the frozen dirt road with small, brown Fannie clopping along effortlessly, the cold wind tingling her nose and cheeks, her gloved hands expertly holding the reins. The fields of Lancaster County lay cold and deserted, waiting till God rolled the season along to spring, when the warm sun would wake up the dormancy of December.

Hester prayed that God would remember her body's own dormant December and would send the sunshine of his blessing into her life. Involuntarily, she set her hat forward with a well-placed grip of her gloved hand. Just in case William's words might be true.

CHAPTER 13

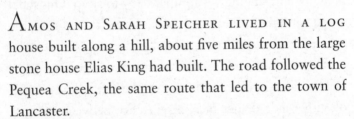

Amos and Sarah Speicher lived in a log house built along a hill, about five miles from the large stone house Elias King had built. The road followed the Pequea Creek, the same route that led to the town of Lancaster.

Hester had traveled this road quite often, visiting friends or going to church, so she only needed a slight bit of pressure on the right reign to turn Fannie onto the small lane that led to the log house.

It was surrounded by pine and spruce trees, the larger deciduous trees having been hacked away. There was a small but serviceable barn, an empty corn crib and a henhouse with one door flapping on its broken hinges, squeaking desolately in the stiff, easterly wind.

Hester stopped the horse and looked toward the house. There was no yellow glow from the small window, but then, Hester reasoned, some people saved their candles or oil till darkness set in. Unhitching Fannie, she looked around uneasily. It was too quiet. The barn door creaked eerily as Hester swung it wide. The smell of raw manure made her nostrils tingle, the stench overwhelming.

A cow bawled. A horse gave a low nicker. A cat slunk around a corner, then slithered along a wall before disappearing. The manure was piled so high Hester could not find a way to open the gate of the empty boxstall, so she tied Fannie to the gate, leaving her in the walkway.

"Stay, Fannie. Good girl." Hester patted the moist neck beneath the heavy black mane before letting herself out, closing the screeching door behind her.

Uncertain now, she hesitated. The flapping henhouse door made shivers run down her arms. Resolutely, she walked to the front door. Wide planks were worn smooth around the heavy latch where many hands had struggled to lift it. The roof was gray, the shingles weathered and split. The chinking between the logs was drying out. Small pieces of it littered the unsown grass surrounding the walls.

The windows were empty of light like a lifeless person. Lowering her head, Hester tapped on the door. She waited, then tapped again. A thin voice called from behind the heavy door.

Hester struggled with the latch, then swung the door wide. A rectangular path of light appeared immediately. The gray shadows returned after she pulled it shut behind her.

"Over here. I'm over here."

Hester found her way to the rumpled bedstead, noticing the weak fire burning dangerously low in the small fireplace as she passed it. She was shocked to find Sarah beneath the covers, her husband, Amos, beside her, and the newborn tucked between them. A foul odor rose from the soiled diapers flung beside the bed, the sour stench of sickness hovering over the small bedroom like a yet undetected whisper of foreboding.

"Sarah?"

Hester's word brought a glad cry, a recognition of answered pleas.

"Oh, Hester. It's you! Thank God."

"Sarah, what is going on? Are all of you ill?"

"Our *maud* went home five days ago. Amos is very sick. Our little Abner is becoming so frail." Sarah began to cry, soft, hiccupping little sobs of shame and helplessness.

Hester was already shrugging out of her coat, flinging her large black hat aside. She rolled up her sleeves and went around to Amos's side of the bed, her mouth grim when the fevered brow burned the palm of her hand. Here was a dire situation. She needed onions. Lobelia. Bitterroot. Small milkweed.

Bending low, she asked Sarah for onions.

"Yes. We have plenty. In the attic."

When Hester found them, she put them in a kettle with water. She poked up the fire, adding the last few sticks of wood. She would get them comfortable, then look for the herbs later. The baby's thin cry sounded from the bed. Amos groaned, tried to rise, but fell back, breathing rapidly.

She found the crock of vinegar and heated it. She bathed their feet and foreheads with cool water, then with the vinegar. She applied an onion poultice and stopped to listen as Amos coughed, gasping and retching. Yes, it was whooping cough, the scourge of every settlement. The phlegm came up. Hester bent to examine it. She needed elecampane now. Also skunk cabbage, horehound, and pignut. She'd boil them together with brewer's yeast.

Her thoughts churned. She must go back home. She had all of these remedies stored in a wooden box. Adrenalin spurred her every motion.

For now, the onions would be sufficient. She brought fresh, cold water from the container on the back stoop. Both Amos and Sarah drank thirstily. She told them of her plans, promising she'd be back, with help.

Hester lashed the reins down on Fannie's back only once. The small horse, sensing the urgency, ran low to the ground, her feet churning with a pace so rapid she seemed to float. The buggy lifted and swung, shattering frozen clods of soil, tilted dangerously, righted itself, and followed the dashing horse.

She slowed Fannie before they reached the King farm. Hester knew she must be careful since Frances did not like to be told what to do. Calmly, she tied Fannie, slipped into the house, found the wooden box, and added potatoes, apples, a wedge of hard cheese, and a slab of bacon. Hurriedly, she put everything into a leather satchel and went back to the buggy.

Good. Frances had not interfered. Likely William was out in the lower cornfields.

Hester drove back at a slower pace, having mercy on Fannie. She gave her a nice pile of hay and a drink of water before returning to the house. The smell of onions, soiled diapers, and unwashed, feverish bodies was hard to bear when she entered, but there was work to be done. Suffering people needed help.

First, she put the herbs on to boil. Then she would mix the extract from the herbs with honey and give Amos and Sarah each a spoonful every hour. After she finished stewing the herbs, she made a warm pot of broth, added potatoes, and brought them to a boil.

She lifted the newborn and bathed him in warm water with vinegar, marveling at the strength in his lungs for one so young. He put up quite a howling, bringing anxious questions from the bed where Sarah lay beneath a plaster of boiled onions.

Hester dressed the baby in clean diapers and a white nightgown of soft homespun. She wrapped him in a heavy blanket and laid him in the cradle, bearing his indignant cries while she washed Sarah's feverish body and put her in a warm, clean nightgown. She draped the hickory chair with warm blankets, thought of Emma and Billy, then helped Sarah into it and put the baby to her breast for a good feeding.

Amos coughed and coughed, sucking in a desperate breath after each racking of his body. He tried to get up again and again. Hester moved among them, quiet, single-minded in her purpose. She would make them feel better. She would heal them with the old woman's wisdom of the earth and its fruit.

She heated water all afternoon. She washed clothes and hung them in the attic to dry. She fed them the fragrant soup, accepting Sarah's sighs of gratitude. While the baby slept, she washed diapers and floors, scrubbed dishes, and changed the rough, homespun sheets on the bed. She shook the dirt from the rugs, swept, and scoured the hearth.

Sarah and Amos swallowed the spoonfuls of medicine obediently, gladly. Hester was alarmed to find the light in the windows turning to darkness, subtly, as if a cloud had passed over the gray curtain that already hid the sun. Breathless now, she gave Sarah instructions, promising to return. She threw hay to the animals. She'd water them in the morning.

Fannie ran low and hard, but night had almost fallen before Hester had unhitched her and raced into the house, her shawl flying behind her through the deepening gloom.

Fortunately, William was late for his supper, so the bean soup was hot and the cornbread baked, golden and piping hot when he came in. He noticed his wife's heightened color, the snapping of her eyes, the renewed energy.

As usual, they bowed their heads. William shoveled large spoonfuls of the bean soup into his mouth and broke squares of cornbread into rectangles, loading them with freshly churned butter.

He asked her about her day, curious about the added energy that radiated like heat.

"Oh, I went to visit Sarah Speicher and baby Abner. Remember, they had a son about six weeks ago? Well, I found them in deplorable shape. All three were sick with what I think is whooping cough. So I stayed, helping them with onion plasters. And I cleaned and made soup."

For a long time, William said nothing. When he spoke, his works were measured, short, as if each one was contained in a very small cup. "That was nice of you. But I hope you won't go back. They need a doctor, not you."

"Oh, I had the whooping cough when I was six years old."

"You did?"

"Oh, yes, we all did. Noah and Isaac and Lissie and Solomon. Noah brought me cup after cup of cold water. Kate said I cried for it constantly."

Hester gave a low laugh, then lifted her eyes to his, seeking his approval, hoping he would agree that she had done the right thing. Instead, he forbade her to return.

"But I have to," Hester pleaded, floundering in the quagmire of his attitude. But he would not relent. He said he was afraid she would become ill, further removing his chances of producing an heir.

She bowed her head and submitted. When William went out to do chores, hot tears of frustration pricked her eyelashes, but not one drop fell on her cheeks. Anger replaced the tears. She gave vent to it by hurling a pewter candle holder into the wall and was pleased to find a nick in the plaster, a small spray of whitewash on the floor.

Word got around, though, probably by way of Elias King, who loved to help his neighbors—or at least organize a frolic, be the foreman of other men's labours, and acquire another pile of honor to his already elevated state. For Elias, like William, was highly esteemed by his fellow Amish. Fortunately, his goodwill included Amos Speichers, and a working bee was held. Hester was allowed to attend.

Hurriedly, furtively, she checked their supply of medicine. She was pleased to see they had swallowed every spoonful. Amos was on a chair, pale, trembling, still coughing, but visibly improved. Sarah's cheeks were pink, her eyes alive with interest. Baby Abner cooed on her lap.

Sarah wasted no time telling astounded neighbors about Hester's concoction of miracle herbs, as she called them. She related in minute detail the placing of the onion plaster, the vinegar baths.

"*Ya, oh ya. Goot. Sell iss goot.*"

Old Hannah Miller nodded her head in agreement, her beady brown eyes going to Hester's face. But skunk cabbage? Pignut? She had never heard of it. Hesitantly Hester spoke. She told them of the old Indian woman. Suspicion hooded eyes and made tongues cluck with caution. These Indians were *behoft* with witchcraft. Perhaps the devil gave Hester the power. Women shivered, thinking of old wives' tales brought across the Atlantic's heaving waters from Switzerland.

The men cleaned the stables and repaired the henhouse. The community brought chickens and placed them in the newly repaired house. Wood was cut, as well as split and stacked beneath the eaves. The chinking between the logs was repaired, as was the fence surrounding the barn.

So much food was brought in the shelves in the cellar bulged with cheeses and hams, potatoes and onions and dried lima beans and cabbage. Honey, elderberry jam, molasses, and cones of sugar were squeezed in. People carried ground cherry pies, green tomato pies, and custards. Amos and Sarah stood side by side with little Abner and thanked everyone *gahr hoftich*. They felt unworthy, they said.

Elias and Frances rode home, confident of having shored up their foundation of good works yet again, followed by William and Hester, whose thoughts of the situation were completely opposite. William insisted that

Hester's *dumb gamach* with those herbs were over, for sure, when Reuben Kauffman said those Indians were all guilty of powwowing. Hester wondered how soon the next call for help would arrive.

She did not have long to wait. Exactly seven days later, in fact. Reuben Kauffman's daughter, Naomi, woke up burning with fever, coughing violently.

Hester cooked the herbs and mixed them with honey. She did not ask William or her parents-in-law. She merely went about her business, hitched up Fannie, and set off to Reuben Kauffmans through the cold, dry countryside. It was almost Christmas, a few days before, in fact.

When the first snow came from the north, the flakes were small and hard, driven by a relentless, moaning wind that howled under the eaves like ghostly wolves. The big oven glowed with heat. The massive fireplace in the kitchen crackled and popped with a lively fire, yet the corners of the house made Hester shiver. She rubbed her arms as she went upstairs for onions and hovered by the fire as chills raced across her back.

She was making medicine again. After the herbs had boiled down, she lifted out the sodden mass, then mixed the extract with honey, bottled it, corked it, and waited for the next household to come down with the whooping cough. By the time Christmas arrived, she was becoming weary of all the sleepless nights and the days spent nursing the sick, cleaning, cooking, and washing.

On Christmas Eve, the snow lay thick and heavy like whipped cream layered over the stone house and barn, the pine trees, and bare branches of the forest. The yellow glow of the downstairs windows made William and

Hester's house appear warm and inviting, a cozy haven of rest for travelers or acquaintances. The people who traveled by on sleighs turned an appreciative eye to the big stone house, so well built that it would last for hundreds of years, a beacon of true workmanship. The son was so like the father. Yes, they were something, weren't they?

William was in a secretive mood, his blue eyes alight with pleasure. He invited Hester to sit beside him on the deacon's bench by the fire. She put a cork slowly onto the last bottle of medicine, washed her hands, and dried them on a flour sack towel before turning to William, who caught her hand in his, so unlike him. Bewildered, suddenly ill at ease, she drew back, hesitating.

"What, William?"

"I have something for you."

"A gift?"

"Certainly. For *Grishtag*." He scuttled to the walnut corner cupboard, boyish in his anticipation. Hester turned to watch as he opened the cupboard door, then extricated an oblong box awkwardly. How had he been able to hide that in such an obvious place? Hester felt the weight of the box.

"Don't drop it!"

Slowly, she unwrapped it, the white paper falling away to reveal a wooden crate containing a set of the most beautiful dishes Hester had ever seen. Blue. A pattern of indigo blue on a white background. Eight plates, eight saucers and teacups. A soup tureen and a serving platter. The china was so delicate, so beautiful, Hester was afraid to touch it.

"Go ahead, Hester. Put it on the big cupboard in the kitchen," he coaxed.

Hester gasped, her eyes wide with wonder. "Oh, I can't, William. It would be too showy. *Hochmut*, you know. I'll place it very carefully in the corner cupboard where no one will see it."

William was clearly puzzled. "But why would you do that?"

"I don't know. Wouldn't it be *grosfeelich* to display the expensive china in my kitchen? Perhaps one of my women friends would become jealous of me."

"That would not be your fault." Sighing, Hester placed the dishes on the cupboard in the kitchen, then felt William's arms about her as he stood behind her. Together, they admired the lovely dishes. They drank spicy eggnog and popped popcorn over the open fire, staying up late to talk about their pasts.

William was attentive, drinking in Hester's rare beauty by the light of the flickering fire. His beautiful wife intrigued him even now, three years after marrying her. She had needed a stern hand at first, but he had taught her well the ways of an Amish wife. He eyed the bottles of herbal medicine. Warily he approached her, bringing up the subject.

Hester listened, then drew away from him. "You do not approve, even after so many people have been helped?"

"What do you mean, 'helped'?"

"The. . . the medicine helps them through the coughing."

"Really? You think so?"

"Yes. It makes a big difference."

"It's only you that thinks so."

Hester shook her head.

"Do you charge them for your trouble?"

"No. Should I?"

"Of course. You could make a tidy profit. The herbs are free. So is the honey."

"But would it be right to charge poor young people like Amos Speichers? They have so little."

"We don't have a lot either. We have land to pay. To my father."

Hester nodded slowly. "How much should I charge?"

Quickly, William calculated the amount Hester could profit, named a sum, and told her to charge that for each bottle.

Hester thought of Lissie Hershberger and the endless hours of devotion she gave to the families around her, for which she received potatoes, a slice of salt pork, some cornmeal. Her payment was more than cold, hard coins. Hester knew love could not be measured. It couldn't be valued the way land or money could. Love kept flowing and flowing until it created a wide river that carried others along with it, straight into Heaven's door.

But William would think her silly if she tried to tell him that. He would say she talked like a woman. *Weibsleitich*. So she agreed. He was surprisingly pleased as he gathered her in his arms, his words of love effusive.

Long into the night, Hester lay awake, pondering her life. So many things were good, and for this she was thankful. For William, for the ability to use her knowledge of herbs far beyond anything she had imagined. So many short years before this, she was only an Indian in hiding.

She was thankful for Emma Ferree. And for Billy.

Quick tears sprang to her eyes, sliding down the sides of her face, but she let them go unhindered. Pillows held secrets well. No one could tell how often they were wet with the heart's sorrows and longings, the sighs of repression.

Sometimes she imagined her life being large and healthy with real love, the way her childhood had been sustained by it. Emma and Billy kept it alive in their good-natured way, as much as any strangers could fill in for real family.

The Indians contributed to the meaning of life and love in their own special way of living.

And now. Was she still blessed with the knowledge of acceptance? Yes, she was. Yes. She told herself this over and over as the warm trail of her tears kept a steady course into her silent, secretive pillow. It was just the way of it, after Kate died.

She was blessed. For a scavenger, a seeker of whatever she could find, she had a good life with William.

She knew, also, that she would gladly break every piece of lovely expensive china to be free of his highly esteemed authority. Always, it was William's way. The belief that a woman should have an opinion never crossed his mind. Did all women feel like she did, whether they'd admit it or not?

On Christmas Day they attended church services at Ezra Fishers, a brother-in-law to Elias. The sun shone with a blinding brilliance. Hester's tears had cleansed her spirit, leaving her with a warm glow that radiated from her dark eyes.

She held little Abner Speicher, whispering with Sarah while the congregation sang the old Christmas hymns from the thick leather-bound *Ausbund*, and was thankful for a home and a husband, the empty cradle beneath the eaves forgotten for the moment.

Frances outdid herself, cooking and stewing, baking, and serving huge platters of festive foods to the extended family. The stone house brimmed with relatives Hester had never met. They spilled over into William and Hester's house, where they admired the dishes. Goodwill and merrymaking poured from every window, the men and women singing lustily, their faces red and perspiring.

The great pink hams were adorned with holly and berries; the turkey lay in a bed of parsley with a display of red apples. The sweet potatoes were lavished with walnuts; the pies were high and sweet and creamy. William's older brothers brought chestnuts, which they roasted over the fire.

Hester glowed in her red dress and moved among her relatives with a renewed sense of belonging. Every man in the room was enchanted with her but remained circumspect, distant, blushing, and bowing when she spoke to them in her perfect, low voice. She possessed a husky quality in her speech, which one brother-in-law found extremely endearing. He was nipping the fermented apple cider in the cellar when Hester opened the door, turned her back, and lowered herself down the steep stairs, the way she would go down the rungs of a ladder.

CHAPTER 14

LARGE, CALLOUSED HANDS CAUGHT HER WAIST tightly like a human vise, the grip forcing air from her astounded mouth. The smell of sour apple whiskey was hot and rancid, flowing past her ear, as she was pulled against the person who held her in his grip.

Instinctively, she began to struggle and pull away, her hands going to her waist, clawing at the disgusting hands that held her.

Slurred words of affection accompanied the sour stench of his breathing. When Hester saw how dire the situation was, she drew up a foot, and kicked backward, the sharp heel of her leather Sunday shoe catching her brother-in-law's shin with a splitting blow.

She was released so suddenly she fell headlong onto the caked red earth of the cellar floor. Before she had a second to recover, the door creaked open and a shaft of light shone on her as she struggled to her feet. Her dress was covered with loose dirt, her eyes were wide and filled with fear.

"Hester! *Voss geht au?*"

It was William, her husband. Before she had a chance to brush off the dirt, he was down the cellar steps, his long legs lowering himself as swiftly as possible. Breathing hard, he grasped Hester's shoulders, his eyes boring into hers from the light of the flickering oil lamp.

Before she could open her mouth to explain, William found the brother-in-law, his hands hanging stupidly by his side, his mouth working as he wrestled with his shame.

The result of that fateful encounter in the cellar were lies the brother-in-law told William in smooth, pious words, punctuated by sighs of righteousness as he explained Hester's descent down the cellar steps and into his unwilling arms. She was an Indian, after all.

Hester remembered very little of the Christmas evening, her eyes large, afraid, furtive.

Nothing was wasted on Frances.

William did his duty, bringing his errant wife to task. Simply, it was her word against Johnny's, the brother-in-law.

Over and over, she repeated her story, her words falling on ears stopped with indignation. William was furious, disappointed. How could she?

Hester sat beside the immense fireplace, the deacon's bench empty except for her quivering form on one end, the soiled red dress in stark relief against the white-washed wall like a Christmas poinsettia someone had trampled upon.

For the hundredth time, she shook her head. "I didn't, oh, William, I didn't. It was him."

William stalked the kitchen floor, his hands behind his back, his head thrust forward in the throes of his anger. "I would believe you if it wasn't for the Indian in you. Indians lie. They don't care, godless heathens that they are."

She stopped then. She gave up trying to tell William the truth. She watched with eyes that were dull and lifeless as he hurled every bottle of herbal medicine into the roaring fire, forbidding her to travel the community with her witchcraft, her Indian powwowing.

He grasped her shoulders, her forearms, leaving dull blue marks that lasted for weeks. He told her that if it ever happened again, the ministers of the church must be alerted, and she would be forced to make a public confession. Perhaps the bishop would then decide to excommunicate her for her sins. He, William, would carry out the required shunning afterward, for the extended period of time the *Ordnung* called for.

The threat drove a numbing fear into her heart. Anything, anything, except public humiliation. So she bowed her head, telling William she was sorry to disappoint him, that she would repent, do better, become more vigilant.

He slept beside her as she lay bruised, her eyes open, tears pooling on the pillow, darkening the dried blotch again where they had fallen before. This was the way of it then. The lineage of your blood, the nature God gave you the day you were born, handed down from generation to generation, was what made you who you were.

Ah, William. So much like Annie, Hans's second wife. What had he said the day he met her at her father's wedding? Be careful, be careful of that family. And he a cousin of Annie's.

Folks went to church, counted themselves Christians, followers of Jesus Christ. Amish, Mennonite, Baptist, Lutheran, all following this man called Jesus. In Hester's battered spirit, she pieced together remnants of her past, filled now with guilt made from the unfairness and cruelty of good Christian people. Each one a dark square of abrasive wool fabric that hurt her fingertips as she threaded the steel needle up and down. She wanted to add a square of color and light, to give William and Annie the benefit of the doubt.

Jesus had been nailed to the cross, and he prayed God to forgive the Roman soldiers as they pounded the rusty nails through his palms. She would try to do the same. Everyone who believed in the man called Jesus was called upon to forgive.

Perhaps William did not know how he hurt her. He was well steeped in the laws of the church, like a pot of tea come to a dark green color of perfection after just the right amount of time, the required amount of tea leaves added at the right time. So important to him, this perfection.

She sighed, prayed to God, begged his forgiveness. Like the petals of an unfolding flower, the beauty of God's love was revealed to her. The luxury of his grace and forgiveness arrived in waves of peace, filling her heart, enfolding it in a kind of pureness, almost like the purity of an angel's wing.

For who could know? Perhaps she had behaved immodestly. Had she fueled Johnny's desire for her? First, there was Hans. And now the brother-in-law.

She cringed, then, with shame and humility that quite effectively eliminated the fresh breath of God's love. Over and over she blamed herself, heaping measures of self-loathing on her own head as she remembered moments with Hans. Now, here again she was to blame.

How much better it would have been if Kate had left her to starve as an infant. Death would have been merciful. Quick. Better. She was forever torn between two cultures, and now, two voices, one enveloping her in the security of God's love, one accusing her of her own heathen ways, the Indian in her, the thorn in her flesh.

Suddenly she remembered a time with Noah when Kate was still alive. They were playing together, brother and sister, one as dark as the other was blond and light-eyed. They were swinging in the barn on the long rope swing Hans had attached to the rafter for them. She could smell the dry hay and see the slivers of light that sifted between the barn boards, carrying tiny pieces of dust, catching the gleam of her straight, black hair.

She had just completed a wide arc, flying high above the hay, lithe, strong, and supple, her hands around the knot at the end with a tight, well-placed grip. Strangely, Noah had reached out, touched her hair, and said she was like "a *schöna* Indian, so dark."

She remembered looking into his pale blue eyes, afraid to blink. She knew then that Noah was special. He was so much like Kate, who found it hard to confront anyone, to demean them with words of rebuke.

Ah, but Noah and Kate had accepted her. All of her. Being Indian had not been a loathsome trait, but an honor.

She would try harder yet again. William might come to appreciate her if she continued with the work of being a healer. She remembered, then, his destruction of her medicines. How like Annie and her goal to destroy the book of herbal remedies.

A stabbing thought about Emma Ferree's premonitions of William suddenly pierced Hester. In one moment, she was face-to-face with the thin film of resistance she had allowed to cover the truth from this astounding little woman. Emma's goodness of heart was sweeter than anything Hester had encountered since she'd left her childhood home. She knew now that Emma had been right. The truth was like a branding iron. If only Billy had let her die in the granary of the livery stable.

Long into the night, a mixture of peace and despair, truth and unacknowledged lies, spilled and rolled around Hester's heart. Her weary eyes were swollen when William heaved himself from bed and went out into the cold, dark, snowy morning to begin the day's milking.

At breakfast Hester was silent and downcast, her white cap pulled so far front on her head that very little of the beauty of her dark hair was revealed. She had drawn the strings up beneath her chin in a large bow of humility.

She had fried the mush crisp and thin, cooked the eggs sunny side up, and finished them with boiling water cooking up furiously beneath the lid, just the way William liked them. The porridge was firm, the tea dark and piping hot. They ate together in silence, the new set of dishes like mocking sentries, a show of love and affection.

William broke the silence only when he poured the steaming tea onto his saucer to cool it. "Hester, I forbid you to leave the house for six weeks now. I expect you to think upon your sins, read your Bible, and repent. It is because of my love for you that I require this. I do love you, Hester, and am glad you are my wife.

"I just need to train you well in the ways of a devoted Amish housewife. I believe Kate was a bit loose with you. My mother always talked of it, wondering how the household would ever turn out with her lack of discipline."

He gave her a sad look of righteousness, a sniff. "I guess this latest episode answers my mother's concerns and questions. You ran away from home and lived English for a while. Noah has gone off to the war, I hear. They say Isaac got on a river barge with a man named Lee who worked on the river."

Hester successfully hid any sign of caring or having heard. She acknowledged his words with a mere dipping of her head, a sipping of her tea. A fierce gladness welled up in her before she could quell it. Let Hans reap what he sowed. Let all his neglect come home to roost. He had never cared for those two boys, and now they apparently did not care for him.

"Why don't you answer me?" William's voice was harsh. He leaned forward, his blue eyes intent, his mouth compressed into a slash of discipline.

"Oh, no, I mean, yes. I hadn't known about my brothers."

"They are not your brothers. You have no ties to them."

"No. I don't."

"Did you know this riverman named Lee?"

Rigid, with eyes downcast, Hester tried to decide quickly. If she shook her head, he would catch the lie, as sharp and perceptive as he was. If she said yes, he would see the past in her eyes.

"Well?'

"Yes. He poled us across the river a few times."

"Is that all?"

"Yes."

Miraculously, he believed her.

Her hands shook as she held the cup, stirred the tea with a spoon.

"I want Mother to teach you quiltmaking."

A sickening thud of her heart was followed by nausea roiling her stomach, churning the food she had eaten. "But I am not skilled with a needle."

"Till the winter is over, you will have learned."

The thought of spending time with his mother, her hands clumsily plying the needle through fabric cut in exact squares and triangles, brought on a cold sweat, an acceleration of her heart.

On the very next afternoon, Frances suddenly appeared in the kitchen like a dark ghost of discipline. Hester was sweeping the hearth and looked up to find her standing by the table.

One eyebrow was elevated, one lowered. "Dishes not done yet?" was her way of greeting.

"Yes, well, not all of them. I overbaked a cake. It's soaking."

"What kind of cake?"

"A molasses. William's favorite."

"He likes *gelbkucken* best."

"He does?"

"Why of course."

"I'll make him one next time."

"He wants me to teach you quiltmaking."

Gripping the back of a chair, Hester nodded.

Out came the tumble of scraps. The scissors flashed in Frances's capable hands as she sliced expertly around the templates, cutting exact triangles and rectangles. Bits of fabric grew into tall stacks as her scissors raced along, keeping time to the staccato words from her thin mouth.

So Hester had overstepped her bounds with Johnny. That's what happens when a woman has no children. Like a cavorting heifer. William was so disappointed. Very generous of him to forgive her for such a wrongdoing.

She, too, could forgive. It was her duty. A Christian was called upon to do this. In time, she was sure that Hester would make a good wife.

Hester acknowledged her words with a humble dip of her head. When she spoke, her eyes were clear, glistening with truth. "I am not to blame for Johnny's overtures. He was drinking apple whiskey. I went down to the cellar, and he caught me about the waist. I struggled."

When Frances met Hester's eyes, the truth in them found its mark, accurately piercing the false lies in her own. But expertly, in the same way she plied the scissors, she cut off the truth and flung it away with contempt. "Puh! They all say that. Every loose woman always comes up with an excuse."

Calmly, her eyes glowing, Hester spoke again, her voice clear, low, and husky, like bells enhancing her words. "Then you must live with what you choose to believe."

When Hester struggled to thread her needle, bending over the triangles she was laboriously bringing together, Frances noticed her long, uneven stitches. Patiently she showed her how to shove only the tip of the needle into the fabric to make one tiny stitch, which immediately helped Hester improve.

Frances soon noticed Hester's eye for color, the way she alternated the blue with the golden maize fabric and the red with the green like a holly bush or a cardinal in a fir tree. But she was careful to withhold praise, careful to keep Hester from becoming *schtoltz*. Words of praise would only serve to give her more free rein than she already had.

Till the week's end, Hester had acquired a new level of quiltmaking. She endured Frances's words of rebuke and her criticism like an unwelcome cold. She dealt with her inability to please, stayed patient, and was rewarded with a perfect quilt top that contained a star pattern, its symmetry so pleasing that her eyes lit up with delight.

Frances almost warmed to her beautiful daughter-in-law.

William was happy beyond Hester's expectations. He praised her work and told her about the verses in Proverbs that lift up a woman who pleases her husband by the work of her hands, then takes her goods to market. She cooked his meals the way he liked them, stayed at home for the required weeks, went to church, and held little Baby Abner. She whispered senseless bits of news and gossip with her friend Sarah, evading her questions about the tinctures and the herbs, saying in winter it was hard to find them. Amos was doing better, but could not stand to do a full day's work yet. Hester said the sun in spring would help.

The snows came often, piling around the stone house and blowing across the Lancaster landscape in great, white, stinging clouds, whipped up by a relentless north wind that created drifts higher than a man's head. Horses floundered up to their bellies in packed snow. Sleds overturned, spilling loads of firewood into deep white drifts. The men shouted and shoveled through the snow, their faces red with cold and irritation, clapping their gloved hands down on the crowns of their black felt hats as the wind tugged at their wide brims.

William came into the house for a scarf that he tied under his chin, tucking his beard beneath it as well. Hester laughed, thinking him very handsome without the long, bushy black beard, and told him so, blushing. He smiled at her, then held her securely in his arms, kissing her soundly before he went outside to join the shoveling crew.

At times such as these, Hester believed she did love him. She did. Perhaps she expected too much from the word "love." Obedience, having no will of her own, brought good times. Weren't her quilts a visual display of her obedience? Wasn't Frances's teaching a blessing?

When the news of sick children reached her ears, a longing welled up in her so intense that she felt she had to go somehow. When a four-year-old succumbed to *lunga feeva* and a ten-year-old to seizures because of an escalated temperature caused by the same disease, she battled with her will to go nurse them, to be allowed to administer the herbs of her foreparents. She fiercely believed that the old Indians carried a wealth of information that they passed down from one generation to the next, and she knew many of these remedies.

Miserable, she stood in the snowy graveyards, her black hat hiding her sorrow, her black shawl wrapped around her desperate longing to save these children. She cried with parents remembering her mother, Kate, and her sister Rebecca. She listened to mothers, looking on helplessly as their children choked on swollen tonsils and thrashed feverishly on soiled beds, the doctor unable to save them.

She baked pies and bread and took them to houses with William by her side. She bent to view yet another child lying white and lifeless, its eyes closed, dressed in white, a life cut off before its time by the dreaded diseases of winter.

One cold winter evening, when the stars hung like little individual icicles, the wind moaning around the eaves, the blowing snow whispering the sadness of the little children's deaths, Hester could bear it no longer. She laid aside the pattern of triangles she was sewing, gathering the ends to fold them into the rye grass basket at her side, breathed in, and turned to her husband. "William, must these children die?"

Astounded by her words, William raised his head from the German Bible he had been reading. "Why, Hester, I am surprised at your question. Have you not heard Bishop Joel say so clearly that their time was up? God needed these children in heaven. They are angels now." His eyes were heavy-lidded with the patience he needed to exercise over his wife's childish question.

Hester shivered and drew the corners of her light shawl around her neck. "But if God put all these herbs on the earth for our use, then gives wisdom to. . . to, um, to people in how to use them, surely there is wasted knowledge somewhere."

"The doctors did all they could."

"The doctors don't know enough!" Hester flung the words into the room with unbridled desperation and the repression that suffocated her spirit.

Instantly, William was on his feet, towering over her with the strength of his anger. "Are you telling me, Hester, that you know more than the doctors? That thought is so preposterous it's laughable."

"No, I don't know more. Just a better way."

"You don't know anything." William grated out his words like a rasp on an oak board.

"But I do, William. I want to help the sick children, just for the love of these suffering little ones."

"Your Indian knowledge is witchcraft."

"No, William, it is not. I believe that viper's grass made into a tea would help these little ones' lung fever."

William was breathing hard now, his eyes containing desperation. Here was his wife rising up again, displaying her own will, just when he thought that the winter months, tempered with the tutelage of his mother, had finally cured her of this nonsense. "Viper's grass! You speak of your medicines in terms of serpents even."

"Ach, William. No. It is merely a grass. It grows in low places by the water. Hence its name."

Frustrated, angered, and without a thought other than the contesting of his will and the need to stop it, he brought back his hand and administered a sharp crack to the side of her face.

Hester's head snapped sideways. The shock in her eyes made William flinch, but only for a moment. He gathered his wits hurriedly and said she must never speak of these things again, ever, in his house.

Hester's face stung, but she lowered her eyes. He gathered her limp form into his arms, whispering words of love, saying that if she rose up against him like a rebellious child, he would have to treat her as one. It was all done out of his great love for her.

Never again did Hester contest her husband's will. That one blow finished any thoughts of changing his opinion about the herbal medicines and her ability to use them.

She spent the remainder of that winter learning the art of quiltmaking. William praised her choice of colors. He built a small wooden frame for her, a clever device to hold portions of a quilt so that she could stitch the pieced top to the bottom layer of homespun fabric. Her needle flashed in the light of the oil lamp, her dark head bent to her work as she immersed herself in the skills her husband and his mother asked of her.

Elias, her father-in-law, was a man of few words, a distant man who kept to himself, minding his own business. He was tall, like Frances, and spare, with the same loping gait as his sons. One evening he asked Hester why she no longer made tinctures. Sam Riehl had asked him the question in church.

Flustered, Hester could not find words to fit the situation properly. William came to her aid immediately, however, telling his father that she had seen the error of her ways, recognized the powwowing of the Indians, and did not wish to continue.

Slowly then, Elias King cracked a chestnut with the nutcracker, popped a portion into his mouth, chewed, swallowed, and then met Hester's eyes. For only a second, a love like Kate's shone from his eyes, warm, soft, and so mellow and approving it was like a balm to a broken heart. He said, evenly, "Well, William, some of these old Indians know more than we do. And I personally don't think the devil has anything to do with it."

No one but Elias saw the look of warm gratitude Hester bestowed on him. And no one knew how Elias yearned to help his daughter-in-law, seeing how caught she was in the net of marriage covered by the deceit of piety, the same as he was.

Chapter 15

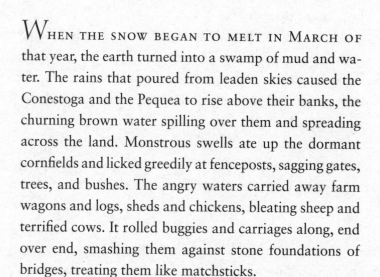

When the snow began to melt in March of that year, the earth turned into a swamp of mud and water. The rains that poured from leaden skies caused the Conestoga and the Pequea to rise above their banks, the churning brown water spilling over them and spreading across the land. Monstrous swells ate up the dormant cornfields and licked greedily at fenceposts, sagging gates, trees, and bushes. The angry waters carried away farm wagons and logs, sheds and chickens, bleating sheep and terrified cows. It rolled buggies and carriages along, end over end, smashing them against stone foundations of bridges, treating them like matchsticks.

The men were called to fill sandbags to keep the town of Lancaster safe. Elias and William rode horses through the fields, skirting flooded, low-lying areas, answering the call for assistance.

Frances and Hester were left alone to keep the animals fed and the cows milked. Normally, Hester did not milk cows. William said it was better for his parents and for him to continue doing the milking by themselves, that it was better for the cows to have familiar and experienced hands working with them. So now, when Hester dashed through the pouring rain, a kerchief tied around her head, she looked forward to milking the cows. She had always milked at home in Berks County.

Frances was beside herself with worry. She was terrified of flood waters. So many people miscalculated and took risks, driving their buggies through waters that appeared to be shallow but were deceptively high, rolling them over and over after the churning waters caught the bottoms of the carriages.

Hester shook the water off her head and shoulders, grabbed a wooden, three-legged stool, and set to work, expertly pulling and squeezing the cows' teats. Thick streams of creamy milk poured into the bucket held firmly between her knees.

Frances was amazed at Hester's ability. She did not allow one word of praise to escape her lips, but her eyes were approving. She asked Hester to spend the evening with her; she was afraid that her worry would undo her if she was alone.

They walked back to the house along the sodden path, the rain pelting them with its fury. Hester looked up at the gray sky as if to calculate the duration of the rain, but had to admit that the heavens appeared the same as they had for three days.

It was awkward, sitting in Frances's kitchen. Hester was required to call her Mother, but had never felt any motherly love coming from her, ever. Only discipline and rebuking. Still, she was William's mother, so she made every effort to be respectful. She helped her set the table for the two of them. They ate slices of homemade bread with good, yellow butter and ladled vegetable soup into big pewter bowls.

Again and again, Frances's eyes appeared wild with terror. Repeatedly, she opened the door, peered out into the cold and the wind, and asked Hester when she thought the rain would stop.

Hester told her the only bit of information she knew. If the wind continued from the northeast, there would be no change.

That seemed to send Frances into despair. "Hester, do you think the men will be safe?"

"Oh, I trust William to be careful. They are riding with a group of men. Surely they'll stick together and use sound judgment."

Frances nodded. But she became increasingly restless. She paced the kitchen. She added sticks of wood to the fire. She shivered when a gust of wind sent hard pellets of rain against the windowpane. She got down her Bible and began to read, her lips moving as she formed the words.

"Hester, do you think the water will come up to the barn?"

"I wouldn't think so. We're up pretty high."

When Frances nodded, Hester was reminded of her stepmother Annie when her hands lost their strength, creating a vulnerability and a loss of power that was hard to watch. It was pitiful, in fact. Clearly this rainstorm exposed a hidden weakness, a lack of faith, in Frances.

"Hester, don't go home to sleep."

Surprised, Hester looked at her. "Where should I sleep?"

"Here."

"Do you have a spare bed?"

"No."

"But."

"Oh, go then, I know you don't want to sleep in my bed with me."

"I suppose I could."

"No, you don't want to. Go home."

Quickly, Hester ran the short distance to her own door through the rain. She let herself in, poked up the fire, washed, and got into her long, warm nightgown. She crawled under the quilts and fell asleep to the rhythm of the rain on the shingled roof, tumbling down the steep incline from one hewn-oak shingle to another, dripping onto the crumpled brown grass that had been covered with snowdrifts all winter long.

She was awakened by a sobbing, wild-eyed apparition that struck terror to her heart. A half-dressed Frances, holding her navy blue dress front together with one hand and gripping a sputtering candle with the other, was calling her name between hoarse cries, a dry, sobbing sound that would not stop. "Hester! *Komm! Komm!*"

Hester sat bolt upright, alarm drying her mouth and her tongue. "It's William. Amos Fisher just arrived. William's horse fell, and he struck his head against a bridge."

Dumbly, Hester voiced, "The horse struck his head?"

"No. William!" Frances was screaming now, hoarsely.

"Where is he?"

"They brought him back. He's lying in the barn."

"Is he alive?"

There was no answer, only the slamming of the door, the rain on the roof, the sound of footsteps as they splashed through the rain.

William's inert form was brought to the house and laid on their bed. His heavy black hair clung to his skull, forming a cap that allowed his ears to show. They were white, bloodless, a sight that seemed alien to Hester. She had hardly ever seen his ears since his hair reached to chin-level. Now he was strangely defenseless, even sensitive, somehow.

Frances moaned and cried, making strange, choppy little sounds of fear and foreboding. Her hands shook as she helped Hester put William into dry clothes, roll him over, and cover him. The doctor would come as soon as the floodwaters receded. Smelling salts brought no response.

Hester worked as the morning light crept into the room, gray, ghostlike, ominous. She glided from the bed to the fire, stroking William's forehead with cloths soaked in vinegar and camphor. She sat by their bed, watching his face for signs of awareness, trying to endure Frances's wet sounds of lip-smacking and crying.

Elias and Ben Hertzler came, peering under William's eyelids and pinching his nose to see if he would gasp.

The doctor came from Lancaster, held William's hand, and said there was little to do except wait to see how soon he would awaken. His heartbeat was good and strong, his pulse lively. He was a young man and healthy. He would probably be fine after he woke up.

The doctor left, and still the rain continued to pound on the roof. Hester was left alone with William. How could she begin to sort out her feelings when so many emotions crashed into her senses, leaving her with no clear direction?

Sad, yes, to see her husband, the William she knew so well, lying inert, unable to move. She was surprised by an overwhelming kindness she suddenly felt toward him. He had been so capable, always following his father's pattern of managing the farm. His profile was so handsome, yet still. His dark lashes lay on his white cheeks, his nose perfectly shaped and adding to his good looks. No wonder she had been visually attracted to him.

The pinched lines between his eyes and his dark eyebrows gave away his capacity for raw and unseemly fury.

The thought of his demise forced its way into her mind. No, he would live. She would be able to bear his children. The farm would prosper, their children would till the soil, and their children after them. God would smile down on her, bless her yet, in spite of her troublesome ways, her uprising against her husband. William would live. It was necessary that he did.

The rain stopped when the northeasterly wind changed to the west. Unbroken gray clouds tore in two on the western horizon, allowing a darker gray, rolling cloud to emerge, followed by churning white ones.

Raindrops skittered from the eaves, were blown sideways, and then fell to the ground with a defeated sigh.

By the time a brilliant blue sky showed behind the gray clouds, the wind was already teasing the tree branches, ruffling the grasses, swaying the weeds that seemed dead.

Hester listened. What she heard was more than the wind. A low roaring swept over the landscape. The wind crashed against the stone walls of the house, seized the windowpanes, and rattled them in its teeth. It lifted loose shingles and let them fall. Floppy gates swung back and forth. Barn doors flapped. Windows shivered as men dashed madly, clutching their hats, their beards split in two. They pushed rocks against barn doors, latched windows and half doors.

Slowly the Conestoga Creek went back to its borders, grumbling and leaving a residue of disease in its wake. Horses pulled carriages through the mud. Mud glued to their wooden wheels, making their load twice as heavy.

Neighbors hopped down from buggies, knocking mud from their boots in the brown yard. They brought biscuits and dumplings, stews and soups. So many remedies from kindly, well-meaning faces. Rub a potato and bury it at midnight when the moon is full. He will awaken. Use burdock root for the palsy or for fainting.

Old Hannah Troyer, bent and feeble, her teeth gone so long her gums were tough as nails, put a gnarled hand on William's forehead and repeated the Lord's Prayer five times in German, the wart at the end of her nose sliding up and down with each word.

Hester met each visitor at the door, thanked them for coming, then took her place beside William on the chair by his bed.

Frances talked and talked, giving each of the visitors a full report of his fall, about the night they brought him home, what an exceptional, well-behaved son he had always been. Each visitor heard an account of his abstinence, how he never touched hard cider or apple whiskey, and how, unlike his father and brothers, he had never smoked a pipe or chewed tobacco.

William was becoming so thin. Hester repeatedly tried to feed him and give him a drink. Still he slept on. She felt almost crazy at the end of seven days. So many visitors, so many good wishes. They flowed and swirled about the room like incense, leaving a blessed odor of love and kindness, along with pies and cakes and loaves of bread.

Everyone agreed that no one could be blamed. It had simply been an accident. The group of men had been riding. Their horses were lively and well behaved when they neared the bridge where the water was churning and roiling only a foot below. But when the henhouse floated down the swollen creek and crashed into the bridge, William's horse lunged to the left, away from the terrifying crash, and unseated William so that he flew through the air. His head hit the side of the bridge.

Amos Fisher said reverently that it sounded like a ripe melon when he hit the ground.

Phineas Stoltzfus said, "*Ach, du lieva.*"

They came and cried with Frances, wrung Elias's hand, shook their heads in sorrow at the sight of his beautiful young wife sitting so stony-faced, so unmoving. A good thing she was barren. The little ones need not see their Dat like this. An *shaute soch.*

The brothers-in-law and sisters came, their voices hushed, their footsteps muted as they rocked back and forth, their hands clasped behind their backs, unable to voice the emotion they felt.

Johnny would not enter the room, saying it gave him the shivers. Hester knew better.

They ate their meals together. The Amish women of the community cooked and did the washing. They spoke of it that the young wife would not cry. Had not cried, ever, that anyone could tell. It was the Indian in her. They didn't feel the things white people did. Death was different to Indians.

Hannah Troyer's voice rose. The wart on the end of her nose jumped when she spoke emphatically, "He's not dead yet."

Eliza Bert's eyebrows jumped, and she said he may as well be.

All of this was only a buzz in Hester's ears. Unable to sleep well, afraid he would wake and call her name, she never slept deeply, which finally caused her days to take on a dreamlike quality. She was finding it hard to separate the real from the unreal.

When gentle souls clasped her hand in both of theirs and cried great quantities of tears, her face remained serene, calm, dry-eyed. Her large black eyes were rimmed with gray shadows. Her skin was dry from the lack of fresh air and much-needed moisture.

Toward the end of the ninth day, after everyone had gone home and Frances had swept the floor, she stood over her son, crying and smacking her lips in the odd way she had. As she bade Hester good night with a touch on her shoulder, the door opened and Elias entered alone.

"Go on home, Frances." He spoke the words with unaccustomed authority. Frances went without a backward glance.

Elias came slowly toward Hester and stopped directly in front of her chair. "Hester."

She looked up, questioning.

"He won't live, you know."

Hester said nothing.

"Not anymore. Tomorrow is the tenth day."

Hester nodded.

"I came to tell you that in spirit, I have stood by you. William is so much like his mother. I don't believe you've always had a good life with my son." In the light of the fire, a teardrop, like silver, appeared, trembled, and dropped, creating a glistening rivulet of moisture on one brown cheek. "God has mysterious ways, but sometimes they are not so mysterious. You will be free to love again, and I believe that is his will. You are a special woman, and I also believe he has plans for you."

He hesitated, then placed a thin hand on her shoulder. "*Herr saya.*"

Silence laden with kindness whispered its way into the room. "You will always have a home here. You may always stay if you want to, my daughter."

His presence and kind words were hard to grasp as a great knot of fear and self-condemnation formed in her throat. "But, I am not worthy of your blessing. I have not always loved William, nor bowed to his will in the way he required. God is punishing me for rising up against him."

"As I have not always loved my Frances, Hester. You and I have done the best we could. I have full trust that we will someday hear the words, 'Well done, thou good and faithful servant.'" The silence was unbroken as Elias laid a hand on Hester's shoulder once more, as if the touch could assure her of his words. He offered a solid, warm caress to comfort and fill her with the same faith he carried deep in his heart, covered only by his humble demeanor.

Then, in a broken cry, Hester breathed. "He must live. He must. So I can have a chance to do better."

Elias sighed, a ragged sound of pity which grew from his own agony of living out his years with a woman devoid of compassion. "You could do your best, and it would fall short every time."

"But God must give me another chance." Her words were heavy with desperation.

For a long moment, Elias stood close to his son, watching the slight rising and falling of his chest. The oil lamp flickered, sputtered, and then resumed its steady glow. The shadows on the whitewashed wall crept after Elias's form as he stepped forward, bending slowly to brush back a lock of William's dark hair. The corners of his mouth twisted as he struggled for control.

"I think *unser Herren Jesu* understands William. I think he knows his nature. He was born with one much like his mother has. He took Jesus as his Savior and tried to follow him, but his exacting nature often got in the way. He did the best he could. I trust God understands this when he reaches the other shore. William loved you, Hester, in his own way."

Why did those words bring her comfort when his previous ones did not? Was she somehow responsible for William's salvation?

"Thank you, Elias, for your kindness."

He nodded once, wished her a good night, and then moved out the door and into the night.

It was only then that Hester lost all reserve. The stone in her heart was smashed to tiny fragments as she bent over, pressed down by the weight of her disappointment. It could have been better. Their marriage had fallen so short of her expectations. She had longed to be cherished and loved for who she was, not for who he wanted her to be, as he tried to mold her into a more devoted, strict, and spiritual wife.

Sobs tore from her throat, dry, rasping sounds of grief and unfulfillment. She rocked back and forth, her hands covering her face, her eyes closed tightly against the awful battle in her heart. If only he would live, she would tell him all this. She would pour out words of love, help him change, teach him compassion somehow. Oh, somehow she would find a way.

As the oil burned low, the smell of the rancid wick stopped Hester's keening. She brought up the corner of her black apron, swabbed her face, and then bent to extinguish the flame, throwing the room into darkness, except for the dying fire in the great fireplace. It was enough.

Hester sat back in her chair and turned her face to William. He was but a slight bump in the white bed, his hair etched dark against the pillow.

"Why must you go now, William? Why did we ever meet on my father's fateful wedding day? What plan did God see?"

Getting up, she placed a hand on his chest and stroked the fabric of his nightshirt, her hand stumbling on the row of buttons. She felt his forehead and his lips, which were dry and parched. Going to the bucket on the dry sink, she poured a small amount of water on a cloth, wrung it into the dishpan, and wiped his mouth lightly. His cheeks were so sunken, so white. She wiped his face all over as if to instill life.

She knew that beneath the caked black hair there was a large, angry bruise that had spread almost the entire way across his skull. She touched it now with her long, delicate, brown fingers. Her lips moved in prayer. Turning down the white quilt, she brought his hand, the large calloused hand that held her so many times, tenderly to her lips. "I love you, William." Her voice was low, whispered, calm.

The storm of her grief had prepared her for God's will. Whether he lived or whether he died, he was the Lord's.

The windowpanes let in a small amount of the night sky. Hester moved to the door, lifted the heavy iron latch, and stepped outside, closing it softly behind her. The air was cold. The chill crept up her arms and across her shoulders. She wrapped her arms around her thin waist and lifted her face to find the familiar constellations. A sliver of a moon hung low in the sky, the remainder of it like a veil trying to appear invisible, but it was there.

Unbelievably, she heard Kate's low laugh. "You know, Hester, the moon thinks it's clever, showing us only portions of itself, but we know it's there," she had said.

Tears of longing rained down Hester's face. She wished to bury her face in Kate's old blue dress, her shoulder warm and soft and forgiving, to feel her soft hands pat her back, her voice crooning, making a terrible world into a perfectly beautiful one.

The shrill cry of spring peepers came up from the creek. It was the seasonal ritual, this beckoning of spring, along with a call for purple violets and yellow, round-faced dandelions. Turning, Hester lifted the latch to go inside. She hesitated at the high-pitched warble of the screech owl. Another one replied, a melodious sound of two of God's creatures.

She slept fitfully, too exhausted to stay awake or to sleep soundly. Just before morning, when the clock's hands on the mantle crept toward five, William breathed his last. Hester didn't know. She had fallen asleep for only an instant. She woke with a start, went to William, and felt the difference immediately. There was no movement; the rising and falling of his chest had stopped. His face was slack, gray.

Quite simply, Hester did not know what to do. The tears that should have come, the grief she should have felt, were replaced by a familiar shroud of indifference, a separation from reality.

When Frances pushed her way in, her eyes wide with fear, her face white beneath the black kerchief on her head, she stopped at Hester's chair, a question in her eyes, her mouth working.

Hester looked up. "He's gone."

Frances nodded and went to William's bed. The familiar sighs and sobs of grief, the wet smacking of her lips, began all over again. She keened, lifting her face, then fell on her knees, her cries reaching levels of hysteria.

Hester stood, helped her up, and patted her shoulder clumsily. She spoke words of encouragement, but nothing could stop the rushing torrent of Frances's sorrow. A mother's grief, Hester reasoned, is a desperate hurt, the tearing away of a child before his time.

And so she comforted, answered questions, shouldered accusations. Yes, she should have stayed awake. She should have, certainly.

But the curtain of death was drawn, and Frances could find no way to push it back.

CHAPTER 16

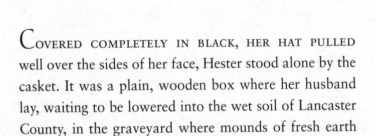

COVERED COMPLETELY IN BLACK, HER HAT PULLED well over the sides of her face, Hester stood alone by the casket. It was a plain, wooden box where her husband lay, waiting to be lowered into the wet soil of Lancaster County, in the graveyard where mounds of fresh earth were heaped over the graves of the children who had not survived the winter.

The singsong voice of the minister reading the *leid* failed to bring any response from the grieving widow, while Frances blew her nose copiously behind her. Elias bowed his head, wept quietly, but remained calm, his face a harbor of peace.

The horses and carriages tied along the fence were in a neat row, the group of mourners all in black. The trees had not yet begun to push their buds, their branches stark and black as well. The grass was olive green mingled with the dead brown of winter, bent over, waiting to be pushed out of existence by fresh, lively, new shoots.

After the Lord's Prayer, Hester stayed by the grave as Frances and Elias turned to go. She felt a tap on her shoulder. Hester turned.

"You can ride back with me." It was Johnny, the brother-in-law. Without Naomi, his wife.

"No."

Without another word he turned away, a deep crimson spreading across his face, his eyes blinking with humiliation at the low-lying fury in her one word of refusal.

The funeral dinner had been prepared by members of the Amish community. Long tables were set in William and Hester's house, then filled with great platters of sliced beef, mashed potatoes and gravy, along with cheese and applesauce. Hester sat humbly with Elias and Frances, William's brothers and sisters, and the family's large, rowdy group of children. She spoke when she was spoken to and acknowledged well-wishers, but nothing seemed real.

She did not want to be noticed. She wished they'd all go away and leave her alone. Yet she did not want to be alone with her thoughts this first evening, with William's passing so close. It seemed as if he should be there sitting by her side, laughing, always glad to be among his brethren.

She was so weary, so bone-tired, and yet she still needed to spend the remainder of the day with William's family, the dreaded Johnny among them. She sighed a small breath of defeat. She was seated on a bench beside the fire, William's sister Amanda holding her infant daughter beside her, surrounded by children, aunts, and cousins. She didn't notice her at first. It was only when a narrow black form sat on the bench beside her and a hand reached over to clasp her brown one firmly in her own that she turned her head to see two bright-brown eyes, like polished stones, peer up at her like an inquisitive sparrow.

"Hester." The word was spoken solidly, well placed, like bricks, square and useful and sensible. The voice was low, accompanied by a dip of heavy eyelids held there, shutting away curiosity, as if she wanted to share a moment of silence, of companionship. Then the eyelids bounced back and the curiosity resumed, brighter than ever.

"I am Bappie Kinnich."

Hester smiled, a slow, hesitant widening of her perfect lips.

"Barbara King, in English. Every old maid in Lancaster Country is called *Bappie*. Don't ask me why." She chuckled, then quickly covered her mouth with her hand, clenched tightly around her chin as if to squelch any humor or unseemly words.

"You are Hester. The wife of my second cousin, William. We have never met, likely because I have been teaching school in Tulpehocken Valley, about twenty-five miles away as the crow flies. As the crow doesn't fly, it's a long arduous trip, hard on the backside."

Hester wasn't sure if she had heard correctly, so she didn't say anything.

"So, Hester, what are your plans?"

Hester shrugged her shoulders, a gesture revealing the blankness she felt, the complete absence of anything called a plan.

"You don't have any, right?"

Hester shook her head.

"I didn't think so."

Bappie leaned back to allow a large uncle to pass. Her eyebrows were lowered in annoyance, but only for a short time. "You don't want to stay in this stone house by yourself." It was a statement, not a question, and not a gentle inquiry either.

"I guess not." Another statement. "No, I don't plan on it, but I hardly know where else to go." Hester spoke so softly Bappie had to lower her head to hear her.

Bappie's head swiveled in both directions as if she were waiting for a passing team or a pedestrian, the way Emma Ferree did in town. Then she lowered her head. "You don't have family, do you?"

"In Berks County."

"Not Amish."

"Yes, they are Amish. Hans and Annie Zug."

Bappie's mouth dropped open. "You're . . ."

Clearly speechless now, she drew back, her eyes wide open, her small mouth open in disbelief. "You're that Indian baby!"

"Yes, I guess so."

"Oh, *siss unfaschtendich*!"

Again, Bappie clapped a hand over her mouth and closed her eyes to stares of disapproval. When the coast was clear, she launched into a loudly whispered account of everything she had heard about Hester over the years. She knew Annie, all right. Couldn't stand her. Mean as a wasp. No apologies were offered after each blunt statement, so Hester took it the way Bappie said it—as an honest opinion that didn't bother to be clothed in masks of righteousness or pride.

"Well, here's my offer. I don't want to teach another year. Those people in Tulpehocken Valley are about the limit. I'm tired of their *gamach*. So would you want me to live here with you? I have my own place, but it's small."

Hester rolled awkwardly into a pit of despair. She searched for words, her eyes large and frightened.

Bappie saw immediately the need to reserve her proposition and said so quickly, grabbing both of Hester's hands and holding them warmly in her own, as her brown eyes filled with quick, glistening tears of sympathy.

"Ach, Hester, I'm not fit. No wonder I don't have a husband. Forget what I said. You barely know who I am."

Quickly, Hester grabbed back Bappie's hands and hung on as if they were a branch in floodwaters. "No. Oh, no. Let's just. . . Bappie, please come visit me on Sunday. I have no one and no place to go. Elias, Father, wants me to stay, but Frances." Her voice faded away.

"Frances? She's a regular scarecrow. Meaner, too."

Hester smiled and lifted her own hand to cover her mouth as Bappie clapped a hand to her chin again. The eyes above the hand sparkled and danced mischievously, rolled in Frances's direction, then closed as she laughed quietly.

"I'll be back Sunday." With that, Bappie got up and made her way quickly through the room, stopping to talk to a few relatives before heading out the door.

Hester held babies, talked to the bashful children, and listened to Frances's account of William's accident and his life with Hester. She acknowledged kind words of sympathy, shaking hands with so many people they seemed to be an endless line of faces and figures dressed in black.

Her head spun with weariness. She longed to lie down anywhere. She seriously thought of sitting against a wall somewhere, wherever she could close her eyes, but knew she could not until the last well-wisher had gone through that door.

The night did come, as it always does, but never was the veil of darkness more anticipated. She refused every offer from kind folks who wanted to stay the night, saying she would be safe here with Elias and Frances.

She fell into bed and remembered drawing the quilt over her shoulders before falling into a deep and restful sleep, the sound of the tree frogs and barking foxes going undetected.

The bedroom was pitch dark when Hester opened her eyes. The soft sighing of a spring rain against the windowpanes reminded her of William's passing, a gray mourning that filled her heart, dripping from the battered portion that remained.

She had never imagined the despair his death would bring, the solid weight of guilt mixed with disappointment, the life-draining inadequacy of her spirit. If only she had done better. She had been unfit to be the helpmeet she had promised to be on the day she spoke her sacred vows. God had not blessed their union with children, heirs to William's family, and it was her fault. Yes, he had been harsh at times, but that was his right. He was the husband, she the lesser vessel, and she had never succumbed fully to his will. Now she must live with the punishment God had wrought. He had taken William, and that, too, was her fault.

Wave after wave of humiliation accompanied the falling rain that blew softly against the dark windowpanes, until the thought of William became a torment. She must never think of marrying again. In her wildest imagining, she had not thought of marriage as the burden it had become, unable to bow fully to the will of her husband and his family.

She had spoken out boldly, accusing him of his lack of love, when all the while it had been her own stubborn will refusing to bend. It was the way the Indians in this Pennsylvania forest refused to bend to the demands of the white man who hacked down their sacred trees, who bought and owned the land they assumed belonged to the Creator they worshiped.

She would never be a white woman.

Somehow, before Barbara King came back to visit, she must leave. She would find her way to the western frontier, to her people. She would speak to Elias and Frances. Perhaps they would understand her sorrow.

The gray light of dawn brought fresh resolve. This time she would ask for a horse. She would plan better now that she was aware of the dangers, the thirst, the hunger that had been her constant companion when she left Hans and Annie's homestead. She had one wish—to see Emma and Billy Ferree. She had never thanked them properly, or enough, for what they had done.

She was surprised to find herself weak, her joints aching, her head spinning dizzily, as she got out of bed, found her clothes, and stoked the fire. Her hands shook as she swung the kettle over the new flames. The room tilted as she brought the cold water to her face at the dry sink.

She was bringing the steel-toothed comb through her heavy, black hair when the latch was lifted with a resounding crack of steel, the door creaked open, and Frances stood in the gray, early-morning light.

"You're up."

"Yes."

"Have you eaten?"

"No."

"Then come eat breakfast with Elias and me. Johnny and Naomi have spent the night. It would be nice if you ate with us."

Hester kept her back turned, her shaking hands twisting her hair into a bun on the back of her head.

"Well?"

"All right. I will come."

There was no reply. Only the creaking of the door and the latch falling into place behind Frances.

Hester finished inserting the steel hairpins. She reached for the white muslin cap, placed it on her head, and tied the heavy strings under her chin. She made her bed, tucking the white quilt beneath the pillows, stroked the top to smooth out the creases, then turned to the corner for the bellows. She clapped them up and down to fan the small flames licking out below the chunk of wood she had placed on the dying embers.

She swept the hearth and carefully replaced the chairs. She would clean the house properly after the men had moved the wooden benches to the attic, where it was customary to store them until the next church service.

The act of carrying out normal, mundane chores was healing and allowed her a sense of well-being, if only in sparse amounts. She threw a thin black shawl over her shoulders and stepped out into the fine, misty rain, then made her way to the addition built onto her own stone farmhouse, hesitating at the door.

She dreaded the breakfast table with Johnny's mocking eyes. Taking a deep breath, she knocked lightly, then pushed up the heavy latch to find the family seated around the table, candles on the mantle shelf illuminating the room, the smell of bacon and fried cornmeal mush hovering thickly around the room.

Frances cleared her throat. "We have been waiting."

"I'm sorry." Quickly Hester shrugged out of her shawl and slid quietly into a chair, her hands clasped in her lap, her eyes downcast.

All heads bowed instantly in silent prayer. Then Elias lifted his head, cleared his throat, and looked around the table. "Everyone help yourselves now."

How could Hester know her own stark, tragic beauty in the flickering yellow light of the candles? If anything, the experience of sadness only enhanced the dark luster of her large, almond-shaped eyes, the thick, black lashes drooping in remembered sorrows. She bowed her long, slender neck in humility, her mouth vulnerable with the sense of past mistakes, a sight that left Johnny's eyes glued to her as he tried unsuccessfully to tear them away.

Naomi, a small wren of a woman, bright-eyed and quick in her movements, helped the four children with their breakfasts, cutting the slabs of fried mush, tying a bib around the one-year-old, completely oblivious to her husband's wandering.

"You have slept well?" Elias asked, his eyes kind.

"Yes."

"That's good. I was afraid you wouldn't sleep after everything was over."

Frances blinked, once, twice. She opened her mouth as if to speak, hesitated, then closed it. She took up her spoon, toying with her bacon. Suddenly she spoke, her words cutting through the kind words of her husband. "I told you, Elias. Death is different to the Indians. They do not feel loss the way we do. Neither do they treasure life."

Naomi looked up, her birdlike eyes darting from one face to another.

Hester's heart leaped within her. She recognized the opportunity to present her case. It took all of her courage, but she folded her hands on her lap, lifted her head, and began. "Yes, Frances, you are right. I am an Indian. I have failed you in many ways, as I have failed William."

Elias raised his hand to silence her. Frances drew in a sharp breath, then laid down her spoon, poised to hear. "If you will be kind enough to give me one good horse, I will leave today. I will ride away from Lancaster County to find my people. I am not fit to be an Amish wife and mother."

Frances hissed, "You can't!"

"Why not?" Hester was calm and composed, drawing strength from her own words.

"How would that make us appear in the eyes of the Amish community? Our son's wife! Riding off to join the. . . those heathen Indians? We would be the ones who failed then. They would excommunicate you." Shrieking now, her voice high-pitched in desperation, her head bobbing in agitation, Frances was clearly horrified.

Elias sat as a stone, unmovable.

Johnny snickered self-consciously.

Naomi broke out. "Hester, why do you say that? You have been a good wife. By all appearances you have been an excellent housekeeper and a learned quilter. William seemed happier than I have ever seen him."

Elias began nodding his head in approval. "I told Hester she can always stay here. She is now the heir to the farm rightfully. She is William's wife."

"*Schtill!*" Frances's command slashed across the table. The children sat up and stopped chewing, their eyes wide with interest.

"I don't know why you would say such a thing. Elias, how can Hester own this farm? An Indian? I certainly hope you have not gone to see a lawyer, unbeknownst to me."

"It is the law, Frances. The wife inherits the husband's share."

"William had nothing!" Frances spat.

Hester listened. She could think of nothing she wanted less than this farm or the great cold stone house that held William's austerity. His rules clung to the whitewashed walls; the shadow of his superiority stained the wooden beams of the ceiling. The wide oak floorboards sounded the echoes of his displeased footsteps; the marriage bed spoke of her inability to conceive. Every corner of the house was rife with the ghosts of her shortcomings.

"I don't want the farm." Soft and low, Hester stated the fact.

Johnny's eyes pierced her face. Naomi saw the look of her husband. "I'll take it," he said quickly.

Elias looked to the eager, flushed face of his son. Frances trembled, then a slow smile spread across her face, the pleasure erasing the anxiety. "Why, of course. The most perfect solution! God be praised!"

Seeing the happiness on their grandmother's face, the children smiled and resumed eating, content.

Elias blew on his pewter mug of tea. For a long while he said nothing. He looked first at Naomi, whose eyes were bright with anticipation, then bowed his head to the turn of circumstances he knew were out of his control. "It is done, then."

Those words sealed the ownership of the farm.

Triumphant, Johnny's eyes seared into Hester's, conveying victory over her. She lowered her eyes. Otherwise, the contempt would have flashed, and Naomi would have seen. Best to let her revel in her husband's acquisition.

"Although I cannot allow you to have a horse. It is simply not safe for you to travel on your own with robbers and highway men about as thick as fleas. Johnny and I will build a cabin for you here on the home place. You can be *maud* to Naomi. We will pay your living expenses."

Hester shook her head before Elias stopped speaking. "No."

Frances breathed out, so obvious was her relief. With shaking hands, she lifted her tea and sipped a tiny portion, blinking rapidly.

"Where will you go?" Johnny's eyes begged her to stay. She was a necessity for him like she had been for Hans.

"Barbara King is coming to make me an offer. But I would rather travel to Ohio, to go back to my people where I belong."

Elias shook his head, his mouth grim. "Hester, you are one of us. You do not belong with the Indians. They are being steadily pushed farther west, becoming more savage and more hostile as time goes on. Or so we hear.

You have been raised among the Amish, you have promised to keep the faith. How could you turn your back to us now?"

Stony-faced, Hester lifted her eyes. "It would be out of necessity that I do this."

They allowed her the good little mare, Fannie, and the top buggy that day. She had only one wish, and that was to visit Emma Ferree, which they agreed to.

Hester's face was flushed with anticipation as she took up the reins, clucked to the little mare, and rode away from the farm in the gray mist of a spring rain. The wheels turned, picking up mud and old withered leaves of winter. Fannie's hooves made a sucking sound in the low, wet places, but Hester saw neither the mud nor the gray drizzle. On this one day she was doing something she had wanted to do for years—return to Emma and Billy.

The surrounding fields were still unplowed. Old wet cornstalks bent low, driven into the earth by the heavy snows of winter. The hayfields were drab, but new growth was sprouting in low places, the promise of an abundance of grass to cut into hay.

An oncoming team of horses made her pull on the right rein, drawing Fannie to the side, allowing the team to pass. Inquisitive faces peered out from the open front of the buggy. Hester nodded, glad when they continued on their way.

On the outskirts of town, the road widened and hardened. The stones from the lime quarry made traveling easier. Fannie pricked up her ears as they passed the blacksmith shop on the right, a low stone building with a wide chimney. Smoke poured from it, created by the hot coals used by the smithy.

She remembered her excursions with Hans, the smell of the horses' hooves as his trimming knife cut expertly into them. His strong, muscular arms pounded the shoes into shape. There was the anvil, the hot coals, the odor of hay and corn and manure. From her perch on the wagon, she would take in all of this, cultivating a love of horses that Hans had taken away when he forbade her to ride. Still, it was an enriching part of her childhood, listening to Hans's voice as he told her stories, bouncing along on the seat of the spring wagon beside him. He had been a good father to her.

Many carriages passed her now. There were poor farmers in clumsy wagons with wide wheels, covered in mud. Drawn by thin mules, their ribs strained against the wet, brown coat covering them. Their necks were too thin, their heads enormous and bobbing, unsightly ears above them.

There were also ornate hacks, polished to a high gloss and drawn by high-stepping black horses, their coats gleaming in the rain. Their drivers were top-hatted and mustached, with long, thick sideburns down their cheeks like squirrels' tails. Ladies protected themselves from the rain with fancy parasols as they cast superior glances at the Amish woman clad entirely in black, her plain, serviceable buggy drawn by the squat, little mare.

A group of children dashed across the road, their hats and bonnets slick with the rain, the girls' skirts like striped flowers, the petticoats beneath them ruffled and sewn by loving mothers.

A lone boy strolled through the rain, rolling a hoop expertly, his white shirt front in stark relief against the gray of his opened coat. For one instant, Hester thought it must be Billy, then remembered that Billy would be fifteen years old now, close to sixteen, and no longer a child.

She drove up the narrow passageway called Water Street, turned left on Orange, and then right onto Mulberry. Everywhere she looked, there was a construction site. Houses were springing up like mushrooms.

The homes were all made of wood. Even the chimneys were slapped together with mud, the way Hans disliked. He said more houses burned to the ground because of shoddy chimneys than for any other reason. Hester knew the wealthy lot owners erected these wood dwellings cheaply, charged a goodly sum for rent, and made a hefty profit. It was only when yet another fire broke out that they saw the error of their ways.

She drew Fannie off to the right and tied her to a lamppost when she neared Emma Ferree's house. Better to walk the last distance, then knock on the door to see if she was home.

Her breath came rapidly as she blanketed the steaming Fannie. She patted her forehead, promised her return, and walked across the street, a lone, black figure, the corners of her shawl spreading out behind her.

There it was. The sturdy house made of stone and wood, the steps going up right off the street as if to welcome any person who wanted to enter.

Hester drew in a deep breath, steadied herself, and lifted a hand to knock. She tried once, then twice. Disappointed, she raised her hand again and knocked harder. When no one answered, she drew back to gaze through the window. On a day such as this, Emma would be burning her oil lamp and perhaps a few candles.

Obviously, there was no one home. She turned to make her way back down the steps when she thought of Walter Trout. It would be better to see him than no one at all.

She made her way to his front door, resolutely, remembering his kindness, his effusive words of praise. Seeing him was the closest thing to meeting Emma Ferree, and it would have to do for today.

Chapter 17

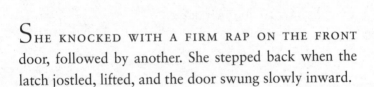

She knocked with a firm rap on the front door, followed by another. She stepped back when the latch jostled, lifted, and the door swung slowly inward.

Hester's mouth dropped open when a ruffled white housecap appeared around the edge of the door, below which shone two beady blue eyes and a florid pink face. Emma Ferree opened her mouth to speak, closed it again, gave up, and threw both hands in the air, her eyes wide and full of recognition. "*Ach, mein Gott im Himmel!*"

Hester started to laugh, but a sob cut it in two. She fell into Emma's soft, plump arms, bending over to lay her bonneted head on her warm shoulder and to let her tears and hiccupping flow for a long moment. Emma's plump hands patted and soothed, her voice crooning as if Hester were an infant.

Somehow Hester was drawn into the dim hallway, the door was closed behind her, and she was enveloped in warmth and the heavenly scent of ginger and molasses and cinnamon and sugar.

"*Ach, du yay, du yay. Meine Hester. Meine own Hester*. How often my prayers went to heaven because of you, *meine Liebchen, miene* Indian girl, still so beautiful." Exclaiming nonstop, Emma reached for Hester's hat strings, yanked on them and removed the hat. Her brilliant gaze swept over the white cap, taking in the severe cut of her black dress, cape, and apron.

"You really are Amish!" she said forcefully.

The back door swung open. The gray light from the doorway was darkened as Walter Trout hove his large frame through it.

"Emma?" he shouted.

Emma held up one finger. "Yes, Walter?"

"Where are you?"

"Here in the hallway. Come look who's here, come quick."

Walter Trout filled up the width of the hallway with his presence, his reaction much the same as Emma's. He began with a polite handshake but pulled Hester into a gentlemanly embrace with one arm, looked down on her face, and proclaimed her his long-lost daughter.

Hester let herself absorb the luxury of their welcome, the love that flowed unhampered by pride or judgment. Her soul expanded with the knowledge that so much kindness was available and that God had not forgotten her after all.

Walter's shirt smelled of ginger and cinnamon, his breath like sugar.

She found herself seated at the kitchen table, a checked cloth covering it. Walter arranged cookies on a platter. Emma put the tea kettle on the stove, and brought out china cups, talking all the while. "Tell us, please tell us,

Hester, how is your life? Does he treat you well? Are you happy?"

"My husband is dead." When she spoke the words, they crowded her consciousness, blotting out the moments of love and acceptance mere minutes before.

Walter became very still. "Oh no! Oh no! What happened?"

Emma sat down heavily, her hands to her face. "The rain? The flooded creeks?"

"Yes. Yes. He rode with a group of men here to Lancaster to reinforce the lower part with sandbags. His horse shied going across a bridge and threw him against the bridge's stone foundation."

"Dead instantly?"

"No. He lived for eleven days. He never woke up."

"Oh, *mein Herr*. An act of God. An act of God."

Hester nodded. Guilt flooded her eyes.

Emma spoke on, freely and openly. "God took him. He did. That's good. He was not for you. It was not his will that you marry him."

Walter came to stand behind Emma's chair. He reached out a hand and patted her round shoulder. "Now, now, Emma, my dear."

Hester's mouth opened in surprise when Emma reached up to clasp the round fingers placed on her shoulders and kept them there. "What?" Hester could not put words to the question, so she gestured toward the clasped hands.

"Oh!" Emma and Walter said with one voice and a great display of merriment. Their pink faces were wreathed in smiles, all the aging lines and wrinkles turning into little trails of happiness. "You don't know! Why, of course not. Walter asked me to marry him after Billy ran off to the war. Oh, and you don't know that, either," Emma burst out.

And so began a long tale, a story spun into emotional clouds of longing for Billy, newly discovered marital bliss, the blessings received from the Lord for their marriage, and spending their days together in gratitude.

"But, you didn't like Walter," Hester stated, laughing.

"Indeed, indeed, were it not for Billy's leaving, I would not have my darling Emma." Walter, always the well-bred gentleman, patted her arm reassuringly.

"That and my washline," Emma chirped. "How I hated the fact that Walter could see my nightclothes flapping on the line! It was downright immodest. And it never failed, I'd hang them out, and there he was like a nosy gopher, up over the top of that fence."

Walter laughed, and his tears ran copiously as he held his rotund stomach. "Now, Emma, I never looked at your washline."

"Puh! That is a *schnitza*!

"Billy got himself in trouble down at the livery. He punched a drunken man in the stomach, then let his horse loose. He had fines to pay after his arrest and couldn't go back to the livery, ever. He almost landed in the stocks on the square." Emma shook her head as sorrow filled her deep-set eyes.

She clucked and lamented, but he was gone now. "Old enough, he was, and fit as a fiddle, that boy. Strong in the legs like a draft horse, he could run for miles without being winded. He'd make a good soldier, but any day, he might be killed." Emma could hardly live with that.

Walter added solemnly that as long as the French supported the Indians to the north, and they fought the English colonists this way, the war would continue. It all boiled down to the lust for land. The Indians had been driven to Pennsylvania from the south, and here they had been wiped out, driven west to Ohio and beyond.

Then Hester began her story. Her marriage to William, her failure to give William children, his stringent rules and exacting nature.

Walter and Emma allowed Hester to continue unhindered, giving no indication of their opinions. They drank cup after cup of tea, snipping off so much sugar with each cup that the solid, white cone was disappearing rapidly, which seemed quite wasteful to Hester. But she must remember, these were English people, not frugal Amish. So she allowed Emma to place a large piece of white sugar in her own tea, sipped it with relish, and pronounced it very good. Frances would have a fit.

The last of her story was her plan to travel to Ohio to look for her people. She presented her case well without seeking pity, stating her inability to be a good wife to William because of her Indian heritage.

The loud ticking of the clock was the only sound in the homey kitchen. The candlelight cast the whole room into the warmth of its yellow glow. The kettle purred on the lid of the cast iron stove. The checked tablecloth was covered with molasses cookies and tea, the cone of sugar, and a white milk pitcher, so much like Kate's kitchen. The only thing missing was children, a baby in the cradle. There had always been babies. And Kate's devotion to them.

Walter sighed, and his great bald head swiveled from side to side. He stood up. "I'll tend to your horse, Hester. She must be thirsty."

Hester nodded. Her eyes were bright with unshed tears, her mouth soft and trembling.

Emma was careful with her words. She chose them deliberately, while letting Hester know that she had done nothing wrong. In fact, she had done well. God had chosen to take William, yes, but not by her sins. Or because of them.

And there was no way on earth she could allow Hester to travel west, a young woman alone. She wouldn't last two weeks before some ruffian would make off with her horse and perhaps even herself.

"Hester, my dearest heart, you must finally make peace with who you are—an Indian, yes. There is nothing wrong with being one. And you were Amish-raised by a loving Kate. And you've lived with Hans, Annie, William, and Frances, all created by God, too, living here by the grace of God. Imperfect, yes; perfectly lovable, no. Blaming yourself has got to go. None of this is a fault of your own. But if you want to hang on to that whole misery, then go right ahead."

Hester cowered beneath Emma's forthright manner.

"Stop running away."

"But I'm not."

"Yes, you are."

"But it's for the best."

"Do you really want to go?" Emma's beady blue eyes shot darts of truth. When they hit their mark, Hester's shoulders sagged and her face relaxed, as warm, healing tears appeared in her black eyes. They hung like silver jewels on the thick, dark lashes, trembled, and then splashed on her cheeks and down the front of her black dress, where they soaked into the fabric, turning it darker than it was.

What followed was a shock to Emma. She had never heard weeping become so forceful. The sobs of anger emitted from her open mouth, the hoarse heaves of sadness and misery propelled by the power of her guilt and misplaced blame, were frightening. In simple language, Emma urged Hester to grasp forgiveness and draw on God's unlimited supply of grace. Slowly, she dismantled all the explanations and resolve Hester had created to explain what she had experienced.

Emma held her, letting her sobs enter her own heart, and cried with her. Walter's small eyes filled up as he came through the door, and he cried as he filled the teacups. He cried as he sliced ham into the frying pan, sniffed as he seasoned the beans, and wiped at tears that plunked into the water in the dishpan as he peeled potatoes. For he loved Hester so much.

She went home in the fading gray light, the rain splashing on the buggy top and the little brown mare named Fannie. She told Elias and Frances of her plans to move into Emma Ferree's house, the empty one beside Walter and Emma Trout. Quite simply, she wanted to be with them.

No, she would not attend church every time, but she would remain true to the Amish faith. Emma thought it would be best.

Barbara King came to visit on Sunday, early, before the hordes of others arrived who would come to wish the young widow well. She came in on the stiff April wind, the kind that bent tulips double, flopping them against the side of the stone house, brushing their delicate petals. She whirled through the door and banged it shut behind her, latched it with a loud ring of iron, and turned to the fireplace, rubbing her hands furiously.

Hester rose immediately, her black dress swishing about her narrow hips as she used the bellows to stir up the fire.

"Chilly out there." Barbara handed her stiff black hat to Hester, loosened the long steel pin so she could slide the black shawl off her shoulders, folded it expertly, and gave it to Hester as well. "How's it going, Hester? I think of you every night."

"Good, Barbara, it's—"

"Call me Bappie."

"Bappie, I went to visit an old friend, Emma Ferree, and her new husband, and she helped me out of a few *dumbkopf* decisions."

"Don't you know the old saying? 'No decisions for a year, when a spouse passes away.'"

"What? A year? A whole year to live here with Johnny and Naomi? I can't," Hester whispered her defeat.

"Why not? You've got it made. Big stone house. Money. Frances at your beck and call."

Hester told Bappie about Johnny and Naomi, and the farm.

"You're not thinking straight, Hester. Take the farm."

"I don't want it."

Bappie looked thoughtfully at Hester, her bright brown eyes polished with understanding. Then she nodded firmly, signaling her empathy. Hester's heart relaxed in the strength of knowing that Bappie, Emma, and Walter all stood with her.

"You're right. You shouldn't accept the farm."

"I'm going to live with—well, not *with* Walter and Emma, but in the empty house beside them. In the town of Lancaster on Mulberry Street."

Up went Bappie's eyebrows. "What will you do for a living?"

"They won't charge me rent. I'll make quilts." She kept her love of herbs and doctoring hidden from Bappie.

"I was hoping you would consent to live with me." Bappie spoke softly, so unlike her.

Hester saw the disappointment in her eyes, the dejection in her shoulders. Hester wavered in her decision. Should she accept her offer first? Indecision cracked the shaky new foundation Emma had placed beneath her so firmly only a few days ago.

Suddenly Bappie sat upright, shrugged her shoulders, and said it was all right, she'd always done well on her own and would continue to.

"I go to Lancaster's curb market, selling garden things. I'll see you on Friday and Saturday sometimes, maybe?"

In that moment, Hester told her of the herbs, her plans to grow them, to bottle tinctures and teas, and to go wherever there was a need. And how William had not wanted her to do this.

Bappie was enthralled. She asked dozens of questions, saying the need for a service such as she spoke of was large and growing.

"Is there room for a garden in the back lot of Emma Ferree's house?" Bappie asked finally.

Hester considered, mulling over the fact that she did not really know this Barbara King, a distant relative of William's. She watched the woman, warily. Reddish hair, a nose like a hawk, observant eyes, a long and lean and narrow face like William's and Frances's. The only thing soft about Bappie was her eyes, bright like polished stones, but guileless, and yes, soft. She was all sharp angles, no womanly curves anywhere, her black dress hanging as if from a coat rack, loose, empty, almost rectangular.

Finally Hester decided the best way was total honesty. She had been betrayed too often. "Are you a cousin of Frances?"

"First cousin not to her, but to Elias."

"So how do I know you're nice, like him?"

At this, Bappie hooted a strange laugh, almost like a screech owl at night or the clumsy squawk of the nighthawk. "Hester, you're odd. You can't go tiptoeing through life afraid everyone is not nice. Very few people are. Don't be so serious. You wear your cap so far over your ears, every bit of your hair is covered. Who made you do that? Or were you always so plain, or whatever?"

"William was very conservative."

"May he rest in peace," Bappie said softly but her eyes flashed without piety. "I can bet a nickel that man was very much like his mother." The words were out of her mouth before she could grab them back. Up went the hand, sideways across her mouth, her brown eyes like glistening river pebbles. "Sorry."

Hester shook her head, a smile curving her lips.

"You know how beautiful you are, don't you?" Bappie asked.

Hester frowned and her eyebrows fell, a straight black line over brooding eyes. "Beauty is a curse."

Bappie stared at her, unblinking. "You really do believe that."

"Of course I do."

"Why?"

"Someday I'll tell you."

"Someday? Does that mean you're asking me to live in Emma Ferree's house in town?"

"Are Amish women allowed to live in town? Does our *Ordnung* forbid it?"

Bappie's eyes turned bright with humor. "We'll never know until we try it, will we?"

When the spring rains turned to the heat of summer, Emma Ferree's house was newly whitewashed, the windows polished, the floors scrubbed. There was new ticking in the mattresses, the fireplace was cleaned and whitewashed. Walter Trout repaired the front door, his face red and streaming in the summer sun.

Hester accompanied Bappie to her house in the country, a low dwelling built of logs, fashioned in a peculiar style without an upstairs. It was extremely small, but sufficient for one person. It was built on the south corner of her brother Samuel's farm, a former hut built by an earlier owner to house slaves.

Bappie had beautiful furniture for a single woman. Fashioned in the old German style with intricate scrollwork, the blanket chests and cupboard doors were painted with delicate motifs carefully preserved from the old country.

Bappie put Hester to work cleaning the furniture with oil soap, then polishing it with sheep's wool. They packed it well with heavy blankets on a farm wagon Johnny loaned them. The massive Belgians stood, their heads drooping patiently as he helped them load the valuable pieces. He remained a gentleman, so impressing Bappie that she became quite flustered when she spoke to him.

Hester sat perched on a wooden chest. The sun had climbed high at the noon hour. Heat shimmered across the cornfields. Bright butterflies hovered among the columbine, delicately feeding on the thin nectar of the lavender flowers, bobbing in the stillness.

A meadowlark sang its lusty song, opening its bill like a pair of scissors. Chimney swifts wheeled in the hot, cloudless sky, dozens of them dipping and wheeling as one.

Today there was a song in Hester's heart, an old tune Kate used to sing while doing the wash. It welled up until Hester was humming softly so no one would hear. She lifted her face to the sun, glorying in the summer scents of the earth and the verdant crops, growing so lush and green. Here men's axes had laid the heavy trees to the ground; then they'd used the lumber to build barns and houses for their growing families, a way of life Hester knew well.

Foreign to her was the way of the nomadic Indian, she recognized. Over and over, gratitude for Emma Ferree's sound advice lifted Hester's spirits.

Elias and Frances sent her away, wishing her the blessing, "*Herr saya,*" as they clasped her hands warmly in their own. Frances was glad to be rid of her, she knew, but still Hester admired the effort she put forth to stand beside her husband and wish her the usual German blessing.

Naomi said she must come often to visit. Johnny shook her hand, holding it longer than necessary, but she endured his touch, shaking off the repulsiveness. To forgive, to let go, was the Amish way, and the way of all Christians who chose to follow Jesus's teaching.

Bappie turned. "You still back there?"

Hester acknowledged her words with a wave.

Walter and Emma awaited them, motioning them to the back alley. Walter helped Bappie guide the horses carefully to the back door, and the work of unloading the furniture began.

They filled the house with the beautiful German pieces. They scattered bright hooked rugs of blue and purple, yellow and red, across polished oak floors.

Hester put her wedding gifts—the towels and table-cloths, doilies and rugs that were made of rushes—with Bappie's things. She placed the set of china with the blue pattern on the cupboard shelves alongside Bappie's set of white dishes.

Frances gave her William's desk and his rocking chair, tears streaming as she presented them to Hester, her mouth compressed piously when she asked her to take good care of them. They put the desk in the living room with the rocking chair beside it. Hester placed one of her glass vases on the desk top, then picked a bouquet of white daisies to remember William. She could picture him rocking by the fireplace, content after supper, his dark head bent over the massive Bible on his lap.

Bappie laid a small fire in the fireplace and made tea for her helpers. Walter and Emma sat side by side on the bench, watching with eager eyes as she cut a strawberry pie. Shoveling huge wedges onto the pretty blue dishes, Bappie winked broadly at Hester as Walter and Emma began enjoying the sweet dessert. Hester smiled, bending quickly to fold a tea towel into the cupboard drawer. She had the distinct feeling that life could become extremely interesting with Bappie, Walter, and Emma.

Every week they drove Bappie's team out to the homestead, as she called the house that was barely more than a hut. There they weeded and hoed the huge vegetable garden, toiling side by side in the blazing sun. They picked the vegetables that were ripe, set traps for marauding raccoons and opossums, then loaded the weeks' supply of vegetables for the downtown market. On the curb they set up wooden crates, then piled the freshly picked beans, red beets, and cucumbers in pleasing mounds, the tops of the beets dripping with fresh water, the way the townsfolk wanted them, Bappie said. Customers came, looked, and voiced their pleasure at Bappie's fine vegetables.

"No," she'd say, "I'll have cabbage next week." Lifting her thumb and forefinger, she squeezed her eyes shut to mimic how very close the cabbage heads were to being the perfect size, but not quite yet.

She was noisy, her voice rising above the cart wheels, the hooves of the horses, the other sellers hawking their wares. She flung her cap strings over her square shoulders. Her coppery hair gleamed from beneath the wide expanse of muslin, her bright eyes never missing a potential buyer.

She sold peas in the pod for exorbitant prices, and raspberries fat and black and luscious with moisture. Wealthy, fair-skinned ladies fought for her smallest cucumbers, her ruffled heads of lettuce.

Hester helped to set up and kept the piles looking fresh and succulent, her large, dark eyes taking in the way Bappie did business.

The men came, staring at Hester, then looked away respectfully, bending to the wishes of their wives, although many discreetly glanced backward at the beauty of the new Amish girl.

Bappie howled with unashamed glee as she loaded up the empty crates. Passersby frowned at the raucous sound, unable to believe their eyes and ears at that unmannerly vegetable seller. But Bappie sold every morsel, every leaf she brought.

She and Hester counted the money at the kitchen table after the sun had gone down. Bappie leaned back in her chair, a pleased expression spreading across her features. "We're all set, Hester. We'll put enough by to hold us over the winter. I never sold so many vegetables. All you have to do is perch on a crate and look at the crowd." She leaned forward, slapped the table, and said Frances would have a fit, now, wouldn't she?

CHAPTER 18

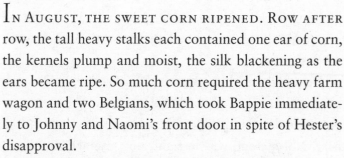

In August, the sweet corn ripened. Row after row, the tall heavy stalks each contained one ear of corn, the kernels plump and moist, the silk blackening as the ears became ripe. So much corn required the heavy farm wagon and two Belgians, which took Bappie immediately to Johnny and Naomi's front door in spite of Hester's disapproval.

When Hester refused to accompany her, Bappie drove off in a tiff, her cap strings flying out behind the back seat of Walter Trout's one-seated buggy. Leaning forward, she rapped the silver mare to a fast trot, muttering to herself about stubborn Indian blood.

Hester watched her go, her arms crossed tightly about her waist, her eyes flashing black heat. If Bappie insisted on hiring that offensive Johnny to haul her corn to market, she'd have to do it alone. Hester was not prepared to work freely in his presence. The moving had been bad enough. That Bappie certainly did have a mind of her own.

The dew was heavy. So heavy, in fact, that by the time Bappie and Hester made their way down the first and second rows of sweet corn, they were soaked. Their kerchiefs clung to their sodden hair, the corn tassels dusted their heads with clinging, yellow pods. The cornstalks were wet and itchy, scraping their necks and faces like rasping claws. They made sacks out of their aprons, holding up the bottoms by two corners until they bulged with ears of corn, dew-laden and heavy. Bappie was frenzied in her movements, yanking the corn off the heavy stalks and filling her apron twice as fast as Hester.

"This corn may as well be made of gold," she crowed, her breath coming in gasps.

"It's about as heavy," Hester called. She was happy, working in the early morning. Johnny had not showed up, thankfully allowing them the use of the wagon without his assistance.

Up and down the rows the women toiled, loading the large green ears on the bed of the wagon. The sun was a pulsing red orb in a yellow sky that already reflected its heat. Not a cloud was in sight, not so much as a small breeze moved the wet cornstalks.

Hester figured that if the wet heat continued, they'd have a thunderstorm. She eyed the perfectly staked tomatoes, the heavy, prickly vines of the cucumber plants, then lifted a hand to shade her eyes as she looked toward the sun. There it was. To the left of the sun was a brilliant flash of light like an uncolored rainbow, the harbinger of rain. The sun dog. Well, if the rainstorm came, they'd dig the vegetables out of the mud, the way Kate used to.

Her thoughts were not on the mundane task of ripping off ears of corn, when suddenly a solid form ahead startled her so that she drew back, her eyes wide with alarm. "Oh!"

His grin spreading widely, Johnny stood at the end of the row, his thumbs hooked in the side pockets of his broadfall trousers.

"Hester! Didn't mean to scare you." His teeth flashed white in his dark face, the straw hat pulled low, his hair as dark as midnight, so like William's.

Hester said nothing, bending her head to her task.

He refused to move, to allow her to step out of the row. His dark eyes glittered, black coals shaded by the filthy straw hat.

He opened his mouth to speak, the black coals turned to slits. "You can't always hide," he sneered.

"Johnny!" Bappie's joyous greeting rang from a short distance away. He turned and patiently hailed Bappie, warmly lifting a hand in greeting. Bappie stumbled over her words, so effusive was her welcome. Johnny grinned, praised her growing of the vegetables, and said he'd never seen nicer corn. She'd get a good price today.

Hester turned down another row. Her apron was bulging with the heavy ears, her dress was soaking wet, and she had no plans to step out for that man's inspection. Discreetly, she emptied her apron in between the rows of corn and kept pulling ears, moving away from their voices.

"Hester!"

Bappie's sharp call stopped her short. Slowly she emptied another apron-load of corn, straightened, and resumed picking furiously. The color in her cheeks heightened; her eyes were dark and brooding.

"What are you doing?"

"Picking corn."

"You're dumping it on the ground!"

"So."

"What ails you?"

Angrily Bappie came stomping down the row, bending to pick up the corn Hester had unloaded. "What got over you?" she hissed.

"Get that Johnny away from here," Hester hissed back.

"Why?"

Hester's face was terrible, her eyes boring into Bappie's with an intensity she had never seen. "Just do what I said. I mean it."

Bappie rolled her eyes, but she obeyed. Quickly she loaded the last of the corn onto the wide bed of the wooden wagon, told Johnny to drive, and hopped up behind him, saying Hester would bring the team.

Shrugging his shoulders, he could do nothing other than obey. He lifted the reins, hiyupping to the big, quiet Belgians. Only when the creak of the heavy wheels sounded in her ears did Hester emerge, watching the wagon until it disappeared behind a curtain of overhanging willow branches. Then she stepped out, smoothed down her apron, untied Bappie's gray horse named Silver, and sat heavily on the open seat of the buggy.

Johnny had already taken the team of Belgians home by the time Hester had changed into dry clothes, the blue dress and black cape and apron, topped by the muslin fabric of her cap, her face freshly washed.

At the curb market, the corn was piled in a high, beautiful bin, green and white at the ends, dewdrops clinging to its dark silk. Carrots lay in bunches, bits of black soil clinging to their thick orange roots. Beside them, the first tomatoes, red-cheeked and inviting, added color to the green, lacy carrot tops.

Immediately the buyers came, pushing, shoving, and carrying away great armloads of corn, wooden crates of it, and cloth bags stuffed full. The coins clinked into the cash box as Bappie yelled and made hand gestures, smiling and dipping her head when the praise became too effusive.

Hester talked to perfect strangers, smiling and handing tomatoes and carrots to fat, overdressed housewives and stick-thin women in ruffles, all sweating profusely in the sweltering heat.

"De corn! De corn!" Beckoning excitedly, her face flushed to a high color, a German housewife plowed through the crowd, elbowing her way through the more well-to-do.

"Step back. Watch it there," came snorts of disapproval and words of rebuke, all to no avail. On she came.

"De corn! De corn! Oy, so fresh! So yellow! Just picked!"

Hester found herself laughing freely, the sound like water rippling over smooth stones. She lost herself in the mad, colorful crowd of pushing people. She heard Bappie's words rising and falling, selling her vegetables. She wasn't quiet, nor circumspect, and certainly not humble.

But Hester was carried along by the gaiety, the high spirits that caused Bappie to talk constantly to her customers. Hester smiled without self-consciousness. She spoke to strangers. And she was surprised to find that they weren't strangers after she had spoken to them. She learned from Bappie to be tolerant, happy to let go of her suspicion, her dislike of certain people. To Bappie, they were all the same. They bought her vegetables.

Too tired to cook supper, and the house holding the heat like a tea kettle, Hester and Bappie collapsed in the backyard beneath the shade of a wilted lilac bush at the end of the market day. Bappie lay flat on her back, her knees bent upward, poking into the sky, all sharp angles and dark colors. She had thrown one arm over her forehead and was saying they made enough money to buy a house today.

Hester lay on her stomach, her chin in her hands, her shoulders shaking as she laughed at Bappie's ridiculous expansion of the coins in the wooden box.

A low rumble of thunder grumbled in the distance. The evening sun shone on.

"It'll rain," Hester said shortly.

"Nah! What's wrong with you? The sun's shining as bright as ever."

"It'll rain."

"Hey, what is up with you and Johnny? You act like he's as lovable as a snake."

"He is."

"Oh, come on. He's much nicer than William was. Sorry. May he rest in peace."

Hester rolled onto her back, shaded her eyes the way Bappie did, and outright told her about Johnny's misdeeds at Christmastime, the lies that followed, and her own bowing to his wickedness.

Bappie pulled a blade of grass, chewing it slowly as she listened. She spit it out, plucked another one, and chewed it the whole way through, then spit it out, too. Finally, she said, "Well, Hester, you in a red dress were probably a sight to see. I'm surprised William allowed it."

"It was his mother's."

Up went Bappie's eyebrows. "Hm. Ain't that something? Well, just goes to show, you never know how men's minds work. I sure never had that problem. No one ever tried to, you know." Her face turned as red as her largest red beet.

"I guess I was too dumb to see."

"Stop blaming yourself. That's why I'm unmarried. You can't judge a book by its cover. You never know if a man is sincere—a good, kind, Christian fellow—or a genuine traitor."

Hester nodded.

They both fell silent. Another rumble of thunder worried itself on the horizon. The red glow of the evening sun disappeared, leaving them in an eerie, grayish-yellow light.

Bappie sat straight up like a jack-in-a-box. Her eyes turned dark and wide with fear.

"Rain's coming," Hester said.

Walter Trout's perspiring face popped up over the fence. "Emma says we have a few corn cakes left. And some molasses and applesauce. If you're hungry, she has a muskmelon cut open for you."

By the time the storm hit, Hester and Bappie sat cozily by candlelight, eating Emma's good food, washing it down with many glasses of cold, sugared, spearmint tea.

The lightning flashed blue, followed by great rolls of heavy thunder that shook the wooden frame of the house. The wind screamed around the corners, howled under the eaves, and lashed the windowpanes with sheets of water. A high sound of pinging ice soon followed. Bappie held her hands over her ears and squeezed her eyes shut tightly. "Oh, my garden, my poor garden," she said swaying back and forth as if mourning the demise of all her vegetables.

"Gott is unhappy with us," wailed Emma.

She believed a storm was God's fury on humankind and all its sins, to bring everyone to repentance.

Hester sat, tired and relaxed, rocking quietly on the armless rocking chair. Her dark eyes watched the rain and ice punish the glass windowpanes. She heard the howling of the wind. Unafraid, she knew all humankind was subject to storms, to the ways of the sky, the sun, the moon, the earth. It was all a part of the universe, so much greater and so much more than one mind could begin to grasp.

Like the eagle's flight, the storm spoke to her soul. All the earth and the things of the earth could not be separated. Like the weather, everything was controlled by the almighty creator. He chose to send storms and heat, cold and wind and drought. If the garden was ruined, they had enough to get by.

The harder the hail bounced off the windows, the more agitated Bappie became, mournfully shaking her head and muttering about the green tomatoes and cucumbers, the green beans and squash. "It'll be gone. All of it ruined. What will we do?" she wailed, rocking back and forth, misery turning slowly to hysteria.

"It'll be all right. Hail is never widespread." These words came from Hester on the rocking chair, her dark eyes untroubled pools of calm.

"How can you say that? You have no idea!" shrieked Bappie, her eyes large and dark with the fear of losing her vegetables and of the wooden box becoming empty of coins before the coming winter was over.

A deafening clap of thunder followed sizzling white light as jagged streaks of lightning erupted from boiling black clouds above the town of Lancaster. Winds increased as the storm moved directly above them. Hail rattled the wooden shingles, attacked windowpanes, jumped on the streets, and nestled in backyard grasses.

Then the rain increased its fury. The wind's force soaked every hand-hewn shingle and brought the rain to seep beneath them, then drip steadily onto attic floors. Meticulous housewives squawked, grabbed wooden buckets, and raced pell-mell up their steep attic stairs to find the dripping leaks, placing the buckets at the proper places.

Rain seeped down mud and stick chimneys and ran down whitewashed walls. Horses whinnied in alarm, kicking and pounding against the sides of their stalls, their eyes rolling in fright as the sizzling lightning became more constant.

A sound reached Hester's ears. She held completely still. A shingle? A loose shutter? Again, the repetitious knocking. She sat up straight.

"Someone is at the door."

"Ach, nay, nay!"

Emma, quite distraught, looked to Hester for assistance. Bappie, forgetting her ruined vegetable garden, sprang into action, tearing open the latch. From the narrow hallway came a shriek of surprise and then an exclamation of sorrow, a sort of mewling edged by the beginning of a sob.

"Hester!"

The command was so forceful she sprang into action, peering around Bappie's narrow shoulders. There in the blinding white flashes of lightning stood a very small boy, holding a bundle almost as big as himself. Drenched, and his sodden bundle dripping water, he turned calm eyes to the incredulous women but said nothing at all.

Behind her, Hester felt the floorboards raise and lower as Walter and Emma lumbered toward them.

Bappie turned, unsure.

Hester reached out and drew the boy in, as water ran off him in rivulets, pooling at his small feet. She took the bundle amid shrieks from Bappie, the usual half prayer, half exclamation coming from Emma. Quickly she unwrapped the sodden blanket, not surprised to find an infant. A baby.

Bappie was squealing about the offensive odor and the rain in puddles on Emma's clean floor and rug.

Walter cleared his throat as he shuffled back to the kitchen for rags, shaking his great pink head with the crown of grayish hair circling his ears. He never could expect a normal day since marrying his Emma, not even during a summer thunderstorm. But that was all right. Anything was better than the life of crippling solitude he had led before he met the boisterous Emma. And she was so loving.

They carried the children into the heat of the kitchen and dried them with the towels. Their smell was like a mixture of manure, sour grapes, and spoiled cream, the stench thick and cloying.

Bappie's anger forced a few surprising words from her mouth. She moved fast, getting down the agate washtub, then starting a fire in the washhouse. Above the howling wind and stinging rain, her voice could be heard commanding and giving instructions. The end result was two shivering children, both like lost kittens, their skin scrubbed, their heads scoured with kerosene, then soaped, rinsed, and soaped again.

Wrapped in rough towels, the boys were terrified of the smell, the powerful soap, the water, Bappie's less than gentle hands. The women threw the stained and torn clothing in the backyard. Bappie said she was taking no chances with the likelihood that those clothes had to be crawling with lice.

When darkness closed in around the wooden house on Mulberry Street, the storm had moved on. Eaves still dripped. Branches and leaves, torn from sturdy trees by the powerful gusts, were strewn across the streets. Small rivers roiled by, then pooled in low places, filling large holes that set drivers' teeth on edge as the steel-rimmed wheels of their carriages hit them.

The quietness that eventually came was a blessing. Bappie rinsed the tubs and set the washhouse in order. Hester wrapped a towel around the baby, who seemed to be about a year old, weighing a bit more than she had thought. The older child was perhaps four. Emma reached for him, rocked and crooned, sang and stroked the small back. Tears came, puddled, then ran down her shining cheeks.

"*Oh, meine liebe Kinder. Meine liebe*," she repeated over and over. "What the *deifel* does!"

She never blamed any person in circumstances such as these. It was always the devil's fault. He stalked around the town, seeking who he could devour, that cunning *deifel*, Emma would say. Why, just look at the women who were slovenly, the men who chose to waste their wages on liquor and became drunkards, leaving their children to starve and eventually be turned into the streets when irate house owners put them there.

When the devil had his way, there was no money for rent, food, or clothing. The women, in despair, turned to the orphanage and left their children there, half-mad with fear and anger and hopelessness.

None of them could get the four-year-old to speak. His tears had dried up, but his light-colored eyes remained fixed, stone cold. Those once glittering eyes went to a place none of them could follow. His face was triangular, with a wide forehead, sunken cheeks, and a pitiful, pointed chin. His mouth, too wide, held decaying teeth that looked like wormy corn kernels.

Hester spoke to him gently in English. She spoke in German, then tried the more common Pennsylvania Dutch.

The smaller one continued to wail, sobbing and sniffing. Walter heated a pan of milk, added molasses, and stirred. He put a small portion in a cup, spread butter on brown, crumbly bread and brought it all to Emma, setting it quietly on the oak washstand beside her rocking chair like a well-trained servant.

When Emma patted Walter's arm, her eyes going to his face, her "*Denke schöen*" was so filled with love that

Hester resolved to someday, if she lived to a ripe old age, feel a love such as they had.

Emma offered the milk to the young boy, who grabbed the cup from her hand, sucking and slurping greedily, straining at the sweet milk. It dribbled down the sides of his face and splashed on the towel as he lifted his face to drain every drop. His eyes begged for more, even as his chest caved in, his shoulders tensed, and he leaned forward to purge every ounce of the nutritious liquid.

There was a sudden flood on the clean floor. Walter and Bappie turned as one. They found a rag and mopped everything clean.

Hester spoke. "That's what happened to me when I was starved on my journey from Berks County. The child is starving like I was. Allow him only a teaspoon at a time. Give him the bread in small bites."

Bappie looked at Hester with a rueful shake of her copper-colored head, the hard, gleaming pebbles that were her eyes disappearing behind lowered lids.

Emma gave the boy small pinches of bread and butter. She waited until he leaned forward, his mouth open wide, before she allowed him more. His translucent eyes were glittering with desperation, the urge to fill his stomach, to rid himself of the torment that was hunger. Small sips of warm milk, more bread. A bowl of porridge. More porridge.

Bappie did not know anything so terrible existed. She was born and raised among the Amish, who lived frugally, and whose food was plain and simple but sufficient. Real hunger had never entered her life. She was incredulous, asking question after question. She pondered the answers. She said that even the Indians, who were supposedly ungodly, provided for their own little ones. This was a shame.

"It's the liquor. The homemade stills, the rye whiskey, the fermented apples, and hops and all the other stuff—they use it to make the devil's brew," Emma said, emphatically.

Both boys' heads dropped, their eyes lowered, and sleep overtook them. The room became still. Occasionally there was a drip of rain, a sighing of the wind, as if the earth was relieved the storm had moved on. Candles flickered. Deep breathing sounds assured them of the boys' slumber.

Emma said quietly, "We'll let them sleep in our bedroom by our bed. Just in case they wake up."

Reverently, as if Christ were in the room, Walter clasped his hands over his rounded stomach and shook his head up and down.

The two women left the hush of Walter Trout's home, returning to the dark, damp interior of their own. They poured cool glasses of tea, and Bappie plied Hester with dozens of questions. Why had she left her family in Berks County? How could she travel all that way? Why wasn't she dead?

Far into the night, Hester recounted her story. She left some of the truth out. She told Bappie it was Annie's dislike of her that finally severed the familial cord.

"Like a birth." Bappie nodded.

"In a sense it was like that. I was free. And yet countless times I have longed to return to the stone farmhouse. To Noah and Isaac and Lissie and Daniel, Solomon, and the baby. I still miss the children."

"Were Noah and Isaac good to you?"

Hester gazed past the candlelight, her eyes drawn to the black corners of the room, as if secrets were hidden best in the dark recesses. Her eyelids grew heavy with sadness as her mouth became soft with remembering. Her voice was husky with fettered pain, a torture that constricted her will to speak.

"Before Annie, they were. They were my brothers. She destroyed the loyalty, the ties that bound us."

"Then they didn't love you for real if they allowed that woman to come between you."

Hester nodded, her eyes somber. "I guess not."

Bappie nodded back, drained her tea, set the glass on the table, and got up a bit stiffly, putting a hand to her back. "It's been a long day. I'm off to bed. Ah, life is crazy, Hester. Don't look back, or your plow will go way off course, the way the Bible says. Not that I'm much of a Bible reader, but that one thing is true." She yawned, stretching like a long, skinny, black cat.

Hester watched and said, "I'm glad you live with me, Bappie."

"Hope you'll say the same thing a year from now," Bappie said, grinning.

CHAPTER 19

THE GARDEN STRETCHED BEFORE THEM, GREEN and flourishing and unharmed. The late-morning sun slanted through the washed tomato plants. The red fruit was mud-splattered, their stalks tossed and showing the lighter dusty shade of green underneath. The corn all lay at an angle, its short roots partly exposed but the ears of corn intact.

They stood, two women shading their eyes with their hands, palms down. One, dressed in dark navy blue, was taller, sharper. The other, dressed in green, was tall and willowy, but possessing the figure of a woman. Their skirts rippled. Cap strings lifted, moved, and fell across their shoulders, the clean, fresh breeze of summer playing with them.

Hester turned to Bappie, her eyes conveying her pleasure. "What did I say?"

Reluctantly, Bappie answered, "Hail is never widespread."

They laughed.

Together, they weeded that day, the cool mud squeezing up between their toes, the hems of their aprons becoming brown with it. The sun shone hot but pleasant. Doves hurried across the blue sky, propelled by their triangular wings. Crows wheeled and flapped, their raucous cries grating and unpleasant, on their way to rob other birds' nests if they could.

Sometimes, Hester broke into song, with Bappie joining in. Mostly though, they remained quiet, pulling weeds, tossing them aside. They spread a blanket in the shade of a spruce tree and opened the lunch basket between them. Bappie cut a ripe tomato into slices, then laid them warm and sun-kissed on squares of new brown bread, spread with plenty of yellow butter, and sprinkled the slices with salt.

They drank cool tea and glasses of buttermilk. Side by side, they reclined on the blanket, resting their backs. Above them, suddenly, a deep laugh, a joyous welcome.

"Well, surprise, surprise!" A lilting slick tone, lifting and falling in all the wrong places.

Without thinking or caring, Hester sat bolt upright, her privacy invaded, her happiness destroyed. Black, hostile lights filled her eyes, and her voice sounded like an assault. "Does Naomi know you are here?"

Johnny recoiled, looking quickly at Bappie for support.

She shrugged her shoulders and kept quiet.

"Go home to your family and leave us alone. You have no business out here with us." Hester did not flinch when Johnny's eyes became bright with anger. She met the light head on, unwavering.

For one wild moment, she thought he was going to hit, to lash out with his fist, helplessly flailing the air between them. Instead he tried to frighten her with his anger, held in check by the regulations of his religion. Still she did not back down. He turned on his heel, sharply throwing his shoulders back, and stalked off with exaggerated steps like an irate schoolboy sent to stand in the corner. Hester would not have been surprised to see a rock come hurtling in their direction.

"Hoo-boy." Bappie shook her head.

"He doesn't need to follow us around. He has wrong intentions."

"But still, Hester. He may be trying to make amends."

"He's not."

"How can you tell?"

Hester shrugged her shoulders and went back to work without another word, pulling weeds like someone possessed, without one backward glance in Bappie's direction.

The child would not speak. Walter and Emma had tried every available resource to get him to at least tell them his name, some sense of where he had come from, who a relative or parent was. But the boy sat, his eyes giving away nothing, only the greenish-yellow light ringed by brown flecks, impossible to decipher.

Both children ate every morsel of food given to them. They were clad in a set of Emma's "necessaries," meaning a small shirt and pants for the four-year-old and a girl's dress for the baby, all made from flour or feedsacks. Emma always kept a wooden trunk well stocked, just in case a hungry or homeless person had need of clothing. The baby crawled, but slowly, pulled himself up by his thin little arms and stood, his thumb in his mouth, his eyes wide and frightened.

Emma showed Hester the stripes on the older child's back and across his legs where a switch had bitten through the flesh. It had healed, then been cut open, time after time. He had angry flea bites and rashes on his elbows and his knees. In the candlelight, they had failed to notice.

Emma sighed. One little victim saved for now.

They gave up trying to find their home after Walter walked to the constable's office, where he was waved away. Repeatedly he talked to the clerk at the desk, who fixed an impatient stare of resentment on his perspiring face. Finally he lifted his hat and wished her a good day, losing no time in getting out of that office.

Hester and Bappie took it on themselves to try to find the children's home. Taking the boy by the hand, they asked him to come with them. They were going for a walk. His terrified eyes glowered at them. Turning, he zigzagged wildly through the house, finally coming to a stop beneath the table, where he curled into a trembling fetal position, his eyes tightly closed.

The baby began wailing, its sobs turning into screams of hysteria. Leaving Emma to comfort the distraught child, they walked out onto the street, more determined than ever to find the source of the children's mistreatment.

The town of Lancaster was newly washed, the storm having given the dusty streets and buildings a thorough rinsing. The evening was warm but not humid, making their stroll a pleasant one.

Naturally, they turned toward the more common section of town where the separate dwellings turned into huts that housed miners, coal-shovelers, and migrant workers. Here the streets were a soup of mud and water.

Tired, unkempt mothers peered suspiciously from doorways, swatting at clouds of mosquitoes that swarmed up from the liquid streets. Yelling children clad in mud shot across the roadways, all thin arms and legs with big feet and hands and bellies.

A youth sagged against a crooked doorpost, smoking a homemade pipe made of a reed and a corncob. He blew a jet of brown smoke in their direction, coughed, squinted, and spat into the mud before lifting the pipe and inhaling deeply.

"Hello?" Bappie said, a question more than anything.

The youth nodded in their direction.

"Do you have any idea if anyone on your street is looking for their children? Two boys?"

A shrug of the shoulders. His too big shirt slid off one shoulder, leaving his thin, white neck exposed, childlike, too vulnerable.

"Is your mother here?"

"Aren't got no ma."

"Your father?"

"Died two days ago. At the foundry."

Bappie perked up, her eagerness bringing her through the puddles of water, the mosquitoes, and the green-tailed flies that buzzed around the filthy doorways.

"Do you have two brothers?"

"A course not."

"Did anyone else die? At the foundry?"

"Two more."

Clearly they were on the right path. They asked him to take them to the men's families. He said no, they didn't have no families.

Defeated, they looked at each other. Feeling dismissed by the disinterested youth, they retraced their steps, lifting their skirts to avoid dragging them through the mud. There were many more streets, but the evening sun was already low in the sky, and both of them had no wish to be here in this corner of Lancaster when darkness arrived. Better to go back home.

The squalor, the odor, and raw poverty of the miners' homes kept Hester awake. She thought of the Indians, their uncanny ability to flourish with nothing except what the earth provided. With the gift of trees, they erected their lodges; with stone they fashioned arrowheads to find food that sustained them. From the wild animals, they fashioned their clothes. They made their tools, in fact, an entire way of life, with nothing except the knowledge handed down from generation to generation. They roamed the land, never hungry, always resourceful.

So who had gone wrong that intelligent white people should let the poor fall along the wayside? Had the liquor and its alcoholic content become a tradition as well?

She considered the Amish, the Mennonites, the Dunkards, the conservative groups who cared for their own. They had the poor among them always, but not like this.

Constantly they gave, they *fa-sarked*, they cared for any less fortunate than themselves.

She supposed she had always been sheltered from the depravity of humankind. The ignorance and unfairness. How could a row of shacks come to be? On that street? What kept the people in poverty? Over and over her mind mulled, searching for a reason that all of God's children were not the same. Perhaps God does love unequally. Otherwise, how could he allow these little ones to suffer untold terrors?

Hans seemed so much better, his shortcomings so different in the way he loved her and ignored the boys, Noah and Isaac. In spite of all that, he provided shelter and food and instilled a work ethic, teaching them to be self-sufficient, to work the land, fell trees, milk cows, and train horses. The list went on and on.

So much of Hans' weakness was her fault. Hadn't she always thought so? As time went on, that idea became firmly entrenched within her. It was easier to handle the past if she lived as the one who had done wrong somehow.

The same with William. She had failed miserably.

Her own sense of unworthiness unrolled like a scroll, the writing not quite legible, but unmistakably there in black and white.

To stay alert, to stay away from men, was her new and immediate goal. It was the only way to fix her past, to stop making mistakes. She would grow herbs and make tinctures with Bappie's help. Together they would tend to the sick, erase the miserable huts, and teach the men and women to clean and cook, to grow vegetables, grind corn, and make their own bread from wheat kernels.

Hester flipped on her side and punched her pillow. She was awake completely now by the passion that drove her thoughts, the tumbled possibilities, the lessons she learned from Emma, good, kind soul that she was. Together with Bappie they would roll up their sleeves and make a big difference in the lives of the poor.

For starters, Bappie did not need to throw away the leftover cabbage leaves or the few tiny carrots half hidden in the loose soil in the bottom of the wooden crate. Red beet tops were very good cooked with salt, pepper, and a dash of vinegar. Bappie threw them away, which Hester found extremely wasteful. But so far she had kept quiet.

Kate had used every last wrinkled pea pod, every little nubbin of corn. She packed away late green tomatoes to roll later in flour and fry in lard. "It'll taste good in the cold winter," she would say, her eyes merry as she shucked that last pitiful ear of corn. This week after market, Hester would crate all the outer cabbage leaves, the red beet tops, anything she could salvage.

She saw the rowhouses every time she closed her eyes. She felt the hopelessness.

Why was the boy lolling about in the late afternoon when he should have been at work the way farm lads were? What caused these people to live in desolate clusters of shacks, when less than a half mile away, wealthy families lived in opulence, black servants seeing to their every need?

She thought again of the Amish and their stringent work ethic. They, the Mennonites, the Dunkards, and many of the more liberal English worked hard to establish farms, clearing entire forests to make room for rolling fields of crops. Maybe no one had taught these poor families how to garden or save money. Hester's heart beat faster. Her pulse quickened with the daring plan that formed in her mind.

Yes. She would start, one family at a time. The summer would soon be over. This is what she would do. With her store of herbs and the wisdom she had learned from the old Indian woman, she would heal the sick children and teach the destitute women to cook, clean, and wash clothes. She hoped Bappie would agree to help her.

Outside in the warm summer night, a figure crept past Hester's bedroom window, tiptoeing stealthily, bent over, a dark figure with his face hidden. He stopped, then slid his hand along the German siding as if to test the sturdiness of it. For a long time he stood, his face lifted, white and featureless in the dark night, with only the ineffective light from the stars overhead.

Hester turned, her dreamlike edge of sleep disturbed by a sound she could not place. A sliding or slithering. A brush against stone? If she were in the forest, she would have known, but here in town, she could not place it. She sighed, untroubled, and let sleep overtake her.

Back in the verdant garden the following day, Hester straightened her back, met Bappie's eyes, and said, "This fall when cold weather approaches, we will go to the poor houses, you and I."

Bappie's elevated eyebrows rearranged her freckles. "We will?"

Hester nodded. She lifted a hand to tuck a strand of hair beneath her cap. "I think God wants me to do this.

This might be why I was led to this town. I have all these herbs and the knowledge of how to use them."

Bappie's face turned a shade darker, obliterating the freckles. Her eyes snapped with anger, black and abrasive. "Hester! You think you're going to solve poverty once and for all with a musty box of stinking herbs? Don't you know the reason those people live like that? They're lazy. The men don't care. They sit down at those taverns and drink away any wages they earn. It's hopeless." Bappie sniffed and mopped her brow with her gray handkerchief.

Hester's mouth turned down. Her nose tingled as her breathing became fast and shallow. "You say that because it leaves you free and blameless. The Amish are soaked with that attitude. You sound exactly like Frances and William."

The words were out before she could think of their consequences. Bappie straightened to her tallest height, her eyes wide and bulging with the scratching truth of Hester's words, an uncomfortable affront to her own righteous life. She stamped one bare foot.

"You! You are such a . . . such an *Indian* in your strange way of thinking!" she burst out, her cap strings flapping, then coming to rest across her shoulders.

Hester faced Bappie squarely. "Yes. I am an Indian. After seeing the squalor and destitution of poor white people, I am glad. Glad. The Indians have no money, only a priceless heritage handed down to them from their forefathers. That's just like the Amish. They are self-sufficient in so many ways, making a good way of life with only the things God has created. I am proud of my Indian blood for the first time in my life, and it feels good."

Bappie's mouth hung open in surprise.

"You can think what you want. I defend my ancestors and the way they live."

Bappie snorted. "I guess you defend the Ohio massacres, the scalping, the savages plundering and burning homes. Those Indians are worse than animals."

"Because they were driven to it by the white men's greed for land."

This Bappie could not truthfully deny.

"The Indians roamed these Pennsylvania woods peacefully, and you know it."

Bappie nodded.

Hester continued, "All my life, I have worn my Indian heritage like an abnormal growth. Ashamed of it. No more. Seeing the little boys, realizing the cruel, depraved way they were beaten . . . ." Hester shook her head.

Bappie looked off across the garden to the woods beyond. She shaded her eyes with a hand, the palm turned down, watching the flight of a meadowlark. Suddenly she turned. "Let's not quarrel about something so unnecessary."

"For you, maybe. But not for me. I know for the first time that I do not have to go through life feeling ashamed of who I am. I want to be able to use the knowledge handed to me by an old Indian woman. Many herbs that grow in these fields and swamps and forests are priceless. They heal. They are good for so many things."

Bappie held very still. "Listen."

From the edge of the woods, by the meandering little creek, came the sound of whistling. At first the women thought it was an unusual bird, till Hester shook her head. Somewhere, she had heard the whistle before. It was more than blowing air through lips, the way Hans and Lissie would whistle. It was a sad, captivating tune. It brought tears to her eyes so many years ago, and it did again.

"Someone is down there," Bappie said, her eyes wide, her hands knotted into fists.

"Sounds like it," Hester agreed.

Warily, they stood still, their ears straining to hear the unusual sound coming from below them.

"Wish we had some sort of protection. Like a gun," Bappie murmured.

"No one dangerous would whistle like that," Hester said, clearly moved by the sound.

They waited, then bent to the task of weeding the heavy pumpkin vines. Soon the green growth would die, leaving the orange pumpkins to ripen in the late autumn sun, one of the last crops to be sold at market before it closed for the season. A few late beets, some lima beans and potatoes, and the days at market would be over.

They worked in solitude, their argument forgotten, each one bent to her own task and her own thoughts.

New life flowed in Hester's veins, filling her with a renewed sense of purpose. She had found her place on earth. She embraced the reason Kate had found her, the reason she left the farm, even the fact that Billy had found her and brought her to Emma Ferree, who had ushered her into the path of the town's needy. The penniless. The weak.

She knew how they felt, the feeling of being an outcast. Hadn't she felt that way all her life? No more. Her soul sang within her. Over and over, the waves of a new understanding lapped at the edges of her own lack of self-worth, wearing it away, creating a sense of peace, of purpose.

Everything—her marriage to William, his death, her senseless servitude and lack of trust in herself and her husband—had prepared her for this venture. Freed from self-blame, she began to whistle, to hum, to break into song, as tears dripped off the end of her nose.

She froze when a figure stood directly in front of her. Straightening slowly, she found a tall Indian, his black hair parted in the middle, a heavy braid down his back, his skin darker than her own. His nose was prominent, his eyes quick and black and restless.

His clothes were the same brown, made of skins, as any white frontiersman. A knife was thrust through the wide leather belt, and he carried a rifle and a gun powder horn slung over his shoulder.

"Hello." He addressed Hester in perfect English.

She met the eyes that were blacker than her own and recognized a part of his face. This was the Indian youth who had moved through the trees like a wraith. She had seen him, heard his whistle. Cold chills crept up her back. The blood drained from her face, leaving her dizzy, light-headed.

"Who are you?" she whispered.

"I am of the tribe of the Lenape. I believe I know who you are. I have watched you for many years. Only now do I make myself known. Your mother was of my tribe. We played together as children. I have come to ask you to go with me to the Ohio River where my people dwell on its banks. I will give you time. I am on my way to the Great Waters and will return in the spring when winter has gone."

Hester could not stand alone. She sank to the ground, slowly folding under this unexpected arrival from her past. Instantly, the Indian brave was beside her, extending his hand to help her to her feet. She shook her head, keeping her eyes lowered to the restless hands in her lap.

"I do not want to disturb you. You have the winter to decide if you will accompany me. You will consent someday to be my wife, I have hoped for many years."

Hester lifted her face to meet his eyes. They were black but kind, gentle, and alive with interest in her alone. A magnetic force rose from his eyes, and she stood, unaware that she had risen to her feet.

The meeting of their eyes could not be broken with so much they recognized in each other. He placed his hand on her arm, taking her trembling hand in his own. She was close enough to see the texture of his skin, the strong cords of his neck. He smelled of animal skins, dust, gunpowder, and sweat. His hair glistened with grease in the ways of her people.

"Thank you for allowing me the winter to decide," she whispered, after long moments had elapsed.

"That makes me very happy," the Indian said. Then, "My name is Hunting Wolf."

"I am Hester King. I was Hester Zug before marrying."

He nodded. "Your husband died."

"Yes."

"Your mother's name was Corn Maiden."

Hester gave only a weak wave of her hand, a dipping of her dark head to acknowledge what he said. She was thankful for his words, but confusion veiled her ability to understand why he had waited all this time, why he had suddenly made himself known.

"You are Lenape."

"Yes." Hester smiled then, directly meeting his eyes.

His face softened, his eyes became black velvet, the longing true, forthright, and honest. "I will return. Think on my words, dearest one. I will take you to my lodge so you can meet your cousins, your brothers. But not without your consent."

"Thank you."

Without another word, he turned and disappeared, blending into the waving grasses and the thick line of trees, as if to hide the sight of her confusion.

Bappie lifted her freckled face to the bright sky and gave a low whistle. "Whoo-ee!"

That was all she said before turning to face Hester with a look that was undecipherable in her brown eyes. Finally she placed a hand on Hester's back, gave a small pat, and said, "Isn't life crazy, my friend? Just when you thought you had it all figured out, along comes a new direction, huh?"

She gave Hester another small pat. "Remember, all your troubles come from men."

Bewildered, Hester turned her face to Bappie, a frightened look widening her eyes. "Are you sure?"

CHAPTER 20

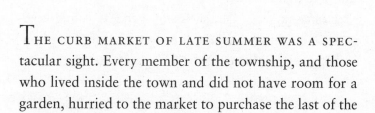

THE CURB MARKET OF LATE SUMMER WAS A SPEC-
tacular sight. Every member of the township, and those
who lived inside the town and did not have room for a
garden, hurried to the market to purchase the last of the
produce to store down cellar.

Farm wagons rattled by, men urging their horses to a
fast trot, their straw hats clamped low on their brows,
bringing in the potatoes and squash and apples. The
smell of cider hung in the air as the steam-driven press
clapped and sputtered while juice ran from a pipe into
wooden buckets.

Carriages that shone like glass, drawn by high-stepping horses, their necks arched like proud swans, their
manes and tails braided with red ribbon, moved slowly
through the crowd, enjoying the attention they received.

Amish farmers sold potatoes and turnips, pumpkins
and squash. But no one's vegetables were arranged quite
like Bappie's. The largest crowd always surrounded her
colorfully displayed goods.

Hester wore a light black coat, just enough to fend off the stiff breeze. She moved as if in a dream, her thoughts certainly not on her duties as she arranged the heavy orange pumpkins, counted the yellow squash, and shooed away a few bees that kept droning around the beet tops.

She stopped working when the hulk of a man named Reuben Troyer threw a look in Bappie's direction as she hawked the merits of her fine vegetables, as usual.

"Someone should tell her to go home to the kitchen where she belongs. No woman should be allowed to sell things in that manner."

Hester smiled. "Oh, she's very good at selling vegetables." She looked at him directly, humor flashing from her dark eyes. His mouth slid up into a wobbly smile, his eyes becoming soft as they caught Hester's goodwill.

"Ach, yes. So she is. Yes, yes."

He moved on, graced by the most beautiful smile he had ever encountered. He told his wife that Hester was like an angel, so beautiful was she. Luckily, the large, big-boned Rachel agreed with him, and he whistled the whole way to the barn to do his chores.

Hester mollified any displeased customers with pleasant words and a frequent smile. When her teeth flashed white in her dark face, two dimples appeared in her cheeks. Her eyes laughed pleasantly as she spoke, universally warming everyone who saw her.

She stored the beet tops in a crate out of Bappie's sight. At the end of the day, she told Bappie she was going to the poor section of town to take some of the day's leftovers. She didn't say what she was taking, just leftovers.

Bappie was exhausted and drained after her long day's work, hunched over her money bag, counting coins, so she waved a hand, and Hester went on her way, triumphant.

For once she did not need to make a decision. For once she could pursue the passion she had so often dreamed of. She carried the crate on one hip, balancing it with an arm flung over top. She walked fast, her long strides taking her down Market Street, then left on to Vine where the street became more narrow. A row of squalid houses sat at the bottom of the incline like blobs of mud someone had thrown.

Strangely, there were no children racing around in the mud, no youth lounging in doorways. An eerie quiet pervaded the street. Hesitant now, Hester set the crate beside the first house, where the door swung crookedly on leather hinges, its wood darker and smoother from so many grimy hands pulling it shut and pushing it open.

Placing her fist on the door, she rapped, loudly.

Immediately, a white face appeared beside her, a mop of tangled brown hair above it, the mouth covered in dirt, the neckline of her dress torn, exposing painfully thin shoulders. The small child glared, her eyes as alert as a chipmunk.

"Hello. May I come in?" Hester asked.

Like a flash, she disappeared.

Hester waited.

Another white face appeared, almost level with her own, blotched and with swollen cheeks protruding below sunken dark eyes. The woman wore a dark dress, matted hair clung to her head, and a thin baby rode on her hip, sucking on a questionable item.

"Vot? Vot you vont?"

Hester smiled, which brought a black look of suspicion from the woman. "I have some greens here from the vegetable seller at market. I thought you might want to cook them for your supper. They don't cost anything."

"We don't eat that stuff."

"Oh, it's good, cooked with salt, a bit of vinegar."

"Couldn't eat it."

Hester sighed. How could she begin if they wouldn't accept her offer? From inside the house, the sound of crying rose to a crescendo until Hester thought she must break down the door to find the cause. "Is something wrong?"

"Oh, my boy stepped on a rusty nail, and his foot swole up so bad I don't know vot to do viss it."

"If you'll allow me, I'll take a look at it."

Reluctantly and offering no other welcome, the woman stepped aside, leaving only a narrow passage for Hester's entrance.

The smell was the worst. Always, from her first step into these dwellings, the odor of grime, spoiled food, unwashed bodies, and earthen floors was the hardest. Breathing as lightly as possible, her head bent, Hester entered the dark room. On a wooden pallet in a corner, she found the source of the agonized wailing. A small boy clutched both hands around a grotesquely swollen foot, angry red streaks reaching almost to his knees, his mouth open in wails of pain and anger.

Hester fell to her knees beside him. She gripped the foot and uncurled the filthy little hands as his wails turned to terrified screams.

"Don't. Don't. Here, don't cry. I just want to see if I can help you. I won't hurt you. Sshh."

The small boy lay back, attaching his gaze unwaveringly on Hester's face.

"I need a light," she said, crisply.

"Don't haf von."

"Yes, you do. Get it." Hester was angry now. She knew they had some source of light, even if it was only the stub of a candle.

Sullenly, a sputtering candle was placed in front of her. She held it to the foot. Instantly the screaming started anew. She had seen everything she needed to know. An angry, festering wound with pus pushing against it, desperately needing to be lanced, drained, and then treated with a fresh poultice of scabious.

She could see the plant, its heavy, soft, whitish-green leaves, their edges ragged, the clumps of pale blue flowers. It grew in meadows and old fields left untilled. She knew where a fine clump of it grew close to the road leading out to Bappie's patch of vegetables.

She rose, her eyes seeking the mother's face. "I will return tomorrow, if you will allow me. The wound needs to be opened and crushed leaves of the scabious plant applied to draw out the infection."

"You aren't no doctor."

"No, but I know about healing with herbs."

"If you come, make sure it's not when my husband is home."

"Please don't tell him if he will become angry."

"No. No." Agreeable now, the woman's eyes sought Hester's face. "Vill my Chon die?"

Hester looked at the sniffling child, his flushed face, and wondered if another day would mean his condition would deteriorate to the point of no return. "No," she said.

The woman nodded stoically, as if any emotion would be her undoing. Life was what it was, and she could do nothing to alter it. To stay alive, to keep her children alive, took all the energy she could muster.

Hester looked around the dim room. Two small windows let in a minimum of light. The small fireplace was black with smoke, soot, and damp air. Cold ashes were piled in a wet-looking heap.

Bits of string, twigs, and pieces of stone lay scattered across the floor. A table, small but sturdy enough, with benches pulled up on each side, a few more pallets covered with colorless blankets, a cupboard, several washtubs hanging on nails, and odd crates containing what Hester guessed were towels or rags or extra clothing, furnished the room.

Where was the food kept? Was there food?

She sat down quickly when the door was flung open and a large dust-covered man entered the room. His heavy eyebrows were drawn down over his eyes, which were only slits in his face. A bulbous red nose stood above a mouth that held a constant snarl. He walked over to Hester and told her to leave, now, in a voice that was both grating and wheezing.

"Heinz, no. The lady vants to help our Chon." The voice of his wife seemed to hold surprising authority. He looked at her, and only for a moment, Hester saw the glint of acknowledgment.

"How is he?"

"Not goot."

Hester spoke. "If he does not get help, he will die of the infection. Do you see these red streaks?"

Going to the child, she lifted the leg, pointing to the angry red marks. "That can turn into poison of the blood. If he turns feverish overnight, he will die."

The big burly German named Heinz turned his eyes on her, mere slits of blue, flashing now.

"Git. Git out. If we need a doctor, we will fetch one. Git." He raised an arm, his long, thick finger pointing in the direction of the door. The ragged edges of his filthy sleeve shook with the force of his anger.

Hester looked at the threatening hulk of a man, then down to the boy, who had curled into a fetal position, whimpering like a hungry puppy. The sound brought an explosion of unnamed emotion in Hester.

She faced Heinz squarely and told him in a level voice ringing with authority that she would be back, and there was nothing he could do about it. His son would die if he did not allow her to help. They had nothing to pay a doctor.

She had heard Emma's tales of the town's doctors treating the less fortunate without pay, perhaps a sack of potatoes, or a chicken, at best. But after years of going into the squalid conditions of these streets, they would no longer venture there. In turn, all sorts of strange practices, old wives tales, myths, mysterious chantings and wailings could now be heard among the sick in this part of town.

Heinz's shaking finger stayed. He shifted his gaze to her face. Slowly he lowered his arm and turned away. The boy on the pallet moaned.

Hester left the red beet tops and the bits of potato, as if she'd forgotten them. She lost no time hurrying home, looking neither left nor right, her long steps taking her to the stable in the back yard.

Bappie called out the back door.

Hester waved but quickly disappeared into the small stable. She yanked a surprised Silver from his stall and without bothering to brush his matted coat, flung the harness on his back, adjusted the buckles, put the bridle on his head, and backed him between the shafts of the serviceable black buggy. She was unwinding the reins when the back door clunked shut and Bappie strode across the yard.

"Hester! Stop! Where are you going?"

"To the meadow to get scabious."

"Can I come, too?"

"Suit yourself."

Bappie attached the britching and traces to the shafts on her side, then climbed into the buggy. She sat forward tensely as if Hester's driving made her nervous, as it should have, the way Hester guided poor Silver. She was requiring the utmost speed from the dependable animal who was never given to fast trots, only a contented clopping along, a regular old farm workhorse.

"What do you need?" Bappie asked finally.

"Scabious."

"What is that?"

"A plant."

"Why?"

"A boy will die if I don't have the chance to treat his infected foot."

"Just one plant?"

"No, if I can find nettles, I'll use them, too."

"Nettles are all over the place."

"Good."

Hester watched the fast sinking sun. She shivered in the cool evening breeze. She hoped the scabious plant would be where she thought she remembered seeing it.

Bappie's lips were grim. For Hester, the knowledge of herbs and their uses was a direct golden thread to her past. A redemption. Proof that her history was retrievable, worthy. She was not only the illegitimate daughter of an outcast young Indian maiden, she was shamed many times afterward, abused by her step-mother, lowered by her husband and mother-in-law. Lowered until she had no idea who she was. More than ever, the passion to pursue the dream of healing rose within her.

Hester turned her face to Bappie. "I want to do this. I know it works. You would, too, if you had met the ancient old grandmother, her face like wrinkled leather, her eyes containing an inward light, so brilliant was she. She knew every plant, every tree, she could name all the barks of the trees, all the mosses, all the mushrooms.

"Every plant has been put on God's earth because of its vital use to us. An important part of life is vanish-ing as Indians flee Lancaster County. You don't have to agree, Bappie. Just give me a chance to honor my ances-tors. It's all I can do."

Bappie was shocked to see Hester's chin wobble, then observe a quick dash of her hand across her eyes, as if when the emotion came, it was unwelcome.

Bappie looked straight ahead, blinked, and swallowed, then cast a sidelong look at Hester, lifted her nose and sniffed. She blinked furiously, before she said, "If you let me, I'll help what I can. Not that I know very much."

"Whoa!" Hester drew back on the reins. Silver lifted his head to release the pressure of the bit on his mouth, lowered his backside, and slid to a stop.

"There. There it is," Hester breathed, handing over the reins. In a flash, she was off the buggy and across the overgrown grasses. Her foot caught on the undergrowth, and she fell headlong, fell flat into the waving grasses as clumsy as on ox.

Bappie lifted her face and howled with glee.

Hester didn't look back, just waved a hand above her head, got up, and kept going. Her face was alive with energy, an inner light radiating from her dark eyes as she held up a clutch of strange-looking mint-green plants with red roots, a passel of limp pale blue flowers on top. "Perfect."

"I thought you needed nettles."

"I have some."

They drove back wordlessly. Silver lifted his head and trotted briskly, as if he got the message and meant to do them proud.

Walter Trout was watching across the backyard fence like a great nosy dog, his liquid eyes filled with love and trust, his face shining pink in the glow of the setting sun. His great slabs of arms lay across the top of the fence, his fingers entwined like sausages below his face. Bappie and Hester both knew he was a cauldron of unsatisfied curiosity. They winked at each other, smiled, and ducked their heads.

Silver, loosened from the shafts, walked obediently away, the sweat staining his silver hair to a dull gray. He lowered his head to drink thirstily from the long cast iron trough that rested on a stone base.

"Hello, ladies." Shrill and energetic, Walter voiced his presence.

"Good evening, Walter."

"Nice evening, now, isn't it?"

"Indeed."

Silver lifted his head, water dribbling from his mouth. He smacked his lips, making the funny sound horses do when they have almost drunk their fill, usually returning their mouths to the water for a few more swallows.

"Too nice for you ladies to stay home, then?"

"Oh, yes."

Hester led Silver through the barn door and into his small box stall, as Bappie turned to close the door to the harness cupboard.

"Market went well, I gather."

"Yes, we had a good day."

"That's good."

Hester reappeared.

"You were off in a bit of a hurry, I saw."

"A bit."

"You got what you were after?"

"Oh, yes."

Without further words, Hester and Bappie headed for the back door, leaving the herbs in the safety of the buggy.

"You'll be over later?" Poor Walter was slowly accepting that he could not extract a sliver of knowledge about where they had been or why.

"Maybe."

With a wave over her shoulder, Bappie opened the back door and held it, allowing Hester to go before her. They laughed freely, deliciously, knowing they would relieve poor Walter's insatiable curiosity later.

Their presence in the Trout home was lauded with many grand bows of welcome. Walter all but ran back and forth, bringing them cups of tea and fresh slices of custard pie sprinkled heavily with nutmeg. He brought a plate of cheese, yellow and pungent, a bowl of popcorn, salted and buttered lavishly.

The two boys, their faces freshly washed, and wearing thin homemade nightclothes, sat up to the table, their eyes bright and alert. The oldest one nodded and shook his head now, Emma informed the women proudly. He did not speak, but at least he was communicating something.

Clearly Emma was in her element. Her eyes snapped with sparks of energy; her face was as pink as Walter's. She bent to the boys, crooning, placing the palm of her hand on their cheeks, brushing back locks of hair that had never been out of place.

She cut their custard pie in small pieces. Walter placed a tin cup of buttermilk at each plate, then watched joyously as each child lifted it carefully and drank thirstily.

They talked of market, about going to church on Sunday. They spoke of William's passing, the time that had already elapsed.

Walter hovered, refilled teacups, inquired whether one small slice of custard pie was enough. Yet his English manners would not allow him to ask them where they had gone earlier.

Emma spoke around a mouthful of custard pie, which Hester could see made Walter cringe to the point of carefully wiping his own mouth daintily. "We have named the boys now. We called them One and Two for so long, until we decided a pet would be named long before these dear ones."

Proudly, Walter said their names were Sebastian and Vernon. Sebastian began to cry, a weak mewling sound at first, which rose to sobbing and hiccupping, sending Emma to his side in great distress. "What? What?" She kept repeating the word, seeming to try to relieve her own guilt, yet taking the blame for his crying entirely on herself.

His voice was only a croak, an unoiled piece of machinery, but they heard his words clearly, in spite of it. "My name is Richard."

Emma's face turned a shade darker, and her small eyes seemed to grow from the folds of her cheeks. She clapped a hand to her rounded bosom, where the row of tiny pearl buttons creased the gray fabric, and said softly, "*Mein Gott! Das kind schprechen.*"

Walter put a heavy arm about his shoulders, smiled into his face, and praised him effusively. Richard looked up into Walter's reddening face, the beginning of a smile forming at the edge of his mouth.

Hester got up. "I must go. I have a few herbs to prepare for the morning."

Walter looked at her, his curiosity buzzing. "Where are you off to?"

"Home." She went around to Richard and hugged him. "Welcome to our family, Richard. We're so glad you are with us." She kissed the small cheek, which brought a definite widening of his mouth.

"Good thing. Good thing." Bappie meant Richard's speech, Hester knew, and accepted her lack of social skill, her inability to convey feelings.

Then Hester nodded to Walter, thanked him for the tea, finally telling him about the herbs in the meadow and that she'd be making poultices, tinctures, and a liquid medicine as well. "I have a sick little boy to tend to in the morning."

Walter was grateful for that bit of information. He sat down heavily and cut a large wedge of pie, thanking his stars that Emma was a talkative woman and gave forth her information readily, unlike these strange Amish.

Back in their own kitchen, Hester stoked the fire while Bappie retrieved the herbs. They boiled the roots, chopped the scabious plant, and bottled some of it in the strong corn whiskey Hester kept for this purpose. They boiled the nettle roots separately and bottled them, too. Darkness had fallen by the time they were finished.

Hester paced the kitchen, straightened doilies, and fiddled with the candle wax. Finally she told Bappie she would never be able to sleep.

Bappie became quite huffy, saying if she was even thinking of going down to that dirty place in the dark, she was going alone.

Hester said she would then. "I have to see him tonight. He may be seriously feverish till morning."

"You are risking your life. It's too foolish. You can't go down there."

Hester nodded. That was all. Already she was putting on her black shawl and hat and pulling on a thin pair of gloves, her jaw set in a line of determination.

Bappie watched her, staying silent as Hester gathered the jars, herbs, and a small knife, some white muslin, and a scissors, then put them carefully into a cloth satchel and let herself out into the dark street.

Bappie called after her. "If you're not back by ten o'clock, I'll come looking for you."

Hester waved, her long strides separating her from Bappie's voice. At midnight she had not returned. Bappie lay cowering in her feather bed, alternately praying and being angry at Hester and her foolishness. Hadn't she warned her?

She tried to summon the courage to get dressed and go find her but could not bring herself to do it. Better one person dead than both of them. At this thought, her heart began banging beneath her ribs until she thought she would surely be torn apart, rib by rib.

When the gray light of dawn finally lightened the dark windows, she got up, tired, miserable, and vowing to herself that she would not go down to those stinking rowhouses, she didn't care if Hester was dead or alive.

As she combed her flaming red hair and scrubbed her freckled face, she considered going to the town constable to tell him about Hester. But as she ate her steaming bowl of cornmeal mush, she figured it would be better to go see for herself what had happened to Hester. She would wear her high-topped boots this time and carry a large walking stick, just in case.

CHAPTER 21

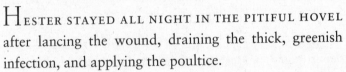

Hester stayed all night in the pitiful hovel after lancing the wound, draining the thick, greenish infection, and applying the poultice.

She spooned up a decoction of the bark of the white oak and the bud of the acorn from the same tree and heated the mixture to a soothing warmth. The child resisted at first, then willingly drained the liquid from the spoon.

Heinz lay rolled in a blanket on a pallet in the corner, his rasping snores settling themselves inside Hester's head until she thought she could no longer keep her sanity intact. At least he was not interfering, snoring like that, she told herself, as the weary night ticked toward morning.

At the first gray light of dawn, she lifted the cover from the sleeping boy and turned his foot toward the flickering candle she held to it. She lowered her head and sniffed the wound. The absence of the sickish sweet smell a revelation, she lifted her face, closed her eyes, and whispered a direct, *"Denke, mein Herr."*

When Heinz rolled out of his pallet onto the earthen floor like a great animal, Hester stiffened and kept her face averted. He rose to his knees, then to his feet, and began scratching his armpits and his filthy hair. He thrust his feet into the shabby torn shoes made of leather, belched, coughed, and let himself out the door without a word to his wife or acknowledging Hester's presence.

His wife's name was Josephine, but her pronunciation of it was funny. She told Hester to call her Finny. She could not speak English well, her German permeating every word, so that they each had a flat sound, mingled with all the wrong consonants. She was sincere, though, and she cared about her boy, Chon.

Heinz worked at the tannery on Water Street, Finny informed Hester, which explained the loathsome odor that followed him like a cloud. The dead animals and their hides piled in stinking heaps to dry, and then be made into leather, were odorous. There seemed to be nothing to do about it. It was a thriving business in the town of Lancaster, a necessary evil, if anything.

Some horses hitched to carriages refused to travel past the tannery, balking and rearing. Others lowered their heads, took the bits in their mouths, and ran at breakneck speed, the buggies swaying and clattering over the stones, the drivers' hats crushed low on their heads, their hands occupied solely by handling the reins.

More than one schoolboy took to loitering about the tannery, gleefully swooping in on an airborne hat and racing off with it before the harried owner could return to retrieve it.

When the first rays of the sun enlivened the street outside, Hester swept the floor and helped Finny stoke the fire. She boiled water, poured some in a wooden bucket, added cold from the crock by the back wall, and asked for soap. Finny shook her head, spreading her hands, palms up.

Hester nodded and set to work with one of the muslin patches in her bag. She scrubbed the table first, then the benches. She swept and scoured the meager hearth while Finny brought out a loaf of coarse brown bread, bought from the fat baker on Queen Street.

Hester's eyes narrowed. For two pennies, Finny could buy a sack of meal, a bit of lard, and some salt. She could make her own bread.

There was no milk, no eggs, no porridge or butter. Only the coarse brown bread torn into chunks. The children sat to the table in the same clothes they slept in, reaching for their share of the bread and stuffing it hungrily into their mouths. Their eyes were wizened far beyond their years, their thin faces colorless and translucent.

"Where is Heinz? Does he not want his breakfast?"

Finny made a sound not unlike an irate horse.

"Nothing to eat?"

"Of course. He eats good down there. But a man has to have his food."

Hester shook her head, brought in the beet tops, washed them with the small amount of potatoes, and put everything in a pot. "Salt?"

Finny shook her head.

When Bappie's anxious face appeared at the door, Hester did not waste any words explaining her night. She sent her straight back to the house with a list of items they would need. Bappie muttered and complained, dis-

gruntled, but did as she was told, returning with a wagonload of supplies.

And they went to work. The scoured the house with
strong lye soap. They washed the thin blankets in tubs
of boiling water out in front of the house, by the street,
where all the neighbors came to watch, their eyes hooded with suspicion and mistrust. Children threw sticks
and called them names.

Bappie lifted her hands from the hot, soapy water and
ran after one especially bold child, caught him by the
suspenders, and tweaked his ear. That brought a loud,
surprised squawk and a scattering of the rest of the by-
standers.

Hester grinned and kept scrubbing the filthy blanket
up and down on the washboard. Leave it to Bappie!

They nailed the scrubbed wooden crate to the wall,
then filled it with meal, a tin of lard, a bag of salt, flour
ground from fresh wheat kernels, a jar of tomato preserves, and a bag of potatoes.

They brought towels and sheets and two extra quilts.
They brought crockery dishes and pewter spoons. Emma
and Walter cried, wiped their tears, and contributed
soap, dried corn, bread, and a hunk of bacon.

Bappie said she was one solid mess of chills climbing
up her back and down her arms. Her nose burned all
day and all she wanted to do was cry. It was the spirit
quickening her, she said.

Embarrassed, then, she lowered her head and asked
Hester what in the world was she thinking, washing these
blankets if they had nowhere to dry? She said it gruffly,
as if that would prove that she was not turning into a

soft-hearted person. Hester remedied the clothesline situation by having Walter string a heavy rope from his and Emma's house to Bappie's, a sturdy line that would hold many clothes for years to come.

Finny held her sickly baby, fed him, then sat on the lone rickety chair and stared into space. She did not offer to help or hinder them. She allowed them to clean and wash, her eyes veiled with an expression of mystery.

When Walter contributed the armless rocking chair, they told Finny to sit in it. She sank onto the seat obediently and began to rock, stiffly at first, then at a slow, steady, relaxed rhythm. She lowered her head as the tears began to fall, dripping steadily, until her arms and hands glistened in the firelight where they gathered.

Little Chon ate his bread. Hester brought him a tin cup of buttermilk and a bowl of salted vegetables. He looked at Hester's face, his large eyes asking her if it was all right to eat it. She nodded, so he bent his head, lifted the spoon, and ate every bit, greedily licking the bowl to get every last bit of salt.

His recovery was imminent now. Pink highlights appeared in his face, and he smiled and talked to his younger sisters. Hester kept the plaster of the scabious plant tied firmly in place, and he had to remain on the pallet.

Hester and Bappie asked Finny's permission to bathe the children, wash their hair, and then dress them in the clothes Emma had given to the family while they washed the ones they were wearing. Tearfully, she nodded.

First, they doused their heads in strong smelling coal oil, with peppermint added to the lye soap, to rid the

children of lice. They did not cry out, sturdily bearing
the hot water and strong fumes, squeezing their eyes shut
as they allowed Bappie's furious scrubbing.

The day was waning into evening when the two
women stopped. Enough had been done.

Finny said she knew how to make bread. But she had
no lard and no money to buy it. Patiently, they explained
about the butcher's back door and the vats of rendered
lard available for taking. She could bring home a large
tin of it that would last for months, for one penny. Finny
shook her head, overcome.

The goodwill that radiated from the cleaned hovel was
infectious, and Bappie and Hester were radiant, fulfilled.
They walked home in the golden glow of early autumn,
pulling the emptied wagon, chattering together like mag-
pies dressed in dark Amish colors, their muslin cap strings
lifting and failing with the rhythm of their steps.

Bappie was duly impressed. She'd never seen anything
work like that crazy plant, that weed that grew all over
the place. You'd think the child would die, drinking that
stuff in the bottle. What was it? Purple wine?

She fussed and waved her arms, quite forgetting to
help pull the cumbersome wagon up the hill to Mulberry
Street, until Hester stopped for breath, leaned against a
lamppost, and exhaled.

Bappie never took notice. She merely stopped with
Hester, lifted her hands, and asked how in the world she
knew this stuff, and what else grew all over the wood-
lands and meadows that she knew had the ability to heal?

Hester laughed, told her she'd see, and went straight
to Walter and Emma's house. Little Richard opened the

door, peering around it like a shy deer mouse, and every bit as cute.

"Do come in," he said, for all the world like a little butler.

"Thank you, Richard," Hester said, smiling, then scooped him up and planted a kiss on his cheek. She was rewarded by a clenching of his arms around her neck like a vise.

With so much happiness and so great a purpose in her life, Hester spoke with energy and enthusiasm, completely forgetting her steaming cup of tea. It turned cold as she related her rewarding day of giving to the poor and helping Finny to climb out of the pit of despair where she had no longer cared whether she lived or died, so great was the burden of staying alive.

Emma lifted a finger. "Hester, I don't mean to lower your banners, but don't be surprised if Finny returns to her old ways. Remember, you two women did all the work. She may not want to continue."

As it was, Heinz proved to be the biggest obstacle. He swore, tore down the wooden crate, said no two Amish do-gooders were ever going to tell him what he could do and what he couldn't, and they were not going to tell him how to raise his family either.

But Finny remained steadfast and calm, going about her days with renewed purpose. Seeing little Chon on his feet, alive and healthy, his eyes shining, was enough inspiration for her to continue to cook the limp vegetables, make her own bread, and buy lard and salt.

Regularly, Hester or Bappie, sometimes both, would visit, encouraging, praising, and bringing her a squash, a pumpkin, some turnips, or potatoes.

One week before the market would be closing because the vegetables were finished, Heinz left the tavern in a drunken rage and smashed all the tannery windows with a club. He was caught, fined, which of course he could not pay, and was thrown into the worst cell in the dank, rat-infested cellar of the town's jail.

Finny was quite unperturbed. "He vill driggle up [dry up], vonct now," she said firmly, pounding and kneading the bread dough as if it was Heinz himself being punished roundly for all his drinking. She stopped, then gave the bread dough one last pat. Like a wise owl, her eyes large and round, she said bitterly, "My Heinz was not always so. It iss the ale. He can't let it alone."

Her words were so infused with the German, her "O's" a total other sound. "Alone" became "aloon;" the "is" a sharp "iss." But the strength of her words was enough to let the women know she loved Heinz still, but he needed to get better, and jail was a godsend.

Hester held the baby, her eyes dark and alive with interest, listening as Hester talked. Finny was strong, an amazing woman, keeping her children from starving in the rawest conditions.

When the winds of autumn became chilly, the leaves of the trees blew through the town and filled the gutters. Rains pounded them into a slimy, brown soup that lay in every ditch.

Finny needed firewood. She burned every stick she could find, her pride keeping this problem from Hester until she was forced to speak to her. The children were coming down with the chilblains, rashes, and angry blisters on their lips.

Soberly the women rode to church, Silver running
along sedately as if he knew this was the Lord's Day.
In their black shawls and bonnets, they rocked together
comfortably in the roofless buggy, the road wet and puddled, brown streaks of water spitting from the wheels as
they traveled.

They did not speak, for Hester's thoughts were muddied and clouded over with the knowledge of winter coming and the decision she would soon have to make. She
thought of the handsome brave named Hunting Wolf and
his true, honest love for her. She believed he came from
the Lenape as he had said. He was not someone who repulsed her. A part of her longed to see her mother, her
cousins and sisters, perhaps brothers. But that was all.

Having been married before, she knew the tremendous effort it would take, the constant work, the drawing on every reserve of love and affection, just to make it
through her days and nights.

She had truly fancied herself in love with William, but
was it love? Was what she experienced all that she was
capable of? Perhaps with her own kind, with Hunting
Wolf, it would be different. She had failed William and
would likely fail the Indian. The thought of marriage
was as burdensome as lugging a wagon behind her, up a
hill from the rowhouses to Mulberry Street. Yet his eyes
had held her, made her feel alive.

To his lodge, he had said. One separate lodge, or a
communal longhouse?

The decision was too monumental, too formidable today with the sky the color of the Indian's turquoise, the
clouds large and puffy like whipped cream, the air brisk
and invigorating, alive with swaying branches and the

smell of black walnuts hidden in wet brown grasses. Squirrels were romping and collecting hickory nuts which still clung to their summer branches, reluctant to fall and become the squirrels' winter staple.

The women were headed north from town on the level road, passing homesteads that were turning into well organized farms, each year making a difference in the amount of buildings and the cleared land.

Hester was grateful, as they drove by the well kept farm where she had spent her years with William, that Johnny kept up the tradition of tidiness. The fields were clean of corn fodder, the woodpile was stacked neatly, the cows looked well kept in the barnyard. Well, you had to give him that credit. He had, by all accounts, forgotten about pestering them, the silly man. He simply had never grown up. Despite having a wife and children, he acted like a youth.

How could he have grown up in the same house and have had the same parents as William? Her sober, conservative, meticulously versed William? A great tenderness rose in her, a memory of William's face and his touch.

"You better get him going or we'll be late." Bappie's voice broke in on her thoughts.

"How far is it to Jacob's?"

"At least another three miles."

Dutifully, Hester brought the whip from under the seat and flicked it lightly over Silver's back. The air whizzed past as he lunged forward. Hester shivered, tugging at her hat.

The women that stood around the kitchen of the stone house shook hands with both Bappie and Hester. Their lips met in a brief kiss of holiness, the traditional greeting among the women.

Jacob Stoltzfus's wife, Veronica, was flushed and "nerved up," the way women were when church was at their house and they were responsible for the comfort of the congregation. Was the house too cold? Too warm? Was there enough food for the dinner table? How many *freme* would show up?

Having made their rounds of greetings, Hester stood to the right of the fireplace, her arms crossed at her waist in a familiar stance, the way most of the women did. She looked around at the typical whitewashed walls, the shelves built on top of the sturdy cupboard that contained all Veronica's dishes.

She admired the embroidered artwork on the wall and noticed the heavy pewter of the candle holders. The curtains which hung on the one window in the kitchen appeared to be very worldly, crocheted along the edges like Emma Ferree's. But then Veronica was said to have a hankering for fanciness, she'd heard from Bappie.

In the center of the heavy oak table was a brown pitcher filled with sumac and goldenrod mixed with foxtails. My, it was so beautiful. Who would have thought that an assortment of plain weeds could be so pretty?

Wistfully she thought of her own blue dishes, more expensive and prettier than anything Veronica owned. The same with the hooked rugs Frances made, too. At the thought of her mother-in-law, she looked for her among the circle of women, remembering now that she had not greeted her. Was she sick?

Leaning toward Samuel Zug's wife, she inquired about Frances's absence in quiet tones. Taken aback, Lydia opened her eyes wide, then leaned close to whisper in her ear. "Hadn't you heard? She requested to be put out of the church."

Hester could not believe it. They had missed church two weeks ago, so they hadn't found out, nor had Hester been to any quiltings or other social events. It would have been far too much like gossip to inquire about Frances's reason for doing this, at her age—a highly unusual happening—but then, she had always been a bit strange, like a . . . Hester tried hard not to think of which reasons her highly critical mother-in-law might have cited for leaving the church, because, well, it was the Sabbath, and she should do her best to live right.

She suppressed a giggle and kept her face hidden from Bappie, striving to keep her thoughts and intentions pure. She sat with the women, singing with a clear and rousing soprano, then listened carefully to the words of Bishop Joel Stoltzfus.

He warned of worldly lusts and the hellfire that would surely rain on their heads, were they to disobey. He spoke of the need to live wholesome lives, upright and honest in all business dealings, to work the land by the sweat of their brow, the women bearing children as was commanded by the Lord.

Oh, how glad, how glad I would be to have children of my own, Hester thought, with a longing so intense she felt a physical ache in the pit of her stomach. Lowering her head, she pictured black-haired, naked little Indian children playing with bones and dogs, running among dusty intestines as the women butchered the wild animals.

She shuddered. She knew she did not want to be alone for the remainder of her years here on earth. But . . .

Joel Stoltzfus's face reddened, and he lifted his fist along with his voice, as it rose and fell in a singsong chant, carried through the generations like a ribbon from the Catholic Mass, their ancestors.

The sound made Hester feel a part of these people, these darkly clad, sincere, spiritually hungry and thirsty people who longed to do what was right. Everyone, in their own ways, did the very best they could, given the nature they each had. Often the children were raised with stringent rules and punishment, so they became their parents, passing the traditions and views on to their children, resulting in a tightly knit group of conservative people.

On her knees in silent prayer, Hester brought a heartfelt petition to God, asking that he show her the way, in Jesus's name.

The second and longer sermon was preached by a fiery old minister named Eli Fisher. His head was bald and shining, his beard in lustrous health, perhaps because he had no hair on his head. The gray beard seemed to come alive, jumping and swaying as he lifted his head, opened his mouth, and expounded on the word of God in all its power. That two-edged sword sliced right through the middle of the congregation and revealed their sinning souls.

Brother Eli clapped a skinny, work-roughened hand to his bald head, then wept and pleaded. He slammed himself back against the wall when the immensity of the seriousness of life became almost more than he could bear. His hands shook. He swayed on his feet. He swung his thin arms and called each person to repentance.

Babies cried and were carried discreetly from the room. A young child was pinched by a frustrated father, the ensuing wail bringing a clap to the face with a hand-kerchief. Somewhere was the sound of soft snoring. The men looked at one another with shamed smiles surfac-ing. Eyebrows lifted, a resounding punch was adminis-tered, and then a loud snort echoed through the room.

Women craned their necks. Who was snoring? Shame on him. Aha, young Willie Zug. Out too late last evening with Fannie.

They sat at the dinner table then, eating bread and dried apple pie, cup cheese, pickled cucumbers, and spiced red beets. There was cold water to drink. Hester longed for a cup of hot tea, but that would be too much work on the Sabbath day.

Bappie approached the ministers about helping to cut firewood for the Heinz Hoffman family. She was told they would not get involved in those lazy Germans' lives, and if she knew what was good for them, she wouldn't either.

Then Joel Stoltzfus told her in authorative tones that Hester and she would better start considering moving back to the country. Some of the *gleeda* were not sat-isfied with the way they lived in town, hawking their vegetables, perhaps being less sober and reserved than the world expected of the pious Amish. They would be better off as keepers of the home, quiet, devout, and not walking the streets of Lancaster, often with their caps untied. Someone had seen them wearing coats without the required shawls and hats. If they did not conform, they would be subject to a visit from the deacon.

It would be better for them to marry, bear children, and look after their husbands, he informed Bappie, not unkindly. He wished her *Herr saya*, and his eyes softened when he looked at Bappie's plain, freckled face. He walked away, aware of the ministers' duties that were not always so pleasant. But he did agree with the lay member that Bappie's voice at market was anything but chaste and humble.

Bappie was furious. She leaned forward and slapped both reins down on Silver's rump until the poor horse flew along the road, the buggy tipping and careening, bits of water, mud, and gravel spitting out from under his hooves until their faces were peppered, and Hester couldn't tell which were mud splatters and which were freckles all over Bappie's face.

Bappie talked as fast as she drove. She said, couldn't he see how homely she was? Ugly as a mud fence and God had made her that way. Was it her fault that no man wanted her for his wife? How was she supposed to go about making a living? Huh? How? She scraped the back of her hand repeatedly across her cheeks, then blew her running nose into the edge of her back shawl.

"And not one of those men will help gather firewood for them!" she shouted into the wind, a strand of brilliant red hair loosening and waving above her black hat like a torch.

Hester assured her that she was not ugly. She just had never met the right person.

Bappie snorted so loudly that Silver broke into a gallop. "You can say that. You with all your beauty."

"I'm not married."

"Puh. Well, I'm going to get a load of firewood, if I have to chop every piece myself. I don't understand. Evidently you have to be Amish to receive any help. Puh."

Hester placed a comforting hand on Bappie's arm. "You won't have to chop firewood alone. I'll help."

Bappie sniffed and looked straight ahead.

CHAPTER 22

WALTER TROUT HELPED. THEY DROVE JOHNNY'S
wagon out to Barbara King's homestead and cut firewood in the brisk, gray day. The sun was a mist-shroud-
ed orb overhead, cold, insufficient, and half-hidden in
the dreary skies. Chopping and loading the wood kept
them warm, their breaths coming in short, white puffs
as they worked.

The great Belgians stood patiently, dozing in the still
November air as the wood clunked into the sturdy oak
wagon bed.

Walter worked alongside, grunting, puffing, and perspiring. At precisely ten o'clock, he announced his wish
for "the luncheon" Emma had prepared. "Ah, yes, a bit
early, perhaps, but to the working man, having a full
stomach is of great and utmost import."

Bappie grinned cheekily and gave the axe a good
whack into the chopping block. She dusted her hands by
clapping them together and said loudly, "Where is this
picnic?"

Walter was already arranging a blanket on the lee-
ward side of the wagon. Giving it a final pat, he happily
dug through the large wicker basket. He brought out a
loaf of bread first, cut into inch-thick slices. Chunks of
fried ham were laid between the slices, after a thick layer
of yellow salted butter was applied with intense concentration. Every corner of the bread was covered precisely.

There was cold buttermilk, spicy little cucumber
pickles, hard-boiled eggs, spiced peaches, sugar cookies,
and wedges of squash pie with cinnamon, brown sugar,
and nutmeg sprinkled over the top.

Walter was in his glory, his eyes shining with the purest delight as he ate. Such large quantities disappeared
from the spread on the blanket that perhaps even Emma
would have become concerned.

He dabbed delicately at his mouth with the cloth
napkin, belched quietly behind it, arranged the belt of
his trousers more comfortably, and humming delicately,
cut a slice of pie that was very nearly half of the whole.
"Fuel for the soul," he crooned, after swallowing
every bit.

"I thought preachers supplied that," Bappie said.

"Oh, they do, they do. But if I had my choice, I'm
afraid the squash pie would prevail, indeed." His shoulders shook with merry giggles.

Word spread among the rowhouses. Something had
happened at Heinz Hoffmans. Finny was working. The
children were clean. They ate green things. Chon survived the infection. Their house was warm.

When, a few houses down, a young girl was tak-
en sick with pleurisy and bleeding in her lungs, Finny

reported this to Hester, who had merely come for a visit, eager to hear how Finny was doing.

Instantly, Hester thought of the red Beth-root, bayberry root, and witch hazel leaves which she boiled in wine, and then stirred in a teaspoon of honey. This was the ancient treatment for pleurisy that she had learned from the book.

Bleeding of the lungs? Or consumption? These were deadly viruses that spread like wildfire. She shivered, with Finny beside her, as they walked to Bessie's house. Bessie was the wife of Joe Reed, a Scots-Irishman who had fallen on hard times, having broken his hip in a farm accident. He was able to walk, but only by leaning heavily on a cane. His wife Bessie was at least twenty years younger and bore him a child each year, with little or no means to provide for them.

The house was bigger than the Hoffmans', if only by a few feet. It was decidedly cleaner, but so bare of even the most basic necessities it was hard for Hester to grasp the Spartan conditions the family lived in.

Joe was a gentleman, proud, kind, and so polite. He bowed over Hester's hand and thanked her for coming in an Irish brogue so thick she could not understand his speech.

Bessie was English, her words spoken precisely. Toothless, thin, and her brown and curly hair riotous, Bessie looked out of eyes that were flat and strained with the impossibility of her days. She was barefoot, her too short dress showing puffy ankles criss-crossed by bulging blue veins.

A baby slept in a broken cradle close to the hearth. A group of thin toddlers were lined up on a bench, either sucking on a thumb or a finger, or holding a corncob as if it were a doll.

The girl with the sickness was propped up against the outer wall by a rolled up blanket, her chest heaving as she struggled to breathe. Her eyes were sunken in her face, her lips apart, cracked and bleeding, a gray pallor spread across her features.

"This is Dulcie."

Hester bent to her line of vision.

"Hello, Dulcie."

A rolling of the eyes and a slow drooping of the tired lids were the only signs that she had heard. One thing was certain. Dulcie was very sick. To Hester, it looked as if she had an ongoing case of consumption, likely well seated, which was, in fact, not curable. Why the smaller children had not come down with it, she didn't know. Perhaps it wasn't the dreaded illness.

Elecampane, pignut, sage, horehound, yellow parilla, Solomon's seal, golden seal, all boiled in rainwater. She had the tincture at home.

Again Bappie accompanied her, cleaning and giving the family food and clothing. When the women had no more extras to give, they went door to door, asking for clothing, food, whatever they had to spare. Bappie said there was no difference between that and peddling wares. Lots of the Amish peddled vegetables, bread, pies, and cakes.

They approached gabled brick houses with ornate white trim, where the front doors were opulent, and there was a brass ring to lift and let fall without smashing your knuckles. Servants, mostly black-skinned housekeepers in immaculate white caps and aprons, opened the doors, shook their heads from side to side, and spoke in low velvety voices. "No, ma'am." "Sorry, ma'am." "Not to-day, ma'am."

When Dulcie breathed her last, Hester cried. Bappie rubbed her shoulders and blinked rapidly, saying she didn't think she would die. They buried her in the common graveyard where the town's poor laid their children. Hester stood in the biting December air, hung her head, and raged at the rich who lived inside their protected brick walls, surrounded by wealth and plenty, their consciences and their money secured by brick walls as well.

She kicked pebbles the whole way home, her nose red from crying, her soul withered within. "I'm going to go with Hunting Wolf. I can't stand another day of this. We did all we could for the Hoffman family, and what happens? He's in jail. Dulcie dies. What's the use?"

Bappie inserted the key into the lock. They let themselves in, shivering and rubbing their hands. Hester poked up the fire, laid small pieces of split wood on the burning embers, and watched it flame up before swinging the kettle over it. They stood in their black shawls and hats, staring morosely into the gray, joyless day, their spirits trampled, as if a giant hoof had staggered all over them.

"I guess there's not much to say, except that the Lord giveth and the Lord taketh away," Hester said softly.

"They have too many children anyway," Bappie said gruffly, slamming her gloves against the stone wall of the fireplace. "Will they all get the consumption?"

"Likely. It's a bad thing. They can cough and spit blood for years. It's hardly ever curable."

They put a handful of beans in the boiling water and added a bit of salt pork from the attic. The rich smell moved through the rooms of the house, warming and cheering their battered feelings, giving them a small degree of comfort.

They made their rounds of the shopkeepers and came away with a wagonload of potatoes, turnips, beef tallow, lard, and cornmeal, heaped on until they had to be careful not to throw anything off.

Joe and Bessie were grateful, the children overjoyed.

Two of the toddlers were coughing, so Hester left some of the same tincture, with instructions for Bessie.

A week before Christmas, when the women were knitting gifts, and green boughs and holly berries decorated the mantle, there was a sharp rap on the front door, then another. Bappie moved quickly down the short hallway.

A gust of icy air moved across the floor. Hester heard Bappie's low voice. When she closed the door, she sighed, relieved the visitor had gone. But then she held her breath as heavy footfalls followed Bappie's lighter ones.

She looked up. A white-coated livery man stood in their kitchen. Tall, dark of face, his eyes light with a greenish flash like a trout in a forest pool, his face was trimmed by a neat beard, a mustache above his lips.

He saw Hester in the gray afternoon light, the crackling fire casting her face in an ethereal, golden glow. Her eyes were large and dark, her mouth slightly open, revealing her perfect, white teeth, her long, slender neck reminding him of a swan.

He forgot where he was and his errand.

Bappie cleared her throat, which severed the spell efficiently.

"I . . . I beg your pardon. You must be Hester Zug."

"King."

"Hester King. Yes. I am employed by the Breckenridges on King Street. Their daughter is indisposed. They have heard of the Amish women and the herbs they have knowledge of. Would you be so kind as to accompany me?"

Immediately, Hester was on her feet.

The livery man was amazed at her height. He had never encountered such charm, such innocent beauty.

"Allow me a minute for my shawl." Her voice was like the call of the whippoorwill, a babbling brook, the trill of a bluebird, the wind in the fir trees.

Hester had acquired a black bag, which she filled with labeled bottles, all in order side by side, along with clean strips of muslin, scissors, a knife, and any small utensil she thought she might need.

As she followed him down to the grand carriage, her heart swelled within her, recognizing this venture for what it was. A dream. A passion.

When he opened the door for her, he saw her face was completely hidden by her large black hat. He wanted to grab the wide black strings and rake it off her head. He mourned the loss of her face.

He sat outside, up high, while she sat alone, Bappie having opted to stay indoors and finish her knitting.

Hester stayed hidden, afraid someone from their church district would see her being borne away to the wealthy section of town. With the stern reprimand of Bishop Joel Stoltzfus still weighing heavily on her conscience, she shrank back against the luxurious cushions.

The carriage stopped. Hester waited. When the door opened, the white-coated man stood directly in her line of vision, his eyes intense, eager. She shrank from his too-familiar look. She lowered her eyes and brushed past him, seeming to skim the steps in her haste to reach the front door.

He mourned the loss of her. She mourned the fact that some things never change.

The brass ring slipped in her hand and crashed against the red door with a splintering sound. Quickly, the door swung open from the inside. A short, buxom woman stood aside, her graying hair piled on top of her head in artificial poufs, containing so many glittering combs her hair seemed to be alive.

"Oh, you've come! You've come! Miranda!" She called quite loudly for a lady of her stature, but was quickly rewarded by the heavy pounding of steps from the wide, oak staircase directly in front of her.

Hester gave Miranda the black shawl and hat. Hester's fingers moved restlessly on the black handle of her satchel; her heart beat loudly in her ears as her eyes took in the sheer grandeur of this house.

The stairway was almost as big as Heinz Hoffman's whole house. The foyer, the hallway with the adjoining library and receiving room, would hold five or six of the poor hovels.

She had not known that wallpaper existed. Flowers and leaves and birds on a wall were unthinkable. How did they get there on that paper? How did the scrolls of paper get stuck to the walls?

"Are you listening?" The woman's voice came from far away.

"Oh, yes, yes, of course."

"I am Cassandra Breckenridge. I am pleased to make your acquaintance. I gather you are Hester King."

"Yes."

"My daughter is very sick. The doctors are puzzled."

Hester nodded.

"You may follow me."

Hester followed at a polite distance, the brilliantly flowered skirt bobbing up the stairs ahead of her, the ruffles sweeping the dust carefully as she moved. A white hand with four short fat fingers trailed along the gleaming banister, each one circled by jeweled rings either gold or what she supposed were diamonds. She had never seen diamonds, or any precious stones, so how would she know?

The room they entered was a vision of pink tulle and huge puffy roses on the wallpaper, as if someone had dreamed of this room and placed it here. The bed was high and deep and wide, the coverlet of white as pure as snow.

The girl reclining on the pillow was short and round-faced, like her mother. Her hair resembled spun gold, with waves that reminded Hester of a pool of water when the wind disturbed it. Her face was flushed, her blue eyes bright with fever, the lids drooping with the weariness of the sick.

A tall glass of water stood on the round-skirted table by her bed, next to a box that held what Hester supposed were confections, a new sweet Bappie had spoken of, which the English brought across the ocean from their home country.

"Cynthia, this is Hester. She is a plain lady from the Amish. She has herbal decoctions to make you better."

A look of sulphuric, hissing blue was cast in Hester's direction. The pink lips blossomed prettily into a pout of steely rebellion. "I won't take it."

Instantly, a fluttering and whining began, a tearful pleading that led to hysteria, the mother hovering and bowing as she begged.

"Won't do it."

Hester stood, waiting till the mother settled down. Finally, she said, "Tell her where it hurts."

"No."

"Darling girl, oh, please, please, please obey your mother."

"I want to talk to her," Hester said.

Dipping and swaying, perspiring effusively, the mother settled herself on a chair, moaning softly to herself.

"Can you tell me?" Hester ventured carefully.

"My stomach."

"Top or bottom?"

The girl widened her eyes, her eyebrows lowered, as she pouted prettily. "It just hurts."

She allowed Hester to feel the swollen abdomen.

What had the book said? The old grandmother? Hester felt the stomach, which was swollen a bit, but not hard. She needed to summon the courage to inquire of this wealthy woman questions only a doctor should be asking.

Hester drew down the girl's soft, pink nightgown, replaced the covers, and gave her a gentle pat and a shy smile. Turning to the still moaning mother, she crossed her arms tightly below her chest and coughed lightly, self-consciously biding her time. She would not be able to ask of her a question so dubious, so personal.

The delicate apparition on the chair had ceased to moan and had taken out a well-used crocheted handkerchief. Flinging it over her nose, she began a wailing that made Hester decide to speak before she brought more sickness to her poor daughter.

"Mrs. Breckenridge, please don't."

From the bed, the fever-bright eyes turned toward the mother and a sour expression came down over her face like a gray, mottled cloud. "Oh, Mother, shut up."

The words were spoken wearily and without respect, her spoiled face turning into a caricature of her mother's weeping one before a triumphant smile stretched across her face.

"Does Cynthia have . . ." Hester hesitated. "Does she, are her, um, are her bowels loose?"

Hester's face flamed with embarrassment. These things simply were not spoken for anyone to hear, except perhaps a doctor.

Immediately the mother ceased her wet, sloppy crying and dabbed indelicately at her eyes, her head held to one side, alert. "I don't know."

From the bed came the angry, "How would you? You never empty the chamber pots. Miranda does."

"Honey, do you have, um, what she asked?"

Indifferently, Cynthia shrugged her shoulders. "Ask Miranda. She knows."

With that, she flipped on her side. Up came the covers over her fever-red face as she burrowed beneath them like a squirrel.

Whimpering, the mother bustled out of the room, her shrill voice preceding her, calling the servant.

She reentered with the fast-breathing, portly Miranda in tow. Hester spent a few awkward moments, unsure of what she should do—go to the bed and question the sick girl herself, or leave it to the housekeeper?

She viewed the beautiful room with appreciative eyes again. She stroked the glossy top of a dresser to be sure it wasn't wet. How could anything wooden shine like that? Her hand dropped to her side as the mother disappeared out of the door with Miranda, and then just as quickly returned with her, urging her to speak.

"Yes, yes, she do. She have the looseness. She sick. Her stomach not right. Course not. The doctor? What those doctors do? Nothin'. They don't do nothin'. They don't know what wrong with her."

Hester stood still. She saw the old Indian woman, her hand going to her stomach. She spoke of the pains, the things to take. So many different ones. So many herbs, and the matter of finding the right one.

She was feverish, this young girl, which spoke of infection. Hester had listened closely as the old Indian woman spoke of the fermented juice of apples, mixed with the salt she gathered at the salt licks by the "waters." Her black eyes had snapped with enthusiasm, and she laughed, a cracked, rough sound of triumph about the taste, but, she had whispered to Hester, the healing would not fail. She had never seen it fail.

Going to Cynthia's bed, Hester gently peeled back the covers. "If I bring some medicine, will you take it, even if it doesn't taste good?"

"No!" The scream was high-pitched, defiant, sure.

"If I mix it with juice?"

"No! The doctors all do that!"

Again, Cassandra, the hovering mother, began picking at the pink coverlet, her voice pleading, cajoling, promising her sick daughter anything her heart desired, if only she would take what Hester asked.

"No!"

Miranda plucked at Hester's sleeve and led her out of the room. "What you need?"

"Vinegar and salt."

"I have both. Come with me."

Together, they moved down the wide staircase, back the wide, gleaming hallway, down another flight of stairs, and into a kitchen that seemed to have no end. A huge fireplace, two cookstoves, a deep sink with a drainer board on each side, and so many pans and pots and dishes, Hester could not imagine the uses for all of them.

Miranda moved to the far wall, opened a wide door to a pantry lined with shelves, and got down a jug. "Vinegar."

Hester found the salt, measured it, then poured in the vinegar, enough to make a liquid.

Miranda's round brown eyes searched Hester's face. "You'll not do the young miss harm?"

"No, this will not harm her."

Miranda lowered her voice, held a palm against the side of her cheek, and whispered, "That little miss is full of worms, that's what. She eat sugar all the time. Breakfast, cookies. Dinner, pie. All day long."

Hester smiled. "This will help."

"How you getting it in her?"

"I think she'll take it."

"Hmph."

They passed two African girls lugging baskets of clothes, their hair done with dozens of colorful ribbons within their braids. They were pretty, their faces wreathed in smiles as they met Miranda.

When Hester and Miranda entered the room, the scene had not changed except for Cassandra's elevated hysterics, her daughter a lump beneath the covers, unresponsive.

Hester felt her patience snap. "Everyone leave the room," she barked in a voice that carried well, brought the mother's face, astonished, toward her, and sent Miranda scuttling from the room, her black eyes rolling in her head, the whites showing her fear and respect for this tall, dark woman.

"I will not leave," Cassandra said, her face a solid mask of resolve.

"Your daughter will not live then." Hester placed the bottle and spoon by the bed, picked up her black satchel, and prepared to leave.

Instantly, two fat, white hands fluttered in her direction. "I'll go, I'll go. Only please, please don't hurt my darling. Don't make her do anything she doesn't want to."

Hester's answer was a steely gaze. Slowly, the mother backed from the room, a hand to her heaving chest, another going to her trembling mouth.

As soon as the door closed behind her, Hester turned, flung off the covers, and said, "Sit up."

"No."

Firmly, Hester grasped the girl's shoulders, turned her, and sat her up. Keeping her hands on her arms, she lowered her face, her dark eyes compelling, and said only one sentence in a voice to be feared. "You have a badly infected stomach."

Cynthia nodded, wide-eyed with fear.

"Take this." Pouring out a measure, she put it to the girl's mouth. Keeping her hand on her forearm, she held it against her lips. When Cynthia turned her head away Hester turned it back. Quietly, and not ungently, she remained firm until Cynthia obediently opened her mouth and swallowed all of it.

"I don't like it," she cried.

"You'll get used to it. I'm staying here to give you this every two hours all night long. You will get better if you obey."

Hester did not praise, neither did she scold. She merely did not relent. And Cynthia took the medicine two hours later and cried again.

The mother and Miranda stayed out of the room, although Hester had to have a conference with them in the hallway, telling them Cynthia would not live if they interfered and the medicine was not taken.

So steady was Hester's trust in the voice of the Indian grandmother, she never doubted the ancient remedy. Not once.

CHAPTER 23

WHEN THE MOTHER DARED TO OPEN HER DAUGH-
ter's bedroom door late that evening, only wide enough
to peer into the room unnoticed, she could not believe
her eyes.

Hester sat on the bed cross-legged, leaning forward in
the soft, yellow light from the oil lamp. She was holding
both hands up, her long, tapered fingers spread with a
length of string wound through them. Cynthia was following Hester's instructions—right then left, over then
under—giggling. Her face was alight with the interest
she felt. When the string was pulled and every intricate
loop loosened in perfect symmetry, Hester clapped her
hands. Cynthia squealed, bouncing up and down on
the bed.

When Miranda tapped on the door, the girl told her
to come in, her eyes going to Hester's face, questioning.

Hester nodded.

The glistening dark face of the housekeeper was followed by the anxious white one of the distraught mother.

They stood side by side, short and buxom, their arms pressed to their stomachs, their eyes wide with the wonder of the scene before them.

Hester stayed the night, sleeping only a few hours on the chaise lounge in the opulent bedroom. Precisely every two hours, she gave the child the bitter mixture, followed by an offering of milk or custard or thin sugar wafers, all of which she petulantly denied.

In the morning, the fever had lessened noticeably, Cynthia's glassy eyes had returned to their normal blue, and her flushed cheeks were pale and smooth.

With strict orders to the mother and Miranda, Hester warned of a recurring infection if the girl's earlier diet was not changed. She could have sweets only occasionally and only after other substantial fare.

Cassandra Breckenridge pressed a wad of bills into Hester's hand. The mother's gratitude was as outsized as the floral wallpaper, resulting in words of praise and flattery tumbling over themselves. Hester quickly put on her large black hat, as if to protect herself from the vanity that could so easily strip her of the humility and submission she was committed to. She was, after all, of the Amish faith and not given to vain words that blew oneself out of proportion, larger than truth.

She pinned her black shawl securely about her shoulders and prepared to be driven back to the safety of Mulberry Street.

"You look like a witch." This observation came from the bed where the child lay propped up.

Laughing, Hester untied her hat, went to the bedside, and kissed the girl's cheek. "I'm not a witch. I just dress Amish."

"I know." As if to make up for the blunt speech, Cynthia threw her arms about Hester's waist, clinging to her as if she'd never let her go. "Come back to see me, please?" she whispered.

Hester stroked the silky, flaxen hair, her hand going to the smooth roundness of her cheek. "I will. I'll come see you soon. And bring you carrots and turnips and parsnips."

Cynthia wrinkled her nose.

Bappie was anxious but resigned to the fact that Hester's comings and goings would eventually be a routine part of their lives.

"After the Breckenridges, who knows what will happen? You better hope the bishops allow this. You know there are quite a few of our members who look on these old healing remedies as witchcraft."

"Ach, Bappie." Hester shook her head as if to erase the threat of being unable to practice the use of her medicines.

"I mean it. Look at the warning *I* got."

"But I'm not on the town square, hawking my wares."

Bappie cast her a level look beneath lowered lashes. "No, you just ride in fancy carriages with lovelorn grooms."

"What does that mean?"

"Exactly what I said."

Hester's face flamed with shame. Her fault again. How could she ever stop this? "I'm sorry," she whispered.

"Sorry for what?"

"That the groom was . . . like that."

Bappie rose from her chair, her movement too quick, too calculated. She went to the window and peered between the wooden panes to the gray, windswept streets of the town. For only a moment, the longing, the dissatisfaction of being an older, single woman, barren and unnoticed, crossed her face.

"Ah, Hester. Dear girl. Of course it's not your fault. You can't help that any more than a dandelion seed can help being torn from its stem and whirled away on fickle April winds. Only God knows where that seed will go and what will become of it."

"I wish I was like you, Bappie." Hester spoke harshly and fast.

"No, you don't. You don't. You will never have to know what it's like to never be noticed, to never be asked to be someone's wife."

"And you, Bappie, will never know what it's like to shrink within yourself when men look at you with that leering expression. I hate it."

Bappie only nodded.

They sat together in silence, each protected by the solitude of her own thoughts. The fire crackled and burned, the steam rose slowly from the bubbling pot on the hook. Outside, a branch scraped against the wooden siding of the house, a brittle leaf was hurled against the windowpane.

"Think you'll always be a widow?"

The words frightened Hester. Like being pushed off a cliff, she was being confronted by the yawning, unknown depths ahead of her. It was much too complicated to answer Bappie's innocent question.

Failing to be a good wife, failing to provide William with sons and daughters, angering Francis, Hans, and

Johnny, and their intentions gone awry, the puzzle was too difficult to figure out.

And yet. She longed for something she didn't fully understand. She wanted the same kind of union she observed with Hans and Kate. That easiness. That toughness, the comfortable happiness. Was that kind of union possible only for special people like Kate? Likely.

In answer, she shrugged her shoulders.

Bappie nodded. Sighing, she said quietly, "Well, Hester, what say we cover the garden really well with about a foot of good horse manure."

"And where do you plan on getting it?"

"From that cranky old Levi."

"You mean Levi Buehler? Surely he'd want to spread it on his own fields, which are lying fallow at this time of year."

"His wife is sick."

"What's wrong with her?"

"Wouldn't know."

Bundled into heavy shawls, scarves, and gloves, they hitched faithful Silver to the courting buggy and drove off down Mulberry Street, past the livery, the wheelwright, and the candle shop, into the open road that led away from the town. Everything was bare and brown and windblown. Every crevice was filled with leaves, every tree branch, etched against the gray sky, moved back and forth, tossed by the stiff November breeze.

Pieces of torn cornstalks whirled across the road, but Silver merely pricked up his ears and hopped across them. The straps on his haunches lifted, then fell with a flapping sound as he ran.

An oncoming team pulled abreast. They both lifted their hands to wave at Frances and Elias. Frances's white face was hidden well by the sides of her great hat. Elias sat stiffly, his black hat positioned squarely on his head, the brim wide and flapping, his hair cut well below his ears.

"Shoo!" Bappie whistled. She looked at Hester. "Your cap tied?"

Hester meant to nod without acknowledging the pious severity of William's family, but a smile played at the corners of her mouth, tugging it into a reluctant smile, and then a wide grin. Finally she burst into a startling laugh that ended up being flung into the air, joined by Bappie's lusty guffaw, and whirled away.

When they turned Silver into the uneven driveway that led to the Levi Buehler homestead, they had to duck their heads to avoid being smacked in the face by pine branches.

"He needs to clip these off. I'm going to tell him," Bappie said, swatting forcefully at the low-hanging branches. Hester had never seen a more beautiful pine forest. Thick and green and dotted with healthy brown pinecones, the evergreens were breathtaking. Redbirds flitted away from the women and horse with their saucy cries.

Hester and Bappie came on to the set of buildings, all weathered and gray, but sturdy and not without charm. The house had a porch on two sides and dormers in the roof, which were quite ornate features for an Amish-designed house. The barn was built into the side of the hill, a sturdy bank barn made to accommodate wagonloads of hay and straw into the top bay. There was a neat henhouse, reliable-looking fences in good repair, and a corncrib with a mended roof, filled to the top.

Silver flicked his ears and arched his neck when a sound, not unlike the baying of wolves, erupted from the barnyard. Immediately, a passel of skinny hounds came around the corner of the barn, their red tongues lolling, their eyes squinting from the effort of the incessant howling. They were so thin every one of their ribs could be counted beneath their scruffy hides.

"Puh. Anyone that keeps those hideous-looking dogs can't be too smart." Bappie snorted her disapproval as her eyes made a sweeping survey, sizing up the management of the farm, or the lack of it.

She reached under the seat, pulled out the sturdy whip, and flicked it in the hounds' direction. "Go on! Shut up! *Schtill!*"

Hester shrank back as the tall form of an Amish man came from the house, his gait easy and lanky, as if he had all day to meet them. He snapped his fingers at the hounds, and they slunk away, looking balefully back at the visitors.

"What do you want with those ugly critters?" Bappie called. Only Bappie, Hester thought.

Amazed, she watched the Amish man adjust his hat, shift his toothpick, and smile broadly, looking directly into Bappie's eyes like a schoolboy, and every bit as guileless. "I make more money with them than I do with my cows," he announced flatly in a deep, rumbling baritone.

"Puh."

"Sure I do."

"How?"

"Coonhounds. Good ones, too. I sell pounds of good-quality furs. They tree a coon, he ain't gonna get away."

"Ain't he?" Bappie said, punching Hester's side with her elbow.

"Nope."

Bappie changed the subject immediately. "We want your manure. The horse manure. We need it for the garden. You told me we could have it."

The toothpick changed directions again. "I did?"

"Yes, you did. Remember? You were at market."

"Can't recall."

Frustrated, Bappie said too loudly, "Yes, you can."

Still he had not noticed Hester, obviously enjoying Bappie's tantrum. Hester was delighted by the unusual banter.

Levi was of medium height and wide, with a good, solid look about him. In a crowd, he would not have stood out. His looks were not striking. His hair was the color of dry brown grass, his eyes clear, his skin medium brown and a bit freckled, his beard unkempt, the way most Amish men's were in the middle of the week.

"How's Martha?"

"The doctor's been out." A cloud passed over his face, turning the clear eyes a stormy gray.

"And?"

Out came the toothpick. He lowered his face, threw it on the ground, and rolled it with the sole of his shoe. "I'd rather not say."

"Why not?"

"You'll find out soon enough."

Hester swallowed. She sat forward, eagerly. "May I visit her?"

Finally, his attention shifted to Hester. His eyes appreciated her beauty in a friendly, offhand way, the way he'd view a pretty child or charming kitten. "You may."

"Hester, no. We have work to do."

Whistling, Levi led the way to the barn. He hitched up two brown mules, attached the flat-bed wagon, put Silver in a box stall, and fed him a generous amount of oats. Then he showed them the pitchforks. "Do what you can today. I'll help you when I can. Martha needs me much of the time."

They pulled rubber boots over their shoes, rolled up their sleeves, and set to work, forking out the acrid, rotting manure, slapping it down on the sturdy, flat bed of the wagon. As soon as they had a load filled, Bappie hopped up on the wagon. Hester followed, standing beside her in the cold air as the mules lowered their heads and tugged dutifully at the wagon they were attached to. The gigantic ears flopped up and down as their heads bobbed. The traces jingled where the chains were attached to the singletree.

Hester braced her legs, shifting her weight with the way of the wagon, breathed deeply of the cold, fresh air, and watched the flight pattern of a flock of snow buntings, flushed from the tall, brown briars.

"What's wrong with his wife? Why doesn't he want to talk about it? Why did he say we'll know soon enough?"

Bappie shrugged. "She's pretty sick. I think it was Enos Troyer's wife, Salome, who said she heard she has cancer."

"What's that?"

"Incurable. Nothing you can do." Bappie's words were hard.

"How do you know?"

"Well, you can't. I don't want you to start with your potions and tinctures and herbs. All that craziness."

Startled, Hester's eyes flew to Bappie's face. She was alarmed to see an expression so painful it changed her features, twisting them into a caricature of Bappie's normally plain, unflappable demeanor.

As if to ease the pain, Hester tried to change the direction of her inquiries. "I don't remember ever seeing Martha in church."

"That's because she hasn't been there."

Suddenly, Bappie turned to Hester. "He . . . he told me, she's not going to make it. God only knows what that man has suffered. They had three babies. All of them died within two years from German measles. They say it got the best of Martha. She's never been right since." Bappie's words were brittle, short, and thrown into the cold November day like rocks pelting against a tree, quickly, one by one.

Ashamed then, Bappie turned her head to watch the brown grasses and the dead cornstalks trampled into the cold, brown earth. A corner of her black scarf flew up into her eyes. Bappie grabbed it, stuck it inside her shawl, coughed, and cleared her throat.

"Looks like we have company," Hester observed.

Sure enough. In the grove of trees by the large garden stood a team of Belgians. The grinning Johnny sat on the oak boards of his wagon, swinging his legs, his hands tucked beneath him. "Well, well. Imagine meeting you young ladies out here."

Bappie leaned back, pulling the mules to a stop. "What are you doing?"

He didn't hear Bappie. His concentration centered completely on Hester, his brown eyes alive with interest, his teeth flashing white as he smiled broadly. "Hester! How are you?"

"I'm fine." Her words were clipped, firm, and without a trace of warmth. Bappie climbed down. Quickly Hester took up the reins, chirped to the mules, and moved off to the center of the garden where she stopped the horses. Then she proceeded to pitch the manure off, flinging it across the garden with monstrous strokes.

Johnny shook his head. "She still doesn't like me."

"Why should she?"

Suspicious, Johnny turned his head and found Bappie's eyes boring the truth from his own. So she knew. Cranky old maid. "It wasn't my fault," he muttered.

Bappie's snort was loud enough to startle the sleepy Belgians.

Johnny sighed, gathered up the reins, and drove away without a backward glance, his shoulders slumped in defeat.

Bappie marched over to Hester's wagon, leaped aboard, and began heaving manure as if her life depended on it.

The baying of the coonhounds heralded their return. Levi helped them load another heaping wagonload. They moved off through the pine forest, back to the garden, bringing more of nature's best fertilizer for next year's vegetables. They worked steadily without speaking. Hester felt the beginning of a painful blister on her third finger, so she shifted the position of her hand and kept forking manure.

A line of dark clouds was forming on the horizon where the setting sun should have been. Like a curtain, it hid the sun's light. Hester shivered as the wind picked up, bending the grasses and rattling the dry branches overhead.

"Too early for snow," Hester observed.

Bappie nodded.

"You want to try for another load before dark?" Hester asked.

"We could finish."

Together they increased their speed, cleaning all the manure from Levi's horse stalls. He came out as they were spreading fresh straw. Hester led the horses back to their cozy pens, clean and sweet-smelling.

Levi whistled his admiration in one long exclamation. "You did good!" he said simply.

Bappie's face was red, as was her hair, strewn about like flames of fire. Her black kerchief had slid off her head, so she let it lie around her neck. Hairpins straggled from the roll of hair on the back of her head. Pieces of straw were caught in the unruly curls that stuck out everywhere. Her breath was coming fast and she was laughing, obviously enjoying the challenge of getting the last load out. "Yes, well, Levi, we can't visit. We have to go. Looks like a storm's coming in the west."

Hester smiled at him, but he missed it completely. He was watching Bappie grab the leather reins and expertly maneuver the mules out of the barnyard, and at a competent pace down the rutted driveway, until they disappeared out of sight beneath the pines.

He stuck his toothpick back in his mouth, called to the coonhounds, and went to the house to tend to his ailing wife before he began the evening's milking.

Bappie kept the mules at a quick trot, the traces bouncing up and down, the wagon lurching over the ruts in the road. Hester's eyes scanned the low bank of black clouds, tumbling and tossing now, as they climbed higher into the sky.

When they reached the garden, they shoved most of the manure off the side, then leaped off the wagon to scatter it efficiently. Overhead, the black clouds boiled and rolled. The first ping of ice hit Hester's nose as she lifted her head to watch the approaching tempest.

"We're in for it!" she yelled, as the wind slammed against her back.

"We'll live!" Bappie yelled back. She lifted the reins, then brought them down on the mules' rumps with a high "Yee-ha!"

The mules lurched into a mad dash. Hester hung on to the makeshift boards that separated her from the mules' pounding hooves, her eyes wide as she watched the fury overhead. Ice pounded the galloping mules, bounced off the wagon bed, pummeled the women's heads, and pinged against their faces. Hester squeezed her eyes shut and held tight. She slanted a look at Bappie, astounded to see her standing upright, her eyes wide with delight, thrilled to be part of this dangerous adventure.

"Ouch! Ow!" Bappie laughed as the ice hit her face, but she stayed on her feet, goading the mules over the rutted road.

Hester was just about to warn Bappie about the steep incline when there was a cracking sound, as loud as the shot of a rifle. The mules were hurled to a standstill as the front axle broke, throwing both women from the bed of the wagon and into the wet, icy grass beside the road. Bappie screamed.

Hester flew through the air, landed on her shoulder with a sickening crunch, rolled on her back, and lay in the cold, wet grass, the ice still pinging on her upturned face. Her shoulder felt as if fiery darts were being shot into it. She squeezed her eyes shut and trembled from the pain.

Gently, she twisted her head, shocked to see the mules standing still, obedient, the only movement the quick flicking of their ears. The wagon was slanted to one side in front where the axle had broken, severing the wheel. It lay in a heap of metal, the ice making dull pinging sounds as it fell against it.

Hester heard a cry. She turned her head farther to see Bappie hobbling toward her, alarm bleaching her face to a chalky white.

"The mules, the stupid things. I never met a mule I liked. Hester, are you all right?"

Hester sat up and gingerly moved her shoulders. She winced, then grinned up at Bappie. "I'm all in one piece."

"It's these *dumbkopf* mules, that's what," Bappie spluttered.

Hester pointed. "Look at them, Bappie. Just look. They're standing there in the pounding ice, hitched to a broken wagon, dutifully waiting until we get ourselves together. You drove them too fast, Bappie. It was your reckless slapping that broke that axle.

"Don't you go on about stupid mules, either. You should have seen Hans when our wagon upset when I was little. The horses ran off for miles, with him floundering in deep snow after them. We walked all the way home without him. I still remember my mother dragging the blanket, with Noah and Isaac wrapped in it, while I watched the redbirds."

Bappie's face changed color again, back to its normal deep pink. "Well, how are we going to get Levi's mules back to him?"

Hester was already walking calmly toward the mules. "Unhitch them and walk them home. The next time, I'm driving." A gust of wind and ice tugged at her long, heavy skirt, but she kept on, resolutely unhitching the traces, remembering a time before when life held only the wonder of a redbird in the pure white snow.

CHAPTER 24

THE HAVEN OF THEIR HOMEY KITCHEN WAS BLISS-
ful as the ice bounced off the windowpanes and water
sluiced alongside, dripping from the eaves and running
down the sides of the sturdy German siding.

The fire leaped and crackled. Sparks exploded up the
chimney each time they added a chunk of wood. The room
was warm, enveloped in a yellow, fire-lit glow. Sputtering
candles on the table enhanced the coziness of their domain.

They had put up Silver first, bedding him comfortably with fresh straw and giving him a good feeding of
oats and corn, then putting down a forkful of hay. They
latched the barn door carefully before checking in on
Walter, Emma, and the boys.

They found them in good spirits, chortling over a
game of marbles as chestnuts roasted on a pan in the
oven, filling the house with the nutty aroma of fall.

"*Keschta!*" Bappie had cried.

"Oh, indeed, indeed. The finest nut of the forest. A
delicacy!" Walter agreed happily, a tankard of warm ale
at his elbow.

The boys lifted their shining faces, elbows propped on the table, their shoulders hunched as they watched the game Emma and Walter were playing. With round cheeks, clean, smooth hair, and warm clothes, the boys were barely recognizable as the forlorn waifs who had appeared on their doorstep months before.

Emma was as round as a pumpkin still. If anything, marriage only served to increase her enthusiastic appetite for good food, which was certainly not lost on her ample partner. Together they bestowed all their generosity of spirit on the two lonely orphans who seemed to blossom like well-tended flowers.

Hester wanted to stay. Walter and Emma's home never failed to fill a need, a certain yearning she had for the goodness of Hans's and Kate's home, and for her childhood, which they had supplied well with the nurturing that children require.

But Bappie wanted to get home. She was cold and wet, with the same temperament as a hen in a similar situation. So Hester got up reluctantly and followed her back to their house.

A hot, steaming bath, a pot of bubbling stew made of salt pork, potatoes, and dumplings, and the warm, cozy firelight, all made Hester sleepy. She was content, thankful for all God had given her.

She looked at Bappie reading by the fireplace, the German *Schrift* opened on her lap, her eyes dark and brooding, her thoughts a galaxy away.

Conversation was not necessary at this hour. They were at peace. The hard labor of shoveling natural fertilizer onto the large vegetable patch had been rewarding. It was good to know, when spring came, that the rich, brown loam would be full of nutrients, enough to feed the tiny plants shooting from the dropped seeds into tall cornstalks, heavy cucumber vines, hardy tomato plants.

"It's not right!" Bappie's pain-filled voice shattered the peaceful atmosphere, slicing it in two like the thrust of an axe.

Hester lifted her face, her eyes wide with surprise. Warily, she watched as Bappie rose to her feet, her movements swift. She slammed the Bible onto the table with a resounding thump, then propped her open palms on top of it as if to derive strength from the bound volume of God's Word.

Hester opened her mouth to speak, but closed it when Bappie's anguished voice rose as she talked. "He's too proud. If he would only talk about her. I don't see how he can keep his wits about him. That's so often the way of our people.

"As long as he can make things appear normal from the outside, no one is going to inquire. I can't understand where his relatives are. He's so alone, looking after that farm and caring for her. I don't know if the doctor has ever been to see her."

"Who?"

"Levi."

"Oh, you mean Levi's wife."

"Yes."

A silence fell, with only the tiny hiss of a flaming candle to break it.

"Should I go see her sometime?" Hester asked finally.

"Of course not. It's not that she has cancer, which your greenery couldn't heal anyway. It's that her mind is

. . . Well, she's like a child. Her good *faschtant* is gone. He has to feed her and dress her as if she were a child. I don't think very many people know how bad it is.

"She hasn't been to church for years. Hardly anyone goes to visit them. Now he has those coonhounds slinking around his buildings. I'm just afraid he's slowly going, as well."

Hester winced at Bappie's mocking word, "greenery." Quickly then, she shook it off, knowing it was only her forthright manner. "Could *we* go visit, do you think?"

Bappie shrugged her shoulders, her eyes dark, hooded. "I'm afraid to," she said, soft and low.

"Why?"

Again Bappie did not answer. The lifting and falling of those angular shoulders was her only response.

Hail continued to ping against the windows. Hester shivered as she watched the rain run down the dark windowpane. She got up to put a log on the fire, stepping back quickly as the flames shot upward.

"I just can't stand to think of Levi going through his days, never complaining or asking for help." Hester eyed Bappie keenly. She had never seen her like this. She was always noisy, sure of herself, knowledgeable, voicing opinions without holding back, and joking easily and lightly. But now, quite unexpectedly, this miserable brooding.

So taken up in the mystery before her, Hester did not hear the gentle tapping on the sturdy front door, closed securely with a large padlock against intruders.

When the tapping turned to raps of a more solid nature, she held very still, her head tilted to one side.

Bappie was so engrossed in her own thoughts she did not suspect anything. Hesitantly, Hester partly rose, her hand on the plank table, her long, tapered fingers trembling slightly.

Bappie looked up unaware.

This time the rapping was harder, more urgent.

"You go," Bappie said.

Biting her lower lip, Hester felt tingling in her nostrils, the acceleration of her pulse. Very unusual to have a caller at this time of the evening in weather like this. With a hand at her throat, and a few light, soundless footsteps, she reached the door, inserted the key, and drew back the latch.

The figure on the doorstep was tall, wide, and dark. Hester did not recognize him until he spoke in the deep, guttural voice of her people. The words were thick, as if he spoke through the swelled linings of his throat.

"May I come in?"

Quickly, Hester stepped aside. "Oh, of course. Forgive me."

As he walked in, the smell of wet deerskin was overpowering. It was the rancid smell of the longhouses, nearly lost to her fading memory of her past. Her heart sank.

His profile was startling. He was every inch the proud brave, the lineage of his ancestors, the Conestoga Indians, running in his powerful veins. His hair hung sleek and thick, parted in the center of his head and braided with thongs of rawhide. Not a hair stood away from his forehead, so well had he applied the rancid bear fat.

Hester swallowed. A choking sound rose in her throat. She put four fingers to her mouth to suppress the cough that would follow.

Bappie stood, startled, as she placed a hand on the chair back in front of her. "Good evening," she stammered, clearly at a loss for further words.

"Good evening."

Turning to Hester, the Indian's deep, unfathomable eyes evaluated her. "I have returned," he said.

"I see. I hope you are well," Hester said, her voice low.

"I am."

Silence crept its uncomfortable way between them. Ill at ease, Bappie spoke too quickly and much too loudly. "Well, you're soaking wet. You're dripping all over the floor." Puzzled, the Indian bent his head to see what Bappie meant.

"It will dry. The fire is warm." He stood closer to the fireplace, his back to the hearth, his silhouette a stance of power, of rigid restraint. His eyes sought and found Hester's face.

"I, Hunting Wolf, have come before I planned. I can wait no longer. Before the snow comes, we will be in Ohio on the banks of the great river. Here, there is much danger for me."

Hester put out a hand as if to stop his words. "But . . ."

"You cannot decline my proposal."

Bappie stepped forward. "Now just a minute here. You can't do this to Hester. She isn't ready to decide."

Like a rock, Hunting Wolf was immovable in his intent.

Hester sank to a chair. The only sound was the crack-ling of orange flames as they licked greedily at the logs. She watched the candle flame dance, shiver, then resume its steady glow. In it she saw the hills and fields of Berks County. The log house nestled beneath the maple trees, the barn below it, the pathway, the split rail fence beside it. She could smell the pies and the bread that Kate baked in the outdoor oven, the homemade lye soap she used for washing, the air-dried clothing that she brought in off the clothesline.

The sun played with the ever-moving shadows of the trees surrounding the cabin. The rain plunked on the ce-dar shingles of the roof when she lay, warm and drowsy, beside Lissie, with Noah and Isaac on the low pallet on the other side of the attic. The scrubbed wooden floor, the sweet smell of raspberry jam on Kate's fluffy biscuits. The hard benches she sat on during church services, the beautiful rising and falling of the German plainsong. All of this was part of who she was.

The smell of the Indian longhouse, the daily slaughter of small animals, the endless pounding of corn, sitting in dust, squatting by the fire, a stone for an oven, a turkey feather for bellows. The communal sleeping arrange-ments. Hester winced.

To stand beside this noble brave, a proud specimen of her people, would be an honor, had she been raised by her blood mother in the ways of her people. She was ap-proaching her thirtieth year of living among the Amish, except for the brief time with the Conestogas.

To live as they did was too foreign. Too distant. A river that flowed too deep and too swift for her to ford. She knew the decision had already been made in her heart, for she belonged to the Amish, the plain way of life, the German heritage she had adopted as her own.

In spite of the trials, here was where her heart found a home. Here in Lancaster County, working the fertile soil with Bappie, working among the poor and the wealthy, but using knowledge the Indian grandmother had passed on to her.

The look she bestowed on Hunting Wolf could only be described as tender, sorrowful, perhaps, but certain. "I cannot go. My heart will remain with my people."

"Your people are the Conestoga."

"The Lenape."

"You belong to us. The red man."

"In blood only."

"I want you for my bride. I desire you as my wife."

Hester lowered her eyes, her head drooping in shame. "I have been a wife. You do not want me."

"Yes. Yes. I do."

"No, I am not a good wife."

"You will be among my people. We will teach you the way of the Indian woman."

Hester knew the ways of the Indian women. She had learned the communal ways, the squabbling, the boldness, the crude laughter. It was good in many ways. There was affection, love, and strength. Yet the culture divided so widely from her own.

"I would be honored to be your wife. But you will find an Indian maiden worthy of your love. I was raised among the Amish and wish to remain with them. I have no intention of marrying."

Hunting Wolf sighed audibly. He opened his mouth as if to speak, then changed his mind. In true Indian fashion, he moved softly away from the fire. Going to Hester, he lifted her chin with his fingers and looked intently into her eyes. He spoke quietly with great respect. "Then I can only wish you the best in the trail you have chosen. I have lost my heart to you. But I will not force you to leave your people."

Like a wraith, a wisp of smoke, he moved away from the kitchen, soundless. The only sign he had even been in the room was the cloying scent of wet deerskin and bear grease.

Quickly Bappie hustled to the door, shoved the latch into the clasp, turned the key in the padlock, and leaned against it. "Whew!" she sighed, heavily.

Hester said nothing. Her hands were in her lap, her fingers intertwined so tightly the knuckles were white. The set of her shoulders gave away the turmoil of her emotions, the pressured burden of making the decision in so short a time.

"Buck up, Hester. You did the right thing."

Hester's smile was only a minimal lifting of the corners of her mouth, but it was a beginning. Slowly the smile widened until it reached her eyes. When Bappie returned to the fire, their eyes met, and Bappie shook her head. "You did good, Hester. For a while, when you sat there like a rock staring at that candle, I declare you were every inch an Indian. Quiet, stern, commanding. I had a notion to get up and wave my hands in front of your face."

Hester sighed, a long sound of expelled tension. "I guess my childhood with Kate as my mother is planted and rooted so deeply in my heart, it's there as sturdy as an oak tree. I will love her always. Everything I am, everything I do, I want to be like her."

Bappie nodded. "As it should be. My mam is dead and gone, but she is the whole axis on which I revolve."

The silence that followed was very deep and comfortable as the icy rain slanted against the cold, dark windowpane.

In the spring of that year, Hester was filled with an unnamed feeling of sadness. In spite of the earth's renewal and the wonder of new life around her, darkness clung to her spirits as if her soul was mired in an unrelenting muck of despair.

The dogwood trees flowered at Easter, and the daffodils and tulips lifted bright, happy faces to the strength of the warming rays of the sun. Everywhere the grasses turned a deep green. It hurt her senses to lift her eyes to the hills as she dropped seeds in the rich, brown earth.

Her feet were bare in spite of the cold, damp soil. A blue shortgown swirled around her ankles, a dull gray work apron flapping above it. She wore a kerchief of off-white muslin, knotted beneath the thick coil of glossy black hair. Tendrils of it blew in straight wisps around her forehead and down the nape of her long, slender neck.

Her eyes were large and luminous, glistening with the strange melancholy that had deepened the light in them.

She dropped one wrinkled pea seed at a time, her heart still, her lips compressed and songless. The butterflies and other insects failed to attract her attention. She didn't hear the birdsong.

Bappie was whistling, breaking into a ribald song occasionally, one that angered Hester. It was simply not a proper tune for an Amish woman, and one who was close to middle age, for sure.

Hester opened her mouth to speak her mind, straightening her back as she did so. Lifting one hand, she shaded her eyes against the strong sunlight and said, forcefully, "Bappie."

Bappie stopped, straightened, and lifted surprised eyes to her friend. She tilted her head at an angle, her eyebrows jumping in the most annoying manner.

"That song is. . . ."

"Oh, get off it, grouch. Just because you aren't happy doesn't say I can't be. Stop pitying yourself."

Hester returned Bappie's glare, the black fire in her eyes popping and crackling. "I'm not pitying myself."

"Yes, you are. It's a beautiful day and a beautiful spring. God has granted us good health through the winter, and are you thankful?"

"Of course I am."

"Then act like it."

Hester dropped the seeds she was holding, turned on her heel, and stalked out of the garden. Blindly, she walked away, faster and faster until she was running, her feet swishing through the tender new grass, her skirts swirling about her ankles, hampering her speed.

Behind her, Bappie watched, lifted her angular shoulders, then let them drop. She shook her head from side to side and went back to dropping the pea seeds precisely. Hester would get over it, whatever it was.

Hester ran effortlessly like a deer, up a slope and through a grove of trees until she reached the top of a rounded hill. She threw herself down in the old growth of grasses, her breath coming in ragged gasps.

She didn't cry. She had no tears within her, but only an ever-widening void, a darkness she could not hold at bay. She felt as if her life held no purpose, and the summer stretched before her as a long, dark tunnel of endless heat and hard work.

Had she made the wrong decision? Should she have accompanied Hunting Wolf to his people? Her people? She tried to pray, but no words would form. She wasn't sure God would hear her prayers if she managed to speak to him.

Alone, bewildered, she rolled on her back and opened her eyes to the intensity of the brilliant sunlight, the blue of the sky interrupted by clouds of white cotton. A shadow passed over her face. Startled, she opened her eyes wide. An eagle was flying so close she could see the white feathers on its head, the distinctive curve of its beak, the great majestic wingspan, and the soaring motion as it propelled itself higher with the graceful lifting of its wings.

Cold chills washed across her back and down her arms. Unbidden, tears pricked at her long, black lashes. She caught her breath as a sob tore at her throat. Leaping to her feet, she lifted her face to the eagle in flight. Flinging out her arms, she sensed the knowledge of God's love swelling inside her, filling her heart and soul with its warmth.

So long ago, it had seemed, and now, a mere heartbeat ago, she had stood on the outcropping of limestone rock and felt God's presence as the eagle soared above her. God was here on this Lancaster County hilltop. He was real, alive. He remembered her. He cared for her.

Over and over, she spoke her praise, her face lifted to the eagle's flight, tears streaming down her face, her arms lifted in supplication.

How long she remained, she didn't know. Finally, like a graceful swan, she folded her arms and sank to the ground. She rested in the peace that had eluded her earlier.

Quiet, her soul anchored once more, she was filled with a new acceptance of her place in life, and gratitude for Bappie, for Walter and Emma, for her home and her work.

Slowly, she got to her feet and began the trek back to the garden. She stopped abruptly when a figure emerged from the grove of trees, hesitated, then swung to the right toward Bappie working in the vegetable garden.

Hester quickened her pace. She had no idea who the man might be, and it was better that Bappie not be alone when she saw him. Turning left, she broke into a run, taking a shortcut by slicing through the woods, so she would reach Bappie before the man did.

Breathless, she slowed herself to a walk. The pounding of her heart was stifling her.

On he came. Tall, immense, his shoulders wide, his body thick, straining at the seams of his clothes.

Hester stopped to watch, mystified now. His gait was heavy, purposeful, the long strides covering ground effortlessly. Where had she seen this gait? The set of those shoulders? Hester stopped, her eyebrows lowered in concentration.

He was in full view now. His hat was brown and pulled low on his forehead. His face was barely visible, so low was the hat's brim.

Hester was motionless, watching, her eyes taking in the familiar walk. Why was this man's gait etched into her memory, branded into her remembering? And yet she could not name him.

He was a stone's throw away. She could not move. When he came on, she stood like a statue, her hands hanging loosely at her side, her skirts blowing gently about her ankles. Her eyes were wide with bewilderment, her graceful neck held taut like the Indian princess she was.

Did he smile first, or take off the hat that hid his features? She didn't know.

When he removed his brown leather hat, thick, straight, blond hair tumbled to his shoulders. His blue eyes were wide and filled with a light that was so glad. Hester lowered hers, shyness overtaking her.

She began to tremble. Her knees shook as if a strong wind was threatening her strength. She drew a sharp breath.

The plane of his cheeks, with weathered lines around his wide mouth, was so even, nearly perfect. He stopped. His eyes were fringed with lashes she had seen before. The cleft in his chin had been there before.

She tried to speak, but could not utter a word. A hand went to her mouth.

Slowly, he came closer. As if in a dream, he reached out, gently grasped her hand, and pulled her toward him. His eyes devoured her face, her eyes, her mouth, still as perfect in their symmetry as he had remembered. Her eyes were the dark jewels he had carried in his heart all these years. Their luster filled the emptiness in his heart. Twice, he opened his mouth to speak. Twice, he failed.

Their gaze locked and held.

When he spoke, his voice was low, filled with years of longing. "I am Noah."

The End

LINDA BYLER

Hester *Takes* Charge

Hester's Hunt for Home
Book 3

CHAPTER 1

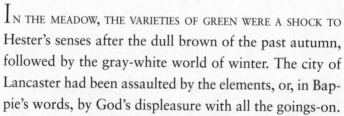

IN THE MEADOW, THE VARIETIES OF GREEN WERE A SHOCK TO Hester's senses after the dull brown of the past autumn, followed by the gray-white world of winter. The city of Lancaster had been assaulted by the elements, or, in Bappie's words, by God's displeasure with all the goings-on.

But now winter was over. The long, dark evenings had faded away; the sound of melting snow and ice was a song. The steady, musical tinkling of raindrops splashing from the eaves formed small streams of water that ran into the streets. There they pooled with the gray slush and were joined by the mud from horses' hooves and steel-rimmed buggy wheels.

Hester's store of herbs and tinctures had fallen to an alarming scattering of almost-empty sacks and a few half-filled bottles of various remedies. The winter had brought much sickness. Hester continued her services with herbal remedies, steadily gaining more knowledge about administering them. The word around town was about a child who recovered from lung fever after the doctor had given up. Some had abscesses heal. For others, sore eyes and flaming, pus-coated throats were relieved by the mysterious tinctures the "Indian lady" carried in her huge, black carpetbag. She dressed in the traditional black shawl and full bonnet of the Amish.

Oh, there were those who held their hands to their mouths sideways, palms inward, rolling their eyes in a pious manner and hissing to one another that this Indian maid was involved in black witchcraft. Look at the color of her outerwear. All black. That bonnet hiding those large black eyes—it gave them the shivers, so it did. They fetched the doctor whom they trusted, not some big-eyed, dark wraith that walked the brick sidewalks of the city without fear.

She held her head high now, they said. Her strides covered the distance efficiently, the long-legged, easy gait of an Indian, but give her a few decades, and she'd be a hunched-over old crone. Then people would see which spirit she possessed.

But to those who knew and loved her, Hester was the beautiful Indian widow who had been married to Isaac King's William, until the fearful, flooding night when his horse threw him against the stone wall of the bridge, injuring his head, and he was taken to the bosom of the Lord.

Now she resided with an unmarried woman, an old maid, Barbara King, called Bappie. Her temperament was as colorful as the wiry strands of auburn hair that eluded her starched white covering. The ever-expanding town of Lancaster, in Pennsylvania, was their home. Theirs was a solid house, and it adjoined a brick-encased one, which housed Walter and Emma Trout and their two adopted sons.

Bappie did not have a solid reputation within the Amish church. Its *Ordnung*, with its stringent rules and regulations in the late 1700s, barely allowed these two single women to live within the town's boundaries. For one thing, Lancaster was a place of the world, where taverns dotted the streets and worldly churches sprang up like mushrooms. There were Baptists and Methodists and Lutherans and those Dunkards who almost drowned the people they baptized, when everyone knew three splashes from the holy cup was sufficient.

No, Bappie was pushing the rules, what with the successful hawking of her vegetables at the farmers' market on the square, even if she grew all of them on her own plot of land.

As for Hester and her practicing of herbal medicines, the ministers left that alone. They were glad when a healing occurred, but they shrugged their shoulders for the most part, saying if it was from God, it would grow and prosper. And if not, the practice of using the herbs would dwindle away since no good came of it.

Hester sat cross-legged, the pleated skirt of her red dress and gray apron holding a large amount of freshly snipped herbs. Here, where the meadow sloped down to a swamp, the moisture stayed plentiful all year long. The abundant growth of plants was far beyond anything she had ever hoped to find.

There was figwort, comfrey, yellow daisies, dandelions, March turnips, dove's foot, elecampane, eyebright, featherfew, and a profusion of artichokes, hemp, and hyssop. The list went on and on, but discovering so many wild artichokes brought an eager shine to Hester's dark eyes.

Many people in the town carried their water from a communal well. But during the winter, rather than brave the cold and driving snow and ice, they drank very little good, cold water, resulting in bladder and kidney troubles. The juice of the artichoke helped immensely with this problem.

Hester had brought three large baskets, lined them with cloth sacks, and labeled each with the herb it would contain. She plied a pair of sharp scissors, snipping away dead leaves and cutting roots from stems, stacking them on a neat pile beside the cuttings. So engrossed was she in her work, with the breath of a song on her lips, that she did not notice a lone figure walking at a brisk pace, until he caught sight of her red dress and white muslin cap.

He stopped, hesitating. The mellow spring breeze ruffled the thick blond hair on his head, moving it gently. He reached up to brush a few stray strands from his vision, then lowered his hand.

His breath came faster, lighter. His one hand clenched into a fist, and then his other one, as emotion shook him. Inner turmoil took hold—a mixture of knowing and wanting, followed immediately by the sure sense that he must be willing to sacrifice his deepest longing. He told himself that he must allow time and patience—God's way—to be his guide. Hard as it was, he believed that God's understanding was far beyond his own. The young man walked on.

Hester hummed, her large, dark eyes liquid with contentment. The unbelievable softness of the day, the vibrating colors around her, enfolded her, healing the cold and the bitter anguish of children dying during the unforgiving winter months. She had felt so helpless in the presence of too many tallow candles, giving only flickering light in the dark and hopeless hovels of the poor.

She looked up just in time to see the tall figure and to watch his retreat, her hands restless in her lap. Slowly she bent her head and lowered her heavy lids as the scissors fell from her nerveless fingers. Would she always wonder? Her heart fluttered, feeling captive within the confines of her body. She had built a protective shell around herself so she could somehow live with her sense of failure as William King's wife. Yet now she felt a rising of hope that she had tried so hard to do away with.

How many months had gone by since that brisk fall day? Whenever she remembered it, the day was filled with color—brilliant yellow, vivid reds, and deep orange. His hair was thick, like spun gold. His shoulders like great oaks. She blushed deeply, thinking of the fine bronzed hair on his forearms, exposed where the gray, homespun sleeves had been rolled up.

"I am Noah."

Involuntarily, she had stepped backward. Always protecting herself. She knew in that instant that she needed to put the hard shell securely in place. The shell grew out of her own shortcomings.

He was her brother. He *was*. Over and over, she recounted their meeting of a few months earlier, every spoken word, every emotion, every light that came from his blue eyes.

Noah belonged to her childhood in Berks County. They had lived together with Hans and Kate, Isaac, Lissie, and dear tiny Rebecca who died in infancy, buried in that stone-cold place. Solomon had been born, and then Daniel. Eventually, ten children in all joined the happy home. Hans and Kate had found her, a wee Indian baby, by the spring, left there by the shame of an Indian girl, her mother. Noah had been born barely a year later.

Now, after all these years, he had come home from the war and found her, his sister. Yet after that day, the sister part was almost laughable. She was not a sister in any sense of the word, but so much more.

And then, like a thundercloud, there came an unwelcome darkening of the glad light within her. In an instant, she had shrunken within herself, leaving her words cold and clipped.

Hester bent over the herbs in her lap, holding the palms of her hands tight to each side of her face to cool the heat in her brown cheeks. She squeezed her eyes tightly as the shame of remembering that day shivered up her spine.

She had not been prepared for the pure rush of longing, the strong desire to lay her head on his solid shoulder, to feel his powerful arms enclose her, allowing her to come home to the safety they held. She had wanted to stay within a place that carried a memory of Kate, who had created her deep sense of well-being. Her mother's love had brought her kindness and generosity, rooted in deep and abiding trust.

She had caught herself, in time, thank God, when the sight of Noah tempted her to believe she had returned to the safety of her childhood world. How close she had come to allowing herself the freedom of revealing any love, even a sister's foolish devotion! How unintelligent was she, she asked herself. Hadn't she married a fine young man? Suddenly the bile of resentment she felt toward William rushed back, rebelliousness against his devout ways. For William had been raised in the strictness of the Amish *Ordnung*, which he took very seriously, keeping every demand to the letter and requiring the same from his wife.

But she had failed him. Not with her outward appearance, and certainly not in the view of his family (apart from his impossibly demanding mother), but with her inward seething. Her strong urge to hurl her mug of tea at his self-righteousness was probably a mortal sin. Only when he was on his deathbed did she come to believe this.

No one could persuade her otherwise, not Bappie nor Emma nor Walter. And so she had thrown herself into her work with passion—gathering and preparing herbs, grinding roots, boiling leaves with whiskey, bottling concoctions, living the knowledge handed to her by the ancient Indian grandmother in Berks County.

When Noah met her that day last fall, she had told him in words covered with cold, hard ice, that she lived with Barbara King, that she was a very busy woman, and that she had no time to sit with him and talk of the past.

In that moment his eyes had turned from warm gladness to a navy blue, then faded to a weary gray of disbelief, and his eyelids drooped low, as if losing sight of her would soften the coldness of her words. When he walked away, his shoulders were hunched in defeat, but only after his kindness had returned long enough to wish her a good day.

Was he able to summon, like Kate, concern for someone else's well-being, even after such a cold dismissal? Instead of firing back, he had collected himself, wished her the best, and without another word, walked away.

It had taken Bappie no more than 30 seconds to make her indignant appearance, raining cold, hard questions, thick and fast. "Who was that?" "What do you mean, 'your brother'?"

This was followed by a snort of disbelief, a swipe of fiery red hair beneath her covering, and a solid planting of her roughly clad feet with her arms crossed tightly in front, covering strings flapping loosely at her back, in disregard of the required bow under her chin.

When Hester repeated, "My brother," Bappie sent another derogatory look her way, along with an expulsion of sound, which left no doubt about the meaning of either the expression or the noise.

"He'd pass for my brother a lot more than yours."

"He's not . . ." Hester floundered, then turned away.

"You mean he was brought up in the same house by the same parents. He wasn't found by the spring with you."

Hester's head dropped forward. She had so wanted to forget Noah's appearance and the hope he had stirred within her. But Bappie's words rang true and strong, reminding her of what she couldn't deny or understand.

Bappie tossed her head, stuck the tines of the manure-encrusted pitchfork into the dry earth, loosened her hands, and dusted them off with a firm whack before rubbing them along the sides of her apron.

"I'd say you were pretty rude to the poor chap."

Miserably, Hester acknowledged this.

"You need to make it up to him. If he comes visiting, I'm going to invite him in, and . . ."

Hester broke in mid-sentence, her eyes flashing. "No, you're not, Bappie! This is my life, my situation, and absolutely not your business. I mean it. You stay out of it."

Bappie's eyes narrowed. "Well, if he's only your brother, you sure are fired up. All right, if that's how you want it. What's his name?"

"Noah."

"Hm. Just like Noah and the ark. He'd make a spectacular Noah. Just like you imagine that stalwart man of God."

Hester felt the color rising in her face and thanked God for the honey-brown color of her skin. At least Bappie couldn't see her reddening, for all her self-effacing shrewdness.

And now almost six months had passed without a word, an appearance, or any sign of Noah again. Over and over, she had told herself, it was not a good sign for a man to leave his faith or disobey his parents, let alone go to war. Had he ever committed himself to the church at all? Perhaps he had been excommunicated. If so, she had good reason to have spoken coldly. She wanted to shun him, keep him out of her life, out of sight. And yet, on this fine spring day, she relived that last meeting with

Noah when she saw a man walking alone, too far away to be recognized with certainty.

She picked up the scissors, then let them drop away. She gathered up a handful of fragrant herbs and rifled through them idly. She smoothed back a few dark hairs, picked up the scissors again, and slowly cut away the stems of a wild strawberry plant.

She thought of all the decaying teeth she had witnessed, the grayish, unhealthy color of so many of the children's gums. The juice of the strawberry root was so good for this foul ailment, but most of the children resisted the bitter taste. Worse still, in Hester's mind, was that the mothers supported the children's yells of disapproval.

She would try mixing in a bit of honey or maple syrup. Motivated now, and inspired once more, she settled her memories. Her sighs turned to quick breaths of anticipation as she resumed cutting with renewed energy.

Back home, in the soft, evening glow of the warm, spring sunshine, Bappie had worked herself into a fever of housecleaning. She had flung open the two front windows that faced the muddy street. The white muslin curtains that usually hung over them flapped softly on the washline in the small backyard.

When Hester dropped the three baskets on the back stoop, she heard windows sliding up and down and the wooden stool being knocked around. She figured if she wanted something to eat she'd have to cook it herself.

"I'm home!" she called.

No answer. Only the scraping of the stool across the oak floors.

Hester shrugged, opened the pantry door, and dug out some dried apples and a bit of hard cheese. She knew there was a ham knuckle down cellar. Her mouth watered, thinking of *schnitz und knepp*, Bappie's favorite and an old Pennsylvania Dutch dish Kate had made so well.

Hester could still see the deep pleats spread over Kate's ample hips, the wide comforting swell of them as she moved efficiently for such a large woman, seeming to float from stove to hearth to dry sink and back again.

Kate's *schnitz und knepp* was one of Hester's most comforting memories. Kate would boil the dried apples to perfection until they were soft and brown, then mash them thoroughly with a potato masher and crumble the ham into the apples, its salt flavoring the sweetness of the fruit and creating the special taste of this dish. The fluffy dumplings on top tasted of both the ham and the apples.

Wishfully, Hester put the ham knuckle in the pot with the dried apples. Wouldn't it be wonderful to see Kate just one more time?

Her thoughts were interrupted by Bappie, holding her arm above her head, leaning on the doorway, her eyes drooping with tiredness. "I didn't know you were home."

"I called out."

"I was cleaning windows."

"Mmm."

"What's for supper?"

"*Schnitz und knepp.*"

"Mm. Good. I'll polish the floor real quick."

"Don't hurry. This takes a while."

Hester sliced a thick slice of dark brown bread, spread a good portion of butter across it, and bit out a huge chunk, closed her eyes, and chewed with appreciation. She was so hungry.

She heard Bappie's maneuvering in the front room, smelled the lye soap, and smiled as she poured boiling water over tea leaves, inhaling the goodness of the spearmint. It was good to come home to Bappie, her friend and coworker, like a mother, sister, and brother, all wrapped up in one.

She had nothing to complain about. Her life here in the city was more than sufficient to keep her comfortable and content. Walter and Emma, kind and accommodating, offered assistance any time, although Hester knew all too well that as the portly couple aged, she and Bappie would need to help them more and more frequently.

The fading light created an aura of gold covering the white plastered walls, the heavy oak ceiling beams, and the well-worn floorboards in a deep, rich color. The stovetop gleamed cozily, the steam from the cooking ham and apples rising fragrantly.

A red and white cloth covered the table, where a brown, earthenware pitcher of purple violets stood in the center. Bappie's sampler, an embroidered piece of fabric with a tree, her family's names, and the words "Home Sweet Home" beneath it, hung on the wall above the bright table.

A rush of sweetness enveloped Hester. For only a moment, she allowed herself the thought of his golden hair and his thick, solid form seated at the kitchen table, infused with warm light.

"His." She could not think "Noah." It was far too intimate, and Bappie might detect a faint blush on her cheeks.

But different memories crowded in then, Hester helpless in their wake. So many meals, so much effort. Lighter bread, crispier chicken, vegetables left boiling too long, or not long enough. Tea that was not strong enough, or harvested too soon. Always after this derision, her husband bowed his dark head, closed his eyes in severe concentration, and moved his mouth with sincerity as he silently thanked God for his food.

Hester often didn't pray at all. She figured God saw the blackness of her rebellion, so he wouldn't want her praise, would he? She was powerless to stop her anger and hurt. She seethed behind her calm, unperturbed face, wanting to throw her heavy ironstone plate at her husband's pious demeanor.

"Her William," he had been, as she was "his Hester." He owned her, possessed her, was proud of her to the world, or appeared to be. It was only when they were alone that he displayed so much criticism. It fell like a shower of bricks, painful, unprotected, crushing. At other times she could manage to wave it away like a swarm of bothersome gnats.

But here it was again. How could she hope to have happiness with any man after having been married to William? Better, much better, to leave marriage and love to those who were truly sweet and good.

With a grunt and a scrape, Bappie scuttled past, a bit bent over as she carried the wooden bucket and scrub cloth, her face contorted and red, her hair only a shade darker, as she went to the back stoop and sloshed the water across the backyard.

Flopping ungracefully into a kitchen chair, she shoved her backside down, sprawled her legs in front of her, threw her arms across the chair back, and lifted her face to the beams across the ceiling. "Whooo!"

"You drive yourself too hard, Bappie."

"It's not as if I had any help."

Hester, mixing the flour, milk, and shortening for the *knepp*, gave her a sidelong look. She decided to say nothing, knowing that when Bappie got into this mood, she became as prickly as a porcupine if you crossed her path.

"Tomorrow I'll be home. We can houseclean the kitchen together."

"But our bedrooms aren't done. You know how long it takes to empty and refill the ticks. It's hard work, getting all that straw to stay in the cover. And it takes them a long time to dry after they've been washed. I was thinking of getting up at five to start the fire under the kettle and to get the bedding on the line as soon as possible. Do we have enough kindling? If we don't, I'll have to split some tonight yet.

"It's hot in here. Why don't you put a window cloth in the window and get some air in here?"

And so they ate their meal while Bappie planned and worried, eating an alarming amount of the dried apples, ham, and dumplings. She soon became quite relaxed, her mood mellowing as she finished up with the sweet spearmint tea. They needed to get out to the farm to check the peas, onions, and radishes, she said. But if they did that, when would the housecleaning get done?

It was important to have the first peas, she stated emphatically, because when the market opened, the wealthy women of the town were always willing to pay an exceedingly high amount for a half-bushel of spring peas. Of course, if they planted the peas too early, there was a danger of frost, which would be no gain at all, if those pea stalks froze. All the profit would be lost, and all they'd eventually have to sell would be some sun-bleached peas that were grown in too-warm temperatures.

Bappie was rambling on.

"We should actually move out there. Emma could find a renter for this house. She would likely be able to charge more then we pay. If we'd live there . . ."

Hester broke in. "Bappie, that house is a hut at best. You know it's not big enough, and it would cost far too much to make it decent. No."

"You're just scared out there in the wild."

"No. No, I'm not."

"Why don't you want to move?"

"I just don't."

"It's your doctoring and herbs and stuff."

"No."

"Yes, it is. I saw all those baskets of weeds out back."

"They're not weeds."

"I know." Bappie smiled good-naturedly, then placed a hand on Hester's forearm.

"You're a gifted herbalist, I know. And I respect that more and more as time goes on. You help me tomorrow, I'll help you Thursday, then Friday we'll go to the farm. All right?"

CHAPTER 2

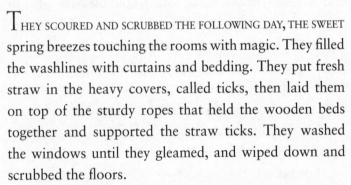

THEY SCOURED AND SCRUBBED THE FOLLOWING DAY, THE SWEET spring breezes touching the rooms with magic. They filled the washlines with curtains and bedding. They put fresh straw in the heavy covers, called ticks, then laid them on top of the sturdy ropes that held the wooden beds together and supported the straw ticks. They washed the windows until they gleamed, and wiped down and scrubbed the floors.

They sang and talked as they worked companionably. Sometimes quiet spread across the room, comfortable and relaxed, an atmosphere that comes only after years of togetherness.

Hester pushed up the window from her bedroom and called to Emma, who was pegging a tablecloth on her washline. "Hey, neighbor lady!"

Emma's shiny, round face looked around, confused, till Hester called again. Looking up this time, the rotund little woman's face broke into a wreath of wrinkles, her eyes almost closing as her cheeks pushed up on them when she smiled. Her white ruffled house cap bounced sideways as she shook her finger at Hester.

"You gave me a scare, young lady!"

Hester laughed, glad to see Emma again. "It's a lovely day, isn't it, Emma?"

"Ya! Ya!"

Although Walter and Emma went to the Lutheran church, she was from Germany and spoke the Pennsylvania Dutch dialect fluently. She spoke English well, but a smattering of Dutch messed up many good and proper English words. Sometimes Hester gave up being serious and attentive and burst out laughing at all the wrong pronunciations.

"Hester, you and Bappie come on over. It's time for *mittag*. Me and Walter have a wonderful goot piece of pork sausage. Come."

Walter, Emma's impeccably mannered husband, bowed and scraped his way down the hallway into the kitchen, his face pink and shining with the pleasure of having Bappie and Hester at his table.

Hester noticed the pull of his wide suspenders, which put an alarming amount of pressure on his trousers. She winced to notice the snug fit around his protruding middle, the button straining at the waistband. His shirt was buttoned properly and was flawlessly white. A ring of gray hair encircled his otherwise bald and shining dome.

"Certainly, certainly, come this way. How grand! How grand!" Pulling back the chairs with a flourish, his pudgy fingers placed lightly at their elbows, he seated first Bappie, then Hester, in his perfect English manner.

He offered them each a white cloth napkin, but Emma waved him away.

"Ach, now, Walter. *Veck mit selly.* We're just plain old Dutch people from Deutschland. We chust eat; we don't need them cloths."

With that, she tucked into her perfectly browned piece of sausage, rolled it into a slice of bread, and topped it with pungent horseradish. On her plate was a stack of fried potatoes, well salted and peppered.

Walter lifted a piece of the fragrant sausage, holding it at different angles to the light that filtered through the small windowpanes, his eyebrows lifted in appreciation.

"Fine sausage, this. The best in Lancaster. I told Harvey, now, 'I don't want any of your lesser quality with too much grease.' I am suspicious that he is trying to elevate his profits somewhat, by adding undesirable portions of the hog to his sausages. I told him of my fears, and I do believe his face took on a red color, although my words were spoken with care toward his feelings."

"Ach, Walter, you're too easy on that butcher. Everyone knows he puts too much of the pig in his sausage. It's good, so chust eat it, and don't be so bothered."

Hester cut a small piece, chewed, and swallowed, but was glad to finish the too-much-discussed piece of meat and eat the fried potatoes. Either way, it didn't seem to harm Bappie's appetite; she seemed to be enjoying her lunch immensely.

"Would you ladies care for some of our sauerkraut? We have the best. It accompanies the sausage in such an excellent manner." Walter rose to bring the blue crockery bowl filled with steaming sauerkraut to each one, carefully ladling huge spoonfuls onto their plates, his eyes shining, his face beaming with anticipation.

It was at that moment that Bappie chose to bring up the subject of moving out to the farm, asking if they could find renters for the house that Emma had vacated when she become Walter's wife only a few years before, since both had been left behind by the passing of their spouses.

"Ach, *du yay.*" Poor Emma was completely taken off-guard, the abrupt announcement almost more than she could comprehend. Walter stopped chewing, wiped his mouth carefully with the snowy white napkin, cleared his throat, and reached for his water glass.

"I don't mean to be impertinent, but why would you do something like that?" His eyebrows shot up in consternation and stayed there, wrinkling his forehead like pleats in an apron.

Bappie explained her case. The garden needed closer watching in the spring, much more than they had given it in the past few years.

Yes, the house out there needed attention, but they would try and do what they could themselves. Perhaps some men in the Amish community would be good enough to volunteer their labor.

"Ach, you Amish. Always for free. You ask too much of each other. They'll want some sort of payment, you watch." Clearly, Emma was unhappy with the thing Bappie was planning.

Hester stayed quiet, surprised that Bappie approached the old couple with her plans quite so soon, although she knew it was her way—think once, then get it done, plowing through life with full determination.

Walter sat back, his chin wobbling as he valiantly fought the overflowing emotion in his eyes. "But, it will

never be the same, you know. No more friendly banter across the backyard fence, no more impromptu visits
like this. My heart would indeed be heavily burdened
were you to carry out these plans."

Emma sighed and lifted forlorn eyes to Hester. "You
don't want to go."

Hester shrugged her shoulders and looked to Bappie
for help.

Bappie took the situation in hand, stating matter-of-
factly that, yes, they did want to go, only because of the
garden, and yes, they would miss them as neighbors, but
it was time. They would have no problem filling their
house, as the town of Lancaster was booming, with
buildings going up so fast. There were always people
needing a home.

There was nothing for Walter and Emma to do but
to let them go, difficult as it was. Bappie and Hester
ate the good, flaky crust of the dried huckleberry pie,
drank their tea, and bade them a good afternoon, promising to stay another month till they found someone to
help them with the renovations of the tiny, dilapidated
farmhouse.

At the door, Walter cleared his throat, drawing himself up to his full height. "My dear ladies, let it be known
that I consider you two as salt of the earth, two of God's
best women ever placed on the face of this earth. I value
your friendship with utmost esteem."

Emma harrumphed beside him, short and squat and
thoroughly disgruntled. "Ya, well, Walter, hush. I'm not
sure I'd say that. I think you're making a mistake. You'll
regret it, living out there."

With that said, she stepped in front of Walter and shut the door firmly.

Hester walked quietly behind Bappie. Neither one spoke as they made their way to the back door.

"Was Silver fed?"

Hester nodded.

"We'll have clean beds and curtains when we move."

"You should have given me a bit of warning. I thought you meant in a year or so."

"And let that pea crop go to waste again? No. I meant now."

Hester said nothing.

They worked silently the remainder of the afternoon, although Hester's heart was no longer in her work. Why clean like this if she didn't need to? Why let someone else enjoy the fruits of their labor? She felt a twinge of the same rebellion she had felt when William berated her, but figured she'd better stay quiet, with Bappie so determined and all.

The truth was, she did not want to live in that little house. It was dark and cold and mildewed. There weren't enough windows. She didn't like the eerie quiet, nor all the hooting and hissing and warbling sounds of the night creatures. She felt alone there and unprotected.

She thought of staying by herself in this good, solidly built house beside Walter and Emma. The safety of the surrounding people, the town police, the passersby, the work she did with the herbs. Could she stand up to Bappie? Did she want to?

She could not generate enough income to pay the rent on her own, that was sure. The people she served with the herbs and medicines so often had very little money, or none. She could not count on her own income to make her way, so she supposed she really had very little choice of her own.

Bappie was good to her, sharing the profits from the vegetables in the summer. They worked well as a team, and as long as they could manage together financially, she had better appreciate Bappie's good way with business. And so she slept in her clean bedroom on the sun-kissed, freshly laundered ticking, grateful for the home she had with a companion she trusted. She only hoped they could make that disgusting little hovel into a house fit for living.

She was awake at first light because of an energetic robin chirping directly outside her half-opened window. She lay a while, breathing deeply of the fresh, crackling straw beneath her, listening to the sounds of the town awakening. Horses' hooves made a dull, sucking sound as they stepped through the ever present spring mud, the rains turning the streets slick with it.

Horses pulled graders across the worst of it and hauled the muck away, but there was still always a layer of mud, sometimes thicker than other times. Men called to each other or to their horses, the early risers who were on their way to their various duties, the menial tasks that kept the town growing.

So many buildings were going up, with endless hammering and sawing and loads of fresh, yellow lumber being hauled in by the great Belgians and Percherons. Many of the Amish preferred mules, hearty, long-eared creatures that worked tirelessly on very little feed, with many of the qualities of a donkey.

Hester heard the gong of a bell, the breakfast call at the hotel for the laborers who worked in construction. Perhaps she could find a job there as a server, carrying great trays loaded with food to the hungry men. She soon discarded that thought though, as she imagined the strange men, the low wages, and the backbreaking work. Better to stay with Bappie, even if she would have to drive Silver into town or ride with the person who came to fetch her when the need arose.

She sat up, drawing a hand through her disheveled hair as a wave of unworthiness attacked her. Despair that was cloying squeezed the life out of the beautiful spring morning.

Lowering her head, she whispered, "Dear Lord, my Savior, be here with me now. You know I need you to revive my spirits. I don't like changes, and now I have no choice. Help me to submit to thy will always."

She whispered the "Amen," then rose, determined to shake off the lethargy. She needed to throw herself into her work, forget her own foolishness, and be thankful.

She dressed, flicked a comb through her heavy, jet-black hair, set the large muslin cap on her head, and went downstairs.

The house was cold, and Bappie was nowhere about. Lifting the lid on the cookstove, she threw in a few small pieces of kindling, watching to make sure the bit of red coals would ignite the dry wood. A thin column of smoke was accompanied by a light crackling, so she replaced the lid and put both hands, palms down, on the welcoming warmth of the cookstove top. She shivered, then added a bit more wood to build up the fire.

Going to the pantry, she brought out the tin of cooked cornmeal mush, found a knife, and sliced a dozen good thick slices. She set them to fry in the melting white lard she had placed in the black, cast-iron frying pan.

Now she'd see if there were eggs beneath the brown hens. Grimly, she drew on a pair of heavy gloves, knowing all too well how every hen wanted to stay sitting on top of her prize eggs in the spring, hoping to hatch chicks. The hens would peck and flog and scratch with their feet, resisting any attempt to gather their brown eggs. Bappie was better at this than she was, but the mush was frying, and there was nothing better than fresh eggs to eat with it. Hester went through the back door with the egg basket, biting her lip and hoping for the best.

Another wonderful day had dawned. The maple tree in the backyard was bursting with delicate, purple buds. Clumps of green grass already grew thickly alongside the fence separating their yard from Walter and Emma's.

A wagon clattered by, the driver perched on a crate and rocking from side to side with each step from the horses, his hat on the back of his head, a piece of hay stuck between his lower teeth, singing at the top of his lungs. He caught sight of her, grinned and waved furiously, his large, farmer's hand flapping madly until he disappeared behind the fence.

Hester waved in return, then shook her head, a small smile playing around her full lips. That was the one thing she would miss the most, moving to the farm.

The inside of the small chicken coop was dry and dusty, with that special, warm chicken smell she loved.

She eyed the eight chickens on their wooden boxes. Every last one sat with their feathers puffed protectively, sitting like queens on thrones, their round, lidless brown eyes watching her balefully.

"Chook, chook, chook." Hester murmured soft words, trying to make peace with these sitting biddy hens, soothing them so they would allow her to reach softly beneath them and steal their eggs. Bappie simply grabbed them by the neck and flung them into a corner, where the poor hens shook themselves, looking dazed and confused for some time, before they gave up and pecked at the cracked corn.

"Chook, chook, chook." Tentatively, she reached out.

Wham! The hen's aim was true and as sharp as a knife. The beak's impact drew blood just above her wrist, where the glove gave way to the soft skin on her arm. After that, it was all chaos as the irate hen left her nest and flew directly into Hester's face, her dusty wings beating and thrashing.

Blinded, Hester screamed as she stumbled toward the door of the chicken coop, swinging the basket back and forth for protection. She stepped through the door, her arm held over her face, then ran into a person, shoving him backward as she reeled to the side. "Oh, oh. My goodness, I'm sorry."

Lowering her arm, her large, dark eyes wide with fright and embarrassment, she looked up directly into eyes that she knew well. Now they were half-closed as laughter welled up, then broke out in a deep, rumbling sound that carried her straight back to Noah and Isaac and the place of her childhood.

"Noah!" Caught so completely off-guard, she let her eyes shine with the gladness, recognizing his laughter, and savoring the warmth that welled up in her heart because of it. But only for an instant.

"What are you doing in our backyard?" The words were only fringed with coldness, but it was there.

The smile never left Noah's face, nor did his eyes leave hers. The unguarded moment was like a cold drink of water to a man dying of thirst, coming at a time when he realizes there is no more strength, no hope of keeping himself alive.

"I'm sorry. I never meant to intrude or disturb your morning." The smile lines stayed around his serious blue eyes, as if the moment of recognition lingered, shoring up his courage.

Ruefully, Hester bent her head, her hands going to the front of her dress, dusting the clinging bits of straw and a few stray chicken feathers.

Noah watched the slim, tapered fingers, the small brown hands that never left his dreams. He could still feel the soft blows of those lovely fists—pure joy—when she lost her temper and came after him with all the fury of a wronged Indian brave. How long had he loved her? Always. Since the age when he understood that she was not his sister in the way that Lissie and Barbara were. Then came years of holding up his head, facing life with the knowledge that a wall stood between them, impenetrable because of his father.

Hans lived in the same house, an upright and pious member of the Old Order Amish church, who taught his children well, led them in the path of righteousness, and loved Kate, his good wife.

Noah and Isaac knew that obedience and hard work were always rewarded by the approval of their father, their taskmaster. They knew nothing else. Hans assigned their duties, taught them to feed the livestock, milk the cows, plant and cultivate and harvest. They were taught to fell trees, dig stumps, haul manure, and butcher the steers and pigs. For a time, they attended a one-room school where the stern schoolmaster, Theodore Crane, led Noah and Isaac into the wonderful universe of books, sums, and knowledge of the wide, unexplored, and unknown world around them.

But always, it was there.

The first time Noah understood his father's feelings toward Hester, he pushed it away, allowing disbelief and denial to make tolerable what he suspected. He told himself that he was the suspicious one, the one who needed to straighten himself out, to stop watching for his father's admiration of anything about Hester that seemed inappropriate.

Hester became the light in Noah's life. His memory of her was like a written journal, the pages turned with the soft sighing of his love. Hester in an old blue dress, the hem torn out, trailing ridiculously in the dirt and the dusty corn fodder, or in the mud bordering the still and brackish waters of the creek on a dry summer's day. Her tightly braided hair like black silk, the dry winds teasing stray tendrils around her brown face. The way she would squint her lustrous brown eyes, puff out her perfect lower lip, and expel a short quick breath to blow the hair out of her line of vision.

Like a young fawn, she was. As quick and graceful, easily outrunning anyone, boy or girl, in a footrace. How his heart would swell to watch her pull ahead every time, her long legs beneath the skirts that hampered them, churning determinedly, her arms pumping out her competitive spirit.

There was Hester sitting by the hearth, tired and sleepy, her heavy eyelids drooping, and still she rocked the cradle with one foot as she sang to yet another wee baby Kate had brought into the world. She had loved them all, her large eyes dark and liquid with awe after another birth, each new, tiny bundle containing the delight of Hester's young life.

She held the babies, bathed them, changed their thick flannel diapers, and carried them to Kate, large and quiet, resting on the high bed, which cracked and groaned under her considerable weight. After Kate had begun to feed the baby, Hester would softly, sometimes hesitantly, lay her dark head on Kate's ample shoulder.

Always, Kate's free arm would leave the baby, slide quietly around Hester's waist, and draw her a bit closer. Hester would lift adoring eyes to her mother. Her mother, not in the true sense of the word, but with love binding them as securely and tenderly as any bond could.

Noah had often felt like an outsider, watching this with the keen eye of the sensitive observer he was. In his young heart, he longed to do what Kate had just done—draw Hester close and let her lay her head on his shoulder. Being too young to fully understand this longing, he dismissed it as jealousy, a childish stirring to be equally as close to his mother himself.

He asked Isaac about his feelings. Isaac waved Noah away as if his longing was only a burst of dust from the cornfield, annoying, unimportant, and soon to end. Slender, brown-haired Isaac, who was a shadow behind Noah, copied his brother's ways, never noticing any difference between his feelings for Hester and for little Lissie.

So Noah figured he must be wrong, allowing these feelings to stir in his body or his heart—he wasn't sure where they came from. He just knew they were there, like a jewel he always guarded securely, but with a painful edge that tormented his innocent well-being.

Hester's restless hands fluttered at her waist, her fingers connecting and clenching tightly there. "Why are you here?" she asked none too kindly.

Hesitantly, Noah looked around, first to the small barn where Silver, the driving horse, tossed his head impatiently, nickering for his morning allotment of oats then to the back stoop, with the oak door leading into the house.

"There is a-a lady, a *frau* who talked to me yesterday. She is in need of a man to help her at a farm she owns. I understood her to say she lived on Mulberry Street, but . . ."

"It isn't here. This is not the right place. We, she, I don't believe your services will be . . ."

CHAPTER 3

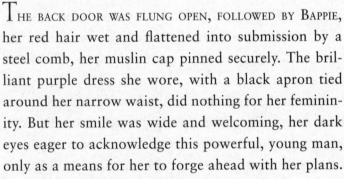

THE BACK DOOR WAS FLUNG OPEN, FOLLOWED BY BAPPIE, her red hair wet and flattened into submission by a steel comb, her muslin cap pinned securely. The brilliant purple dress she wore, with a black apron tied around her narrow waist, did nothing for her femininity. But her smile was wide and welcoming, her dark eyes eager to acknowledge this powerful, young man, only as a means for her to forge ahead with her plans.

"You found me! Good."

"Yes, good morning, Barbara? How are you?"

Bappie became flustered then, blinking furiously, color washing over her face, a pink tide that gave away her fierce denial of any attraction for men, any man. In her mind they were all alike, and she didn't need them. She waved a hand in front of her face, as if his manners were a mosquito whining about her head.

"Doesn't matter how I am. How soon can you start?"

Noah remained quiet, then looked at her.

"Well, I'm working for Dan Stoltzfus right now. He's building a barn west of town. I don't know his plans from one week to the next."

"You mean Bacon Dan?" Bappie asked.

Hester, remembering the frying mush, slipped away across the yard to the back door.

Noah exercised all the willpower he possessed to keep his attention on Bappie's question without turning his head to watch Hester enter the house, his whole being willing her to stay with him.

He nodded. "Flitcha Danny."

"He doesn't say two words a day, hardly, does he?"

Noah shook his head. "He's a man of few words, that's for sure."

Bappie's lips compressed into a firm line, and her eyes narrowed as her thin hands curled into a fist and came to rest on her narrow hips. Noah could see her mind was churning. "So we need to get out there. You tell Dan we need you for the next two weeks at least. He can get someone else to help him. I'll pay you double what he does. I can about guess you're not getting very high wages. Why are you here? Just home from the war or what? Are you Amish? Are you staying around? Not married. No beard. Where are you staying? Out at Dan's?"

Noah laughed. "Whoa, whoa. I'm a man. One question at a time. You know we men have to think a while before we answer."

"How come you know Hester?" Bappie asked, charging ahead to get all her questions out there so her curiosity could be folded away and disposed of before planning his work schedule.

"She's my sister, from my childhood in Berks County."

"She's not your sister."

"No, well, yes. My mother, Kate, found her by the spring."

Bappie waved impatiently. "I know all that. So you're Noah."

"Yes."

"I heard so much 'Noah this, Noah that.' What was the other brother's name?"

"Isaac."

"Yeah. That's it. He was younger, I guess, right? Sort of an afterthought, as far as Hester's concerned. It was all Noah."

Bappie untied her apron in the back, then retied it, as if that would prepare her a bit better to finish the conversation and move on to a solid commitment from him.

"Do you know how to repair a shake roof? We need an addition to the house and a porch. I need gates repaired and doors, and a new floor put in."

"In two weeks?"

"Well, I'm going to make a frolic for the neighbor men. They can erect the walls for the addition and put the roof on in a day. You can do the rest."

Noah thought he might be able to but said nothing, only shaking his head slightly from side to side.

"I think you can. Me and Hester will help. Hey, she's in there frying cornmeal mush. Why not come in for breakfast? I'll probably have to get the eggs. Go on in."

Noah hesitated.

Bappie entered the chicken coop, extracting chickens from their boxes with an expert flick of the wrist, grabbing their necks, and flinging them across the floor. She gathered eight large brown eggs while he stood and watched, terrified of entering the kitchen alone. Hester would not want him at her table, of that he could be certain.

"Thanks for the invitation, Barbara, but. . ."

"Oh, don't start. You're hungry. You haven't eaten. Two eggs for me, two for Hester, and four for you. Come on."

With an upward arc of her arm and an inclination of her head, she led the way across the yard.

Noah was a coward. His stomach roiled; his breath came in quick, short spurts. "No, I'll . . ."

"Oh, come on. I'm making *panna kuchen*."

Noah followed her hesitantly, then made the inward decision to listen to Bappie and go in. It was, after all, a business meeting, and surely Hester would be civil, or at the least, distantly polite.

He was right. The kitchen was pleasant, sun-filled, clean, and cheerful. The violets in the pitcher on the red and white tablecloth reminded him of the large stone house in Berks County. Unbidden, he felt his throat tighten, his eyes stinging. Too much had happened since then. He didn't know if he could ever risk remembering those days.

Hester did not look up when they entered. She was placing knives and forks on the table beside two white ironstone plates.

"Add another plate, Hester. He's staying for breakfast."

Hester said nothing. A slight nod was her only acknowledgment. Irritation flickered across her perfect eyebrows, then disappeared.

Bappie drew a bowl from the kitchen shelf, measured flour, and melted lard, all the while talking faster than her hands moved.

"It's because of the early crops in the garden that we're moving out there, Hester and I. Put your hat on that hook by the back door. You can wash up in the bowl there. There's water in the bucket. Soap's there somewhere."

Noah turned, removed his hat, and placed it where he was instructed. He poured some lukewarm water into the bowl, rolled up the sleeves of his blue shirt, and soaped his hands.

Hester glanced in his direction. His eyes caught hers in the small oval mirror above the dry sink, but she stepped aside as swiftly as a frightened moth. He lowered his head and resumed his washing.

"Here, Noah. You sit here. Right here by the door. Hester, you fry the eggs, and I'll finish the pancakes. Noah, do you mind pouring the buttermilk?"

Hester set the pitcher on the table quickly before she slid away to the stove, turning her back to him immediately. Bappie watched, pursing her lips.

"For people who knew each other as brother and sister, you two sure don't have an awful lot to say to each other, do you?" she blurted out with all the tact of a sledgehammer.

Noah said nothing. Hester remained at the stove, rigid with annoyance.

"Oh, well, whatever dumb fight you had, you may as well forget about it now."

Hester began to breathe again when Noah said easily, "Oh, no fight. It's just strange, having known one another all those years, and now, we're grown up. We've experienced living and found out the world is a lot more complicated than we could have imagined."

"Yeah, yeah, well, get over it. Get on with your living. Life isn't easy. Nobody's going to carry you around on a satin pillow, careful of your comfort, or lack thereof, mind you. The way I see it, you have to stay ahead of the wolves—meaning hard times, unkind people, death, disease, whatever God slaps in your direction."

As if to add emphasis to her basic wisdom, Bappie flipped the pancakes high, letting them settle back into the pan with a dull sound.

"Get the maple syrup, Hester. Is there any butter?"

Wordlessly, Hester obeyed, lifting the iron latch on the narrow cellar door and disappearing through the opening like a ghost.

They bowed their heads in silent prayer and folded their hands in their laps, the way they had done since they were two years old.

Hester had no idea how she would eat anything, although she planned on doing it even if she choked. He was not going to have the satisfaction of seeing her completely ill at ease and painfully aware of him seated at this too-small table.

Noah was tall and wide and powerful, completely filling his chair. His hair was blond, clean, and well cared
for. His face was as she remembered it, except now it
was a man's face, tanned by his days in the sun and chiseled by the strength of his work. His blue eyes were calm
and nearly closed as he smiled, the light in them the same
as the light Kate had possessed.

Kate was interested in whatever the world around her
had to offer. And she felt kindness toward all living creatures, not only her husband and children, but aunts and
cousins, the elderly and the wayfarers, and most of all,
the animals, even the wild ones that ate the strawberries
and the beans.

Oh, she would say, the bunnies needed those beanstalks. It was probably a mama bunny with a whole nest
of little ones at home. Or the birdies needed a few strawberries to take home to their young.

Hester cut her fried egg with the edge of her fork,
swallowed, then softly laid the utensil beside her plate
as she reached for her glass of water. She sipped, keeping
her eyes lowered.

"Hester, pass the bread, please." Bappie stopped
talking to Noah long enough to ask this, her eyes wide
with a question in them.

Noah sensed Hester's misery immediately. Laying
down his fork, he looked directly at her. "Hester, if I'm
making you uncomfortable by being here, just say so. I'll
leave and not put you through this. I know it seems odd,
the way I show up so suddenly."

Hester looked at Noah, searching his face for sarcasm
or loftiness, the tones William used when speaking to her.

When she found only blue earnestness and kindness, it was her undoing. Quick tears welled in her dark eyes. Taking a deep breath, she calmed the beating of her heart.

"No, no. You're welcome here at our table."

Noah acknowledged her well-spoken words with a dip of his blond head.

"Thank you, Hester. I heard you are widowed. I knew your husband only slightly. He was older than I. That must have been very hard."

Hester nodded.

Bappie snorted, lifted an alarmingly high pile of pancake pieces into her mouth, chewed, swallowed, then sat back, lifting her fork for emphasis. "Well, Noah, don't think she mourned too long. Hester was married, yes, but not in the way most folks are. William King is a nephew of your stepmother, Annie King, before she became a Zug, when she married your father, Hans. So what does that tell you? There's a mean streak in that family, you mark my words. Just like a breed of horses that bites and kicks, you ain't ever gonna get it out of them, and that's right."

Noah's eyes widened, as what he had heard changed and softened his features. Hester looked up at that moment, but her eyes fell away quickly, unable to fathom the tenderness she witnessed in Noah's blue eyes.

Bappie completely failed to see all this. She was squeezing her eyes shut tightly and flapping her tongue in the most eccentric manner after scalding it viciously with her cup of boiling tea. "Shoo, this is hot!"

The spell was broken, but Noah was rewarded by a soft laugh from Hester, her perfect eyebrows lifting in

the way that he still remembered. If only he could somehow win her trust.

What was William like? Had she suffered? Why had
she left Berks County? He told himself he needed to take
one moment at a time, one day, one week. But he could
never leave her now. He had to find out more about her
life after she had disappeared, leaving Hans in a state of
wildness, a fury he could fully understand.

"Well," said Bappie, after cooling the afflicted
tongue in her water glass, "William wanted a whole
bunch of children, that's what it was. They never had
any. It was hard on his pride and rode on that Frances's
back like a growth."

"Bappie, it's all right. It's in the past. Noah, William
was very devout and held fast to the tiniest requirements
of the *Ordnung*. So I was not always obedient. The Lord
couldn't bless us because of my rebellion. The marriage
would have been good otherwise." Hester's voice was
soft and low, the words thickened by the constriction in
her throat.

Bappie reared back and placed her cup of tea on the
table with a bang, so that some of the scalding liquid
splashed over the side, wetting her fingers, which she
rubbed across her apron.

"See how she is? That's like saying the snake wouldn't
have bitten me if I would have stayed out of its way. She
blames herself, and that is simply not truth."

Noah knew there was not much he could say to this,
so he drank some of his tea, biding his time. He knew
Hester well enough to know her mind was not easily
changed. He also knew Bappie would be the help he

needed and wanted, if he could ever hope to tell Hester of the love he carried in his heart all these years.

But she had spoken to him and called him by his name.

"Well, Hester, I can't say. I wasn't there with you. Unfortunately, after you left I joined the French cavalry to fight with the Indians against the British. I was young, wild, rebellious far beyond anything you can imagine. Nothing in my life mattered much at all. Isaac stayed home on the farm. Annie's hands got so bad, Lissie had the whole work load, and Dat, well, he become demented, of sorts. He was never the same after you left. They say he is better, but shakes with the palsy. Isaac pretty much runs the whole farm now, with the younger boys' help."

An expression of raw longing passed over Hester's face. "I miss the farm in Berks County," she whispered.

Noah swallowed, feeling mist rising in his eyes. He had never loved her more completely than at this moment. How long would he need to wait?

The days after Noah was a guest for breakfast passed in a haze of remembering for Hester. Dreamy-eyed, she walked absently from room to room as the rain fell steadily on the house on Mulberry Street. It was a good rain, a cold rain that soaked into the earth and brought plenty of moisture to the energetic growth of the new spring plants. It fell relentlessly from scudding gray clouds and turned the small, meandering creeks into swollen, brown torrents of dangerous, swirling currents. The streets of Lancaster became avenues of mud, the dirt clinging to wide, steel-banded wheels and the hooves of the horses.

Bappie hitched up Silver in the pouring rain and drove the distance to the farm as determinedly as she did everything else. She wore her shawl and bonnet, sniffed righteously when Hester refused to accompany her, and returned with a severe headache, sodden clothes, and a bad temper. If this rain kept up another few days, the garden would be drowned, she informed Hester gruffly as she shed her clothes on the back stoop and ran barefoot through the kitchen and up the steps, her wet petticoat clinging to her narrow form. Like a stick, Hester thought, holding her hands to her mouth to stifle the giggle that rose in her throat.

"Start a fire!" Bappie bellowed down from the top of the stairs, followed by a tremendous sneeze, a quick intake of breath, and then another sneeze. "Ah, shoot! Must have run on to some goldenrod."

"Not in the spring," Hester called back.

"Start a fire."

"There is one."

"Well, poke it up. Get it going. I'm cold. I'm so cold my teeth are chattering."

Ah-hah! Hester was delighted. For the first time since Bappie had come into her life, she was coming down with a cold. At least Hester sincerely hoped she was. Bappie merely tolerated the herbal remedies that Hester was so deeply convinced of, no matter what she said.

Oh, Bappie pretended to support her, but now if she came down with a fever or a severe cough, Hester would have the opportunity she had so often wished for. She smiled impishly, rubbing her hands over the increasing flames as the rain splashed against the window panes and slid to the sash, ran down the clapboard siding and into the street, where it joined the brown puddles and piles of dirt turning into mud.

Bappie come down the stairs, blowing her nose into a large square handkerchief, warm brown socks on her feet and a clean shortgown pinned down the front, but no apron. Going to the hickory rocker, she yanked it as close to the stove as possible, lifted a small nine patch quilt from the basket, and covered her shoulders securely, clutching the two ends with her hands.

She shivered. Her feet flew off the floor as another sneeze racked her body. "Whew! It's freezing in here."

"Want some tea?"

"What kind? Not that stuff you make for sick people. Horsehair, or whatever it is."

Hester's laugh rang out loud and true, an honest laugh of happiness and humor, appreciating Bappie's unsuccessful attempt to hide her discomfort.

"You're getting sick, Bappie."

"Puh! You wish I would."

"How did you guess?"

"Well, you can forget it, Hester. I'm not going to swallow those foul-smelling tinctures and teas and rub that greasy stuff all over myself. I just got wet, that's all."

In the gloomy light of late afternoon, as she sat wrapped in the quilt, sunk into the depth of the rocking chair and glaring balefully out of the folds of the cover, Bappie looked like a trapped raccoon.

Once, Noah and Isaac had set a snare beside the Irish Creek in Berks County and caught a large, furious raccoon. When they found it, it was well on its way to chewing through the rope that held its two front feet and was glaring at them with brown eyes that closely resembled Bappie's. Hester had cried and made them let it go. She wasn't sure if Isaac ever forgave her.

Now Hester smiled. "I'll make you comfrey tea."

"I hate that stuff."

"How about fennel?"

"Worse."

"Spearmint?"

"Only with sugar."

So Hester brought Bappie a cup of tea and a slice of toasted bread. She crumbled some ham into a pot, added beans and water, and set the mixture on the back of the stove to simmer. As she swept the kitchen and dusted the cupboard, she was surprised to see that Bappie's head had fallen forward on the quilt. She was fast asleep, snoring lightly.

Hmm. That was strange. Bappie had never taken a nap as far as Hester could remember, not even on Sundays. She must be exhausted after that long, wet ride.

The kettle hummed quietly, the fire beneath it popping and crackling. The gloom in the kitchen deepened, so that Hester got up to light a few candles. She shivered. It felt just like the night William was thrown from his horse—that awful, rain-filled night, with the wind howling around the eaves, lifting loose wooden shakes with a mournful, whirring sound, sending shivers of foreboding up her spine.

She had prayed for William's safety. She wanted him to return out of harm's way, having carried out another selfless deed that aided in the growth and well-being of the fledgling Amish community. Her William, strong, dark, and highly esteemed by the ministers, an exacting and noble young man, if ever they saw one.

Why, then, had she rebelled so bitterly against him in her heart?

Oh, she didn't do it outwardly. She was absolutely the picture of humble submission, her hair sleek and controlled, her muslin prayer cap large, covering her ears and tied closely beneath her chain, her mouth kept in a demure, straight line. When she spoke, her voice was well modulated; she never spoke an unkind word to anyone.

For the most part, the Amish were kind and accepting of the Indian girl who was William's wife. There were some, of course, who shook their heads, compressing their lips and speaking quietly of William and Hester's inability to conceive. Well, of course they would have problems. *Der Herren saya* was withheld, likely, because Hester was an Indian. It wasn't the way God intended *vonn anbegin*. They were sure Isaac and Frances hadn't blessed the marriage. But then, that William was smooth. It was easy to tell he had a way with his mother. With her "wearing the pants" the way she did, what was Isaac to say? Not that he ever had very much to say to anyone, poor man.

Hester had desperately wanted William to live, to wake up from that agonizing sleep that hovered so close to death. She did not understand why, when his heart beat so strongly in his chest, he could not wake up.

The guilt of her rebellion held her by his bedside, keeping a tormented vigil, her whole being crying out to God in groanings that could not be uttered, as the *Heilig*

Schrift taught her. She felt the rain and the wind, the howling, the dangerous waters in her soul, a chastening so firm and exact from a God who was angry, taking William as a sign of his displeasure.

Wretched and regretting the day she was born, Hester lived in anguish those ten days that her William lay unable to wake from the battering of his head.

Had Kate lived and been there to hold her, to tell her those thoughts were not good, to bind her to the comfort of her great, soft dress by the sweet arms of her love, Hester would not have had to endure those days of self-inflicted torture. But Kate was dead. There was only Frances, William's mother, appearing like a tall, dark ghost, bearing displeasure and blame in the form of her own sorrow. Frances's keening reached to the rough-hewn beams of the bedroom and swirled around Hester's ears like the high, raucous cry of the crows that battered her senses.

Some semblance of peace had been restored by the quiet voice of her father-in-law, the hesitant Isaac, who spoke quiet words of assurance, urging her not to lay blame on herself. He, too, had lived many years with the pious Frances, having had no choice but obedience to her harsh will. He felt his subservience might bring *der saya*, recognizing his sacrifice for loving a woman who was so often held aloft by the sails of her own grandeur.

"*So gates. So iss es*," he had spoken softly, shaking his head as he urged Hester to accept the situation. His words to Hester had partially healed the raw wound of William's disapproval, but never entirely.

CHAPTER 4

IN HER HEART, HESTER RESOLVED NEVER TO LOVE AGAIN. SHE was not a good judge of what was true and kind in a man. And so, because of her past, she clung to Bappie, the strong and independent spinster.

She would never return to Berks County, the home of her heart. Her father, Hans, had made life unbearable after she finally realized the affection he felt for her was not what he wanted her to believe, but a kind of love that was unacceptable. She found it hard to fully forgive him, since she felt she had to leave the only home she had known.

Hester stood, stretched, and yawned. No use getting all dark and gloomy like the kitchen was. Lighting two more candles, she set one on the high shelf, filled a bowl with good, hot bean soup, and sat down at the table.

She lifted a spoonful, pursing her lips to blow on the steaming soup. In that moment, Bappie fell sideways in the rocking chair, mumbled, righted herself, and then looked at Hester, her dark eyes glistening with an unnatural light, her face almost as dark as Hester's. Lifting a hand, she clapped it weakly to her forehead and said that her head felt like one big potato.

Quickly, Hester rose. She felt the heat before her hand touched Bappie's head. "Bappie, you have a fever. A high one."

"It's from the stove. It's too hot sitting here with this quilt. I'll be all right. Just get me a drink of cold water."

Hester did. Bappie gulped it down thirstily, then promptly leaned forward and deposited it all over the clean oak floor. She groaned and held her head, apologizing gruffly before sagging against the back of the rocking chair, her eyes closing again.

"I'll clean the floor," she whispered, her pride carefully in place.

"I'll get it." Hot, soapy water and a clean rag were all Hester needed. It was a job she frequently did, having been to numerous bedsides of the sick.

She tried to persuade Bappie to go upstairs to bed, arguing that the rocking chair was no place for a person with a fever. But Bappie would have none of it. Stubbornly, she sat upright, refusing to take anything Hester suggested.

Bappie's coughing began around midnight, a tight, scratching sound that wouldn't stop, ejecting Hester from her bed as if someone had dumped it sideways. Holding the hem of her thick nightgown in one hand, the handle of the pewter candleholder in another, she made her way down the stairs to Bappie's side.

Again, she felt the heat before she touched her forehead. Instinctively, she knew Bappie was very sick. She had to get her out of this rocking chair and into a bed, but there was no possibility of maneuvering her up those narrow stairs.

Coughing furiously, Bappie waved her away. "Go back to bed." She simply dismissed Hester with a wandering wave of her thin hand.

Her mouth pinched in a determined line, Hester went to Bappie's cedar-lined wooden chest and began to remove the heavy sheep's-wool comforters. Stomping down the stairs, with the candle flame flickering, she wrestled Bappie's pillow, her large heavy nightgown, and more warm socks to the first floor.

She stretched out the blankets on the floor, put the pillow on the end away from the stove, then approached Bappie with one purpose. She would help her out of the quilt, her dress, and the rocking chair, and get her onto the floor where she could lie down. Then she would spoon some medicine down that stubborn throat.

Taking a firm grip on the quilt, she dragged it away from Bappie's shivering form, as she grabbed at it weakly. "I'm cold, Hester. Stop it. Stop taking my quilt."

"Get up." Hester's words were as solid and unmoving as a stone wall.

Bappie shook her head, then reached down for the quilt.

"Get up." Hester began removing the straight pins that held her dress closed as Bappie fought her hands.

"Stop it, Bappie, you're sick. This is not your choice this time."

When all the pins had been removed, Hester raked the dress off her thin shoulders and immediately lowered the good, heavy nightgown over her head. She stuck the now unresisting arms into the sleeves, like dressing a child, and buttoned it securely under her chin. She smiled to herself as she thought Bappie might have elevated her chin only a fraction, like an obedient youngster.

Well, that was just fine. Bappie had never experienced this side of Hester. She helped her to the bed she made on the floor, lowering her carefully, then covered her with the warm sheep's-wool comforter, adjusted the pillow, and slid a cool hand expertly across her brow. Hot! Bappie was so feverish. Somehow she must get this fever down.

Going down cellar, Hester opened the wooden plug on the small vinegar barrel, held a cup underneath till it was partially filled, and went back upstairs, closing the door softly behind her. She tore a clean portion of white muslin from the length in the lower cupboard drawer, soaked it with the cold vinegar, and approached Bappie. Lowering herself to her knees, she leaned forward, speaking quietly, "Listen, I'm going to apply vinegar compresses to your forehead and the tops of your feet. Just lie still, all right?"

"Phew! You're not putting anything anywhere. Go away."

In answer, Hester clamped a cool, vinegar rag on her forehead. Bappie promptly ripped it away with her thin fingers. Hester put it back, holding her head in a vise-like grip.

And so it went all night until the light of morning appeared, gray and ghostly, creating squares of color where night had erased them, Hester resisting Bappie's pride and ignorance of the dangers of a fever as high as hers.

Hester dozed in the rocking chair next to the fire, which was now only a few bright embers, and beside Bappie who had fallen into a restless sleep. Hester was suddenly awakened by the sound of a polite tapping on the front door. At first she thought it was only the wind, but when the tapping became more pronounced, she went to lift the cumbersome cast-iron latch.

"Yes?" she asked, peering through the gloom and a heavy, swirling fog that was cold, wet, and so thick she could see only a form.

"Is Bappie here?"

"She is, but she's indisposed at the moment."

"I would like to talk to her."

"Who is calling, may I ask?"

"Levi, Levi Buehler."

"Oh, yes. We borrowed your team of horses and wagon last fall."

"Yes." He seemed hesitant, unable to state his purpose, yet unable to leave. He shifted his weight uncomfortably, looking around as if searching for a clear direction somewhere in the dank, swirling fog.

"Can I be of any help?" Hester asked.

"Well, no. Bappie knows my wife well, or used to, before she got so bad. She's not doing so good. I thought maybe Bappie could come sit with her, talk with her, as she often has in the past."

"Bappie is very sick with a cough and fever."

"Oh, is that right? Well, then I'll go."

"There's nothing I can do?"

"No, no." Without another word, Levi turned, made his way down the steps, and disappeared into the vast gloom and fog.

Slowly, Hester closed the door, wincing as the dreaded coughing began in earnest. This was not good, Bappie being so sick in this wet, heavy weather. She had to get something down her throat, or things would only go from bad to worse.

Scabious would be first. This odd-looking plant, with thin, hairy leaves and a long, bare stem holding a blue flower in the time of blossoming, was the best for a cough or any disease of the throat and lungs. The clarified juice, given with plenty of liquid before an infection settled in, was without fail.

She woke Bappie, telling her she must swallow the liquid she would bring. If she refused, she might very well have permanent damage. She must take water and allow Hester to continue with the vinegar compresses, as well as an onion and sugar syrup.

Bappie glared. A grimace changed her features, but it seemed as if all the wind had gone out of her sails, leaving her compliant and rocking lethargically in the waters of her sickness.

For two days and nights neither one had very much rest. The cough persisted and the fever remained high. Finally, on the third day, after a poultice of cooked onions was applied to Bappie's chest, her fever broke; the cough became loose and rattling. Hester gave her a decoction of mallow, an herb that was good for pleurisy. A few hours later, Bappie rolled over, opened one eye, and asked if they had any oat cakes left. Then she pulled herself up, wobbled over to the rocking chair, squinted at the afternoon light, and whooshed out a long expulsion of air.

"I was pretty sick, huh?'

"You were."

"Guess I'm still here for a purpose. God spared me good and proper."

Hester smiled. "I'm glad he did, Bappie."

CHAPTER 5

NOAH RETURNED.

Bappie was still weak, but eating like a horse and drinking copious amounts of steaming spearmint tea laced with honey. Sometimes she added a generous dollop of homemade whiskey, grimaced, sneezed, coughed, and sputtered, but said they always had it down cellar at home. It was good for fevers.

Hester let Noah in through the back door, the brilliant spring sunshine blinding her for a moment. As always, he inquired about her well-being, quickly noticing the dark circles under her eyes, her pinched look of exhaustion.

Without looking into his face, she assured him she was fine as she led the way to the rocking chair beside the stove, where Bappie sat with a quilt around her knees. She held a cup of steaming tea in her hand, her hair a disheveled riot, freed from any moisture, comb, or cap. Her face was peaked with weakness; a certain exhaustion clouded her eyes.

Noah was quick to notice this. "You must have been sick, Barbara," was his way of greeting.

Flushing brightly, Bappie waved it away, his concern like an affront to her pride and determination. "I'm better. It wasn't anything. Bit of a cough."

"Well, I hope you had the doctor out."

"No, of course not. That's costly. I had Hester."

"Hester?"

"You know, all the weeds she bottles. She poured them down my throat. Against my will, mind you." Lifting one long, skinny, finger, she began to shake it, but the weakness in her arms made it droop, so she quickly curled it around her mug of tea.

Noah turned, a light of recognition slowly dawning. "Hester, you . . ." Speechless, he searched her face.

Hester turned away, hiding her face and refusing to meet his eyes.

"I remember the old Indian woman and the book she gave you. I had forgotten all of that."

"She treats a bunch of people. Especially down in the poor section of town. Not too many Amish yet. They're all afraid of witchcraft."

"Well, Barbara, I'm glad you're feeling better. Now that the rain has cleared, I'm ready to begin, if you're well enough to accompany me out there."

"Sure. I'll go. Let me get my shawl and bonnet."

Noah watched Hester's back, the lovely slope of her shoulders, the black apron tied snugly against her soft form, but he decided not to try to engage her further. She had opened the door and glanced at him only for a second before closing the door behind him. But she had let him in, which meant she must approve of Bappie's hiring him.

Elation waved its warmth through him as he thought of this. He still had a chance. No use pushing her or requiring more than she was ready to give. If she did not want to talk about her herbs or the use of them, perhaps she would another day. For there *would* be another day, and that was all that mattered.

Hester urged Bappie to remain at home, afraid the damp, spring air would be too much for her delicate lungs.

Noah pretended not to hear as Bappie told her it was all right to boss her around while she was sick, but now that she was well, if she wanted to ride out to the farm with Noah, she would.

"Put a scarf over your mouth."

"Yes, Mother." Without another word, Bappie pulled her bonnet over her scraggly hair, pinned the black wool shawl across her shoulders, and, minus the scarf, left with Noah in Dan Stoltzfus's top buggy to review the renovations at the small farmhouse.

Frustrated, Hester wandered through the house picking up vases, pitchers, pin cushions, and small dishes, and setting them back down. Her mind raced, full of bits and pieces of her past, including the torment that the book containing the herbal remedies of the Indian tribes of Pennsylvania had brought.

Well, she was not going to tell Noah that their stepmother, Annie, had threatened to burn the book. He didn't need to know all that. Besides the deep wound of failing William and his parents, she couldn't bear to go back to the time of Annie's hatred, which had been brought about by Hans's infatuation, or whatever was the right word to call it. Much better to leave that stone unturned. Noah did not have to know anything about her past from the moment she stepped into the woods in Berks County and traveled the vast distance across mountains, fields, creeks, and rivers. If he wouldn't have taken Annie's part, and then come to dislike her and want nothing to do with her, things might have been different.

Hester decided to do the washing. She'd take the covers off the comforters, wash them and the pillowcases, all the muslin clothes and rags, the dresses and socks, washing away all the sickness that had hung about the kitchen like a pall. Hester knew the scabious plant had again proved its worth. How amazing that God had provided for humans' diseases in the form of plants of the earth. Now, slowly, people were losing this knowledge.

Only the simple and the ignorant retained it. The red people, the Lenapes, the tribe of Indians whose blood ran in her veins. And yet she knew now that she would never return to them. She was steeped in the culture of the Amish. It was all she knew.

She recalled Noah standing in the warm spring air, the sun at his back. Her heart swelled. She put up a hand to cover it, ashamed of its beating. If she could still it, she wouldn't need to be reminded of how she felt. She could not give in, ever. It was too misleading, this thing called attraction, which tempted her to believe that it would grow into love and marriage. No, no, she couldn't bear a whole new set of deceptions.

She threw kindling underneath the brick oven that held the great copper kettle. She pumped as if her life depended on getting all the water she could to fill the buckets and then slosh them into the kettle before setting fire to the kindling.

A roaring fire took hold, and soon the water was steaming. Using a bucket, she filled the tin tubs with hot water, shaved a portion of the white lye soap into it, and then threw in the covers and pillowcases. Taking up the smooth, well-worn stick, she swirled the items in the steaming, soapy water until it had cooled enough so she could rub them up and down across the washboard.

The day was perfect, so she swung open the back door, then bent to wring the covers out, twisting them securely with her strong hands before pegging them onto the sturdy rope washline. Droplets of water were flung from the clean squares as the spring breezes caught and flapped them. Good! They'd be dry by sundown.

She paused on the back steps, inhaling the sweet fragrance of April. Here in town she detected the smell of mud and dirt and squalor from the poor section, but over top was the scent of hay, of new green lumber, of horses, and of whatever else makes up the people and houses that are a living town.

Hester longed to ride in an open buggy out away from the town, if only for a few hours. The garden in spring was like a tonic to her soul, but to live in the little house that Bappie wanted was an idea she could not imagine.

She'd wait and see what Noah accomplished. She had no plans of going out there while he was working. That would only be inviting trouble, the kind that required too much effort to control. Better to stay here and let Noah and Bappie figure things out.

She wondered where Walter and Emma Trout had gone. Their horse and carriage had been away from the shed already. She'd love to sit at their table the way they always used to do, but Emma was unhappy about their plans to move out to the farm. She had never been capable of displaying the good manners of her husband, so there was no use going over there only to be shoved out the door by her disapproval, her face red with it.

Hester ate a molasses cookie, then sat in the rocking chair by the fire. Just enough warmth radiated from the kitchen stove to make her eyelids droop, and sleep overcame her quickly. Her nights of tending to Bappie's needs had taken their toll.

The loud knocking on the door failed to waken her at first. Repeatedly, the sound entered her consciousness until she sat bolt upright, her eyes wide. She heard the sound again, more urgent than ever. Back door? No, definitely the front.

Hurriedly, she walked down the hallway, pulled open the oak plank door, and looked into the wild stare of the same visitor of a few days ago.

"Is Bappie here?"

"No, I'm sorry. She accompanied uh . . . our worker out to the farm."

"I need help. My wife, Martha, is gone. She's disappeared. I have searched every corner of our farm, and I thought perhaps Bappie could understand her ways better than I."

"How long since she's gone?"

"This morning. She was in her bed when I went to do the feeding."

"Have you asked anyone to help? The town constable? What about your hounds?"

"No, I haven't. I wasn't sure if our bishop would approve of having English people searching for my wife. Yes, I used the hounds to find her scent, but . . ."

Here Levi stopped and his voice choked. He lowered his eyes and shook his head, as if he meant to hide a thought that was too fearful to contemplate. Denial seemed best. "Bappie had a way with her."

"But I don't remember Bappie visiting Martha ever."

"She did. More than you know. She was very good for Martha's feeble mind."

"Is there anything I can do?"

"No."

Hester listened. She thought she may have heard the clatter of buggy wheels.

"Come in, Levi. I am going out the back door. I think Bappie may have returned."

Together they hurried through the house and out the back door to find Noah throwing the reins across the sweated horse's back. Bappie had already climbed off the buggy.

Levi pulled his hat down over his head to keep it securely in place. His eyes immediately sought Bappie's face.

"Levi Buehler."

"Hello, Bappie."

"What brings you?"

"My wife is gone missing."

Bappie stopped short, the color leaving her face, her dark eyes wide.

Noah remained in the background, tying the horse to the hitching post, although he glanced at Levi a few times.

"How long?" Bappie asked, curtly.

"This morning, early."

"Did you get help?"

"Not yet."

"Why not? You need to round up a bunch of men. She can't be very far. She's not strong enough."

Levi nodded.

Hester tried to convince Bappie to stay in the house, but she would not hear of it. Martha was her friend. She had been ill in body and mind for far too long, and lately without the aid of a doctor.

On her last visit, Martha had been disoriented. Some of her talking sounded more like a dream, as if she lived in a world of her own creation. Bappie felt caught. If she revealed her worries to Hester, she'd want to try healing through herbs. But the doctor was unable to diagnose her illness as her mind steadily weakened, along with her body.

Martha talked incessantly of the children she had lost as infants, one after another. Sometimes Bappie listened without trying to stop her. At other times she tried to have her think about something else by speaking forcefully, as if chastening a young child.

Martha railed at Levi from her twisted confinement, blaming him for the loss of the babies. Patiently, he absorbed her disgruntled cries like a sponge. He closed

his eyes in an effort to squeeze out the bitterness, telling himself she couldn't help it. He fed her, changed her
clothes and her bed, and did the washing and most of the
housework with the aid of a *maud*, a young Amish girl
hired out to help.

Some days she would cry and beg his forgiveness,
which he gladly granted, for she was his wife, and he
had promised to care for her in sickness and in health.

Bappie thought she must have a cancer growing in
her head, which was damaging her brain. She was an
innocent victim, beset by a disease, an *unschuldicha
mensch*. Bappie's loyalty stood firm. Let people say what
they would, she would not bend. She'd told Josiah sei
Esther that if she kept on judging poor Martha Buehler,
she'd end up worse than Martha if she didn't watch out,
which pretty much set Esther on the straight and narrow,
what with that Bappie Kinnich's flashing eyes and red
hair and her splattering of freckles.

It was a situation in the small Amish community of
Lancaster County that few people understood. The doctors called it nervous affections and treated her with different medicines that brought on sleep or stupors, but
she always resumed calling out to Levi, her husband.
Now she had disappeared.

"Well, here is a horse. Levi, I'll go with you now. Perhaps she's hiding, and when she hears my voice, she'll
come. Noah, you and Hester hitch up Silver. Go to the
blacksmith shop and spread the word. All able-bodied
men will be needed."

Noah nodded and turned to go to the small barn.
Levi sat in Dan Stoltzfus's buggy like a man in a dream,

weary of the tension, the demands placed on him, and now this. Bappie wasted no time in seating herself beside him, picking up the reins, and taking off at a fast trot.

Hester did not want to go. Her first instinct was to run into the house and hide upstairs where Noah could not find her. Let him go by himself. She didn't want to sit beside him in the buggy.

Noah threw the harness across Silver's back, then adjusted the straps quietly and efficiently. Silver's ears pricked forward, then slid back, ready to listen to any command Noah would require.

Hester stood, unsure of herself.

Noah looked up. "Ready?"

She shook her head. "I will need my shawl and bonnet."

"I'll wait."

CHAPTER 6

OVER AND OVER, WHILE SHE PULLED ON HER OUTER CLOTHES, she told herself that this was only Noah, the brother from her childhood. She yanked her hat forward, well past her face as a protection, a wall between her heart and this blond giant.

He helped her into the buggy, a gesture she was unprepared to accept. Amish men did not normally do that, so she became flustered and unsure. But when he stayed on her side of the buggy with his hand extended, she had no choice but to place hers into it, the mistake already done before she could retrieve it and place it beneath her black woolen shawl where it should have stayed in the first place.

Holding his hand, even lightly, was not something she could do ever again. The touch of his hand broke straight through the barrier of her strict resolve. They were at the blacksmith shop, and he had already climbed off the buggy before she could even begin to gather the fragments of the shell she had built around her heart.

Her hat helped. Like blinders on a horse, she could look straight ahead without seeing him. That was good. She had gotten her resolve firmly back in place again. She focused on Silver turning, leaving the blacksmith shop and taking the well-traveled road out of town.

Noah remained quiet, driving with one hand. Hester watched the tip of Silver's ears flicking back and forth. The muddy road stretched before them, and nothing else.

Suddenly, Silver shied away from a groundhog that had popped up from its hiding place, his haunches lowered as his hooves dug into the muck. When he took off running, a large portion of the mud flew out from under his hooves and landed on her face. Hester let out a bewildered sound before reaching up to brush away the offending dirt.

Noah brought Silver under control, then put the reins between his knees, turned, and placed a hand on each side of her hat. His fingers found the strings, untied them, and slid the hat off her head. "There, now maybe I can see your face."

He brought out a square men's handkerchief and wiped the splatters of dirt off her face, smiling directly into her eyes. "Better?"

He returned to his driving without waiting for an answer.

Hester was deeply ashamed and wildly elated as she nearly choked on her beating heart. She wanted to get down off the buggy, tell him she wasn't six years old, and stalk away. She also wanted him to wipe the mud off her face again and smile at her one more time. What she did do was say, "You used to do that a lot."

"Did I?"

"Yes, you did. Remember when I cut my face on that corn-husking knife?"

"It wasn't really your face, was it? More a cut just above your temple. Is there still a scar?"

Hester shrugged and looked sideways at him without meaning to. Certainly without wanting to.

But Noah was intent on his driving, watching for the almost hidden road that was Levi Buehler's lane. By all accounts, he had dismissed Hester in favor of remembering more important things, which was the matter at hand—finding Levi's wife Martha.

"Did you know Martha very well?"

Hester shook her head. "Not at all. I only learned about her when Bappie spoke of her, which wasn't often. I don't believe I've ever seen her."

"It's very sad. Levi has had his share of sorrow."

"Oh, he did. He took to coon hunting with a pack of hounds. He sold his cows. Says he makes more money raising the hounds."

Noah nodded.

They rode side by side, her shoulder jostling against his sturdy arm, both thinking their own thoughts about the sadness that was Levi Buehler's life, as well as Martha's slide into unreality, caused by something so mysterious even doctors could not begin to figure it out.

"Perhaps someday we'll understand diseases better. Or how our brains work," Noah said quietly.

They had to duck their heads to get past the low hanging branches that hung over Levi's drive. When they arrived at the buildings, Hester was surprised to see that things were in order—well-kept doghouses, repaired fences, the garden plowed, harrowed, and planted.

The baying of a dozen hounds brought Hester's hands to her ears, a pained expression on her face. Noah reined in the horse, then climbed off the buggy amid the milling of the dogs, each one wagging its tail, a friendly gesture in spite of the baying.

Levi and Bappie stood by the fence uncertainly, facing this unfortunate nightmare head on, as was Bappie's way.

More buggies clattered in, men throwing the reins, their faces grim.

Bappie stood with Levi as Hester turned to Noah. "I'll go inside, do what I can. I won't be much good searching with the men. It would be unseemly."

Noah's eyes were kind as he found hers.

"Of course. I'll go."

He walked off as she turned to enter the front porch. More women stepped down from the buggies that kept arriving.

Enos Troyer's wife, Mamie, was crying copiously. Great tears slid down her cheeks, lining the folds around her mouth. She held a fresh handkerchief at her nose, which had already swelled to a mammoth size.

"*Oh, mein Gott. Bitte dich, bitte dich,*" she moaned over and over, as she reached out to shake Hester's hand firmly. "*Vie bisht, meine liebchen?*" she choked, which brought forth a fresh burst of tears and a wobbly sob.

"I'm all right, Mamie. As well as we can be on such a sad occasion."

"*Oh, ya, ya. Gewisslich, gewisslich.*"

William's mother, Frances, was the next one to arrive, her tall, thin form propelled by her long feet moving her up to the porch without much of an effort, her walk a study in efficiency. "Mamie, Hester."

A curt nod, a slanted look, and she drew her shawl tightly about her scrawny form and pushed open the door that led to the kitchen. "You may as well come in. Chilly out there."

Bappie walked with Levi, calling and calling. When the men felt they had depleted that plan, they set the hounds on Martha's scent.

The men and dogs disappeared to the swollen waters of the Pequea Creek, where the animals ran constantly back and forth, milling about, whining, their wagging tails whipping with pent-up energy. But that was as far as they would go.

Men and boys from the town took up the search— English, Irish, Lutherans, Catholics, barkeepers, livery men—it made no difference this afternoon, each one having the same goal—to find Levi Buehler's wife.

Henry Esh's wife and daughter, Emma and Katie, brought a roast of beef. Frances brought a pound of butter and one of lard. Mamie, two dried apple pies. Ezra Zug's Elam brought three loaves of freshly baked bread and dried mulberry jam.

The hotel owner, the one who built that new structure on the corner of Queen Street, sent a pot of pork and beans and a pot of sauerkraut.

Evening fell. The sun lost its springtime splendor as it slid close to the farmland and woods of Lancaster

County, casting a shadowy gloom around Levi Buehler's buildings.

"*Ach, du yay,*" said Mamie. "*Ess vort dunkle.*"

Around the circle, the farmers and their wives traded glances discreetly. Each person was afraid to say what the curtain of evening would bring. Or if they said aloud what they were thinking, it might come to pass.

Bappie entered the kitchen, pale and shaken. She went to the hearth, held out her hands, then sank into the small armless rocking chair Hester had vacated. "It's just so hopeless. I can't imagine she could have gone far. I just can't."

"How was she in the past few weeks?" Mamie asked.

Bappie shook her head without speaking.

So they stood, this small knot of Amish women finding comfort in the fact that they were together. Dressed alike in almost every detail, their faces grim with the sense of awaiting disaster, they still believed there was reason to hope, as Mamie said.

The fire burned low, and the light in the windows faded from a sunset of orange and yellow to a dull twilight. Shadows climbed the log walls of Levi Buehler's house as the women moved about dully, speaking in quiet tones, as if any ordinary conversation would be unholy at a time when they all whispered prayers for Martha's deliverance.

When Levi's brother Amos's wife, Rachel, Martha's sister-in-law, came through the softly opened door, she shook hands solemnly, graciously, her eyes wet with unshed tears.

"Bappie." Rachel greeted her with emotion, knowing she had been the one who helped Martha most. Bappie bestowed kindness in her gruff, forthright manner, but she delivered kindness nevertheless. For Bappie took the time to be with her when others turned away or lost patience with her declining health.

As the night wore on, the women prepared a *schtick*, some simple, handheld food to tide the men over until the morning. Many of them went home to their wives, while a few lit blazing torches and continued the search. Now and then they entered the house exhausted, wet, and puzzled, drained by the tension of not knowing, of wondering that was almost too much to bear.

Late in the afternoon of the third day, almost two miles away from the Buehler homestead, a group of men from town came upon the body of Martha Buehler, carried downstream by the swollen current and caught in a wide eddy beneath the roots of a large sycamore tree. They were ordinary laborers who offered their assistance from the goodness of their hearts and because of their respect for the "black hats."

It was a miracle she had been found, the white of her nightgown the color of the sycamore's bark. God had shown those men where poor Martha had been taken.

When Levi Buehler met the men carrying the form of his ailing wife—when he knew there was no hope— he placed his hands on either side of her poor swollen face and lowered his head. Gentle tears rained down his unshaven cheeks and into his straggly beard.

Each one of the men turned away, their shoulders shaking. Then they laid her gently on the tender green grass where the April sun had warmed it after the rain. They stood, their hats in their work-roughened hands, their heads bowed, as they gave their respects to Levi Buehler and his deceased wife, may she rest in peace.

One of the Irish Catholics from the livery stable crossed himself, while the buggy driver rumpled his hat and whispered his prayer, "Lawd have muhcy." The Lutherans and the Mennonites, the Dunkards and the Baptists, all the groups were united as one in that moment.

Faced with the way of all humankind—the finality of death—every doctrine and disagreement fell away, leaving everyone in awe of mortality. Love sighed in the April afternoon, from the west breezes to the east, and the people stood united in sympathy and in death.

The women up at the house received the news in disbelief, then each stood alone in varying degrees of mourning. Mamie cried, giving herself up to great heaving sobs, with a good supply of white handkerchiefs to soak up her grief. For hadn't that poor Levi suffered enough? Why, the poor man already had an awful rough row to hoe, and now this.

Hester stood by the fireplace, her eyes wide with the tears that would not come easily, not here where the other women would see. She had not known Martha well, only hearing some things from Bappie. She had often longed for the chance to treat her with some of the herbs that may have helped, and yet, she had no way of knowing what caused Martha's mind to worsen. Some things were beyond knowing, and that was that.

In her black dress Hester was more beautiful than Noah had ever seen her. He tried hard to remain in the background and never glance in her direction. Yet he was always aware of exactly where she was.

Many visiting ministers came. Many relatives from Berks County traveled as swiftly as their wagons and horses could bring them. Some chose not to make the trek, sending their sympathy in letters that arrived a few weeks later.

Noah helped care for the horses with the other young men, although there were those who asked why that young man was even in attendance. Wasn't he a Zug from Berks County? Wasn't he the one who ran off and fought in the war? Well, he's dressed Amish enough, some said. Others watched him with suspicious eyes, saying he walked like a *grosfeelicha* soldier and shouldn't be here.

Dan Stoltzfus, his employer, said he was as good as any of the rest of them. "Let him alone. He's not hurting anyone." It was quite a speech for Dan, the man of few words, but it shut them up properly.

The sermon was preached by Ben Kauffman, a brother to Martha. Hester sat on the hard wooden bench, her feet on the fresh, yellow straw that had been spread on the barn floor, her head bowed as the loud chants of the minister settled in her heart.

Death was so real at a funeral. The end of time had come for the individual who lay before them. God had cut the golden thread of Martha's life, and now her bewildered suffering was over. No one would ever know what had happened that fateful evening. Naturally, everyone thought of suicide, the desolation of her poor brain finally taking its toll, but no one knew so no one judged. Let Levi have the benefit of the doubt. He had been so good to her through all the years of her declining health. And so it was not spoken of.

The minister preached *an gute hoffning*, the hope that her soul would be taken to heaven, while tall, gentle Levi bowed his head and nodded it slightly, the hope in his heart in tune with Ben Kauffman's.

The funeral reminded Hester of Kate's, a blur in her memory, the heartbreak almost too much to bear. Even then she had depended on Noah's companionship to get her through the days that followed.

It was Noah who carried the wood, dumping it carefully into the wood box without creating dust or unnecessary splinters on the floor. He spent hours at the chopping block, ensuring that he cut pieces of wood that were not too long or chunky to fit through the round lid of the cookstove.

They talked of Kate's death. At 14 years of age, Hester knew the finality, the separation of body and soul. She believed in heaven, in God and his son, Jesus Christ, who saved believers by his suffering on the cross. *Heilandes blut*, the Savior's blood. And so she could find snatches of joy in the midst of the dark fog of grief, thinking of Kate in heaven with the angels, and of Rebecca, the wee child who died of the dreaded lung fever.

Hester's faith had been like a fledgling sparrow, fed by Kate's love, her kind ways, and her care. After her death, Hester was forced to fly on her own. But now, sitting here in this sad service for Martha, she knew Noah had flown beside her in spirit, shielding her from the worst blows, the responsibilities that seemed too heavy.

He had protected her from Hans's worst days when he lay around the house awash in his grief, unable to accept the fact that the pillar of his life lay beneath the soil in that lonely graveyard. When Hans would shout in frustration at the little ones, Noah would speak kindly to them, getting down on the floor to build a tower of blocks until the children's tears turned into smiles of happiness.

Hester lifted her head and looked around at the benches filled with Amish, her kinfolk, all dressed in the black of mourning. Her people. She was accepted by them as she lived among them, although not all was perfect. There would always be those who were stingy in spirit, giving little and judging harshly, who would never fully approve of *sell Indian maedle*.

But with the Lenape, the people of her blood, would it be different? God-given natures were just that, given by God, and weren't folks much the same? They all aspired to goodness in their own way, some much less than others, but who was to judge but God alone.

A wave of gladness and contentment, an emotion she could hardly define, made her lower her head in gratitude and self-acceptance. Let it be so, Lord. Let me accept the kindness of these, my people. Let me accept myself for who I am. Guide me now that Noah is back in my life. If I need a shell to protect my heart, then help me to keep it in place.

Hester stayed behind at the house with those women of the community who were not relatives or close friends of Martha's. Friends and family joined the procession of carriages to the graveyard for the burial.

She helped with the meal, setting the table with apple butter, bread and butter, kraut, pickles, and cheese, while other women prepared the potatoes and gravy. There was the usual running commentary about the merits of making the smoothest gravy.

Old Suvilla Buehler shook her head, smiling in spite of herself, and beckoned to Hester with one crooked forefinger. "*Komm mol.*"

Quickly Hester obeyed, holding a fistful of knives and forks. Bending low, she looking into Suvilla's lined face, the wrinkles and deep crevices there speaking of years of labor, of sunshine and rain, drought, heat, winds, snow-storms, grief and joy, love and laughter, all etching the map of her countenance.

"Hester, tell me. Did you ever hear the story of the Tower of Babel?"

Hester nodded, smiling.

Suvilla inclined her head toward the black knot of women, all talking at once by the cookstove.

"Right there you have it. They're all talking at the same time, and no one knows what the others are saying."

Hester laughed and lightly smacked the old arm with an affectionate pat of understanding, leaving old Suvilla with the light of shared humor in her eyes, her shoulders shaking with her own cleverness. Hester continued placing the knives and forks on the table, then looked back at Suvilla who gave her a wide grin, the gaps in her teeth a sign of the wisdom of her years.

Hester went to stand at the cookstove, peering through the black-clad shoulders at the large kettle of bubbling broth.

"What do you think, Hester?" asked Butter John sei Lena, a tall, thin woman who held the wooden spoon and was, therefore, the boss.

"About what?"

"Do you mix the *schmutz* with the flour? I know the chicken gravy is best that way, and I thought beef was, too. But they say not. They say beef is too greasy. But how else will you get the rich flavor? Huh?"

Hester shrugged her shoulders. "I'm not good at making gravy. But when I do, I use the fat—chicken, beef, or pork."

Hannah Weaver broke in. "Well, I don't. My man is fat enough without feeding him all that grease. Gravy is good without it. Save the grease to make soap."

Mamie Troyer inserted this put-down with all the ease of an axe: "We don't all have fat men."

Hannah's comeback was just right. "Well, with a little *Schpeck*, my man can work in winter, unlike your Ezra, who looks like a fencepost, his teeth chattering as he sits by the fire on cold days."

From the rocking chair, old Suvilla cackled her glee. "That's right, appreciate your man. When he's gone, you'll miss him so *hesslich*."

Hannah shrugged her shoulders, and Mamie nodded, yes, yes. Lena went right ahead and mixed the beef *schmutz* with the flour and made the gravy her way, with all that rich flavor.

Hannah and Mamie tasted it carefully, pursing their lips and blowing on the large spoon they had filled—they were hungry; it was past the noon hour—then nodded their heads in approval. "*Sell is goot dunkas*," they both declared, handing the gravy-making prize to Lena, who lifted her chin and closed her eyes as she proudly accepted this verbal trophy.

"*Siss gute, gel?*"

Ah, yes, the gravy was good, they all agreed. This recipe should be written in a small book for future reference, they said, eliminating the need for constant bickering over the bubbling broth.

Hester knew the funeral meal would be delicious, the way all big kettles of food cooked by many different hands were.

The big pots of potatoes would be whipped by a few strong young men. Suddenly it dawned on Hester that Noah might offer. Wild-eyed, she glanced around the kitchen, looking to see if the women had put anyone to work. She hoped to watch him hang his hat on a hook and see his bright hair, knowing he was here at this service with her. Ashamed of her thoughts and afraid of the longing, for that is what it was, she turned away, straightening a corner of the snowy white tablecloth. No one could see her thoughts.

She heard him, then, speaking to the women, his voice low and well modulated, as befitted a funeral service.

She heard old Suvilla from the rocking chair. "*Na, do, veya iss deya fremma?*"

No one seemed to know who Noah was. An awkward silence settled over the kitchen, the women at the stove without the answer Suvilla wanted.

"Hester, who is the *unbekannta?*"

There was nothing to do, but turn, face the women, and tell them it was Noah Zug from Berks County.

Noah was busy sitting astride the bench, a large pot of steaming potatoes shielding his vision. Across from him, Levi's Jessie had taken up the second potato masher with his own large kettle of cooking potatoes.

Mamie Troyer stood, fists resting on her hips, a dish towel clutched in one hand, watching Noah with a light of curiosity that would only result in a loudly spoken question: "Noah Zug. Who is your father?"

"Hans. Hans Zug."

"That Hans. Married the second time to Annie Troyer?"

"Yes, that's right."

The cogs on the wheel of Mamie's quick thinking caught, and she blurted out in that resonant voice that carried so well: "Well then, you must know our Hester. Wasn't she *au-gnomma* by that Hans and his first wife? What was her name?"

"Catherine. Kate," Noah supplied.

"Yes, yes. That's right. So you are Hester's brother. Or something."

The "or something" brought quick smiles, but everyone saw how flushed Hester was, so they righted their smiles into deference, displaying the reverence that befitted this solemn occasion, and said no more.

Hannah added the butter and salt, while Mamie Troyer poured the hot milk from the dipper, viewing Noah's blond hair unashamedly and making a few lilting remarks. For here was a *schoena yunga*, and it didn't hurt to get a smile from him, or at least some recognition.

Noah smiled and lifted his head, but only for a quick second as he looked for Hester. She stood behind the cookstove, away from too many knowing eyes. She was watching Noah's wide shoulders, his white shirt too small and tugging at the seams, the too-short sleeves rolled up as he plied the potato masher. It looked like a toy in his hands.

"Oops. Ach, oops. Ooops!" Mamie Troyer stepped back as she dropped the dipper of hot milk. It splattered across the bench, over Noah's and Jessie's pant legs, eventually pooling on the oak boards in a white, steaming puddle.

Hester grabbed a clean cloth, lowered herself, and began mopping up the spilled milk as Mamie clutched her cheeks, apologizing profusely for such a *dummes*.

Hester swabbed the milk—luckily, the dipper had only been half-full—and assured Mamie there was plenty of milk, it would be all right.

As she got to her feet, Noah and Jessie sat back down. Noah met Hester's eyes. "Thank you Hester." Hester nodded, her smile for only a second, her eyes only for him. But they all saw. These women were sharp. They'd raised large families, were in fact still raising them.

A beautiful young widow, the long lost brother, but not a brother at all. They lifted their hands to their mouths, thinking, *Siss yusht*.

Old Suvilla, from her rocking chair, felt the familiar prick of goosebumps up her arms. She rocked a bit to hide her nodding. *Ya, dess gebt hochzich.*

In Gotteszeit. In Gotteszeit.

CHAPTER 7

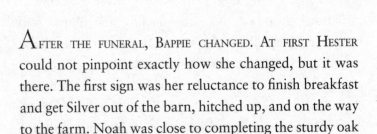

AFTER THE FUNERAL, BAPPIE CHANGED. AT FIRST HESTER could not pinpoint exactly how she changed, but it was there. The first sign was her reluctance to finish breakfast and get Silver out of the barn, hitched up, and on the way to the farm. Noah was close to completing the sturdy oak floor, and he had only a few directions from Bappie.

The house was even more desolate than Hester remembered. She could not see how Bappie could improve very much with only two weeks of Noah's labor, but she didn't say anything until the second week, when Bappie expressed no more enthusiasm or ideas.

They were finishing up a breakfast of fried mush and eggs, with coffee soup, a rare treat. There had been a few coffee beans left over at the funeral, which Bappie asked to take home, mincing no words and offering no apology. She wanted coffee soup for breakfast.

Hester liked it, remembering it as a treat at Christmas, when Doddy Zugs would bring coffee beans. Kate would brew coffee, while they all inhaled the rich, brown fragrance. She would add hot milk and brown sugar to the drink, and they would pour it over toasted bread, enjoying every spoonful of the soggy, sweet, coffee-flavored soup.

Bappie scraped her spoon carefully across the heavy dish, put it in her mouth to savor the last bit of soup, slid down in her chair, yawned, stretched her arms above her head, and whooshed out a breath of air.

Hester eyed her from the opposite end of the table. "Either you're not sleeping well, or you're plain lazy."

Quickly, Bappie sat up. "Oh, no, no. Nothing like that. Come, Hester. Let's get these dishes washed. We need to get out to the house. Noah's probably been there since sunup. Nope, nothing wrong with me, Hester. Why?"

"It just seems as if you've lost interest in fixing the house."

"What? Me? No, never." With that, Bappie jumped up and cleared the table so fast she was like a blur rushing past. She scalded herself with the hot water she dumped into the dishpan. She threw the harness over Silver's back with so much power it almost slid down the other side.

The faithful horse's sides were lathered with sweat by the time they reached the farm, goaded on by Bappie's burst of high spirits. She was like a whirlwind all day.

Noah pushed back his hat and watched her carrying boards. He sat down in the shade of the maple tree in front of the house, opened his lunch bucket, found the cheese, bread, and butter, and began to eat.

Here he was, on the tenth day of the twelve he would be hired, and he had had not one chance to talk to Hester, other than the usual banter or talking about the job, and with Bappie present every time. He thought perhaps she might not show up one of these days, the way she seemed to lack direction or energy after the funeral. But then, he guessed it was because she had lost a friend and she felt defeated.

The addition was well on its way. The walls were up and the rafters set. Now all it needed was the roof, which Bappie had bought from the lumberyard in town, saying they had no time to make their own.

Noah sat against the trunk of the tree, his gaze roaming to the garden where the fine pea stalks climbed up the low fence. He had watched Hester put in stakes close to the roots and then tie hemp rope from stake to stake. With all the good rains, they should have a bumper crop of peas to sell before the middle of June.

He could not imagine a woman being so enterprising, but then he thought, this is a new age, a new generation, and some things do not always stay the same. He was so proud of Hester making her own way. He wished she would talk about her healing with herbs, but she never once mentioned the subject.

He finished the molasses cake, tipped the crockery jug of water, and swallowed gratefully. The sun was overhead, already showing the strength of the sizzling days of July and August.

He was surprised to see Hester walking in his direction, carrying the two-handled lunch basket they filled every day. Her pace slowed as she came near, placing her feet timidly, as if she was afraid she would waken him. Surely she would not sit beside him on the grass beneath this tree. But that is exactly what she did. Settling herself comfortably about a foot away, she lifted the lid of the basket and extracted a slice of bread. She opened a brown paper of cold, cooked bacon, laid a few slices on one side, folded the bread and took a small bite. Still, she said nothing.

He could hear the dull hammering of his heart, a pounding in his ears. His breathing quickened; he hoped she would remain unaware. He prayed for Bappie to stay busy, to stay away.

Hester broke the silence abruptly. "Is Hans . . . are Annie and Hans still alive?"

Noah's heart fluttered, then sank, when he realized that was all she wanted from him.

"Yes, as far as I know. I think the people in Berks County know I am here in the Lancaster settlement."

Hester nodded. "You mean, if they, if one of them would pass away, they would let you know?"

"Yes."

"Are they well? Hans and Annie?"

"I believe they are."

She ate in silence then. "Do you understand why I left?"

His throat constricted with unexpected emotion, closing off the words he wanted to speak. He shook his head from side to side.

"If I tell you, will keep it quiet?"

He nodded, the constriction worsening.

"It was Hans. His love for me should have gone to Annie. She hated me for that reason."

Still he could not speak.

"It was my own fault."

Without thinking, and feeling only rage that pushed back any obstruction in his throat, Noah burst out, "What are you talking about? None of that was your fault."

Hester dropped her head. She bowed her long graceful neck in humility and lowered her eyelids. The profile of her face was unbearably sad.

"Hester, look at me."

Her only answer was a shake of her head.

"You can't mean what you just said."

"But I do."

Suddenly, she raised her head to face him squarely, her chest heaving with the force of her words, her eyes flashing the dark fire of the intensity she felt. "Noah, you don't know what a sinner I have been. I was accosted by my own husband's brother in the cellar at Christmastime. And I was rebellious to William, as well. So how could I blame my life and its trials on others, on men? Things like this occur so often, and, Noah, it is all my own fault. William said so."

Noah took a deep breath to steady himself. He realized his hands were shaking, jarring the lid of his lunch bucket.

"Hester, you must stop thinking this. It is a lie. God gave you your beauty. These . . . those . . . the men, my own father . . ." His voice faded away as the words fell over each other, a stone in his chest replacing the warmth of his beating heart.

Now her hands went up to cover her face as she began to cry, unable to control the years of pent-up fear and self-loathing.

Noah's longing to take her in his arms was so strong that he got to his feet in one swift upward movement and in two long strides, separated himself from Hester. Only now did he begin to grasp the enormity of his undertaking. To win her, to have her, was not possible at this time—and maybe never—with her mind so set on William's accusation, his blaming her.

Of course, Bappie chose to make her appearance just then, waving and striding quickly in their direction. "Where's the basket? I'm hungry. Have you eaten already, Noah? No use rushing off. Stay sitting. Let's have a picnic here under the lovely tree."

Noah smiled and said thanks, but reminded her that he had only one more day, and it would take the rest of the afternoon to finish the one side of the roof. Hester gathered herself together as best she could, partially hiding her face by looking at the fast-growing pea stalks.

Bappie plopped down, opened the lunch basket, wrinkled her nose, and said something in there smelled odd. What had Hester packed?

Hester sniffed, got to her feet, and said if she didn't like what was in that basket, why then she could pack it herself.

Bappie lifted her chin and watched Hester stalk off in one direction and Noah in another. It was too bad, she thought, the way those two simply couldn't hit it off. But then, often that was the way. She'd heard Mamie Troyer talking to Lydia Esh about how *au-gnomma* children often had bad natures, and it didn't work out. Not that Hester wasn't good. You just had to be careful about these things.

That Noah was a looker, though. Made you wonder, the way he seemed to avoid talking to Hester. Bappie guessed they simply didn't like each other too good. Too bad, because they made quite a pair. Well, no romance in the air where those two were concerned, so that was that.

She shrugged her shoulders, bit off a piece of over-cooked bacon, rolled a hard-boiled egg to remove the shell, added a pinch of salt, and popped half of it into her mouth. She chewed contentedly, watched the crows flapping overhead, and thought about living here with Hester. Much better than in town. So much better.

The sun was too hot for the month of May, she observed. These sorry little buds on the trees did nothing to keep the striking light of the sun off her face. Bappie reached for the water jug, wiped her forehead, and thought a storm was likely brewing with this extraordinary heat from the new spring sunshine.

Hester stopped drilling the floorboards, sat back, and looked out the door. Sweat trickled down the middle of her back. Her dress felt too snug; her face was flushed with the heat. It seemed like August when the corn and tomatoes were ripe.

One side of the roof was finished, throwing shadowed light across the yellow plank floor. The opposite side offered only strips of shade, so the heat from the sun was finding its way between the laths Noah had nailed across the rafters.

Hester returned to drilling holes where the wooden pegs would be pounded. This would be a good, solid oak floor that would never wear through. Around and around, her one arm swung the drill, while her other arm pushed down on its top. Oak lumber was hard, the best choice for a floor, but in the heat of this day, Hester was wearing out and her patience was growing thin. It didn't help that the conversation with Noah had gone wrong, veering off into a disagreement.

She had meant to alert him of her inability to be a wife. He had to know. He had to understand that she could not possibly return to her Berks County home.

She could never forgive Hans. That was not possible. She hated him with hatred that ran in her blood. She felt the agonized cries of the Lenape, pushed from their homes and denied their birthright by the white people who moved into Pennsylvania like a swarm of locusts. Like Pharaoh's plague in the Bible. *Diese hoyschrecken.* These grasshoppers.

She know the hatred was wrong. It was so wrong to remember Hans's behavior and to think of Annie's cruelty. It had become much easier to shift the blame onto herself and to set Hans and Annie free from judgment.

Only sometimes on the darkest nights, the tears would seep from her eyes and pool in her ears as she lay staring at the underside of the ceiling, the hewn logs rough and dark, the way her heart felt when she remembered. Yet she longed to return, to feel the safety of the familiar pastures, gardens, and roads of her childhood, to soak up the security of the innocence that was no longer hers.

Yes, God had given her this beauty, but to what end? A curse was all it was, the way the men in her life behaved without being respectful. At least some of them.

If only she had learned to behave in a more careful manner. She had been too free with her smiles, the flash of her dark eyes, allowing herself to enjoy William's company and Johnny's attention.

She had loved Hans and adored him as a child, accompanying him on his horseshoeing forays, becoming the delight of the Amish settlement. Large, swarthy, dark-haired Hans and his astoundingly beautiful little Indian daughter, who handed him his nails and his tools and was never afraid of the spirited horses or the hooves that could strike out with the speed of lightning.

Kate had always been free with her affections, smiling easily, placing a warm hand like a crown of approval on Hester's dark head, softly singing German hymns that Hester absorbed like melting sugar.

She sang boisterously, sometimes, too, her blue eyes laughing, her head nodding in time to the silly words, but only when Hans was safely out of hearing distance.

> Her hair is so *schtrubbly* in the wind
> Her eyes so big and brown,
> I often see her on the road,
> When I drive into town.

At the washtub, mostly, she would sing the songs of her youth, when Hans was tall and dark and she was the slim, blue-eyed *schtrubblich maedle*.

The hatred she felt for Hans as she grew older was a canker sore in her soul. If she gave in to it, eventually the canker would burst, poisoning her with its infection and spreading through her whole being with its dark and sinister promise and pushing out God's healing love.

It wasn't possible to harbor hatred and healing love at the same time. They could not coexist. But on some dark nights, fear and remembering would come back. She determined it was far better to blame herself. She wanted Noah to know this, although she wasn't exactly sure why it was important. Well, now he knew. He could disagree if he wanted, but she would never let her guard down.

Late in the afternoon, the water jugs were empty and the sun's heat was like a wet blanket. The air was moist and much too hot after the cold of winter and the bone-chilling breezes of April that had bent the old brown goldenrod and the stubbles of wheat and had matted the grasses in the fields.

Bappie threw herself down along the north side of the house where the damp earth held cool moisture and cold earthworms dug along the base of it. She pulled her skirts up to mid-calf, then untied her sturdy black shoes and kicked them off, each one landing with a thunk in the new grass. She rolled down her heavy socks, then leaned forward and tugged on the toes, slid the itchy garments over her heels, and flung them after the shoes.

She sat back against the log walls, dug her heels into the cool, damp earth, and wiggled each toe, liberating them from the heat of the socks. She closed her eyes, took a deep breath, and let the tension roll off her shoulders and down her back.

The only sound was Noah's steady hammering. She had never seen anyone slap on wooden shingles like that. *An begaubta mensch*, for sure.

Perhaps he'd be like his father, Hans. But then, they said Hans didn't become prosperous till he married

Annie. She was the one that set the gunpowder under Hans's britches and managed like a man. She knew when the moon turned in July and you dug thistles, when to plant corn, which horse could easily work all day and which one should be sold. That's what they said.

Bappie was not the first one to notice the cloud in the northwest. She was sitting in the moist shade, so the fading yellow light went unnoticed by her as she thought about that Annie Troyer wearing the trousers the way she did.

Noah stopped and looked off to where the line of trees met the flat grassland of the meadow. A fast moving line of clouds had already swallowed the sun. Without its heat, the air turned brassy, and a yellow pallor fell over the surrounding fields.

Hester straightened, laid the drill by the wall, rubbed her back, and went to the door, wondering where the light had gone. She lifted her head and sniffed the air. Not a whisper of a breeze. The new leaves on the trees hung as still as lace doilies on a shelf, their pattern constant.

She did not like the brassy atmosphere. There was a storm brewing—ominous, a black panther of the sky stalking the earth below, ready to unleash its power of sizzling lightning and great earsplitting crashes of thunder. This would be a big one.

Her eyes went to the garden and the steady green growth of the pea vines. Healthy tendrils reached toward the top string that Hester had stretched between the wooden stakes. Ah, surely God would spare them. Hard, knife-like sheets of rain, strong winds, and the heavens crashing and rumbling about them would be fearsome, but none of that would have the power to damage like the dreaded hail and its large balls of ice. She took another deep breath. She could smell the rain, the moisture that would fall from that black, boiling bank of clouds.

Bappie came around the corner of the house, her eyes dark, every freckle visible, the blanching of her skin revealing the depth of her fear. "Storm coming, huh?"

"Looks like it."

"Is it bad?"

Hester shrugged. She lifted her eyes to the horizon, watching.

Bappie watched Hester's quiet face. "How bad?" she repeated.

"It's a good-sized storm."

Hester had been born with the uncanny ability to sense the coming of different changes in the weather, an Indian skill and knowledge that had been a part of her since birth. She had no fear of any of nature's forces. She was calm and unhurried in the face of storms and winds.

Noah scrambled off the roof, threw his hat on the ground, and ran his hands through his blond hair, turned dark with the sweat of the day's heat. "Think we should head back?"

Bappie searched Hester's face for reassurance, anything. She swallowed the fear rising in her throat, her breath coming in jagged puffs.

"I wouldn't." Hester spoke quietly, nodding her head toward the black cloud. Noah looked at her dark eyes that were intent, curious, eager. Without a trace of fear. "It's coming fast."

"What about the garden?" Bappie asked, her voice quivering.

In answer, Hester shrugged slightly, her eyes never leaving the clouds.

They stood in front of the house, the small log hut with the unfinished addition, the new shingles a lighter shade than the dark, warped ones on the original roof. The small front porch would give them a bit of shelter when the storm hit, but for now, it was comfortable to stand in the new grass surrounding the house, feeling the air change to a more seasonable temperature as the storm approached.

Noah, looking around, decided to push the buggy into the small barn with Silver, then latch the door securely, as he had always been taught.

The first rumble could soon be heard, even before any lightning was visible, which was unusual. A prickle of apprehension raised the hair on Noah's arms. He crossed them across his chest and absently drew a palm across his forearm. "Let's go inside."

Bappie's teeth were chattering as she sat on the edge of the porch to put on her socks, now a welcome warmth. Noah watched her, seeing that she hated a storm. A quick stab of sympathy softened his eyes, and the lines around his mouth softened, as he thought about how alone she was and how responsible, without a husband, father, or mother to care for her.

Hester lifted her arm, pointing a finger in the direction of the storm. Small, orange streaks, like trailing threads, appeared as a fringe on the fast-moving clouds. As they watched, the streaks' size and color changed until they appeared as white, hot, jagged streaks of lightning, powerful and breathtaking in their fury.

Ahead of the boiling mass of clouds, the blue of the sky had changed to a dirty yellow, as if the hissing clouds had spewed their tepid breath before the onslaught they contained.

Still, the new leaves hung unmoving; not a blade of grass whispered. A large brown spider scuttled across the bare spots, disappearing beneath a wall of grass. In the barn, Silver whinnied, a high, lonely sound, as if the static in the air reminded him that he was in a solitary pen, deep in the surrounding walls of the barn.

"He wants out. He's afraid," Bappie said, quite unexpectedly.

Noah shook his head. "He's better off in the barn."

The first sign that the storm had come closer was a soft rustling of the new leaves, a subtle rearranging of their pattern. The small grasses waved, disturbed by an undercurrent of the winds that were about to sweep through.

Noah rubbed his palms across his forearms as the wind increased, lifting the wet hair from his moist brow. Hester reached behind her back, found the wide, white strings of her muslin cap, and tied them securely beneath her chin.

Bappie whimpered like a child as she watched the heavy pea crop begin to shiver, the tender shoots waving slowly like tiny, slim dancers moving to invisible instruments, the prelude to the approaching storm.

CHAPTER 8

As the wind increased, Noah dashed beneath the maple tree to gather up the lunch basket and water jugs. He laid the ladder flat on the ground right next to the wall, picked up his hat, and pitched it through the door.

The last row of shingles hummed, as if an unseen hand was rifling through them. In a matter of seconds, the wind rose, a wall of power that ripped the tender new leaves off the purple stems and sent them whirling through the thick yellow atmosphere, followed by dead growth from all trees and bushes. Grasses were flattened in a minute. The garden became a mass of undulating movements, the plants twisted and tortured by the power of the storm.

When Hester shouted and pointed, Noah reached her side, then followed the direction of her finger. Where the clouds were darkest, in the middle of the restless, roiling mass, a lashing tail appeared, a dark, terrible tunnel of fury, whipping as if building its strength for the moment it would hit the soft green earth beneath it.

Bappie screamed a sound of rich terror as gigantic hailstones hit the earth in front of them. As one, they turned and raced for the safety of the four log walls. Noah slammed the door, breathing hard, but Hester yanked it open, yelling that being watchful was what they needed to do. She stood at the door, her hands bracing her body, as the wind roared and hailstones sharp as knives whirled onto the porch floor.

The roars and moans reached a shrieking crescendo. Bappie's screams of terror were lost among the intensity of the wind.

Suddenly, Hester turned, flattened herself against the wall of the house, and cried out for Noah and Bappie to do the same. Like three fenceposts, they lay prone against the sturdy log walls. Hester stopped her ears with her fingers, the pressure in her head almost unbearable. Bappie no longer screamed, and if she made any sound at all, it was lost in the roaring and gnashing that were the wind and hail, the torrents of water and ice.

All they knew, then, was a ripping, tearing sound, as if a giant piece of fabric had been torn in two. And then the hail—and cold, wet pain—hit their bodies. Noah yelled as a bough of the maple tree hung on the log wall where the roof had been, toppled, and fell on top of him, the weight of it smashing into his back and taking his breath away.

As he fought to regain it, out of the corner of his eye he saw the opposite wall shudder, then fold out and crumble, the logs falling haphazardly. Dust, thick and brown, was instantly soothed by a biblical deluge from the moaning, roaring sky.

Hester pressed her body to the ground, praying the wall would hold. If the logs came dislodged and rolled, they'd be killed, if even one fell on top of them. She had never known such fear, didn't know it existed. She pressed her face into the cracks of the lowest log and breathed in the splinters and sawdust, dirt and dust of years of neglect in this little old hut they meant to call their home.

She was aware of being soaked through, of being cold and shivering, of being accosted by sharp blades of freezing rain, by the clamoring wind, and by a high keening sound like the howling of a thousand demons left helpless in the storm's wake. Her tears were unde-tected as her soul cried out for deliverance. She knew only that the grace of God alone could save them all from this untamable fury. She was as helpless as the day she was born.

A great ripping, tearing sound rose higher than the wind. She heard the splintering of some object she could not identify. Sobs rose in her throat, along with the knowledge that they would all surely die.

A great sadness for what might have been welled up in Hester. But suddenly she throbbed with anger at the rip-roaring elements that had turned her into this dirty, wet, sniveling heap. She was not going to die. If a log fell off this wall, the wind could just place it beside them. A cry of deliverance emerged from her throat as she felt, rather than heard, an easing of the shrieking wind. The worst must be over. But better to stay here than risk the deceiving lull in the wind.

Rain still pounded against their bodies. The log wall shivered but held. The wind moaned around it; the clouds boiled like black porridge over their heads. Piles of ice were scattered across the floor of the hut, banked against the tree trunks, and whooshed into the air and flung out of sight by the power of the gale. And yet Hester knew the worst was past. She could sense the storm's weakening, its defeat.

Noah was the first to sit up, painfully, his shirt soaked with blood where the branch had jammed into the muscle of his back. The dark reddish color turned pink where the rain and hail had lashed at the cut. He winced, then put his head in his hands to steady himself as the world tilted and turned black.

Bappie had fainted dead away. Hester leaned over to place a hand on her narrow, sodden back. The heartbeat was there, strong and sure, but she slept on.

Hester rolled over and got to her feet. Quickly, she surveyed this new world. Only two walls of the hut remained standing. The maple tree was twisted off and flung across the garden, a sentry fallen in its prime.

Her throat tightened. The roof was gone. It had simply disappeared, the new one and the old one, like a grandfather and a newborn grandson joining hands and melting into the horizon. The barn was a pile of debris, everything misplaced, the buggy somewhere inside.

Silver. The dread of discovering Bappie's faithful horse injured or dead made her nauseous. Oh, surely not.

She turned to Noah. She was shocked to see his bent head. Dirt, wet, puddles of filthy water, splinters of wood, sodden leaves and dead grasses, branches—destruction was everywhere.

She nudged Bappie, then tried to speak, but only croaked. She cleared her throat, turned to Noah, and reached out to touch his head. "Noah?"

He lifted his head, the pupils of his blue eyes black with pain and shock, his face the color of new muslin.

"Are you hurt?"

"My back." He spoke the words around a block of pain. The effort to speak took his full concentration.

"Can you move?"

In answer, and with heroic effort, he leaned forward, wincing. The muscles in his face worked, but he got to his knees and turned.

Hester remained calm, having seen so much suffering when she treated the poor in the low section of town. The soaked shirt that clung to his pooled blood was not too alarming. So she said nothing at first, quietly bending over Noah's shoulder. Then she asked him to move forward a bit so she could see.

He complied, but sank to the floor, his legs folding beneath him as he fought waves of darkness.

His shirt was torn and mangled, so when Hester lifted it away, she was not surprised to see the massive lacerations. The extent of his wound was beyond her knowledge. She bit her lower lip to extinguish the gasp that rose in her throat.

Bappie moved, whimpering.

Hester straightened and looked around. Noah had lost too much blood and was still losing it, so that made it impossible to move him.

She shouted for Bappie to wake up, nudging her with a wet shoe. "Bappie. Wake up. Come on. Up."

She groaned, opened one eye, rolled over, and covered her face with her hands. "Oh, dear Lord. Dear Lord. What have we done to deserve this, your *tzorn*?"

"Bappie, listen, Noah is hurt, bad."

"Why?" Still dazed and uncomprehending, Bappie lay on her back, as wet and bedraggled as a drowned rat.

And worth about as much, Hester thought. Well, it was off to Levi Buehler's, the closest farm. She'd have to walk. She told Noah to stay there and not to move, ignored Bappie, and headed in Levi's direction, stepping over destruction, trying not to think of Silver somewhere in that heap of lumber that used to be a barn.

When it became evident that the power of the twisting, grinding wind had been a narrow swath, she broke into a steady lope, her feet settling easily on the wet ground, the only hindrance her heavy, sodden skirts that clung to her legs like cold, wet flaps of leather.

Everywhere branches were torn off trees, and broken limbs lay on the ground, leaving yellow wounds in the steady coat of bark that protected the tree. Some of the older, weakened trees were toppled, pulling down more branches of healthy trees, but nowhere was the destruction as bad as at Bappie's small place, the old hut, the small barn, and few surrounding acres.

She slowed and came to a stop, her breathing in short rapid jerks, when she saw an approaching figure. Tall and thin and surrounded by his coonhounds, Levi Buehler was on his way to see how they had fared during the storm.

His hat was floppy, the brim coming loose from its base. One side was higher than the other, giving him the appearance of someone rather pitiful, a poor person needing help. His shirt was clean but old, torn in places and patched, or patched on top of a patch.

His eyes were kind, the laugh lines called crow's feet deep and pronounced from squinting in sunlight, or straining to see through the dark nights when he went coon hunting. His beard was gray and thin, like an afterthought of wispy hair.

"Hester!" He flung up a large, knobby hand, like a fly swatter, a long flat growth on the end of a thin handle.

"Levi."

"I was on my way to make sure you're all right out there. Never saw clouds like that. Figure you had hail."

Hester gave a short, rueful laugh. "A lot more than hail. Listen, Levi, Noah Zug was working on Bappie's roof, and he was hurt. We need a doctor. Can you help us, please?"

Levi had already turned, his hounds like an appendage of himself, and was gone, calling, "Be there as soon as I can."

The desolation was hard to describe. Bappie's small holdings were flattened except for the south and west walls of the hut, the barn was in splinters, the garden ravaged, the crops all lost, and the buggy buried somewhere. Faithful Silver lay beneath the capsized walls, a mound of beautiful silver horseflesh with no life at all. He had gaping wounds on his head and neck; one leg was almost severed, impaled by the beam from the door.

Bappie said it was just as well that he died, because they'd have had to shoot him with that busted leg. She didn't cry, only sniffed and blew her nose, blinked rapidly, lifted her head, and said, "That's how it goes. You never know."

Noah was soon stitched together, bandaged, and taken back to Dan Stoltzfus's, where he lived. The kindly doctor, George Norton, did his work efficiently, giving Noah a healthy dose of whiskey to help with the pain. The flying limb had cut his back so that it looked like great raw chunks.

Only Levi Buehler, Bappie, and Hester remained in the aftermath of the storm. The countryside looked washed clean, in spite of the ruined buildings. The sky rippled with shades of rose, lavender, deep orange, and yellow. The sun had emerged from still grumbling clouds that were neither gray nor white, like dirty sheep's wool before shearing.

Bappie bit her lip as she lifted shreds of ruined pea vines. She kicked the sodden growth, gouged a hole in the mud with the toe of her shoe, and looked at Hester. "You know I have nothing left."

"You have your things. Your furniture and dishes."

"I can't start another garden. I have no money to rebuild. I don't know what I'm going to do."

Levi Buehler stuck his hands in his pockets, leaned back, and eyed Bappie with one eye. The other one was covered by the floppy hat brim. "The church will help. When the men hear about this, they'll be out."

"Who's going to pay for the lumber, Levi?"

"Well, maybe I can."

"With what? Your skinny hounds?"

Levi lifted his face and laughed, a great sound of merriment that he had not made for too long. The wispy gray hairs on his chin waggled, his yellow teeth were in full view like even ears of corn, as he kept up the sound that made even Bappie smile.

"Ach, Bappie, I forgot."

"You forgot what?"

Levi shook his head.

Levi drove them home to Lancaster. Bappie jumped unceremoniously off the buggy, never said a word of appreciation, and disappeared through the back door, a thin stick of a woman, dirty and wet, but efficiently containing all her pride and well-being.

Hester thanked Levi, then turned to follow Bappie. She had already yanked the tub off the wall and was filling the kettle with cold water from the pump, as she barked at Hester to get some kindling made, they needed to wash.

They didn't eat anything, only drank warming cups of tea, holding the heavy mugs in both hands, each one appreciating the warmth, the roof, and the walls that enclosed them.

Walter Trout popped in unannounced with news of storm damage throughout the town. He took the news of Bappie's ruined farm with great soft sighs of sympathy, his swollen fingers entwined over his massive stomach. He pursed his lips and rolled his eyes, dipped his head, and grimaced as they told their story.

Emma stayed home and nursed her solid grudge. She told Walter he could prance over there and make amends, but she wasn't going to. But when she was told of their loss, she threw her hands in the air and cried, "*Ach, du lieva! Du yay! Die arme mäed!*"

She covered her fresh *Ob'l Dunkes Kucha* with a white tea towel and told the boys to stay out of mischief, that Vernon and Richard, the dear ones she'd taken in from the street. They could be a handful, they could.

The scent of the warm applesauce cake followed her, the short, wide woman who rocked from side to side when she walked, the pleated white housecap like a large blossom on top of her head, her beady dark eyes like boiled raisins.

She cried, "*Voss hott Gott getan? Meine arme liebchen!*" She patted their shoulders and kissed their cheeks and said, "No rent, no rent, just stay here with me and Walter," then had to sit down and lay a hand over her heart to still it, to slow it down. "More than a person can imagine. More than these *meine liebchen* can take."

But Walter said the Lord does not give us more than he gives us strength to bear, and he most assuredly had a plan somewhere. Emma nodded so hard her housecap slid forward over one eyebrow, then settled up farther on one side than the other.

Bappie ate three squares of applesauce cake and made another pot of tea, nodding her head in agreement with Walter's words of encouragement. Her eyes had narrowed though, and a new light glinted in them, as if the brown irises had been polished like silver with a damp cloth.

Hester saw this, she knew Bappie so well. Something was churning inside that mind like the dasher on the butter churn—*kalunka, spaloosh*. When she saw Bappie concentrating and chewing her nails, her eyes still holding the same gleam, she became concerned.

They ushered their effusive neighbors out the door with many cries of "*Gute Nacht. Denke, denke.*" Then they went to bed, each to her own room, sleepless, sighing long into the night as they relived the nightmarish event of the day. Never had they seen anything like it.

The following morning Bappie dressed in her Sunday clothes, her black cape and apron, the best muslin cap, and only a sliver of hair combed into submission visible. She told Hester she was going to borrow Walter and Emma's horse and carriage, that she would return right after this errand.

Hester nodded, sleepily frying sliced potatoes and onions in the heavy black skillet, knowing Bappie would eventually inform her of the nature of her morning errand. She'd likely be off to the lumberyard, although she was surprised Bappie had not asked her to accompany her.

Hester spent the forenoon resting, often dozing by the cookstove, attending to the bumps and bruises that kept making an appearance. Her back hurt, and one elbow burned. After viewing it in a mirror, she found a raw-looking scrape, almost like a burn. The back of her head was sore to the touch as well.

When Bappie came home, she opened the back door softly, closing it as if a baby might be awakened. Her face was serene, so peaceful it seemed almost waxen, like a candle.

Hester looked up, her eyebrows lifted in question. When Bappie offered no information, Hester asked what her plans were, how she was going to rebuild.

In answer, Bappie clapped her hands reverently as a rush of color suffused her cheeks, her eyes half-closed with piety. "I won't rebuild."

Hester sat up straight, her eyebrows rising in shock. "Why not, Bappie?"

"I just asked Levi Buehler to marry me."

Hester gazed at Bappie, speechless.

Immediately, Bappie found her voice. "Hester, it's not what you think, really it isn't. I just did what made sense. Levi has not had a wife for a very long time. He is a sad and lonely man. We have known each other for years. I did things for Martha. I tried to help them, but I realized now why I did it.

"The storm, the loss of everything I worked so hard to build, left me without pride. So I did what I thought made sense. I asked Levi if he wanted me for his wife. I told him I could just be like a *maud*, you know, not a real wife. I would clean the house, the garden, and yard. Did you ever see his garden? *Siss unfaschtendich*.

"I could have my room upstairs. We would get cows, raise pigs, have a nice flock of chickens. The hounds must go. But of course, I didn't tell him all this. I just drove up to the fence, tied the horse, knocked on the door, and asked him. I think I said '*Guten Morgen*' or something about the weather. I don't know. Can't rightly remember.

"He never said much. Didn't bat an eye. Just cleared his throat and said that sounded like a good idea. But he said he didn't want any of this *maud* business. He wanted me for a real wife, that he had planned on asking me but not till fall. Any earlier would be unseemly.

"So if people ask why I'm not building, tell them we're not raising produce anymore. That's all they need to know. See, I didn't want to spend money to get those few acres in shape if I'm not going to need the buildings."

Bappie paused for breath. "What's for breakfast? I'm about ready to collapse from hunger."

While they ate, Bappie told Hester she could stay with them, help around the house or teach school, perhaps further her studies of the herbs.

Hester listened, nodding, catching the hopeful tone in Bappie's words, knowing she wanted rid of her, and soon. She cut the pancake on her plate with the side of her fork, her eyes downcast, her shoulders slumped forward, as if it made her weary to lift them.

Slowly, she began to shake her head from side to side. "You won't want me, Bappie. I'd be like a third hand you didn't need. I'll stay here and find some place of employment. Something will work out."

"You should charge the people you treat. Make them pay."

"They don't have anything, Bappie."

"You've treated rich people."

"I know. But they all return to the doctor. They have more faith in him than my jumble of herbs and tinctures."

Bappie nodded. "At any rate, we need to find employment for the summer. I must sew my wedding dress, make tablecloths, and crochet doilies and embroider pillowcases. I know Martha had all that, but I want my own stuff.

"I am getting married, Hester! I'm no longer going to be skinny, red-haired, single old Bappie Kinnich. I am going to be called '*da Levi sei Bappie.*' Think about it. A place to be, close by Levi's side. And he is not wearing that hat. It's *schrecklich mit,* that hat."

She laughed, a sound that welled up from the triumph in her lonely, middle-aged heart. "I'll be a good wife. Just think how I'll keep house and the garden. The barn, I'll help him, show him what it takes to have a nice herd of cows that *faschpritz* with milk. My father was a good herdsman. I learned it all from him."

Hester nodded, smiling. She could see this. That Buehler place would be the picture of good management, now that Levi had the ambitious helpmeet he needed, the push to get him going. After years of having Martha to care for, how must he feel, looking forward to a new beginning?

After wondering what God had done, venting his anger in allowing that storm to lay desolation to Bappie's small buildings, here, like a phoenix from the ashes, arose a brand new life for Bappie. She only had to get rid of her pride.

Of course, in years to come, Bappie and Levi's story would be told and retold, how the old maid became desperate and asked the widower. Embellishment, that added-on packet of spice, would provide entertainment around tables, knee-slapping hilarity, all in good fun. Among the Amish, although the story was true, the telling of it met with open-mouthed disbelief, generation after generation.

CHAPTER 9

TOGETHER THEY WALKED TO THE DRY GOODS STORE ON QUEEN Street. The bell above the door tinkled, announcing their arrival. The proprietor, an aging, slight man, wore a white shirt and cravat. His mustache, clipped and tidy, bobbed above his small, pink mouth like an ancient caterpillar, or one dropped in lye.

The shop was empty. "Everyone's cleaning up after the storm," he said. They asked to see the blues first. The royal blue was so beautiful, the color of the indigo bunting.

Hester was not expecting the desolation she felt, the need to gather every ounce of strength to be happy for Bappie when she held the color to her face and twirled a bit, jubilation following her every move.

"Do you think it will suit me?" Her brown eyes in the narrow, freckled face were so eager, so anxious.

Quickly, Hester pushed back the thought that she looked like a horse, her face so long and narrow. She felt so wretched inside she turned away, grabbing moments to compose herself. "I think it's perfect. We're allowed blue and purple for weddings, so purple would probably be a bit bright with your auburn hair."

"You think?"

The caterpillar spread out, elongating as the clerk bowed and dipped with pleasure. It was a big sale of very expensive fabric. Hester could not believe the price, but said nothing when Bappie produced the cash from the deep pocket in her skirt.

"What do you think, Hester? Would I be too fancy if I bought black velvet ribbon to sew on the bottom of the sleeves? It looks so nice, the way the young girls do."

Hester nodded, urging her on quickly before Bappie would see the shadow that darkened her eyes. She remembered William's disapproval the time she had purchased a yard of black velvet to sew on the deep purple sleeves of a new Sunday dress. No woman of his would be seen with such finery, for shame. What would Mother say? If this is how she was becoming, then she needed to stay out of that worldly dry goods store. The peddler would be around, and he knew what Amish housewives needed.

Her eyes bright with the anger that infused her, she had said levelly, "The peddler has black velvet ribbon. Your mother bought some for Suvilla."

"Enough!" thundered William.

Lowering his voice, he brought his face close to hers and quoted a verse from Proverbs, about how a woman cloaked herself with righteousness. How could she even aspire to be a woman worthy of the King family and their Amish heritage if she lusted after strange, worldly objects?

Hester had slunk away from him, threw a shoe at the door he passed through, then sank into the armless rocker and cried her frustration at never being allowed to be heard. *Just once let him see that I am capable of making choices, even small ones. Let him acknowledge I am a person with a mind of my own who thinks like other people.*

Bappie paid for the velvet, then fairly danced out of the store and down the street. She waved to passersby, folks she knew who bought her fresh spring onions and small green peas.

"Not this year," she told Hester. "Someone else will have to take my place at market. Someone else will fill my shoes. I have to sew. I'm getting married."

She walked sedately, but her spirit skipped and hopped and danced, visible only by the quick darting of her eyes, the flashing smile, the greetings she called so loudly and easily. Hester had never suspected this of Bappie, her all-encompassing joy at having a man of her own.

She told Hester she had never had a date. No one had ever come to court her. Now she was going to be Levi's wife, and still she had never been courted.

"Whoo-ee!" And on and on, the whole way home.

Bappie spread the richly hued fabric out on the kitchen table, dug out the paper pattern she would need, then fetched the big scissors from the cupboard drawer. This dress would have to be perfect, so she could not make a wrong cut. She hovered over the table, breathing heavily, talking nonstop, cutting slowly, a brick weighing down the pattern.

Hester wandered outside, sat on the back stoop, lifted her burning elbow, and grimaced. She wondered how

Noah was doing. She felt bumped and bruised, sore and aching in every joint. In a way, the storm had been good. She had never looked forward to moving out there, unsure exactly why she wasn't excited about it. And now she wouldn't need to.

Well, one thing was certain. She would not live with Levi and Bappie. She would not intrude into their happiness. Perhaps Walter and Emma would allow her to stay here without paying the rent she could not afford.

The atmosphere was clean, newly washed, and fresh since the storm had cleared the air. Spring breezes wafted around her like an elusive scent she could not name, bringing a longing she could not define or understand. The sweetness and fullness of life was found in God, and in him alone, of this she was sure.

Unlike Bappie, she had been married and failed. God did not give second chances to those who acted as miserably rebellious as she had. She wished her friend a long and happy life, but fervently hoped that Levi was as good as his word. How could Bappie go about making all these plans without consulting him? Thinking of Levi and his kindness to Martha, his love of the people around him, yes, Bappie had a good chance at happiness, she believed.

As if God knew Hester needed a distraction, a vicious cloud of influenza settled over the town of Lancaster and its surrounding areas. Without the cautionary hand-washing, or even the frequent washing of their bodies, people suffered the dreaded virus that spread like a plague, which is what a few of the doctors named it.

"A curse," cried the devout. "God has cursed us with this plague."

Superstition prevailed in many of the homes and neighborhoods where a rich jumble of cultures all came together. Many immigrants were from the German-speaking areas of central Europe, from Switzerland, Germany itself, and the old Austrian Empire. Many of them carried the old fears of a "hex," a word pertaining to witches or witchcraft.

Some were deeply embroiled in the practice of *braucha*, certain rituals for eliminating diseases, because they believed that every sickness was a sign that witches had played their mischief. *Hexerei* was frequently heard, as the old covered their heads with their hands, repenting and declaring themselves unworthy of God's mercy.

Entire families took to their beds, their intestines cramping with pain. A clamping nausea emptied stomachs. And when there was little the doctors could accomplish, they sent for Hester.

The first request came with a firm knock, just when Hester had set a pot of potatoes to boil for the evening meal. Bappie opened the door, alarmed to find a neighbor man, pale and shaking, as if he had encountered a terrible fright. His hair was unkempt, a week's growth of unshaven hair like a scattering of dark, prickly splinters stood out from his cheeks, the ashen color beneath them signaling that he could fall in a heap on their doorstep.

"I beg your pardon. I hear this is the house where the Indian woman abides."

Bappie nodded, thinking *"abides"*?

"We need help. My family is all abed with the sickness."

Bappie stepped back, the sour smell from his mouth assailing her from the distance between them. Turning, she called, "I'll get her for you," and closed the door with a decided clunk of the latch.

Going to the kitchen with swift steps, Bappie focused her eyes on Hester's, then jerked her thumb in the direction of the door, and mouthed, "Go."

Hester slid the pot of potatoes to the back of the stove, wiped her hands on her apron, and went quickly, lifting the latch and opening the door cautiously.

Her practiced eye took in the pallor, the weak, rheumy eyes, the steady tremor of his hands, the chapped lips, and knew this man was indeed very sick.

"Where do you live?" Hester asked, immediately taking stock of the situation, knowing words of advice were useless.

"On Water Street. The second house. Stone. A white door."

"Very well. I'll be on my way. Will you be able to go back on your own?"

"Yes."

Not waiting to see how he fared, Hester was already closing the door. A sense of purpose swelled in her veins, as though her calling was singing her on, to lay her hands on suffering, fevered brows, to find good, cold water.

Going to the cupboard containing the bottled tinctures, she took down different ones, pursing her lips in concentration. Plantain and almond water. Red poppy syrup made with molasses. Bran, flaxseed infused with beer as a poultice for stomach pain. Oil of chamomile.

Her mind churned as she dropped the fruits of her gathering into a basket. Her labor of love filled her hours with wading in swamps, the watery mud sucking at her bare feet like a strong catfish's mouth. Sunny meadows were her favorite place—dry and clean, with easy access to dozens of plants and the herbs she knew so well, although learning their properties was a constant challenge. The origins of her treatments were all written in the old pages of the Indian woman's book. There was the priceless wisdom about the application of poultices for external use, the herbs to be gathered, dried, and then mixed with liquor, although whiskeys and brandies were so hard to obtain for these internal remedies.

At first, after her move to Lancaster, her friend Walter Trout had been able to purchase them for her at one of the many taverns that were sprinkled throughout the town. "Like rotting boils on healthy skin," Emma Feree had said, in clipped, judgmental sentences, hating even the thought of the devil's brew in her pure house.

But the liquor was a necessity, Hester had pleaded. Emma never allowed it after poor Walter came home, stuttering half-lies to cover his mission of procuring the *opp schtellt* liquid for her. So there was nothing left for Hester to do but bargain with the tavern owners herself. She would dress in her most rigid clothing, pull her large hat forward well past her face, and drape a woolen black shawl across her shoulders, obscuring all of her womanly charms.

She had entered through the back door that first time, slipping into a dank and steaming kitchen, filled with an immense cook wielding a wooden spoon the size of a pitchfork, her face red and perspiring. She rushed from dough table to oven, squawking orders at rebellious handmaidens who shrugged their shoulders in resistance, bringing a hard cuff to the offending rebels.

Hester almost turned and went back the way she had come, willing to enlist the service of some young man. But the thought of suffering children kept her from it.

Trying to get the attention of one of the maids, Hester extended an arm from her black shawl and called out a greeting. The girl spied Hester from the corner of her eye, shrieked, and dropped a bowl of boiling hot gravy on the brick floor, shattering it into tiny pieces of crockery that floated in the thickened, greasy puddle like sharp fangs.

She pointed a shaking finger, her mouth covered with her other hand, bringing the cook with the wooden spoon, now turned into a weapon of defense. Quickly, Hester removed her bonnet, bringing into view the white of her cap, flattened beneath the hat.

"Hello. I beg your pardon." She spoke in a well-modulated voice, addressing the woman courteously, the features in Hester's lovely face revealed by the flickering coal oil lamps on the shelves.

Slowly, the cook lowered the spoon, her dark eyes alert, cautious. "State your business, young lady."

"May I speak to the owner of the tavern, please?"

The cook turned and barked an order at one of the girls, who replied with bald insolence, "Get him yersel'."

The cook screeched a volley of words while powerfully waving the wooden spoon, which soon had the girl scuttling through the thick swinging doors that opened to a dark and cluttered area. Smells of leather, sweat, horses, grease, and food wafted into the room after the opened doors closed after the girl.

Hester shuddered, knowing she could not enter the tavern itself, the front room where the men lounged, ate, and drank their bitter ale. She waited, shifting her weight uneasily, fingering the fringes of her black shawl.

There was more shouting from the enormous cook, bringing a thin boy, who darted past her like a trout in a cloudy stream, and who took down a black dust brush and began to clean up the broken bowl, goaded into hurried movement by more threats and scoldings.

The maid returned through the swinging doors without the owner. Hester followed her movements hopefully. She was eager to return to the streets outside and into the purity of moving air.

"He'll be back." The girl spoke in Hester's direction, her sullen eyes sliding away without meeting her gaze, her lips pouting as she turned away. She almost stumbled over the thin boy who was bent over, swiping the dust brush through the mess, the broken crockery jangling into the bucket he had brought. She landed a kick in his ribs, rolling him across the floor, with no more thought than if he would have been a hungry dog lapping at the gravy.

Hester gasped as the boy leaped to his feet and brought the heavy dust brush across the girl's legs, leaving a thick splatter of grease on her skirt. Whirling, she caught him by the ear, her face grimacing with the strength of the twist she put on the appendage, bringing a howl that sounded like the high wail of a wounded cat.

They were both sent scuttling by threats from the cook, followed by the appearance of the tavern's owner, a tall and stately man with the bearing of a gentleman.

Hester breathed a sigh, relieved to find someone who seemed completely accessible. "Good afternoon, sir."

Immediately, the tavern owner's hands began to flutter, two white birds flapping, ludicrous in their movement. Hester took two steps backward, feeling the cold, hard door latch through her shawl.

"My lovely lady. And what, pray, may I do for you?" His face was level with hers, his mouth red and fleshy like the carp that hid beneath tree roots in shallow water. His whiskers were thick and black, so much like William's, his eyes dark and greedy and glittering.

Hester kept her poise, telling him levelly, and, she hoped, coldly, what she needed and why. Instantly, the owner of the tavern changed his approach, becoming the perfect gentleman in every way. He sold her two jugs, one of whiskey and one of brandy, took her money and promised to fill them whenever there was a necessity, wishing her godspeed and blessings in her venture.

From that day forward, he kept his word, recognizing her as the Amish medicine frau. She was always treated with respect and kindness, by the tavern owner, anyway.

Hester told Bappie where she was going, bringing only a nod and the waggling of one finger as she bent over her pattern.

She walked down the street clutching her black satchel, her purple dress offset by the black of her apron. Her long, easy stride, the tilt of her head, the elegance of her graceful neck, made more than one passerby turn for a second look, of which she was completely unaware.

Because it was a lovely day and she had a mission to accomplish, thoughts of her troubling future evaporated like thin smoke. A sense of well-being rode lightly on her shoulders. She smiled and waved as Walter Trout's nephew, Jacob, rode by on his brown horse, cutting a striking figure. Vaguely, Hester wondered if he would ever become as large a man as his uncle.

She arrived at the second house on Water Street, a narrow stone dwelling with a white door, a brass knocker centered in its middle. She grasped it and rapped strongly, eager to begin.

When there was no answer from within, she rapped again and was rewarded by the door opening only a foot, with one pale, tousle-haired little boy staring bleary-eyed into her face.

"May I come in? I am Hester Zug."

There was no answer, only the pulling back of the heavy, whitewashed door.

The odor was stifling, the room she entered in disarray. There was the distinct sound of retching coming from the recesses of a hallway, followed by a groan of misery. The room was dimly lit, so at first she was unaware of the piles of blankets and children strewn across the floor like afterthoughts. As her eyes adjusted to the light, she counted six piles of bedding, the pillows all containing varied sizes of dark-haired children. Some were sleeping fitfully, others lay awake, and a few had thrown up on the floor the watery, yellow bile that comes after the stomach has been emptied of its contents.

Hester jumped when the shadowy figure of the father emerged from the darkened hallway.

"You are here."

"Yes."

"My wife is sickest. I believe she has swooned. The baby is lying very still."

Immediately, Hester brushed past him to the hot, suffocating bedroom. She found his wife hanging over the side of the bed, her face like a waxen doll, her arms like white rags draping to the floor.

Going to her side, Hester placed a hand on her forehead, not surprised to find it burning hot. When she found the white chamber pot, she saw the fullness of it, lifted it and held it sideways to the light. As she had feared, dysentery might be present. Were they all drinking well water? Was there a communal well? If so, this outbreak was not influenza as the doctors thought.

She lifted cold hands to her burning cheeks. But who am I? Oh, who am I to overstep my bounds?

Well, she would do what she knew worked—have everyone who was sick swallow walnut oil, the extraction of the walnut, beaten together with rose water; then fast for two hours; then drink a bowl of boiled milk with salt. It was always a quick relief. Quickly, efficiently, she found the two bottles, stepped over the sleeping children, and located a spoon in the drawer of the blue cupboard by the dry sink.

She went to the woman's side, shook her, called her, all to no avail. Going to the baby's cradle, she bent to touch the child's head. It was cool to the touch, the baby asleep and breathing normally, but the stench of soiled diapers spoke of long neglect.

Nothing to do about that now. She resumed her efforts, finally waking the man's wife, who rolled back on the bed, her head flopping like a rag doll, before she began gagging and heaving violently. The husband made clicking sounds of sympathy before turning to the chamber pot and heaving silently himself.

There was a loud cry from the front room, so Hester hurried out to find a small child rolling in agony, clutching his stomach, grasping and desperately scratching with his small white fingers.

Hester stooped and gathered him into her arms, soothing him by rubbing his back. He laid his head against her breast and wept bitterly, as an older child began to vomit with such force it took her breath away.

Carefully she spooned the mixture of walnut oil and rosewater into the child's mouth, crooning to him as she did so.

One by one, she helped all the children, in varying stages of distress, to sit up. She gave the same medicine to the parents in larger amounts, saying if they couldn't keep it down, she had more.

When the baby awoke screaming, and three of the children vomited, crying out with the misery of it, Hester knew she had to have help. She spoke a few curt words to the father, then walked as fast as possible, without running, up the street to their house. She burst through the door, calling out for Bappie, who accompanied her to Water Street with strident complaints. Her stiff-legged gait gave away the reluctance she was determined to convey.

"I'm getting married, Hester. A houseful of vomiting people is about the limit. I don't know how you stand it. How am I going to get my sewing done if you keep this up?"

Hester stopped, grabbed Bappie's arm, yanked her back, and thrust her face close to her freckled one.

"You stop whining, Barbara King. You are selfish, thinking only of yourself and Levi Buehler. How can you have a blessing in your life when you act like that? Huh?"

"You stop acting so self-righteous, Hester. When you grab that black bag, it's like you think you're God. Or at least his right-hand helper." Bappie stamped her foot for emphasis, like a cow protecting her newborn calf, then stomped off, her arms held stiffly away from her body, her hands rolled into stubby fists.

Hester scuttled after her, so furious that tears welled in her eyes. But when they entered the house, both women forgot the angry words and got down to work. Bappie heated large quantities of water, added yellow lye soap, rolled the beds on the floor out of the way, and began scrubbing.

Hester kept shoveling in the walnut oil with rosewater, the children grimacing, even crying, but she remained resolute.

After they had all been dosed once, she took up the baby, holding him away from her body while Bappie, her mouth a grim line and a clothespin propped firmly on her thin nose, peeled away the soiled diaper that had been on the sick child far too long.

They lowered the howling baby into a tin of warm water and bathed him well, wrapped him in a clean towel, applied a tincture of lobelia to his poor body, then spooned in a small amount of medicine. When his crying resumed, they boiled milk, added salt, and offered him a portion in a bottle.

They replenished the candleholders, trimmed the wicks of the coal oil lamps, and lit them.

Darkness came suddenly, as the sun disappeared behind the buildings, and still they labored. When someone couldn't tolerate the medicine, the heaving began anew. Hester waited, then spooned in another small amount.

Bappie swiped viciously at the soiled floors and carried the chamber pots to the privy out back, her eyebrows lowered, her upper lip slightly lifted with distaste, her smallest finger extended, holding the pot gingerly as if it was red hot. In passing, she muttered, "I guess you know we're not all created the same, Hester."

Hester answered, "That's right," and kept on going. By one-half hour past midnight, the vomiting and heaving had stopped. There was deep breathing from the bedroom as the parents finally found rest from the torturous, heaving pains that had roiled their stomachs like boiling water. The children remained restless, some of them sitting up and crying out, the fear of pain stabbing at them like unseen claws.

Hester was always there, talking softly, giving them more medicine. Bappie, however, stopped in her tracks, fell on a blanket, rolled over, and began snoring almost at once. She was tired, so she slept.

Hester laughed softly to herself. In Berks County, Hans Zug owned a horse that reminded her of Bappie. He was a good worker and pulled the plow, or the wagon of hay, for hours, but once he was finished for the day, there was no use trying to rouse him. He would not budge. It was as if his huge hooves were nailed to the floor of his pen. He was done.

Hester sat and rocked the hungry baby, gave him watered milk from a rag, burped him, and sang softly. As her eyelids fell lower and lower, the rocking chair eased to a standstill and she laid her head gently on the baby's.

A deep ache of remembering filled her then, a slow trickling of longings coupled with despair, as she recalled those days of unfulfillment, of never being able to give William what he wanted most. Children. Heirs to the farm. Generation after generation, carrying the seed of William King, just the way God had promised Abraham in the *Heilige Schrift*.

It never occurred to William that he may not have had the blessing. He had found favor in God's eyes, he felt sure. He was honest in all his dealings, kept the *Ordnung* to the letter, worked hard, rose early to read God's word, and prayed and prayed for Hester, who, it was plain to see, was the one who erred.

Oh, she knew, she knew his thoughts. She asked him one night in the intimacy of the bedroom, "What if neither of us has sinned?" She quoted the verses from the New Testament, where the people asked Jesus who had sinned because a child was blind, and he answered, "No one. Now the glory of God can be revealed." And hadn't it been?

The glory of God was here, too, when she was left alone. God's ways were so mysterious, but his glory so perfect. For would she have even been allowed to think that she could practice this medicine, these forgotten Indian remedies, if she was a widow with many little ones to care for?

CHAPTER 10

A<small>ND SO HER THOUGHTS WHIRLED, AN ENDLESS VORTEX OF</small> wondering with no definite answers, always just bits and pieces she would never understand.

She stroked the baby's back and thought she didn't need to know. To understand everything was not exercising faith, the faith of her culture, the faith of her people, the Amish. She knew her faith was firmly rooted, and she deeply appreciated it as she grew older. She was certain the Almighty was watching over her like the brightest star, guiding her into the future.

Hester's eyes snapped open, sensing a figure standing close by. It was the mother, dressed in a clean gown, her hair held away from her face by a freshly tied ribbon.

"I'll take him," she whispered, her white hands reaching for him in the semidarkness

"How are you?" Hester whispered back.

"Thirsty."

Hester shook her head. "Do you mind drinking left-over milk? When morning comes, I'd like to bring water from a different well. I'm afraid this well may be causing the sickness."

Quickly she added, "Though I don't know."

Weakly, the mother nodded her head. "I'll do anything you want. I have never been so sick, even when I was with child."

Even before the day arrived, Hester was on her way, Bappie in tow, chilly and grumbling, attacking her back with darts of threatening words. "Hester, I'm hungry. Now you can't expect me to eat anything in *sell cutsich haus*. I'm not eating a bite. I'm skinny as a pole, so I can't take much sickness. I have to eat. I didn't eat yesterday. Well, last night you know those potatoes on the stove got ruined. What a waste."

And so she railed against Hester, who walked swiftly to their pump in the backyard and pumped two buckets full to the brim without speaking.

"Help me carry these to Water Street, then you can come straight home and start frying mush," she said, the words as hard as pebbles.

"Use a yoke."

"All right."

Bappie ran to the stoop, got the wooden yoke, settled it on Hester's shoulders, attached the buckets, and shooed her away.

She was going to make soft-boiled eggs and, if she was still hungry, *Schnitzel Eier Kuchen*, with the old bacon hung in the rafters and new eggs that the chickens laid this morning. If she felt like it, she would make *panne kuchen*, too. With maple syrup.

Hester threw up a hand and was on her way, balancing both wooden buckets with her hands, striding easily. She swallowed more than once, thinking of bacon, eggs, and pancakes.

As it turned out, her work had just begun.

The first family she helped, the Lewises, were able to be on their own that afternoon. They pressed a few coins into Hester's hands and thanked her with genuine sincerity, over and over, as the large-eyed children sat up and watched her, still feeling weak but rid of the clawing nausea.

She had closed the door behind her softly and was on her way home, her head spinning from lack of sleep, grateful to be able to put one foot in front of the other. She heard footsteps, then.

"Ma'am? Beg pardon, Ma'am."

Turning, she looked into the eyes of a child, a boy with a thatch of whitish-blond hair, eyes like saucers, his chest heaving.

"Were you at the Lewises'?"

"Yes."

"Would you come? My mum's sickern I ever saw her."

"Lead the way."

Only a few houses from the Lewises' stood a wood-sided house, its door well built, with two fairly large windows facing the street, heavy curtains draped on each side.

Wearily, Hester climbed the stone steps and entered the house, surprised to find her feet cushioned on soft rugs, and a low reclining chair, unlike anything Hester had ever seen, placed below the windows. Luxurious pillows, stitched with a rose pattern, were set along its back. Various pieces of ornate furniture sat tastefully along the walls with brilliantly hooked rugs scattered in front of them, as if each one had its own little flower patch. *Ein English haus*, she thought, as she followed the boy to the bedroom.

An exact replica of the Lewises' illness sent Hester's heart plummeting. The husband, moaning feverishly from the high sleigh bed, the wife like a plump porcelain doll sunk into voluptuous pillows, the telltale acrid smell of sickness—it was all there.

Quickly, Hester checked the room for a cradle, a trundle bed. Turning to the small boy, she asked, "Do you have sisters or brothers?"

"Yes. Four."

"Where are they?"

"My grandmother came to get them. They weren't sick."

"Where does your grandmother live?"

"Just down the street."

With a sinking heart, the weight like a stone in her stomach, Hester realized she could not handle this alone if it was dysentery from the well water. She needed to talk to a doctor, someone who would support her theory, her speculation.

She bent over the people in the bed, touching their foreheads as they groaned in pain. She asked for cool water, which the boy brought gladly, then wiped their faces with a cool cloth. She spoke to the man when he awakened and asked him and his wife to swallow the bitter herbal tincture.

After deciding this situation was not as grave as the Lewises had been, she asked the boy if he knew where Doctor Porter's office was.

He shook his head.

"Are you feeling sick?"

"No."

"Have you already been sick?"

"No, ma'am. Just my mother and father."

"Do you drink the water there?"

Hester pointed to the bucket, the one on the kitchen dry sink.

"No. I never do. I drink milk. That water is yellow and tastes like sand. I drink coffee though. And tea."

Hester could feel the excitement rumbling along her veins. Was her guess the correct one?

She had no time to think as the front door burst open and a large, wild-eyed apparition barreled into the room with the force of a runaway bull.

"Ah needs help!" The poor Negro woman was clearly alarmed, her hand going to her huge heaving dressfront, the whites of her eyes like little half-moons on each side of her dark irises. Her mouth opened and closed as she struggled to gain her breath.

"De little 'uns, is sickern' calves. Like little babies, dey spit up, dey cryin'. De missus too old for dis."

"Did you call Doctor Porter?"

"Yes'm. Ah done sent ma man a few minutes back."

"Good."

Hester accompanied the heaving figure back out the door, down the street, and into another house, almost identical to the one she had left. An older woman rose to greet them, her bearing regal, stiff, and condescending.

"An *Amish*? Royal, I didn't know the woman was *Amish*." She said the word as if it tasted bitter on her tongue. Hester stood tall, unbending, too sleep-deprived to care.

"Yes, 'm, she Amish, I black, you white and English. S' far as de Lawd go, we look zactly alike." Royal was in no mood to take any airs from her mistress, who had puffed up like Bappie's hens, ready to strike out.

"Well, I beg your pardon, but I don't believe an Amish girl . . . woman will have enough knowledge to know what to do with these children being ill all at once."

The piteous sound of gagging and retching, the high, thin wail of a terrified child, and Royal moved out of the room like a large ship, her skirts riding the floorboards efficiently.

Hester was left facing the taut face of the older woman. Up went the chin, the nostrils dilated, the lids of the eyes slid lower. She crossed her arms at the waist, drew a deep breath, and spoke, the words like scalding steam. "I would ask you to leave. No Amish is going to minister to my grandchildren. Your people have no idea about sickness or health. No schooling, no knowledge. You are a fraud. Do you hear me? A fraud."

The last sentence was spat in Hester's face.

"You will not enter my son's house again. Leave. Now."

Hester drew up her chin, bent to pick up her black bag, and spoke slowly, "As you wish, ma'am." She let herself out, walked up the street heavily, the weight in her legs from exhaustion, but also from defeat. So be it. Perhaps she was a fraud.

Hot tears welled up in her eyes as she walked past the Lewises, past houses where others would become sick, or were already gripped by the stomach pain and nausea. She went past the round, brick well in the small courtyard without seeing any children pulling up buckets of tainted water.

What had the Indian woman said? If the spring run-off produces an ill stomach, it must be boiled to sweeten it. Now the illness was called dysentery.

Well, it was up to the doctors to figure it out. She would go home to Bappie, get some much needed rest, and see what occurred in the following days.

She stumbled into the house, her face pinched and drawn, slammed her black bag against the wall in the hallway, and grumbled to herself, ill humor escaping her mouth.

"Bappie!"

"What?"

"Can't you ever get this rug straight inside the door? I always stumble over it when I use the door from the street."

When there was no answer, she walked into the kitchen. Noah was seated at the table, watching her face with his blue eyes squinting in delight. Hester did not see him at first, her vision clouded with the mist of exhaustion, her temper short because of it.

When she looked up, her eyes widened. She became flustered, but desperate to hide the mixture of feelings, she hung up her shawl, straightened her windblown cap, and tucked an imaginary stray hair behind her ear.

"Hello, Hester."

She nodded, short and curt, without meeting Noah's eyes. Still, his eyes twinkled with good humor and something more. "Rough night? Bappie tells me you think there might be an outbreak of dysentery."

Whirling, her fists clenched, Hester faced him, her eyes like polished black stones. "Bappie has no right to tell you anything. I don't know what's wrong with the people who have been taken ill."

She turned, yanked open the narrow door that led to the small, twisted stairway, and disappeared, her feet sounding dully on the stairs, the floorboards creaking in her room.

Bappie watched, raised her eyebrows, and pursed her lips. "Whatever brought that on?"

Noah shook his head, the light of humor replaced by a dark brooding, an unfathomable shadow in the depth of his eyes.

"It's all right, Bappie. You forget I spent my childhood in her company. I know her much better than you have any idea. She'll tell you what's bothering her, then you can let me know. I have a hunch she was put down pretty badly by someone."

Bappie looked up, puzzled. "You think?"

He nodded, then got up to leave. "I'll be back."

Before Bappie could protest, he had slipped silently out the door, leaving her shaking her head. Like a puzzle with most of the pieces missing, those two.

Noah had collected his pay from Bappie, although he cut the amount to less than half. He smiled at her announcement that she would not rebuild, a very good move, as he had seen Levi Buehler and figured there would be a public announcement when the time was right.

The storm had been an act of God, yes. There was a time when he wasn't sure he believed in God, and certainly had no faith at all in the goodness of the Christian faith when it was carried in a pious manner behind a veil of deception that hid a hornet's nest of sins. It had shaken him to the core when he discovered that folks around him were not always what they professed, but he learned to shrug his shoulders and judge no one unduly, knowing it was a part of life.

When Hester left, disappearing into the forest one golden evening, every suspicion he had tried to dispel came roaring back, setting him back on his heels. He had helplessly watched Hans thrash through the surrounding woods in a fever of agitation, driven by a passion he could not understand. At first.

He had been forced to search for her with Isaac and his father, torn by the wild hope that she would escape the cruelty that dogged her life—Annie's jealousy of her a rampant misery—and the unbearable fear that he would never see her again.

He had lived the ensuing weeks in bouts of utter emptiness. Joining the cavalry became a way to escape the loss of his faith—not only in God, but in his father and his stepmother, Annie, too, whose wrongs multiplied by the hour. But he had come to realize that he, too, had chosen to betray her. By trying to keep the peace, he had ignored the depth of Annie's cruelty to Hester.

Yet he carried an all-consuming love for Hester like a torch held aloft, the flame burning with an endless supply of oil like the vessel in the Bible. Hidden away in his heart, it burned steadily.

Riding with the men of war astride a powerful horse, he cared nothing for his life. Like a rotting log, his life was crumbling and bitter, without foundation, his hatred of his father corrupting his own soul. He rode into battle recklessly and without fear, not caring whether he lived or died. He forgot Kate, his gentle mother, along with her love and her upbringing, his mind clouded with the untrustworthy deeds of his father.

The only thing he knew for sure was the torch he carried for Hester. Images of her put him to sleep on cold, rocky stretches of earth. She walked softly through his dreams and was there in his thoughts when he awoke. He wasn't sure if it was real love, or if he had an obsession with the child of his boyhood. He just knew she was the only thing that mattered, and since she left and he would never see her again, he saw no use in living without her.

And so he rode, shot his rifle, marched along, steadily losing sight of the person he had been. Isaac, his brother, followed him, as devoted as he was when they were children. They had two years of being in the war, two years of unbelievable sights and sounds, experiences they would never fully forget.

Then Isaac was killed. Hans and Annie gave him a decent burial at home in the graveyard among the pines. That loss broke Hans completely, aging him in years as well as wisdom. He believed it must have been his own personal atonement, a payment to God for his wrong fascination with his adopted daughter, Hester, his downfall. In spiritual sackcloth and ashes, he sat for days as tears of remorse cleaned his soul, washing away the dust and the dirt he had been unable to overcome by himself.

Hans wept unashamedly over Isaac's coffin, gathered his children round and loved them, making amends for the past. He had come to love Annie, whose palsied hands worsened. Tenderly, he cared for her, helping her with household chores. He kissed her cheek and squeezed her shoulder affectionately when yet another pitcher or serving bowl crashed to the floor, her poor afflicted hands shaking and fluttering.

And then Noah decided to go home.

Slowly, his faith was being restored. God came to him in a dream one dark and weary night when his body and soul knew no rest. He blamed himself for Isaac's death. Isaac had been the younger brother, following his older brother's footsteps straight into the devastation of war, and he could not forgive himself.

He dreamed the sun rose, blackened by sin, and made an arc across a blood red sky, all the way to the western horizon where it hung without sinking. There was no power in him to change this, and he knew he was doomed. Then God spoke and reminded him that though his sins were dark and heavy, God's mercy is as sure and present as the sun rising in the east and setting in the west. Noah saw the red sky change with a swipe of a dazzling white hand, bigger than he would be able to grasp and larger than the universe, and wash the landscape clean. Whiter than snow, as pure as the angels.

He awoke, sobbing, flattened into his bed by the force of God's love. He was nothing, an empty shell, and only God could give him life. His faith was restored, his soul fed by the knowledge of God's mercy and the sacrifice of Jesus for him, for his sinful, empty soul.

When word came from Bucks County about the chance to make quick and plentiful wages as a builder in and around the town of Lancaster, he left almost immediately, thinking of the money he would need to buy his own acreage.

While there, he heard of the Indian woman named Hester, plunging him back into the world of his first love. Despite all he had known and experienced, had he ever really lost that love?

Wryly, he shook his head as he rode home from Bappie's house. He was sure he'd made some progress with Hester, but about the time he thought she would speak to him, and resume a childhood friendship at the least, she became abrupt, aloof, and so alien she may as well have not even been an acquaintance. It was like trying to tame a deer.

He knew she had been with sick people, and of her ability to heal with the plants she bottled and dried. He believed in her talent, but she could get herself into situations where holding those unconventional truths about healing would be risky. Hester hated being put down. It stemmed from her own low account of herself, being an Indian in a white Amish world.

Teased mercilessly in school, she had never joined
the group of youth during the time of *rumspringa*—for
hymn singings, for buggy rides home through the darkened forests, furtively holding hands, or going for dates
during weekends.

Noah winced, the pain in his back irritated by his
horse's movement. He thanked God for sparing his life
through the storm. He dared to hope he was here for
a purpose—mostly being Hester's husband—a thought
that brought a wide grin to his face as he lifted his hat
and whistled back at the crazy mockingbird on Levi
Stoltzfus's fencepost.

Hester slept till the sun cast a wide band of light across
her face, then got up, dressed, and went downstairs. She
washed her face at the dry sink, combed her hair, pinned
on her muslin cap, and marched resolutely to the black
bag she had dumped in the hallway. She grabbed it, took
it outside to the outhouse, and began uncorking bottles
as fast as she could.

With the bottles lined up on the wooden seat, she
grabbed them, one by one, and emptied them down the
hole, the glugging and splashing satisfying. No more of
this. She replaced the corks, pitched all the bottles into
the bag, then walked back to the house, her mouth set in
a stubborn slash across her face.

She emptied the tea kettle of hot water into the dishpan, added a generous sliver of lye soap, swished her hand
back and forth till the suds appeared, and began to wash
the offending glass bottles, now emptied of her failure.

Fraud, the woman had said. Fraud meant a deceiver,
a cheat, a fake. Well, that was one thing she would never

be. Hans was a fraud. But she was not. So there, you English lady, you just get the doctor to fix your problem. I will not spend one minute of time wasting these herbs on people who think I'm a liar.

Her anger was like brute strength, and a sharp pain shot through her thumb. Quickly she lifted her hand from the water, already dripping with blood, the gash deep but clean.

Hester snorted with frustration. Now who would wash the bottles? Where was Bappie? Annoyed, she tore clean muslin into strips and went to the cupboard for dried comfrey. Without thinking, she laid the leaf in a small bowl of hot water, then lifted it, patted it dry and draped it across her thumb, winding strips of cloth around it. She'd keep some comfrey for cuts.

She was sweeping bottles of tinctures off the shelf when Bappie returned from Walter Trout's house, where she had gone to borrow a cup of rye flour.

She stopped inside the back door, watching Hester with suspicious, dark eyes, her eyebrows lowered. "What are you doing?"

"What does it look like?"

"You're not emptying those bottles, are you?"

"I sure am."

Two giant steps of her large, bare feet, and Bappie thrust her outraged face into Hester's surprised one. "You're not getting away with this. Whatever are you thinking?" Bappie spread her hands, palms up. "You can't let those sick people fall like flies down there on Water Street. I'm sure you're right, that it's the well water."

In answer, Hester swooped all the remaining bottles of medicine up in her arms and carried them to the sink. "The doctors can figure it out." Then she pulled the cork from one bottle and upended it above a wooden bucket. Bappie grabbed her hand, shouting at her to stop this silliness. "What in the world has crawled over you?"

Hester drew back, the backs of her hands on her hips, her fingers curled into fists. "She said I was a fraud, Bappie. That's one thing I will never be."

CHAPTER 11

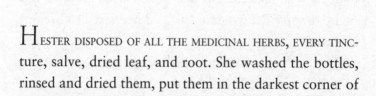

HESTER DISPOSED OF ALL THE MEDICINAL HERBS, EVERY TINC-ture, salve, dried leaf, and root. She washed the bottles, rinsed and dried them, put them in the darkest corner of the large, oak kitchen cupboard, and never looked back.

Not once did she inquire about the well-being of the people who lived on Water Street. If there was a funeral, she did not know it, figuring the doctors could decide what to do. If the well water was unclean, so be it. For the last time, she had been called a liar.

Bappie shook her head, paid the rent, and prepared for her upcoming nuptials. She suggested many different types of employment to Hester, even buying swatches of muslin and embroidery thread, putting down a pattern and tracing an intricate design for Hester to work, but she would have none of it.

Hester cleaned the house, did the washing, tended the small garden in the backyard, and avoided Noah and Levi Buehler—and every other man—going about her days in silence, an injured ghost.

Bappie shrugged her shoulders, made small talk, and ate the meals Hester cooked. But she spent most of her time out at Levi's farm, cleaning, washing the walls, the floors, the blankets and quilts, avoiding the hounds as best she could, tagging after Levi, and making bold statements where the management of the farm was concerned.

Levi indulged the peppery Bappie with slow humor. Ripples of laughter rumbled deep in his chest, but Bappie never heard them as she spread her thin arms, gesturing to make a point. Levi nodded, his eyes twinkling and dancing with unaccustomed amusement, so gratified was he by the spirited woman who had promised to become his wife.

It was the evening he asked her to go coon hunting with him, that he kissed her—a slow, gentle expression of his love, his admiration, and the wish that she should know this. Bappie was taken completely by surprise, the gentle kiss knocking all the speech out of her as thoroughly as a faint. She put two fingers to her lips and would not look at Levi the remainder of the evening. She went home with a silent demeanor and an unusually humble, "*Gute Nacht.*"

She sat at the breakfast table with Hester the following morning, her brown eyes large and limpid, saying nothing, eating very little. Hester eyed her friend discreetly, finally asking what was wrong, she was so silent.

Bappie lifted shamed eyes to Hester. "Levi kissed my mouth. Now I'll have to make my *socha* in church." Hester looked at Bappie and her shoulders began to shake. She laughed clear, delicious merriment that welled up from her stomach, worked its way through her chest, and was finally thrown into the air like visible music notes, bouncing and jostling against the ceiling where they sparked the day with pleasure.

"Ach, Bappie, no. No. It's very much a part of his love for you. I'm surprised he waited this long."

Bappie's eyes turned from dark suspicion to shame to acceptance to ribald humor, flavored with relief and capped by gratitude. "You mean, it's not wrong?"

"For some, maybe, but it's up to you."

Bappie clasped her hands reverently just beneath her chin, let her eyelids fall as demurely as a blushing bride, and sighed with pure contentment. "I'm glad I'm getting married," she whispered.

They went coon hunting. It was a warm evening when the sky was moonless, and only a scattering of stars, like pinpricks in the dark sky, was barely visible through the thick canopy of trees.

Bappie was prepared, wearing sturdy, black, leather shoes. Hester wore only the soft moccasins she used around the house.

They drove to the farm with Walter Trout's horse, the brown mare they borrowed frequently after Silver had died in the storm.

Hester was alarmed, then dismayed, to find Noah standing in the barnyard, the coonhounds roiling around him and Levi like a current of dogs. Her breath quickened and her head spun with dizziness, as she clutched the handle of the buggy with whitened knuckles to lower herself to the ground. Angry at the rush of anxiety that sped up her senses, she helped Bappie unhitch the brown mare without glancing at either man, who walked over to offer assistance.

Bappie blushed furiously but met Levi Buehler's gaze with open appreciation, the twilight a kindness to her reddened complexion.

Hester stayed behind the horse, her head bent, unclasping the britching as slowly as possible. She felt exposed when the brown mare was led out of the shafts of the buggy and taken away by Levi, with Bappie walking beside him to put the horse in the barn.

Noah stood on one side of the shafts, Hester on the other. If the twilight was kind to Bappie, it made Hester look enchanting. Like a vision, she stood, her head bent, her eyes lowered.

Noah could tell by the droop of her shoulders that she struggled with failure inside her, the feeling that she was nothing, an outcast, and now, a liar, a sham, and worth less than nothing. Bappie had told him what happened.

A love welled up in his chest, unrivaled by anything he had ever felt for her. This lovely, lovely woman, so battered by life, by experiences that drained the small amount of self-worth she did have, threw her gift away like a used shell, broken into a thousand pieces.

One high step, and he was across the shafts. Up went both hands to her shoulders, which he gently clasped, and then drew slightly toward himself. He could find no words to express what he felt, so he applied a bit more pressure. His chest exploded when she came willingly. A stifled sound of defeat emerged from her lips, a small, entreating sound of pain, a gentle begging.

Noah had never held Hester. Only in his dreams did he allow himself the thought of perhaps, someday, being able to take the liberty. Far beyond his imagining was the feel of her, and the thought that she allowed herself to stand in the circle of his arms, if only for a moment.

Hester laid her head on his firm, rounded shoulder, closed her eyes, and let the delicious encounter with the broad chest close over her like a warmed quilt on a cold winter night.

They stepped apart, Noah relinquishing her to the wide space that was the remainder of the world, the great atmosphere that now seemed an eternity, a million miles between them.

He gathered his senses, called in his thoughts. "I'm sorry to hear of your . . ." Almost, he said, "refusal to practice the use of your herbs," but he caught himself and said, "loss of the herbs."

Hester nodded, a slight movement of her head, but the large eyes, fringed by the beauty of her lashes, stayed on his. She wondered how he knew and what he thought, yet she wasn't ready to ask and risk hearing his opinion. She pulled away and lowered her eyelids, the thick dark lashes sweeping her cheeks like the delicacy of a bird's wingtips.

Out of the corner of his eye, he saw Levi and Bappie return, so he said quickly, "Hester, it was one woman. One opinion. You are not a liar."

"How do you know? Who told you?"

"Bappie."

Again she inclined her head, with only the whisper of acknowledgment.

Levi was jubilant and in his glory. This night was his chance to show his Bappie the thing he loved most. On a dark night like this, the marauding raccoons that inhabit the fields and streams of southern Pennsylvania became unaccountably bold and daring, breaking into henhouses, eating eggs, chickens, and hatchlings, plus corn from the fields, pulling down ear after ear. They'd eat a small amount, then leave the year's profits to waste in the frozen mud of autumn.

For once he hoped to display the reason he kept all these lean dogs, unattractive perhaps, but worth their weight in redeemed corn and the contents of henhouses. Simply put, they were his passion. Now they set off, the men shouldering their guns, the rifles thick and heavy, as deadly as Hester remembered of Hans and the boys bringing in wild game in winter.

Down the small incline behind the barn they went, the creek next to it gurgling full and glinting in the starlight where the ripples roiled over the boulders hidden beneath.

Levi lifted the kerosene lantern, telling Bappie where to put her feet, pointing out the three smooth rocks placed at proper distances to step across the stream, proud that he had so much forethought. Bappie, on the other hand, was thinking, *Here's something else that needs attention—building a decent footbridge going to the cornfields.* How did he think she was going to bring him dinner, or a cold drink of ginger tea on a hot day, if she had to leap across from stone to stone?

A bit huffy now, she started across, becoming distracted by the splashing, surging hounds. She slipped, stumbled, and remained upright, but she was in the water up to her knees now, her long skirt dragging in the dark creek.

Levi gasped, laughed, and kept on laughing as she clambered up the other side, her fury evident in the shrieks, grunts, and volley of grumbles that came out of her.

"You all right, Bappie?" he shouted, after he saw her reach the opposite side.

In answer, she plopped down on the bank, lifted her sodden, dripping skirts, shook them, and yelled, "Levi Buehler, now what am I supposed to do?"

A whoop from Levi, a bent-over figure slapping his knee, and his hilarity sparked a shout of anger from the bedraggled figure on the bank.

Bappie took off first one shoe, then the other, dumped the creek water out, and pulled her socks off as if shedding a second skin, all the while mumbling about coon hunts and creek stones. She wiggled her slippery toes and glared at Hester, who came bounding across, her arms outstretched for balance, the toes of her moccasins curling around the stones. Noah followed, striding across easily, a bit of mud on his boots the only evidence he had been close to water.

Levi dried his eyes, made his way across, sniffed, then stood above Bappie, asking if she wanted to go back and dry her feet. But Bappie regained her pride, grabbed hold of her shoelaces, stood up, and stalked off. Levi stumbled after her with the lantern bobbing like a misplaced moon, the smirk still not completely wiped off his face.

Noah looked at Hester. She lifted her chin, and they started off. Noah reached for her hand, but only in spirit, restraining himself, unsure of the outcome if he touched her. In silence, they followed the bobbing light, Hester as light and quick on her feet as she had always been, like a fawn, her footsteps effortless and easy.

The silence was not uncomfortable, yet it was there like a garment unneeded but tolerated, a bit too snug, a slight tension between them.

Hester wanted to ask him why he had come, if he planned more of these forays, and if he was here in Lancaster County as a permanent resident. A thousand questions, quenched by her pride.

The need to break the silence was eclipsed by the unearthly howl from one dog, and then the eerie baying joined by ten more voices, as each dog took up the scent.

"Coon! Co-oo-n!" roared Levi, immediately bounding after the dogs. Bappie dug her toes into her sodden leather shoes and hustled after him.

Laughing, Noah reached for Hester's hand. He wasn't thinking when he did it. He just wanted to be sure she wouldn't stumble and could keep up. She placed her hand in his, as natural as breathing. Together they hurried after the leading lantern and the baying, yipping, frenzied pack of dogs.

They plunged through the dark woods on spongy moss and wet earth, through puddles, tripping over tree roots, righting themselves, and resuming the dash to keep up. Ahead, the trail dipped down a steep incline. Noah gripped her hand tighter, his breathing fast.

"You all right, Hester?"

She nodded, then remembering the dark, said, "Yes."

They slipped and slid. When Hester's feet lurched out from under her, she sat down hard, her hand yanked loose from Noah's. He stopped immediately as Hester's laugh rang out.

"Like a mule, Noah!"

He laughed.

She got to her feet, the bobbing lantern below them, the hounds setting up an unearthly ruckus. Hester had never heard anything like it.

"Co-oon!" Levi yelled, in a high crazy pitch.

They reached the giant tree on the banks of a wide, still creek bed. Levi bent over backward, his hat tilted up on his head as he searched for the elusive raccoon, the dogs leaping, falling back, howling like banshees.

Bappie stood staunchly, the coonhounds knocking against her bedraggled skirts. She took no notice of them, her head tilted at the same angle as Levi's as she stepped in one direction, then another, helping Levi find the raccoon.

Hester and Noah reached the melee but chose to stay back, observing how this was done.

"There he is!" screeched Bappie, her voice only snatches between the sound of agitated dogs.

Immediately, Levi was by her side, his long neck stretching out of his shirt collar, the wispy gray beard like old moss. Lifting his rifle to his shoulder, he pointed it at a ridiculous angle, squinted, and fired off a deafening shot. Hester heard the rustling of leaves as the heavy body of the raccoon tottered, then fell down through the branches, snapping off small ones, loosening twigs and leaves, till a dull splat sounded and the animal was on the ground.

Amazingly, the hounds stayed back. Their baying ceased almost instantly, but not quite. One young dog had not been taken on a hunt more than a few times, the yipping sound from her a testimony to her inexperience. Levi bounded over, cuffed her sharply, and shouted, "No. No." The small hound lowered herself to her stomach, as another smart blow landed across her nose.

"You listen to me, Baby. When that coon is down, you hush up." Bappie watched as Levi picked up the fat raccoon, rolled it onto its back, and made a swift incision down his stomach. A few flicks of the curved knife, an order for the dogs, and a pelt hung on his pack. The remainder of the coon was torn apart by the snarling, fighting pack of hungry dogs.

"Onward, ho!" Levi shouted. The hounds took the cue to resume howling, their noses to the ground, first in one direction, then another, tumbling over each other and snapping, as quarrelsome as tired children.

Another coon, and Bappie sat down on the floor of the forest, her legs straight out in front of her, propped up by the angle of her arms. "That's it, Levi. My feet are soaked inside these shoes, and I have at least a dozen blisters."

"You sure, Bappie? We can get another, maybe two."

"Well, you just go right ahead. I'm staying here."

Undecided, Levi hesitated. He had never taken a girl coon-hunting and certainly never his wife, so he guessed if Bappie was tired, it would be the honorable thing to take her home.

He cleared his throat, then scratched his head by tilting his hat back over his head. In the light of the lantern, Hester saw his eyes soften as he watched Bappie yank off a sodden shoe and rub her toes, grimacing with the pain of the raw blisters that had formed there.

"We'll have to carry you home, I guess, won't we?" he said, gently. Bappie became so frustrated she put her shoe on again, got to her feet, lifted her chin, and set off, calling back, "Of course not. I can get home. What makes you think I can't? It's not that bad."

Noah smiled and turned to follow with Hester behind him. Levi brought up the rear, the lantern bobbing as he hurried to catch up to his indignant bride-to-be.

Back at the house, they were amazed to find it was past midnight. Levi stirred up the fire and put a kettle on, while Bappie threw off the offending shoes, yanked off her socks, and turned her head to hide the pain of the raw blisters.

Hester saw them. If only she had chickweed, comfrey, perhaps a burdock leaf. But she stashed that idea away and didn't say a word. She would not go back to that, ever.

Every ounce of her pride intact, Bappie got to her feet, padded lightly to the table, then hid her poor, injured feet in the safety of the shadows beneath it.

Noah sat in the lamplight, wide and solid, his white shirt open at the throat, his blond hair a halo of light that reflected the yellow flame from the lamp. His blue eyes were lined at the corners, his mouth wide with the kindness he carried in his features, a soft revelation of his feelings. His eyes left Hester's face only occasionally when he was brought back to the present by a spoken word from Levi or Bappie.

Bappie got to her feet, moving cautiously, the blisters a riot of pain. Levi noticed, gently took her shoulders in his large, gnarly hands, and stopped her.

"Sit down, Bappie. I'll get the tea."

Bappie looked at him, opened her mouth to resist, closed it, let herself be guided to a chair, then sat down heavily, her face flaming.

Forgetting Hester's purging of her medicines, Noah said, "Don't you have something for her feet, Hester?"

She hesitated, keeping her eyes lowered. Pouting only a bit, she shook her head.

That exchange twisted a knife in Bappie's ill-concealed humiliation; she so hated being the weak one. "Puh!" she spat.

Levi turned, watching her.

"You need a mother to tell you to get off your pitiful self and stop acting so childish, Hester," Bappie ground out.

Hester's eyes widened with surprise. She felt the heat rise in her face and was glad for the color of her skin. "Yes, well, my mother is dead, the only mother I knew. She would not have said that to me."

"Well, she should have. Stubborn girl."

Noah interjected, unable to watch Hester miss Kate. "She was hurt too many times, Bappie. It would be hard to practice medicinal plants if people made fun of your ability."

Bappie snorted, "Oh, get over it, Noah. Which one of us sitting here at this table has not had their ears clipped by negative words? Huh? Who hasn't been told where they're wrong? It's weak to throw out a lifetime of knowledge. It's stiff and proud and self-centered. Think of others, Hester, not yourself and how you are a poor martyr, persecuted by awful people. Fight back. The only thing that will prove your worth is the bedrock of the whole idea—people who get well after all the different illnesses you've worked with. Sores and fevers and poxes and rashes."

She pulled her feet out from under the table, lifted one, spread the toes, and winced painfully. "And these blisters."

Noah looked at Hester for only a second before he looked away. Hester's face registered pain and the fury of emptying all those bottles, but there was something else. Bewilderment? He didn't know and he didn't try guessing.

After that, a somber mood hung over the room. No matter how many lighthearted remarks Levi attempted to dispel it, the atmosphere didn't change.

Noah hitched up his horse, and Bappie and Hester climbed into the buggy. They left Bappie's borrowed brown horse till another day, allowing Noah to transport them since they had no lights on their buggy.

When they reached their backyard, Bappie clambered off the buggy, mumbled a word of farewell, and hobbled into the house, bent over by the blisters, stepping gingerly as if walking on pins.

When Hester got out to follow, Noah stopped her with a hand on her arm. "Will you wait and listen to something I have to say?" In the light of the flickering kerosene lamps attached to the buggy, her luminous eyes were dark with a polished sheen of yellow, a reflection from the flames mirrored there.

He turned to look at her, losing himself in her eyes. "Hester, I know you're having a bad time with the herbs and all. But I do believe you need to reconsider. It's a shame to throw all that wisdom, or whatever you call it— the knowhow—to throw all that away." Hester sat quietly listening, the only sound the dull whacking of her pulse.

"Summer and its heat will soon be here. So I'm asking if you'd consider going with me to a few places I found on the Dan Stoltzfus farm. I want to show you something."

"What?"

"It's a secret."

Hester smiled, a small lifting of the corners of her mouth. "We used do to it all the time."

"What?"

"Roam the woods and fields. Snare rabbits, find birds' nests.

"Remember my slingshot?" Hester asked. "I still have it."

Noah laughed, a deep sound that shook the shoulder resting against hers. "You were a dead shot."

"I still am."

"Take it when we go."

"I haven't said yes."

"No, that's right. You haven't. But please come with me. Just a day out as old friends."

He could not bring himself to say "brother and sister." He was afraid that was all he would ever be to her. A big brother. Never a man.

"I have no need of plants, herbs." She spoke the words quietly, without conviction.

"You do, Hester. Don't let one woman's opinion . . ."

He was cut off by her passionate words. From her side of the buggy, the sound of her voice was surprising. "More than one. Often, over the years, there were those who made fun of me, our own people, as well. They think I am *behauft mit hexerei.* Even some children hold their hands sideways over their mouths, lean in, and whisper, rolling their eyes. 'An Indian,' they say. 'Mixing her weeds with whiskey.' They may as well spit in my face, it hurts the same. It will never amount to anything, this healing. The doctors know more. Every day they are learning, making pills and medicines with plants that are grown in foreign countries, better cures."

"But among our people, Hester, surely you can practice what you know among those who love you and know who you are."

"Sometimes, they're the worst."

"Who? Name one."

Hester refused, crossing her arms and leaning back against the seat, the flame from the lantern flickering and losing her.

Suddenly, Noah said, "If we were small the way we used to be, I'd pull you out of this buggy and beat you up good and proper."

There was a small sputter from the recesses of the buggy, then a sound of merriment and a whoosh, followed by a genuine laugh. But something like a sob stopped the laughter, a choking sound, and Hester was crying, muffling the sound with the handkerchief she fumbled to produce.

Frightened and unable to stop it, Noah sat, his hands drooping helplessly, thinking he had said something terrible. He had never heard Hester cry. And he certainly didn't know how to stop her.

He spoke miserably, his voice edged in pain. "Don't cry, Hester. I'm sorry."

"It wasn't you."

Noah didn't know what to say. He felt big and dumb and completely at a loss.

She shuddered and blew her nose so delicately, he wasn't sure if that was the sound he heard. Then she said, "Sometimes I wish we could go back and be children, when life was good, carefree, easy."

She took a deep breath, as if clearing the air between them. "All right, Noah, I'll go. You can come with your horse and buggy, but don't ask me yet if I'll gather plants. I have not decided if I'll go back to herbs and medicines."

She placed a hand on his arm. "I'll make molasses crinkles. Our mother used to make them all the time because you and I loved them so much."

CHAPTER 12

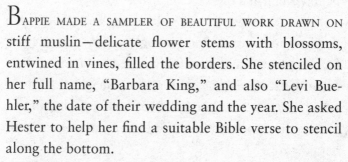

BAPPIE MADE A SAMPLER OF BEAUTIFUL WORK DRAWN ON stiff muslin—delicate flower stems with blossoms, entwined in vines, filled the borders. She stenciled on her full name, "Barbara King," and also "Levi Buehler," the date of their wedding and the year. She asked Hester to help her find a suitable Bible verse to stencil along the bottom.

Hester was in the cellar sprouting the old, wrinkled potatoes that had been gathered the previous August and stored in the potato bin since then. Now some of the sprouts were two or three inches long, like waxen white worms. Hester snapped them off, threw them in one bucket and the potatoes in another.

"My wedding sampler says, 'What God has joined together, let no man put asunder,'" she called up the stairs.

"Perfect," Bappie said.

Hester repeated the verse, and Bappie set to work. She would keep the sampler in a small basket with the embroidery thread, needle, and a wooden hoop that would stretch the fabric for better sewing, and take this with her when they went *yung kyat psucha*.

After their wedding, the bride and groom were expected to visit every invited guest, sometimes for a meal, other times for just a call to collect their wedding gift for the *haus schtier*, the start of housekeeping. It was a time-honored tradition; newlyweds were held in high esteem. How Bappie looked forward to this time, when she could enter the homes of her friends, now married with a husband, able to feel like one of them and not just Bappie Kinnich alone.

Oh, she'd always been able to converse, keep up a good argument, serve food in high spirits, to be the perfect hostess welcoming the newlyweds and giving them useful gifts. Never once had anyone imagined how she ached to be a newlywed herself. Unflappable, no one had ever seen beneath the facade, her mask of energetic happiness.

Now she could sit with Levi and partake of all the special dishes made for the *yung kyaty*. There were no common dishes for visiting newlyweds. No brown flour soup or potato cakes. There were butter *Semmels*, *Krum Kuchen*, German bread, soft gingerbread with whipped cream, beef brisket with sauerkraut and dumplings, sweet and sour tongue, and stuffed beef heart. The flavorful, traditional dishes were spread on the company table fit for a king.

She would feel like a queen. She was a queen. Humming the old wedding song, Bappie burst into song, a loud rendition of the plainsong, the slow chant sung at each wedding. Bent over her work, she tapped her foot in time, nodding her head slightly with each word.

"*Schicket euch, ihr lieben gäschte.*" Thump, thump, nod, nod. "*Zu des lammes hochzeit fest.*" Thump, thump, thump. At the third line, Bappie's voice rose to a shrieking pitch, "*Schmücket euch aufs allerbeste.*" Thump, thump.

She bet anything Enos Troyer sei Mamie would make her three-layer hazelnut cake with boiled icing when she and Levi, the *yung kyaty*, would come to visit.

She started in again, singing raucously, tapping her foot with all the grace of a wooden pestle.

"Hey!" Hester shouted.

"What?"

"I'm down here, you know. You're loosening the whitewash and cobwebs. Stop your stomping on the floor."

"All right."

The singing resumed, louder than ever, and jerkier, but the thumping stopped. There were footsteps overhead; the cellar door squeaked open.

"Did they sing that one at your wedding?"

"I'm sure they did."

"Brings back memories, huh? Good ones, though, on your wedding day, huh?"

"Yes." Hester acknowledged this, mostly to get rid of Bappie's questions. She had been in love, she supposed. And yes, happy to become William's wife. She wondered vaguely if the sense of doom that hovered around the edges of her conscious thoughts had all been her own unwillingness to surrender to William's stringent rules even then.

He had spoken of this the week before the wedding. He had asked if she knew the verses in the Bible about giving over her will to him, and she had said yes, she knew. This was expected.

But was she ready? he had asked, digging for straightforward answers of complete obedience. So total, he had swallowed her own life or may as well have.

May he rest in peace. William was gone, and there was no use gathering senseless memories that only served up fear of the future like a plate of unappetizing, moldy bread.

Her senseless feelings of agitation when she was with Noah would only dissipate with time. Noah, too, would expect that life-sucking submission, the authority over her so complete it was like a hood, stifling, allowing one to cling to life by short half-breaths, just enough to stay alive.

What had he done last night? Tried to tell her to start over with the herbs. That was very likely only the beginning.

No, she could not trust him. She could not begin to imagine that any form of friendship, and especially marriage, would be safe. It would be like stepping off a cliff, never being able to tell the outcome. She would be either dead, half-dead, or somewhat alive.

She had to stop thinking about Noah. She could not continue to harbor any thoughts of love or even attraction. Nothing. His touch, the way he smiled and looked at her, the sheer force of him as he sat at a table, drove a buggy, walked away or toward her; eventually she would be able to banish any feeling of wonder or amazement. If she stayed aloof, the thrill would fade.

If only she had done that with William, she would not have had to endure the marriage, the death, and all the hideous ghosts of self-blame that still haunted her at night.

Yes, good for Bappie, her dear friend. Levi was captivated by his ginger-haired sweetheart, the secret of their friendship only making it more precious, more sacred. But Levi had suffered in his life, had shown he was willing to give his life for his beloved, even if she was given to him with a weakness of the nerves. And who could have foretold the dying of the dear babies?

Bappie's raucous singing continued as Hester snapped the sprouts off the potatoes and threw them in the bucket. She had found only a few very small wrinkled ones in the corner of the bin.

She was conscious of Bappie's footsteps, and then heard the back door hinges squeak. Someone had entered the house.

A man's voice.

Bappie's voice. Her footsteps, quick, light.

"Hester?"

"Yes?"

"Someone to see you."

Hester straightened, dusted her skirt with the corner of her apron, and climbed the steep stairway to the kitchen.

A man of medium height, a youth, stood inside the back door, framed by the blinding spring sunshine at his back. Hester walked toward him, puzzled.

Dressed in the ordinary street clothes of the English, he looked like dozens of young men milling about on the streets of Lancaster. His face was pleasant, vaguely familiar, but she had to admit, she had never seen him. Until he removed his hat.

All the red hair, that copper-hued thatch as thick as a bird's nest, came tumbling down about his ears and over his forehead. An impish grin followed, and Hester's hands went to her mouth.

"Billy!"

"Yep!"

"Billy Feree."

"Sure am."

They shook hands, Billy's face turning as red as his hair.

"Oh my," Hester breathed. "Look at you. All grown up."

The light from the back door was darkened as a beaming Emma, with Walter in tow, entered the room, the pride in her son so evident. It was unbelievable, the way Emma's face seemed youthful, even radiant. Walter dipped and bowed, smiled at everything Emma said, and ushered little Vernon and Richard into the room where they stood, gazing up at Billy with amazement.

Bappie rushed around, produced more chairs, and put the kettle on, while Hester explained Billy to Bappie, if she held still long enough to listen.

When Hester was taken from the Indians, that dark and fearful night, and left for dead in the livery stable, it was Billy, Emma Ferree's adopted son, who had found her. He loaded her on his sack wagon and brought her home to Emma, who nursed her back to health.

Then, when Hester married, he ran off and joined the war. It was just an awful blow to his mother, who meanwhile, had married her neighbor, Walter Trout. Now here he was, a youth, hardened and seasoned by the terrors of one battle that led to another, a senseless clashing of bayonets and rifles. But he'd stayed and was only released when he lost a leg.

Proudly, he rolled up the cuff of his trousers. The women gasped to see a wooden peg where his shoe should have been. "Ain't much wrong with me now. I strap this thing on and away I go."

His grin was crossed by delicate shadows of remembering though. The pain of it clouded the exuberance of his eyes, too, but only Hester saw that.

Bappie produced a plate of cinnamon cookies and *smear Kase* with new brown bread, hard-crusted and filled with whole grains of wheat and oats. She set out a pat of butter, a glass jar of plum conserve, and a large, heavy bowl filled to the brim with pickled pears.

A stack of plates, a few knives, forks, and spoons, and the midmorning *schtick* was spread.

Walter pulled up his chair, happiness creasing his cheeks, which pushed up against his eyes and squashed them flat, the prospect of a snack so pleasurable, there was no hiding it.

Emma said, "Now, Walter, we just ate our breakfast."

"Ah, my good wife, I agree, certainly, and good porridge. It was the best. But porridge speaks of a lightness to the meal, unlike scrapple and ponhaus or puddins.

Although, Emma, I do acknowledge, porridge is so much better for the constitution, is it not?"

Emma raised her eyebrows. Frowning prettily and patting his arm, she told him they were in the presence of ladies, and perhaps that was more information than they needed to know.

Billy laughed outright and said it was good to be home. When Emma smiled indulgently, Walter took this as a good sign, spread an enormous chunk of the butter on the thickest slice of bread, and chewed, enjoying the delicious flavor with his eyes closed.

Emma handed each of the boys a cookie. They each murmured their "thank you" and ran outside to play next to the henhouse, where they terrorized the chickens so badly, they declined in their egg-laying.

Billy told them many stories of his years away from home, peppered with his quick grin and infectious laugh, the Billy they remembered so well. If the years had taken their toll, his good humor and frank outlook were still intact, which was so good to see.

Hester found herself caught up in his stories, listening with rapt attention, her large eyes never leaving his face. Indeed, he had met some interesting characters and seen so many new places, including plenty of things he had no wish to speak of.

"There were these two brothers, though, that stand out to me. I rode with them for awhile and I'll never forget them. The oldest, Noah, was magnificent. Ain't no other way to describe him. Can't forget a name like that, huh? Straight off the ark. Oh, he was a sight. He rode with the colonel. He was put up in the ranks, the way some of 'em are. Never saw anyone ride like that. That build, that hair. He had wildness about him. Didn't care if he lived or died, that one. He saved my life, but he couldn't save his brother. Forget his name."

"Isaac," Hester whispered before she could stop herself.

Billy snapped his fingers and sat up straight. "You knew him?"

"I did."

"How?"

"They are my brothers from Berks County."

"That's right! You told us that. You mean, these guys are . . . you were raised with them?"

His face fell, folding in on itself as memories attacked him. "You know Isaac's dead."

Hester nodded.

"It was vicious cold that winter, so cold our breath froze to our mustaches. Tears froze on our faces. It was Noah, Isaac, me, and maybe a few dozen others ridin' into camp, mindin' our own business, when one of the younger men—those often don't think, just act—shot into this bunch of whacked Injuns to scare them off. Stupid little skirmish, nothing any commander knew about, just some Injuns drunk on some kinda poison someone sold them, must be.

"It was terrible. Savages didn't seem human. Painted faces, half-starved, their minds half gone with the slop they were drinking, acting out of revenge, knowing they was being chased outa Pennsylvania.

"Isaac took an arrow through the chest. He died in the snow, with Noah holding him like a baby. Just sat in the snow and cradled him. He was talking in Dutch, I guess, or German. Singing. Noah was singing. He laid Isaac down, real gentle-like, then tended to me, with an arrow through my shin, bone splintered like a chunk of wood. He packed me to camp like a bedroll, where he took care of me till the doctor could take off my leg. The infection I got after a few weeks couldn't be stopped. That's how come they had to take it off.

"Noah sang sometimes. Hummed, whistled, kept talking about his sister back home in Berks County. Said she was something. Could shoot a slingshot better than anyone he knew or ever heard of. Said she was good with the children. I forget everything he said, but he sure thought a lot about his sister. So that musta been you, Hester. He never mentioned your name. Didn't say you was Indian."

Hester was blinking back the tears that pricked her eyelashes and trying to swallow the lump that rose in her throat. "He probably meant Lissie."

"No, he talked of her, too. Said she was a loudmouth."

Hester said nothing, clearly ashamed of this, afraid what Bappie would say.

Walter cleared his throat and looked around for a napkin. He would never get used to these Pennsylvania Dutch and their eating habits. How was he supposed to wipe his mouth if they did not supply a good cloth napkin? He wiped a finger across his buttery mouth, quickly slid it beneath the table cover, and rolled it back and forth a bit. There, much better.

He raised his head, tilted it back a few inches, and lowered his eyes to view his shirt front. As he had feared, it was

scattered with crumbs, an embarrassing plop of plum conserve, and a wet spot at another place, no doubt a splash
of pickled pear juice. This was annoying. He had tried and
tried to impart to his dear wife the importance of a napkin,
but she waved him away like an irritating mosquito, saying it made too much wash. This, when he so gladly built
the fire, heated the water, even shaved the soap.

Quite in despair he sat, the plum conserve and pear
juice glistening on his shirt front, his face heated with
consternation, his stomach only half full, the loaf of
bread sliced and so inviting.

"Walter, would you like to have a napkin?" Oh, the
redemption in Bappie's voice! "Why, yes, dear girl, if
there is one available, I would be enormously grateful."

Billy watched as Bappie brought a stack of snowy
white cloths embroidered on one corner with the letter
B and crocheted delicately on the same corner. She was
blushing all the way to her ears, the high forehead the
same color as her hair.

"There you go," she said, her voice thick, her face
flaming. Emma smiled up at Bappie and put her hand
on the long, thin forearm. "How nice of you, Bappie. I
know napkins make so much wash. Did you embroider
and crochet these? B for Barbara, lovely. These napkins
are lovely."

Hester said quickly, her eyes dancing. "The B is for
Buehler."

"Buehler? But her name is King, I thought." Emma
was confused, sitting in the sun-filled kitchen, her round,
wrinkled face glistening with the excitement of Billy's

arrival and too many cinnamon cookies dipped in her steaming, heavily sugared tea.

"It will be Buehler in November," Hester said, enjoying the mystery.

"Buehler? But how?" Emma was completely flummoxed, till Billy's grin gave him away and he whooped and pointed. Walter looked up from tucking in the blessed napkin and smiled, his eyes closing in delight.

"You are betrothed, Bappie!"

Bappie reveled in the moment, floating in the delighted stares, luxuriating in the drama that spread across the table, as her guests swooped up their hands in disbelief, full of pure happiness for her.

"I am marrying the widower, Levi Buehler. He asked me, and I have consented to be his wife."

Hester slanted a look at Bappie and pinched her leg at the white lie. Bappie grabbed Hester's thumb and twisted until her mouth went slack with pain. Bappie's shoulders shook, but she steadied them quickly.

Congratulatory words, pats on shoulders, hand-wringing, even a few maudlin tears from Emma, brought a festive air to the kitchen that forenoon in the early summer, when the sun-kissed room held so much joy.

After that, Bappie held forth like a royal monarch raising her scepter, with tales of Levi and his long-suffering wife, the farm that languished, raising no profit, his coon hunting, the dogs, everything.

Emma was amazed, so Walter figured if she was occupied in this manner, he may as well take advantage of it and proceed with the bread and butter, seeing as it was almost the noon hour.

Billy and Hester wandered to the back stoop, allowing Bappie her time with Walter and Emma. They sat side by side talking about old times, about how short a time it actually was.

Hester told him about her marriage to William, the grief, the loneliness, but hesitated about telling him more.

"No kids? I mean, children. You had no children?"

Hester shook her head.

"Well, good you didn't. They wouldn't have a father."

"I know."

After awhile, Billy shook his head. "He must of thought an awful lot of you."

"Who?"

"That Noah."

Hester didn't know what to say to this, so she said nothing. She lifted the hem of her apron and twisted it into a roll across her legs, over and over, while Billy looked out across the cramped space of the backyard. He squinted, his little boy's face turned into the square-jawed, undimpled face of a man. He was clean-shaven, with too-long hair tumbling in untamed strands over his forehead and down his back.

Not unattractive, Billy had a strong face with good humor lurking beneath the surface. Hester watched him sideways without his being aware of it.

"He wanted to write to you. Said you'd left. Never said why. Just that you'd left. I don't think many evenings went by without his talking about you, mentioning things."

"Like what?" Hester clasped and unclasped her knees.

"Oh, just stuff. You know, the kinda stuff you do with your sister. Shuck corn, make hay. He said you could drive a team of horses like a man. He said you used to chew on clover and then eat the whole stalk, even the purple blossoms. Stuff like that. To me, seemed as if he loved you a whole lot more than most brothers, but then, he ain't your real brother.

"In fact, I think he loves you the way grown folks do, not some kinda brotherly thing that he tried to make me think it was. But then, Hester, *I* always wanted to marry you. Remember? So maybe I shouldn't tell you all this."

Hester laughed. "Is this a proposal? You still want to marry me, Billy?"

He turned to look at her with the frank good humor of the eleven-year-old he was when he had saved her life.

"Yeah, I do. The only thing is, you're Amish, and I don't like them big caps you all wear."

Hester tilted back her head and laughed. It felt good to be with Billy who had not changed so terribly much. Bless his heart. She would have hugged him, but that would never have been proper, so she leaned her shoulder against his, and said, "Dear Billy. I would have you, although I'm at least nine or ten years older than you."

"That's not too old. You're still a beauty. Never saw anyone prettier, I don't think."

"You don't think! Oh, come on. There've been quite a few."

Billy shook his head, resolute in his spoken declaration. "Nah, I'll have to see if I can find that Noah. What was his last name?"

"Zug."

"Oh, yeah, funny name. But guess that's yours, too, ain't it?"

"Yes."

Then, because she felt like a traitor, she told Billy that Noah had found her, that they were friends, and that he'd come back to the Amish again.

"Noah's Amish? I don't believe it."

"Yes, he is."

"He wasn't Amish when I knew him."

"No, he wasn't."

"So what's going to happen now?"

Hester remained quiet for some time, then shook her head. "I don't know."

She told Billy more about having been married to William. She described it as less than perfect, trying to avoid the issue that stayed with her, the lack of restraint on her part.

Billy looked at her. "But I guess you of all people— you know, bein' Amish and all, you know, taught to be good and righteous and all that stuff—should know that marriage goes well if you're good people, don't it?"

His words, the wisdom in them, were a blow, a hard whack below the ribs that took her breath away.

There it was. The whole thing. Placed in her lap in all its monstrosity. She shuddered and clasped her hands tightly in her lap, interlocking her fingers until the knuckles turned white from the pressure she applied.

"William was good. It was me. I was rebellious toward him. I have suffered remorse. Wished it would have been otherwise."

"I can see that."

There it was again. Billy could see it, and he knew her well. The upcoming event, this going with Noah on a picnic or an adventure, a secret, he had said, would have to be stopped. Her mind churned, her thoughts of the future caterwauling about, unsettling every semblance of peace she may ever have held.

They got up, speaking their goodbyes. Walter and Emma gathered up the boys and went home to their own house.

Hester let herself in the back door, numb and reeling with the words Billy had spoken. She found Bappie jubilant, glowing, and fairly walking on her tiptoes, caught up in the heartfelt congratulations Walter and Emma had strewn about the room like confetti.

"Walter loved my napkins," she sang out.

"Good."

Hester pushed past Bappie, clomped up the steps, and sat on her bed, staring dead ahead, not seeing anything. Her hands hung loosely from her knees, her feet thrust in front of her.

She felt like a desert, dry, unforgiven, without life. First, the vegetable garden was taken, then the farm, and next the herbs, her lifelong passion thrown into a bucket and dumped in the outhouse. And now Bappie was going.

There were no tears; she felt no emotion. Only an emptiness, a lifeless landscape of sand and cold wind, a barren place in her soul.

It had all started, all her misery, when Hans behaved unseemly. That's all it was. It was Hans. Unsure about how she could ever forgive him, she set her lips and planned the remainder of her life without Noah's or any other man's help.

CHAPTER 13

On Saturday afternoon Noah arrived, driving Dan Stoltzfus's new buggy, the one he had built for his son, Ezra. It was a topless carriage, glistening black as if it was wet. The seat was upholstered in blue; the floor of the buggy was carpeted as well.

The black gelding horse had lots of fire, his neck arched proudly, his tail flowing in a graceful arc.

The harness was new by all appearances, without a trace of dust or grease. Because it belonged to an unmarried young man, a few silver rings and other splashes of fanciness popped up here and there.

Hester had become completely undone as she bathed, washed her hair, and put on the clean, freshly ironed blue dress. Its indigo color matched the spring buntings, those elusive little birds that appeared too infrequently, singing their hearts out from high places.

If only her head could convince her heart to quit slamming around in her chest. Her anticipation of seeing Noah had driven away all the resolve she had shored up against him, like sandbags along a flooded creek, placed there to save the low-lying village that was her life, her future.

Then there was the remorse about her marriage to William, and hatred—yes, a raw word, but it seethed in her veins now—for Hans, and nothing better for her spindly cruel stepmother Annie, or her sister Lissie who was always favored.

When she had put on her black apron and slipped her feet into the brown moccasins, her face was still not calm. Agitation played across her features, darkening her eyes and turning her mouth into a hard slash, as she thought of telling Noah that she had no plans to ever become any man's wife again, if that was what he was after. She would be his friend, but nothing more. As far as those herbs, she guessed that was her business as well and none of his.

Luckily, Bappie was out at Levi's farm whitewashing and cleaning. Walter and Emma had taken Billy to visit aunts and uncles, so Noah's grand entrance caused no fuss among Hester's acquaintances.

He stood beside the buggy as imposing as a general, his bearing almost regal. He was well over six feet tall and built like a workhorse, this Hester could not help but acknowledge. When he watched her walk toward him, he smiled, the kindness so like Kate's that Hester felt the beginning of a lump in her throat, a breach in the dam of her resolve.

Oh, Heavenly Father, stay with me. The prayer was like armor. She had to stay strong to resist this giant of a man who was not her brother at all. Not at all.

"Good afternoon, Hester. I hope you are well."

She acknowledged his kindness with a curt nod and averted eyes, her mouth dry with the acceleration of her heart and her senses.

Noah's heart sank. So this was the way it would be today. He took her hand lightly, helping her into the buggy. He leaped in after her as the horse lunged. Noah grasped tightly at the black leather reins, hauling back while the horse reared, shaking his head and trying to rid himself of the unwanted restraint.

Hester watched as the horse rose, up, up, his back long and black and powerful. She thought he would surely topple over backward, crushing them, but then he lunged forward, turned right, and came down running, hard. Dogs scattered and a child in a wagon watched them with awe as Noah struggled with the reins. The town required a lot of a driver, with other teams and pedestrians everywhere, and a horse that was clearly uncontrollable.

Once they reached the open road, Noah let him run, slowly releasing the reins through his hands until the wind tore at Hester's muslin cap and pried loose the black strands of hair she had so carefully combed with water and a fine-toothed comb.

They did not speak. Noah knew this was not the time or the place to make small talk. The day seemed to be unraveling before him, his anticipation and hope of reintroducing Hester to her medicinal herbs darkened by her lowered brows, her mouth a thin line, her face a map of her stubborn mind.

Today there was something else about her, an aura of rigidness in the way she shrank away from him, as if he was too big, too real, too loathsome. By the time they reached the Dan Stoltzfus farm, the black gelding was shining with sweat. There was no white lather, however, which meant Noah had been careful to wash him before throwing the harness on his back. That was good.

Noah drew back on the reins, and the horse came to a standstill. Noah leaped down, tied the reins to the ring on the side, then came around to Hester's side, extending his hand, his eyes searching her face. She barely touched his hand, landing lightly on her feet. She averted her eyes again, and stepped a dozen paces away, holding her hands stiffly by her sides.

Noah unhitched the horse and rubbed him down, then turned him out with the rest of the horses in the green pasture that led to a line of thick trees.

Hester turned to survey the new barn. She had been careful to avoid looking at it before, not wanting Noah to start an enthusiastic tour of it before she told him what was on her mind. It was the most magnificent building she had ever seen, including the stores and hotels in Berksville or Lancaster. Built into the side of a hill, the front of the barn was immense, as high as two houses built on top of one another. No, it was higher. The stonework was amazing, the grayish-brown stones cut to size, exquisite in their handiwork.

Six heavy doors, with the longest black hinges she had ever seen, were built into this stone wall, rectangles of perfection.

Above this first floor rose a sheer wall of boards, attached vertically to the massive oak beams with hand-hewn wooden pegs. The boards were still yellow, the new lumber retaining its original color before the elements, the sun and wind, the rain and snow, turned the boards a dark gray.

Above the doors in the stone wall, on the next story, were five shorter doors that could be swung open at haymaking time. Intricate arches, the wood shaped into half-moons above these doors, made Hester wonder what builder would put that kind of workmanship on the second story of a barn. She felt Noah approach.

She lifted her eyes to the third story, which was probably the fourth or fifth story on the other side of the barn, and saw windows on top of that, with half-moons of trim above them. The eaves from the roof were deep and wide, casting shadows on the window glass. Without thinking, she said, "What a wonderful barn!"

When Noah said nothing, she turned sideways, afraid of what her blanket of silence had done. Perhaps she'd overdone it.

She saw him lift his shoulders, then drop them.

"About a year's work."

"Who did it?"

"Dan and I. You want to see the inside?"

"Of course."

He led her through a side door and into a wide bay where harnesses hung on long pegs and water troughs lined the walls. The stables were so well-built and so clean that Hester was amazed.

The interior of the barn was dark and cool, the air hazy and thick with smells of corn and oats, cured hay, and glistening yellow straw. The acrid undertone of manure was a sweetness to Hester. Her sharp pang of remembering felt almost physical as she recalled the barn in Berks County where she had learned to milk cows, clean stables and harnesses, sweep the walls of cobwebs, and bring baby lambs from the cold windblown pastures of early spring, when the air was still raw and unforgiving to the shivering little white bundles.

She wanted to tell Noah this, but how could she, with the job she had chosen for today? She must not waver.

Noah let her breathe in the smells and run her fingers over the water trough and the pegs that held the harnesses. She went to the stable doors, bending over them to talk to the piglets and calves. She found a baby colt, lying in the straw alone.

"Why isn't he with his mother in the pasture?" she asked.

"Dan and Rachel went away today to her sister's house. They have a frolic to build a springhouse."

Another memory was suddenly upon her—the springhouse Hans had built for Kate, the rocks dripping moisture, the water smelling like dew in the morning, the crocks of cheese and new butter, the lard and peppermint tea they stored there. She saw Kate's pleasure like the sun through the storm clouds' aftermath, her round face beaming with the inner light she always carried, magnified now, as she praised Hans.

Hester turned to Noah. "I'm ready to go."

They left the barn with the memories that threatened her resolve and went back to the buggy, where Noah lifted out the basket of food Hester had prepared. He held the gate for her, and she walked through without meeting his gaze. Silently they walked across the pasture, her strides matching his, the basket between them.

The sun was already well past noon, throwing their shadows into chubby caricatures of themselves behind them. They climbed a fence where the flat meadow turned downward into a much lower level. The thick border of trees was beyond this low pasture. The closer they came to the trees, the more spongy the ground became. A familiar smell, a woodsy, decaying odor rose from the low ground.

It was not a swamp like the one Hester would wade in with water up to her knees, collecting skunk cabbage and bulrushes. She'd gather bits of mosses, too, that were good to pack around other plants, keeping them wet till she replanted them in Bappie's garden.

"You'll have to walk behind me now, please. There's a narrow trail here that leads into the woods."

Hester stepped back, letting Noah lead the way. She knew there were no plants growing in that dense forest. What was he thinking? But he'd said he wanted to show her something, so she would see what it was in spite of her mistrust.

"Careful." Noah held aside blackberry brambles, branches of wild roses and thistles, holly bushes, and nettles. They walked swiftly, their long strides covering the distance easily. The woods turned darker, the trees overhead a roof of leaves, shutting out the sun's light. In shafts, light broke through, pinpoints of dust-filled light that created an otherworldly atmosphere. Rotting leaves, new growth, moldy logs, crumbling bark—the familiar smells of the forest rose and filled her senses with another form of remembering, the woods her only home after she left the Berks County farm.

She swallowed and lowered her face as quick tears rose to the surface. Instantly, she bit her lip and kept her eyes on Noah's back, refusing to give in to the scents, the dank, heady odors around her.

Suddenly, without warning, even before she could sense the changing of the light, they broke out of the dense woods into a sun-dappled circular ring without a single tree in its midst.

The grass was brilliantly green, the new grass the color of premature peas, the older grass like just-cooked broccoli, a beautiful deep green. Peppered among the glorious green, in a profusion of delicate color, grew small flowers in pink, soft dainty yellow, and white. Bluebells nodded over the smaller flowers. The most amazing thing was the fact that this profusion of beauty grew in a perfect ring.

Hester's hands came slowly to her mouth as her eyes widened. She leaned forward a bit, as if her spirit was being led to its home. She dared to breathe, but only softly, for fear this vision was only that, a mirage that would disappear.

Noah watched her face from a polite distance, putting his hands firmly in his pockets. She walked swiftly then to her right, fell to her knees, her hands reaching out to touch but not to gather.

There was an abundance of spearmint, lush and heavy, a growth of the wonderful tea unlike anything she had ever seen. Leeks, wood sorrel, lily of the valley, mullen, so many plants, all growing in abundance, a patch of nature's gift to mankind, unspoiled, pristine.

Murmuring, she got to her feet, only to bend back and exclaim softly, as she stroked the spikenard that some called petimoral. It was so good for the elderly who had aches and pains of the joints, and for anyone with unhealthy kidneys.

Her thoughts went to the victims of nausea, how they would need fresh water and tea made of herbs. Without sufficient drinking water, the bladder and kidneys would ache.

A hand went to her heart, a painful sorrow for the sick children pulsing there. When she had denied this and left them to the doctor's care, she felt nothing. The sadness vanished, leaving her cold and dead inside.

As she walked among the wondrous profusion of plants, Noah remained silent. He watched her bend to caress the healthy plants and followed the movement of her lips. He saw the inward battle. He knew how determined she could be, how impossible to persuade. And so he said nothing.

The sun slanted through the trees, casting a rosy glow across the flower-gathered clearing, making it appear almost heavenly. Like a paradise on earth, in a way you could feel more than see.

Finally Hester stood, her hands crossed at her chest. She took a deep, painful breath.

Noah waited, observing her face.

When she lifted her large eyes to his, they were like dark wells of torture, filled with the suffering of her inward struggle.

He met her gaze with the only thing he was capable of, his long and undeclared love which he had carried within himself as long as he could remember. It was a flame, tended by the angels themselves, after he had accepted that it would never go away. It shone blue from the depth of eyes, so much like Kate's, a love that was the strongest emotion, the most powerful force on earth. It broke barriers, crashed down defensive walls, a glorious Roman gladiator of the soul.

The gaze held as their two spirits clashed, sword against sword. Hester panicked when she felt his power, the love in those blue eyes. Turning, she cried out, a soft, strangled cry of defeat, and took off running across the flower-filled clearing.

It wasn't that Noah even thought about a choice, he only knew he had to keep her. Lunging after her with a dozen quick strides, he caught her shoulders before she reached the thicket of trees.

She wrenched free, crying out for him to let her go. He held her in his powerful hands and turned her toward himself. He felt her resistance weaken as sobs, thick and deep, rose in her throat. He thought she was choking, strangling, and so held her away, searching her face.

Her eyes were closed, her mouth open, anguish written in bold letters in the way her eyebrows were drawn down. It was as if the pain in her soul would render her unable to breathe or to live.

"Hester, please don't."

With a groan, he brought her into the circle of his arms. He held her so powerfully, it was hopeless for her to resist.

She wasn't sure if she wanted to. His arms tightened slightly, and her own crept up slowly, hesitantly, until they were placed about his waist. She told herself this was only for comfort. Like a child she stayed there, afraid to breathe.

Then she felt a quietness, not a void, just a silent place of rest where there was nothing. A place of pure peace where no thoughts could enter. William King, the herbs, Hans and Annie, her Indian heritage, the pain, nothing, not one semblance of her past, had the power to enter this place.

Noah remained still, neither asking her to speak nor speaking himself. He simply held her, allowing her to tell him when she was ready.

Hester sighed but had no idea that she did. When the rest became so calming, and all the railing of troubled thoughts were banished, she sank forward and laid her head against the thickness of his chest. The sobs rose, quietly then, the anguish melting away by the flow of her tears. He pulled her closer, closer still, as she cried. And still they spoke no words.

When her tears soaked through the homespun fabric of his shirt, he felt as if he was anointed. Hope welled in his chest.

Vaguely, calmly, Hester thought Noah might release her, then lift her chin to kiss her the way William used to do. How would this be different with Noah?

Suddenly she was overcome by a longing that Noah would kiss her. That he would gently lower his mouth to seek hers, an affirmation of his caring, his wanting.

When he loosened his arms, it was all she could do not to clutch at his waist, a needy child who searched for safety. The haven of Noah's arms was a known place now. She knew there was rest there, and she could never not want it.

He released her.

She was jolted to bare, stark reality. He handed her a clean square of white linen, saying something she failed to hear.

They stepped apart, each one stranded now, knowing they were alone, when moments before they had not known this.

Noah said, "Would you like to share the picnic lunch? I am suddenly quite hungry." He laughed softly when he looked at her. "It's all right, Hester."

That was all he said. She knew what he meant.

He used to say that when she missed a target or the cow kicked over a bucket of milk that they had to have, or when some other unfortunate episode happened. He had always used those words to help her set her life right. So she followed the pattern of her childhood, believing it *was* all right, including the tears and her love of the plants in this hidden glade. It was all right.

They ate ravenously, the cloth spread on the brilliant carpet of green. The sandwiches were filled with the best roast chicken and with spring lettuce from the tiny back-yard plot they called a garden. The molasses cookies were crinkled with rivulets where they separated in the heat of baking, then sprinkled liberally with white sugar. They ate, their eyes like magnets now, finding each other, knowing that they could return to this place just with a glance.

Ordinary food had never tasted like this. The cold peppermint tea was like ambrosia, liquid stars in their mouths.

Noah smiled and asked if she wanted to gather any plants, perhaps fill the picnic basket? He spoke easily, ready to accept a No, or an unwillingness to bend or to allow herself freedom from her wounded pride. She bowed her head, slowly moving it from side to side.

"You don't want anything?"

"No."

Then, "Noah, this place is magical. If I would believe in fairies, I would have to say I saw a real fairy ring. These thousands of little flowers are like stardust, sprinkled over the grass by the tips of the fairies' wands. You know, Kate used to tell me stories about elves and fairies and Saint Nicholas, always telling me first that none of it was true, but her stories always took me places. I imagined these things. Then she would hold her finger to her lips and say it was our secret, that I was not to tell anyone, especially not my friends in school. The other Amish mothers would be shocked, such *unwort*.

Noah laughed. "Yes, our mother was a bit adventurous with her songs and poems and the stories from the old country. I often wondered about her parents, our grandparents, and if they were truly Amish. Did they belong to the church?"

"She never said."

"I know. But Mother was different; not as exacting as Father."

"Don't you call them *Dat* and *Mam*, the way you used to?"

"Sometimes, Hester, I don't know who they are." A note of bitterness crept in his voice.

"After our mam died, a part of me died with her. I loved my mother so completely. Dat was different. He never cared much for Isaac and me. We were his hired help. If we didn't do our work to his expectations, we were whipped with the buggy whip. I can still feel the burning welts. It drove us to do our best, but so often the best was not good enough. By the time we were teenagers, after 14 years of age, we were worked far beyond anyone can imagine.

"I remember felling trees at a young age, well before others our age did. I tried to spare Isaac. He was smaller and lighter, and he used to weep with weariness."

Noah's smile was gone, his kindness absent, now replaced by a harsh light, his mouth set by the anger in his remembering.

"But that physical part, the hard work, the endless labor, was nothing compared to the time after our mother passed away. That was when . . ." He stopped, emotions washing over his face like churning storm clouds.

"That was when I had to face what I tried hardest to deny. Hans loved you more than as a daughter. We were insanely jealous, Isaac and I. To hide his feelings, Hans became rigid in discipline, forbidding you everything, the horses, the rides to town. You remember."

Hester nodded, hanging on to Noah's words like a drowning man thrown some form of hope.

"As I grew taller, stronger, Hans, Dat, Father—all the same, but sometimes I am unsure of who he really was—carried a certain fear of me. I'm not sure when it actually happened. I just know it did.

"He saw the trees I felled with an axe, the amount of hard labor Isaac and I accomplished, and he knew his days of whipping us were over. Annie was a bitter disappointment, which created fear as well. He was consumed, then swept away, by his obsession of you, Hester.

"Why did I stay? I don't really know. Perhaps the whip had driven undivided obedience into me. Fear of disobeying must have been stronger than my will to turn against him. At any rate, I stayed, watching the way Annie treated you, knowing there was no way out.

"If you will forgive me for telling the truth, my love for you was destroying me. I had two choices—to stand against my father to protect you, or to get rid of any feelings I ever had, any fondness for sure, to try to destroy the love I imagined I had. I was unsure, ashamed, and feeling it was as wrong for me to love you as it was for Hans. I drove you out of my mind, my conscience, and my heart. I became a dead, empty shell, a living, walking, breathing person who was left with no emotion, no love, no fear, no anxiety, and, as I practiced daily, no caring."

He watched Hester's face, the drop of her bent head, the long dark lashes that lay so close to the golden, burnished cheek.

"I was just inside the house, listening to you and Hans on the porch that evening. I heard his speech."

Here, Hester's eyes raked his face, widening in disbelief. She watched his cheeks contract, the muscles turning his mouth grim and taut as he fought with remembered outrages.

"When you spoke, my heart swelled, my tears ran freely. Goosebumps raced up and down my spine, the hair on my arms stood straight up with the thrill of the truth you pounded into him.

"'My Hester,' I thought, 'you keep going. Please tell him all of it.' I was shaking, alone as I listened. My bones turned to water; I think I prayed. I remember that God felt closer than he has ever been. I was sure this was the end, and perhaps we could leave together. And then you were gone.

"Hans became like a person demented. We had to follow you, but I went only because I could not bear the parting, knowing that you were gone forever. I was not afraid of your ability to survive; I knew you would do it. But to think of the years stretching ahead without you, even to see your face from a distance, was more than I could bear."

He stopped, quieted now, and looked off into the distance.

"At war, the outward world around me was in real chaos, but there was a spiritual war just like it in my mind, my heart, my whole being. The only way I knew to survive was to spend all my energy riding, building forts, digging ditches, not caring if I lived or died. Through all of it, including the worst times, I carried one of the smooth stones from your slingshot in my breast pocket. It was like my image of you, the only real thing in my life."

CHAPTER 14

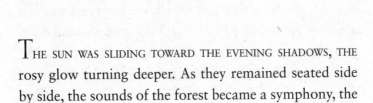

THE SUN WAS SLIDING TOWARD THE EVENING SHADOWS, THE rosy glow turning deeper. As they remained seated side by side, the sounds of the forest became a symphony, the glade of fairy flowers their theater.

Hester's eyes were filled with emotion as she listened to the voice beside her, bringing back all the events she had tried to dispel, or blame herself for, which was easier. But now it was clear that neither one had worked.

She watched the antics of two black and orange monarch butterflies, flitting in their dizzying, uncharted spirals, drunk on the nectar of so many flowers, so much color and profusion.

Noah breathed in, a deep cleansing of his emotion, then let the breath out with a quavery sigh, as if the beating of his heart had interrupted the clean breath.

Hester said, soft and low, "I had no idea. I thought you hated me. Along with Annie, with everyone."

"No Hester, never. It wasn't possible. I loved you. I just felt it was wrong, somehow, and did what I had to do to survive."

The Indian blood in her veins held her silent as Hester pondered deeply every word he had spoken.

Finally, she ventured, "You did love me back then. But now it's different for you. Isn't that what you're saying?"

"Look at me, Hester."

She would not turn to him, so great was her fear.

"I have never given up the love for you that I carry within. I never will. But I know you are like a trapped bird, caged by your past, your own sense of failure."

Hester nodded. Then she turned, her eyes soft with gratefulness. "Thank you, Noah. You do understand. If I would not have married William . . ." Her voice drifted off.

Noah let her have all the time she needed to think how to say what was on her mind.

Finally, she said, "I am not a good wife."

Noah let this sentence hover between them before he attempted a reply.

"Why do you say that?"

"In so many different ways I failed William. His mother, too. My cooking, my rebellion. Sometimes, I hated him. As I might come to hate any man I marry. That exacting obedience, that rigid control, Noah. It takes away your mind, your thoughts, until you don't know who you are. It's like a giant leech that drains away your life. And still, you keep up a perfect outward appearance, looking as if you're happily obeying so that the community around you keeps up their admiration for William and Hester King."

She flung the last words into the idyllic little forest clearing, destroying the holiness of God's handwork, the venom rising in her throat.

Noah nodded, choking when he tried to speak, so he let her continue.

"I believe in God's Word, Noah. I believe in submission, a woman's place, giving up her will to obey her husband. And this is right and good. God ordained it. But the husband is to love his wife, giving his life as Christ gave his for the church, so is that really any different from what a wife is to do? Doesn't that mean William had no right to insist on everything he wanted, to say anything, no matter how hurtful? No matter what I did, Noah, it wasn't good enough. But I wasn't holy."

Her voice rose. "Do you have any idea the crushing weight of being unable to produce a son? Barren, Noah. I am barren. I was told repeatedly that the Lord could not bless my womb because I was rebellious. I believe this is true. Please forgive me for speaking boldly, but I know no other way to let you know who I really am—an unfit person, someone who should never marry again."

"Hester, stop. Those two things are not related—whether you are rebellious or not able to have children. There is a love that transcends that, overlooks it, or doesn't see it at all. I knew you since you were a child. Do you think I should not love you because you are not perfect?"

"Yes."

"But that's not how it is. We love all the imperfections in each other. It is who we truly are."

"That's just the English way of thinking. We're Old Order Amish, Noah, you and I. Frances and William have beaten every aspect of the marriage vows into my head, believe me."

Noah decided, then, to end the conversation, seeing how Hester was clutching with determination her own shortcomings and that she would not relinquish them. She was like that. As bullheaded as a mule, once she decided something. His eyes twinkled, shining very blue, as he thought about how angry she would be if she knew his thoughts just now. She'd likely take off her shoe and throw it, the way she used to do when he and Isaac threw a wet, slimy frog at her.

No, he would not push her. He had the rest of his life. In spite of himself, he burst out laughing. He tossed back his head, opened his mouth, and laughed until he was finished.

Hester turned to him, glaring, her eyes black with misunderstanding. "What?" she asked.

"Oh, you! I can just imagine. I bet you took off your shoe and threw it at your poor husband." Again, great ripples of movement sounded through the meadow.

Hester leaned over and hit his arm solidly with her fists. "You can't laugh, Noah. It's not funny."

He caught her hands, held them firmly, looked into her eyes, and said he would love to have a wife that threw shoes at him.

And then, because of the feeling that rose in his chest, and because of how much he wanted her, he released her hands and bent to gather the remains of the picnic lunch, leaving her standing alone again.

Noah drove her home in silence, thanked her for accompanying him, and drove off as she stood in the backyard. The town's buildings rose up around her, tall and dank and suffocating. She felt trapped, or as if she was wandering aimlessly. She wasn't sure which. She only knew that Bappie irritated her and that the streets were dirty and filled with far too many people, carts, and filthy old farmers' wagons with slovenly drivers.

Often, she wondered about Noah's injury and how it had healed. She wondered if she should have inquired about it, but that seemed too personal so she had let it go. She had noticed him grimace, and observed a stiffness in the way he had carried himself across the pasture. It seemed his back was still bothering him somewhat.

If he thought he could show her all the lovely plants and persuade her to change her mind, he would discover otherwise. This time she meant it. There would be no medicinal herbs in her house. She would never make tinctures again. As time went on, doctors would find many more plants in other countries, hire men to explore those places, and cultivate and gather many more growing things than Hester could ever begin to name. Even now, there were many more cures available from companies called pharmaceuticals. Walter Trout had read to her from the *Intelligencer Journal* about this booming industry.

So what was puny little wisdom from the old Indian woman really worth? Very likely next to nothing, as medical wisdom grew by leaps, and highly educated men who went to colleges learned about the body and about plants they could turn into pills to heal it. And so her thoughts swirled about, filling her mind with the noxious fumes of defeat.

One morning, however, she had had enough. The sun rose red with pulsing heat at eight o'clock. She threw out the dishwater, rinsed the tubs, swept the kitchen carefully, went to the mirror and smoothed back her hair, set her muslin cap straight, walked out the door, and did not stop till she came to the biggest house on Duke Street. It was immense, with white pillars cast on either side of the massive doorway, the door itself so large and ornate, Hester had a moment of indecision.

The walls of the house were built of quarried limestone, smooth and blue-gray, and laid to perfection by the finest mason the town could find, the mortar thin and straight without chinks. The windows were tall with numerous small panes, and heavily draped, with ornate moulding at the top. Set back from the street far enough to allow the growth of a few cultivated hedges, trimmed conifers and holly, it was the home of someone who was wealthy, the group known as the "gentry."

Hester had made up her mind to seek employment in the only way she knew—going door to door, asking if those who lived there needed servants in the kitchen, the laundry, or with housecleaning. She knew it was not allowed by the Amish church, this employment outside of the home, but she was becoming desperate with Bappie getting married and her savings dwindling. She needed some source of income.

Lifting the brass knocker, she let it fall repeatedly, with no answer. The door remained closed. She had just turned to go back down the steps, when the door was opened from the inside.

"Yes?" The voice was level with Hester's face, the interior shadows making it difficult to see the person framed in the doorway. When the door opened wider, Hester saw a large woman, her hair tied into a white cloth, a white apron covering her dress front, immaculate in her appearance.

"Hello. My name is Hester Zug. I am seeking employment as a cook or housekeeper."

Before she could finish, the woman rolled her eyes, shook her head from side to side, and closed the door with a whoosh, a clunk, and the decided snap of the heavy latch.

Hester wiped her face gently with the palm of her hand as the sun climbed the midmorning sky. She had walked far, she was thirsty, and could only do one thing—keep knocking on doors.

The neighboring house was made of stone like the first. The only difference was a deep porch on two sides of the house, setting the side windows and doors into a cool shaded area. A strip of cut green grass bordered the steps, and some coneflowers and iris nodded in the sun's heat as she made her way up to the front door.

She knocked, lifting the brass ring and letting it fall. Immediately, Hester looked up into the haughtiest face she had ever seen—the butler, she guessed, wild-eyed.

"My name is Hester Zug. I am seeking employment." Before she could finish, the butler spoke in clipped, icy tones: "The house is fully staffed. Good day." The door creaked and banged, the latch fell, and that was the end of that. Hester felt like knocking again to tell him the door needed to be oiled, and perhaps they could use a door oiler, but she went back down the steps, her pride intact, and kept on trying.

From house to house, always asking the same thing, Hester met with varying degrees of politeness, but she was always refused.

Discouraged, hungry, and thirsty, her feet throbbing in her black shoes and stockings, Hester couldn't stop thinking of Bappie's garden out on the farm, the ruined, storm-ravaged garden, her place of previous employment. Digging in the good earth with her hoe, pulling weeds, harvesting vegetables—she had never appreciated the job enough, those sun-filled days with Bappie, even that pest Johnny King, who finally realized they simply didn't want his company.

That was all gone now. Her bottled tinctures, along with her dreams of helping people, healing, and curing— which she believed in strongly, along with the wisdom of the Indians—had been thrown into the outhouse in the small Lancaster backyard.

She stopped in the shade of a deep eave on the north side of a brick building. She needed only a moment to get out of the sun, to wipe her face with the edge of her apron, then she'd continue home.

There was no use trying to find a job. These homes were all filled with Negro servants. Hester was curious if they were slaves or free. Likely they were free, working in those grand houses, perhaps having relatives in the South who were in bondage. It made her shiver. At any rate, these well-to-do landowners' houses were fully equipped with capable people, so that avenue to employment had just been closed off.

She bent over to tie a loose shoelace, then continued on her way, stepping smartly, her mind on the cool mint

tea down cellar, along with bread and cheese and perhaps a slice of apple pie waiting for her at home.

The sun was merciless, straight overhead, the tall
buildings on either side shutting out the faintest whisper
of a breeze. But she marched toward home, resolving to
forget this forenoon and to never try such a foolish thing
again. If all else failed, she could always move in with
Levi and Bappie.

She heard a horse approaching from behind and
wondered vaguely who would be in such a hurry in
the downtown. It was foolish, besides being downright
dangerous.

She turned and froze. Noah sat astride an impressive
horse. He was a commanding presence with his way of
sitting on the saddle and looked completely in control.
For years he had ridden in that position on a horse the
cavalry provided.

Time stopped for Hester. The heat of the sun, the
teams passing by, the sparrow's chittering music, everything slid out of her senses. Only Noah filled her world.

He reined in the magnificent animal, who tossed his
head and fought the bit, slewing his head from side to side.
Then he rose on his hind legs as his front ones pawed the
air. Hester remained beside the street but shrank away,
afraid the animal's hooves would flail in her direction.

"Hey, whoa, whoa, there," Noah called, his teeth
flashing white in his face, his eyes squinting beneath the
brim of his straw hat. His white shirt was splattered with
mud and splotched with grease, along with his trousers
and boots. The horse danced, stepped sideways, snorted.
When Noah spoke again, the animal's ears flicked back

and forth, but the whites of his eyes did not show, speaking of a quiet temperament. He was merely too full of energy to behave.

"Good day, Hester!" Noah said, tipping the brim of his hat as his smile spread wider. The blue of his eyes reflected the blue midday sky.

"Hello." The word was choked, her happiness at seeing him an obstruction in her throat.

"I was on my way home from the blacksmith. This horse needed new shoes, and it appears he needs a good long run on them now!"

Hester smiled up at him openly, her eyes alight. "He's beautiful."

"I have two. A matched pair."

"Both black?"

"Yes. They're part Percheron, a cross. Bred for hard work and endurance. I should put them in the plow, but part of me doesn't want to make regular work horses out of them."

"I can't say I blame you."

Noah's eyes held hers. "What are you doing out and about in this heat?"

"I was on a fruitless search for employment." Hester lifted her shoulders, spread her hands, palms up, to show Noah the defeat she felt after the responses from behind the grand doors she had knocked on.

Noah acknowledged this with a disbelieving stare. "You were what?"

Hester felt the color rise in her cheeks. "Looking for work." She spoke quietly, the humiliation suppressing her words.

"Why?"

"Noah, why do you think?" she burst out. "I'm a woman alone, now that Levi and Bappie will be married."

With that, she turned on her heel and walked stiffly away, bouncing a bit by the pace she set for herself, getting away from Noah as quickly as possible.

She kept walking rigidly, her arms pumping as her long strides covered the heated dust of the street. She heard the hoofbeats, heard his call, "Hester, wait!"

She increased her speed, turned the corner, and ran, where there was no one to see her lift her skirts, allowing her leather-clad feet to pummel the street. Her breath soon came in hard jerks, and perspiration dripped from the end of her nose, making glistening rivulets of salted liquid down the side of her face. Still she ran, not stopping until she reached the doorstep of their house, let herself in through the front door, and collapsed on a kitchen chair, her chest heaving.

She did not cry. The only emotion she felt was the fierce pride that caused her to run. He was not going to sit on that horse and look down his regal nose at her, making her feel like the beggar she was. She may as well have been sitting by the gate of the orphanage with her tin cup when he rode by in all his finery. She wished she could take back the words she had spoken, unashamedly telling him what she had been doing. A fine example, she was, of speaking before thinking.

Ah well, the deed was done. Luckily, he didn't follow her. And Bappie was nowhere around, inserting her nosy questions like pesky starlings fighting over potato peelings.

Bappie was a bit too full of herself these days, Hester mused, as she wet a clean rag in cool water and mopped her face. She drank a glass of tepid water, longed for the cool springhouse in Berks County, considered buying ice from the ice house on Strawberry Street, then thought better of it. Much better to keep the small amount of cash she had in the carved wooden box on her dresser upstairs.

When Bappie returned, her face was glowing, every freckle darkened by her exposure to the midsummer sunlight. The crow's feet at the corners of her eyes gathered a few freckles and pinched them in the folds when she smiled and laughed, which she alternated with words. She strung her sentences together with fervent enthusiasm, punctuated by exclamations of a future so bright she could hold nothing back.

Levi was digging the foundation for a tobacco shed. She had helped him haul limestones up from the low fields by the creek. Did Hester have any idea how lucrative tobacco was? Buyers would come from the north; they'd even get orders from overseas, Levi said, like the gentry from England. There were some problems with tariffs and laws, whatever in the world Levi meant by that, but yessir, Hester, we'll be rich.

Acres and acres of tobacco. They would make ten times the amount of money that little truck patch brought in. They would have to hire help in the summer. Cows were out. They didn't need to get up early and have their lives ruled by five o'clock milkings. Sheep. They'd graze sheep in the pastures, raise coonhounds and tobacco, and keep the barn for the sheep.

On and on she went, as she built a small fire to heat some potato soup, peppering it with a heavy hand. She brought out the apple pie, bread, and elderberry jam, stopping midsentence to ask why Hester hadn't thought to make lunch.

Hester mopped her face and glared, halfway through thinking that the coonhounds might eat the sheep, and there would always be drought or hailstorms or flooding to take care of the tobacco and all the future wealth Bappie envisioned. She was warm and without any hope of a future even a portion as amazing as Bappie's, and she wasn't about to sit here and goad her on with exclamations of wonder. Bappie had plenty of wonder gathered and stored.

"I was too hot to think of eating. Why do you need to built a fire for soup on the hottest day of the year?" she asked testily.

Undeterred, Bappie informed her it would taste good and she was hungry, then launched into a ribald account of hers and Levi's plans, their conversation on the wagon, how pitiful his straw hat was, and how she just had to get that thing off his head somehow. And on and on and on.

It wasn't until the sun burned the edge of the sky red, losing its power as it slid below the Lancaster County fields and woods, that Hester washed in cool water, dressed in an old, thin, cotton dress, leaving off the black apron and white muslin cap, and sat on the black stoop as the twilight spread its promise of comfort across the backyard. The maple leaves looked spent, drooping with retained heat, the waxen grass like melted candles below.

The chickens lay in low corners of their dusty chicken yard, their wings spread out, trying to find a bit of cool, damp earth to relieve themselves from the heat of the day. The rooster strutted around, his thick, red comb wagging in a princely fashion, the clucks' low, homey sounds like backyard music as he bent to pick at a stray ant or bug.

She could hear the distant, muffled clopping of hooves, a child's cry, a door swinging shut, the deep barking of a large dog.

She felt a contentment settle around her, chasing off the anxieties of the day. Lancaster was her home; this is where she would stay. Some form of employment would show up somewhere.

One of the barn cats, the large gray one, came out from beneath the steps and rubbed along Hester's bare toes, emitting a long, healthy purr. Hester reached down to stroke its back, then laid her cheek on her knees, talking softly to the animal, telling her what a pretty creature she was, what a fine mouser, and that when Bappie left, she could stay with her.

She heard footsteps come close, figured it was Bappie, and stayed in that position. When she heard a deep voice above her, she sat up so fast the cat bolted, streaking across the yard and disappearing underneath the wooden fence that separated their property from Walter Trout's.

Yes. It was him, and here she was with no covering on her head, wearing no apron, her feet bare.

"Noah!"

"Just me once more," he grinned.

"How did you get here?"

"I walked."

"All that way?"

"It's probably less than five miles."

Hester didn't know what to say to that, as clearly he was right, and, clearly that distance was likely soon covered with his long, powerful strides.

"Beautiful evening," he said. She heard the kind smile in his voice, his way of speaking that was tender yet careful, as if each word was meant to portray goodwill toward the world.

Hester blinked and pulled the hem of her skirt down as far as she could to cover her feet. That task accomplished, she didn't know what to do with her hands or her eyes, so she clasped her fingers tightly and leaned over them, as if this movement would help with the part about meeting the blueness of his eyes.

Noah tried again. "Really warm today."

When no response was forthcoming, he took stock of the situation, noticed the bare step beside her, and sat down, the length of him brushing against her as he did so.

"I think, Hester, that there is a very real possibility that the cat got your tongue."

He didn't know for sure whether she had heard this stab at conversation, until he saw her shoulders become more rounded, then begin shaking as she started laughing.

She sat up then, and turned to face him. Unprepared, his closeness undid her battered pride and broke down her self-applied tower of resistance. The scattering of her thoughts, and the need to lay her head on his shoulder and weep like a child with a skinned knee, made her turn away so quickly, that Noah sighed.

And then he spoke, his words thrown out into the mild summer evening, without fear or caution. They were merely a question. "Hester, would you consider accompanying me to Berks County? Annie is not well. I have a team of horses that would benefit from that long trek. I think that before we step further into the future, that we need to step back into our past. Will you do that with me?"

CHAPTER 15

H IS WORDS WERE ASTOUNDING.

Oh, she wanted to go. As the crow flies, her spirit had soared countless times, far above the trees, the patches of corn, the barns and roads and gardens. Over the mountains that lay between them, the rivers and creeks and puddles of water, over every tiny thing and every large thing that kept her from seeing her home one more time.

But to go with Noah?

To retrace her footsteps by herself, her memories wrapped around her head like a turban, would be effortless compared to sitting beside him on a wagon, to be in his company every day. It was too hard work to keep the barrier up, protecting herself from the dizzying encounters with the blueness of his eyes. She always started out firm, serious, steadfast, but after a few hours she would fall away, forgetting to guard the feeling of severity, of distance, and there she'd be, as helpless as a newborn lamb.

No, she could not go. She told him so.

He did not say anything for a long while. When he spoke, his words were raw and devoid of kindness. "Listen, Hester. Why don't you try, just this once, to forget about your foolish pride? You know you want to see your home."

She nodded. "I do."

"Well, then."

"What would people say?"

"We're brother and sister."

"Like Abraham lied about Sarah, entering that town, huh?"

Noah looked at her and was met only by the tops of her lowered lids. He turned away, sighing. "I'd like to leave in a week or so. It will be a bit warm for the horses, but I figure it will be better to spend the night, in case we need to camp somewhere."

"Camp?" Hester breathed, the thought alarming.

"There are inns along the way, but they're not always a place for an Amish woman who's been sheltered from many things."

When Hester had nothing to say to this, he got to his feet and stood over her. He took in her black hair, darker than the surrounding twilight, the part in the middle the divide between a raven's two wings. She looked small and childlike. But underneath he knew there lurked a will of iron, a stubborn mind of honed steel. Neither made him change his mind. They only presented a challenge, an obstacle he would enjoy, given enough time.

"I look forward to seeing the Berks County mountains," he said. "Hopefully, you'll be willing to accompany me."

With that, he was off, his long strides covering the backyard in a few seconds, leaving Hester with one hand extended, her mouth open, the call for him to come back balanced on the brink of her voice, then pushed back and swallowed by the force of her pride.

So great was her turmoil, she slept only a few hours that night, flipping from side to side, punching and rearranging her pillow, angry, sometimes mellow, and crying, praying into the blackness of the night, unsure if God heard her or not, wondering why he withheld answers when she so desperately needed them.

In the morning, Bappie was off to the farm. Hester knew that according to tradition, it was highly unusual for a single woman to be spending full days with a widower. Hester told Bappie so, waking into the gray morning with a temper so short, Bappie stayed out of her way.

"Yeah, well, tradition is fine in its place, but Levi needs me out there. Nobody sees me going so early in the morning, and if they do, it's no business of theirs, so that's that."

Hester made porridge but left it uneaten to congeal on the dry sink, deciding to see if they would hire her at the dry-goods store. Perhaps the milliner might. She smiled to herself, thinking of an Amish woman fashioning the outrageous hats and bonnets of the wealthy women who sailed the streets of Lancaster on Sunday. Their hoopskirts swayed, their fans swished, their arms firmly tucked in the stalwart, richly clad, top-hatted gentlemen's, who walked slowly to accommodate the showboats beside them.

Sometimes Hester wondered if her best answer would be to leave the plain, restricted life of the Amish, the life where humility and hard work, fear of God and the denial of all frivolous things were the bedrock of their faith.

Oh, she knew, Jesus Christ was the cornerstone of the plain people. This fact she never doubted, hearing the ministers speak of it every two weeks. And it was true.

She could always hear the words of Ben Kauffman, his visage dark with effort, his long white beard wagging with the vehemence of his words. The commitment to deny oneself all worldly pleasures, along with the sins they brought, to take up the cross of self-denial and follow our Lord, was serious.

Sitting on the hard wooden bench, Hester had bowed her head with shame and guilt as she remembered her marriage. Ben's words pressed against her heart, weighing against her breathing like a stone.

On good days, when the sun shone and life stretched before her with all its uncertainties, she was glad for her faith, glad for the belief that one's happiness lies in serving others—Jesus first, yourself last, as her mother Kate would say.

It was good to be afraid of sin and good to seek humility, but when Kate spoke of it, she seemed to fulfill the law the way Jesus said he had come to do. It was not hard, not an insurmountable chore, not something that felt like repression. Kate had truly found joy and happiness in the life she led—in simplicity, in a homey kitchen filled with praise and laughter and new babies, a fresh blueberry pie cooling on the windowsill and a pot of stew bubbling on its hook above low coals, sending out an invitation to contentment.

The world and its ways meant nothing to her. Every stray cat or dog was fed and cared for, every bird and butterfly adored. She explained to Hester the reason for plain clothes: not to be superior to worldly fashions, not to appear self-righteous, but to be clothed with humility and obedience to the laws of the church, which would benefit the soul throughout life.

Hester was filled with a longing so great she felt it physically in the region of her heart. She clasped both hands there, her eyes swimming with quick tears, blinding her for an instant. Ah, Kate, if only you were here.

She thought again of Noah. So much like his mother, was he God's way of leaving Kate in the world through her son? This oldest son of Kate received so little from her husband, except reprimands and stinging slaps at the supper table. Kate would wince, and a certain shadow played across her face.

Hester wondered if she should go with Noah. She wanted to so fiercely. In fact, she had not longed for anything ever quite like this. But was it her own will, or God's? How could a person know?

Ah, but she knew. She knew. Ben Kauffman had explained it clearly. If we sacrifice ourselves to God, we can discern the will of God. If we empty ourselves and give up our own will, then we will know.

She wanted to go. She wanted Noah. She wanted to marry him, to be his wife, and live in Berks County among the beloved hills and forests, next to the streams that played clear music as the water rushed over the rocks, then eddied in deep pools where the tree roots hung low above the dark brown water, covered with moss and sprouting with lichens. The smell of the damp, muddy creek bank was ambrosia, a heavenly perfume in her nostrils.

She wanted to watch Noah build a small house, a log one, with a barn just the way she remembered. A sturdy fence would surround the barn, making a yard where the cows would wait to be milked, the barn cats would purr and stretch around the posts, and violets and wild irises would nod and play in the breeze.

To have Noah, to have and to hold him, to live among the beauty of the hills of Berks County, the home of her childhood and his, was a dream, a mirage, shimmering on the horizon, conjured by her imagination. It was not to be. How could it be meant for her if she deserved nothing, not even a small portion of such happiness?

No, she would remain firm, resisting her selfish desires. Once she had been attracted to William King's dark, good looks and swayed by his confession of great love.

And now this. This blond giant who was her brother. So great were the differences between them, so unbelievable, so far beyond her imagination. Even the lights in their eyes couldn't have been more opposite, one as dark and forbidding as the other was light and pure.

Hester stood by the kitchen table, her hand lightly on a chair back, staring through the narrow, wooden-paned window. She saw nothing as these thoughts ran through her mind, all connected one to another in sequence, as if the order of her mind had been freshly cleaned and organized. She had questions, too many of them, but they could not all be answered now. She would remain on course, deny herself the pleasure of going with Noah, and see what each day would bring.

She had just dropped her hand from the kitchen chair and turned to go to the backyard to gather the eggs, when the front door burst open, followed immediately by "*Eppa do?*"

Hester hurried through the short hallway leading to the front door and found an Amish man standing inside, the sweat on his hatband grayer than the darkened old straw of his well-worn everyday hat, his beard long and black, the hair hanging in greasy tendrils. His clothes were slick with dirt and grease as well. An unwashed aroma hung in the small hallway.

Without thinking, Hester's hand went to her mouth and two fingers covered her nose. A short cough followed.

"*Ya, ich bin* Amos Stoltzfus."

"Hello."

"*Doo bisht* Hester King?"

"*Ya.*"

"*Die vitfrau?*"

"*Ya.*"

"Well, I came to ask for a *maud*. Our girl fell from the hay wagon and broke her back, we think. My Frau had a *bupply*. She is in bed. We have now 13 children, and no one to do the wash. The peas are overripe. The beans are coming on, and there is no one to hoe corn or potatoes."

Hester nodded, wide-eyed. So here stood God's answer in all its soiled form. She had never in her life smelled anything like this man, except perhaps in the houses in the poor section of town when she still occasionally practiced with medicinal herbs. She glanced at his feet, then swallowed when she saw the telltale stain of liquid cow manure spread up between his knobby bare toes.

She nodded again, swallowing quickly as she looked away from his toes.

"How soon can you come?"

"Well, I need to tell Bappie, do some washing, pack my things. Can you come back tomorrow morning for me?"

"Ah, I don't know. I was hoping you'd ride back with me."

"Well, do you have any business in town?"

"I was going to buy my wife a new copper pot, for the washing."

"Go ahead. Give me about an hour to get my things and leave Bappie a note."

"*Goot. Goot. Sell suit mich.*" Clapping his filthy hat on his head, he let himself out. Hester stepped up to the door quickly, caught the latch, and peered out at his form of traveling.

As she had figured, a two-wheeled cart was pulled by a pot-bellied mule, every rib showing above the distended stomach, the blinders on the harness wobbling outward, revealing the eyes of the animal, half-closed in laziness. The cart was splattered repeatedly with untold layers of mud.

Hester shut the door quietly, sagged against it, laid her head against the moulding and closed her eyes. She let out a long, slow breath of acceptance. "Here I am,

Lord. Truly, here I am. Completely given up to do your will. This family needs me, and I am willing to go. Just provide strength for every day, every hour."

She leaned away from the door and sprang into action. Her movements were fluid and quick. She ran upstairs and grabbed her two extra work dresses, the oldest gray aprons to tie over them, and a fresh cap. She decided against shoes. Summer was here, so there was no need. She'd come back every two weeks to attend church.

She sat at the kitchen table with a square of brown paper, an inkwell, and quill pen. Slowly, she dipped the pen into the ink, spread the palm of her hand across the paper to smooth it, and bent her head to the task.

Dear Bappie,

Amos Stoltzfus came for me. His daughter is ill, and his wife is in bed after childbirth. I will be back to go to church.

My regards,

Hester

That was all. No indication of her whereabouts, or how long before she'd write again, or any more information. When Bappie found the note, her face turned as red as her freckles. She crumpled the paper and threw it on the floor.

There she went in all her righteous martyrdom, very likely without telling Noah what she was doing or where she was. Sometimes Hester made Bappie so mad she saw red. If she could only move past that Hans and William once and for all, instead of nearly throttling herself on her rope of grudges. She took better care of her self-pity about her past then she did of the chickens.

Bappie often wondered what that Billy Ferree told Hester. It seemed to give Hester a fresh hold on some past wrong. Oh, well, so be it. She'll come to her senses soon enough, if it's the Amos Stoltzfus Bappie thought it was.

Hester sat beside her newfound employer, perched on the edge of a hard wooden seat that slanted backward, her bare feet planted firmly on layers of dried mud and dust, bits of twine, pieces of hay, and something that looked very much like a snakeskin.

The mule's flapping haunches seemed to be only a few feet from her knees, the cart bobbing and wobbling along behind it. The wheels seemed to be strangely oblong, coming around each time with a thump and a sideways shift of the cart, leaving Hester scrambling for a steadying grip, so as not to be thrown against the less than clean Amos.

The cart was so low, and the mule so huge and loose and flappy, Hester sincerely hoped they'd make it to the farm before nature called for the mule and they were splattered.

Amos rode in silence, his beard and face a stark profile. He looked like Daniel in the lion's den, so serious was he. The picture in Kate's Bible storybook of the unfortunate prophet looked so much the same, with a long black beard, a square cut of bangs on his forehead, and hair so unwashed it hung in sections over his protruding ears, smashed flat here by a discolored hat.

She turned her head wistfully to view the low-lying meadow, that patch of swampy ground with an abundance of herbs and plants all lush and green, ripe for drying or boiling into healing tinctures.

She looked away.

From his trouser pocket, Amos produced a grubby, homemade pipe made of corncobs. He tamped down the half-smoked bowl of blackened tobacco, lit it with a match, then sucked away on it until the bowl glowed red and tiny sparks rained over his shoulder, plumes of smoke decorating the air between them.

Hester's mouth was a grim line. He had a match, those expensive little wonders that even Bappie refused to buy. She bet his wife had no matches for her cookstove.

When the mule slowed to a tired walk, Amos hit him across his skinny haunches with both reins, accompanied by a loud yell of, "Come on, *du alta essel*. Git up there."

When that endeavor brought no change, Amos bent low and scrabbled under the seat, searching for a whip. Amos brought that down with a vicious crack on the bony back, and the mule lunged forward, throwing Hester back with a hard jerk. Fortunately, she had driven carts and wagons and was prepared, tucking her legs beneath the seat and hanging onto the edge of the seat with both hands as the mule broke into a run, the cart bobbing and swaying behind him.

Hester noticed the absence of a copper pot and was just about to ask Amos about it, but then thought better of it. She was a new *maud* so it wouldn't have been proper to ask.

The sun shone down, spreading heat across Hester's black hat, its power felt along her shoulders and down her back. The mule's haunches were stained dark with sweat, and a thin band of white foam appeared on his legs where the harness jostled along the back of his legs.

Amos lifted his hat, the pipe clenched in his yellowed teeth, and let the breeze blow through his hair, which did not move at all, so hardened by weeks of not being washed. Hester swallowed and looked away.

It was no surprise, when the road shifted downhill, to find a farm nestled along a forest, the ground low and uneven around it, dotted with rotting stumps. Trees had been felled and the wood cut and taken away, but the stumps were still there, sentries to Amos and his dreaminess, his unwillingness to finish a job he started.

As they approached, the mule, with a final burst of speed, sensed the presence of home. Hester was appalled to discover an Amish farm quite like this one. She had not known it was possible, or even godly, to live in such squalor. The farm lay in another church district, a natural border dividing it from her own church, perhaps a creek, a road, or a band of trees, so she had never met or known about this family.

The house was built of lumber and had grayed to a nondescript color since the once-new boards had been allowed to face the elements without the usual coat of whitewash. There was no porch, only the square, unadorned two-story house with only one window on each side, small ones with even smaller panes.

The barn was small as well, surrounded by a split-rail fence in varying stages of disrepair. The vegetable patch was a growth of solid green, the weeds as high as the potato plants, the beans and yellowing pea vines barely visible among the thistles and crabgrass, burdock and red root.

As they approached, a small group of children, each barefoot with clothes torn and filthy, their hair uncombed, came around the corner of the house. They stopped and stared, the youngest sucking on thumbs, their knobby little knees showing through the holes in their trousers.

Stiff, yellowish-brown diapers, tablecloths, and towels had been thrown across the decaying yard fence to dry in the sun. Without a washline, that was suitable, Hester supposed.

The weeds and clumps of dry grass that was the yard around the house contained firewood, broken wheels, bits of cloth, buckets upended or lying on their sides, cats as thin as pieces of slate, and red-eyed chickens with all their tail feathers missing, pecking belligerently at any remaining bits of food or bugs not eaten by the whole hungry flock.

Washtubs and a scrubbing board stood close to the door, the bare earth around them wet and gray from being sloshed repeatedly by the water containing lye soap and dirt.

"Here we are, Mrs. Stoltzfus!" Amos sang out.

Hester felt her mouth widen into a polite semblance of a smile, an acknowledgment, before she stepped down from the cart, lifted the valise containing her clean clothes, then picked her way gingerly between the broken pottery and angry chickens to the front door. The wide-eyed children stayed rooted in place, nothing moving except for the soft motion of their mouths, drawing comfort from the thumbs inside them.

Taking a deep breath, Hester knocked at the faded gray door, noticing the broken board where the thin shadowy cats had easy access to the interior of the house.

"Komm rye!"

The voice came from what Hester supposed was the bedroom. As her eyes adjusted to the dim light, she saw a pallet made with graying covers in the corner beside the blackened fireplace. A slim form lay inert, the small face turned to the wall as motionless as a doll. This must be the injured daughter.

It was the smell that stopped her from going into the bedroom. Thick and cloying, the rancid stench colored the air around her with images of unwashed diapers, overfull chamber pots, spoiled food, unswept floors, unwashed beds and bodies. Hester almost turned and fled.

She imagined herself running, her feet skimming the earth as she flew down the hot, dusty road, finally reaching the shade of a heavy forest, and never stopping until she reached her home in the town of Lancaster.

From the hearth, a teenaged daughter glared at her. She was holding the newborn infant wrapped in a gray blanket, her eyes petulant and unwelcoming. Hester directed a faltering smile in the vicinity of the fireplace, swallowed, and made herself enter the bedroom.

A low bed stood against the opposite wall. The only light came from an uncurtained window that was stark and yellow, trapping sunshine and shimmering heat. A woman was propped up by two pillows, both stained and brown. A light quilt was thrown across her legs. Her face was large and square, the jaw as prominent as a man's, but her eyes were kind, in spite of being so small they appeared to be two black dots in the big face.

"So you are the *maud*."

Not a question, no inquiry about her well-being, not even a request for her name. Only a recognition that the *maud* was here, which, Hester supposed, was a lifeline thrown to a drowning person.

"Fannie is hurt, we don't know yet how bad. Amos thinks her back will heal."

Her voice became strident, then, impatient with what Hester supposed was her lot in life. "I know it's *shreck-lich*. We didn't start out this way. I'm going to ask you to just take ahold, do whatever you see needs to be done, which is everything. I've been in bed for six days, so I have four more to go, I'm afraid. I'll get milk fever if I get out too soon. Had it last time. Put the girls to work. They don't always listen to me. Amos is so easygoing with the children."

Here she paused.

"I'm awful hungry," she soon said. "Dinnertime is past, but it seems Rachel didn't know what to make."

Grimly, Hester set her lips, glanced at the valise clutched in her white-knuckled hands, and asked where she would sleep so she could put her things away.

"Oh, upstairs somewhere. We supposed you could sleep with Rachel since Fannie hurt her back."

Turning, Hester made her way upstairs and into the acrid smell of stifling rooms filled with sheets used by a horde of little bedwetters. She had no way of knowing which bed was Rachel's, so she set the valise down and made her way downstairs.

Looking around, she took stock of the situation. The hearth was unswept. Rachel and the baby sat rocking on gray ashes and bits of burnt wood. The long trestle table was piled with unwashed dishes and bits of leftover food, all on top of a tablecloth that appeared to be stuck to the table in its own grease.

A cupboard on the opposite wall contained more dishes, so Hester piled all the soiled ones on the dry sink against the other wall. When she tugged at the tablecloth to remove it, she found it stuck so tightly, she had to unearth a knife to scrape at the substance that held it to the tabletop.

Rachel sneered, "Leave it on."

Hester pretended not to hear and kept right on scraping until she lifted it off, stiff with weeks of food and mold. Holding it away from her body, she flung it out the door close to the washtubs, then turned to go back in, determined to get food on the table somehow.

Slowly, the small kitchen filled up with children trickling in through the doors. They were wide-eyed and silent, filthy and painfully thin, with sores around their eyes, mosquito bites, and angry-looking rashes, their hair stiff with dirt and the lack of a comb.

This home was no different than those in the poorest section of Lancaster. Perhaps worse. How could they live like this, having been brought up in the hard-working expectations of Amish culture? Hadn't they arrived from spotless farms in the Rhine Valley in Switzerland? Weren't they successful landowners in Germany?

Quite clearly, something had gone awry. Maybe it was a rebellion against a harsh parent or simplemindedness, marrying a girl who didn't know any better or who had given birth to such an overwhelming number of children in so short a space of time that she had given up and gradually, without noticing, had succumbed to hopelessness.

CHAPTER 16

Hester did get dinner on the table, but not without snapping at the insolent Rachel, telling her to give the infant to her mother, then sending her to the garden for beans, scattering the other children with orders to help their sister.

There was no bread or cheese, so Hester stirred up a panful of biscuits. By raking the coals, she unearthed a few red embers, so she could set the biscuits to bake after bits of kindling flared into a fire.

She found a cloth, spread it on the soiled table, and covered it with dishes, including using some tumblers that were half-clean. Since there was no meat to be found, she boiled a pot of cornmeal, then took Rachel's beans, which she handed over disdainfully, and set them to boil as well. She used only salt to flavor them since she was unable to find even a bit of salt pork or bacon.

Amos was fetched, and the children scrambled to their assigned places. Five boys appeared from the barn, in varying stages of adolescence, pimply-faced, sullen, and as thin as rails. They watched Hester with small, narrowed eyes, like trapped ferrets.

At the sight of the enormous pan of biscuits, the vast pot of cornmeal mush, plenty of milk, and enough green beans to go around, their eyes glittered with hunger and something close to happiness. They smiled tight smiles, jostled one another, poked stick-thin elbows into prominent ribs, and whispered, "S, *gukt vie blenty.*"

There was plenty, and they ate ravenously like starving wolves. Amos grinned, smacked his lips, and ladled large portions out for the children. Hester took a plateful to his wife, inquiring now about her name, which was Salina. She seemed to be embarrassed to pronounce her own name, blushing pink and blinking her eyes rapidly. Hester felt a stab of pity in spite of the nauseating stench surrounding her, which made it impossible for her to eat. She tucked a cold biscuit into the pocket of her skirt, knowing she would need her strength later.

That whole day remained a blur of motion as she barked orders and pushed the angry Rachel and her sister Sallie to the dry sink with orders to wash and to keep washing until every dish was clean.

Behind her back, they stuck out their tongues, giggling, but they set to work while Hester emptied pots, swept, scrubbed, and built a roaring fire in the yard. Then she scrubbed and washed and boiled clothes and bedsheets and towels some more until it was time to prepare yet another huge meal.

She threw open the door and the windows, preferring flies to the smell that seemed to cling to the walls of the house, to live in the floors, and to dangle from the ceiling like cobwebs.

Rachel grudgingly offered that there were potatoes and salt pork down cellar, and some turnips and carrots if Hester wanted them, but she refused to go down the ladder to get them.

"There's a black snake down there. I know it," she said forcefully.

Hester growled, "Well, then, I guess we won't eat."

"I'm going to tell Mam how you talk to us."

With that, she did, followed by the whining voice of Salina asking Hester to go down cellar, that Rachel was very afraid of snakes.

Hester grabbed a reed basket, backed down the ladder into total darkness, and groped her way to the potato bin. She reached into sprouts and decayed matter, the nauseous mushiness of spoiling turnips, spiderwebs, and finally, the greasy barrel of salted pork. She guessed if there were snakes down here, they'd likely slither away with all the banging and scraping she was doing, partly because she was so angry and partly to do just that, scare the snakes.

She was greeted at the top of the stairs by Rachel's triumphant eyes alive with mockery, knowing full well she could get away with anything she chose, fortified by her mother's sympathy. Twelve-year-old Sallie, it seemed, had a whole other relationship with her mother. Salina snapped at her from the bedroom for the slightest misdemeanor.

Hester lowered her head, refusing to acknowledge Rachel's superiority, and set to scraping carrots, peeling potatoes and turnips, adding more beans to the mix, and then setting the immense pot over the fire, sweat trickling into her eyes as she turned to making more biscuits. While they baked, she fried thin slices of salt pork and then made a milk gravy, thick and smooth and filling.

With that meal, she won the heart of each thin and hungry boy around the table, their empty stomachs a way of life. Now filled and sated, they were comfortable, their moods and energy given a boost they didn't know was possible. Shyly, with eyes averted, thumbs hooked in trouser pockets, and shoulders squared for courage, they said, "*Sell vowa so goot. Denke.*"

Hester blinked the wetness from her eyes, smiled, and said, "*Gyan schöena.*" They were so welcome. It was a joy to fill those stomachs.

A low moan from the pallet alerted Hester to Fannie's needs. She had had no time before this to check on her. Rachel had fed her. And between them, Amos and Rachel had helped her to the outdoor toilet, Fannie's face a mask of pain and suffering.

Hester went to Fannie's pallet, sank to her knees, and asked what was wrong.

"It hurts."

"Has the doctor been here?"

"No."

"Where does it hurt, Fannie?"

"Low in my back."

"Can you roll on your side?"

"I believe I can."

Despite Rachel's disapproval, Hester helped her, easing her gently as Fannie took a deep breath, then began crying softly. Quickly, before Rachel went to her mother with tales of more martyrdom, Hester opened the back of the soiled nightgown. Feeling along the painfully thin spine, she found a bulge of grossly swollen vertebrae and peered closely at the discoloration, the blue fading to red, the sickening yellow and green.

Hester's soft hands explored lightly and tenderly. When she felt the heat and inflammation, she knew what to do. Nettles and plantain leaves, cooked with wood ashes and white wine, would act as a liniment.

She stopped, straightened, and focused her mind as Fannie's soft crying continued. She would not give in. She had vowed, making a silent pact with herself, that she would no longer practice using medicinal herbs. Instead, she put a pillow against Fannie's back to ease her suffering, filled the wooden tubs with warm water, and proceeded to wash the children's heads with loads of shaved lye soap. Amid plenty of rebellious yells, threats, and grimaces, she sloshed and splashed, showing no mercy as she scrubbed, then parted clean hair to check for lice or fleas from those bilious-looking cats that slunk in and out like an evil vapor.

When darkness fell, nature's curtain of privacy, she built another fire, heated more water, and bathed every one of the little ones. She gave orders to the boys, who promptly informed her that they bathed in the creek every month or so, and the month wasn't up yet. Whereupon she informed them they should be bathing every week, with a bit of hysteria injected into the word "week." She sent them off with a chunk of soap and a bundle of clean clothes and told them not to come back till everyone was thoroughly washed and had clean clothes on, as well, *Denke schöen.*

Rachel and Sallie staged a rebellion, which Hester quelled in a hurry. She was close to total exhaustion and her patience was in short supply. She longed to lie down anywhere, even on the bare floor, and close her eyes.

Hester lowered her face into Rachel's and gripped her shoulders, her eyes exuding the black fire of her outrage. She told her that she was an Indian, and if she wouldn't do what Hester wanted, Hester was not afraid to call the *schpence* of her Indian heritage. Old ghosts of the past, she said.

Hester's shoulders shook with laughter as the girls disappeared, casting wide-eyed glances over their shoulders as they went. Maybe it was not the best form of discipline, but it worked on Rachel.

Far into the night after the children were in bed, lying on straw ticks without sheets, their bodies washed, their hair clean, Hester stayed up, retrieving clean laundry from every fence and bush available. She would wash the ticks tomorrow and ask Amos for clean straw. She would address the bedwetting as well.

From her corner, Fannie cried softly, her cries turning to moans, then back to sighs. Her small, soft sobs wrapped themselves so tightly around Hester's heart, she felt as if she could not go on living or breathing.

Finally, when the washing was folded in neat stacks on the table, she heard Fannie pray in the only way she knew how.

"Ich bin Klein,
Mine heartz macht rein,

Lest niemand drinn vonnen
Aus Jesus alein."

A great and terrible conviction gripped Hester's soul, and she could not stand against its righteousness. All that firmness she had built around herself would have to melt away. She would forget all this focus on self and think only of poor, suffering Fannie in the way that Jesus healed the suffering, knowing full well not everyone approved of what he did.

She stopped, shaken to the core, with this new understanding. Well, she wasn't Jesus, not even close, but if she could spare this suffering, she would.

She didn't feel very holy, when she told Rachel she'd send her Indian ghosts on her, that was sure.

Quickly, her exhaustion forgotten, she took down the oil lantern, lifted the chimney, and lit it with an ember. Where were Amos's matches? Likely filched away somewhere, handily brought out to light his odorous pipe. She heard his snores, and Salina's soft ones, as she let herself out the door. No need to stir up another cauldron of protest or chunks of unbelief.

The night was dark with only a sliver of white light from the moon. The stars blinked from their dark space, little pinpricks of soft, white, midsummer light. Crickets chirped an occasional goodnight tiredly. The more gutsy katydids filled in with their energetic tempo.

The grass was already wet with dew. Hester's bare feet felt washed by the coolness as her long strides took her to the fencerow at the end of the winding uphill lane. Her muscles ached, but in a good way. She would sleep well in spite of the dirt and the smell in the house.

The flickering yellow light from the lantern cast a comforting arc around her, catching the winking dew on the tips of grasses. She had no problem finding nettles, as she knew she wouldn't, but the broad-leafed plantain was harder to locate. She finally climbed an unsteady rail fence, hoping there were no bad-tempered cows or a bull to chase her off. She settled for a dry hilltop where the cows had eaten most of the grass. But they had left piles of dung in the almost bare pastureland, and thick grass grew around them, including the plantain, which bovines don't eat.

She grabbed two tough leaves, then beat a hasty retreat when she heard the lowing of a cow, answered by the high bleating of a calf. Sometimes a mother cow protecting her offspring was as bad as an ill-tempered bull, or worse.

Almost running now, the lantern light bobbing up and down with her rapid footsteps, Hester hurried to the house, the pure clean smells of the summer's night giving way to the scent of filthy living. As she entered the house, she knew she would never become accustomed to the wall of pungence that enveloped her.

She boiled water, then added the plants, letting them steep like good tea. Lifting the lantern, she slid noiselessly backward into the cellar. She searched among the half-rotten vegetables for wine or vinegar, but found only dusty bottles of aged whiskey, which would have to do.

She found an empty, small glass jar and returned to the kitchen, washing it quickly. Then she bottled the whiskey, the extract of the plantain leaves, and the nettles and shook the mixture vigorously. She liberally soaked a half-clean rag with the warm liquid. Then she spoke softly to Fannie, who was lying wide-eyed in the semidarkness, her hands crossed on her chest, silent tears sliding down the sides of her face and pooling into wet spots on her pillow.

Gently, she lay Fannie on her side, then applied the cloth so softly Fannie hardly knew Hester had touched her. On top of the cloth she laid the wet plantain leaf, put another cloth on top, and then let her roll gently back, lying against the poultice. Fannie sighed and turned her head to the wall.

Hester slept on the floor rather than sleep with the belligerent Rachel. She fell into a deep sleep without dreams, her head resting on her outstretched arm, the air warm and acrid around her.

When she heard Amos call the boys to do the milking, she pulled herself up into a sitting position, her muscles sore and stiff.

Why wasn't Rachel expected to help milk? Spoiled child.

Hester had been too taken up with last evening's tasks to think of the morning meal. She suddenly knew her first job was to find some sort of food for breakfast. First, she bent over Fannie's pallet, alarmed to find only a slight rise in the quilt and fearing she wasn't there. So slight, so terribly thin, these children.

She resolved to talk with Amos and Salina about finding more and better food for their growing offspring, and with special concern for the new babies which they added with such regularity. Well, if they didn't cooperate, she would do what Bappie did—march right over to John Kauffman, the bishop, and alert the church to this family's needs. If something was not done soon, the church would have to place these children in other, more capable homes. This was done at times, Hester knew well.

Fannie opened her eyes. A new sensation dawned in her eyes, and they opened wider. A small, shadowed smile clung to the corners of her too-wide mouth, a slash in the pale, peaked face.

"How do you feel, Fannie?" Hester whispered.

"It's not so bad."

"Isn't it?"

Fannie shook her head. Then, "I'm so hungry."

Hester patted the thin shoulder. "I'll hurry up with breakfast."

She found only ten eggs, hidden under pieces of unused lumber, wheels, and a broken wagon. She took a garden rake and swung it fiercely if one of the red-eyed chickens came close. She beat the eggs, added milk, salt, and plenty of flour and baking powder, making an *egg kuchen* of sorts. She stirred up more biscuits and put a big pitcher of milk on the table. That was breakfast. It had to be. There was nothing else, unless some new potatoes could be salvaged from that vast sea of solid weeds called a garden.

As usual, Amos was jovial, his good spirits infectious, lighting the sleepy eyes of the little ones and making the boys smile shyly. Salina ate all her breakfast in bed, thanked Hester, and went back to cuddling the wee bundle, who had not been bathed at all. Hester planned to do that as soon as possible.

She told Amos she needed the boys that day to clean the vegetable patch, or they would not have anything to put down cellar for winter. Amos nodded agreeably, saying he had to go to *schtettle* anyway.

Hester said if he went to town, she had a list of things for him to buy. When he frowned, she told him in firm, clipped tones that if he was going to be too tight-fisted to see that his family was fed, then she was going to see the bishop, John Kauffman, and not the less decisive Rufus King.

Amos blushed a furious red, put on his sweat-streaked hat, and let himself out the door, closing it none too gently behind him.

Instantly, the boys spoke as one. "Would you? Are you going to? What would he say? Is someone coming to talk to Dat and Mam?"

Questions pelted Hester like a hailstorm and were every bit as painful. Could it be true that these boys actually lived in deprivation, leading lives of hunger and repression? Hester came to believe it as the boys kept asking questions.

Of course there was the matter of Fannie, too, told to lie on her pile of blankets in the corner, without sending for the doctor. The monstrosity of the situation was like a multi-layered disaster. You took off one layer, only to keep discovering other layers underneath.

Hester said nothing. She wrote the shopping list, then ran to the barn and handed it to Amos. She reminded him that the house contained very little to eat, and if he wanted to avoid public shaming in the church, he would need to bring back everything on that note. *Everything.* Coffee would be nice, too. Oh, Amos said, that was far too expensive. Hester quickly told him then, that he needed to stop buying tobacco and matches, too.

Afterward, Hester found she was shaking, although she felt empowered and alive in a good way. A mountain of work lay ahead of her, but adrenaline flowed through her veins, fueled by her newfound purpose in setting things right. She hadn't once thought of Noah or his invitation to travel to Berks County. Not for at least two hours anyway.

She set Rachel to churning butter, Sallie to washing dishes. She accompanied the boys to the vegetable patch and instructed them in the proper technique of pulling weeds and cultivating the soil with a hoe. They picked the overripe peas; they'd be all right cooked with sliced carrots in a cream sauce. Rachel and Sallie joined them later, setting to work at picking the green beans. They harvested the late radishes and the wilted lettuce. Nothing went to waste, not even the tops of the red beets.

Hester left the children to their work and went to take care of Fannie. She was softly crying, but only because she had accidentally soiled the bed. Hester crooned to her, assured her it was all right and that she should have come sooner.

When she changed the bed, boiled and washed the bedding, then bathed the thin body, the great angry bruise on the girl's lower back felt like a vise around Hester's heart. Fannie said she would like to try walking now.

First, a fresh poultice needed to be applied and tied in place. Then Hester lifted her gently, her hands cupped beneath the bony hollows of the child's underarms. Fannie grimaced, then gasped, but Hester held her steadily, smoothly lowering her weight onto her feet when she was ready.

Fannie took two very small steps as she rested her hands on Hester's extended forearms and leaned into the smiling encouragement on Hester's face.

"My back is not broken, is it?" she whispered.

"No. Oh, no. Only bruised very badly."

"It will heal?"

"Yes. I believe it will. Do you want to show your mam?"

"She probably won't want to see me. When she has a new baby, she doesn't want us for a while."

"Oh, she will. Come."

Hester refused to believe Fannie's statement, knowing Salina would be so comforted by the sight of her daughter standing upright.

"Salina? Are you awake?" Hester called softly.

"Oh, yes," came the soft reply.

"Look!" Beaming with excitement, Hester led Fannie to the doorway. Intent on the face of her newborn, Salina afforded Fannie only a short glance, saying, "I figured it wasn't broken," and went back to the baby.

Fannie remained stoic as she followed Hester out to her pallet where she was willingly lowered, a sheen of perspiration along her upper lip, testimony to the pain still present in her lower back.

"You're a brave girl, Fannie. You really are."

Hester smoothed back the hair on her forehead, then caressed the thin, pale cheek, softly stroking her face, before bending to kiss her.

Fannie's brown eyes opened wide, sparkling with amazement. "I often wondered how a kiss would be," she said, smiling fully for the first time.

What an astoundingly pretty face, Hester thought, like an underfed little fairy. A feeling of so much love that she could barely contain it swept over Hester like a life-giving rain to a parched and barren desert. She had never imagined such a sweetness of love and life and living, that had little to do with her personal desires and didn't begin by serving her own selfish happiness. She was suddenly exploring the unending possibilities of life, triggered by a wellspring of something she could not explain. She felt privileged to care for this broken-down little soul who was living in the corner of a room on a pile of blankets, whispering a child's German prayer through her tears.

Hester laid the palm of her hand against Fannie's cheek, so tiny and pale, for what she guessed was an eight-year-old.

"How old are you, Fannie?"

"I'm eleven. Sallie is twelve."

With that pronouncement, Hester knew without a smidgen of doubt she would be going to see John Kauffman before the week was up.

In the meantime, Hester cooked and baked, washed endless tubfuls of dirty clothes, scoured and scrubbed, lectured, and taught the children how to be useful, to care about the appearance of the yard, to pen up the chickens, to build nests where they could lay their eggs.

Amos remained agreeable and good-humored to a fault. He even bathed in the creek one evening, although he then dressed himself in the same clothes he had worn for almost a week.

Salina left her bed, dressed, combed her greasy hair filled with flakes of white dandruff, put on a limp, whitish-gray kerchief, and settled herself into the hickory rocker by the hearth.

The little ones climbed on her lap, clamoring for attention. She ladled it out sparingly, but it was there. Salina remarked on the house's order, the freshly baked bread, the good butter. Rachel told her almost shyly that she had done all the churning. But when that brought no praise, the hooded, sullen look replaced her hope of a few words of praise from her mother.

Hester was quick to notice. She touched Rachel's shoulder, telling her she could not have done it without her, with all the washing and cleaning she had to do. Rachel's eyes flashed a quick grasp of Hester's thanks, but then turned away just as quickly, before Hester would see her tears.

That evening Hester boiled the last of the sweet potatoes she found down cellar, made a brown sugar sauce for topping them, cooked beets with sugar and vinegar, and split a ham into two pieces before boiling one part in a pot on the hearth. Then she instructed Rachel about how to make a sponge cake and set Sallie to bring in the washing and fold it, while eight-year-old Eva set the table.

Salina took this all in, observing the way Hester put these girls to work, and her small, black eyes filled with hope. Was that the way other women got their work done, when she never could? Aloud, she said, "If I had a cookstove, I could make better meals."

"Ask Amos," Hester remarked.

"Oh, he doesn't like to part with his money." She lifted the baby to her shoulder, patting the tiny little back, the baby's legs scrooched in under his stomach like a baby squirrel.

She watched as Rachel whipped the cake batter, her strong, young arms never tiring of the effort.

At the supper table, the family ate and ate, enjoying every spoonful of the good, wholesome food. By now, the row of older boys almost worshipped Hester, the saving grace sent into their lives in the form of a *maud* to help out for awhile.

Hester looked at Amos and told him his wife needed a cookstove, and a good one, now that they had 13 children, and it wouldn't be a bad idea to build her a washhouse either. No wonder the clothes didn't get washed if she had to do it out in the cold of winter and heat of summer. And did he ever think of putting up a washline?

"Oh, this stuff costs money!" he exclaimed. "*An lot gelt.*"

"You have money, people say," she replied quickly, knowing nothing about it but hoping it would bring the desired response.

Amos lifted his shoulders and inhaled, clearly enjoying the thought of other people thinking he had money. "Well, I have some put away."

Startled, Salina looked at her husband. She could clearly not believe the words from his mouth. "You need to buy these things. Take a bit of pride in this place. The boys can paint."

Amos narrowed his eyes and looked at his row of sons, who were already losing the furtive, hungry look that ruined their faces so much of the time. His gaze went to his daughters, slim, capable young girls, who were so unaccustomed to attention from their father that they all blushed deeply, lowered their faces to their plates, and kept them there.

One thing kept the family together, sparing them the pain of being separated, with some of the older ones being put into other homes to be raised—Amos's good humor. He was too unconcerned to be harsh; he just didn't think. It had never occurred to him that they needed more money for staples like flour and sugar and oatmeal, or a cookstove and a washline. He thought a fireplace and a fence was just all right for Salina, and she was too simple or too afraid to ask.

Hester still couldn't understand her. What woman would be so taken with yet another baby, leaving an eleven-year-old crying silently in pain?

How Kate would have gathered little Fannie to her immense bosom, crying freely with her! Immediately, a new thought formed. Would Noah, like Kate, love Fannie, too?

CHAPTER 17

Hester entered a whole other world when Amos took her home on Saturday afternoon. She would attend church on Sunday, and he would return to fetch her on Monday morning. She'd have two blissful nights in her own clean bed, resting her battered muscles. She was bone-weary and had not had a decent bath, so being at home was a luxury that filled her with happiness.

The house was cool, orderly, and so clean. Hester ran a hand along the scrubbed oak table, the gleaming cookstove, the dishpans turned upside down in the dry sink. Even the glass-paned doors on the cupboard seemed to beam and wink with cleanliness. And the smell! The scent of soap and spices, of warm air flavored with growing things, the summer sun, even dust from the street, all of it seemed pure and sweet and unsullied.

Bappie was gone as usual, so the first thing Hester did was spread all the food on the table that she could find, pour a glass of cool buttermilk, and begin to eat. She had brown wheat bread, the crust hard and chewy,

. spread with good butter from Emma Ferree, plum preserves, dried venison, hard white cheese, new strawberries, a slice of custard pie, then another one, and more bread and butter.

She built a fire in the washhouse and filled the large iron kettle with water from the pump so she could wash her clothes first, followed by a good, long, Saturday-evening soak behind the curtain in the corner of the kitchen. Then she would visit Walter and Emma.

Hester was humming, her spirits revived by the waves of joy that broke over her, swelled around her senses, and filled her heart. The week was over. She was here now.

She sang as she scrubbed her clothes, wrung them dry, and hung them reservedly in a corner of the washhouse. No good housewife, or old maid or widow, would hang clothes in the backyard on a Saturday evening.

She filled the iron kettle again, upended the large tub, pulled the curtain out on its string, and was shaving the good scented soap into a bottle, when the door was pushed open, followed by a raucous cry from the ebullient Bappie.

"You're back!" she yelled, her hands clasped to her skinny chest.

"I am! Oh, I truly am!" Hester sang out.

"Well, it's good to see you, Hester. Leaving a note on the table and being whisked away by some Amos Stoltzfus was pure nonsense. What in the world, Hester?"

"I knew you wouldn't understand. This man had a wife in bed with a new baby, thirteen children, and a daughter with a broken back. Or so he thought. It isn't broken, only bruised."

Bappie's eyes narrowed. "How do you know?"

"I checked."

"You gathered herbs."

Hester's eyes twinkled, a dimple appearing on one cheek when she smiled only slightly. "I did. But, oh, Bappie! You have no idea. I hardened my heart and turned away, determined not to give in, but she cried so softly and is so painfully thin and repeated '*Ich bin Klein*,' the children's prayer, over and over, until I just lit a lantern and went to gather nettles and plantain."

"That is a good thing. God's ways aren't so mysterious sometimes, now are they? What about Noah?"

"What about him?"

Hester looked straight at Bappie, the twinkle in her eye erased, the dimple flattened by the grim line of her mouth.

"Does he know about you being out at Amos's?"

"Of course not. Why would he?"

Bappie turned without another word and let herself out the back door, slamming it harder than necessary on her way out. Hester shrugged her shoulders and began the ritual of her Saturday night bath.

Later she was welcomed and fussed over, with questions popping from Walter's and Emma's mouths. They made her sit down and have a glass of grape juice, cool and sweet from the cellar.

Walter said the butcher had a new product called Lebanon bologna, which was a tad spicy, heavy on black pepper especially, but if you ate it in small quantities, accompanied by buttered toast, it was exquisite. In spite of the heat remaining in the kitchen at this hour of the evening, he lit the kindling in the cookstove, brought out a cast-iron skillet, and proceeded to fry slabs of Emma's good bread in copious amounts of melting butter. He sprinkled the fried bread with bits of thyme and rosemary before serving the crispy slices with round, thinly sliced portions of the new bologna.

Richard and Vernon had gone to the neighbors, Mr. and Mrs. Amesly, to play with their children in the back alley, returning as the light in the windows began to fade and Emma got up to light the coal oil lamps. Richard had grown into a strong-limbed, towheaded little boy, his face round with cheeks like apples, gleaming with good health. Vernon was taller and thinner, but like Richard, the picture of health and contentment.

Hester's throat constricted as she watched Vernon grasp Emma's heavy upper arm in both hands, smiling up into her round, dimpled face before laying his head on her plump shoulder, her arm bringing him close to her side.

Richard grunted, the effort of pulling himself into Walter's lap turning his face dark with his maneuvering. Walter, so intent on placing a slice of bologna exactly in the center of the buttered toast, failed to discern this.

"Walter," Emma said, sharply.

"Oh, oh, goodness, Richard, goodness."

He quickly placed the eagerly awaited food on the plate, licked his heavy red fingers, and bent to help Richard onto his lap.

Hester smiled to herself, wondering what had become of the English napkins. Or was he slowly being converted to the more relaxed style of the Pennsylvania Dutch?

She watched as he bent sideways to cut the delicacy in half and handed one section to Richard before finally closing his mouth around his own portion, closing his eyes in appreciation.

It was so good to be home here with Walter and Emma, to have good food, and to relax in the luxury of being clean and rested and well fed.

Already, Sunday was almost here, and so soon it would be over.

Church services were held in the home of Danny and Lydia Miller, who had a prosperous farm east of Lancaster, only two miles from the town.

Hester dressed in a blue shortgown and pinned the traditional black cape and apron over it. The many layers of fabric were designed to disguise the womanly charms of her figure. Plentiful gathers in her black apron discreetly hid the curve of her hips. The hem of her long, full skirt fell to her shoe tops. The cape hung slightly over her shoulders and was pinned loosely down the front. She tucked the ends beneath the thin band that was the belt of her apron. The sleeves were long, all the way to her wrists, and loose without adornment. She tied her muslin cap beneath her chin. The cap was large and shielded most of her hair and her ears.

In spite of the austere dress code, there was no hiding Hester's grace and beauty. Even from a distance, her gait was lithe and fluid, her steps easy, befitting the Indian princess she was. Her face was small, oval, and well proportioned, her big, dark eyes pools of light and dusk, twilight and night. Womanly thoughts and secrets were stored away in their depths.

As Hester aged, her beauty increased from winsome girl to a woman who had suffered, having experienced life and its imperfections. Her spirit was like the gold that can emerge from refining, when bitter dross is burned away. She believed that a greater being was in control of her destiny, which lent her an aura of restfulness, of quiet contentment.

Beside her, Bappie strode along with her choppy gait bobbing her up and down, her arms swinging vigorously. She was shorter, but the brown dress she wore covered her identically, including the heavy black cape and apron, the large cap, black shoes, and serviceable stockings.

Her hair was like tamed fire, combed severely for now. Her brown eyes danced and the freckles traveled along. They had been stamped on her fair skin the day she was born. The summer sun always deepened their color, even as it heated the skin beneath to an alarming pink that would turn into an attractive copper hue as the summer waned.

Bappie's sheer happiness could easily be accounted as beauty, or at least radiance. She was betrothed, promised, wanted by the one man she had both pitied and admired. Now, given free rein, her love was like a tropical flower, lush, watered, a thing beautiful to behold.

At the Miller farm, a few buggies were parked along the barnyard fence. The horses had been led into the cool interior of the barn, given a cool drink at the trough, then tied to a stall to wait till church services were over. The barn itself was similar to Dan Stoltzfus's barn, the one Noah had worked on for almost a year.

Painted white, it had louvered windows on the gable ends and fancy trim along the front, where glass windows gleamed in the hot morning sun.

Freshly painted board fencing outlined the rectangular garden, a showcase of beautiful vegetables. The dark earth between the rows had been loosened with a hoe, a testimony to hours of labor. Already, the sweet corn was higher than a person of medium height. The potato plants were dotted with white, star-shaped blooms, the harbinger of large, brown-skinned potatoes growing underneath.

The beans and beets looked lush. The wide bare spot where the pea vines had been pulled was now tilled and planted with lima beans or late corn. Along the garden fence, the huge, red-veined leaves of rhubarb plants thrived; the frilly tops of the carrots showed off like a decoration of lace.

Bappie said this was what her garden would look like after she and Levi were married. She had serious *zeitlang* to work in such a garden. Looked like Lydia didn't grow turnips, which was something Bappie would not do either. The sheep would eat them.

Hester saw Levi Buehler drive past, his buggy grayish, splattered with bits of mud, and coated with dust, his horse a bit ungainly. He held his neck out at a tired angle, not high with a spirited stance, the way some horses did. It was just the way Levi was—relaxed and happy, never competitive, nor trying to make a show of his own good management. If the buggy was less than clean, well, no one would notice or care.

Unfortunately, Bappie did.

First she said, "There goes Levi."

Then she followed it with, "He should have washed his buggy."

Followed by, "After we're married, I'm getting rid of that horse. He runs like a cow."

Hester smiled. Levi climbed down from his buggy, caught sight of his future bride, and beamed like a ray of sunlight before turning away quickly, busying himself with the reins. But it was enough for Bappie, who had caught Levi's shining look of happiness, which seemed to take away her dissatisfaction with the less than clean buggy and cow-like horse.

Hester smiled wider but lowered her face before someone caught her being bold or brazen on a Sunday morning. It was bad enough that Bappie had persuaded her not to wear a hat that day. A hat was a Sunday requirement. Large enough to cover all of one's hair and the sides of one's head when it was pulled front, a hat did its part to obscure a face, so that a woman's appearance was mostly a shapeless, black figure, the rustling of skirts on shoe tops the only distraction from the severity.

Bappie refused to wear the thing on hot summer days, stating briefly that if someone didn't like it, they could come talk to her. She had once gone barefoot to church, which was met by drawn eyebrows and mouths turned down like upended bowls of disapproval. Whispers and head-wagging were of course followed by a visit from the deacon, Abner Esh, from south of town.

Bappie wouldn't admit it to Hester, but she was plenty shook up by the visit, ashamed, humiliated, and even a wee bit sorry after being rebuked in Abner's loving, godly manner. Her face was white as a clean pillowcase when she came back into the house, after he had spoken to her on the back stoop. She wouldn't say much to Hester, but she didn't need to, as her face flamed and her eyes blinked rapidly and she told Hester she didn't care what anyone thought, she wasn't going to wear shoes to church in this humidity. But she did care. She was ashamed of her own boldness, and she wore her shoes and stockings to church from that day on.

In the Millers' house, the furniture had all been put in the bench wagon or stacked against the back wall of the bedroom to make way for long lines of wooden benches. Copies of the thick, chunky *Ausbund*, the black hymnal filled with German hymns that had been written centuries before by prisoners who languished in the cells of a Swiss castle for their faith, were scattered over the benches.

Some women stood in the kitchen, all dressed similarly in modest clothes, their arms crossed, talking, smiling, and greeting one another with firm handshakes and holy kisses, as they believed the Bible instructed.

Little girls were in blue, purple, or green, with plain and unadorned white pinafores. Their small muslin caps were tied beneath their chins with wide strings; their bare feet peeped out beneath the hems of their dresses.

As always, Hester was glad to see all the members of the church, especially the women she met regularly every two weeks. She knew them all, their names, their children and husbands, where they lived, who would be having a new addition to the family, and many other facts about their lives. When there was a barnraising, she was there, cooking and sharing community news, trying not to gossip but enjoying a few hair-raising bits of it. When a child died, or an elderly person, she was there, helping with the food, cleaning, and cooking some more.

Weddings, funerals, accidents, barnraisings—each was a calling to pitch in, to willingly give what she could, even if it was just a few loaves of bread or a pie, babysitting or cleaning the house, raking the yard or quickly sewing black dresses. It was all about being part of a body of people, cultivating bonds of love and belonging.

And yet she longed to return to Berks County, at least out of curiosity, as she wondered about the welfare of her people beyond her family—Theodore Crane and Lissie, her friend Amanda—all of the folks she could picture so clearly in those times when she felt the tugging at her heart.

But first she would finish at Amos Stoltzfus's, delaying until they were in a better situation. She would wait.

And so it seemed right, this waiting, as the first lines of the song rose and fell around her. She felt a settling of her spirit, a sense of balance as she was finding her way. She could help with the singing, her throat swelling with an emotion that felt good, the words tumbling over her parted lips like a clear brook of sound. Doing the right thing was no longer a burden. It would materialize out of life. All she had to do was wait.

Noah was not in church. She had not seen his bright hair among the darker colors but figured he might only be late. She felt a sense of depletion, a vague uneasiness. Had he been to Bappie's house, only to find her gone with no explanation? She found it unlikely. With a jolt, she wondered if he may have gone to Berks County alone. The thought brought a sense of failure so sharp it took her breath away, leaving her with only short, shallow breaths of panic.

Where had all the rightness gone? One minute peace wrapped itself around her; in the next, Noah had destroyed it the way he always did. Well, she hoped he did go to Berks County without her. It would be better if he went by himself and stayed there, and she stayed in Lancaster, always. He scattered her senses, raced through her mind, churned it all up, and confused her. Just like now.

But the voices of the preachers were comforting. They delivered their sermons in a kind of traditional chant carried over from the Catholic church where the priests would elevate their voices, the Latin rising and falling, a singsong way of speaking that was both comforting and regular, like the sun's rising or clouds giving way to summer rain or birdsong in spring.

Under the sound of the Amish minister's German words going up, then down, her choppy and distorted thoughts quieted, rested, and slowly absorbed words from Scripture. She heard admonishments, encouragement, and sometimes a story from the Old Testament, simplified in Pennsylvania Dutch for the children's benefit. As the voice droned on, Hester's eyes and thoughts roamed around the room. She wondered why Noah had not come to church.

Thinking about the upcoming week, the endless hard labor, planning and cooking of large meals, and with only a limited amount of food available, drained her energy and her spirit of joy and contentment if she dwelt on it. Better to let it go, if only for this afternoon.

It was when she was helping to serve the dinner that she caught sight of Noah's well-groomed blond hair, sitting in the row of single men and boys. Hester's stomach roiled one hard lurch, her breathing became quick and short, and the room spun sideways before righting itself. She almost dropped the dish of sweet pickles she was carrying. Quickly, she set it down on the farthest end of the table, turned, and exited the suddenly stifling room.

She wanted to talk to him. She wanted to walk beside him and tell him she would accompany him to her home in Berks County. She wanted to go now worse than ever. It was raging in her breast, this desire to return, if only to be seated beside Noah for two whole days, or three, however long he chose.

She did not want to go back to Amos Stoltzfus's, back to the smell, the beds that needed to be washed of their acrid odor, the children clamoring for only a shred of attention from the preoccupied Salina, to Fannie with her injured back and her lack of love, so gamely accepting the fact that her mother was done with her now that she wasn't needed because she had a new baby, that her brothers and sisters were all she had.

But were they?

She was on her way to find Bappie. Her head hurt. She wanted to go home and lie down in the coolness of the living room just for an hour, until her headache went away.

From the corner of her eye, a shadow came near. She turned. Noah whispered, "I'm coming to talk to you this evening." He had merely walked by, so casually and so quickly no one would have noticed. It was simply not acceptable, a single man speaking to a widowed woman in broad daylight.

It wasn't a question that he asked. It was a telling, the stating of a fact.

Hester bowed her head and walked away quickly. She found Bappie, and together they walked out the lane in the hot afternoon sun.

The heat was a shimmering, white cloak cast over the land in midsummer. But Hester noticed only the blue of the sky, the wild rosebushes, the white columbine growing in profusion along the road, the butterflies and meadowlarks, the song of the mockingbird that hopped along beside them like a raucous escort, trilling one mocking note after another.

The dust puffed up, coating their black shoes and the hems of their skirts, the hot winds tugged at their caps and riffled the edges of their capes. Hester talked, spreading her hands in emphasis. She laughed, trying to keep from skipping and throwing her arms wide, to restrain herself from lifting her face to the sun and saying, "Thank you, thank you."

Bappie eyed her sideways. "Sermon must have done you good."

"Oh, it did, it did."

Bappie let out a wee remnant of a snort, which Hester failed to hear. She knew it wasn't the sermon, but as skittish as Hester was about any mention of Noah, she chose, wisely, to keep her mouth closed, if only for this once.

They spent the afternoon sitting in the backyard, a bowl of popcorn and glasses of peppermint tea between them, talking.

Bappie sensed a new willingness in Hester to share her life, so she listened, only occasionally nodding or opening her eyes wide in acknowledgement of Hester's words.

She spoke of the mysterious Salina, of Amos and his lackadaisical view of the world, his farm, all those children, multiplying each year.

"Bunch a rabbits," Bappie said, straightforward.

"But, Bappie, I honestly think that is his pride and joy—to have a house overflowing with children. I imagine he sees all those hired hands and *mauda* out earning money which they'll bring home to him, the time when he can sit at the blacksmith shop in town and smoke that nasty old pipe to his heart's content."

"Well, maybe he is inclined to believe the Bible and is just so happy to have his quiver full. Just as Proverbs says, you know."

Hester nodded. "At any rate, I'm going back tomorrow morning to work all week, and probably several weeks after. If I could only get Salina motivated to teach Rachel and her sister to work. Can you believe, after every meal I still have to tell them to do the dishes? Then they slop around in lukewarm water with hardly any soap. They simply aren't taught."

"Do you dread going back?" Bappie turned her head, upended her glass of tea, and dumped the contents with a splash beside the steps.

Hester's shoulder shrug went unnoticed as the two women sat in the comfort of each other's company, not speaking. The quiet clucking and pecking of the chickens was a homey sound, as was the distant yell of a child, followed by the deep barking of a dog. Heat hung over the town. The shade of the maple tree, the occasional restless movement of its leaves, stirred by a muggy puff of air, did nothing to relieve the cloying warmth.

Bappie picked up her skirt and flapped it madly, her knobby white knees like startled white birds. "It's uncomfortably hot."

"It usually is, midsummer."

Bappie grinned, punching Hester's forearm. "Is Noah going?"

"Going where?"

"To Berks County?"

Hester's irritation showed by the flicker of fire in her dark eyes. Now how did she know anything about this? Eavesdropping, likely. She faced Bappie, squarely. "How do you know?"

"Oh, the birds were singing about it."

"Don't add a white lie on top of your other trespasses, namely, hiding somewhere and listening to Noah talking. You do that, you know."

"Do I? Nah, not me. No, never would, never will."

Hester glared at her till Bappie's words cut her off. "Well, miss secretive lady, let me tell you something. We choose to be happy, we choose to be miserable. But when unexpected love comes along, we don't brush it off. We grab it and thank our Heavenly Father.

"We take it, Hester, because it enriches our lives. Yes, you think, what does she want with that odd-looking Levi Buehler? You know, there was a time when I probably wouldn't have chosen him, and he wouldn't have wanted me either. I'm older now, a bit baggy and wrinkled, but then so is he. And if God wants us to enjoy the rest of our days together, well, then, so be it.

"I'll always cherish these years with you, Hester. Your friendship has made me into a better person, and I'll always carry that in my heart like a fulfillment. If you do go with Noah and you don't come back, let's never forget each other. You must write to me always. And Levi and I will visit."

Hester sat very still. Then she whispered, "That is so sweet, Bappie, my friend."

They sat together, the moment a lovely comfort of feelings.

"I'm so frightened of Noah, of marriage," Hester whispered finally, a sort of clutching, choking sound overriding her words.

"I guess you have reason to be, Hester. I can't make fun of your fears. But maybe, just maybe, you've suffered enough, and God knows you deserve better. Maybe he has a great, big, happy surprise for you, and you won't open that wonderful gift because of your fear. You're always looking back over your shoulder, hanging on to past mistakes, carrying them around like a sack of horse feed."

"You think?" Hester asked.

"I know."

They both stopped speaking as Noah's tall form rounded the corner of the barn, his bright hair tousled, his straw hat in his hand, relaxed, smiling, genuinely happy to see them both.

CHAPTER 18

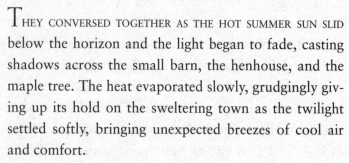

THEY CONVERSED TOGETHER AS THE HOT SUMMER SUN SLID below the horizon and the light began to fade, casting shadows across the small barn, the henhouse, and the maple tree. The heat evaporated slowly, grudgingly giving up its hold on the sweltering town as the twilight settled softly, bringing unexpected breezes of cool air and comfort.

Bappie yawned and stretched, saying she was going to bed since she had to be up early to go to the farm. "Sheep fence," she said, in a voice anything but humble, wanting to convey to Noah her anticipated prosperity. Sheep would need a large pasture, good water, and a solid fence, so she planned to help Levi with the acreage and the planning.

Hester knew Bappie would plan and Levi would follow, but she said nothing, hiding her grin in the dusky evening light.

After the door closed behind Bappie, a silence settled, an uncomfortable stillness. Hester felt the urge to say something, anything, to rid the air of prickliness.

She cleared her throat, picked a blade of grass, and wrapped it around her thumb, pulling it tight before breaking it.

Finally Noah spoke, inquiring about her week. Startled, Hester groped for the correct word. He didn't know she had gone to be a *maud* to the Amos Stoltzfuses.

"I wasn't here, you know."

"Oh, Amos Stoltzfus from east of here, close to Bird-in-Hand, needed a *maud*, so he came to see me."

"And?"

"I went."

"How was that?"

"All right, I guess."

"Hester, why did you go?"

"They needed me."

"There are plenty of single women around. The countryside is full of large families with girls loaned out for hire."

"I wanted to go."

Noah didn't reply. When he finally did speak, the kindness had returned, his voice softened by it. "I don't mean to be critical of your choices, but it has to be terribly hard work. Terribly. I know the Amos Stoltzfus family. The church is often called to help them out with food donations, labor, or handing over money from the collected alms to fish him out of yet another fiasco he got himself into. I know you meant well, Hester, and I'm sure you were great for that family, but I wish you would not go back."

"I need to go."

"Why?"

"Salina is not recovered from childbirth, Noah, and Fannie is hurt."

"Fannie?"

"The third daughter. She's eleven years old. She fell and hurt her back." Like the beginning of a slide down a snow-covered hill, Hester's halting first sentence gained momentum until she described in rich pathos the feel of that too-thin spine, the skeletal little body lying on a heap of filthy quilts, crying softly to herself when the pain became unbearable. She told him of her plant-gathering at night, all of it. Salina and her disconcerting way of looking up from her newborn, and Fannie's innocent acceptance of the fact that her mother didn't need her or much want her, now that she had another baby to care for.

"Hester, you surely know what will happen to her, don't you?"

"Well, I know some destitute families give their children to more well-to-do families to raise, don't they?"

"Yes, they do."

"Really *give*, to keep forever?" Hester whispered.

"It's a fact of life, Hester. It's sad, but when a father like Amos does his best and is not able to feed so many mouths, some actually do give their children to another household."

"I can see Salina doing that."

"Amos, too."

"He's always good-humored, though. He doesn't seem cruel. He says he has some money put by. It just never occurred to him that Salina might want a new cookstove or a washline."

"He has money?"

"That's what he says."

Noah sighed, "At any rate, you are not responsible to keep that household running smoothly. They have older children to carry on without you."

"But I need to go back. What will happen to Fannie? They'll put her with another family, and she won't be loved. Noah, please listen to me. She's so painfully thin, so disarmingly accepting of the few crumbs of caring she does receive, so content, asking nothing more from life but a bit to wear, a bit to eat. All her life, people will take advantage of her goodness. She'll be a slave, a white Amish slave, no better."

Hester's words rose with the passion she felt. Noah remained quiet, his legs stretched in front of him on the cool grass, the darkness now hiding his features. Only the lightness of his face and hair were visible. Down by the henhouse fence, a katydid began its clamoring call, the unsettling rhythm, the urgent squawk of its cadence. The answering call of another katydid rose high and sure, a beckoning. Still Noah did not speak.

She heard him get to his feet, felt, rather than saw, him bend in front of her, his thick arm and hand extended.

"Come, Hester, let's walk for a while. The fresh air and change of scenery will make us appreciate the coolness of evening."

She hesitated, then placed her hand in his. He never let go of it after that.

Hand in hand, they walked out of the short drive, the back alley, down Mulberry Street past the Lutheran church, then on to Vine Street, past the haberdashery, the wheelwright, and out of town, without speaking at all.

The silence was no longer prickly, but a kind of soothing quiet. A million white stars blinked above them. A half-moon allowed shadowy light, the merest whitewash of silver bathing them in the midsummer night's glow, spraying pearls of luminescence.

Noah's hand was wrapped firmly around her own, claiming her hand. When he dropped it suddenly, Hester did not understand, feeling cut off. It was as if the hand was an extra unwanted appendage, and she had no knowledge of what to do with it. She put it behind her back where it was safe without his hand.

When Noah spoke, his voice was garbled, as though coming from underwater or from a distance. "One more time, Hester, I will ask you. One more time I will lay everything at your feet. I know you hold my future in those perfect dark hands."

Hester's breathing stopped but her heart beat on, dull thuds of life suspended between her own desire for Noah and what she felt was God's will for her, a confusing mixture she could never quite understand.

"I will tell you again one more time. I love you, Hester. I love you. I always have loved you, and my love only grows with the passing of time. Will you accompany me to Berks County, our home, to make peace with our father and his wife?"

Suddenly Hester was tired. She was drained emotionally from building her fortress of pride and mistrust. It was too much effort. The wall would not stay. Repeatedly she built it higher and stronger, only to have it crash around her, leaving her standing exposed in a heap of rubble, smoking debris, and dust that shut off her vision.

It was dangerous business to bare her soul, to tell Noah what she felt. How horribly awry things could go afterward. She wanted to warn him that they could both be stranded high and dry with nothing to sustain themselves except bitterness and self-loathing, that they could each feel stupid and unable to acquire the Lord's blessing. She had experienced being dry and barren, never able to meet requirements, never being enough.

When she started talking, her words were whispers caught on short, soft sobs, like hiccups. Noah had to bend his head to hear, and then he was able to understand only a portion.

She wanted to go with him. She wanted to see her old home. But what if she did? The future was not safe. It was like crossing a frozen lake, never knowing when the ice would cave in. How could she know if her desire was God's as well?

Did he fold her in his arms, or did she wrap herself around him? In the starry night, with the insufficient light of the half-moon, they found the comfort of each other, the melding of two bodies that drew together, instinctively seeking comfort and assurance, needing trust. They stood, one taking comfort from the solid form of the other, and it was enough. More than enough.

Noah bent his head and whispered, "Does this mean you want to go? You said you have a desire to go, so may I assume you mean just that?"

In answer, Hester released him and stepped back.

"Noah, there is nothing on earth I want more. I want to be with you. I want to go home."

"Then why are you stalling? Why go to Amos's?"

"I don't know if it's God's will or just my own."

"You are afraid."

"Yes."

"Of what?"

"The future. You say you love me, but will you always? What is love?"

That last plea was Noah's undoing. That cry from the depth of her wounded heart had come from years of living with a man who was capable of cruelty. She had shared the marriage bed and could still ask that pitiable question. He wanted to have Hester believe that his love for her was like a pure jewel which he wanted to give to her tenderly.

His strong arms drew her close, closer. With a sigh, a groan, a sound coming only from the gentle kindness of an overflowing love, his hand touched her chin and brought the beautiful beloved face to his. He bent his head, his cool, perfect lips sought hers, found them, and stayed there until her arms went around his neck. She pressed him closer to her loneliness, her sadness of a past gone wrong.

In this brief space of time, she understood the meaning of God's will. God's will was one with the purity of a person's own will, after that person bowed to God supreme as Lord and King. It wasn't something other, it did not require a martyrdom or an act of deprivation to obtain it. It was not harsh and brutal.

It was this: God's love of people, of man and woman for each other. It was all true love. A blessing beyond all understanding. A love that was not earned.

When they finally moved apart, they were both crying. Tears like healing rain wet both of their faces. Noah gathered her back into the haven of his arms, kissing the tears on her cheeks as they mingled with his own.

"I love you so much," he whispered.

He waited, holding his breath.

When her words came, rich and full of meaning, he was filled with indescribable joy. Floodgates long closed, opened, allowing his love to flow.

"I love you, Noah."

He could not speak.

When she said, "But I didn't always. You and Isaac were mean to me sometimes," he let out a great whoop of laughter and held her so close she struggled to breathe.

"My precious, adorable Hester. I have a hard time believing this night is real. That you are here, and that this is not all a dream and I must wake up to my usual life without you."

Hester smiled, softly parting her lips. She knew this was different. This was not a dream.

Far into the night, they talked, sitting on the back stoop in the sleeping, quiet town of Lancaster. Even the hens did not make a peep. The summer's night was soft and warm as a newborn lamb, the air mellow, caressing them with the newfound expression of their love.

Hester went back to Amos Stoltzfus's in the morning, transported in the same rickety cart pulled by the same pot-bellied mule.

Amos was in high spirits, the gray smoke trailing behind him in regulated puffs, as if the mule and cart were partially run by the power of the tobacco. He said the boys were cutting hay, Fannie was in the garden, and

Rachel was helping with the baby. Everything was going great, he said. Salina was gaining her strength.

Hester scowled. Fannie in the garden? What was Fannie doing in that hopeless patch? She compressed her lips and shoved her anger into silence.

When she entered the house, an acrid stench almost made her gasp. As it was, her hand went to her mouth and she struggled to breathe. As her eyes adjusted to the dimly lit kitchen, she saw a half-dressed, uncombed Salina sprawled in the rocking chair by the blackened remains of the fire on the hearth, gray ashes mixed with charred wood scattered all the way to the creaking rocker. Her feet were bare, her dress front soiled, stiff with grease and remnants of dried milk from the baby held across one shoulder. She had on the large white sleeping cap she had worn to bed, which was faded to a cloudy gray and torn across the ears, one pink lobe protruding out the side.

Salina was smiling, glad to see the capable Hester again.

"*Goota mya*, Hester!" she sang out, in a strong voice.

"Good morning," Hester replied, then swallowed quickly as the nausea rose in her chest.

"Did you have a good Sunday at home?"

"Oh, yes."

How insignificant that answer. She could not begin to tell Salina of the wonders of Noah's love, which he had offered and she had taken, two hearts melted together, searching and insecurity things of the past.

"Well, that's good. Now you're back. I'll let you begin with the washing. I think the cloth on the cradle needs attention; perhaps our bedding as well. And, oh, you might want to empty the pot in the bedroom and the slops on the table. Rachel saw a maggot this morning. The flies seem to be extra plentiful this year. Seems as soon as a bit of food stays on the table, the flies are laying eggs on it."

"Where are Rachel and Sallie?"

Salina gazed absently at Hester. "Around here somewhere."

Hester eyed the piles of dirty dishes, the food congealed in puddles of grease, the black houseflies droning above it, the greenish bodies of the blowflies settled quietly to deposit the eggs that would produce the loathsome maggots.

"Why did no one attend to yesterday's dishes?" Hester ground out, her thinly veiled disgust unnoticed completely by the slovenly Salina.

"I have an awful time with Rachel. She doesn't like to do dishes, and sometimes I just don't have the strength to keep telling her. It seems Sallie takes after Rachel. I don't know how to handle them, I suppose."

"What about Fannie?"

"Oh, she's in the garden. She is supposed to be picking beans. Amos said the beans are overripe, so we need to get them."

"Why is Fannie picking beans alone with her back injury?"

Salina waved the question away with a flopping wave of her large white hand. "She's better. She always was so childish, so *bupplich*, with aches and other trivial pains."

"The way she hurt her back is not a trivial pain."

"She'll be all right."

With that, Salina lumbered to her feet and came over to the table, where she lifted a piece of cold fried mush amid a flurry of disturbed flies and stuffed it into her mouth.

Hester turned away, sickened by the gulps as well as her dismissal of Fannie's injury. She pumped water with energy generated by her anger, dumped it into the copper kettle, and built a roaring fire underneath. Then she marched off to look for Rachel and Sallie. She didn't care if it was dinner-time till she got the washing started.

The lone figure of Fannie, sitting in the long rows of green beans, her thin body twisted sideways to find and pick the endless clusters of beans, fueled her anger even more.

When she finally located the two older girls by the corncrib, absentmindedly shelling corn and throwing it across the loose rails of the fence to the horses, Hester had no hesitancy or fear within her. She walked up to them with solid steps, grabbed one arm of each girl in a grip that did not convey gentleness or goodwill. "Get up," she hissed.

Startled, Sallie stumbled clumsily to her feet, her eyes wide with alarm. Rachel swung her head in Hester's direction, her eyes hooded with insolence, and she tried yanking her well-muscled arm out of Hester's grip.

The years of hoeing, mulching, and hauling manure for the huge vegetable patch, along with the strong muscles of her Indian lineage, had honed Hester's arms and hands into solid strength, her grip like a man's. When Rachel saw she would not be able to free herself, she got to her feet, pulled back one leg, and placed a solid kick on Hester's shin. Pain shot through her, but she chose to ignore it, increasing her hold on both girls until their mouths opened with howls of frustration.

"Let me go!' Rachel bellowed.

"I will not. You come with me, both of you. You ought to be ashamed of yourselves. Why have you left the dishes unwashed till there are maggots crawling on the table?"

"Mam doesn't mind a few maggots."

"Well, I do. And as long as I am the *maud* here, you will wash dishes, or I will tell your father."

"Dat? Puh! What does he care?"

"If he doesn't, then I'll have the ministers pay you a visit, and I can guarantee that some of you children will be given to other families to raise."

"Dat and Mam wouldn't let that happen," Rachel said petulantly. "Let go my arm. You're hurting me."

Sallie began crying, opening her mouth wide, her yellow teeth protruding as wet sobs and wails rose from her throat.

"Now look what you did. You made Sallie cry."

Rachel's own face had taken on a quality of surprise, a mixture of disbelief and fear upheld by a fading brashness.

"I don't want to be given to someone else," Sallie wailed, gulping and hiccupping, a thin stream of mucus trickling down her nose.

"Be quiet. You'll scare Fannie with that howling. Stop it now."

"What do we care about Fannie? Mam doesn't like her. She's *bupplich*," Rachel sneered.

When Hester entered the house with the two girls in her grip, Salina glanced up, then as quickly looked at the girls' faces, the traces of Sallie's tears and Rachel's white-faced rebellion.

"Hester! My goodness. You made Sallie cry!"

"I did, yes. These girls need to be disciplined if you are expected to live in a decent manner."

"Oh, but they would have washed the dishes without hauling them in that way."

Rachel's sneer of triumph told Hester what the actual situation was here in this hovel, this decrepit caricature of an Amish household. Others were brought up to believe that cleanliness was next to godliness. The children were expected to obey, to learn a solid work ethic as they grew up in a family that was organized, to hold good morals and develop a strong Christian foundation.

How could Hester hope to achieve her goal of getting this family on a solid footing, teaching the children to pick up and pull their share, if their mother frowned about any discomfort experienced by her older daughters, the ones who could carry the bulk of the workload? She dared not think of Fannie, faithfully picking the green beans, very likely humming the children's tunes in German to herself.

As she scrubbed the soiled bedding and diapers, the dresses and shirts and trousers, repeatedly changing the dirty, gray water with fresh clean hot water, stirring and scrubbing, rinsing and wringing every article of clothing out by firm twists of her capable, brown hands, her anger was replaced by a daring plan: she would ask for Fannie, to have this small, unloved child.

Hester's heart beat swiftly and strongly. Her veins sang with the beauty of it. To give one small, injured soul a new kind of life—wasn't that what Hans and Kate had done for her? Without *their* love, for, yes, there had been that from both of them, in spite of Hans's feelings gone awry—where would she be? She would have died there at the spring. There were times when she wished she could have perished as an infant, but not now. Oh, no. Her whole life had not been in vain.

She had not lived or suffered without a reason. She had never been alone or forgotten or unloved, in spite of it seeming so at times. A thread of purpose had been woven into every event—with the birth of Noah, Kate's death, her own leaving, finding William and Bappie, everyone—all of it.

Her whole life led to the perfection of Noah's love, an undeserved but richly abundant gift straight from the throne of God. To relinquish her hold on the castle of resistance she had built and to release her fear, the deep, dark moat around it, were gifts as well. She knew that Noah's and her love was only a beginning, that a draw-bridge back into the castle of fear was easily available if she chose.

But now with the beauty of having Noah in her life, wouldn't it be richer, indeed, to include Fannie? The knowledge of her barrenness, that dry place that knew only suffering, was something she needed to recognize. Thank God she had told Noah in her outburst of soul agony.

He had accepted her in spite of it. He said it didn't make a difference in his love for her. Hester's heart overflowed in salty tears that ran down her cheeks and pooled in the corners of her lips, her hands busy scrubbing and wringing the clothes in the steaming water.

She would spend the week cooking, cleaning, and tackling the endless cycle of hard work, till Amos took her home. She would try her best with Rachel and Sallie. Then she would propose her plan to Noah.

Somehow he should meet Fannie before actually giving his consent. The thought of little Fannie, so thin and undernourished, seated between them on the way to Berks County, her brown eyes taking in the wonders of another world outside the squalor of her own, was so inspiring it brought a song to Hester's lips.

"*Mein Gott ich bitt*
Ich bitt durch Chrischte blut,
Mach's nur mit meinem
Ende Gute."

Over and over she sang the chorus of the German hymn till she had the washing all strung on the line, pegged firmly with wooden clothespins. It flapped and danced in the summer breeze, the noon sun already high overhead.

When Amos and the boys came in at lunchtime, they were disappointed to see the fire was out, the kitchen soaked with strong lye soap, every dish washed and put away, but without a smidgen of food to be seen anywhere.

"*Voss gebt?*" Levi asked, his good humor intact.

Salina shrugged and lightly slapped the gurgling baby, letting the milk he had spit up settle into the fabric of the dress she wore, already stiff with previous milk, hiccups, and burps.

"I guess Hester thinks cleaning is more important than eating."

Hester turned, her eyebrows lowered, her face dark with effort and the heat of the day. "We can't eat if we don't have dishes to eat from," she said, her words clipped and sharp.

"*Ach, ya, ya.*" Amos nodded, smiled his benevolent smile, reached for the sour-smelling baby, and settled him contentedly in the crook of his elbow. He lowered his face, clucked and crooned, coaxing a small smile out of the alert little newborn, so well cared for and cuddled.

The older boys crowded around, eager to catch sight of that fleeting little smile. Reuben reached for the tiny fist, waiting till the perfectly formed, pale, little fingers wrapped themselves instinctively around his forefinger.

And out in the garden, in the blazing heat of midday, little eleven-year-old Fannie continued her bean-picking, waiting until someone called her for dinner and a glass of cold water.

CHAPTER 19

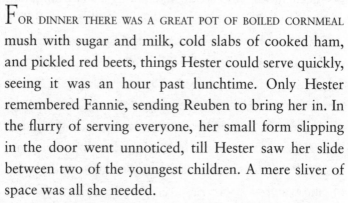

For dinner there was a great pot of boiled cornmeal mush with sugar and milk, cold slabs of cooked ham, and pickled red beets, things Hester could serve quickly, seeing it was an hour past lunchtime. Only Hester remembered Fannie, sending Reuben to bring her in. In the flurry of serving everyone, her small form slipping in the door went unnoticed, till Hester saw her slide between two of the youngest children. A mere sliver of space was all she needed.

Fannie reached for her water glass first, drained it completely, then looked around for the tin pitcher of water. When she was unable to find it, she didn't ask, merely waited till her bowl was filled with mush and milk.

The children bent their heads, then lifted spoons of dripping mush to their mouths without speaking, intent on filling their cavernous stomachs, which hadn't been fed well for breakfast or the night before.

Two of the smallest boys, their mouths ringed with dirt, squabbled for the last two red beets. The smallest one set up a howling after being roundly smacked by his peer. Amos looked over, said, "Here, here," then resumed shoveling mush and milk into his mouth. Salina never noticed, tearing at the tough, stringy ham with her teeth, chewing contentedly, glad to find her family so well fed with a minimum of effort on her part.

Hester ate a bowl of mush but chose to forego the ham, unable to forget the flies and eggs she had seen laid in leftover food. Again and again her eyes went to Fannie, watching her eat, taking in the sweet way she conversed softly with Ammon, the six-year-old boy, not asking or seeming to want anything. She took only what she was given and asked for nothing more.

By all accounts, with a meal on the table and clean laundry on the line, this was an ordinary family, raised with Amish values, but Hester knew that the minute she would leave, chaos would resume in a few hours' time. This she acknowledged—that there would be no change, no permanent turn for the better. She could scrub and clean till her hands were raw, cook and bake and sew, but what she did was only temporary, a quick fix that would disappear the minute she walked out the door.

As in all things, there was some good with the bad, and this Hester easily recognized. There was companionship, caring, and a family structure, and if a few of the children were haphazardly neglected along the way, that was not overly alarming to anyone. If Fannie was a bit poorly and went unnoticed much of the time, it was simply the way of it.

Hester watched, narrowing her eyes and biding her time. She joined Fannie in the garden after putting Rachel and Sallie to the dishes, so she could include her fully in her plans. She talked about many things with Fannie — her back, school, her parents, anything she could think of, trying to draw this little closed person closer.

Fannie sat on the weed-choked earth, her dress carefully pulled to well below her knees, her thin, blue veined legs straight out, the soles of her feet brown with dirt, bits of earth clinging to her toes. Her hair was brown, her eyes set wide apart in a small, pointed face, as brown as old honey, almost golden, but darker. She was so thin and narrow, Hester could hardly find the shape of her body in the loose, ill-fitting dress she wore, also brown, mended many times with dark colored patches of various nondescript colors.

She reached out her thin arms and pulled the beanstalks as close as possible to grasp handfuls of thick succulent beans, way past their prime but edible. These would be nourishment for the family in winter after they were put in jars and sealed by boiling them in a hot water bath, usually the same pot that was used to heat water for the washing.

Hester watched as Fannie became sleepy, her eyelids drooping, her hands slowing in their constant scrabble for beans.

"Fannie, what would you say if I asked you to go away with me for a while?" Hester asked, very softly.

Fannie watched Hester's face curiously without a trace of fear, ready to accept anything Hester might say.

She shrugged her thin shoulders, causing the neckline of the too-large dress to slide to the right, exposing a painfully thin, blue-veined shoulder. "I don't care."

She caught Hester's eyes and smiled, a small lifting of the corners of her mouth.

"Would you miss your family very much, if we went away for awhile?"

"Where would we go?"

"To a place called Berks County, where lots of Amish people live."

Again, a small shrug, an even smaller smile. With one hand she pulled her dress back into place. "I guess I could go. If my mam and dat said I could."

"Do you want me to ask?"

"I don't care."

"Only if you want to, Fannie."

"I don't have good dresses and only one Sunday apron and no shoes."

"That's all right. We'll sew for you before we go."

"Will you bring me back?"

"Do you want to come back?"

Like a quizzical little bird, she tilted her head sideways, put one finger to her chin, and pondered this question, all the wisdom of her eleven years weighing the question.

Finally, she said, very soft and low, "I guess they don't need me much now that Mam has a baby to play with. Once, I was a baby; then Mam liked me, too."

Hester quickly assured her that her mother loved her now, too. Fannie nodded, her eyes alight.

"When she has time."

That evening, without the usual amount of dishes to wash, having served only cold fruit soup, Hester approached Amos and Salina, telling them she would only finish the week. They needed to find another *maud*. The reason was her trip to Berks County, and would they consider allowing Fannie to accompany her?

Salina agreed immediately, stating as fact that with fifteen mouths to feed—thirteen children and two parents—with Fannie so puny and all, she certainly wasn't worth much as far as the work went.

Amos cleared his throat a few times and swallowed, a pained expression crossing his face more than once. He glanced at his wife, as if her decision would help him decide as well.

"But, Salina, she's ours," he finally said.

"I know, Amos, but we have thirteen now. My Uncle Ezras gave their Samuel and Jonas to his brother Joe. Not that the boys had an easy life after that, Joe was so hard on Jonas, but I guess it didn't hurt."

"Oh, I would never mistreat Fannie," Hester said hurriedly. "I'm only asking her to accompany Noah Zug and me to Berks County to visit family. I think it would be a good thing to heal her back, maybe have her get some rest."

"Who is Noah Zug?"

As quick as the darting of a butterfly, and as subtle, Hester's answer was true but void of much content.

"He is my brother."

"You were a Zug?"

"Yes, before my marriage to William King."

"Oh, yes, that's right." Nodding easily, Amos remembered her as Isaac King's William's wife. Salina looked pleasantly blank, her face as smooth and untroubled as the moon when it was full.

"*Ya, vell don*. I guess you may take her along and see how everything goes," Amos said finally.

"I think she'll be just fine. She's so easy to have. Doesn't say much, won't cost hardly anything to keep."

And so it was decided.

The week was filled with work, hard work that made Hester's muscles ache at night and put dirt under her fingernails and toenails. Her hair was filled with the dust that never quite settled on the beaten paths surrounding the house, where children's feet stomped down any weed or plant that tried to raise its head and flourish.

She butchered those red-eyed chickens. With Amos's permission, she caught them early in the morning on their roosts, using a long wire hook. Then she grabbed them by their feet and hauled them squawking and screeching with that doomed sound captive chickens will make. That was fine with Hester, who hated those ill-tempered chickens only slightly less than the family's slovenly lifestyle.

She laid each chicken so its neck was positioned between two nails. Hanging onto both feet with one hand, she brought the hatchet down with a solid whop with the other, severing the head cleanly. The chicken felt no pain, it was so quick.

While their bodies flopped around headless in the dirt, she carried buckets of scalding water and set them close by. When the blood-soaked carcasses stopped their carrying on, she grasped the feet again and dipped the bodies in the scalding water to loosen the feathers. Then she set about plucking them, grasping handfuls of soaking wet feathers and yanking them out until each chicken wore only its skin, sprawling on a board in all its unadorned baldness.

Hester summoned Rachel and Sallie to help clean the pin feathers, those annoying little growths that needed to be pulled out with a knife blade. They groaned and grimaced simultaneously, then made a great show of pretending to throw up, while Hester glared at them between lowered brows, perspiration dripping off the end of her nose.

Finally, every last one of those hateful chickens was cleaned, cut up, put to cool in cold water, stuffed in a glass jar, cold-packed in the iron kettle, and put down cellar with the beans.

Salina mourned the loss of the eggs, saying she wanted eggs more than she wanted all that chicken meat, so Amos brought home twenty poults, half-grown peeps that ran around the yard on legs that seemed much too long for their bodies, with feet splayed like turkey feet, pecking wildly at anything within reach. Cats, worms, frogs, children, any moving object was easy prey. Hawks circled overhead, waiting to zoom down and grab a tasty lunch, but the poults remained safe, probably saved by the many children and toddlers that ran around among them.

Hester cleaned the cellar, carrying up decomposing potatoes and half-rotten bacon. She coughed when she wiped green mold from the vinegar barrel and rolled the crock of salt pork to the cellar's doorway to check for spoilage, then rolled it back. She carried out rotting boards and sour carrots, turnips bloated with decay like wet sponges. She swept and scrubbed while Rachel carried buckets of hot water, grumbling and making nasty remarks, which Hester chose to ignore.

Finally, when Rachel could get no response from Hester, she asked her outright why she was named that different name, "Hester." It wasn't in the Bible, she said, lifting her brows piously.

Hester chose not to answer, feeling guilty for the anger that rose up in her over a question as harmlessly spoken as that.

"See, you don't know," Rachel goaded.

Hester was carrying a heavy crock filled with spoiled turnips and in no mood to put up with Rachel's craziness, so she said she was found by a spring as an unwanted baby, and the lady that found her named her Hester.

"Was she Amish?"

"Yes."

"I bet."

Hester shrugged her shoulders. *Believe whatever you want*, she thought.

"She wasn't, was she?"

"Yes, she was. Her name was Kate."

"That's not an Amish name."

"Catherine."

"Oh."

Then, still determined to get the better of her, Rachel kept going. "Where is she now?"

"Buried in the graveyard in Berks County."

"Why? What happened to her?"

"A bear mauled her. She died later of infection."

"You're making that up."

That was the communication she had with Rachel, with Sallie nearby like a shadowed twin, placing an emphasis on every word. The girls were not endowed with their father's good humor. Their mother's lack of caring or discipline or love, or perhaps a combination of all three, left these girls without social skills.

They whitewashed the cellar, then pulled the carrots and dug the potatoes in the garden. They carried the root vegetables down cellar and placed them carefully in clean bins. Amos was grateful, chortling over his good fortune. Finding a *maud* like Hester had sure set him free of the responsibility of managing the cellar. Salina said it was all right, either way, but would Hester make a few cakes yet before she left? She was hungry for black walnut cake, and Amos had brought eggs from Abner Hershbergers.

So much for her appreciating a clean cellar. That lack of recognition solidified Hester's decision not to return the following week. She had baked the cakes, done the washing, cleaned the house, scythed and raked the yard, and had harvested and canned all that was possible. Now it was time to go.

Fannie was ready—bathed, with her hair rolled, braided, and twisted into a coil on the back of her head. She had no valise or haversack; only one change of dress, a blue one faded to a splotchy gray, and one black apron. No comb or brush, no shoes or stockings, and no underwear.

When Amos handed Hester two five-dollar bills, her wages for two weeks, she thanked him, feeling well and fairly paid. She pocketed the money, smoothed her hair, and said as soon as he was ready, they could go.

Salina was on the rocking chair, the baby flung across her lap face down, like a bundle of blankets if you didn't know any better. She watched Fannie with an expression Hester could not discern. A blank look, but not exactly a scowl, more of an acceptance, a lack of caring.

Did Salina know she was overwhelmed and, like a mother pig, a sow with a large litter, realize that the smallest, hungriest in the litter, the runt, might not survive? Pushed back, without proper nutrition, would Fannie fall easy prey to childhood diseases that crept up on her in the cold of winter when the house was full of sniffling siblings? Salina may have known this—a primal wisdom, the way of nature—when the babies kept coming and there was never enough energy to feed and clothe and nurture them all.

Hester placed Fannie's small bundle of clothing in her own valise, then straightened and caught Salina's eye. She stepped across the room, extended her hand in a formal handshake, and said, "Thank you for everything, Salina. I'm glad I had the opportunity to be your *maud*." More a formality than truth, but there it was.

Salina smiled widely and said she'd miss her, but she guessed Rachel and Sallie could *fasark* things. Amos's mother would come on Wednesday, but she couldn't wash, the way her hip was hurting.

Finally she asked Fannie to come over. She complied, standing close to her mother, her wide eyes searching her face, an eagerness about her as if she was aware this moment was special. Now she would know how much her mother wanted her to stay, how much she was loved.

But Salina pushed her back with a palm flat on her shoulder, said, "*Ge bacht*. Don't touch the baby."

Quickly, Fannie stepped back, her hands knotted behind her back, an expression of shame and bewilderment erasing the eagerness.

"Now don't you be a bother to Hester. Bye." Salina lifted a large white hand in dismissal, her face as bland and expressionless as a large wheel of cheese.

"Bye," Fannie said, the word coming out hoarsely. Embarrassed, she cleared her throat and tried again. "Bye."

Salina nodded, bending her head to the baby.

Hester looked at Fannie, a fragile, almost lifeless sparrow, then reached for her hand, encircling her thin fingers.

They walked out the door without looking back.

Amos smoked his pipe with a vengeance without speaking. The day was hot, the heat suffocating and shimmering above the dry pastures. The trees stood stiff and unbending, their leaves lifeless as the heat withheld even the comfort of one stirring breeze.

The afternoon was waning, bringing the promise of evening and its cooler air, a luxury that made the heat bearable. The mule walked tired and discouraged, so Amos reached under the seat for the usual whip to slash across the thin rump. A good thwack, a lurch, and they lumbered uphill and down, the cart rattling and heaving in its craziness.

Fannie was stuck between them like a wedge, and yet there was barely room for her. She showed no emotion, simply sitting quietly, her hands in her lap, even when they approached the town with all the buildings, the horses and carriages, the many pedestrians. It must have caused her at least a bit of surprise or bewilderment, but her face remained impassive, inscrutable.

When the mule heaved to an ungainly stop, Amos crawled out over the wheel, tapped his pipe on the steel rim of the buggy, and said, "Well."

"Thank you for the ride home," Hester said, going around to shake hands with Amos, a formal parting.

"*Gyan schöena.*"

Amos became quite agitated, shifting from one foot to the other, his eyes going to his daughter, only eleven years old, but leaving home.

"Fannie." Awkwardly, he extended a hand.

Fannie took it, and he shook the limp white hand once. She tucked it behind her back, keeping it there.

Amos blinked. His face worked. He swallowed, once, twice. When he cleared his throat, his mouth twitched downward, as if emotion was dangerously close to having the upper hand.

He looked at Hester. "It shouldn't be like this. She was always *schpindlich*. Salina had a hard time."

He shrugged his shoulders. "Bye, Fannie," he said quietly.

"Bye," Fannie said, obediently.

"You'll be back," he said.

Fannie looked at Hester, a question in her eyes.

"We'll see how things go."

"*Ya, vell.*" Amos turned to go, climbed into the cart, lifted the reins, and chirruped. When there was no response, he brought the reins down across the mule's loose-skinned haunches. That brought up the ears, then the ungainly head, and a half-hearted pull on the traces. Amos waddled off on the rickety old cart.

Fannie watched her father go without a word. The only sign that Hester noticed was her hands clasping and unclasping behind her back. Her thin shoulders were almost square, her eyes expressionless.

Hester looked down at her and smiled. Only the beginning of a smile teased the corners of Fannie's mouth, but her eyes were alive with wonder.

"So, here we are, Fannie."

Hester grasped the valise in one hand and Fannie's hand in the other. Together they made their way through the back door to find an eager Bappie, her eyes quick and bright, her curiosity sizzling, waiting to meet this child Hester had brought home.

"Well, hello, Fannie!"

Fannie looked steadily at Bappie with no response.

"Fannie, this is Bappie. Her name is Barbara King. She lives here with me."

Fannie nodded, but said nothing.

"Did you have supper?"

"No, we are both starving, aren't we?"

Fannie nodded.

"I fried chicken and made mashed potatoes."

Fannie looked at Hester, checking her response. When she saw Hester's smile of approval, she smiled widely.

Bappie watched Fannie's face, then wiped her eyes with the back of her hand, her only response to the child's lack of certainty.

They sat down to their meal, bowing their heads in silence, as was their custom. Fannie, taught to fold her hands beneath the table, waited reverently till Bappie lifted her head, the signal to begin serving the food.

When a crispy portion of chicken was placed on her plate, Fannie had no idea what to do with it, so she ate her mashed potatoes and gravy, then placed her spoon quietly beside her plate and waited.

Hester leaned over and asked if she didn't like the chicken.

Fannie's mouth trembled as her eyes filled with tears. She whispered, "I don't know what it is."

Bappie and Hester exchanged further looks.

"It is chicken, fried. You can use your hands. Here." Hester showed the child the procedure, biting into her own.

Fannie shook her head.

When Noah arrived, he greeted Fannie warmly, bending over the hesitant child and telling her he was glad to be able to take her with them to Berks County. He let her know in his kind voice that he was Hester's brother.

Fannie watched him warily, her eyes turning dark with some unnamed emotion that puzzled Hester. When Levi arrived a few minutes later, she disappeared into the front room where the fading light of evening obscured her, giving her a measure of safety.

Bappie's eyebrows went up and she mouthed a rapid question, followed by a hiss of "*Voss iss lets mitt sie?*"

Hester shrugged her shoulders, spread her hands with palms upward, and shook her head.

They moved to the backyard where the air was turning cooler, sitting on chairs they brought from the shed. Levi said the child was only frightened, likely never having been away from home. She'd come around. He had heard of the Amos Stoltzfus family, had helped them shuck corn in the fall.

"Amos is a real nice man. Not much ambition, but I am not sure about the wife. She seems a bit slow."

"They are nice, as far as that goes. I don't think the children are treated unkindly. The parents just don't have much insight as far as the children's needs, never giving the ordinary attention and caring most families are accustomed to showing. Fannie is so quiet, so used to going about life unnoticed, that going away and meeting strangers is too much for her tonight," Hester said.

"So what are your plans?" Levi asked.

Noah looked at Hester, his eyes questioning. Finding the joy he sought in the warmth of her eyes, he told them of the upcoming journey to the home of their youth, the hope of keeping Fannie with them.

Bappie, as sharp as a blade, connected the dots saying loudly, "With you? With both of you? Or just with Hester? How is this now? You're traveling together as brother and sister, but when you get there, who is going to live with whom? Huh? I mean you're not getting married or anything, the way Levi and I are, are you?"

With this, she reached over and grabbed Levi's hand proudly, possessively, her face radiating happy ownership. Levi's face shone in the twilight as he reached over with his other hand, covering Bappie's with both of his own.

Completely at ease, Noah responded. "Oh no, we have no plans. We are brother and sister, so I'm sure our parents will welcome us and allow us to stay as long as we want."

Hester got to her feet, saying she was checking on Fannie. There was nothing to do or say to this, out of respect for the Amish tradition of not announcing a wedding until just a few weeks in advance, in spite of Bappie's unladylike snorts of disbelief.

A romance was always kept well hidden, even if the truth was stretched by small white lies at times in order to keep it a secret. Courting was done in the late hours of a Sunday evening, after the traditional hymn-singing that usually ended an hour or so before midnight. The secret was well kept by both sets of parents, too. Typically, a young man accompanied a girl into her house, well hidden from her parents, who had already gone to bed. In fact, it was not unusual for a young man to court a young woman for a few years without actually speaking to either of her parents until he asked to marry her.

Only after the engagement was announced publicly in church did the young man show his face at the home of the bride-to-be, freely coming and going in broad daylight. At that point he became an honored *hochzeita*, a prospective groom, a son-in-law-to-be, already welcomed warmly into the family.

Noah pulled it off seamlessly. Levi was completely clueless, or if he wasn't, he respectfully didn't show it.

Chapter 20

And so on Monday morning, Hester packed her clothes into a small wooden trunk, along with some of her most cherished possessions—a few linens she had embroidered, the set of fine china William had gotten for her, the figurine Emma had given her as a Christmas gift.

When Noah pulled up to the backyard with his team of pawing black horses and a canvas stretched securely on bands that arced above the sturdy spring wagon, Hester's heart beat crazily in her chest. A myriad of emotions overcame her, fluttering butterflies of every color that confused her, magnified by the sheer number of them.

How to describe how she felt? Anticipation, wonder, fear, trepidation, sadness, a sense of loss. But also a great swell of love and adoration for Noah, now released and allowed to flow unfettered, her wall of refusal a faint and dimming memory. This love overrode all others like a leader, a giant who strode forth with an impenetrable armor.

When Walter, Emma, and the boys appeared, a lump rose in Hester's throat and quick tears blurred her vision. Emma. The rotund little woman with a heart of gold. She was the angel of mercy, the one who had nursed her back to health after the white men's destruction of the Indian village on the banks of the Conestoga Creek. In her memory, Emma would always shine with a pure light. And Walter. Dear man, so devoted to his food, his impeccable English manners, and his wife. Richard and Vernon, the homeless waifs, would grow up to be good, solid citizens under their tutelage.

Billy had not returned yet, which saddened Hester, the longing to see him before she left surprisingly real.

Hester stood, clothed in a shortgown of summery blue, her black cape and apron pinned over it, her muslin cap strings tied beneath her chin, her black shoes and stockings worn according to the *Ordnung*, but a cumbersome bother. Her feet were already uncomfortable, longing to be free from the stiff leather.

Fannie stood beside her watching warily, taking in the pawing horses and the strange people with the small boys. She was dressed in her one presentable shortgown, a gray color that may have been purple or blue at one time, covered with her black Sunday apron, pinafore-style and buttoned with two black buttons down the back. Her feet were bare, which was acceptable in summer, even for Sunday services, to spare the use of shoes, which were expensive.

Noah loaded the trunk, then stood politely as Hester said her goodbyes. She was enveloped in long, hard hugs by both Emma and Walter as tears flowed unashamedly, their bodies as soft as pillows and as comforting.

Hugs were unaccustomed among the Amish, a show that was much too physical, but Walter and Emma were English and displayed their love freely.

When it was Bappie's turn, she and Hester simply stood facing each other, their eyes speaking what their throats would not allow, lumps of emotion cutting off any words that formed in their hearts.

"Good-bye, Bappie," Hester whispered, a strangled sound that was met by a sob. Bappie threw her long, skinny arms around Hester, two bands of love as sturdy as leather straps on a harness.

"I'm going to miss you terrible," Bappie sobbed.

Hester's eyes were closed but her cheeks were wet with tears that squeezed from beneath her heavy lids. "Thank you, Bappie, for everything. I'll write," she choked.

"You have to come back for my wedding in November."

"I will."

"You mean, *we* will."

They stepped back, both of them fumbling in the pockets sewn to their skirts, lifting their black aprons, blowing their noses, then beginning to laugh through their tears.

Noah lifted Fannie first, seating her on the cushioned seat. Then he gave Hester a hand, looking gently into her streaming eyes, his touch a reassurance of his love, his caring so great he could not fully convey it.

From her perch on the wagon seat, Hester waved and called out her good-byes, promising to return in November. She turned in her seat to continue waving as the horses pranced off, pulling the wagon behind them.

"Good-bye, good-bye," the small knot of friends called in unison as the buggy rumbled out of sight.

The air was thick and sultry, the sun's intensity cloaked with a veil of haze. The air that moved past them as the horses trotted along was wet and stale, as if it had smoldered over the town all night.

The trees were limp and discouraged-looking, as if they knew their heyday was in the past and fall was imminent. The cornstalks were heavy and green, the ears of corn weighing them down, brown streaks along the stalks speaking of the end of the growing season. Soon would come the crisp, cool air of autumn, when the fields surrounding Lancaster would ring with the cries of the cornhuskers as wagons moved slowly through the fields of rustling brown corn, and the hard, yellow ears were ripped from the stalks and thrown on the wagons.

Most of this bountiful crop would be stored in corn cribs and then fed to the livestock. Some of it would be ground into cornmeal at the mill, then cooked with salt and water, a staple of many Amish families' diets. Fried mush, mush and milk, cornpone, cornbread. Virtually free, these corn-based dishes were nutritious and filling, fueling the children as they ran off to school.

Meadowlarks opened their beaks like scissors, lifted their heads, and trilled their country song, singing from fenceposts and stone fences.

Crows wheeled overhead. A convoy of blackbirds circled through the sky, scrabbling hurriedly through the air on busy wings as if they were late to an important meeting. A bluebird flitted ahead of them, its wings beating frantically.

Noah didn't speak, his attention on the eager horses, allowing Hester time to dry her eyes and remember her friends.

Fannie didn't move a muscle. Only her eyes showed her interest as she watched oncoming teams and the road opening to the countryside.

Hester squeezed her shoulder. "Are you all right, Fannie?"

Fannie looked up, nodded, then added a small smile like an afterthought.

"You'll be all right with leaving your home? If you're afraid of *zeitlang*, we can always take you back if you want to go."

Fannie's silence made Hester feel uneasy. What if the poor child would want to return? In spite of the squalid conditions, it was her home, after all. Who was she to think Fannie's life would improve with her and Noah?

When Fannie spoke, Hester had to bend low to hear the words.

"Maybe I will get *zeitlang* for Ammon, but they won't miss me. Not my mam."

"Oh, she will miss you, Fannie. She'll think about it that you're gone."

"I don't think so."

She spoke breathlessly with a wisdom beyond her years, so Hester did not try to correct her. She merely slipped an arm around the slim figure and pulled her close.

"It's all right, Fannie. What would Noah and I do without you?"

Fannie tilted her small face upward, looked into Noah's face, then Hester's, as the slow light of understanding crept across her features, bringing up the corners of her mouth. "That's right, isn't it? You don't have any other brothers or sisters, do you?"

"We do, but they are all in Berks County. At home. But none of them is you. They don't have a Fannie among them."

"They don't?"

"No."

Fannie pondered this for some time, then opened her mouth as if to speak. But she closed it again, choosing instead to lay her head against Hester's arm and breathe deeply.

The two horses trotting together formed a sort of rhythm that made its way into Hester's senses, a cadence not unlike the night sounds of insects. Sometimes the hoofbeats were synchronized in perfect unison; other times there was a mishmash of off-beat thumps until they gradually returned to the same orderly beat.

The harnesses flapped on the glistening backs of the horses. The traces pulled taut on the upgrade, then flopped loosely going downhill when the britchment surrounding the haunches drew tight, holding back the covered buggy they rode on.

The horses' black manes rippled and shone, streaming with every footstep. Their tails arched proudly, the long black hair spreading evenly behind them. They held their heads high, their ears pricked forward, flicking back occasionally in response to a command or an instruction from their driver.

The sun had unwrapped itself from the fog, its red, blazing light shimmering across the backs of the horses. A thin, white band of sweat appeared around the britchment on each animal. The hairs along their backs turned slick with it. One of them, the horse on the right, slowed visibly, lifting his mouth until the bit rattled the reins, then letting it fall. Over and over he did this, till Noah looked at Hester and said he believed Comet was tiring. They'd pull off at the next shady spot.

"Comet?" Hester inquired.

"Comet and Star."

She smiled. Finding his eyes, their gazes held.

"Good names for these beautiful horses."

"Yes, I am fortunate to have them. However, they aren't nearly as beautiful as my most prized possession."

Puzzled, Hester asked, "You have more horses?"

"Oh no, she's not a horse."

When Hester met his eyes, she blushed furiously and wished she had a hat to yank forward over her heated face. As it was, she turned her head to the left until her cheeks cooled.

She said, "I am not your possession."

"Almost. Someday soon."

"Does a man possess his wife?" asked a small voice between them.

They had forgotten Fannie. Hester gasped.

Noah lifted his face and laughed aloud, a great freeing sound without embarrassment, just the joy of finding something extremely funny.

Hester fumbled for words, made a few very bad starts, gave up, and stared ahead without speaking. Noah took the situation in hand, saying Hester was not his sister, except in name, and they hoped to be married someday, although he had not yet asked her. That would all come later, after they visited their parents, Hans and Annie Zug.

Very firmly the words came, put into the atmosphere with meaning, an expression containing so much wisdom for a child of eleven, it took Hester's breath away.

"I didn't think Noah was your brother. His hair is almost white. Yours is very black. But Abraham said that about Sarah, his wife, and since you are traveling like they were, well, it's almost the same thing."

This speech coming from the timid Fannie left Hester speechless. Noah began humming and turned his face to the right, away from Hester's unease. There was only the sound of the buggy wheels on the wide dirt road, the dull hitting of iron clad hooves on packed earth, the jingle of buckles and straps, the flapping of leather against the horses' wet legs.

Evidently Fannie was not uncomfortable with her speech left unanswered. She sat against Hester, her eyes bright and alert, watching the ever changing landscape.

When the road led downhill to a clump of trees, an appendage of a large tract of thick forest, Noah reined in the tired horses and pulled off to the side of the road. Unsure what was expected of her, Hester remained seated till Noah asked if she wanted to unhook the traces for Star and lead him to the creek with him and Comet.

The horses lowered their heads, snorting and snuffling, blowing out their breaths on the surface of the water till thirst overcame their distrust and they lowered their mouths and drank.

Noah watched Hester's face as she looked at Star drinking from the tepid little creek. She felt his eyes on her face, looked up, and smiled.

"They are good horses," she said.

"They sure are. I got a bargain when I bought these from Dan."

"Are you planning to hitch them to the plow?"

"Oh, my, no. It would ruin them. They're far too highstrung to wear them down in the plow. That's for draft horses or mules."

Hester nodded.

"Will you be buying a farm?"

This question startled Noah. He was surprised Hester asked him, because she was so shy about many other things.

"I am hoping to persuade Hans to let me have about half the acreage he owns. I don't want to live close to them. First, I need to see how things are, how Annie is, the children, just everything. We need to be very careful, Hester, with the way things were in the past."

"Oh, I am not implying anything. I am just going for a visit. Not that I have any concern as far as your buying a farm."

Hester ran her hand through the heavy, tangled hair in Star's mane, keeping her eyes averted, her face taking on a deeper, darker hue.

Noah said, "Look at me."

She would not, finding the safety she needed in the horse's mane, as if the most important task in the world had presented itself to her.

Noah clipped a snap from Comet's harness to Star's, came around to Hester, and put his hands around her waist, hidden from Fannie's bright gaze. He stood behind her and spoke soft and low.

"We have spoken of our love for one another, my darling Hester. You are the love of my life. Hopefully God has many years planned for us together. But first we need to take care of this business with Hans and Annie, my parents and yours."

"Hans is not my parent, and neither is she."

Hester flung the words into the air, her language portraying her long-remembered hatred and the grudge she carried within herself. This was the one thing Noah was afraid of, the reason he had not yet formally asked her hand in marriage, coupled with the fact that he was unsure how he felt about Hans and Annie himself. That was the reason for this all-important trip.

Hester's words were like a dagger in his back, as painful and as dangerous. He knew forgiveness would not come easily for her, if ever.

He also knew they could not step into a holy union as husband and wife, while still carrying the baggage of past hurts and unforgiveness. Even if their love was a thing of brilliant splendor now, with time, it would tarnish if these past ruptures were not dealt with. Noah felt it was important to forgive and honor their parents. Only then could they be blessed with a real and lasting love that came from God alone.

He believed he loved Hester enough to carry both of them through any trial that came into their lives, his need to have her for his wife sometimes overpowering his solid common sense. He longed to tell Hester that she needed to forgive but figured it would do no good.

All he could do was take her to these two aging people, watch her reaction, and wait to see what occurred. If God had a plan for their lives together, it would all fall into place like pieces in a child's wooden puzzle.

They ate in the shade of enormous oak and sycamore trees, nestling in the grass by the side of the road. Noah allowed the horses a long tether so they could graze, biting off the lush green grass and chewing contentedly.

Fannie was confused when Hester handed her a sandwich. She finally took it, then lifted the top slice of bread and ate it dry before grasping the cold, baked ham and eating it separately as well. She drank the water obediently, then got to her feet, wandering among the blue bells and white columbines, humming softly to herself, her small face alight with happiness.

Noah lay back in the grass, his hands beneath his head, his knees bent, his shirt unbuttoned at the neck. His blond hair was in disarray from passing his fingers through it, his eyes closed, the heavy lashes sweeping his tanned cheeks.

Watching him, Hester thought his face looked lined, perhaps even older than his years. Had the war taken its toll on him, or had some hardship in his life chiseled the features, like storm winds on a rock or a cliff face, wearing away the perfect symmetry after years of time?

Noah could not have had a carefree childhood without the ease and acceptance found between most fathers and sons. Hester's mind retained vivid pictures of growing up in the little log house in Berks County when Kate was still alive.

The heavy plank table, Noah's and Isaac's chins barely reaching to the table top, being cuffed on their shoulders as Hans's great red hands came down in punishment for something as insignificant as a giggle or a forbidden burst of laughter at the table, where children were to be seen and not heard. Once Noah had spilled a half-tumbler of water, resulting in a ringing smack across one cheek, then the other, his head spinning in both directions.

He never made a sound. Always it was the same. Noah's eyes would be a brilliant blue, the color enhanced by unshed tears. His mouth would tremble once, slightly, and that was all. Hester always winced, feeling the slap on her own cheek. But she had learned to squelch her pity, folding it away where no one would see.

Now, thinking of Salina, she suddenly wondered. Had Kate been a bit simple? Overwhelmed? Or was she only obedient to her husband's wishes, honoring him to the point that she had no will of her own, leaving the discipline of the children to him?

That Kate had loved her husband was without doubt. She had loved him, made him laugh, helped him through his anxiety and fits of depression. And Hans had been good to her, the way most husbands were.

Watching Noah's face, the craggy, chiseled planes of his features so striking, Hester remembered him as a baby, a toddler. Much larger than most babies, his head was big and almost bald till he was well past a year old. His wide mouth was almost alarming when he cried, which seemed to be his favorite thing to do.

Did some fathers find themselves having a secret aversion to a newborn son? Hester only knew that Hans had often been unfair, even cruel to the two sons, born so quickly after they brought her home from the spring and nursed her back to health with goat's milk.

All her life Hans had been good to her, as well as to Kate. She had been favored even above Kate, but she had been too young to know. She had found security and happiness in Hans, the perfect attentive father.

Until he wasn't.

Then her privileges were taken away and she was forbidden to ride horses, as Hans became harsh in his expectations of how she should follow the *Ordnung*. He was strict and unyielding where her clothes were concerned. After Kate's death, he married thin and frigid Annie, who was merciless in her contempt for Hester. She treated her, the adopted Indian girl, with a coarseness that sprang from dislike, fueled by her jealousy.

With a groan, Hester turned away. The unfairness of it, the patience of Noah and Isaac, the shame of Hans's unrighteousness. She loathed Hans. She felt a deep and abiding humiliation, the knife edge of the wrong Hans had harbored in his ill-concealed heart.

Why, then, did she feel as if she herself was tainted, soiled by the knowledge of his fatherly love and affection gone wrong? How could she hope to find even the smallest measure of peace by returning? How would she face him, the robust, swarthy man who had been her father, a figure of security? As she grew, she had been the *dum-kopf*, the simple girl in school. But she skipped through her days with innocence, until Kate died and Hans married Annie, followed by the sense that something had gone very wrong. She could relive the intense glittering of Hans's eyes, but how was she to know how wrong it was, never having encountered anything of that nature?

She sat beside Noah, her arms wrapped around her bent knees, and let the misery overtake her. How could she have been so naïve, so uncomprehending, when so much was at stake? She could not go on, blindly riding into the Amish settlement and being among so many acquaintances after all she had gone through in the years since she left.

How was she to know Noah would be any different than Hans? Here she was, taking Fannie, her pity for the thin, neglected girl overriding her common sense, perhaps into the same trap she herself had been caught in.

A soft movement caught Hester's attention. A whisper, "Here."

A bunch of white columbine, mixed with lacy ferns and waxy bluebells, was thrust into her lap.

Hester looked up into Fannie's face, her white cheeks flushed with embarrassment.

"Fannie! These look just like a garden. I can't believe you arranged these flowers to look so natural. It's amazing. How did you do it?"

Fannie lowered her eyes, blushed deeper, and shrugged her thin shoulders. "I don't know."

"Thank you. I love these flowers. I think it's the nicest bouquet anyone ever gave to me."

"Oh."

Noah awoke, sat up, and smiled immediately, as if kindness slept and woke with him. Fannie watched him warily as Hester showed him the flowers and laughed when he shook his head in disbelief, banishing Hester's dark thoughts like a sunrise on night waters.

They traveled steadily through the afternoon, the two black horses trotting faithfully, sometimes walking, the canvas top flapping in the breezes, Fannie content to sit between them.

Noah observed the gathering clouds like dirty sheep's wool rolling into dark colored bundles. He did not like the stillness in the air or the oppressive heat. He chose to say nothing, so when Hester questioned him about the approaching clouds, he simply nodded his head, taking in the surroundings, his gaze sweeping left, then right.

They passed farms dotting the countryside, homes of the Amish, Mennonites, and the more liberal English, all dwelling side by side, forming neighborhoods of diversity and, for the most part, enjoying a life of peace, if not exactly spiritual unity. That part was accepted and acknowledged, as each family traveled to their respective house of worship on Sunday mornings, passing each other with friendly waves.

The Mennonites had their meetinghouses, while the Amish met in homes. The English attended massive stone or brick churches scattered through the towns. Each chose to worship the same God in many different ways, following the Scripture according to their own understanding, love, and tradition. These were the ties that bound each one to family and congregation, the strongholds of their own individual faiths.

Noah had spoken of his desire to stay in Lancaster. He thought it was the only sensible thing to do. With the soil so fertile, the crop yields were higher than anywhere he had ever been. But the land was costly, three times the amount per acre than it was in Berks County. He could purchase a tract of land without borrowing very much, if any, if he chose to buy in his homeland.

Hester had been too shy to ask or to add to the conversation, certainly not wanting him to feel as if she had any part in his future.

In her heart, she couldn't imagine a future without Noah, but perhaps she was only being irrational and not thinking clearly.

She also recognized that she had never cared for William the way she did for Noah. As each day passed, each week an eternity if she was not with Noah, her growing understanding of what love actually encompassed was staggering.

Why had she married William? Did everything have a reason? Had it all been in God's plan? If this is what real love is like, then perhaps she shouldn't blame herself for her lack of obedience or her fiery rebellion.

Her thoughts were unsettling, her spirit tumultuous, as she sat in the deep grass beside Noah. She glanced at the approaching clouds, wondering if a coming storm was causing her mind to produce all these endless, senseless thoughts.

Noah suddenly suggested they hitch up and try to make it to an inn by nightfall. He got to his feet and reached for her hands, drawing her up with him. He would not let go of her hands, looking into her eyes until her vision blurred and her head swam. Wise little Fannie looked over her bouquet of flowers and nodded once to herself, then sighed softly.

CHAPTER 21

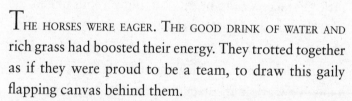

THE HORSES WERE EAGER. THE GOOD DRINK OF WATER AND rich grass had boosted their energy. They trotted together as if they were proud to be a team, to draw this gaily flapping canvas behind them.

The road made a few turns, dipped down once, then steadied into a gradual incline up to a higher level. A steep ridge lay ahead, and then a small mountain.

The clouds moved in steadily from the northwest, a low bank that seemed caught above the line of hills. The sun shone hot and brilliant, turning the backs of the sweating horses into polished glass.

Noah said he remembered an inn at Black Creek at the foot of the ridge, which was a line of small mountains called Eagle Rock.

Hester said they would be fine beneath this canvas, that she was afraid it was simply too expensive to stay at an inn. A waste of money.

In answer, Noah pointed to the approaching storm, shaking his head.

Toward evening, the light turned gray with a cast of yellow-orange.

They passed a barn so new the lumber shone golden in the haze of the approaching bad weather. The house had been painted white and shone like a beacon of solid workmanship, the white sheets and towels and tablecloths dancing on their clothespins. A buxom woman clad in purple came hurrying out of the house, a wicker clothes basket balanced on one hip, glancing at the dark clouds. The hammering of nails reverberated from the barn. Children dotted the yard, colorful little characters running and tumbling about like birds.

They waved when the woman set down her basket, stopped, and raised a hand to her forehead like a salute. Shading her eyes from the glare of the sun, she lifted her hand in a wave immediately.

The wind was getting up, stirring the summer's old leaves, rustling the dry grass by the side of the road. It lifted the horses' manes, riffling through the thick hair. The breeze felt refreshing as it blew a few of Fannie's *schtrubles* across her face.

Far away, they heard a low muffled sound of thunder. Noah peered through the trees as they approached the ridge, muttering under his breath.

"Don't worry about an inn, please. When I traveled alone from Berks County, I slept in the rain more than once. If we get wet, we'll dry out."

Noah smiled at her, flicking the reins across the horse's back, goading them forward a bit faster as another low muffled sound came from the distance.

The road wound in and out of the forest, the trees giving way to cleared land repeatedly, but always on a steady incline. The horses were tiring, their steps flagging, the neck reins stretched taut as their heads went lower, no longer held quite as high by their own accord.

The distant rumblings were no longer muffled but a solid, rolling sound, followed by thin, jagged appearances of bluish-white light. These were powerful storm clouds that could send balls of fire through buildings and light barns with their ferocity, a thing feared but not understood. Lightning was the power of God on full display.

The first raindrops that hit their faces were carried by powerful winds that swelled the canvas, whipped green leaves from thrashing tree branches, tossed the dusty roadside grasses, and flung the horses' manes and tails to the right.

The inn was nestled against a high bank of trees, built of solid gray limestone that had been carved and set, creating a building that would withstand the elements. The door was wide and thick, its boards painted a dark blue. The shutters beside each many-paned window looked like solid sentries, guarding the patrons within.

Noah pulled up to the door, leaped off the wagon, and went to the horses' heads without offering assistance to Hester or Fannie.

"Get inside. I will be in," was all he said.

Hester walked up to the inn, lifted the heavy, cast-iron latch, drew back the massive door, and stepped inside, her eyes lowered and her face averted as she kept a steady grip on Fannie's frail hand.

The interior was dim, cool, and smelled of strong drink and burned food. The odor was thick and stale, clinging to Hester like a sticky vapor, a cloying scent she could not dispel. She stood uncertainly, gasping slightly as her senses became accustomed to the stale air.

Immediately, a man came from behind the counter, a white dish towel tucked into the belt of his apron. He was about Hester's height, thick and muscular, with a mustache and a full beard covering most of his face, his small black eyes like two dark beetles.

"Yes, ma'am?"

"We're waiting for my brother. He's seeing to the horses."

"Oh, indeed. Indeed. Welcome. Welcome. You may be seated at any of these tables while you wait. May I bring you sustenance?"

Hester shook her head. "We'll wait."

Bowing deeply, the dishcloth lurching forward, he straightened and moved quickly behind the counter.

Curious stares directed their way made Hester uneasy. She longed for her big hat which she could pull forward, obscuring her face. She felt exposed since her muslin cap did nothing to hide her features, so she lowered her eyes, keeping her gaze directed on the tips of her shoes and the floor beyond.

Slowly the hush lessened, voices rose in their usual crescendo, and conversations resumed as the inn's customers lost interest. Hester was relieved when Noah appeared, his eyes sweeping the room with a practiced gaze before he dropped into a chair.

Blue lightning flashed against the windowpanes, followed by lashing rain and deep but muted growls of thunder. Candles were lit by long matches, the flames large and unsteady till they gained the full wick. Then they burned steadily, throwing a homey light across the greasy, smoke-filled room.

The bearded man hurried over, the two dark beetles glistening, his eyes small and close to his nose. But a friendly smile showed his teeth somewhere in the recesses of all his facial hair. "Yessir. How do you do, sir? I welcome you to Black Creek Inn. How may I be of service?"

Hester thought of Walter Trout, and a lump formed in her throat.

"We'd like two rooms for the night, please. And an evening meal as well." Noah had risen, extending a hand, a towering blond giant but given to a gentle demeanor, an air of kindness about him. He viewed the innkeeper with the same charity as he held for all the rest of the human race. Hester's breath caught, a sensation of love and admiration quickening her heart.

Of course, Noah held the innkeeper in high esteem. Condescension was not an attitude Noah practiced. He clearly thought well of the stranger and received his welcome with sincerity.

"Two rooms indeed, sir. And just in time, the weather affording you no welcome," the innkeeper said, indicating the violence of the storm with a wave of his hand.

Their food was brought by a comely young woman dressed in a manner that made Hester blush, her eyes on Noah as she served their supper. He remained as polite and kind as he had been to the innkeeper.

The heavy plates were heaped with roasted sausages, mounds of boiled potatoes and turnips, slices of summer squash and chunks of tomatoes and parsley. She brought glasses of dark frothy beer, which Noah asked to have replaced with hot tea and tumblers of water.

Fannie's eyes became big and round in the flickering candlelight as she eyed the mountain of food. Her cheeks were pink, her brown eyes full of light, as she dipped her head and put a hand to her mouth, trying to suppress a giggle.

Hester caught Noah's eyes, smiled, and leaned over. "Just eat what you can, Fannie."

And she did. She enjoyed a large portion of the potatoes and turnips, but only tasted the sausage delicately.

Hester found the food delicious. The sausages were browned to perfection, the potatoes creamy, the tomatoes rich and satisfying. The shoofly pie that followed the meal was heavy with the rich brown sugar and molasses concoction that made up the two-layered filling, all baked in a thick, flaky pie crust.

Noah ate two platefuls and three slices of pie with his tea. Hester finished her serving of food but felt overfull and uncomfortable after eating her piece of pie.

Outside the storm continued, a summer thunderstorm that would cleanse the whole countryside of the cloying heat and humidity. The inn seemed a haven now, a warm, dry place to be, the horses stabled and fed, the wagon pushed into a wide bay on the top floor of the bank barn.

Hester had never been served food at an inn. She had no idea how to go about ordering a meal or paying for it afterward. She had certainly never slept in an inn. She hoped the night would prove restful, imagining the misery of riding on the high seat of the spring wagon while sleepily clinging to the side of the seat.

"Would you like to retire to your rooms?" Noah asked after draining his tea.

"It's still early, isn't it?" Hester wondered.

"I'd say nightfall is only a few minutes away, although it's hard to tell on account of the storm."

"At any rate, I am tired, and I'm sure Fannie will be willing to lie down after the long ride."

Noah went to make arrangements, brought the valise from the wagon, and led the way up a steep narrow stairs that opened to a long hallway with closed doors along each side. Towards the back of the hall, he opened a door to the right, gave the candleholder to Hester, set the valise on the floor, and asked if she and Fannie needed anything else.

The wide, white bed shone like a beacon of rest; the washstand beside it held a large pitcher and bowl, along with clean white towels. Hester had all she needed. Weariness crept over her, a numbing sensation as she nodded, telling Noah that everything looked more than sufficient, and she was extremely grateful for these luxurious accommodations.

For a brief instant his eyes stayed on hers, containing all his love, his longing as well as restraint. In his kindness, he bid her a good night's rest before bending to take Fannie's hand in his and putting a hand to Hester's shoulder. Then he was gone, the door closing behind him with a soft click of the latch.

Hester and Fannie both fell sound asleep almost the minute their heads touched the pillows, the distant hum of the activity in the tavern below only a minor distraction.

The rain beat steadily on the good, sturdy roof as the storm stayed above the ridges and hills bordering Berks County. The moisture seeped into the soil, boosting the corn and hay crops, the gardens, and surrounding creeks and ponds. Frogs chugged in the bulrushes, the voice of the crickets stilled on this rainy night. When the storm passed, a thin half-moon shone weakly through the clouds, its silver light illuminating the darkness of the quiet inn tucked beneath the trees.

Hester was awakened by a soft mewling sound, piercing her senses with the force of a scream. At first she thought a kitten may have found its way into the room. She got fully awake when she realized that Fannie was crying soft, muffled sobs, restrained by a hand across her mouth. She had drawn her knees up to her chin, a thin coil of humanity, obviously suffering some pain or loss, and perhaps both.

Hester rolled over and gathered Fannie into her arms, holding her as she smoothed her hands down the back of her linen nightgown.

"Fannie, please don't cry. What is wrong? Shh. Don't cry." The sobs increased until the small body shook so violently, that her teeth chattered.

"Can you tell me?" Hester urged.

When no words came, Hester began to hum, keeping up the soft stroking. Almost immediately the shaking subsided and the sobbing slowed, then stopped. An occasional sniff, a whimper, and then Fannie's deep breathing continued. Her coiled body relaxed as sleep overcame her, as if nothing had happened.

Hester released her, sighed, burrowed into the pillow, and fell into the sleep of a child, untroubled, resting completely.

In the morning, Fannie was bright-eyed, fully awake, eager to get on with the day.

When Hester inquired about her misery during the night, Fannie's large brown eyes met hers, deadpan, owllike. She spoke with the same wisdom she had displayed before. "I was crying because thinking of Ammon gave me an ache in my throat. He would have liked to have one of my sausages."

Quickly, Hester was at her side, hunkered down, looking into her eyes as Fannie sat on a stool, tying her apron. "Fannie, we want you to be truthful. If you want to return, we'll take you back. You know that."

Fannie held very still, her head tilted to one side. "No, I can't go back. There's no room for me there. They don't always have enough to eat."

She stopped and spread her hands, palms up. "And my mam doesn't care for me much."

Instantly, Hester assured her of her mother's love, but was stopped halfway by Fannie's quiet, "Stop that. You know it's not true. I'm eleven years old. I should know by now."

Then she paused, before deciding to continue. "What would be the difference, do you think? A mother finding you at a spring, or a *maud* asking to have a half-grown girl?"

"Oh, Fannie," Hester cried, throwing her arms around the small frame and holding her close. "None. There is no difference. If you want me to be your mother, then that is exactly who I will be. I will take you as my own foundling, just as Kate took me."

Fannie sighed, then pulled back to look into Hester's eyes with a direct gaze. "Well, then. Now I will never cry at night again."

But Hester cried then, while she combed her hair and braided Fannie's. A fountain of tears welled up and ran over, a seemingly unstoppable flow, like an artesian well of more minute volume. Quietly she wiped them away, and quietly they continued to fall.

Noah was alarmed at the emotional display of tears, but Hester whispered to him on tiptoe, close to his ear, that she was quite all right and that she would tell him the reason for her tears when they were alone. His arm gathered her close for a stolen instant and he left, satisfied with her answer.

Hester decided that morning that Fannie was sent into their lives for a purpose. Perhaps it was for a small reason, if providing a home, love, stability were small things. God directed lives for a reason, and here was the miracle of Kate's large heart, with her never-ending kindness passed to her son, the love of her little foundling's life, and now a haven for one unwanted little girl. Love was the chain that threaded through the generations.

Each link added was a golden one, enriching the lives of families like a beautiful gem, passed on to the next generation.

The morning was what Hester imagined a portion of paradise to be. The air was achingly clear. Freshly washed grasses and leaves held drops of diamonds glittering on their backs. The woods were alive with a choir of birds, trilling the jubilance of the morning, glad to welcome the arrival of a brand new day.

In the early evening, Hester had recognized landmarks, forests, the rolling of the land. In the golden light, they entered the Amish settlement by way of Berksville. They passed the school and then Amos Ebersole's farm.

Hester gripped the seat. Her throat worked.

The horses trotted gaily, the harnesses tapping out a rhythm. Every hoofbeat was the echo of her heartbeat, timing the minutes. She had forgotten the blue of the mountain, the vibrant green of the ridges, how rolling and magnificent the undulating landscape.

There was the grove of birch trees. There, the great white sycamore. The ache of coming home was a weight in her chest. She put up a hand to still the tumult there, as if she could quiet the emotion that threatened to spill over.

Noah watched her face. "Another mile and we'll be home."

Hester nodded as her throat constricted.

The road had been packed down, graded, and widened, becoming a good serviceable one. Hester noted the new fields, where someone—maybe Hans?—had cleared more of the forest.

And then the farm itself came into view as they rounded the final bend.

The house had not changed, the stone still as she remembered it. The barn, however, was painted white, with a new addition, judging by the still-yellow lumber. There was a new corncrib and a wagon shed.

The pasture was dotted with black and white Holsteins, the cows she could remember milking. The fences were in good repair, the maple trees, one on each side of the house, trimmed and healthy. So Hans and Annie had continued to prosper. The children who remained at home were taught well in the ways of farm management.

This was home, Hester thought. This farm is my home. Why, then, did the surrounding hills and forests bring more emotion than this homestead? Too many thoughts fought for control. Too many bad memories suppressed what she might have felt—true happiness upon returning to this childhood home.

When the horses came to a stop, real fear pervaded her soul. She was rooted to the seat, her eyes wild with the rush of all she recalled.

Noah's eyes questioned her. "Would you rather go with me to the barn first?" he asked.

Hester nodded. It was all she could do to keep her teeth from clacking against each other. She folded her hands in her lap to still their trembling.

"No one seems to be home," he stated.

She searched his face for signs of the anxiety she was experiencing, but if he felt any, he did not give himself away. He merely sat solidly, his eyes searching for signs of life from within before telling the horses to go, heading them to the barn.

They came to a stop at the forebay, the wide empty area containing the stone trough and harness racks. Noah leaped down, threw the reins across the horses' backs, and was turning to help Hester down, when a door banged open. Footsteps pounded across the yard, and a grown man, whom Hester could not name, came running, out of breath, his face wreathed in welcoming smiles, clearly delighted to see his big brother Noah.

"Noah!"

"Solomon! Sollie, old boy!"

Hester grimaced as she watched the energetic pumping of their handshake.

"How are you, old chap? *Eye due lieva, mon,* you're riding in style." Solomon gave a low whistle as he circled the black horses, his practiced eye taking in the horses' deep chests, their long muscular legs, the fact that they were barely out of breath after their long run.

"Let me help you wash them down."

He noticed Hester and Fannie then, and stopped in his tracks, a comical expression crossing his face.

"Who do you have with you? Are you? Wait a minute. It's Hester. Hester, is it really you?"

Noah helped her down and Hester stood, her knees so weak she was afraid she would crumble onto the hard packed dirt.

"It's me," was all she was capable of saying.

Solomon came to Hester, his eyes as blue as Noah's, and bent over her hand, shaking it warmly in the old traditional manner. "Welcome home, Hester, welcome back to Berks County. But I don't understand. How did Noah find you? And who is this?"

Hester introduced Fannie Stoltzfus, an *au-gnomma Kind*.

Solomon nodded, then reached up to help her down. Fannie came to Hester's side immediately, shrinking against her when Hester reached to draw her close.

"How is Dat? And Annie?" Noah asked.

"Oh, they are both poorly. You heard, didn't you? Isn't that why you came?"

"We know nothing about our parents."

"You don't? I find that rather hard to believe."

Solomon kept talking as he helped Noah unhitch, telling them of Hans losing his strength, his weight plummeting, his being wracked by constant stomach pain. Annie was stronger but a victim of the palsy, the only thing the doctors could find to explain her constant shaking.

"Where is everyone?"

"Oh, they don't live here. My wife, Magdalena, and I and our two children have taken over the farm."

"Where are our parents?"

"They live about half a mile out the road. Only Barbara, Menno, and Emma are at home. Daniel is newly married and moved to his wife's brother's farm, and John, well, John ran off with an *Englischer*. He was always the wild one. Lissie's married."

"And what's Emma doing?" Hester asked.

"She's at home and going to school."

"What about Theodore and Lissie?" she asked.

"They're both well. Still living in Lissie's house and tutoring pupils. She quilts, helping out whenever there's a need, but she's aging. They're both a great influence on the community with their unselfish ways."

The horses were stabled and fed a good portion of oats and hay. Noah put his hand on Hester's elbow, and together they went to the house, where they were greeted by a tall, thin, young woman with a friendly smile of welcome, her face round and pleasant, with interested brown eyes that held no suspicion or animosity.

Hester held her hand warmly, glad to meet her first sister-in-law. She followed Magdalena through the house, guided by her memories, the house so much the way she remembered and yet so different.

The kitchen was the same, large and pleasant, the crackling fire on the hearth absent, the fireplace cleaned, brushed, and scrubbed, waiting for the cool nights of autumn. Most of the cooking was done on the stove now, although in summer they'd sometimes build a quick fire just for mealtimes.

Magdalena's furniture took the place of Hans and Annie's well-built cupboards and rocking chairs, making the place appear new. The walls had been whitewashed recently. There were new curtains in the windows. Rag rugs in brilliant colors added sunshine to the otherwise dull floors.

It was a good, substantial house, the house Hans, Noah, and Isaac had built, the product of months of back-breaking labor. It was a monument of hard work, good management, planning, and forethought—the closets, the wall space with hidden nooks that were used for storage, the root cellar, the well-built fireplace that rose all the way through the second story to the roof, with an enclave that housed red-hot coals to help heat the upstairs bedrooms in winter.

As Hester moved through the rooms of the house, she was wrapped snugly in nostalgia, a warmth of memories that flooded her soul. Here was where they sat to eat as a family, such as it was, after Kate's death. But it was home, and here is where she had felt secure, if not always loved. Home was a haven with a repetition of comforting daily duties, the days measured by their required tasks.

She suddenly recalled the routine of milking cows, the creamy milk directed into the tin pail, the froth building up the sides as the pail was filled, the handkerchief tied firmly across her forehead as she rested it on the cow's flank.

Breakfast was served on old homespun tablecloths of various hues. The menu was porridge, fried mush, and eggs in spring when they were plentiful. There was always good hot tea, freshly churned butter and bread, the family gathered together, their heads bowed in silent prayer, both before and after the meal.

Washing, bread-making, butter-churning, scouring, scrubbing, and cleaning filled the days. But there was always time to stop and soak up the birdsong, allowing it to elevate your spirits while pegging white sheets and tablecloths, and grabbing toddling little Menno by his suspenders and sitting him in the clothes basket made of reeds that Kate had woven together.

In the afternoon, when the weather was fine and Hans allowed it, Noah, Isaac, and Hester would race pell-mell to the creek with their homemade fishing poles and a can of fat, juicy earthworms they dug from the base of the manure pile. Yelling, racing each other, and sliding down the steep bank at the edges of the water, they'd dig around, come up with a round, wriggling worm, impale it on the cruel hook, then fling it out into the water, knowing where the fat, sleepy bass lay under a fallen log or tree root.

Hester could smell the filet of bass rolled in egg and cornmeal, then fried in sizzling lard in the two cast-iron skillets, sprinkled with salt, and fried to a golden crispy goodness. Hans always praised their ability to supply these wonderful portions for the dinner table. Or, he mostly praised Hester, the boys turning their faces to him, eager to absorb a few crumbs that might fall from the loaf he shared with his eyes on Hester's face. That was simply the way it was.

She had to give herself a mental shake, now, to pay attention to Magdalena's words as they moved from room to room. She had been nodding absently, her eyes taking in what she was showing her, but her thoughts lagged ten years behind.

"So, that's it," Magdalena was saying. "Oh, and you can just call me Lena. Everyone does."

She bent to pick up the baby from the large oak cradle, who yawned and stretched contentedly, his pink cheeks like patches of cherry blossoms.

"This is Hans," she said proudly.

"Oh, you've given him a namesake. That's nice."

"Yes, it is. He was pleased. That was one thing I told Solomon we should do, as it doesn't appear as if he will be gaining in health."

"Really?"

"He's not well. I'm afraid you will hardly recognize him."

Hester said nothing, her stomach immediately in knots of anxiety. She could not tell this loving woman about the fear that lay in her stomach like bile, the sour taste Hans brought to her mouth, the plague that sickened her soul. Tomorrow she would have to face him, look into his eyes, and wish him well.

Magdalena watched Hester's face with curiosity and benevolence, but no suspicion. How would she even understand? She could not know anything about the past, the unforgiven, the unforgivable sins of the fathers.

Hester froze when Magdalena said, unexpectedly, "Solomon told me about your leaving. He remembers the argument. He remembers Annie being cruel and threatening to burn your book. He told me much about your life here, Hester."

Hester kept her back turned as she fought to control her anger. She felt a soft hand on her shoulder and heard the words Magdalena said. They were kind words, encouraging ones, but they rained about her head with all the consolation of fiery darts.

Hester whirled and faced her sister-in-law, her eyes black with fury. Magdalena stepped back, clutching her baby tightly to her chest, her eyes wide with alarm.

"Yes, well, it's good of you to say all the right things. It's good of you to give Hans a namesake. But you didn't live through any of his slimy deceit, his lies. You were never splattered with the mud of his hypocrisy. You have no idea what I have to face tomorrow, so don't give me a package of smooth words," she hissed. Then, with a strangled cry, she disappeared through the back door of the kitchen, moving like a wraith across the backyard and into the woods.

CHAPTER 22

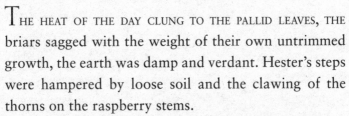

THE HEAT OF THE DAY CLUNG TO THE PALLID LEAVES, THE briars sagged with the weight of their own untrimmed growth, the earth was damp and verdant. Hester's steps were hampered by loose soil and the clawing of the thorns on the raspberry stems.

She swung her hands beside her skirt, raking back the briars, sliding back one step for every several steps she went forward. She had no idea where she was going; she was simply filled with the blind urge to get away from prying eyes and people who knew and remembered.

How could he? How could Solomon have told his wife? How many people had *she* told? Hester had always thought that her past, that pit of despair, the smudge of shame that lay on her face like a birthmark, was hers only. Not even Noah knew who he should blame nor could he comprehend her feeling of having been sullied, even if she never was physically.

Sobbing harsh sounds that ripped from her throat as she climbed up the ridges, her breath came in ragged gasps. She knew nothing but an urge to hide, to remain hidden. She could not face tomorrow.

The cliff was too high. Her strength to scale it was gone, taken away by remembering Hans.

Crowding out her sudden weakness was her desperate recognition that she had allowed herself to fall in love with Noah, when she should have known it could only turn out badly. He would forgive his father out of reverence for him. Noah was so good. He was kind like Kate. And here she was, born an Indian, with the proud blood of the Lenapes flowing through her veins. She would not bow to that man Hans, even if he was on his deathbed.

Here it was again. All her life she had tried to fit in, to be a white Amish woman, when all she was, all she ever would be, was an Indian, a red-skinned person of the earth who belonged to an entirely different culture.

She felt herself slip, then let go and fell to the ground, heaving sobs tearing from her throat, dry and hoarse, until she was spent.

She sat up when the light through the woods turned rosy, a covering of beauty she couldn't notice as her eyes swelled with the pain of her tears. She caught sight of the outcropping of limestone, her girlhood place of worship. Tears ran unchecked down her face as she rose and fought her way upward to the place of her youth.

When she finally reached the flat surface of rock, she saw, through streaming eyes, a heavenly vista before her—the late summer sunset a blaze of glory, painting the sky in magnificent shades of red, fiery orange, and yellow, fading into the restful hues of lavender and blue.

Berks County, her home, spread out before her, a land of rippling green, shades of blue, rivulets of black, sparkling with yellows and lighter greens. Below her lay the Amish settlement, the people she loved, remembered, and cherished.

But it wasn't enough. She could not forget the blood-red stain of Hans. She would have to give up and release Noah, release her love. It would never work.

With a groan, she flung herself down, shutting out the beauty of the evening. She closed her eyes, willing herself to keep them closed. She felt the need of prayer, of joining her thoughts to God.

God? Did she believe he cared about her at all? Here she was in this last hour, her life of happiness stretched before her, and she could not close the gap, she could not cross the bridge of forgiveness. Maybe, just maybe, she could try talking to the Great Spirit, the god of the Indians, her foreparents. Did he care?

Here on this rock she had found God. She had found him in the eagle's flight. She had taken God into her heart and fully realized that he was one with her own self. She would wait on him, she would renew her strength, she would run and not walk, she would rise up on the wings of an eagle.

But now she could not pray, so great was her inner battle. She lay face down and became quiet; deep in her soul, she became still and waited.

Her tears ceased and her heart slowed, as the warm breezes played with the high branches of the sycamore trees and spun the pine needles, wafting the sharp, gummy scent across her spent face. A chipmunk dashed across the edge of the rock, disappearing beneath a few brown weeds, their swaying the only sign he had been there.

When Hester heard the bird's cry, she waited, tensed, straining to hear. Surely it could not be. She sat up, held a hand to her forehead, straining her sight, searching. The sky was empty, a panorama of heavenly brilliance. She heard it once more. Twisting her back, she let her swollen eyes rake the sky.

Like a mirage to a man dying of thirst in a desert, the silhouette of an eagle, his wingspan magnificent, his white head visible, soared across the sky, followed immediately by his mate. Together they sailed their vast empire, the evening sky, floating on unseen pockets of air, swirling currents that carried them on the evening, slowly away from her and into the beauty of the sunset.

Hester stood then, tears coursing down her face. She lifted her arms, flinging them to the sun and the beauty of the pair of eagles. She called aloud, "Here I am, oh, my Father, my God."

He had sent not one, but two eagles, her symbol of strength.

She remained in that position until the eagles disappeared into the sunset. She slowly folded herself onto her knees as the sun slid behind the Berks County mountains.

Then, like the softest whisper, a mere stirring of her senses, she recognized her own lack of power. On her own strength, she was helpless to forgive, to forget, to love, to live triumphantly. She could not do it. But with God, the white Amish version of God or the Indian version of the Great Spirit, the God who created everything—the earth and its inhabitants—with him and in him, it was possible.

Unexpectedly, Hans became very small, a dot that was disintegrating fast, where before he had been a huge stain that kept her focused on her own self-loathing. Life before her was imperfect, filled with trials and troubles, but God within her was perfectly capable of renewing her strength each morning, every morning fresh and new.

And so she stayed on the rock, her tears slowing, her body and spirit both entering a place of tranquility.

In the sun's afterglow, in the golden evening light the shape of a white cross appeared, shimmered for a few seconds, and disappeared.

Had she imagined the cross? No, she couldn't have. It was the way of the cross that would lead her home. She was learning not to make herself the center of the world. Jesus would be her model, giving the ultimate sacrifice as he did.

"*Mein Yesu*," she murmured.

She heard the cracking of brush and tensed, remembering the youth who had slipped through the trees, watching her. The shadows were deepening and the woods were becoming dark, and still the cracking sound continued. Someone was coming up the ridge. She remained seated, listening, watching the treetops in the direction of the breaking brush and the scuffled leaves.

In the fading light, his blond head hatless, his eyes round with fear, Noah stood just below the rock, his face lifted, searching.

Ashamed, Hester remained seated, huddled in the safety of her own personal chapel. On he came, until he stepped to the base of the rock and caught sight of her. With a glad cry he moved swiftly. He stretched out his arms, but with a question in his eyes.

"Hester! I was sick with worry."

She gave him her hands, and he drew her to her feet. His eyes searched her face, taking in the swollen eyes, the tear stains, the emotional havoc on a face so beautiful. And yet fear kept him from taking her in his arms.

"What is it, Hester?"

She lowered her eyes, feeling guilty.

He put his hands on her shoulders and gave her a gentle shake. "Please tell me. Is it just too much, this returning to your home?"

Hester drew in a deep breath, then turned her head to look away from the searching eyes. "You'll think I'm *kindish*. Out of my mind."

"Never."

With a small cry, she flung herself into his arms, into the solid warmth of the man she loved. She wrapped her arms around him, clung to him, and buried her face in his chest. "I love you so much, Noah. I love you, I love you."

With a muffled cry he kissed her swollen eyes, the tearstained cheeks, her trembling mouth. He held her as he had never held her before with a newfound possession, gladness in having her, so afraid of this great love gone wrong.

Finally he let her go, searching her face in the fast ebbing twilight and asking if she was ready to tell him. Side by side, his arm around her waist, they sat as she talked in low words of her struggle.

He listened, rapt, as she spoke from the depth of her shame about feeling tainted, in spite of Hans never having touched her.

Noah's jaw tightened, the muscles in his cheeks moving rigidly. He nodded, mutely understanding, absorbing her misery.

She told him of the eagles and of God's message to her heart.

"Hester, do you believe God wants us to be together as man and wife?"

Suddenly Hester's shoulders began to shake. Thinking he had made her cry again, he quickly took back the question, stammering some nonsense about not meaning it.

But Hester was laughing. Great cleansing waves of merriment. "You never asked me," she chortled.

So he did. There, on Hester's rock, on the stone floor of her personal outdoor chapel, he asked her to be his wife, to walk beside him all the days of his life. He knew he was not worthy of her, but he hoped to love her and care for her as long as God gave each of them the breath of life.

Hester could only bow her head to absorb the beauty of his words.

Then she whispered, "Yes, Noah, I will marry you. With joy."

When they reached the house, Solomon and Lena showed their relief, visibly able to relax now that they had returned. Lena apologized effusively for having said the wrong thing and for hurting her feelings.

Fannie's eyes were large and so afraid that Hester went to her immediately, took her in her arms, and held her there, explaining that she needed to take care of some unfinished business in a place she had to go to. That seemed to be sufficient. She helped Fannie put on her nightgown and led her upstairs, tucked her into their bed, and said she'd be up soon.

"Poor little Fannie," she crooned, smoothing back the fine, brown hair. "I'm so sorry I left you like that."

But Fannie smiled and sighed, adjusting her head on the thick, goose-down pillow, already fading into the land of a child's dreams. "If I cry during the night, it's your fault, you know," she whispered.

Hester kissed her cheek, and tiptoed quietly down the stairs.

They told Solomon and Lena about their engagement, knowing the secret was safe with them.

Solomon whooped and shouted, saying he figured there was something going on, coming back like this out of the blue without telling anyone ahead of time. Lena smiled widely and congratulated them sincerely.

She served hot tea with sugar and milk, slabs of cold cornbread with honey, a bowl of purple grapes from the vines beside the garden, and slices of cheese with a bold, nutty flavor, the thick slices full of holes. Solomon said it was Swiss cheese from Ohio, made here in America now.

Far into the night, they talked of farms and land, the price of an acre here versus in Lancaster County, which was where so many were migrating and paying crazy high prices for smaller plots of land.

But the yield there is tremendous, Noah argued, although he couldn't imagine that the Amish could last very long in Lancaster. How could they keep their conservative ways while living so close to the worldly people—that whole hodgepodge of Irish and Lutherans and Dunkards and Germans—a vegetable soup of people.

"So why don't you buy land there?" Solomon asked.

"I like these ridges."

"It's my home. Our home," Hester said.

Solomon nodded. "Such as it was after Kate died. My mother. She was the best."

Noah nodded. "Remember how mad she used to get when we teased you, me and Isaac?"

"Your fault. You showed no mercy."

Noah's eyes became soft with the memory of Isaac. They talked of his death, of the fruitlessness of war. Noah thought that if life and love were somehow different, wars could be eliminated. But he supposed that as long as people had natures of greed, hate, and jealousy, there would be war. That led to a long discussion of whether there was ever a war that was right in God's eyes. Or should everyone be nonresistant, like the Amish and Mennonites?

"Isaac was nonresistant in his heart. He was much too gentle in his spirit to be a soldier. He should never have followed me. Or rather, I should not have gone in the first place. And yet it was a good experience. I learned and lived so much more than I would have, had I stayed home."

"Why did you go, anyway?" Solomon asked.

"Hans. And Hester leaving. Dat made me mad. I was wild inside. Rebellious. I didn't care if I lived or not. Reckless."

"Do you blame Dat still for Hester leaving?"

Silence hung over the kitchen, the only sound the ticking of the clock on the wall, the sleepy sounds of tired crickets, the shrill screech of cicadas.

"I did for a long time, but how can I still, if I say I have forgiven him for what he did?" Noah finally said.

"Things were never right between him and Annie, right?"

Noah shook his head. Hester lowered her eyes, keeping her gaze on her hands. Solomon and Lena exchanged meaningful glances.

Noah saved the conversation by saying, "She was plenty bossy, for someone accustomed to Kate."

Solomon nodded. "That's about right."

When morning came, with its special, sun-dappled light filtering in between the maple leaves, Hester was dressed and ready to go when Noah called for her at the doorway.

Her hair was combed neatly, the muslin cap pinned over it, the green of her dress bringing out the olive tones of her skin. Her eyes were still slightly puffy but clear, containing a new confidence. She held her head higher, she straightened her shoulders with new purpose.

Fannie wanted to stay with Lena and the babies, having taken to the toddler, Levi, immediately. Her natural love of infants and her sweet, unassuming ways captivated Lena, who was happy to have Fannie till Noah and Hester returned.

Noah looked at Hester and told her he had never seen her more beautiful. The green of her dress made her seem like a princess of the forest, stepping out from the trees.

Hester held his gaze, returning his love without a spoken word.

Every step of their walk was the old path to school, down past the barn, a left turn onto the road, through the woods, and past Amos Fisher's to school.

The morning was clear and already warm, the dust swirling at their feet. Dry, dusty grass waved in the summer air. A box turtle ambled across the road, heard their footsteps, and pulled himself into his shell.

Hester bent down the way she had always done, picked up the turtle, and carried him to safety by the side of the road.

Noah smiled. "He'll crawl right back, likely."

"No, he knows better."

They laughed, walking on until they came to a small clearing where a wood-sided house had been built by the side of the road, along with a barn and a few outbuildings. "This must be it," Noah said softly.

Hester's heart beat thickly in her ears, the blood pounding as she took a steadying breath, then another.

"You all right?" Noah asked, searching her face.

"Just frightened. Scared terrible," she whispered.

"Shall we turn back?"

"No."

A wide porch was built along the front. Firewood was stacked on one side of the door; a chair sat on the other side. A rain barrel caught the water from the edge of the porch. The house was small but substantial, built by Hans, and sturdy. Each window was encased in heavy trimwork, the door thick and solid. The yard was scythed and raked, the fence around the garden well maintained.

Hester noticed the chicken coop, with the chickens contained inside the fencing, and thought of Amos Stoltzfus's vicious hens.

She gripped Noah's hand for one last shoring up of strength, then tilted her chin up, her eyes holding his.

Noah lifted his hand and knocked firmly.

After the second knock, the door was opened slowly by a young woman, her eyes as blue as Noah's, her hair streaked with blond, her face round and sweet—so like Kate that Hester's breath caught in her throat.

"Hello. *Kommet rye.*"

She stepped back to allow them to enter.

"Emma?" Hester asked.

"Yes, I am Emma. But I don't know you."

"Hester. Remember your older sister?"

Emma shook her head, bewildered. She looked up at Noah without recognition. Then she gasped and pointed at him, saying, "Noah?"

Noah laughed and gripped her hand.

Emma led them to the right into a sitting room, lighted well by two large windows. Hester immediately recognized the rugs, the oak sideboard, and the armless rocking chair, before she noticed the person lying on the bed in the corner.

He was only a thin rail beneath a small blanket that covered him from the waist down. A muslin nightshirt was draped over his skeletal frame, his hair gray and matted to his head, the thick black beard now turned gray as well.

His face was white as parchment, his once full, robust cheeks hollow and sunken below prominent cheekbones, the full, protruding nose thin and beaklike. His eyes were closed, his bony hands resting on the top of the blanket.

"Dat is not doing good, as you can see. He sleeps a lot. The doctors have done all they can."

Hester was aware of someone at the doorway and turned to face her stepmother, the thin, cruel Annie of her past. She was thinner, even, than before, her dress hanging as if on a rack, the black apron circling her waist loosely, the gathers below the belt the only thing that kept her appearance from resembling a pole. Her face was drawn downward, as if the pull of gravity enabled her normal expression to appear more sullen than ever.

"Mam, Noah has come back!" Emma announced. But Annie had not heard. One hand went to the doorframe, another to her mouth. Her thin, claw-like fingers shook violently, her eyes wide, now, with fear. She pointed one unsteady finger at Hester. "You!" she spat.

Hester stood facing her stepmother squarely without alarm or shrinking. "Yes, it's me, Annie—Hester."

"What do you want here? Have you come to worry me with your Indian ways and your *hexarei*?"

"No."

Noah stepped forward.

"Annie, we have come to see our dat. We didn't know he was ill until Solomon and Lena told us."

"What do you care now? You left us to fend for ourselves. Why bother coming back now when he is too weak to know you?"

"Mam," came the whisper from the bed. Then, louder, "Mam."

Quickly Annie went to him, bending over her husband to catch every word. Her hands shook so violently she could not lift the blanket to cover his hands. But Hans had seen the two visitors. His black eyes, sunken deep into his face, were large, alight, keen with interest as he struggled to see them clearly.

"*Henn ma psuch*, Mam?" he whispered.

Annie nodded.

Noah stepped forward, went to his father's bedside, and placed a strong hand on the shriveled, weak ones of his father.

"It is me, Noah," he said.

Hester shrank back, the room spinning with her dizziness. From the bed, the dark eyes searched the face of his son before Hans opened his mouth, trying to speak. But the only sound was a dry, hacking sob, one harsh intake of breath followed by another.

Hester had often heard Hans cry. He had cried loudly, sobbing in despair when Kate passed away and crying at little Rebecca's death, but never like this. It was the crying of a man who was almost too weak to breathe, a sound so pitiful it brought quick tears to Hester's eyes.

Hans lifted a thin hand. Noah took it, held it.

"Noah, *unser* Noah. Kate's and my Noah," he whispered. "*Ich bin so frowah.*"

That Hans was glad to see Noah was pitifully evident. He clung to his oldest son, his eyes alight with pleasure. He asked for more pillows, which Annie provided, putting him in a semi-seated position. His eyes found Hester. He blinked, then blinked again.

He relinquished his hold on Noah's hand and waved the hand weakly in Hester's direction. "Have you brought a wife, Noah?"

Hester stepped forward, buoyed by a calm that was not her own. "I am Hester."

Again, Hans's mouth opened, but he was soon wracked by fresh dry sobs, his eyes closing by the force of his sorrow. Over and over he raised his hand as if to speak, but the rasping sound continued.

Noah came to stand close to her, wanting to support her in the only way he could here in this room, with Annie like a specter of disapproval. Finally, Hans gathered some weakened control over himself.

"Ach, Hester, Hester, Hester. *Komm mol.*"

He waved a feeble hand. Hester caught it and held the hand as light as air.

"How I have prayed!" Hans gasped for breath. Annie rushed over, saying it was too much.

"No, no," Hans shook his head.

"God heard the prayers of a sick man. Over and over I prayed that you would come. Ach, my Hester. My *liebchen maedle.*"

He stopped and asked for water, which Annie supplied from the kitchen, holding the tumbler to his cracked, dry lips gently, as if for a child.

"*Danke,* Mam," Hans whispered.

As if the water revived him, Hans seemed to gather strength. "First of all, I owe you an apology. I am sorry, Hester. I was a man possessed by you. I allowed the natural affection of a father to turn into something that nearly destroyed me, my faith, you, and many more members of the family. You have suffered on my account, Hester. Annie has suffered. Noah. And my Isaac, gone to his eternal rest. Oh, how I hope he remembered his teaching."

Noah broke in. "He did Dat. He was saved at the end."

"*Preist Gott.* We are not worthy of such grace."

Hester lifted the black apron to find the white lawn handkerchief in her pocket, blew her nose gently, and dabbed at quiet tears.

"As I was saying, my unnatural affection, the lust of my heart, caused great hardship, and I have reaped many times over what I have sown. Isaac's death, your disappearance, Noah going to war, but worst of all, the ferment of my own conscience. I begged God to forgive me day and night, yet I found no peace. I felt I had to make it right with you, my dear Hester. I know I am lower than the worms that burrow below the earth's surface and do not deserve to be forgiven. If anyone ever deserves to burn in hell for all eternity, I do. Will you try, at least sometime in your life, if not now, to forgive me? I know I'm asking for more than you can ever grant me."

By now Hester was crying freely, her lower lip caught between her teeth, the lawn handkerchief catching the tears that welled up and spilled over. It was the pure, jeweled releasing of a festering sore, finally opened and beginning to heal by the miraculous hand that healed so many people before.

She stepped up and bent over his hands as she caught them in both of hers. She spoke clearly in her low voice. "I forgive you, Dat."

For a long time the only sound in the room was the awful, dry sobs, the sound of a broken man, crushed to bits by his own failure, completely repentant, honest, and finished. Annie blinked repeatedly, pursed her lips, scowled, and made all manner of strange faces to keep her tears hidden. Emma merely stood at the foot of her father's bed, sniffed occasionally, and wiped her eyes with the back of her hand. She was a child and could not grasp the full impact of her father's confession.

When the sound of his crying ceased, he drew a deep, ragged breath and spoke again. "I won't be here long, so let me say this. To make restitution, Noah, you shall have two hundred acres to the south. It is all surveyed and posted. I am leaving you five thousand dollars to build on the land. That is my wish. Solomon has the home farm. Daniel and John will also inherit land."

Suddenly, he smiled. "But Menno, I'm afraid, won't require land. He has inherited my love of horseshoeing. So be it."

Instantly Hester was at his bedside again. "Oh, Dat, I have many good memories of going with you on the spring wagon, shoeing horses. Those were the best years of my life. I do thank you for allowing me to go."

Those words brought another smile and a new light in his eyes. But he was tired out, completely exhausted by the force of his confession. Before anyone could say anything more, he was asleep, breathing slowly but deeply.

Noah turned to Hester, took her hands, and held them, as Annie watched with disapproving eyes, scowling, and pinching her lips.

"How do you feel, Hester?"

"As light as a feather. And very hungry."

Annie erased the scowl, led the way to the kitchen, and said stiffly, "Well, you should have said something."

"Oh, no. You shouldn't go to any trouble."

That was the way of tradition, the polite answer, but in truth, Hester was ravenous and unreasonably happy, her great burden lifted. She suddenly remembered Annie's baking, especially her molasses cakes, the oversized sugar cookies sprinkled with brown sugar, the huckleberry pie and butterscotch pudding drizzled with clabbered cream.

Annie spread snow-white tablecloths on the plank tabletop, turned, and said, "I just made a fresh molasses cake."

She scowled immediately after saying that as her hands shook fiercely. She made two or three attempts at placing the tablecloth, but so much had happened. At least she had made a molasses cake.

CHAPTER 23

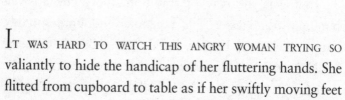

It was hard to watch this angry woman trying so valiantly to hide the handicap of her fluttering hands. She flitted from cupboard to table as if her swiftly moving feet would make up for her ill-disposed hands. She was nervous, which Hester assumed made the shaking much worse.

The knife wobbled as she sliced through the perfect layer cake. The tumblers clacked wildly as she brought them to the table. She asked Emma to pour cold buttermilk, and Hester could easily see why. Annie would not have been capable. Now, more than ever, Hester would so have liked to try the Indian remedy for palsy of the hands, but she chose not to speak of it.

While they were seated, there was a clatter on the back porch and two more children burst through the door, their faces red from exertion, their hair plastered to their foreheads, perspiring freely.

"Barbara. Menno," Annie said sternly.

They stopped, two adolescents, the picture of good health and vitality, smiles fading from their faces as they struggled to recognize these people who were seated at the table.

Barbara's voice burst out, "Noah! Hester!"

Noah beamed, hugging his sister and then his brother. Hester gathered them into her arms immediately, laughing, teasing them, and saying they certainly hadn't grown up much at all.

They were both dark-haired and dark-eyed like Hans. They exuded the same ambition, the lust for life, the boundless energy, never quite able to sit still for any length of time. They were clearly delighted to have Noah and Hester here at the house and were soon swapping tales of childhood shenanigans.

"They're probably pretty much the same way we were, Hester," Noah laughed, punching Menno on his upper arm.

"I can't shoot a slingshot the way you could, Hester," Barbara said. "You killed the rooster once."

"Did I? Oh, I remember. I guess I did. Well, don't blame me. He had it coming. Roosters can't go through life flogging people!"

Noah laughed heartily. "That's not the only thing you shot. I still remember that rumor about the ghost in the hollow. I think you climbed a tree and shot Obadiah's hat off one morning on our way to school."

Hester's eyes danced. "You will never know, will you?"

Through all this banter Annie moved stiffly. She seemed determined to hide any show of interest in Hester and Noah, intent on heating water in the polished kettle, sweeping up a few crumbs, straightening the curtain by the dry sink. Hester watched, wishing there was a way of getting to know her better, a way of understanding her.

Annie moved fast, checking on Hans, going to the back door to pull the latch, and back to the stove. Then she was again at the dry sink, always with her mouth pulled down in a perpetual scowl, a sort of repressed, upside-down smile.

Was her life a bitter potion? After Hester left, had Hans loved her? Had he been good to her?

A sudden pity welled up in Hester. Surely Annie had some reason to be so hard-hearted. The cruelty Hester remembered had bordered on uncontrollable surges of anger. Only after she had demeaned Hester to a mere scrap heap would she let go of her taunting.

Now that all this time had passed without Hester in her life, had she, too, felt badly, perhaps remembering the unfairness of her hatred? Or was this woman simply not aware of having done anything wrong?

It was when Annie dropped the butter dish that Hester's pity became real and deep. She determined within herself to find some way of tunneling into her good graces, if any such thing existed.

She watched Annie bend to retrieve the broken butter dish piece by piece, her hands shaking so badly Hester felt sure she would cut herself. When she offered to help, getting down on her knees, she was elbowed aside so rudely she was almost knocked on her backside.

Embarrassed, she straightened and went back to her chair. Noah caught her eye and winked, smiling widely. *Some things never change*, he mouthed.

Hester sat up to the table, aware of the flush stealing across her face. As Noah kept up a lively conversation with his siblings, Hester remained quiet, watching Annie's determination to hide any form of disability, her mouth drawn in concentration. She set her shoulders and worked stiffly and persistently, as if she, all by herself, could exert control over her shaking hands.

Hester got up, went over to the dry sink, asked Annie for a clean tea towel, and began to wipe dishes without saying anything further. Instantly Annie became terribly ill at ease. Her nose twitched, her mouth worked, her movements became so jerky that water from the dishpan splashed on the floor. She fought the tremors, but eventually, after repeatedly attempting to lift a heavy white plate from the slippery water, she clutched the edge of the sink and stood still until they passed. Then she turned, her tortured eyes sparking with animosity.

"I guess you came to dry dishes so you could see my *aylend*." Her words were quick, harsh, and as dry and scaly as a rattlesnake crawling over a rock at midday.

Hester felt herself shrink, an involuntary need to get away from the words that brought back memories of her overwhelming anger, the tongue-lashings she experienced as a girl. But now she was a woman. A person in her own right, who had been married, loved, and rejected, who worked among people in the world and knew a few things about life in general.

So she said, "That is not why I came to help you, Annie. I think you are managing very well with your difficulty."

"No, you don't."

Hester watched her ailing stepmother, saying nothing.

Annie clenched her hands as she stared out the window. Her words tumbled thick and fast, like quiet hisses from a swarm of angry wasps attacking Hester.

"You think you're so much better than me. You sailed through our house like some queen, swinging your hips at my Hans, you did. Your big eyes are so bold, and here he lies dying, apologizing for something you brought on yourself, you Indian. You never were anything, and you still aren't. I was glad when you left, glad."

Hester absorbed the viciousness of her words quietly. They were merely words, flung out by her mouth from the dark recesses of her heart.

Then Hester spoke. "Annie, you know as well as I do, that you are not speaking words of *wahrheit*. I did nothing to get any of this attention from my father."

Here Annie broke in. "He's not your father."

Hester turned to look at her stepmother, hoping to meet her eyes, to convey some sort of feeling. Annie presented her profile like a brick wall, and as impenetrable.

From the corner of her eye, Hester saw Noah herd his younger siblings out the door and thanked him silently.

"You are right, Annie. He is not my father. If he were, none of this would have happened."

"Yes, it would. You brought it on yourself."

Hester sighed. She polished a glass tumbler until her towel became stuck, then continued to twist it round and round, buying time, desperately seeking a response that was not an argument, a continued clash of senseless word-dueling.

"Annie, I don't believe I ever tried anything intentionally. Hans was a good father to me. I adored him as a child, as he loved and adored his wife. I had no idea there was anything amiss, growing up."

Here Annie snorted, a derisive, mocking assault. "You were dumb. Indians are. He married me merely to cover up his feeling for you. I saw it the first week of our marriage."

This silenced Hester. All too well, she remembered the tight-lipped Annie, the tension between Hans and his new bride, Annie's refusal to meet his eyes, her angry movements like a puppet on a string when she served him at the table. Yes, Hester had seen it, believing that their newlywed bliss had gone far wrong. But never once had she thought of herself as the cause.

Extending the olive branch of peace, Hester bowed to Annie the way Abraham of old bowed to his brother Lot, offering him the choice of the much better land. Hester conceded, allowing Annie her valued opinion.

"Yes, I was dumb, innocent, naive. All of that. Whether it was because I'm an Indian, I'm not sure. Perhaps it's just me being me. I never did very well at numbers and letters in school.

"But, Annie, you must believe me when I say I never did anything to intentionally come between you and Hans. I wanted a mother, someone like Kate."

When Annie turned her head, Hester met her eyes, completely unprepared for the raw pain and the bottomless vulnerability in this thin, spare woman. She saw only for a moment. Then Annie drew the curtain of anger, sparking a dangerous round.

"I'm not Kate," she spat.

Hester remained quiet, set down the polished glass, then picked up a fork and dried it.

Annie launched herself away from the dry sink with quick, staccato steps, marched through the kitchen, her shoulders stiff, her arms like pokers at her thin hips, and disappeared into the sick room to check on her husband.

When she returned, she sat at the table, her hands clenched in front of her, her head bent over them. "Come sit with me," she ground out.

Hester sat.

"All my life my father was cruel. Not just to me, but to everyone. The sting of the whip across my legs was nothing unusual. I needed it. I did most things wrong. I was the small, spindly one, the runt."

Here, Hester thought of Fannie.

"My father always had money. Our farm was well managed. Yet he gave me away to a family who needed a *maud*. A maid.

"Rebecca was a good enough stepmother, but I was not her child. I was on the outside looking in. She held the other children, kissed them. But she never touched me. My heart often hurt, but I found strength in anger. In not caring. I decided it wouldn't hurt me. I became strong. I never complained, I did my share of the work. I had it nice, really. *Ich hab es shay Kott*. Plenty to eat, clothes to wear.

"About five years after I entered *rumspringa*, I realized that I would likely not be chosen to marry. My face was plain. I was thin and already angry most of the time. I lacked charm. It was the other girls who smiled, laughed, spoke clearly, and won the attention of the boys at the hymn singings. One by one, my friends were all courting. And one by one, they were married."

Annie reached into her pocket, produced a spotless square of white linen, wiped her nose with a few swipes, sniffed, and returned it to her pocket. "When Hans asked for my hand at the age of thirty-nine, I was overcome with gratitude. I had returned to my family as a house-keeper, and since I was an adult, Dat could no longer ply that whip. So he used words, as hurtful as the slash of the leather thongs.

"Never once did I imagine I would become like my father. I had always imagined that I would be kind and loving to my children. I would never stoop so low as to lash out with words or a whip. So why did I?"

The kitchen was bright with the late morning sun-shine streaming through the windows, dust motes hover-ing on shafts of it, the polished floor gleaming where the light fell. The ornately carved clock on the wall ticked loudly. Somewhere, the pinging of heated and cooled metal sounded.

"Why did I?" Annie repeated.

Hester opened her mouth to answer, to tell her it was all right, to make her feel better in an urge to convey sympathy.

"I became my father."

Again, Hester took a breath, a soothing reply on her lips. Annie held up her hand.

"Don't. Let me finish. I married Hans with complete happiness. I loved him and looked forward to the time when I would be his wife in every sense of the word."

A long silence ensued, after which Annie lifted her head and met Hester's eyes, revealing another painful glimpse of those tortured eyes.

"He never touched me, Hester," she whispered, a ragged sound so pitiful, it shredded every ounce of painful memories in Hester.

"We lived under the same roof, sharing our meals and our bed as brother and sister. You are the only one who knows. Can you understand my frustration? Although I had no right. As I was treated cruelly, so I treated others. You especially. I hated you. I wanted you gone, out of my life. Away from Hans.

"When you left, he blamed me. He became like a man possessed. It was terrible to see. But life went on. Outwardly, we prospered. We acquired acreage. The crops did well. The children worked alongside us. Hans developed a distant fondness for me, his second wife. If it was all the love I would ever receive, it was enough. I stayed strong, bolstered by work and the harsh words that gave me my strength.

"Then, Hans's strength began to fail. Last July he began losing weight. The doctors tried everything. Bloodletting. Laudanum. All to no avail. He asked about you often, wondering if there was no word as to your whereabouts. These questions were always a dagger to my feelings, robbing me of the tiny smidgen of love I could glean from my husband.

"As he weakened, he became kind. He wanted me by his side. He often held my hand, caressing the back of it with his thumb as he spoke words of praise to me. He thanked me often for being a mother to his children, for being the good worker that I was. It filled my empty heart, this outpouring of his love, for that is what it was, a cup of sweet ambrosia to my scalded self."

Annie became quiet, her fluttering fingers placed in her lap. Once there was a derisive sound of laughter, a mocking note forged with the always present anger.

Suddenly she held up her hands like freckled claws, thin and bony, calloused by the hard labor that had always been her lot, the days of her life spent performing the menial tasks that kept the wheel of farm life smoothly oiled. "They look like the hands of a man."

Tentatively, her fingers went to her mouth.

"My thin, homely face has never been kissed, never." She shrugged, straightened her shoulders, and remarked, "It doesn't matter. It won't hurt me. Never did, never will."

Hester sat in her chair dumbfounded, stunned. In all her life, she had never seen such an example of lonely courage. How could she have known this hateful, cruel woman's deep well of unfulfilled love?

Hester stood, hesitated, then bent slowly to the thin, freckled face. Just before her lips touched the dry, papery skin, she whispered, "Now you have been kissed."

She folded the thin form gently against her breast, one hand stroking the cheek on the opposite side. "Annie, you have been in my life for a purpose. If I would not have left, I would never have met all the people I did, wouldn't have married William or been through so much of what God has given me."

When Annie's thin shoulders began to shake, warm, wet tears coursing down on her fingers, Hester's sob caught in her own throat. Oh, the pity of it.

Annie cried quietly. Then whispered, "*Ich vill au halta fa fagebniss.*"

Hester's throat was so constricted she could not speak for a moment, so she gathered Annie into another warm embrace and said softly, "I do forgive you, Annie. I do. I mean it with all my heart."

"*Denke.*"

The sun shone into the kitchen just as it always had. But now the walls, the floor, the oak table, everything seemed warmed by the presence of angels hovering just out of sight, hosts to the king of forgiveness, the one who gave his life for all of humankind's ills and iniquities. These angels sang the same chorus they always sing when there is redemption and forgiveness. On this day, two women, one so beautiful, the other so unattractive, both designed and created by God, and loved with the same love sent down through the ages, forgave each other.

Again, Annie said, "*Denke*, Hester."

Words were meaningless, unnecessary, with the aura of God's presence so near.

The comfortable silence was broken when Annie asked if there was anything between her and Noah. Hester blushed a deep, charming shade of red. She nodded.

"I thought there might be. Has he asked you yet?"

Hester nodded again.

Annie placed a hand on Hester's knee. "Could we have the wedding here?"

"Oh, Annie," Hester sighed, "That would be a dream come true. I would never be worthy. It would be wonderful, but you know, we have to wait till Noah sets a time."

"Yes, that is true. And we have to see how many days God will allow Hans to be with us."

As it was, Hans slipped away faster after finding peace in Hester's forgiveness. He shook his head, refusing food or water on the second day after their arrival. Often his weak, quavery voice could be heard breaking into an old German hymn, the words barely audible, the frail humming a continued version of the song in his heart.

It rained on the fourth day, a Saturday, a warm summer rain without thunder or lightning. A bank of clouds from the east had been ushered in by strong afternoon winds the day before. Hester woke to the sound of steady rain on the shake shingles, accompanied by a constant drip from the eaves. Low clouds scudded across the sky. Moisture in the form of warm raindrops replenished the good brown soil.

Noah said a rain like this so late in the summer was priceless. Menno looked up from his plate of fried eggs and toast and asked what that word meant.

"Without price. Worth a lot," Noah answered, taking a long drink from his teacup.

When Menno said he'd have a hard time bottling the stuff if he wanted to sell it, Noah choked on his tea, spluttered, and coughed, and carried on until Annie smiled along with everyone's laughter.

Till late afternoon, the rain was still coming down steadily, water splashing from the roof and ripping across the yard. Two white ducks waddled through the grass by the front porch, quacking happily, the short white feathers on their tails wagging with energy, their flat webbed feet slopping along from side to side.

Hester was shucking corn on the front porch, her strong brown hands ripping off the outer husks in two deft twists before breaking off the short stalk and chucking all of it in a reed basket. Her fingers brushed the silk absently, her mind wandering across the unbelievable events of the week.

She whispered a short prayer for wisdom and understanding, asking that she never judge anyone harshly, especially without knowing their upbringing. She looked up when Annie called her name softly.

"Hans is calling for Lissie and Solomon. You had best find Noah." Hester got up, brushing the corn silk from her apron, a question in her eyes. "Is he worse?"

Annie's lips quivered, but she only nodded.

Hester splashed through the rain down to the barn, the barn of her childhood, now enlarged with two different wings. The original cow stable and a small barnyard fence had been taken away and replaced by a larger stable. She found Noah brushing the workhorses, oiled harnesses on a heap beside him.

"Annie says Hans is calling for the children," she said quietly.

Lissie's arrival raised quite a stir, her being as noisy and opinionated as ever. Hester would not have recognized the round young woman had it not been for her strident voice and the take-charge way with which she burst into the house, followed by a passel of toddlers and little children.

Her husband, Elam, entered later, a beanpole of a man with a quiet, good nature, a patient man, happy to let his effusive wife be the center of everyone's attention.

Soloman and Lena arrived soon afterward, followed by Daniel and his new wife, a blond, trim beauty, with eyes so blue Hester found herself staring.

They all gathered by the bedside of their father who was slipping into eternity, drawn by the bands that tie us to the Heavenly Father, whose final call of death is feared by all mortals, but is sweet rest for those weary of life and suffering.

And Hans was weary. His dry, parched lips moved as he asked for Annie who sat by his side, his hand in both of hers. "Mam?" he whispered.

She bent low.

"I love you."

She nodded, pursing her lips in the old way to keep emotion in check.

"Noah?"

Quickly Noah went to his father.

"*Ich segne dihr.*"

"Thank you for the blessing, Dat." Noah spoke thickly, as if he had to push the words past an obstruction.

Hans's breathing was so soft, so faint, that it was hard to tell if he was still with them. When he seemed to gather strength, his breathing becoming stronger, he raised one hand partway, only to let it fall. He sighed deeply and never breathed again.

Each member of the family mourned in their own way—with quiet reverence, a few audible sobs, and tears coursing down grieving faces. They placed his hands on his chest, closed his eyes and his mouth, then left Annie at his side as they filed into the large room to make plans for his funeral service, the burial, and whatever else needed to be attended to.

Neighbors, church members, and all other available members of the family showed up within a few hours. Some cleaned; many brought food, preparing for the days of mourning and burial. The women wore black short-gowns, capes, and aprons. They took over the kitchen, making meals for the family in mourning. Kindness and sympathy flowed freely through soft handshakes and shoulders gripped in empathy, all of it a wonderful way of uniting each person in the bonds of love.

When the rain stopped, the air felt fresh and new. Sunlight speckled the buggies, drawn by all the different horses as they trotted obediently in the funeral procession, driving through the woods to the fenced-in graveyard on the hill.

There, Hans was laid to rest beside Kate and little Rebecca in the soft moist soil of Berks County. The large group of family and friends was dressed all in black, their heads bent, softly weeping as the minister read the *lied*. When the prayer was said, the men held their wide-brimmed hats in their hands, their uncovered heads bent in reverence.

Later, after the graveside service, Noah stood with Hester, their heads bowed as silent tears flowed down their cheeks, at Kate's grave, the small, plain headstone of Catherine Zug, their dearly beloved mother. In blood for one; in spirit for the other. It was a moment Hester would cherish forever, this unspoken bond birthed by the single most loving person she and Noah had ever known. Her memory and the goodness of her spirit had helped Hester through countless times in her life when despair had threatened to sink her.

The rolling green hills of Berks County were still the same—gentle and lovely, a vibrant green refreshed by the rain. This was the place they had spent time together as children, dotted with homes and farms of the Amish. The forest continued to be tamed into submission, giving way to fields and roads, which crisscrossed the ridges and swamps. Here in this land of Pennsylvania with Noah by her side, Hester's life contained a sense of new promise, the possibility of a life fulfilled, until death would part them.

CHAPTER 24

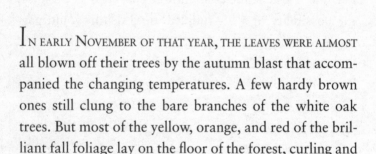

IN EARLY NOVEMBER OF THAT YEAR, THE LEAVES WERE ALMOST all blown off their trees by the autumn blast that accompanied the changing temperatures. A few hardy brown ones still clung to the bare branches of the white oak trees. But most of the yellow, orange, and red of the brilliant fall foliage lay on the floor of the forest, curling and turning brown, compost for the thick bark to thrive on for yet another winter.

Chipmunks scurried frantically, gathering seeds and nuts. Their larger counterparts, the gray squirrels, chirred at them from their perches high in the branches. Raucous crows teetered on boughs too thin for their claws, their beaks open and giving vent to their haunting cries. Red-headed woodpeckers tapped busily at the bark of trees, their tongue slivers darting to catch the grubs and insects inside.

The bashful fawns still trailed along with their larger mothers, coming to the edge of the fields at twilight, their large sensitive ears held forward to catch every available sound.

Along the border of such a field two figures strolled hand in hand, the muslin cap on the woman's head in stark relief against the surrounding trees. The man wore a yellow straw hat, his white shirt front visible between the black coat front on either side. The woman's shawl was pinned securely, its corners waving in the evening breeze.

Noah stopped, held both arms out pointing east and west, his eyebrows raised as he asked Hester what she thought of having the house built facing south, with the forest hill to the north behind it. Hester asked how she would ever see a sunrise if they did that. Why not face the east?

"And catch all the rain and snows?" Noah countered.

"What about a porch?" Hester proposed.

And so they bantered, planned, and dreamed, until Noah caught her up in his arms and told her he was marrying one of the bossiest women he knew, and Hester kissed him solidly to hush him up.

Hester felt a new freedom these days. She had been released from the troubling past, a blessing that was like the mighty flow of a waterfall, as unstoppable and as inspiring. With forgiveness came closure, bringing days of bright energy, a new spring to her step, a sense of purpose and fulfillment.

They had settled temporarily into the large stone house with Fannie, who had become fast friends with Barbara. They roamed the hills and fields of the Zug farm, trained the stubborn ponies, played church with the barn cats, and walked to school with Emma. It was as if little, deprived Fannie had never known another life. She bloomed like a wan flower, the sunshine and rain of the whole family's love allowing her to grow in ways no one had thought possible.

She even asked for a slice of cake, another molasses cookie, or a second cup of buttermilk, please. Every day brought a wealth of discovery as she saw the world around her through her friend Barbara's eyes.

Hester and Noah made a quick trip back to Lancaster to attend the wedding of Levi Buehler and Barbara King, a solemn affair that was held at the Buehler farm. The place had been painted, raked, cleaned, and trimmed until it was no longer recognizable. The hounds were now housed in their designated area, the chickens were cooped in their own yard, and there was the beginning of a profitable sheep industry. A flock dotted the green hillsides like balls of cotton.

Hester sat demurely, her head bent, her eyelashes brushing her cheeks, the twinkle in her eye completely controlled as the minister asked Barbara the usual wedding vows in German, and she answered in a less than humble—actually quite strident—"Ya."

After the service and seated at the wedding table, the place of her dreams, Bappie radiated an inner loveliness. Everyone agreed they had never thought of her as attractive, but that purple dress with her red hair gave her quite a shine, didn't it? Bappie and Levi ate their *roasht*, mashed potatoes, and the cooked slaw hungrily, enjoying every morsel of the wedding dinner.

Bappie opened her gifts, becoming quite boisterous when she received a set of green dishes from her Aunt Barbara, a namesake gift that far surpassed anything she had ever owned.

When she finally had a few moments with Hester, she gripped her hands and told her meaningfully that this was, without a doubt, the best day of her life, and did she see Levi's new hat? Whereupon, she opened her mouth and laughed in a most raucous manner. Hester joined in, thankful that Bappie had not changed at all.

While in Lancaster, Noah and Hester visited Walter and Emma Trout and Billy, who had arrived home a few weeks before. They left for Berks County that afternoon, full of hopes and plans for their own wedding.

Annie stood at the door of the stone farmhouse, shading her eyes from the glare of the evening sun, watching the advance of the two matched horses pulling the carriage behind them. The expression in her eyes was unfathomable. The Annie of old had changed in subtle ways, not yet noticed by anyone except the couple who was now approaching. A strange thrill, a sort of renewal, surged through her body.

Here was this couple, her children, brother and sister, and she was their mother. Anticipation beat happily in her breast as she looked forward to the responsibility of making a wedding for them as she had done for Lissie.

Hadn't that been a time of battles lost and won, though? Lissie is so powerful in words with a will of iron, and she is the same. Shameful. Absolutely shameful the way it went. But that was long before the time

Annie had spent with Hester, telling her of the dark past. Embarrassing the way she had told her so much.

Annie shrugged her shoulders, lowered her hand, and went to meet Noah and Hester, an unaccustomed gladness welling in her heart. As she neared the buggy, she hesitated. Would it be the same? Would they have discussed her and decided that none of that scene in the kitchen meant anything?

So she stood, her hands held loosely at her side, her back stiff and unbending. She had put on her usual scowl and wore it firmly, the armor that protected anything soft or insecure within.

But here was Hester now, her arms wide as she walked towards her, a gladness softening the black depths of her large eyes. Annie surrendered to the embrace, then stepped back with a soft, wobbly smile and examined Hester's eyes to make sure this was real and not some false follow-up to make her feel all right. For Annie was now a fledgling, a baby sparrow dependent on the food of love that Hester and Noah would continue to bring her. On her own, the old wounds and the anger that made them bearable would return, leaving her to starve, unable to grow.

Such a long and painful past could not be erased in one day. But with each day of their presence, and unknown to Noah or Hester, Annie received the bits of sustenance she needed. Mostly it was little things. Acts of unselfishness and kindness. Annie had never known kindness to have such an impact on her days.

Hester had brought a wrapped parcel, the brown paper tied securely with string. She handed it to her with a smile, her soft eyes shining.

Annie's hands began to shake, in spite of clenching her teeth, as she went to the cupboard for a scissors. Self-conscious now, she shook more until she dropped the scissors, which clattered loudly to the floor. "Ach," she said, impatient.

"I'll open it if it's all right," Hester said.

When the string was undone and the brown wrapping paper fell away, she saw four yards of beautiful blue fabric for a new Sunday dress.

"Why would you waste your money on an old ugly lady?" Annie croaked, emotion like sandpaper in her throat.

"Oh, Annie, it's the color of my wedding dress! You are the mother of the bride, so you and I will wear the same fabric."

"Ach." Annie held her mouth in a straight line, blinked furiously, and looked at Noah to avoid Hester's eyes. Then not knowing what else to say to hide her wellspring of pleasure, she scolded, "It's unnecessary. Too much money spent."

"Not for the mother of the bride, Annie . . . Mam," Noah said softly.

For Fannie, Barbara, and Emma, there was another large piece of blue fabric, along with yardage of black for their aprons. Peppermint candies were hidden in the folds, which created shrieks of excitement, a wild elation as the three girls scrambled onto the kitchen floor to retrieve them.

Hester watched Fannie, her cheeks pink, her large brown eyes alight with the joy of living, her dress stretched taut across her shoulders, which could not have been called thin any longer. Even her brown hair seemed to have thickened and taken on a luster. Her teeth had whitened from being vigorously brushed with bicarbonate of soda. With Barbara and Emma on either side, they resembled a trio of sisters, eager to live life with the carefree abandon of children.

Only occasionally at night, Fannie would waken, crying softly to herself until Hester pulled her close. She'd smooth back the tendrils of hair moistened by her tears and let her cry for whatever reason. After Fannie felt Hester's arms about her, she would become calm, a deep cleansing sigh would finish the tears, and she'd fall into a deep sleep.

Who could tell the loneliness of this little person? In a sense, she had been an orphan in a family of thirteen children, her parents mere shadows that passed over her.

And so wedding planning began in earnest.

Annie was a superb manager, saying, "First things first." The sewing would have to be taken care of immediately. They asked Magdalena to make the white shirts, as she was an accomplished shirt-maker. In the days following, they cut and sewed aprons, capes, dresses, and coverings in quick succession.

The date of the wedding was set for the thirteenth of November, too late, in Annie's opinion, but who had ever heard of getting ready for a wedding in less than a month? They even had to buy the chickens from Enos Yoders. She had never heard of not raising your own for a wedding. But there was a smile lurking in her eyes, Hester could tell.

The acreage that Hans had given them was an undeserved gift, a glorious remembrance from an imperfect,
tortured man, who had lived out a terrible penance,
suffering because of his sins, but redeemed by the grace
of Christ. He had given the land out of his love and as
restitution.

The land included acres of beautiful forest, lush and
green in the summer, with brilliant foliage in the fall.
Now, with winter's beginning, the cold winds whipped
the trees, leaving them etched against the sky and surrounded by a carpet of curling, brown leaves. Although
the grasses were yellow and brown, they still held the
promise of a new life ahead.

Noah staked the house facing southeast, the way
Hester wanted. The barn was to the left and set against a
hill, which allowed access to the top floor. Wagons could
also be pulled onto the barn floor by a team of horses to
ease the unloading of hay and corn fodder.

They would leave a few oak trees to provide shade in
summer. The pastures would fall away below the barn
where the incline was gentle. The cow stable would be
on the underside of the barn. The stones that would be
laid would provide sturdy walls to keep the animals
warm in winter and cool in summer.

They would rent the small house on the Henry Ebersole place for the first year, while Noah built the house
and barn. With neighborhood frolics and the help of
their brothers, they should be able to move within the
year.

Hester did not want a house made of stone. Noah
planned on a stone house, but Hester had wonderful

memories of the little log house with Kate, her mam, the babies, the fire on the hearth, and she wanted only that for the rest of her life.

"A small house, Noah, for we will have only Fannie," she said, a hint of sadness passing over her eyes.

Noah had seen this and quickly gathered her in his arms, kissed the top of her head, and assured her that Fannie was all they would ever need. He was getting far more than he deserved by having the chance to be her husband, to care for her all the days of his life. If he never had children of his own, that was as the Lord wanted. Hester was a gift, and enough.

She had remained in his strong arms, tears wetting the front of his shirt. How could she ever live up to this kind man's expectations? She told him this, felt his chest rumble with laughter, and smiled through her tears when he told her she'd have plenty of opportunities to throw her shoes at him.

As the days of preparation went by, their love grew more steadfast, more deeply rooted in the admiration they had for each other. Hester never failed to notice Noah's many acts of selflessness, how he gave of himself, not just to her, but to everyone he met. Especially to Annie. He seemed to understand the wounds she hid away from them, her eagerness to maintain a stance of strength, when in reality it was only a mask, and an ill-fitting one at that. Often as the days went by, the mask slipped, giving them a glimpse of the Annie that was to come.

The barn cats had always been a source of irritation to her. Woe to the cat that attempted to rub itself against her wicker laundry basket. Always, the cat was booted out of her way, sent into the air with a swift kick, and a firm "*Katz*!" If Annie had her way—except for the necessary extermination of rats and mice—no cat would have been on the farm.

So now, when Hester rounded a corner of the house and found Annie at the washline, bent over tickling a startled cat's chin before trailing a gnarled, shaking hand the length of its silky back, she stopped and reversed her steps soundlessly. She knew that if Annie was exposed, she'd resume her old ways and kick the unsuspecting cat for the benefit of her pride.

There was also the Fannie surprise. Fannie had developed a firm hold on Annie's affections. To see them together was a heartwarming vision. Fannie still hummed or sang softly, the way she always had, but now, Annie would join while they did dishes together. Annie's rough, patchy baritone pitched in to join Fannie's high angelic notes. Annie always stopped when Hester walked into the room. But it was all right. It was good to know that Annie cared for Fannie, took her under her wing, and kept her there.

The matter of her shaking hands came to a head, like a sore and throbbing boil, one morning when the tea kettle fell out of her grip, splashing boiling water on the floor, across her skirt, and all over the stove, sending water sizzling onto the hot stones of the hearth. With all the gathers in her skirt and the added protection of a heavy apron, Annie was not scalded, only frightened into a lip-trembling silence.

Hester had been folding wash, and with a shriek of fear came to her side, her eyes wide. "Annie! Are you all right?"

Grimly, with her wet skirts held out and bent at the waist, Annie nodded.

"You must do something, Annie. You will hurt yourself even worse as time goes on," Hester pleaded. She handed her a towel, which Annie used vigorously, rubbing the wet spots on the front of her apron. She turned away to lift the long heavy skirt and check for burns, but said it was only enough to redden the skin.

"What? What should I do?" Annie asked desperately. "The doctors all say the same thing. They call it palsy of the hands, and there is nothing to do for it."

Quietly Hester whispered, "There is something,"

What passed between them could only be called painful, a humiliation that could be felt, a nearly physical force.

Who could forget the agony of the past? Forgiveness was one thing—over and done with. But to forget completely was another. In a flash, they each relived the roaring sound of Annie's hatred as she refused Hester's remedy for palsy, forbade her from making any more tinctures, and nearly succeeded in burning the book of remedies above open flames, the precious book containing all the knowledge of her ancestors. Had Hester not torn it from her hands, Annie would have destroyed the priceless gift Hester had been entrusted with. The whole scene sat between them, thick and cloying, threatening to choke the life out of the flower of their forgiveness.

Annie lowered her eyes and turned her head away.

Hester felt the sting of remembering.

Silence hung between them, dense with unspoken words that were too loaded with danger to be uttered. Hester almost turned away and left the room, leaving

Annie to the demons of her past. That one incident had been the most cruel, and now to open that old sore and review it again in the light of day was almost more than Hester could do. She was afraid to try, but she was just as frightened to forsake Annie now.

Hester went to Annie and got down on her knees by her side as she sat slumped in a kitchen chair. She reached out, took her hands, and held them softly. She could feel the tremors.

Annie did not pull away.

"Let me try," she said simply.

Annie kept her face averted. Her throat worked as she swallowed. Hester kept her peace, watching Annie's face. When the glimmer of a tear appeared on her lower lash and hung there, trembling, before slipping down her papery cheek, Hester still did not speak.

Finally, Annie said, "Don't make me remember this."

"We won't. We will not remember together."

"What will you do?

"First of all, since it is November, I suppose we'll have to pay Theodore and Lissie Crane a visit. Does she still have her store of herbal plants?"

Annie nodded.

"Then come with me."

"Now?"

"Now. The work will wait."

"I'm too ashamed. Lissie Crane knows what I tried to do."

"Lissie will be too happy to see us. I have not had the reunion with them that I wanted. I could only barely acknowledge them at the funeral. They are so old."

Annie turned. Unexpectedly, a smile lit up her face. "Not old, if you listen to Lissie."

Hester laughed outright, imagining the hefty Lissie moving about her house like a ship in full sail. "Does she still glide like that? Sort of float along on her tiny feet?"

"Oh, yes. She gets around."

"Then let's go see her."

They bundled into their heavy black shawls and bonnets, hitched up the trusty brown driving horse, and rode through the blustery November winds. The road wound in and out of the forest, past Sam Ebersole's and Crist Fisher's, the scenery so familiar, so dear, so recognized, Hester mused.

This was home. These rolling hills and cleared acres. These skies that were blue, scudding with gray and white clouds, like layers of freshly shorn sheep's wool. The air was pure and unhurried, the farms familiar, the new dwellings signs of prosperity. The very air carried an aura of acceptance, the hills and trees receiving her, protecting her, bringing a sensation she knew meant belonging. This was where she was meant to be.

She was home. Home in Berks County, close to the grave where Kate lay, and soon to be married to her son, the incarnation of Kate herself. Hester had been raised in kindness, with the gentleness and good grace of Kate's heart, cared for by her soft hands.

Theodore opened the door, his long, thin face wreathed with delight. Lissie lumbered across the floor behind him, her hands extended. Hester laughed, then cried a little, finally sitting at their small table with Annie beside her. She marveled at the vast person Lissie had become. Marriage must have given her a good appetite, as she was quite a bit larger than Hester remembered. Theodore wasn't thin either. A good portion of his stomach overlapped his broadfall trousers.

Hester and Annie could not get a word in at all. Lissie's face became an alarming shade of red as she talked, moving from stove to table, bringing hot cups of tea "to warm them," she said, along with a whole pumpkin pie, plates, forks, tumblers of ice-cold water, soft cup cheese, and slices of bread.

"*Schmear Kase! Frisha schmear Kase*," she yelled in a stentorian voice, punctuated by Theodore's vigorous nodding and repeating, "*Frish, frish*."

Annie's hands shook so badly that her teacup clattered against the saucer, almost upsetting it. Quickly, both hands went to her lap.

"So, a wedding, I hear. A *hochzeit! Ach, du lieber*. You and Noah? Who would have thought it, years ago? You and Noah and Isaac all running around, with Lissie trailing on behind like an unwanted pup."

Hester nodded, smiling, and helped herself to a slice of bread and fresh cup cheese, that soft, pungent, spreadable cheese made from squeaky milk curds.

Theodore told them of his life with Lissie, the years going by so fast. He worked at tutoring the hard learners while Lissie kept the house clean and warm and put food on the table. He reported experiencing contentment and happiness he had never thought possible. His story was heartwarming, but out of respect for Annie and her disappointments, Hester switched subjects as soon as possible, asking if Lissie had sage and mustard seed on hand, which led to Lissie lumbering off to her storeroom and returning with two tin canisters.

"Now you have to be careful with the sage. You don't want too much. It can give you a bilious stomach. Lots of gas and cramping."

"No, I won't need it to be taken as a medicine."

"Oh?" Lissie lifted her eyebrows, a pained expression along with them; her curiosity made her miserable. Hester gave nothing away. She knew keenly Annie's pride and her reluctance to admit her one weakness, no matter how laughably obvious it was.

She paid Lissie for both herbs, and they were on their way home as soon as they could untangle themselves from the web of Lissie's talk. It never stopped, following them out onto the porch, down the walkway, and into the buggy. She was still calling out words they couldn't hear after the horse pulled the buggy away from the hitching rack.

Hester shook her head, laughing. Annie smiled and said, "That would be awful to have all those unnecessary words tumbling about in your head."

But they both loved Lissie, so they said nothing further about her.

At home, Hester boiled the sage and mustard seed into a decoction, the smell of it permeating the entire house. Annie busied herself with the sewing, keeping her eyes averted and saying nothing. When the mixture had cooled sufficiently, Hester asked Annie to place her hands in the liquid while it was as hot as she could possibly stand it.

She said the words quietly, forming a question more than a command, knowing how very hard this was for Annie.

She said nothing. She just sat at the table with the shallow basin of hot water and placed both hands into it, her face expressionless. The steam from the decoction alarmed Hester, who watched for any sign of discomfort, but there was none, not even a mere knitting of her brows or a flinch.

They repeated this quite often during the day, always being careful to avoid being seen by Noah or the children, for on that first day, Annie's furtive glances gave away her wish for privacy. But over the next few days, after mentioning what they were doing to the rest of the family, Annie felt comfortable enough to remain seated, no matter who walked into the house.

The children wrinkled their noses at the smell but said nothing much about it. Noah knew how much the effort meant to Hester and praised her deftness, saying that if she could accomplish a healing for Annie, imagine where this might lead! Perhaps that was why she had never borne children, that God had other plans for her with this gift of healing.

Annie was discouraged on the third day when she dropped half the pumpkin pie, and the custard slopped down the side of the table. Hester thought she might not be willing to continue further treatment, but Annie said she'd keep going till after the wedding.

As time went on, Hester developed a deeper respect for Annie's tenacity and her ability to keep trying in the face of doubt.

She also knew what this cost Annie—her pride, her painful memory, her admission of wrongdoing. It was a huge order for someone who had been as injured as she had been.

Meanwhile, the wedding preparation work continued—the cleaning and whitewashing, the raking and window-washing. Even the barn windows were rubbed to a gleaming luster, the furniture waxed and polished.

The baking took days—the loaves of bread, trays of cookies, cakes made with walnuts and molasses, ginger cakes, and white cakes decorated with icing and dried cranberries.

Through all the days of preparation, a sense of happiness stayed with Hester. She wore her sense of belonging like a rose-colored dress, confident in the way she went about her tasks, addressing every person with love.

CHAPTER 25

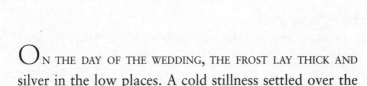

O N THE DAY OF THE WEDDING, THE FROST LAY THICK AND silver in the low places. A cold stillness settled over the surrounding landscape, the promise of an early snow in the air.

The sun melted away the frost on higher ground as the black buggies with brown horses hitched to them made their way to the Hans Zug farm. Excitement was in the air, everyone bathed and scrubbed and wearing their Sunday best, even if it was not the usual big event.

This wedding was not a full-sized, 200-guest wedding, customary for youthful couples. This was a widow marrying an older man, so there was no bridal party, no one to sit beside Noah and Hester.

Hester did not wear the customary white cape and apron, but black ones, signifying the fact that she had been married before. The blue dress she wore was a beautiful, tightly woven fabric, costing far above anything she had thought reasonable, but Noah insisted. It reminded him of the blue she wore when he met her and Bappie in the garden that day.

She had been a dream for him, belonging to his imagination and memory. But when she stood there, he knew his memory of her paled in comparison to the deep, black depth of her eyes, the deep, brown, toffee color of her skin, the blue sky matching the deeper blue of her dress.

If he lived to be a hundred, he would never be worthy of her, he said. Her beauty radiated from within. She was as sweet and unspoiled inside as she was beautiful on the outside.

Hester sat quietly and believed him, for that was how she felt about him. She would never tire of watching him move—the powerful swing of his shoulders, the height and breadth of him. Never had she imagined that the plane of someone's nose could thrill her. The way he talked, always with a half-smile of kindness and a chuckle at the end of so many of his words, belying a nature that was good.

Yes, they believed in love. In a love that could endure arguments and irritations, that was greater than trials and troubles. They had both come through so much and been blessed richly. Their forgiveness of each other was made sweeter as time went on. Now on this day, the love that was hampered in the past was given freedom to flow, a tumbling, rolling brook of purest water.

Annie had proved to be a capable manager, with everything listed and checked off as the days went by. On the *risht dawg*, the day of preparation, relatives and friends arrived early and plunged into the work, making the day festive with jokes and teasing, which was the custom.

It was Noah's job to behead the twenty plump chickens, safely housed in the coop. The fact that they had been bought was a well-kept secret. Enos Yoder pocketed the cash, his eyes twinkling, saying his lips were sealed.

First, the brothers hid Noah's hatchet. Six o'clock on the morning before his wedding, and Noah thought he had misplaced the carefully sharpened hatchet. He looked everywhere while the water bubbled away in the *eisa-kessle* and the *roasht-leid* arrived, and still he could not find the hatchet.

Hester had never seen her beloved Noah quite so rattled. She began to wonder if it was a bad omen, when she saw Solomon streak across the yard with Noah in pursuit, his powerful legs pumping. When he caught Solomon by the tail of his coat, he flung him to the ground and straddled him as Solomon screeched, "Uncle! Uncle!" The women clapped and cheered as Noah raised his fist, ready to pummel his brother, till in the knick of time, he yelled, "*Da cha shunk!*"

Noah released Solomon, ran off to the cupboard in the forebay of the barn, retrieved the hidden hatchet, and began to chop off the twenty chickens' heads, amid friendly ribbing from the *roasht-leid*.

That done, it was Noah and Hester's job to remove the clumps of celery, banked in long lines of raked-up soil, and bring them to the *kesslehaus* to be washed and sorted.

Alone in the garden, the cold, still air around them alive with the magic of the *risht dawg*, they worked in the freezing air, stealing kisses and laughing, the wedding day a beacon of joy over every task.

And so they were married in the great stone house Hans had built for Kate. Every piece of furniture had been stored in the shed to make way for hard, wooden benches, creating a wedding chapel, plain and austere, but warm with the love between them.

The service opened with the rousing German wedding song and closed with another song, also a traditional wedding hymn.

They stood side by side, Noah taller, his blond hair gleaming, cut and combed in the *Ordnung* of the Amish church. Much care and concern had been given by the church to this special day of being given in marriage.

Dressed in a snow-white shirt, black trousers, vest and *mutza*, he was indeed an *schöena bräutigam*, a young man who had waited longer than most to take a wife.

Beside him, Hester's beauty had never been more pronounced. Her face radiated true goodness from within, framed by the perfect line of her eyebrows, the perfect symmetry of dark lashes sweeping her golden cheeks.

They spoke their vows solemnly, as befitted the sobriety of the occasion. They never lifted their eyes or smiled until the last song had been sung. As the guests filed out, only then did they dare meet each other's eyes, speaking volumes to each other in their new freedom to love.

They said Annie smiled and laughed that day more than anyone could remember. And who was that young girl who sat with the bride and groom at their table?

Oh, that is Fannie Stoltzfus, others said.

Selly glay Fannie. Ach, ya. The women nodded, shaking their heads. That was the way of it, then. Her parents' house was full with too many mouths to feed, *arme leit,* yes, yes. She'll have a good home with *Hansa ihr Noahs.* But isn't it something how these two got together? Raised in the same house.

And so the day brought them many blessings, well-wishers, folks who wanted them to have a long and happy married life. And wasn't it so nice they had an *au-gnomma kind. Selly glay Fannie, gel*?

They praised the cakes, made a fuss about the cookies, said that Annie was something, now wasn't she? They shed tears thinking of Hans, barely cold in his grave, and here his son went getting married without him.

Only Lissie, Theodore's wife, had the nerve to say what many of them were thinking.

"It's a good thing," she said, her words clipped with disdain. Then she stretched her neck, her large head swiveling, and asked why it took the *freundshaft so hesslich* long to eat. She was hungry for *roasht.*

"Don't they know there are people here who didn't eat yet? Likely that ginger cake with brown sugar frosting will be gone till I get there."

She sat up straighter, her beady eyes peering worriedly from rolls of flesh. "Look at that Annie. She seems like another person. Laughs all day."

"Not all day," Elam Fisher *sei* Rachel said sourly.

Lissie turned to look at her. "You're hungry, too."

At dusk, the last buggy wound its way down the curving driveway. This had been a small wedding, so no eve-

ning meal was served, and there was no singing far into
the night.

Annie, of course, was in the kitchen washing dishes.
Solomon sat on a bench enjoying one last cup of coffee
while Magdalena finished a slice of walnut cake.

The children were playing tag, dashing between the
benches, fueled on an endless supply of cake and cookies.
Daniel broke into song, his voice strong as he climbed
the notes.

They cleared benches from the kitchen, then brought
in the table and the cupboard. Annie said it was quite
enough, they would be back the following day to clean
up. She sat with them then, poured herself a cup of coffee, and talked about their day. Noah and Hester joined
them, both radiant.

"We want to thank everyone for what you did, helping us prepare for our special day. We really appreciate
it," Noah said.

Solomon waved a hand in dismissal. "It was nothing."

They had decided to spend the night together in the
small rental house, and because it was a still, frosty evening, they walked.

Fannie stayed with Barbara and Emma, although
Hester had warned them that sometimes she cried at
night. They took this very seriously and promised to be
very careful with her.

The night was dark with no moon. Only an occasional star
shone from the black night sky. The silhouettes of the stark,
leafless trees were even blacker, the road barely discernible.

Close by, an owl hooted its ghostly sound. The screech of a nighthawk followed, then another more drawn out one.

There was no need for words.

Both of them walked in perfect comfort, grateful for the holy moment. God had led them together, and now he was here to guide them, to give them strength, and to see them home by his grace.

Noah took her hand in his. "My wife, my love," he said.

"My husband, my love," she answered, releasing his hand to step into the circle of his arms.

Freed from the pain and confusion of her past, shedding it along with Noah's rebellion toward his now deceased father and the bitter Annie of his youth, their love was like a tropical flower, opening to the wonders of soft warm rains and brilliant sunshine.

After all they'd been through, neither one of them took their union for granted. As they continued their walk through the still night air, they talked of the times when they were apart, the times they suffered, missing their old home here in Berks County.

Hester told Noah that she had come home now. "This is my home, Noah. This place on earth is mine to call home. You are my home, my dearest husband. I love you for all time, here in these hills of my childhood."

The kiss they shared as husband and wife was sacred.

Annie's hands healed to a degree, enough that she was able to perform duties she had no longer been able to accomplish. She continued the treatment all winter, often thanking Hester quietly, with a touch of shame.

Noah and Hester brought Fannie to live with them in the cozy little rental house. She walked to school with Barbara and Emma every day, the same route Hester, Lissie, Noah, and Isaac had walked a generation before.

Fannie swung her little tin lunch pail as she ran to meet them in the morning, dressed warmly in her black coat, shawl, and bonnet, sturdy boots on her feet.

Hester spent her days arranging her furniture in the small, cozy house, the fire burning cheerily on the hearth. She thought often of her wedding day, of Bappie's tears, her raucous congratulations, and more tears at her parting.

She fixed a small bed upstairs under the eaves for Fannie, making sure there were plenty of quilts and sheep's-wool comforters so she would never be cold. She cooked good, nutritious meals and packed her tin lunch pail with honey sandwiches, dried apples, cookies, and canned pears.

The snow came early that winter, hard, biting bits of ice that pinged against the windowpanes and piled around the south side of the house like sugar. Hester threw logs on the fire, cooked a bubbling beef stew, and felt fulfilled.

Only sometimes she'd sit on their bed, the soft ticking crackling beneath her, silently stroking the white quilt Annie had given them, gazing out the window, her eyes seeing nothing. She would wonder, if only for a minute, how it would feel to be able to tell Noah they would soon have a child of their own.

Then she would turn away, scolding herself. It was not to be. Hadn't she been grateful, God giving her far more than she deserved? Here she was with all this happiness, longing for a child. Then she would refuse to dwell on this one small spot in her heart that yearned for a little boy who looked just like his father. Fannie's presence helped immensely—her humming, the way she never wearied of schoolwork or of Barbara and Emma.

The farm became a reality. The barn was every bit as magnificent as Dan Stoltzfus's in Lancaster County. The house made of logs with a steeply pitched roof was a true Dutch dwelling with a spacious kitchen and clever little nooks hidden away, to store extra linens, bedding, and towels.

A year passed. A year of happiness with Noah a constant source of joy, his love never once disappointing her. He had a love for her that he nurtured every day, always concerned for her welfare and Fannie's.

Which came first, then? The nausea or Annie's marriage to the widower Elias Lapp? She could never quite remember.

All she knew was that she woke one morning and thought surely someone had cooked onions during the night. The house smelled awful, just awful. She fussed and fumed, opened widows, and still that evening something smelled in this house, she said.

When she staggered outside very early in the morning, gagging and making horrible noises, Noah became alarmed and rushed to her side. He was elbowed quite sharply in the ribs and told to get away from her. This continued all week, till Noah stood stock-still in the barn, his eyes lighting up with a jolt of sudden knowledge.

Could it be? He remembered Kate. Tears sprang to his blue eyes as chills raced up his spine.

He couldn't tell her. It would be too great a disappointment if it were not so. A month went by before it dawned on Hester as she lay alone in their bedroom one rainy day, crying for no reason other than being so tired of this choking nausea. She called it a spring sickness at first. Or spring fever. Some vague ailment.

Could it be? Oh, she couldn't tell Noah because the disappointment would be too great to bear. She wouldn't say anything.

And so as she cooked, she almost always ran to the privy, the nausea in her throat, while Noah sat in the house wondering what to do.

They both became quite irritable with each other. She told him he needed to change his socks more often, and he said he was getting tired of potato soup.

One morning, Noah had had enough. He took Hester in his arms and whispered something in her ear.

"What?" she asked.

"Kate, our mam, used to be sick before another child came. Do you think it could be possible?"

She leaned back in his arms, her eyes wide and dark and fearful.

"Oh, Noah. She did, didn't she? Oh, Noah."

Then she cried, because tears came so readily these days.

Their baby girl arrived one still, frosty night in December, a dark-skinned little girl with a thatch of blond hair and the bluest eyes Hester had ever seen. Noah cried great sloppy tears, his emotion unchecked as he looked down at this perfect child of his and Hester's. A miracle.

Lissie Crane handed him a less than clean handkerchief and shooed him out of the room. She gave the baby to Hester, and Noah went.

They named her Annie.

Annie and Elias came to see her, pronouncing her the most beautiful child they had ever seen.

"You didn't have to name her after me," Annie said gruffly, so visibly pleased her eyes danced.

And then, like Kate, Hester bore many more children. She learned to laugh at the nausea, her soul fulfilled with the arrival of each one. Little Hans, all black hair and eyes. Albert, with only a sliver of dark hair, and blue eyes. Kate, the tiniest blond-haired one with black eyes.

Hester gained a bit of weight with each one. She rocked them all in the armless rocking chair, loving Noah, Fannie, and each of their children all the days of their lives.

The sun rose and set over Berks County in the late 1700s, the seasons came and went, the old passed away in due time, and the babies grew to become the children of the next generation.

The clock on the wall ticked away the hours, the house was filled with the happy cries of Noah and Hester's children, and God in his heaven looked down on what he had created and, someday, would return unto himself.

The End

GLOSSARY

A Hochzeit! Ach, du lieber! — A wedding! Oh, my goodness!

Ach, du lieva. — Oh my goodness.

Ach du lieva. Grund a velt! — An old, High German exclamation of amazement. Translated literally, it means, "Oh, you love. Ground of the world!"

Ach, du yay. — Oh, dear.

Ach, mein Gott im Himmel! — Oh, my God in heaven!

Ach, mein Herr Jesus, Du Komm. — Oh, my dear Jesus, please come.

Alta essel — old mule

An begaubta mensch — a talented person

An gute hoffning — a good hope for one's departed soul

An lot gelt — a lot of money

An schöena bräutigam — a good-looking bridegroom

An shay kind — a nice or beautiful child

Arme leit — poor people

Auferstehung — resurrection

Au-gnomma — adopted

Au-gnomma Kind — an adopted child

Au-gvocksa—tight, sore, aching muscles, which relax when massaged

Ausbund—The hymnbook that the Amish sing from during church services. The old German book was written by their foreparents during a time of persecution and imprisonment.

Aylend—trial

Behauft mit hexerei—mixed with witchcraft, or containing witchcraft

Behoft—has, or has to do with, or possessed

Boova Shenkel—beef-and-potato-filled pastries

Bund der lieva—bond of love

Bupplich—babyish

Bupply—baby

Da cha shunk—the dish cupboard

Da Levi sei Bappie—Levi's wife Babbie

Dat—name used to address one's father

Deifel—Devil

Dein villa geshay, auf Erden vie im Himmel.—Your will be done, on earth as in heaven.

Denke, Gute Mann.—Thank you, good Lord.

Denke, mein Herr.—Thank you, my Lord.

Denke schöen.—Thank you very much.

Der Herr—God

Der Herren saya—God's blessing

Der saya—a blessing

Die Englische leid—anyone whose first language is English

Die freundschaft—the extended family

Die gichtra—seizures

Die vitfrau—the widow

Diese hoyschrecken—the grasshoppers

Doddy—grandpa

Doddy haus—an addition to the main house, built as living quarters for the grandparents

Doo bisht, Hester King?—Are you Hester King?

Du, yay.—Oh, dear.

Dumb gamach—chaos, or chaotic

Dumbkopf—dumbhead

Dummes—dumb thing

Egg Kuchen—egg cake

Ein English haus—a house belonging to someone whose first language is English and who is, therefore, not Amish

Ein maedle ein shoe maedle. Oh, du yay, du yay.—A girl, a beautiful girl. Oh, my, my.

Eisa-kessle—cast-iron kettle

Elam Fisher sei Rachel—Elam Fisher's wife Rachel

Englische leit—people who aren't Amish or Native American

Englische schule—a school run by people who aren't Amish or Native American

Englischer—someone who isn't Amish or Native American

Eppa do?—Is someone here?

Ess vort dunkle.—It gets dark.

Eye du lieva, mon.—An old German expression, which translated literally, means "Oh, my love, man."

Fasark—to care for, look after

Fa-sarked—to take care of

Fa-sarking—caring for

Faschpritz—burst

Faschtant—sense

Faschtendich—common sense, or sensible

Fishly—the best cut of deer meat fried in lard

Fa-shput—mocked

Fore—leading the song in church

Frau—wife

Freme—visitors

Freundshaft—extended family

Gaduld—patience

Gahr hoftich—very much

Gamach—chaos

Geb acht.—Take care.

Geeda—members

Gel?—Right?

Gelbkuchen—yellow cake

Gewisslich—for sure

Gile chplauwa—blacksmithing

Glay Indian maedly—little Indian girl

Gook do runna, Mein Herr und Vater.—Look down here, my Lord and Father.

Goot—good

Goot. Goot.—Good. Good.

Goot opp—better off

Goot. Sell iss goot.—Good. That is good.

Goota mya!—Good morning!

Gott im Himmel—God in heaven

Gott sie gelobt und gedankt.—God be praised and thanked.

Grishtag—Christmas

Grishtag Essa—Christmas dinner

Grosfeelich, or Grosfeelicha—proud, cocky, or vain

Gute Nacht. Denke, denke.—Good night. Thank you, thank you.

Guten Morgen.—Good morning.

Gwundernose—curious nose; nosey

Gyan schöena.—You're welcome.

Hans sei Kate—Hans's wife, Kate

Hansa ihr Noahs—Hans's Noah and family

Harrich mol sell.—Listen to that.

Häse—hot

Haus schtier—wedding gift

Heiland—Christ, or Savior

Heilandes blut—the Savior's blood

Heilig Schrift—the Holy Bible

Hembare! Oh, meine Hembare!—Raspberries! Oh, my raspberries!

Henn ma psuch, Mam?—Do we have company, Mom?

Herr Jesu—Lord Jesus

Herr, saya—God bless you

Hesslich—very much (as in extremely dark or cold, etc.)

Hexarei—hexes, curses

Hexary—witchcraft

Hinkle dunkus—gravy

Hinna losseny—the ones remaining after a death

Hochmut—pride

Hootsla—a bread and egg dish

Hulla chelly—elderberry jelly

Ich bin Klein, / Mine heartz macht rein, / Lest niemand drinn vonnen / Aus Jesus alein.—I am small, / My heart is pure, / Let no one live in here / But Jesus alone.

Ich bin so frowah.—I am so glad.

Ich hab es shay Kott.—I had it nice.

Ich segne dihr.—I bless you.

Ich vill au halta fa fagebniss.—I want to beg for forgiveness.

Ich vinch da saya.—I wish a blessing for you.

In Gotteszeit—in God's time

Ins ana end—a small addition built onto a homestead to house the older generation

Josiah sei Esther—Josiah's wife Esther

Katufla—potatoes

Keschta—chestnuts

Kindish—childish

Kinder—children

Knabrus—buttered cabbage and onions

Knecht—a young hired man

Komm—come

Komm mol—come now

Kommet rye—come right in

Krum Kuchen—crumb cake

Leberklosschen—dumplings filled with chopped liver and onions

Lebkuchen—a loaf cake

Leid—verses

Liebchenmaedle—lovely girl

Lied—song

Lunga feeva—lung fever

Mam—name used to address or refer to one's mother

Maud—a young Amish hired woman

Mein Gott! Das Kind schprechen!—My God! The child talks!

Mein Gott, ich bitt / Ich bitt durch Chrischte blut, / Mach's nur mit meinem / Ende Gute.—My God, I ask / I ask through Christ's blood, / Provide for my end of life / To be good.

Mein Gott, ich bitte dich, hilf mir—My God, I ask you to please help me.

Mein Gott im Himmel.—My God in heaven.

Mein Gott, vergebe mich meine Sinde.—My God, forgive my sins.

Mein Himmlischer Vater, Ich bitte dich hilf mir.—My heavenly Father, I ask you to please help me.

Mein Kind—my child

Meine Liebchen—my dear one

Meine liebe Kinder—my dear children

Mit-dienner—fellow ministers

Mit-tag—lunch

Mol net die Annie—certainly not Annie

Mutza—coat, or Sunday suit coat

My grund! Die fees. See Fa-freer.—"My grund" is an old High German exclamation of amazement. "Die fees" means "the feet." "See fa-freer" means "they freeze."

My gute frau—my good wife

Na, do, veya iss deya fremma?—Now, here, who is this stranger?

Nay—no

Net heila.—Don't cry.

Ob'l Dunkes Kucha—apple gravy cake

Oh, Gott Vater, in Himmelreich, / Un deine gute preisen—Oh, God our Father in heaven, / We praise your goodness.

Oh, mein Gott. Bitte dich, bitte dich.—Oh, my God, please, I ask you, please.

Opp shtellt—forbidden

Ordnung—The Amish community's agreed-upon rules for living, based on their understanding of the Bible, particularly the New Testament. The Ordnung varies from community to community, often reflecting leaders' preferences, local customs, and traditional practices.

Panna kuchen—pancakes

Paradeis—Paradise

Pon haus, or Ponhaus—Scrapple, a dish made with ground pork, broth, and cornmeal. After it congeals in a loaf pan, it is sliced and then fried.

Priest Gott.—Praise God.

Risht Dawg—day of preparation at the bride's home, just before the wedding

Rivels—small dumplings made of eggs and flour

Roasht—the traditional main dish served after an Amish wedding, made of cooked and cubed chicken and stuffing

Roasht-leid—the people making the roasht, the main wedding dish made of bread filling and cooked, cut-up chicken

Rote birdy—red bird

Rumschpringa—a young man who is overdue for a wife

Rumspringa—A Pennsylvania Dutch dialect word meaning "running around." It refers to the time in a person's life between age sixteen and marriage. It involves structured social activities in groups, as well as dating, and usually takes place on the weekends.

S, gukt vie blenty.—It looks like plenty.

Sage mihr.—Tell me.

Schicket euch ihr lieben gäschte. / Zu des lames hochzeit fest. / Schmücket euch aufs allerbeste.—Behave yourselves, you loved guests. / To the Lamb's wedding feast. / Dress yourselves in your very best.

"Schlofe, Buppli, Schlofe."—a lullaby; "Sleep, baby, sleep."

Schmear Kase! Frisha Schmear Kase!—Cup cheese! Fresh cup cheese!

Schmutz—fat or grease from meat

Schnitz und knepp—a main dish of dried apples, ham, and dumplings

Schnitza—a lie, a falsehood

Schnitzel Eier Kuchen—cut-up egg cake

Schnuck—cute

Schnucka galena—cute little

Schöena yunga—a good-looking young man

Schöna—beautiful

Schpeck—fat from meat

Schpeck und bona—ham and green beans

Schpence—ghost

Schpindlich—thin

Schput—mock

Schrecklich mit—frightening with

Schrift—Scripture

Schtettle—town

Schtick—snack, or piece

Schtill!—Be quiet!

Schtinkiche menna—smelly men

Schtoltz—proud

Schtrubblich maedle—girl with the messy hair

Schtrubles—loose hair

Schtump—dull

Schtup—room, or living room

Seck veggley—sack (or bag) wagon

See iss an chide kind.—She's a sensible child.

Seeye, der brautigam kommet; / Geht ihm entgegen—
the lyrics of a wedding song; "Watch, the bridegroom
comes; / Go now to meet him."

Sell cutsich haus—that house full of vomit

Sell Indian maedle—that Indian girl

Sell is goot dunkas.—That is good gravy.

Sell suit mich.—That suits me.

Sell vowa so goot.—That was so good.

Selly glay Fannie—that little Fannie

Semmels—I have no idea. I'm sorry.

Shaute soch—a pitiful thing

Siss unfaschtendich!—This is unbelievable! or It makes
no sense!

Siss yusht.—It's just.

Smear käse—spreadable cheese

So gates. So iss es.—So it goes. So it is.

Socha—things

Sodda schnuck—sort of cute

Souse—congealed cooked and seasoned meat from pigs'
feet and heads

Tzorn—anger

Unbekannta—the unknown person

Unfaschtendich—unbelievable

Unglauvich—unbelieving

Unschuldicha mensch—innocent person

Unser Herr—Our Lord, referring to God

Unser Herren Jesu—Our Lord Jesus

Unser Jesu—Our Lord Jesus

Unser Vater—Our Father, referring to God

Unwort—untruth or lie

Veck mit selly.—Away with those.

Vell don.—Well then.

Vesh pettsa sock—clothespin bag

Vie bisht, meine liebchen?—How are you, my young friend?

Vonn anbegin—from the beginning

Voss gebt?—What's going on?

Voss geht au?—"What's going on?"

Voss hat gevva?—"What gives?"

Voss hot Gott getan? Meine arme liebchen!—What has God done? My poor children!

Voss in die velt?—"What in the world?"

Voss iss lets mitt sie?—What's wrong with you?

Voss sagsht?—What do you say?

Vossa—water

Wahrheit—the truth

Weibsleitich—having to do with women

Wunderbahr!—Wonderful!

Wunderbar goot—wonderful good

Ya—yes

Ya, dess gebt hochzich.—Yes, there will be a wedding.

Ya, ich bin Amos Stoltzfus.—Yes, I am Amos Stoltzfus.

Yung kyat psucha—newlywed visiting

Yung kyaty—newlyweds

Zeitlang—homesick

Ztvie dracht—tensions, or divisions

ABOUT THE AUTHOR

LINDA BYLER WAS RAISED IN AN AMISH FAMILY AND IS AN active member of the Amish church today. Growing up, Linda loved to read and write. In fact, she still does. Linda is well-known within the Amish community as a columnist for a weekly Amish newspaper.

Linda is the author of several series of novels, all set among the Amish communities of North America: Lizzie Searches for Love, Lancaster Burning, Sadie's Montana, Hester's Hunt for Home, and The Dakota Series.

Linda has also written five Christmas romances set among the Amish: *The Little Amish Matchmaker*, *The Christmas Visitor*, *Mary's Christmas Goodbye*, *Becky Meets Her Match*, and *A Dog for Christmas*. Linda has co-authored *Lizzie's Amish Cookbook: Favorite recipes from three generations of Amish cooks!*

OTHER BOOKS BY LINDA BYLER

Available from your favorite bookstore
or online retailer.

"Byler is Amish, and the authenticity of her narrative shines on every page, as do her impeccable research and skillful plotting. This tale will captivate readers looking for clean Christian women's fiction with a dollop of romance."

—*Publisher's Weekly* review of *The Homestead*

"Author Linda Byler is Amish, which sets this book apart both in the rich details of Amish life and in the lack of melodrama over disappointments and tragedies. Byler's writing will leave readers eager for the next book in the series."

—*Publisher's Weekly* review of *Wild Horses*

LIZZIE SEARCHES FOR LOVE SERIES

BOOK ONE

BOOK TWO

BOOK THREE

TRILOGY

COOKBOOK

LANCASTER BURNING SERIES

FIRE in the NIGHT

LINDA BYLER

BOOK ONE

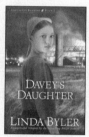

DAVEY'S DAUGHTER

LINDA BYLER

BOOK TWO

The WITNESSES

LINDA BYLER

BOOK THREE

LINDA BYLER

Lancaster Burning

TRILOGY

Three Bestselling Novels in One

TRILOGY

SADIE'S MONTANA SERIES

WILD HORSES

BOOK ONE

KEEPING SECRETS

BOOK TWO

The Disappearances

BOOK THREE

LINDA BYLER

Sadie's Montana

TRILOGY

TRILOGY

HESTER'S HUNT FOR HOME SERIES

Hester on the Run

LINDA BYLER

BOOK ONE

Which Way Home?

LINDA BYLER

BOOK TWO

Hester Takes Charge

LINDA BYLER

BOOK THREE

LINDA BYLER

Hester's Hunt for Home

TRILOGY

TRILOGY

THE DAKOTA SERIES

BOOK ONE   BOOK TWO   BOOK THREE

CHRISTMAS ROMANCES

THE LITTLE AMISH
MATCHMAKER
A Christmas Romance

THE CHRISTMAS
VISITOR
An Amish Romance

MARY'S CHRISTMAS
GOODBYE
An Amish Romance

BECKY MEETS
HER MATCH
*An Amish Christmas
Romance*

A DOG FOR
CHRISTMAS
*An Amish Christmas
Romance*